Haven

Also by Joel Shepherd

A TRIAL OF BLOOD & STEEL

Haven

JOEL SHEPHERD

an imprint of **Prometheus Books**
Amherst, NY

Inquiries should be addressed to
Pyr
59 John Glenn Drive
Amherst, New York 14228–2119
VOICE: 716–691–0133
FAX: 716–691–0137
WWW.PYRSF.COM

15 14 13 12 11   5 4 3 2 1

Library of Congress Cataloging-in-Publication Data

Shepherd, Joel, 1974–
    Haven / by Joel Shepherd.
        p. cm. — (A trial of blood and steel ; bk. 4)
    Originally published: Sydney : Orbit, 2010.
    ISBN 978–1–61614–363–3 (pbk. : acid-free paper)
    ISBN 978–1–61614–364–0 (e-book)
    I. Title. II. Series.

PR9619.4.S54H38 2011
823'.92—dc22

2010050959

Printed in the United States of America on acid-free paper

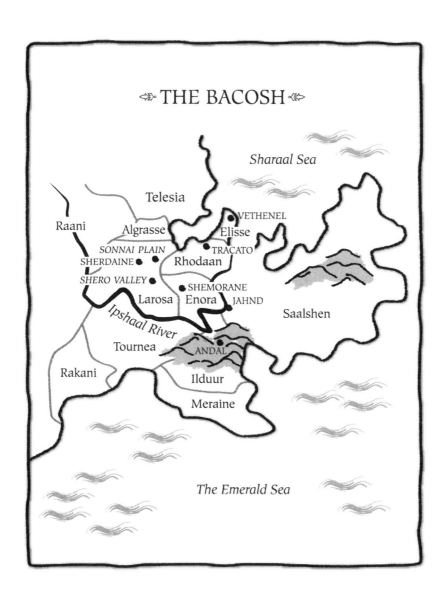

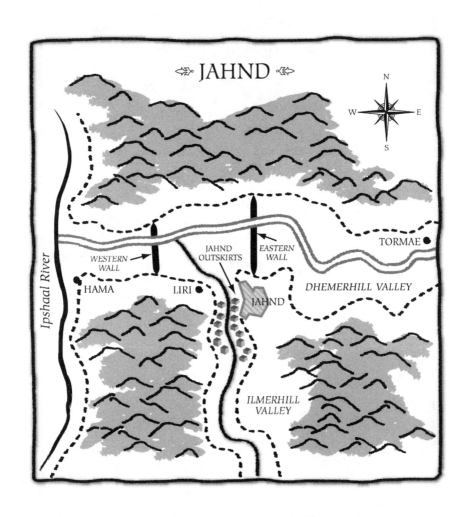

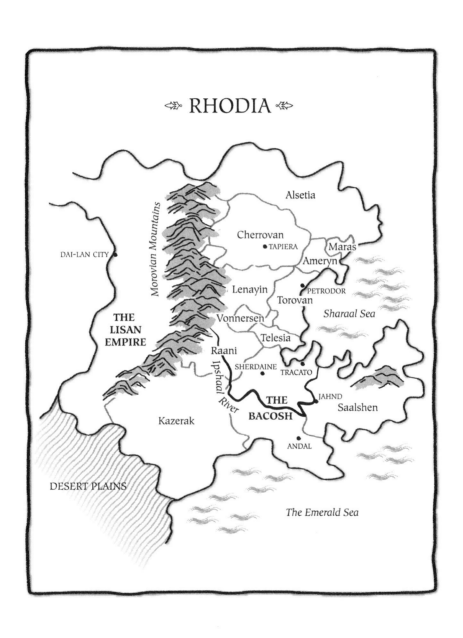

One

Kessligh galloped his horse up the field beside the tree-lined avenue, and saw that he was too late to save Hershery. He swung down from the saddle and scrambled along the embankment between the trees, staring at the flames that rose from the old town's little cluster of rooftops. Men rode about the town on horseback, pointing and talking. Several put their heels hard to their mounts and tore off in pursuit of something unseen.

"That one's the leader," said Errollyn from Kessligh's side, stringing his huge bow with a heave and twist of powerful arms. He nodded to the apparent captain on his horse. "I could have him."

The captain was at least sixty strides away, in heavy chain armour, but Kessligh did not doubt Errollyn's certainty. Kessligh shook his head. "Wait." He looked back across the field, and waved his arm toward the tree line, pointing for an encirclement.

"I count twenty," said Errollyn. From within the little town came wails and screams, and the barest sound of fighting. In the villages of Rhodaan, safe and happy behind their defensive wall of Steel for two centuries, there was rarely any more than that. Several nearby houses were now going up in flames. "If we're fast we could save more."

"I know," said Kessligh. He wasn't here to save Hershery. These villagers had been told to evacuate and hadn't listened. From that refusal on, their fate had been beyond his power to alter. He could, however, do something about the Regent's advance raiding parties . . . for whatever good it would do.

The captain and his one man departed at a gallop.

"Let's go," Kessligh told Errollyn. As they accelerated down the slope to the village, a dismounted soldier appeared from a little lane between brick walls. Errollyn's bow thumped, and the man took a shaft through the eye. Errollyn did not so much as blink as they dismounted for a second time, and tied their horses' reins loosely to a post.

Errollyn's arms beneath his loose sleeves were crisscrossed with scars, and the gleam in his inhumanly luminescent eyes was different from what Kessligh remembered from their first meeting. The mischief was gone, replaced by something implacable and deadly. That Errollyn had always seemed surprised by his own proficiency at killing, and faintly apologetic about it. This Errollyn apologised to no one, and regarded his victims with cold disinterest.

Kessligh led the way, controlling his ever-present limp enough to make a decent pace up the narrow, weaving lane. Smoke billowed from a doorway. At a gate, an old man lay dead in his own blood. Within a second gateway, Kessligh glimpsed more bodies. Footsteps gave him warning of an approach, and when the soldier appeared, Kessligh shoved his serrin blade through the man's chest—mail and bone parted like butter and the man sank with a burbling, spluttering protest.

A man of Meraine, Kessligh noted, not of Larosa. The Larosans were now the kingly province of the Bacosh, and led the invasion of Rhodaan beneath the command of Regent Balthaar Arrosh, soon to be High King Arrosh. As soon as he reached Shemorane, and the Enoran High Temple. Kessligh had known warfare since his late teens, and he knew that it could not be stopped now. He only hoped to slow the Army of the Bacosh down, in order to organise further defences.

The path opened onto a little stone courtyard, picturesque with flower boxes, a small well, and the end face of a chapel with a little iron bell. Limp figures were now being hung from the branches of an oak that spread beside the chapel. Three men were heaving on a rope, while another supervised. Hung by the neck, the bodies were already dead, but disembowelled and gruesome, they hung as sentinels or warnings.

Errollyn shot the supervisor through the back of the thigh, reloaded fast, and, as the three holding the rope began to react, shot one through the neck. The two remaining dropped the dangling body, which hit the stones with a horrid thump. Those two tried to retreat, in shock and fear, then attacked when they realised they were trapped against a courtyard wall. Kessligh took one attacker through the hand when he presented a poor guard, sending fingers spinning. The other presented a more commendable attack, which Kessligh sent sliding past with a high elbow and downward angle that whipped into a cut whilst the attacker was still in his follow-through. The man split and hit the stone in a gush of blood.

Errollyn took guard while Kessligh stood over the arrow-shot man, struggling on the ground, trying to half-limp, half-slither away. "How many in this party?" Kessligh asked him.

The man grimaced, unreasonably attempting to escape. Kessligh put the blade to his neck. "Mercy," the man muttered, tears leaking from tightly shut eyes.

"Oh, I don't think so," said Kessligh, looking at the carnage around him. "How many, and I'll make it fast."

The man said nothing. And was knocked sprawling by Errollyn's arrow through his chest. Errollyn strode over to him, put a boot to the dead man's chest, and retrieved his arrow with a yank. The armour-piercing head was intact, barely scratched, to the satisfaction of Errollyn's critical gaze.

"Twenty," said Errollyn, placing the arrow back in his quiver. "I told you." And he set off down the narrow lane, looking for men to kill. Kessligh thought about cutting down the hanging bodies, but decided against it. Better that his men all saw. A few had not yet been persuaded of the necessity of the action he proposed.

From the fields came the sound of galloping hooves and the cries of battle. Errollyn climbed a short stairway to a wall beside a rooftop, and Kessligh joined him with a little difficulty. From there they could see the trap this party of Meraini had stumbled into. The land here was a depression, a small basin amidst fields and trees, with limited escapes and one obvious approach for a sweeping counterattack from Rhodaani cavalry.

Now those cavalry came, on Kessligh's command, while other light cavalry approached Hershery on Kessligh's flanks to cut off any escape. Meraine cavalry scattered before barely thirty oncoming horsemen—there were twenty more ahorse, in addition to the twenty Errollyn had counted in the village. Their positioning poor, they tried to flee and the Rhodaani cavalry cut them from their horses. Several came rushing toward the town, to find some safety within its walls. Errollyn stood, drew firmly, and shot a man from his horse. He pulled another arrow immediately, fitted it . . . and was surprised when Kessligh yanked on his bow, throwing off his aim.

"They're dead anyway," Kessligh explained to Errollyn's nonplussed gaze.

"But not by me," said Errollyn, as though offended.

"Exactly," Kessligh said grimly.

They were finishing with the bodies when a captain of the Rhodaani Steel came galloping across a field, five soldiers at his flanks. He rode to where Kessligh was examining bodies and horses, looking for clues. Errollyn had little interest in corpses and captured horses. Kessligh had a war to win, and was a general once more. Errollyn was glad Kessligh had found a purpose. He wished he had one like it.

Errollyn swished his hand at some tall grass. Wild wheat, escaped from nearby farmers' fields. Thirty terms for it in Saalsi occurred to him. This wheat was a crossbreed of human lands; it had not existed here before the serrin had brought it from Saalshen. Like so many things.

He could overhear the captain and Kessligh arguing. The captain was General Geralin's man, and Geralin was a stern and proper soldier of the Rhodaani Steel tradition. The Steel had never lost a war in two centuries of constant testing, yet now they fled across the fields of Rhodaan, with the soon-to-be King Arrosh in hot pursuit. Geralin and his higher officers thought themselves still in command, yet Kessligh of the Nasi-Keth, and similar-minded soldiers of a less formal battlefield tradition, insisted on taking the fight to the enemy in this unorthodox manner.

The captain now insisted that Kessligh cease to waste men in this way. Kessligh replied that he hadn't actually lost anyone today. The captain remarked acerbically on the scale of Kessligh's achievement—thirty dead Meraine cavalry, against the hundred thousand plus that advanced on them. Kessligh barely bothered to answer, bored with the whole debate and disdainful that he even had to answer to the likes of Geralin and his men, who understood not a thing about this kind of warfare.

Or no, Errollyn corrected himself . . . not disdainful. It was too strong a word for Kessligh, in speaking of his interaction with people for whom he had limited respect. Such people Kessligh merely looked past, as a master composer might regard some insignificant student, barely hearing a word they said while, in his head, already composing his next great music.

The captain rode off in frustration. Kessligh set about explaining some things to several of the younger riders—one of them Daish—escapees from the Tol'rhen in Tracato. He beckoned to Errollyn too, with some annoyance.

". . . all men of one house," Kessligh was telling the youngsters, pointing to the bodies on the ground. "That's the problem with feudal forces: the division of responsibility falls along lines of lineage and power, not of capability. These are men-at-arms and a few half-nobility from the same lands in Meraine; they're after spoils, probably they volunteered."

"They're just trying to sow terror," Daish muttered, looking back to the still-burning village of Hershery. "Arrosh himself ordered this."

Kessligh nodded. "But it's the opportunists who volunteer to carry out the orders. We've an opening here; such men are not natural scouts, they cling to their groups for protection rather than strategy, and don't understand the advantage of the land as Lenay cavalry might. Now let's be off before their friends come to check on the delay."

There were three prisoners, on their knees still with hands on their heads. There was no possibility of taking them along, they had not the forces to spare for guarding them. And from the terrified looks on their faces, it seemed they knew it. Errollyn took his bow in hand, but Kessligh issued the orders elsewhere, and gave Errollyn an irritated gesture to mount up.

"It's easier to do it from range than let the kids get their hands bloody," Errollyn explained as they rode away from Hershery.

"You've killed enough," Kessligh said shortly.

"I don't mind."

"I know," said Kessligh. "That's the problem."

It was the kind of thing Sasha would have said. Or rather, it was the kind of thing a certain Sasha would have said perhaps a month or two ago. Lately, Errollyn didn't think she'd have minded any more than he did.

Sasha rode with the Army of Lenayin. Those were her people. Kessligh's too, if pressed on the point. The Army of Lenayin were allied to the Merainis they'd just killed. They marched now some distance behind this main force of the Army of the United Bacosh, but not too far now, considering how much lighter Lenays would travel.

Verenthane gods and Lenay spirits forbid that they ever catch up. Errollyn did not know what he would do then. His people's very existence was threatened, for this enormous army that came down upon them was motivated not merely by the reconquest of Bacosh lands, but by the prospect of ending all serrin life in the world, forever. Yet he could only think of Sasha, and how he would rather let anything happen than be forced to fight against any number that contained her as well.

It was a preposterous sentiment, and one worthy of self-loathing. But he did not loathe himself for it. Not really. He just killed every enemy Kessligh pointed him toward, and tried to think on other things. Kessligh worried for him, he knew . . . which was odd, because Kessligh was a general who saw things from the broadest possible perspective, and spared his personal concern on very few. Possibly Kessligh was concerned for him on Sasha's behalf, because in his odd human way, Kessligh felt for Sasha as a daughter, and for her lover as some kind of son.

Which was nice, Errollyn supposed. And unnerving, because he no longer believed any of them were going to make it out of this alive. Not on his side of the fight, anyhow. On Sasha's side, there was a chance. He hoped she would stay precisely where she was, and that her brothers would place her far at the rear of any fighting. It did not seem likely that they or a thousand wild horses could keep her there, but he could hope. He would never see her again, of course. But she'd live a full life, and grow old to tell her children of fond memories of the strange serrin man she'd once loved. That was better than an early grave at his side, unmarked upon some foreign field, far from her beloved Lenay home.

Even viewed from the head of an invading army, Rhodaan looked beautiful. Sasha rode in the second group of the column. Ahead rode the cluster about her brother Koenyg, King of Lenayin, comprising of several northern great lords, the southern Great Lord of Rayen plus the princes Damon and Myklas. Ahead of them, a short vanguard of Royal Guardsmen in gold and red, flying the royal banners most prominently.

The second group was led by bannermen of Isfayen, Valhanan, and Taneryn. Behind, the respective great lords of those provinces, Markan, Shystan, and Ackryd. Each had several loyal lesser lords for companions. Sasha, for her part, had Markan's sister Yasmyn and Jaryd Nyvar.

Ahead on a bend of road, Sasha spied a scout, waiting as his horse grazed. The man remounted as King Koenyg approached. Koenyg joined him on one side, Prince Damon on the other, while the scout described something up ahead. Koenyg gave orders, and one of the lords peeled away to fetch men from further back in the column. Damon halted his horse until Sasha drew level.

"There's a town," he explained. Damon had always been the most dour of King Torvaal's children. "By the river ahead."

"The Larosans didn't burn it, did they?" Jaryd asked darkly.

"No. The scout says it seems an important post for river trade. Best we go and check."

Sasha detected that he was not making a request. There was something else, then. She nodded.

"I would come," Great Lord Markan declared.

"No, brother," said Yasmyn. "The entire noble vanguard does not ride on scouting missions."

"If the king shall demean himself on scouting missions, why should I not also?" Markan said stubbornly. Yasmyn scowled, and switched tongues to Telochi, the primary native tongue of the Isfayen.

Tempers were short all along the Lenay column. Only in the last few days had Koenyg declared mourning for King Torvaal over. Since then, banners had flown high instead of low, and the white of funereal mourning taken down from the column's head. Moods, however, had not improved.

The Army of Lenayin marched in disgrace. The opening battle of what the Larosans now named The Glorious Crusade, had been fought in two parts. The massed armies of the so-called Free Bacosh, led by the most powerful feudal province of Larosa, had mustered north, before the border of Rhodaan. The Army of Lenayin, with some assistance from Torovan, had mustered south, to assault the border of Rhodaan's neighbour and steadfast ally, Enora. The assault on Enora had been primarily a diversion to keep the Enorans off the Larosan's southern flank. The Enoran Steel, like the Rhodaani Steel, had never been defeated in all its two centuries of warfare, but nonetheless, most hotheaded Lenays had expected to win. Lenayin fancied itself a nation of warriors, and the greatest exponents of the martial arts in all Rhodia. It had been the first time ever that all the disunited and squabbling provinces of Lenayin had fought together as a single army, united for a common cause.

They had been defeated, sent running before their foes, leaving perhaps a third of their number, four of their provincial great lords, and their king dead upon the field. Instead of the great victory to bring glory to Lenayin, there was nothing for Lenayin on this lowlands crusade but unbearable shame.

Now the Army of Lenayin marched in the wake of the victorious Army of Larosa. That rankled all the more, to walk behind a foreign army, allies though they were. All knew well, in the theory of such things, that this victory was as much Lenayin's as Larosa's. Lenayin had engaged the Enoran Steel with only a little advantage in numbers, and fought them harder and bloodier than the Enorans had ever been fought . . . indeed, if not for the heroism of a last, suicidal charge by serrin *talmaad* of Saalshen, who fought on the Enorans' side, outcomes might well have been different.

Lenayin had retained enough force, and rocked the Enorans back on their heels hard enough, that the Enorans had been unable to make a direct march north to assist their hard-pressed allies in Rhodaan. Without such support, Rhodaan had fallen to the vastly superior numbers of the Larosan Army.

Koenyg rode out from the head of the column behind a cluster of Royal Guards, Damon at his side, and several younger lords as well. Sasha followed with Jaryd and Yasmyn, and no few scowls from the northerners as they passed them. On such short scouting rides, it had been agreed that numbers about the king should be limited, as speed was the greater defence, and too many riders on narrow roads would only get in the way should there be an ambush. The great lords, to Sasha's relief, remained behind.

Sasha could not see any life in the fields they passed. She knew this land a little, having lived several months in Tracato during the troubles there, before abandoning everything she'd thought she was serving to return to the only cause she had left—her people, and her nation. Always the farmlands about Tracato had been full of life, farmers working their fields, children playing around the farmhouses, carts and shepherds with their animals on the roads. Now, there were only the birds in the trees. Even the animals were missing from the fields.

Soon the village came into view on the far side of the winding river. It was pretty, as were most Rhodaani villages, its yellow brick and red tile structures standing tall on the bank, making a line of colourful reflection in the gently flowing water. A low stone bridge crossed the river, another scout waiting at its end to signal the way was clear. The Lenays clattered across, banners high. The village had the look of a ghost town.

"At least they didn't burn it," said Jaryd. Several villages further back along the road had not been so fortunate. Sasha had been surprised at the strength of Jaryd's disgust back then. Jaryd had been a nobleman once, the heir to the Lenay central province of Tyree, no less. A fall from grace had led him to convert from the grand, noble faith of the Verenthanes to the rural paganism of the Goeren-yai. Sasha had thought him largely done with the trappings of nobility, and indeed he seemed quite happy to dress in the rough cloth, leathers, and skins of a Goeren-yai warrior, grow his hair long, and own little besides his horse and sword. But now, he seemed in great distress at the wanton destruction of lovely buildings and works of art in the little court-yards that seemed to occupy the centre of every Rhodaani village.

"It is too pretty to burn," said Yasmyn. "Even the Larosans must have some standards." From Yasmyn, such remarks surprised Sasha even more than from Jaryd. Yasmyn was Isfayen, daughter to the Great Lord Faras, slain in the Battle of Shero Valley, as the great conflict against the Enoran Steel was known. She had ridden with the Army of Lenayin as handmaiden to the Princess Sofy, Sasha's sister, now safely wed to the Larosan Regent Balthaar. Her parting from Sofy's service had not been amicable, as Balthaar's men had raped her in retaliation for her attempted defence of her princess.

Yasmyn now wore the red scarf of the *angyvar*—or "the impatience," in translation from Telochi—with dark markings of ancient symbols, and fading, self-inflicted scars on her cheek. Two gold rings in her left ear indicated some success so far, representing the heads of two of her attackers, delivered to her father as proof of honour restored. Sasha understood that there was still one left.

But Sasha was surprised all the same to hear any concern from Yasmyn for a mere village. The Isfayen were renowned as uncompromising warriors even by the standards of Lenayin. Whatever Yasmyn's hatred for Lenayin's allies in this war, Isfayen honour would not typically allow sympathy for an enemy, even an enemy who fought against Larosans.

As they came upon the far bank, Sasha saw waterwheels slowly churning the river currents. The riders turned onto the main road, past the buildings that flanked the river. The road was narrow between tall stone walls, and hooves made a clattering racket on the cobbles. There were no people in sight, but no destruction either.

"Perhaps they all ran away," said Jaryd. It seemed likely.

"Perhaps the Larosan raiding parties finally missed a village," Yasmyn added. That seemed less likely. The Larosans knew Rhodaan well enough, having plenty of Rhodaani spies who had drawn maps for them. They seemed to be hitting every village anywhere near their army's advance, and many that were not near at all.

Sasha did not reply. She knew that she had not been talkative company lately. Much of the time, she simply did not feel like speaking . . . which, amongst those who knew her before, was regarded with grave concern. Her father King Torvaal had died at Shero Valley, though she had neither known nor loved him well. Far worse, her dear childhood friend Teriyan Tremel had also died, and her even dearer childhood friend Andreyis had never been found in the aftermath. She retained a faint hope that he had been taken prisoner.

And her lover was on the other, Rhodaani, side and the Army of Lenayin now marched toward him. Kessligh Cronenverdt, truly the closest thing she had to a parent, was also on the other side. Fighting against Enora had been one thing, where she knew that neither Kessligh nor Errollyn would be numbered amongst the enemy. Fighting the Rhodaanis would be another matter entirely. There were times at night, as she stared at the stars, when she wondered if she would not rather have fallen at Shero Valley. At other times, she wondered if it would not be too dishonourable to fall still, by her own hand.

Sasha saw the Royal Guards ahead reach for their swords. Then the shock, and the staring. She had suspected it would come, eventually, as they drew deeper into Rhodaan, and encountered villagers who had perhaps, for whatever reason, thought not to run.

The courtyard was a temple courtyard, with a big tree, gnarled and swollen before the temple steps. Hanging from the tree were perhaps twenty corpses. Some had been disembowelled, entrails swinging in glistening tangles. Some were women. Several were children. An older man was tied to the tree, his corpse and much of the trunk feathered with arrows, where soldiers had used him for target practice.

"Get them down," ordered Koenyg. No one moved. Koenyg stared at one of the young northern lords. The youngster, no more than eighteen, looked offended.

"My king," he said, with a thick Hadryn accent, "you surely cannot expect such work to fall to me?"

"I expect," Koenyg said sharply, "that a Lenay man marching to war will follow his king's instruction." In any land but Lenayin, such a firm tone from the king would have been followed by rapid obedience.

"But my lord!" the youngster protested. "Find me a formation of Rhodaani Steel to charge single-handedly, and I shall gladly do it! But to perform such rank and lowly duties as this, I should be dishonoured before my peers."

His accompanying lordlings nodded their agreement. "Get the guardsmen to do it."

Koenyg ground his teeth. "They have the distinction of actually being useful," he growled. Sure enough, the Royal Guardsmen now ringed the courtyard, swords drawn in defence of their king and Prince Damon. "Go then and ride back to the column. Tell them not to ride through the town, tell them on my order to stay to the northern bank, and follow the road there until we can rejoin this road further ahead, perhaps at the next bridge."

"The road on the northern bank is inferior to this," another lordling said, doubtful. Koenyg's glare saw him swallow the rest of his protest.

"No," said Damon, gazing up at the grisly, swinging bodies. "Have them come through the town. It is quicker, and safer. The north bank is better ambush country."

Koenyg turned on his brother, half-wheeling his horse. "I swear, does no one in this column take my orders? We hold them to the north bank."

"Something to hide, brother?" Damon suggested.

"Something they need not see," Koenyg retorted. Their stares locked. Predictably, it was Damon who looked away first. His expression was that of a man who had swallowed something foul and could find no place to spit.

"I'll ride back and find some men to come and clean up this mess," said Sasha. "I think perhaps fifty of the common cavalry should do it."

Koenyg turned his glare on her. "Sasha, no! Don't you dare." Sasha's return stare held none of Damon's uncertainty. Hers held utter unconcern for anything her brother might say. Koenyg opened his mouth to command further, then closed it again in frustration. He knew that she would not listen. He saw that she barely cared if he tried to kill her.

Sasha turned and rode away without awaiting a dismissal. Once away from the clattering road and onto the dirt road beyond the bridge, Yasmyn had questions.

"Why was he upset that you'd ask the common cavalry?" she asked.

"Because it's a mixed mob behind the vanguard that have all mingled and become friendly whatever their province," Jaryd answered for Sasha. "They roam the length of the column, carrying messages back to their respective provincial commands, and they're the worst gossips in the army. They'll tell the whole column what they saw in the village."

"Ah," said Yasmyn, as she understood.

"Some of those Larosans will be held to account for this," Sasha muttered. "One day they will."

It was a struggle to find a place to train in the evening. Sasha finally found a spot down by the reeds at the river's edge, where she performed her taka-dans, and found some interest in the poor footing. A warrior craves a perfect footing, Kessligh had told her often. Deny him that, and your advantage increases.

As usual, some men came down to watch. That was not an uncommon thing amongst Lenay warriors, who could talk swordwork from sunrise to sunset. This audience was remarkably silent as she performed her strokes. Many Lenay warriors found the svaalverd style of Saalshen discomforting, almost supernatural. Sasha's blade and body described ethereal forms in the dying light of evening, a shadow in the mist, movement both precise and fluid to a degree that appeared, to the superstitious, barely human.

Finally she sheathed her blade over her left shoulder, tucked the tri-braid behind her right ear, and stood with head bowed. Respect toward the river reeds; respect for the resident spirits. She thought of her sister Alythia, whose spirit had been freed in the city of Tracato, toward which they presently rode. Alythia whom she had hated for so long, then recently come to love, only to lose her to those she had once been urged to consider as friends. Those people, if she found them, she could kill happily. If only the Army of Lenayin would be fighting them.

She turned, and walked from the reeds toward the camp. Her audience faded respectfully away, save one man, a young Isfayen who kneeled before her path, and presented her with a red cloth. The cloth was inscribed with curling Telochi script, and decorated with braiding, no little effort gone to, considering the deprivations of camp. Sasha sighed, and took the offered cloth. She could not read Telochi script, but she considered the markings anyhow, and found some admiration for the quality.

The young Isfayen warrior said something in Telochi, and then, in halting Lenay, "Please will you consider." He rose. His gaze was not worshipful; Lenays of any stripe did not do worship. But the respect was blazingly intense.

Sasha smiled sadly at the man, folded the cloth carefully, and tucked it within her jacket. She had a pocket there, in the inner lining, that pressed against her heart, and her breast. The young man seemed pleased with that. Sasha patted him on the arm, and continued back to camp in the rapidly descending dark.

She found Yasmyn a short distance from the big tents, the only tents in the entire Lenay column. Lenays slept rough, and disdained basic comforts while marching to war . . . all save the nobility and royalty, who required some tents for status, and private consultations. Yasmyn sat beside her brother Markan, eating roast meat and bread. A warrior at her other side saw Sasha coming and made space. Sasha put a hand on his shoulder in sitting to thank him—his name was Asym, she recalled, and he had no special title to gain him access to the great lord's campfire save that he was known as a great warrior, and had fought ferociously at the Battle of Shero Valley.

Yasmyn handed Sasha a plate of food, and she ate. Most conversation was in Telochi, of which Sasha understood only the occasional word or phrase. It had been Damon's idea to place her with the Isfayen. The northern provinces despised her. The Verenthane nobility (as all Lenay nobility save Taneryn was Verenthane) of most of the rest of Lenayin disliked her nearly as much. In Valhanan's case it saddened her; she had spent most of her life in Valhanan, and if she had a provincial loyalty, that was where it lay. The Great Lord Kumaryn was dead at Shero Valley, but his place had been taken by another just as loathsome. The Taneryn would have taken her, but she had ridden with many Taneryn against their old enemies the Hadryn in what was known as the Northern Rebellion, and it would not do to have those old rivalries stirred once more.

But the Isfayen considered themselves almost a separate nation, and cared little for the opinions of fellow Lenays. The Great Lord Faras's opinion of Sasha had been dramatically improved by his daughter Yasmyn's friend-ship with the Princess Sofy, Sasha's dearest friend of all her royal siblings. And the Isfayen, Damon had reckoned, thought all things secondary to skill at warfare. If Sasha could find acceptance amongst the nobility of any Lenay province, it would be amongst the Isfayen. And so, after the Battle of Shero Valley, it had proven to be.

"Another bloodwarrior just proposed to me," Sasha told Yasmyn. She gave Yasmyn a faintly accusing look.

Yasmyn smiled. "Tyama. He told me he would. He is the son of a herdsman, from near the village of Uam, in the west. A brave and skilled warrior." Sasha sighed, and ate her food. "How many is that?"

"Seven," said Sasha. She shook her head. "I don't know what they're thinking. I mean no disrespect, but I'm not inclined to marry anyone. Do they think I'll be a farmwife in some homestead on an Isfayen mountainside?"

Yasmyn shook her head. "The problem is that they don't know what to think. Isfayen men are rare amongst Lenays in that they like a strong woman. It is in our culture." Another reason, Sasha reflected, why Damon placed her with the Isfayen. "But though Isfayen women can fight, rarely is it expected they could match a man in battle. For an Isfayen woman, fighting is a victory of courage over common sense. Isfayen admire that, and Isfayen men find little more attractive than a pretty girl who dares to snarl to a great warrior's face. Tremendous sex often follows."

Sasha managed a faint smile. "It has a certain logic."

"But now they see you," Yasmyn continued. "You fight not merely with courage, but with unmatched skill. And with the svaalverd, that makes you nearly unbeatable. The young men find themselves struggling with a feeling they had not known before—both unmatched respect, and great lust. They do not know how else to express this feeling if not in a proposal. None of them expects you to accept. If they did, you'd have had hundreds of proposals by now, not just seven. They just do not know how else to express what they feel."

Sasha nodded slowly, gazing into the fire.

Yasmyn smiled slyly. "I envy you greatly."

"I hadn't thought you were struggling for proposals yourself."

"Not in that. I mean that you could have your pick of these men tonight, and other men the night after. Isfayen women are dishonoured to have more than one man at a time, but you! You best them all, and they have no grounds for complaint."

Sasha smiled. It grew to an outright grin. Yasmyn laughed. The Great Lord Markan saw their humour.

"Aha!" he said loudly, pointing at Sasha. "The great Synnich finally smiles!" Men about the campfire paused conversation to look. "Of what do you smile?"

Sasha shook her head faintly. "Sex, what else?" Men laughed.

"My sister is obsessed with sex," said Markan. "It is a disease of the mind. I should send her to a holywoman to have her cleansed with smoke and ash." He put an affectionate arm about Yasmyn, and kissed her head. Yasmyn shoved him away, scowling but good-humoured.

Markan had barely twenty-two summers, a year more than Sasha, but he was a very big lad. With Yasmyn's looks, his father's shoulders, and a cheerful disposition when not in battle, Sasha found herself reflecting that if she could have any man in Isfayen, she'd probably rather it be him. And she shoved the thought aside, as she knew it could lead nowhere good. Markan had been Great Lord of Isfayen for several weeks now, following his father's death. Sasha did not think the bloodwarriors of Isfayen had yet come to accept him entirely, and Isfayen being Isfayen, there were always grumblings of possible challenge from rivals. But Markan would have to stumble first, to provoke such a challenge. Sasha hoped that he would not.

There came a shout from somewhere beyond the camp. Then a yell, and a war cry. Sasha leaped to her feet and drew her blade. "Defence!" she yelled. "Defence!" About the camps men leaped up with weapons in hand. There was no mad rushing, for they had practised this, on Sasha and Damon's insistence.

Men made formations, but crouched low, not presenting a target to archers. Some oil was thrown on several campfires, making them flare brightly. Sasha herself did not join the line formations of the men, but ran to a near tentside and crouched there, peering past the support ropes. Yasmyn joined her, similarly ill-equipped to fight shoulder-to-shoulder with the men, her forearm-length darak gleaming in hand. Sasha thought she heard an arrow's hiss. Someone cursed. Then, more distantly, some shouts and directions.

"They're probing," said Sasha, in a low voice. Out beyond the ring of fire-light, shadows danced upon the trees, and made a luminous glow in the campfire mist. Here in Rhodaan, one did not post sentries beyond the ring of firelight and expect them to remain alive by morning. Even the hardy, far-ranging Lenay scouts returned to the safety of camp each night before sunset. Men with knowledge of woodlore set traps for wild animals, or suspended lines of string in the undergrowth, attached to pots and utensils to make a noise if disturbed. It seemed to help somewhat, for nighttime losses so far remained light. But all the same, every night someone died. After a time, it became unnerving.

"They fight like cowards," Yasmyn fumed. Again distantly, Sasha heard a clash of steel, and another battle cry. Numbers were greater tonight, if fighting was hand-to-hand.

"They fight with what they have," Sasha murmured. "A snake will always strike from below, a hawk will come from above. Serrin learn from nature. Complaining because they refuse to fight as we can beat them is pointless."

At a further campfire, Sasha saw a man stand up higher to peer into the mist. His neighbour pulled him down. Behind, an arrow whistled, and Sasha spun to see a man falling, struck through the eye.

"Stay down, you fools!" someone shouted. Further back along the column, past the tents, Sasha could faintly see figures moving, edging to the trees at the flank. Only here, surrounding the royalty and nobility, did men remain in fixed ranks, making a defensive wall against the death that lurked in the dark. Serrin saw well by night, but many Lenay men had experience hunting, and knew how to ambush an alert prey. Some had had success in such attacks taking shelter at the perimeter, and letting the serrin stumble across them.

This attack was coming from the south, and the river, Sasha realised. It was the less obvious direction, considering open fields to the north. Where would a serrin ford a river, at night? Somewhere shallow, with lots of cover. Like water reeds.

Sasha caught the eye of a nearby warrior, and gestured. He ran to her at a crouch. Too late, Sasha realised he was Hadryn, his scalp nearly shaven, a slim goatee on his chin, and a large Verenthane star hanging around his neck. But still, he had run to her when she summoned.

"Have you an archer?" she asked him.

"Crossbowman," said the Hadryn. Lenays did not fancy archery much, but the northerners used them more than most. "What of it?"

"I think I know where they came across the river."

The Hadryn considered her for a moment. Then turned and ran crouched back along his line of men, to tap one on the shoulder.

"I'll come," said Yasmyn.

"You're a fighter," said Sasha, "but you're not a warrior. There's a difference."

"I'm no use here!" Yasmyn retorted. "If not here, where else can I be useful?"

"*Mey'as rhen ah'l*," said Sasha in Saalsi, with a shrug. "Such is life."

The Hadryn crossbowman arrived, and Sasha set off at a low run for the cover of a nearby tent. Soon she was at the furthermost camp, near the river. Here men crouched attentively, blades in hand, some shields at the ready. Sasha spied several further from the firelight, low in the undergrowth against the tree trunks.

"Anything?" Sasha asked the man there. He was Fyden, Sasha could tell by the tattoo on his cheek. The Fyden man blinked at her, perhaps less surprised at her sudden appearance than with the company of a Hadryn crossbowman at her back.

"Not a sign," whispered the Fyden man. "You're going down to the reeds?"

"Aye," said Sasha.

"I'll come. There's a way through the trees, good cover. We've no more archers, but I could find one over with the Yethulen—"

"Three's enough," Sasha replied. "Any more, we'll be spotted for sure."

They moved silently forward, Sasha following the Fyden man's lead, the Hadryn bringing up the rear. The mist closed in, thick with the smell of evening cooking. Sasha concentrated more on speed from tree to tree than on maintaining silence; serrin eyesight was far more dangerous than serrin hearing, which was no better than a human's. From the column came the steady rise and fall of calls and shouts, as men from different sections called to each other. The Fyden man pushed through thicker undergrowth as the trees closed in, then onto a patch of open ground before a fallen log.

They took cover there, and peered over. Ahead lay more open ground, and then river reeds. Beside Sasha, the Hadryn steadied his crossbow on the mossy trunk of the fallen tree, and waited. Stillness followed, broken only by calls from the column. Sasha strained her ears but heard nothing. The Fyden man seemed more alarmed, eyes wide as he stared into the mist, breathing hard. Sasha was mildly surprised to realise that her own heart, whilst quickened, remained steady. Somewhere along her travels, she had lost much of her fear. Perhaps in Petrodor, though more likely Tracato.

Perhaps that was not all she'd lost in Tracato, came the more alarming thought. Perhaps she'd also lost the ability to care, and to feel.

She glimpsed movement. Barely more than shadows in the mist, down by the reeds. Lean shapes, all wielding bows. The Hadryn steadied his arm, lifting himself for a good aim. Sasha felt a stab of alarm that the man was about to shoot at serrin. And then a further alarm at herself, for even being here. Why had she volunteered to rush out here in the hope of hunting serrin at a possible river crossing? What had she been thinking? She loved the serrin. And now, as Lenay honour commanded, she fought them. But that did not mean she should volunteer to rush headlong into a fight. Her own actions baffled her.

The Hadryn's crossbow thumped. Amidst the reeds, one of the shadows flailed and fell. Sasha heard the rush from her left before the others, and leaped to her feet with a warning shout . . . but the Fyden man sprang up into her path and brought his blade flashing at the shadow that came at them from the trees. Sasha danced back for space as steel clashed briefly, and the Fyden man fell with little drama, just a face-first thud on the turf as an evil-sharp blade tore him open.

The figure that killed him wove sideways, slim like a woman, and tall for one, spinning a silver blade. Sasha glimpsed snow-white hair beneath a tied black scarf, and emerald eyes that blazed in the night like green fire. Familiar eyes, widening now with recognition. Sasha's heart, recently accelerated, nearly stopped.

Rhillian swung first, or nearly first, as the svaalverd forbade hesitation. Steel met steel and slid fast. Sasha, reversing that first cross into the low second, met firm defence, and pressed on that contact, just a little. A small slide of the front foot, a pressure of wrists, and the blade angle changed, and Rhillian took a step back to adjust. A moment's balance, a moment more time. Sasha led with the left shoulder for the high cut to follow, and altered the angle viciously at the last moment . . . and Rhillian abandoned defence for a desperate spin beneath, and out of trouble. Sasha's blade took off her white braid in passing.

Rhillian spun into the path of the Hadryn man, who had abandoned crossbow for sword. Sasha yelled warning even as he attacked, not that a Hadryn would have listened. Rhillian recovered to a near-perfect up-slanted deflection rotating into an utterly perfect beheading, in barely the time required to blink. And stood above the fallen, headless body, staring at her old friend past the bloody edge of a silver blade.

Sasha stared back. Her strokes had been all reflex. Had they stood further apart at the moment of recognition, she doubted she could have swung, had Rhillian not attacked. But she had. They had. Another moment between them, nearly the last.

Sasha had seen the ruthless precision of Rhillian's technique before. In battle, Rhillian feared little, because in style, she had little to fear. Her expression now was not fear, but rather . . . acknowledgement. She'd have been dead, had she not abandoned the contest. Perhaps, had she not known precisely whom she'd faced, she'd have shown more confidence, and died. She acknowledged that now, with her eyes. A wary, sombre green blaze.

"Don't do it," Sasha wanted to say. Her lips could not move. She had to watch Rhillian's centre, where her vision could catch the entirety of any rapid motion in hands, feet, and balance, but her eyes were drawn back to Rhillian's face. Those familiar eyes, that expressed so much in friendship, but not in battle. Only now, beyond the recognition of death barely avoided, there was anger, and shock, now all settling to a brooding, grim fatalism.

Her eyes flicked to Sasha's boots. Always the feet, in svaalverd. Sasha knew her old friend well. Selfless to the last, she was sizing up the threat, and wondering how many of her own comrades would die at Sasha's blade if she did not attempt to remove this threat now. An impulse seized Sasha to throw away her blade, and kneel, and have Rhillian be done with it all. But her hands did not twitch upon the well-worn grip, for Lenay honour could not conceive of such a thing. She wondered if Rhillian would still strike, should she kneel, unarmed. She wondered what could have possibly gone wrong, that they should arrive at this moment.

More footsteps were running, but softly, from the river. Sasha took a step back. Rhillian did not follow. Another step. For a moment, Sasha thought Rhillian might call to those approaching, and tell them to stop, and buy time for her escape. But Rhillian's face barely twitched, her stare intent, her weapon ready. When Sasha took another step back, Rhillian tensed as though about to pursue.

Sasha took off sprinting, through the undergrowth and between the trees, hoping against hope that her foot would not catch and trip her. It did not, and after a short, mad dash, there were fires ahead, and lines of Lenay soldiers crouched low and peering into the gloom.

"It's me, I'm coming back!" Sasha yelled in Lenay, so that her men could hear her voice, realising too late that many serrin attackers were women, and spoke Lenay flawlessly. Luckily her Lenays erred on the side of caution, and she hurdled their crouching line, and stopped to lean her back against a tree.

A Fyden man came to her. "The others?" he asked.

Sasha shook her head. And slid down the tree to crouch on her haunches. "That was stupid," she muttered. "I shouldn't have done that." Two men dead, because she'd had some crazy urge to purge her demons, or whatever that had been. And suddenly she was furious at herself—here she was, scared of the personal trauma of fighting a friend, and two brave comrades were dead by that same friend's blade. She should have killed Rhillian in an instant, to avenge their deaths. Lenay honour trumped all, wasn't that the decision she'd made, in leaving Tracato to come here in the first place?

"That was brave," the Fyden man corrected her. "Did you kill any?"

"Our Hadryn friend hit one," said Sasha. "*He* was brave, fighting serrin in the dark. And your man." She, at least, had some confidence of surviving such a fight. Spirits, she'd been stupid.

She got to her feet, and ran back toward the vanguard. Her progress was met with some cheers and approving gestures from those about. It made her angry at her own people, that they so easily confused stupidity with bravery, and thought it good.

Yasmyn greeted her with a flask of water by a tent, and Sasha took a long drink. "Crazy woman," Yasmyn told her, surmising well enough what had happened without needing to be told. "You must be blessed, to still be alive."

"I'm not blessed," said Sasha, after a hard swallow, "I'm cursed." She felt dizzy. "I need a moment."

She pushed past a tent flap, into the privacy of lordly quarters. From outside came calls of an all-clear, and a trumpet to tell the column. Damn trumpets, everyone was using them now, she'd never liked them. She sat on the edge of a cot, and put her head in her hands. The moment she closed her eyes she saw Rhillian, but it was not their recent meeting she saw. She saw emerald eyes asparkle with laughter, teasing her over some misunderstanding of the Saalsi tongue. She remembered the feel of Rhillian's hair in her hands, braiding it as they stood before the windows of a *talmaad* mansion, contemplating the view across Petrodor Harbour, and talking of their childhoods. And she recalled Rhillian's arms about her, when she'd once felt miserable, and thinking herself alone in her homesickness had leaned in a doorway and dreamed of Lenayin . . . only for Rhillian to approach unbidden from behind, and embrace her, and rest her cheek against Sasha's head.

"Unlike a stone," she'd murmured in Saalsi, "the burden of sadness can be lifted with a smile."

Sasha had smiled, then. Now, she cried.

Two

Sofy rode at Princess Alora's side, and watched the passing countryside.

"I do think the translator has it wrong," Princess Alora declared, shoulders straight in elegant sidesaddle atop a silver mare. Ten ladies of the court rode here, just behind the head of the column, protected by advancing armour in all directions. "Fifty-three deklen cannot equal ten gold sovereigns. I think it more likely they equal five."

Beyond the trees at the end of the field, a line of smoke was rising into the blue sky. Sofy watched it and wondered what burned at its source.

"The translator was quite adamant," Lady Mercene insisted. Mercene was from Elisse, the lone Bacosh Peninsula state, recently defeated by the Rhodaani Steel, and now about to be liberated once more. Mercene, her family and country folk were eager at the prospect. "One gold sovereign equals five and a third deklen in Tracato, the price is well established."

"But dear Mercene," said Alora, "the ledger books we recovered from that little riverside village stated that farming income from a single acre was seventy-nine deklen, about fifteen sovereigns. And that in a less-than-average season. A farmstead in the most fertile regions of Larosa makes no more than four-and-a-half sovereigns in the best seasons."

Sofy spied a farmhouse behind the line of trees. It had pretty brick walls overgrown with ivy, a chicken coop, and a pigsty. The house was of a stonework quality sufficient for minor nobility, yet far below the size demanded by noble honour. Could it be that such dwellings belonged to common folk? The ladies had nearly concluded such several days ago, and now changed the subject whenever it threatened to stray back.

These farmhouses clustered into not-quite-a-village, sharing a common series of little irrigation canals, with movable gates and good stonework. Where they had passed crops, all had seemed unusually lush and colourful. Sofy had no difficulty imagining that these lands, farmed by Rhodaani farmers using serrin-inspired methods, were at least three times more productive than what the Regent's allies liked to call the "Free Bacosh." It would explain, for one thing, why the Steel armies of the Saalshen Bacosh were so well equipped, and the roads, bridges, and buildings of such high quality.

"Sir Teale," Sofy announced, and one of the knights riding before the ladies' party reined back to Sofy's side. "I would like to know what village burns yonder."

"Perhaps not a village, highness," said Teale. "Perhaps a wood, or bales of hay, set to fire to deprive us of it."

"Whatever the source," Sofy repeated with certainty, "I would like to know it."

Teale nodded within his scarred helmet. "Of course, Your Highness."

Sofy bit her lip in frustration. About her the great army advanced, looting and burning as it went, as great armies would. Her husband, the soon-to-be High King Balthaar, assured at her insistence that the destruction would not be too great, that the lovely towns would not be burned unless enemies used them for defence, that artworks would be preserved, and families allowed to return to their homes, in time.

But they would not allow her to visit the towns that the column passed, claiming the region was thick with serrin, whose long bows could kill an armoured man from a hundred paces, and an unarmoured man from two. Now she was reduced to sending Sir Teale to enquire into the fate of passing towns, knowing that he lied to her when he returned, and hoping only that he did not lie too much.

The ladies rode in awkward silence. At times they spoke amongst themselves, of noble claims to these lands, and lineages long suspended. Two hundred years it had been, since the feudal ways had ruled in these parts. Many in the conquering army claimed ancestry, or argued for the suspension of whatever title now existed. But they did not argue the point too loudly in Sofy's presence, as they saw her worry for the fate of traitorous locals, and made snide remarks—when they thought she could not hear—that the queen-in-waiting worried more for serrin half-breeds than the lives of Bacosh outriders.

"I would speak with Lord Elot, if you please," Sofy announced loudly to a nearby servant, who turned his horse to gallop to the rear.

Soon Elot appeared at her side, astride a large horse. Sofy's mare was a little taller, allowing her to view him almost eye to eye. Lord Elot bowed to her. He was a big, bearded man, a native of Rhodaan. A traitor, perhaps, though not in his eyes. He was a noble, believing in all those things the serrin law had denied nobility for two hundred years. Upheaval in the Rhodaani capital of Tracato had led him here, with Sofy's sister Sasha at his side—her to join with the Army of Lenayin, and him to join with the Army of the Bacosh, and reclaim his noble birthright, and those of all his fellows.

Now, however, and in spite of heroism in a glorious victory, Elot looked far from content with the fates.

"I sent Sir Teale to investigate the smoke yonder," said Sofy. They spoke Torovan, the trading tongue of the Sharaal Sea routes, and common amongst the noble classes of Lenayin.

"He will find nothing," said Elot, grimly. "He never finds anything."

Sofy gave Elot a sideways look. He did not seem pleased to see his nation invaded. What had he expected, if not this? "Whose land is this?" Sofy asked.

"Family Miel," said Elot. "A well-established claim, the title documents remain hidden, Lord Miel knows where, if he survives in Tracato. Yet Family Junae of Larosa now informs me that their claim through a defecting cousin is superior."

Thus the grim look, Sofy thought. She'd been gathering something of these developments, and was not surprised.

"And your own family's lands?" she asked the Rhodaani lord.

"From Siadene to the north of here, all the way to the sea. Similarly challenged." Sofy just looked at him. "Your Highness, I would be in deepest gratitude to you if you would speak with your lord husband, and put a stop to these frivolous claims. This should be a time of celebration for the forces of honour. We should not be divided against one another so early, before the final victory is even won."

"It seems to me, Lord Elot," Sofy said mildly, "that you have misunderstood the nature of the feudal society that you have idolised for so long from the isolation of Tracato. Gratitude and allegiances come after the acquisition of land, not before. If you have land, many wish to be your friend. Today, in Larosan eyes, you are landless, and in no position to make demands."

"There are laws!" Elot insisted with anger.

"That can be reissued at my husband's single word," said Sofy. "I understand that laws are a somewhat more permanent and serious matter in Tracato. Or they were, until your little internal war burned the law houses down."

"That was not us," Elot muttered. "That was the peasants."

"And were you so sad? Given that those laws denied you the noble title that you seek as your right?"

"I can prove my claims," said Elot, stubbornly. "When we reach Tracato, I shall do so, with our records."

Sofy remained silent, and Elot met her gaze. Her eyes held warning. She was young yet, and recently naive in the ways of the world. No longer. Elot nodded slowly, noting the warning. His gaze held thanks. She dared not speak her fears, yet Elot was not a stupid man. If he should fail to reach Tracato alive, or his records could be destroyed before presentation to the soon-to-be king, it would be as though Elot's claims had never existed.

They had ridden a short distance further when Sir Teale returned at a gallop, silver armour shining in the sun.

"Highness," he said, with a nod to her in the saddle. "I bring word from your husband, the Regent. He is aware of your concern, and wishes that you ride to see this town in person."

Sofy blinked at him in surprise. A glance at the ladies of her party showed them similarly surprised, and some scowling.

"But of course, Sir Teale!" Sofy exclaimed. "Let us go at once! Lord Elot, would you join us? I would appreciate your insight."

"An honour, Princess," said Elot.

The ride to the town was a short canter across ploughed fields and men-at-arms stood ready at open gates. Even as Sofy marvelled at the beauty of the countryside, she spotted gleams of armour from amidst the trees, and the shuffling movement of horses. Her path was guarded, with some preparation. What was her husband's game?

By a little stream that meandered between fields and forest nestled a small village of stone walls and red tile. There was a barn afire in a nearby field, the source of the smoke. Cavalrymen milled in the fields, and watched as the princess approached.

"The rebels put the barn to fire rather than allow us the fodder within," Sir Teale explained. "The town itself is utterly deserted. The rebels spread lies of our intentions, and many flee in fear. Many shall die of exhaustion upon the road who would have lived, had they stayed and not believed the lies."

Sofy reined to a halt near the town walls and dismounted before Sir Teale or the waiting men-at-arms could assist. She walked quickly past sties and pens to a narrow alley through the village centre. All was quite clean, she noted. Small villages in Lenayin were always dirty, not that Lenay folk were unclean, but more that the Lenay hills were rugged, with winds and rain that washed mud and dirt onto all paths after a time.

She peered into an open doorway and found a neat little space within, with simple furnishings, a floor rug, and a stone oven. All seemed in order save for empty spaces on the wall hooks where pots and pans would typically hang. Those were a common farmer's more valuable possessions, those and livestock. Probably they'd have taken them on the road, piled onto some cart or mule.

Sofy hurried further along the lane, looking into other cottages, and finding things much the same. Soldiers followed her, and all these cottages had been searched in advance, she was certain. The absence of blood and fire relieved her, and yet, the scene had the feel of a show.

She arrived in a central courtyard, where a small, pretty temple was fronted by a well, and green creepers smothered the walls. Sofy admired the well, which had a small statue atop a pagoda roof, erected to keep leaves and bird droppings from falling in. The statue was of a naked lady, her long hair in one hand, a water jug in the other. It looked like Cliamene, Verenthane goddess of fertility . . . only this lady was far more sensuously carved than Sofy had seen, with bare breasts and one suggestive hip. And her face and eyes seemed . . . could she be serrin?

Lord Elot, she realised, had entered the temple. Sofy scampered to follow him, holding her skirts to clear the rough paving steps to the door.

The space within was larger than it seemed from the outside, perhaps large enough for sixty or seventy people at a very tight squeeze. Small, high windows let in the light, and there was even a circle of coloured glass in the wall above the altar. Lord Elot stood in the middle of the aisle, hands on hips, and gazed up at that window. It showed the Verenthane gods and angels, in remarkable detail.

"What craftsmanship," Sofy said admiringly, coming to Lord Elot's side in the gentle hush of the temple. "For such a little village."

"Serrin made," said Lord Elot, in a low voice. They were alone in the temple, save for a guard at the door . . . but sound echoed. "The serrin made many crafts for small temples like this. To build goodwill amongst the people." Sofy might have expected a man of Elot's leanings to be bitter at the practice. But Elot seemed subdued.

"Lord Elot, is something the matter?"

"The star is still here," said Elot, pointing to the simple, eight-pointed wooden shape hung upon the wall behind the altar, below the coloured window. "Townsfolk would not willingly leave it behind. Perhaps they left in a hurry."

Sofy frowned, and walked to the altar. A good Verenthane always, she took a knee and made the holy sign. Rising, she examined the star. It was simple wood, polished to a varnished gleam, all edges and joins worn away with careful attention. No wider than a man's shoulders, it would not be difficult to carry. Her attention settled on a discoloured mark, against the wall. An oil stain? She rubbed at it. It came away and soiled her finger. She sniffed it. It smelled nothing remarkable. Yet suddenly the cosy little temple felt cold, as though someone had thrown the doors open to a winter's wind.

She walked quickly to the doors, and stopped upon the steps. There in the courtyard before her, amidst a retinue of lords and knights, stood the Regent Balthaar Arrosh. He smiled at her, his regal cloak slung dashingly over one shoulder. Tall, and quite handsome, hair and moustache slightly curled.

He spread his hands to her. "Well, my dearest?" he asked. "Are you quite satisfied?"

Sofy forced a bright smile. "Quite satisfied, my husband." She trotted down the steps, curtseyed, and came to kiss him chastely on the cheek. The nobility in the courtyard all smiled at that. Balthaar's relatives, some of them. Others, his allies, lords of the powerful provinces of the "Free Bacosh," men who commanded great armies in their own right. All together, on this grand crusade. And her, the Lenay princess whose marriage secured the allegiance of Lenayin, without which current victories would never have been possible, however little those assembled here would like it admitted.

"We are not all barbarians in these lands," Balthaar assured her, to the further amusement of the courtyard. In all the lowlands, of course, Lenayin had been known for centuries as the land of barbarians . . . and perhaps not so unfairly. "We wish to return these lands to their rightful state of rulership, to the natural order of men, not to see them turned to ash."

"I understand, my husband," Sofy said with a further curtsey, in apology. "I never did doubt you. I merely wondered at the temper of some of the men. Losses were great in the Battle of Sonnai Plain, I had feared some would seek revenge. . . ."

"And surely some shall," said Balthaar, "as such things occur in all wars. But trust me that I shall endeavour to keep such happenings to a minimum, and punish those who go against my order. These lands are ours now, and to destroy them is to cut off our own limbs."

"I understand," said Sofy. She did not entirely meet his gaze. Balthaar took her by the arms, and for one nervous moment, Sofy feared he had guessed her thoughts.

"Dearest," he said instead, "I come because I have a favour to ask." Sofy met his gaze now, surprised. "I would ask you to ride to Tracato. I cannot— I must ride with the army to pursue the Steel into Enora, where they must be defeated for once and all. But Tracato's nobility have risen against the serrin devils. Much power resides there, and wealth, and a link to our Elissian allies. My interests are there, even as I cannot be.

"But I would send a trusted emissary, with wit and guile to match any man, and a stout heart too, to see my interests represented. Would you do this for me?"

Tracato? Sasha had just ridden from Tracato, and told of horrors there. And, more reluctantly, of wonders, of learning and civilisation greater than anything in all the lands of Rhodia. Ride to Tracato, to see its wonders preserved, its heritage protected, its people saved from the slaughter that Sofy feared could still descend across all these lands? To try and find a new balance between the invaders and the invaded?

Sofy's heart leaped at the prospect.

"My lord," she said gladly, "I would be honoured." And she hugged him, for all to see.

The wagon was a misery. Andreyis sat propped against its hard side, and tried to keep his bandaged, splinted arm from jolting. Low cloud scudded across a gloomy sky, and showers cast a grey veil across distant Enoran fields. The wagon's one coat had been given to Ulemys, the Ranash man who lay upon the floor. Ulemys was dying, and his groans were more painful than the wagon's jolting upon Andreyis's arm.

Four others shared the wagon with Andreyis, besides Ulemys. One, Sayden, was a fellow Valhanan, though from a village to the north that Andreyis had never heard of. The other three were from Hadryn, Tyree, and Yethulyn. There had been two more, when the journey had begun ten days before. One of those had been buried in a shallow grave, and the other, a Taneryn, had been burned on a pyre, as Taneryn customs dictated. It had been a struggle to gather enough dry wood in the unseasonal midsummer downpours. Andreyis knew that Ulemys would soon join them, as his gut-wound was smelling foul despite the serrins' medicines, and his deliriums grew worse. But for now, he could have the coat. It made the smell more bearable, for one thing.

At lunch an Enoran rider threw some bread, fruit, and cheese into the wagon, and they ate. Soon after, Andreyis decided he would rather walk, and slithered one-armed off the wagon and onto the muddy road. He had always liked to ride after a meal, but with horses unavailable, walking would do. He recalled now those afternoon rides at Kessligh and Sasha's ranch in the hills above Baerlyn, sometimes with Lynette or Sasha, sometimes alone, with always an eye out for game or intruders, or a sudden change in the weather across the rumpled, sprawling landscape of Lenayin.

He felt unutterably homesick. He had fought bravely at Shero Valley, but was now horrified at his own unmanliness when he awoke in sweating, heart-thumping horror in the dead of night, thinking the battle still raged about him. A prisoner on the trailing wagon swore that he'd seen Teriyan Tremel, Andreyis's good friend and father of fellow ranch-hand Lynette, fall upon the field. Worst of all, he was a prisoner, and still alive, when most Lenays would rather die than yield to such a fate. At times, Andreyis envied his comrade Ulemys. For him, at least, the torment would soon be over.

A serrin rider held to the side of the road, perhaps ten steps behind him as he walked. It was the girl again, the same girl who always rode guard along this stretch of the procession. With serrin, one could always tell. This girl had shocking red hair, swept back with a comb to one side and several odd braids, and sparkling blue eyes. She was pale, with a lean face and fine cheekbones, and utterly striking to look at. Several days ago, when Ulemys had been more aware, he'd cursed her when she'd given him food, and called her a demon, and thrown the food onto the muddy road. Andreyis knew better than to think the serrin demons, but he could see how a devout northern Verenthane like Ulemys might mistake her for one.

She carried a bow, strung at all times. That was not good for bows. Andreyis was fortunate amongst the Lenay prisoners that his legs were unhurt—it was his arm, and a blow to his head, now healing though tender. He wondered if he dared take on the girl's bow, and make a dash for passing woods, or perhaps try and knock her off her horse. He recalled Kessligh saying that serrin women tended not to favour the bow as much as men . . . ironic, as Lenay men considered archery an unmanly skill, that it was the serrin women who favoured swords instead. Serrin bows required great strength to draw. It was serrin swordwork, the svaalverd, that found more use in technique than muscle.

A Banneryd man two wagons ahead had tried to run on a wooded hillside the other day. Another serrin rider, a man, had shot him in the leg before he'd gone ten strides. For now, Andreyis bided his time. Walking at least would keep him from wasting away in the back of the wagon. Yet it was unnerving that the serrin did not mind, and did not insist the least-wounded prisoners be tied or restrained in any way. They merely held their distance, and kept their bows handy, as though daring the Lenays to try and run.

Camp that night was a village, and the wounded were given a barn. As one of the few able to walk freely, Andreyis assisted the movement of those who were less fortunate from the wagons to the straw. Some of the Enorans helped too. These were mostly older men, in mail and armed with long swords, which Enoran soldiers rarely used. They were Enoran militia, some Lenays had surmised—formerly soldiers of the Steel, now retired, but mobilised to assist on less vital matters such as the transportation of prisoners. No match for a Lenay warrior in single combat, Andreyis was certain, but they were all armed and healthy, where every Lenay carried an injury. And they were smart, and experienced, and not about to let their guard down. Andreyis wondered what his little band could even do, if they did somehow manage to wrest control of the column away from their captors, and arm themselves. They were deep into Enora now, halfway to the capital Shemorane. There would be no hiding from ordinary Enorans, some of whom were also former Steel, and many of whom had horses. Soon the Lenays would be run down by reinforcements, and all pretence at civilised conduct toward prisoners in wartime would surely cease.

Andreyis took a place by the barn door, nearest the draught, and ate the food that the Enorans brought to them from the cooking fires outside. Militiamen talked with local villagers by the barn doors as the prisoners ate, the villagers peering in with curious eyes. Neither Andreyis nor any of his comrades understood more than a few words of Enoran, but it seemed clear what the villagers were saying.

"So these are the fearsome men of Lenayin." A few of them joked with the militiamen, stifling laughter. Clearly they were not so intimidated, and made jokes at the Lenays' expense. Andreyis knew that he ought to be angered, but he could not muster the energy.

After the meal, the serrin began their rounds of the wounded. Some men allowed treatment, now accustomed to this evening ritual. Others refused, and the serrin simply gave medicines to their comrades for them to apply. There appeared to be six serrin in the column, Andreyis reckoned. Four seemed old; two definitely were, and two more moved as though they might be—with serrin it was often hard to tell. The last two seemed young. One was a tall lad with hair so black it shaded, astonishingly, toward blue. The other was the red-haired girl.

She knelt before him now, as he looked up in surprise, lost in thought with his back to a hay bale. "Show me your arm."

Andreyis showed it to her. She unwrapped it and checked the splints. The forearm had fractured, but would heal well enough in time. Her hands were firm, but caused little pain.

"You walk like one accustomed to riding," the girl said as she worked. She spoke Torovan, Andreyis's only second tongue.

"I ride," said Andreyis.

"Horses are expensive in Lenayin," said the girl, dubiously.

"Are you calling me a liar?"

The girl snorted, and said nothing. The angle of her chin suggested . . . contempt. Her eyes were cool. Andreyis realised that she was very young. He had nineteen summers. She might be considerably younger than that.

"How old are you?" he asked.

"Seventeen," said the girl. Andreyis knew from Sasha and Kessligh's tales how fast some serrin grew up. There was no reason not to believe her.

"That's why they make you guard prisoners," he guessed. "Instead of doing anything exciting."

"Exciting," she said scornfully, rewrapping his arm. "Were you excited in battle? Does all this suffering excite you?"

"We're not barbarians."

"Hmph," said the girl, utterly unconvinced. "I'm sure you don't even think a woman should be performing these duties."

"For a serrin," Andreyis said drily, "you seem awfully certain of things you can't know. One of my best friends is a girl who could best your entire column single-handed should she come to rescue us."

The serrin girl frowned at him, finishing her wrapping. And sat back on her heels for a moment. "You're that one." Andreyis just looked at her. "The friend of Sashandra Lenayin." She said something in Saalsi, and to Andreyis's amazement, looked a little flustered. "I am *as'shin sath*," she explained, a little awkwardly. "You have made me . . ." She waved a hand, searching for the right word, and slightly embarrassed that it eluded her.

"Wrong?" Andreyis offered.

The girl frowned. Then shrugged. "Perhaps," she conceded. "Though it is *yilen'eth*. Indelicate."

"But accurate."

The girl rolled her eyes in exasperation. "You argue like my brother. What kind of a girl is Sashandra Lenayin?"

Andreyis frowned. It seemed an odd question, from a serrin. "Most serrin seem to know all about her. You didn't know I was her friend, though you knew her friend was in this column. And you know nothing about her."

"And?" the girl challenged, eyebrows arched.

"I'd heard serrin were curious."

The girl's eyes flashed. "I'd heard humans were arrogant. You seem to presume that my lack of interest in you or your friend is some kind of failing."

Andreyis found himself smiling, just a little. "You really do think we're barbarians, don't you?"

"So?" she said, defensively. "You march halfway across Rhodia to attack Enora, you fight in the service of bloodthirsty murderers, and your culture seems to love nothing but war."

"And how much of Lenay culture do you know?" Andreyis retorted.

"Deny to me that Lenays love war!"

Andreyis shrugged. "I can't. But we also love music and dancing, and good food and family and weddings . . . you shouldn't judge a people so narrowly."

"When that narrowness threatens my people's very existence, I see no reason why not," the girl snapped. "Your arm is fine, it should heal straight and you can take off the splints in another five days." She got up. "*My* people have a love of healing, even our enemies."

Andreyis sighed, and leaned his head back against the hay. "Thanks," he murmured, and closed his eyes. "If you only knew how much I'd rather we fought with you than against you."

He opened his eyes to watch her walk away, but found instead that she was crouching once more, staring at him. She'd heard him. "Why don't you?" she asked him, faintly horrified. As though she simply did not understand.

Andreyis felt very sad. "I don't know," he murmured. "Perhaps we're barbarians."

The girl looked disgusted. And confused. And . . . she got up, and stood over him, looking very odd indeed.

"What's your name?" Andreyis thought to ask.

"Yshel," said the girl.

"I'm Andreyis."

Yshel stared a moment longer. Then shook her head in disbelief, and stalked off.

Three

At midday the Lenay column paused at a lake. Sasha dismounted, removed her boots, and, barefoot, led her horse into the shallow water. As the gelding drank, she looked about at the shore. Upon the far bank, fields climbed a slope to a village on the crest. To the right and west, a stream meandered to the lake edge, framed by an old stone arch. To the left and east, virgin forest, lovely green and dappled shade.

Men and horses joined her in the shallow water, hooves churning the shallows. Damon left his horse to another man, and stood on the lakeside talking with Jaryd . . . some matter of politics, Sasha presumed. Today Damon was aggravated that the Great Lord of Ranash would not hold his place in the column, and instead wandered to pursue rumours of serrin in the nearby hills. Yesterday, Damon had been upset that the Great Lord of Yethulyn refused to discipline several of his men for the killing of a villager who had insulted one of them. Sasha was certain the true source of Damon's frustrations lay elsewhere, and left Jaryd to deal with him. Better him than her.

She removed her bandoleer, and then her jacket, and hung them on her saddle horn. She stooped to wash her arms and face in the cold water. The chill was lovely, and reminded her of Lenayin.

Something hit the water in front of her, and splashed her, startling her horse. Sasha turned in suspicion and saw nearby her youngest brother Myklas, closest to her of a new group of riders. He tucked his thumbs in his belt and looked nonchalantly elsewhere. But several men were grinning, which gave the game away.

Sasha pulled a rotting piece of wood from the lake bed and threw it at him. It hit before the young prince, showering him with water.

He looked aggrieved. "What was that for?"

Sasha gave him a warning look, and went back to washing. She was in no mood for play. Myklas splashed over to her. He had celebrated his seventeenth birthday just last week, muted and solemn though the celebration had been. Not yet at his full height, he would never grow so tall as Damon, nor so broad as Koenyg. But to hear the Hadryn tell it, he would soon surpass both as a warrior, if he had not already. It was Hadryn he rode with now, pale men in black cloth and armour astride big horses, the famed northern cavalry of Lenayin.

"Sister, I'm wet," said Myklas as he approached.

"Oh, the injustice."

"I demand recompense."

Sasha ignored him. Though now a blooded warrior, Myklas still found the world a game. Perhaps he felt he could recapture an earlier innocence. Sasha wondered how long it would be until he discovered he could not.

Myklas sighed, sensing her mood, and put an arm about her shoulders. "How do you heal?" he asked.

"Well enough," said Sasha. "Even the scars are fading."

"Let me feel," said Myklas. It was hardly the place for it, with men all about watering their horses, but Sasha had long ago decided that the moment she demanded ladylike exceptions from these men, they would put her in the rear and suggest she exchange her sword for an embroidery needle. She unlaced the front of her shirt, pulling it back to her throat so that the collar fell down her shoulders. Myklas put his hand down her back, and felt at the old scars.

A month ago, those had been terrible, great welts and scabs from cuts, canes, and burns. Now, Myklas's hand felt only faint unevenness on her skin.

"No pain?" he asked her.

"It's odd," she admitted. "The new skin feels too sensitive, almost sore. The burn marks are the worst." Those had been from a red-hot poker. She'd killed the man who'd done it, but not the one who'd ordered it done. There was great competition amongst her brothers and friends to be the one who severed that man's head . . . after perhaps several limbs, and various other appendages. "But no, no pain."

"It would take more than a dozen torturers to leave a mark on you," said Myklas. He withdrew his hand, and put the arm back around her. Sasha sighed and rested her head on his shoulder. He was just now getting tall enough that she could do that. He kissed her on the head, put a foot behind her own feet, and tripped her over backward.

Sasha hit the water with a freezing splash, cursing herself for an idiot, but not at all surprised. She grabbed Myklas's legs, braced her feet, and drove a shoulder into him. He came down on top of her, and then they were both splashing and flailing in the water, her nearly gaining the upper hand to shove his head down, then he taking her arms and twisting her over sideways. Sasha got a knee into him, and a fistful of belt, but he was too strong and lithe, and grabbed her into a bear hug from which she could not escape.

"Victory!" Myklas yelled. "Victory for Lenayin!" Cheers and laughter came from the shore.

"I'm Lenayin too, you idiot!" she snarled at him, struggling vainly.

"We Lenays should fight each other more often!" Myklas laughed. "No matter the outcome, a Lenay always wins!"

"And one always loses," Sasha muttered, ceasing her struggles. Myklas picked her up and dumped her in the shallows. He was wise enough to escape quickly to avoid further retaliation, and walked up the lakeside with arms raised to the cheers of watching men.

Sasha picked herself up from the water. "Sparring tonight!" she demanded of him. "No pads!"

Myklas turned to give her a reproachful look. Lenays always wore pads when sparring, not from cowardice, but because sword practice, even with wooden stanches, was not something done with restraint. Without pads, one of them would get seriously hurt. All present knew it was not likely to be her.

"Sister, truly, there is no need for violence."

"Perish the day when a Lenay should say such a thing," Sasha retorted, to more cheers from the observers. Myklas laughed. He bowed to her, and walked off. He knew her temper, and knew not to take such threats seriously . . . when directed at *him*, at least.

Sasha sighed in disbelief and shook water from her hair like a dog. Her heart thumped hard from exertion, and the pleasure of a hard yet harmless contest. For the first time in a long time, she felt nearly . . . good. She smiled. Annoying, naive brat though he was, he knew how to cheer up his sister.

Behind Myklas, a line of Hadryn cavalry looked on. They seemed neither as impressed nor amused as she.

Sasha recovered her unnerved horse from the Isfayen man who held him and checked the animal for any sign of strain. As she did so, she noticed a new commotion on the shore, a rider in Bacosh colours dismounting amidst the royal party.

Sasha handed off her horse once more, reclaimed her sword, and splashed dripping from the lake—luckily the sun was bright and the sky clear, and in another hour she would be dry. Isfayen men gave her bemused looks as she passed, perhaps intrigued to see that the great Synnich-ahn was, after all, just a girl whose brothers treated her as poorly as any other.

She arrived at the conversation with the messenger, sword and bandoleer hitched over a soaked shoulder, and edged through the small crowd. Koenyg and Damon stood at the gathering's centre, talking to the Bacosh man.

"What's going on?" she asked shortly, with no qualms about interrupting the conversation. The messenger looked at her warily, eyeing sodden clothes and bedraggled hair.

"The Regent sends Sofy to Tracato," said Koenyg, less annoyed with her interruption than he might have been. "He offers for you to go with her, as a guardian." Sasha just looked at him. Koenyg waited until he realised he wasn't going to get a response. "I had thought to agree."

Sasha waved the messenger away. He looked affronted. Sasha stared at him, and adjusted the bandoleer on her shoulder. Koenyg scratched his forehead, and indicated the messenger to leave. Sasha considered waving the others away also, but they were Lenay great lords and officers, and would hear of this discussion anyhow. One could not just dismiss such men in Lenayin.

"No," Sasha said to Koenyg. "I won't go."

"I would like Sofy to have a protector," Koenyg replied, his gaze hard. "Wouldn't you?"

"Brother, if that nest of scorpions wishes Sofy or me or both of us dead, there is little we could do . . . unless you spare me twenty guards and an entire personal staff."

Koenyg frowned. "You think Sofy's life at risk from her own people?"

"*We* are her people," Sasha said firmly. "Her married family are not. The Army of the Bacosh is confident now they've won their major battle, they wonder if they need us anymore. Already they bicker over how they will divide these lands amongst themselves, and we are not party to any of that. We become a distraction, brother . . . and so the Regent sends Sofy to Tracato, to get her out of the way. And he'd love to have me out of the way too, no doubt."

"So important you've become in your own mind," Koenyg sighed, with faint disbelief.

Sasha did not bother replying. She had a following in the Army of Lenayin—she was Nasi-Keth, and some men's sympathies lay with the serrin. She did not wish to state so boldly what the leaders of the Army of the Bacosh feared from her, not here. No doubt they felt the Army of Lenayin would be a far more predictable ally beneath Koenyg's sole control, with Sashandra Lenayin elsewhere.

"I could order you to go," Koenyg suggested.

"You could order pigs to fly," Sasha said flatly. "Sofy is under more threat with me than without me; she doesn't need all my enemies coming after her as well. My place is here, with the Army of Lenayin."

"Fine," said Koenyg, dismissing her with a word. "Sofy will go to Tracato. I would send someone with her, though. I will think on it."

He walked off, and the small gathering dispersed.

Jaryd approached her and Damon, and beckoned them aside to the lake. "There is some word of resistance ahead," he said. "The Army of the Bacosh is beset by skirmishers; it seems their forward light cavalry suffer defeats."

"That will be Kessligh," Sasha said quietly.

Damon nodded. "Men of this army will not be happy to hear it."

"Some say Kessligh has betrayed Lenayin," said Jaryd.

"Others say Koenyg leads us on a fool's errand," Damon countered. "I do not like this mood the men are in. We are not only defeated, we doubt ourselves."

"Kessligh can't slow the entire Bacosh Army for long," said Sasha. "He's being a nuisance, buying time for the Rhodaani Steel to get back to Enora. But if he keeps it up, we'll be gaining on the Bacosh Army in a few days."

A silence followed. Gaining on the Army of the Bacosh would put the Army of Lenayin into direct conflict for the first time since the Battle of Shero Valley. Against forces led by Kessligh. Sasha looked at the ground. She wished she did not feel anything, that she could make herself like stone.

Damon left to attend to other matters. Jaryd remained with Sasha. Sasha guessed his thoughts.

"Sofy will be fine," she said quietly.

"You know I don't believe that," said Jaryd. Sasha gazed at him. There were four rings in his right ear now. His light brown hair was approaching collar length, haphazard about his face. In past weeks, he'd grown to become Damon's most trusted advisor, a young man who shared Damon's distaste for lordly pretension, and favoured the most direct solution to every problem.

"Yes," said Sasha, "but unlike you, I have concern only for her safety, not her chastity." Jaryd's look was reproachful. Sasha sighed. "I'm sorry. Jaryd, Koenyg must send a party of Lenays with Sofy to Tracato. It's the proper form, for an alliance between armies—Tracato is important, Lenayin should have representation. Would you like to go?"

"Is that wise?" Jaryd asked.

"Most people would think that a fine joke," Sasha said wryly. "You, asking that question of me."

Jaryd snorted. Then laughed, humourlessly. "I'll go if you tell me to," he said.

"Jaryd." Sasha stood close to him, and stared him in the eyes. "Do you love her?"

Jaryd looked away, across the lake, and sighed. "Woe befall me if I do."

A landless ex-lord could have no hope of consummating such a love, he meant. Such a man could throw his life away in pursuit of dangerous things that were beyond him by the gods' own law.

"Jaryd, Koenyg's right. Sofy would be safer with some protection, at least. Just not mine. And if not you, then who? Who would do it better?"

"When I was a young man," he said, "I thought women were the toys of men. Now I find they are our masters."

Sasha smiled. "Oh come, the world is not ending as fast as that, surely?"

The column resumed shortly after, Sasha taking her place with the Isfayen contingent in the vanguard. Great Lord Markan talked with an Isfayen scout, who spoke of a curious town several folds away that the Army of the Bacosh had passed through.

Ahead, the main vanguard climbed a small rise. Behind stretched the entire mass of the Army of Lenayin, tens of thousands strong. Finally, she grew tired of her own silence.

"Who would like to go for a ride?" she asked loudly. All Isfayen men in the group paused their conversations to look at her. Great Lord Markan broke off his discussion with the scout, and wondered at this curious humour. "Our scout tells us of a village, just over the hill yonder. I would like to see it."

"The Bacosh forces occupy it," countered an Isfayen lord. They had won their battle, he meant. Lenayin had lost its. Lenayin now suffered the shame of marching second in the column, and the Bacosh forces gained the privilege to occupy whatever town they liked.

"Nice day for a ride," said Markan, squinting up at the sun. "What do you think, sister?"

"I tire of staring at the backsides of Rayen horses," said Yasmyn.

Markan nodded, and gave a signal. Isfayen horses wove to the right, then accelerated to keep pace with their lord. In the main column, surprised faces looked across at them. At the column head, Sasha saw Koenyg, similarly surprised. He made a gesture, and someone pursued.

Koenyg's rider came racing across in front of them, signalling them to stop. Markan only smiled, long black hair and braids flying, and galloped his horse a little faster.

"What the hells are you doing?" Sasha heard Koenyg's rider yell above the noise. "The king orders you to fall back in line!"

"Isfayen tire of marching in line," Markan said cheerfully. "We shall return shortly."

"You shall return at once!" yelled the rider.

Markan's stare informed the rider that if there had been any chance the Great Lord of Isfayen could be persuaded to turn around, it was now gone. The rider slowed up in frustration, and the Isfayen thundered on.

Soon the pace slowed, and they rode across fields between small farmhouses. Tall hills rose in the near distance, with sheer, dark cliffs that reminded Sasha of Lenayin. Further along the hillside rise there perched a village, emerging above trees and orchards that covered the hills. As they came closer up the road, Sasha saw why the scout had found the town curious— there were larger buildings here than the typical little cottages. One was a temple, with grand spires. Several others appeared to be clustered together, and boasted ornamental spires or crenellations.

The approaching road wound through orchards as it climbed, and finally arrived at the gates of the town walls. As they rode within, Sasha began to recognise the buildings. "These are like the Tol'rhen in Tracato," she said. On the walls were friezes of men building things and consulting maps. And on plinths within the walls, statues of learned men, and a woman. The woman was Maldereld, the serrin general who had led Saalshen's conquest of these lands two centuries before, and ordered the construction of these great institutions of learning. "Only far smaller than Tracato."

Soldiers had been here. The statue of Maldereld was faceless, stonework smashed with deliberate effort.

"What manner of place?" asked an Isfayen, frowning up at the high walls as they rode.

"A place of learning," Sasha replied. "Students come here from across the lands, to learn skills for their people. Medicines, building, farming, languages, history."

"Fighting?" asked another man.

"Yes, these are Nasi-Keth," said Sasha. "They learn to fight like me." And the men of Isfayen looked far more impressed to learn that, and considered the walls with renewed respect.

A search of the buildings' echoing halls revealed signs of fast departure, and no sign of life. But an Isfayen lord's intrusion in the temple revealed signs of recent activity.

"There is blood on the paving," he said grimly. "Pews have been overturned, and rear rooms searched. There are wagon tracks outside and hoofmarks. There was food left in the temple, and blankets . . . I think perhaps someone was using it as a refuge."

He handed Markan a wooden doll, with a head of long horses' hair intricately embedded in the wood. A child's toy.

"Someone did not leave fast enough," Yasmyn said solemnly. Sasha looked away, biting her lip. Like stone, she told herself. Be like stone. Yasmyn tucked the doll into a pouch at her belt.

"The tracks lead away, quite fresh," said the lord who had discovered it. "We can catch whoever made them, I'm sure."

"Interesting," said Markan with a nod. "I should like to see this latest conquest of our grand allies, against a ferocious, doll-wielding foe."

Some of the men smiled or laughed at that. Sasha did not. Nor, with a concerned look her way, did Yasmyn.

The road from town led them toward the looming cliffs seen earlier. These odd tombs of rock seemed incongruous with the surrounding green landscape of gentle hills. The Isfayen scout followed the trail easily enough, and soon informed them all that a wagon party lay ahead.

They came to it on a rutted trail by a stream. There were four wagons, accompanied by ten men on horse. All wore the colour and armour of Bacosh warriors, and peering now behind them at the Isfayen's approach, they seemed relieved but wary.

"We thought you might be serrin!" one horseman shouted back at them in Torovan, which Sasha, Markan, and Yasmyn alone of their group understood. "We're making double time to reach the column, don't want to be caught out here past nightfall!"

Markan rode forward. Sasha could see men with crossbows peering from the rear flaps of the wagons. The Bacosh horsemen seemed wary too, of this big man with slanted eyes and flowing hair, clad in patterned leather, chain armour, and steel-studded gloves. The curved sword drew many looks to his side. One did not need to talk to an Isfayen warrior to know his nature, one needed only look.

"You come from the town back there?" Markan asked, pointing back the way they'd ridden.

The horseman nodded. "Weird place, yes? Too many damn weird places in this land, I'll be happy to get home to Meraine, myself." He looked at them with some suspicion. "I bet you Lenays don't find it so weird, though? Men say you folks don't mind the serrin?"

"In Isfayen we've had little to do with them," said Markan.

"Ah," said the horseman. "Isfayen." Clearly he had no idea where that was. In most of the lowlands, a Lenay barbarian was a Lenay barbarian, no matter what region.

"What manner of soldiers are you?" Markan asked, with clear disdain.

"Men-at-arms," came the reply. "Tasked with foraging."

"Foraging what?" Sasha asked.

The horseman stared at her, only now seeming to notice her presence. He blinked rapidly, perhaps realising who she was.

"Things," he said defensively. "Food. Supplies."

"Mind if I look?" Sasha asked.

"It's ours!" scowled the horseman. He backed up his horse, clearly worried. His reaction made her cold. If he recognised her, Sasha reckoned, he no doubt knew something of her conflicted allegiances.

Like stone, she told herself. Like the hard granite of the looming cliffs.

The crossbowmen in the back of the wagon were readying their weapons, as horsemen along the column grasped at the hilts of their blades.

"There are a handful of you," Markan said contemptuously. "There are many of us. We are the Isfayen, the bloodwarriors of the western mountains, and all Lenayin has feared us since we first walked in the world. I think it best that you let us look."

The horseman thought about it. A nervous shifting passed along the wagon column. Then the horseman backed up, and crossbowmen leaped from the back of the wagon.

"There was a bounty," the horseman explained nervously. "A gold piece each. We just wanted to bring something back to our families."

Sasha dismounted, strode to the back of the wagon, and threw open the rear flap.

The wagon was filled with small bodies. Little shapes, arms and legs askew, entangled in dreadful heaps. She saw little faces, and widened eyes. Saw a flash of inhuman colour, the gleam of serrin sight. Crossbred children. Part human, part serrin, like her good friend Aisha. Like she and Errollyn would have had, given the chance, and the assurance that their offspring would not end up like this, piled in some forager's cart like . . .

The wagon floor was awash with blood. The smell was dreadful.

Sasha did not know how she hit the ground, but suddenly her knees were gone, and she was curled against the wagon wheel, her body torn with sobs. From the Isfayen behind her, there was consternation. Markan dismounted and peered into the wagon. And cursed in shock.

Then Yasmyn, who said nothing when she looked, but her grip on Sasha's arm when she crouched at her side was painfully tight. Other Isfayen lords came to look, now guessing the wagon's contents, but horrified all the same.

"Sasha," said Yasmyn, perhaps as distressed to see the great Synnich-ahn curled and sobbing like a child as she was at the wagon itself. She put a hand to Sasha's face, eyes pleading her to stop. Sasha barely noticed. She had tried to make herself like stone, but stone was not her nature. She was water, free and wild, and she could not bear this weight.

She could not be a party to this. Her land and her people were all she had that remained, and she marched with them into the very gates of Loth . . . but she could not be a party to this. She would rather die. She *had* to die. She had no other choices left.

A time passed, and Sasha was barely aware that the men of the column had been rounded up, and the other wagons searched. Men about her muttered of an orphanage, a special place for abandoned children of mixed blood.

They must have been late to leave, they said, and taken refuge in the temple, praying that their gods would save them. Sasha sat against the rear wheel, face in her hands, and wished the world would end.

"Sasha," came Markan's voice at her side, more gentle than she'd ever heard him. "Synnich-ahn. We have found one alive."

Sasha raised her tear-streaked face and looked at him. Then another lord came, carrying a bundle that he placed on the road beside her. It was a little boy, perhaps six years old. His face was pale, yet his eyes were sharp, emerald green. Like Errollyn's.

Sasha gazed at him. The boy seemed sightless, and Sasha wondered if he were blind. But she passed a hand before his face, and he blinked, and moved back a little.

"Hello there," she murmured, in Torovan. "What's your name?" There was no reply. Torovan was a tongue learned at later ages, if at all. Most likely the boy spoke Rhodaani . . . and perhaps one other. "What is your name?" Sasha tried again, this time in Saalsi, the language of the serrin.

The boy blinked at her, as though noticing her for the first time. Sasha nodded.

"I do speak that tongue," she told him quietly. "I see you know a little."

The boy's green eyes shimmered with tears. Sasha hugged him before the sight of his face could make her lose control again. She held him tight, as Isfayen about them wondered at the location of a grave and what to do for a ceremony.

"What do we do with the prisoners?" one man asked Markan. Markan made a gesture of thumb across throat, as careless as a man might decide to cast away food gone bad. The other nodded, and left to do that.

"Ask them who demands the bounty," Yasmyn called after that man. "If he will not answer, make it slow."

Sasha picked up the boy, and carried him away from the wagons. He was not going to watch this, nor the burial of his friends.

"Will you tell me your name?" she tried again as she walked.

"Tomli," came a faint murmur against her ear.

"Well, Tomli," she said, still in Saalsi, "I have an idea. Likely it will get all of us killed, and destroy the Army of Lenayin. But it's the best idea I have, because it is the only thing I'm still certain is right."

The more she thought about it, the more certain she became. She climbed the slope off the road, to gain a view of the cliffs, and wait for her party to ride once more.

Four

Burying even little bodies took time, when one took proper care. By the time the Isfayen returned to the column, dusk was falling, and the Army of Lenayin had halted to prepare its nighttime defences, and distribute the day's foraged food.

Sasha carried Tomli before her on the saddle, and cared not how many men stared at the pair of them in passing. She left her horse at the stable of the farmhouse commandeered for the night's lordly retreat, and took Tomli inside to the washroom. There she booted out several lords, and set about seeing Tomli washed, well aware of the building commotion outside the washroom door. She emerged only once to ask if anyone had clean children's clothes, and a search of the farmhouse did bring a clean pair of breeches and a shirt down to the washroom door. They were a little too big, but Sasha rolled up the pants, made cuffs of the sleeves, and wondered if some skill in much-despised needlework might not be useful after all.

Then she emerged, ushering Tomli before her, into a main room full of Lenay captains, lords, two princes, and one king. Lamps lit the wooden floors and smooth stone walls, and food lay arrayed upon a long table. The men were all in sombre conversation, knowing what lay within the washroom, and awaiting its emergence.

Koenyg now rose from an armchair, and conversation trailed away to silence.

"Markan told me," said Koenyg. Markan stood nearby. "How is the boy?"

"Traumatised," said Sasha. "His name is Tomli. He is five, and he speaks Rhodaani and some Saalsi. He was born to a single mother who gave him to an orphanage. Saalshen keeps them well funded, Tomli seemed happy enough there."

The horror of it nearly stole her sanity once more. She swallowed hard.

"A Verenthane orphanage?" asked the Great Lord of Rayen, curiously.

"I think," said Sasha, nodding. "He said he was cared for by priests. He called them all Papa."

"Those men you found did a grave crime," Koenyg said grimly, "and their punishment was just. But from now on, all Lenays shall stay within the column. We cannot be enforcing our laws onto every criminal act. Enmities between the Free and the Saalshen Bacosh are two centuries old, and there will be many crimes. It cannot be our place to intervene, and strain the allegiance further."

"The Black Order of Larosa placed a bounty upon the heads of all serrin and half-breed children," Sasha said quietly. "Word passes across the land. What we saw was not a crime. It was policy."

Koenyg's stare darkened. "Sister, I will not have you sow dissension against our Verenthane allies. . . ."

"I state only fact," said Sasha. "Ask Markan to deny it." No one looked at Markan. To question the Great Lord of Isfayen's honesty was not wise. "And brother, I cannot be party to any army that supports such acts. These are our allies, and they murder children by the wagonload. Little girls and little boys like Tomli." Her hand was firm on Tomli's shoulder. Even in the face of this fearsome gathering of strangers, Tomli did not flinch or shake. He had seen far worse than this. "I do not appeal to your sympathy. I appeal to your honour. There is honour in victory against warriors in battle. To murder small children for gold . . ."

She gazed at each of them in turn. Men met her eyes for a moment, then looked aside. Others would not look at all. She did not complete that last sentence. She could not. For even the rough men of Lenayin, there were no words.

Save for the northerners. The Hadryn, the Ranash, and the Banneryd stood to their own, separate side of the room, and stared with unflinching calm. With them stood Myklas, frowning.

"I recall that you have played this game before," said the Great Lord Heryd of Hadryn. He was a wall of a man, blond, tall, and undecorated. Pure, in the image of his faith. "In the rebellion, you used orphan children to tug at the hearts of nobles and ladies in Baen-Tar."

"Not orphan children, Lord Heryd," Sasha told him, unblinkingly. "They currently reside with their parents in the Udalyn Valley. Their parents live, thanks to me, and your glorious defeat at my hands."

Lord Heryd steamed. Great Lord Rydysh of Ranash muttered an insult in his native tongue that Sasha did not understand.

"We do not speak of past conflicts," Koenyg said sharply. "Each part of Lenayin has fought each other part of Lenayin so many times in history, and our losses and grievances outnumber the stars. Here we are one army, and we will not sacrifice future glories on the altar of past hatreds."

There was nothing "past" about this hatred, and they all knew it. The north was not merely Verenthane—they were devout, and pure. Most Lenay provinces rode in this battle for the allegiance of the great Verenthane lowland powers, and the promised future glory of Lenayin. But the north rode for the sheer religious pleasure of smiting evil, and in northern opinion, that evil had gleaming eyes and oddly coloured hair. They did not care if ten thousand half-breed children were murdered, they were going to heaven, climbing on the piled corpses of the serrin race.

"She has sung this tune before," Lord Heryd repeated. "One orphan child proves nothing, save that she has few new ideas for luring strong men with women's cowardice."

"Every time the likes of you go to war," Sasha told him, "helpless children escape your slaughter to fall into my hands. The only thing proved is that you lot would rather kill children than warriors."

Koenyg had to intervene, physically, as Lord Heryd stepped forward quickly, a hand to his hilt.

"Do it," Sasha invited him. "Draw the blade. I've killed so many of you northern lords. Let's make it one more. See if your gods punish me worse than they did when I killed the others."

Silence followed in the room. The northerners hated her, but they were no longer stupid enough to challenge her. They knew her to be a hothead, prone to shouting and rash displays of temper. Now, she did not shout. Her words were clipped, firm, and calculated.

Amongst the nobility of Lenayin, it was occurring to Sasha, an unchallengeable duellist possessed a frightening advantage not merely in blades, but in debate as well. One dared not push her too hard, for duelling was the law, and cowardice as fatal as death itself. The men in the room feared not for their lives; they feared for their honour, and that of their families. They feared that here was a girl who could twist them to her will and, if they retaliated in anger, issue a challenge they could not win.

Such a woman could become a queen. A terrible one.

Sasha had no doubt they'd kill her first, honourably or not.

"I will take the boy," said Koenyg. He came to Sasha. "I will see that he is . . ."

Sasha drew her sword, and took her opening stance, blade at quarter check behind her head, raised for the strike. Koenyg stopped.

"Any man," said Sasha, "who attempts to remove this boy from me shall die. Tomorrow, I shall demand before this army that the priests of the Black Order be brought to account for their actions, and their bounty upon the heads of half-castes be withdrawn. *Selith'en to tamathy, elish'an so valth'mal rae, y'seth lan as'far.*" Evil grows in the dark, while good men lie, and snuff out the light. It was a saying well known in Saalsi. None present understood it, yet the mere fact of Saalsi spoken proudly in this room caused more eyes to widen.

Sasha grasped Tomli's hand and strode from the room, out into the night. Markan followed.

"Well that you bed with the Isfayen tonight," he said. "Even the great Synnich-ahn cannot defeat foes in her sleep."

"Very well," Sasha agreed, following Markan's lead to the Isfayen camp.

"And better still should you bed with me tonight," Markan added.

Sasha glanced at him in surprise. Then smiled. "I shall be the death of us all, Markan."

"I know," said Markan, a gleam in his eye. "It is arousing."

Sasha sighed, and grasped little Tomli's hand more firmly.

She was awoken that night by a kick at her boot. Her eye flicked that way, unalarmed, despite the sudden grasp of her hand for the knife beneath the bundled cloak she used for a pillow. It was the safe way to wake a warrior, when nerves were on edge in the constant nighttime harassment of the serrin.

A dark figure crouched by her boots, backlit by the orange glow of coals.

"Sasha," Damon murmured. Sasha turned to look and found Tomli, sleeping soundly alongside. She did not know how he slept. Perhaps it was exhaustion, or shock.

Sasha patted the thin bedroll, and shifted over for Damon. He slid in alongside her, an arm about her shoulders. It was no longer just affection between them, but habit. They had not been close for most of their lives, Sasha and Prince Damon, but lately that had changed. It was nice to have family, that was all. And Sasha thought of her sister Alythia, murdered in Tracato. She embraced her brother, and put her head on his chest.

"I know what you're doing," Damon said quietly.

"I'm glad one of us does," said Sasha.

"Don't play the fool with me," Damon replied, but there was no anger in his words. "This is very dangerous, Sasha. Koenyg will not allow it. Nor will the northerners, nor most of the lords."

"I know," said Sasha. What was left of the fire crackled, and about it men snored. The camp seemed calm, and Sasha did not think they had been attacked tonight. "It's this or die, Damon. By my own hand. I can't live with this, and I don't think much of this column can either, once they know what's happening."

"Koenyg is trying to stop them from learning," said Damon.

"I know. But the king's power to prevent the men of Lenayin from knowing what they know has always been limited." Sasha looked up at him. "Can *you* live with it?"

Damon said nothing for a moment, staring at the stars. Then he shook his head. Sasha guessed his thoughts, and what remained unsaid—however much he hated the situation, he did not know that he could stand up to Koenyg either.

"Sasha," Damon murmured finally. "What would you have us do?"

"Switch sides," said Sasha. From Damon's sigh beneath her cheek, she registered his unhappiness.

"It's always that simple with you," he murmured with exasperation.

"I'm only interested in the destination, Damon. You worry too much for the state of the road."

"If all you watch is your destination," said Damon, "you may fail to notice the ravine that has opened between you and it."

"Build a bridge," said Sasha.

Damon pinched her ear. Sasha jabbed his ribs.

"It'll tear the Army of Lenayin apart," said Damon.

Sasha raised herself from his chest and stared at him. "Damon," she said firmly, "who fucking cares?" Damon gazed at her. Dumbly. "Who would take their side, if all who share our sympathies come with us?"

Damon thought about it. The north. The nobility . . . or many of them. He nodded, slowly. They were not people Damon wanted on his side any more than Sasha did. But . . .

"Koenyg," he said. "And our father's memory. His spirit. This was his war. . . ."

"It was Koenyg's," Sasha snorted. "Father believed that the fates would show him the way, and the gods watch over us. All the actual decision making he left to Koenyg."

"The purpose of this war was to unite all of Lenayin within a common cause," Damon said stubbornly. "We've fought each other for all history, this is the first time we've fought all together, on a foreign campaign. . . ."

"Aye, for the glory of a faith less than half the population shares," Sasha interrupted. "Damon, you're arguing like Sofy—she always thinks it's better to make peace and bring people together. What about the men who murdered those children? Would you like to make peace with them? Forge a common destiny? Me, I say any common destiny with people like that is a destiny not worth having. I'd rather see their heads on pikes."

"Or yours on one," Damon warned.

"Yes," Sasha agreed, adamantly. "Better that, too."

"And what of the great Verenthane alliance that would sustain Lenayin for centuries to come?"

"What of it?" Sasha asked. "When did either of us believe in that? That Lenayin needed civilising, needed to become more like the lowlands? Those were always the dreams of men who never *liked* Lenayin, those whose greatest hope for their homeland was that we should become like someone else.

"Damon, the great hope of lowlands alliance is not the Verenthane faith. It's the serrin, it always was. . . . This . . . this land we invade, it's not perfect, but there is so much here that they got right. *This* is what we should be copying—education, tolerance, the abolition of the special rights of nobility, equal laws for all, the creation of wealth and trade. . . ."

"Wait, wait." Damon looked at her grimly. "These are the people who tortured you and murdered Alythia, and . . ."

"Some of them," Sasha agreed. "Not all."

"And even little Tomli was abandoned by his mother," Damon persisted. "Are things so perfect here that . . ."

"Not perfect, no! But that's the point, Damon, the starting point is that we all must accept that humanity is not perfect, and never will be."

"Any civilisation inspired by the serrin will never make an empire," Damon said with certainty. "And only empires are any use to us, in allegiance. We're too far away, otherwise. This war is only worth the price for Lenayin if we gain in trade, or materials, or treaties of common interest. Grand treaties with hermit kingdoms do us naught, we'd do better to invade them ourselves and gain their benefits directly."

"We'll see," said Sasha. "If the Saalshen Bacosh survives this, they'll have had an awful shock. They never thought they'd lose, and for two centuries they were right. Kessligh has argued for a long time that they should have expanded, instead of simply ceding ground and time upon which their enemies can grow stronger. If they see the other side of this, they may well see Kessligh proven right."

Damon thumped his head back upon Sasha's improvised pillow. "It's all fantasy talk anyhow," he murmured. "If, when and maybe. We're just two people, dreaming at the stars."

"From such beginnings do civilisations spring," said Sasha.

Damon looked at her for a moment. "You really are Nasi-Keth, aren't you?"

"I think I may be," Sasha said quietly.

A moment later, Damon got up and left, leaving Sasha to gaze at the stars.

"They will not attack tonight," said Tomli, a small, Saalsi voice at Sasha's side. Sasha rolled over and looked at him. "Who will not attack?"

"The serrin." Tomli gazed into the night, his emerald eyes distant. It seemed to Sasha that he was listening to something that only he could hear. "They know you have an *en'vel'ennar* with you."

"One with *vel'ennar*," that meant. It was the serrin collective "we." A consciousness shared by all serrin, and unknown to humans. When Sasha had first learned of it, she had assumed the meaning was figurative or poetic. Serrin were frequently poetic, as was the Saalsi tongue. But experience had taught her to doubt whether the *vel'ennar* was quite that simple.

"Tomli," she murmured. "Can you hear them?"

Tomli shook his head. "I feel them. They are sad."

"Because you are sad?" Sasha asked. Tomli nodded.

"And because so many of us are *tuan'sli*." There was no direct translation in any tongue Sasha knew. "*Tuani*," Saalsi for "phrase." Or "words," but more than words. Elided to "*esli*," meaning "to move beyond," but not physically. To move as thoughts moved. Or as conversations shifted, from one topic to another.

Tuan'sli . . . to move beyond words? To shift from the realm of the living to dreams unknown? Serrin had more euphemisms for death, and indeed most things, than Sasha knew in all other tongues.

"They'll have found the graves," Sasha murmured, mostly to herself. Serrin finding those graves would know what had happened. Though Sasha suspected that somehow, through Tomli, they'd have known anyhow.

It was a mixed formation that plunged toward the Bacosh camp, Rhodaani cavalry in the middle, with serrin *talmaad* on the flanks. Errollyn found little joy in the ride down the wild hillside toward the pocket of wood below, and the camp nestled within. His attention was fixed solely upon the further ridge, where the land rose up above the Bacosh camp.

Errollyn cast a glance across to the head of the formation, where Kessligh crouched low before a charging mass of Rhodaani cavalry. There were nearly a hundred and fifty in all, much to the displeasure of General Geralin, who remained furious at Kessligh for using so much of their precious strength on "needless diversions." Kessligh's stare seemed also focused upon the far ridge. Kessligh had fought and won entire campaigns in the highlands of Lenayin, and if anyone could judge mountainous terrain, he could.

Below, the pocket of trees grew closer. Errollyn glimpsed tents amidst the trees, and moving horses, and steel. He waved his left arm out, indicating the line he wished the *talmaad* to establish to that side.

With perhaps five hundred human paces to go, horses began crashing through the trees of the camp below. They came pouring out, in their tens and twenties, heavily armoured and in the full colours of armoured house cavalry.

An ambush. The trees had hidden far more men than the camp at first appeared to hold. Kessligh swung away to the right, the formation following him, as though startled. Errollyn followed, his left flank trailing behind, now forming a line-astern, archers firing left across their bodies as they raked across the advancing Bacosh line. Arrows streaked downhill, aiming mainly for horses. Animals fell, and men with them, but the mass was now turning to follow—slower, and hindered by the slope, but determined and furious, yelling and waving swords.

Kessligh's formation rounded the woods and smashed through some riders who had emerged on the far side. Bacosh men were cut tumbling from their horses, whilst others reined back downslope, and more sensibly awaited the strength of their pursuing friends.

Only now, with a new roar, there emerged atop the far ridge a new mass of Bacosh riders, plunging down the boulder-strewn slope to the right. Not merely an ambush, but a trap.

Had Kessligh been right about that slope? Errollyn stared above the heads of the racing Rhodaanis, and watched the descending wall of Bacosh cavalry. Too many rocks, had been Kessligh's opinion.

The Rhodaanis thought now only of speed, and hurtled across the bottom of the valley with the *talmaad* at their rear, determined to pass the base of the rocky slope before the descending Bacosh cavalry did. Behind, Errollyn's *talmaad* spread out, turning to loose arrows at the first pursuing group, making more horses tumble. Errollyn galloped past the foot of the slope just as the cavalry reached the bottom on his right, and made sharp turns to follow them. The first group of pursuers wove across the valley floor to avoid them, and then there was a great, galloping wall of riders behind. They fell back a little in the face of deadly accurate archery from the *talmaad* ahead, but not too far.

Kessligh's formation rounded a bend in the valley, holding to the right of the small stream that emerged from trees to the left . . . and ahead, Errollyn could see the valley narrowing sharply, with small cliffs and thick trees, impossible for the rapid passage of so many cavalry. The first in their formation could ride into that and escape, but the rest would be held up waiting while the big, heavily armoured formation behind chopped them to pieces.

The Bacosh men roared in triumph, and spread out further for the final charge. They did not at first notice the sudden increase in arrow fire into their front and then their flanks. Until suddenly the smattering of arrow fire increased to a deadly rain, now felling men more often than horses, with the confidence that came with advantage. Errollyn could see the horror on the riders' faces, as they realised that the entire valley was bristling with serrin archers. The Bacosh formation reined to a halt, milling and spinning to face the new threat that poured onto them from the narrow valley's forested hillsides. Errollyn reined up his own formation also, and they turned back to join in the volleys of fire.

Yells and commands echoed off the valley sides, and Bacosh men split their formation to go charging up the slopes, and in amongst the trees on one side, and across the stream and up the far slope on the other. The *talmaad* cavalry positioned and waiting, evaded before them, abandoning the protection of the trees on lighter, more nimble-footed mounts. Heavier Bacosh cavalry chased them, only to find themselves under fire from serrin standing or half seated on tree roots, calmly shooting one man after another off his horse, bodies tumbling back the way they'd come.

Surviving Bacosh cavalry plunged back down from the murderous slopes, and clustered once more on the valley floor, milling in panicked groups. Others chased serrin *talmaad* in circles, the *talmaad* dodging aside like naughty children teasing some slower, dimwitted child. Then bows would twang, and another man would fall, then several at a time.

Suddenly there were too few targets, and any surviving Bacosh cavalry were retreating rapidly up the valley, with more *talmaad* in pursuit. Errollyn found himself alongside a Rhodaani officer, who looked utterly astonished at the ease and speed of the victory. Before him, the valley floor was littered with arrow-spiked bodies, and bewildered, riderless horses.

"Their tactics against us have a little way to improve," Errollyn said drily.

"They'd best leave playing in hills and valleys to us," the officer agreed. The Bacosh ambush had at least been a sign of tactical thought, but Kessligh had seen through it in an instant, looked over the surrounding terrain, and seen a possibility for counterambush that the invaders, in their focus on setting up their own, might have missed.

The Rhodaani cavalry were yelling now, saluting Kessligh with swords raised high. He had been playing cat-and-mouse with the forward elements of the advancing Bacosh Army for weeks, with Rhodaani and *talmaad* forces decidedly in the role of mouse. Thus far, the mice were winning, and this was their biggest victory yet.

Errollyn noticed a serrin rider heading for Kessligh, and there were cheers and salutes from the Rhodaanis for her, also. The ambushing force had been hers, here in the valley. As Kessligh's successes grew, so did the numbers of his forces, as others fighting rearguard actions against the advancing Bacosh masses abandoned their own small battles, and came to join his.

Errollyn urged his horse forward to join the gathering of commanders. He was in command of those serrin who rode with Kessligh from the beginning. At Kessligh's side now, surveying the scene, was a captain of the Rhodaani cavalry.

And the new serrin arrival, Rhillian.

"One of those knights is Lord Hilsen of Meraine," said Rhillian with satisfaction, nodding toward the body-strewn valley floor. "A close friend to the Chansul of Meraine. We make the Meraini so angry at us that they throw their senior lords into our pursuit."

The Chansul ruled all Meraine and, as such, was a contestant for King of all Bacosh. Meraini forces seemed particularly keen on foraging and sending advance parties ahead of the main column, perhaps eager to claim their share of new lands before others arrived. Kessligh's previous, much smaller, successes against them appeared to have caused some anger. Now they had sent a larger force, and lost them.

"The Regent will put a stop to it now," Kessligh told them. "Or he will try to. I suppose we will learn from this how much command he actually has over the individual provinces of the Free Bacosh."

"Either way, we've gained some space between our retreating army and their advance," said the Rhodaani captain. "They are a huge force, and they advance like one. As we enter the hills on the Enoran border, they will be slower still."

"It's still not enough," said Kessligh, grimacing slightly as his attention moved onto problems far ahead. "Enora is no place for decisive battles, and with the border now unprotected, there's no telling what uncommitted elements are racing toward us to lay a claim with the new king. We need the Ilduuri to commit, and still we hear nothing."

"We cannot plan on the Ilduuri coming to our aid," said Rhillian. "We must plan on defeating Regent Arrosh on our own."

"Whilst still aiming to increase our forces at every opportunity," Kessligh added, at once agreeing and disagreeing with her. Rhillian shrugged.

Those serrin travelling with her told that she had been probing the Army of Lenayin, greatly concerned about how the battle would go once those forces arrived in full. Errollyn wondered if that were all there was to it. She looked different now, her white hair short, the long braid that Errollyn had never known her without, missing. Something about the cut was odd, too—it was slightly longer on one side of her face than the other. If there was a story behind it, Rhillian was not telling, and none of her travelling companions professed to know.

A serrin woman interrupted them, to introduce a messenger. Kessligh beckoned the messenger forward, and a serrin lad of no more than sixteen rode to join them.

"I come from Coromen," he said. Kessligh frowned—Coromen was in the path of the Army of Lenayin's advance, still two days behind the Army of the Bacosh, to hear the latest. "An orphanage was slaughtered there, thirty-two children and their carers."

Rhillian's hand went to her mouth. "We missed one?" she murmured, aghast.

The lad nodded. "We came across the bodies buried by a roadside. The Bacosh men responsible had been hauling them to the army column, to collect their bounty." Rhillian's eyes gleamed with tears. It was the nightmare that all *talmaad* had striven the last two centuries to avoid. "But those men, we found killed and left to rot. From the manner of ritual execution, we think it was Isfayen men, of Lenayin. And given the closeness to the head of the Lenay column, it must have been Isfayen lords from the vanguard party—the main body of Isfayen ride too far back in the Lenay column for it to have been them."

"And they buried the children's bodies?" asked the Rhodaani captain, frowning.

"The Isfayen are not all you've heard," Kessligh said quietly. "They think warfare is sport, but there is no sport in killing children. People who think otherwise will anger them, and angry Isfayen are uncompromising."

"Sasha rides with the Isfayen vanguard," said Errollyn. All looked at him. Kessligh was silent, almost unreadable. And Errollyn found himself swallowing against a sudden tightness in his throat.

"We cannot hope that dreams and wishes shall save us," said Rhillian. "First we hope for the Ilduuri, now we dream that Sasha may turn her people against this war. She may have had vengeance upon those murderers, but she rides with an army of their allies that makes such slaughter possible. Sasha is my enemy. She is the enemy of us all."

Five

Sofy was kneeling before the shrine in her tent, maids daubing her hair and hands with scented oils, when another maid entered to tell her of the new arrivals. Sofy scowled, and gave her reply.

"It is not proper for the Princess Regent to receive a male visitor within her chambers," announced Sister Mardola from beside the shrine. She sat with a book of scripture upon her lap, paused now in her recital of the verse of Harienne.

"I must see him," said Sofy, still frowning. "My Lenay family have sent him, he is to be my protection."

"You have twenty knights of Larosa to your personal guard," the sister reprimanded. "You have no need of any other."

"It is the gods' will that one cannot change one's family," Sofy said firmly. Sister Mardola looked severely displeased. She did that a lot.

Sofy remained kneeling for the rest of the recital, then took a sip of holy water in consecration and was blessed by the Almin Star. The star was then placed about her neck, and she rose and took a black silk shawl in which to receive her guest.

Jaryd was admitted through the front entrance of the tent. He looked up and about in amazement at the sheer size of the interior. Silk drapes divided the living space into sections, drifting in a slight breeze. There were furnishings too, light but expensive, and great rugs for the floor of grass.

Jaryd dressed as a Lenay warrior would, and a high status one at that—a leather jacket over a chain vest. The jacket had thick shoulder guards, his riding gloves bore steel studs, and there were spurs on his boots. His sword was a big Lenay two-hander, and the knife through the front of his belt was nearly the size of an Isfayen darak.

He looked at her now, and stifled a laugh. Sofy folded her arms crossly.

"What?" she snapped.

"No, you look good," Jaryd managed. "Nice stones." Meaning the jewellery. "And the, um, other stuff."

"What the hells was Sasha thinking to send you?" Sofy retorted.

"Damon's idea too, and Koenyg agreed."

"Aye, couldn't be happier to be rid of you, I'm sure."

Sister Mardola cleared her throat. "The gentleman will kindly speak in a lowland tongue in my prescence," she announced. They had of course been speaking Lenay.

Jaryd frowned at the sister. "Who's the old bat?" he asked Sofy in their native tongue.

Sofy rolled her eyes in exasperation. "The gentleman does not speak a low-lands tongue," she lied. "I will speak with him as we can both understand."

She gestured impatiently for Jaryd to come and sit on a leather-upholstered chair. Sister Mardola followed, and maids rushed to attend them, and offer drinks, fruit, and biscuits. Jaryd accepted all, hungry as ever, with more disbelieving mirth at all the activity.

"Well, this is a lovely arrangement," he remarked.

"Will you just stop it?" Sofy retorted. It didn't help that he looked so . . . well, good, she admitted to herself in frustration. His eyes were alive with unreasonable cheer for these circumstances. Seeing him so carefree, she could feel resentment building. "Why are you here?"

"Because neither Sasha nor Damon feels particularly comfortable with you being here all alone."

"As you can see," Sofy said coldly, "I am very far from alone."

Jaryd glanced about, and sipped his tea. "That's a matter of opinion."

"Jaryd, I don't know what *you* think you're doing here, but I'm on a very important mission. Tracato is a treasure, and I intend to see it saved. I hear the Lord Alfriedo Renine is being proclaimed the new lord of all Rhodaan and Tracato, and I hear that he is a very intelligent boy. I will negotiate with him and I will find a way to bring him and all of Rhodaan into my husband's fold, with as little damage to all parties as possible."

Jaryd's expression sobered a little. "And what does Prince Dafed say about this?"

Sofy smoothed the dress in her lap. "Dafed is a warrior," she said. "He will negotiate military matters. He has little interest in other things."

She was not pleased that Balthaar's brother Dafed had come too. He was not pleased, either, to be sent away from the advancing army in order to collect this trophy for his brother's new crown. But Tracato was close to Elisse, and the Elissians had not been destroyed as a fighting force in the recent war against Rhodaan. There were alliances to forge, and Dafed was here to forge them, then to lead the Elissians south, to rejoin Balthaar in his advance. Dafed, Sofy was reasonably sure, would not get in her way.

Jaryd shook his head in faint disbelief. "Sofy, your husband's priests want all of this destroyed. You've ridden in the Bacosh column, you've seen what even the common soldiers are doing to Rhodaan. . . ."

"They appeared quite restrained from what I saw."

In an instant, Jaryd's good humour vanished. He regarded her with something she had not seen him direct at her before. Not quite contempt, but a distinct lack of respect. Perhaps pity.

"It may look that way from safe within your gilded cage," he said coolly. "I can assure you otherwise."

Sofy felt cold. She looked about in distraction, and hugged her shawl closer. And suddenly, in desperation, she came to the edge of her chair. "Oh, Jaryd, I know it's hard! These two peoples, they've been separated by so much hatred and mistrust for so long . . . but I have to try, Jaryd! I've always been a good peacemaker, I've done it between my siblings, I've sometimes even done it between Lenay lords, and they're no easy mark. Surely I can find some common ground between my husband's new rule, and the old ways of Rhodaan . . . and possibly Enora and Ilduur too one day!"

Jaryd sighed. He nodded to her jewellery, and the Idys Mark on her forehead. "You observe the Idys too. The old Lenay ways."

Sofy nodded enthusiastically. "There was some opposition, but I told them that whatever my new title, I am Lenay and I shall practise the old Lenay traditions also. All new Lenay brides observe the Idys, and I shall too."

The Idys Mark was a dark oval spot on her forehead, in the shape of an eye. The Idys was one of the old spirits, thought to bring fertility and wisdom alike.

"Do you see, Jaryd?" she continued. "I'm trying to bring peoples and customs together. I am Princess Regent of the Bacosh, and I observe their customs, yet I am also a princess of Lenayin. I can show by example that two such different peoples and cultures can exist side by side. And if I can bring that example to Tracato, perhaps I can save that great treasure, and it can enlighten all of the Bacosh and far beyond!"

Jaryd said nothing. Sofy did not think that she had convinced him. But she could see that he was not surprised at her passion, and indeed, wore that familiar look of wry defeat. He knew her so well. Perhaps it would not be a bad thing to have him on this trip after all.

"And how about you?" she asked more kindly. "You've been spending a lot more time amongst the Goeren-yai of late. Do you feel yourself a true Goeren-yai now?"

Jaryd shrugged. "I don't know," he sighed. "And that's the wonderful thing about it." Sofy frowned, not understanding. Jaryd smiled. "No one cares. My Goeren-yai comrades, they don't quiz me about my beliefs, they don't threaten to expel me if I don't know all the words to their tales or all the beats to their rhythm. They know me as a warrior and as a man, and that's enough for them."

"But there are many customs and practices amongst the Goeren-yai," Sofy pressed. Jaryd could be so naive in his lack of understanding these complexities, and she was suddenly worried. "If you are to call yourself Goeren-yai and be accepted by them, you must take their beliefs and customs seriously, Jaryd. . . ."

"I take it as seriously as they do," Jaryd said with amusement. "The ancient ways aren't about reciting this text or that song, it's about heart." He rapped himself on his armoured chest. "I may not have much, but I have that."

"So you're happy then?"

"I think I am. I don't miss all of this shit, I can tell you that." He nodded toward the temporary shrine. Sister Mardola cleared her throat, disapprovingly. She did not understand his words, but she knew a look of contempt when she saw one. Jaryd ignored her. "Sofy, you can't change the world, you know. Some people are shit. You can't make them nice by setting a good example."

"Jaryd, you Lenay men always think that violence is the only solution to everything. Why don't we try ending hatred with love for a change, instead of always using swords?"

"Because it doesn't work," said Jaryd, unruffled. "Men don't plough fields because they're violent to the soil, men plough fields because lovingly asking the soils to part does nothing. Besides which, it's not only Lenay men who think so, there's Yasmyn, and Sasha."

"Both of whom could use a little more feminine sensibility," Sofy sniffed.

"And where would that have gotten Sasha or the Udalyn against the Hadryn?"

Sofy rolled her eyes. "The serrin agree with me," she said stubbornly.

"Aye, they did—look where it's gotten them. Backs to the wall and a sword at their throat. They showered these lands with love and your husband repaid them with invasion and slaughter."

Sofy found herself blinking back angry tears. Jaryd was from that other life, the one now lost to her. It wasn't fair that he should come here and do this to her. She had to make *this* life work, but he, apparently content in the other, kept crossing that divide and shattering all her carefully constructed dreams.

Jaryd left the Princess Regent's tent in frustration, and made his way back to his camp. Knights stood in full armour about the tent, and would do so all night in shifts. Jaryd did not envy them, just suiting up could take such men an age. The rest of the camp was clatter and activity, and far too many servants and wagons for Jaryd's liking. There was a firm perimeter set against any serrin attack, and they camped in the middle of a wide field so none could sneak up on them. But if the serrin were to attack in force, he did not know if there were enough defenders to stop them, and all these cooks and maids would not help.

His campfire was near the perimeter beside a wagon, where they could shelter if it rained. There sat Jandlys and Asym, and a noble girl in a dress.

She stood up as Jaryd approached, and stuck out her hand. "You must be Jaryd Nyvar. I'm Jeddie. Lady Jelendria Horseth of Tournea, daughter of Lord Horseth, anyhow. I'm pleased to meet you."

She spoke Torovan, which Jaryd had only just pretended not to know. He shook her hand cautiously, and invited her to resume her seat on a saddle.

"I'm a friend of your Princess Sofy," Jeddie continued earnestly. "She is quite amazing, isn't she? My father is a grand patron of the arts; he has always wanted to see Tracato, and he was quite taken with Sofy. He is riding with the Regent at the war of course, but I did pester him, and he sent me. He said that the Princess Regent would need a female friend amongst so many men."

Jeddie was quite young, perhaps Sofy's age. She had a narrow face and a large nose, not especially pretty, and her manner was a little odd. Jaryd had seen one or two girls like this amongst the noble families in his home of Tyree, girls given a good education who, in the absence of real work or responsibilities, had fallen in love with matters of academics or arts. He recalled his own father, the late Great Lord of Tyree, complaining that such girls became unmarriageable and useless, more interested in their passions than in their duties as noble ladies. Proof that women should not be educated at all, he'd said.

"Why were you riding with the army?" Jaryd asked, as Jandlys forked him some bacon from their pan, and passed it over with a hunk of bread.

"My father made rather a large commitment of men to the war," said Jeddie, matter-of-factly. "The household was weakened, and he wanted his family with him."

"And you want to help Sofy to save Tracato?" asked Jandlys from around a mouthful of food. Jandlys was even larger than his father, Great Lord Krayliss of Taneryn, had been.

"Well, yes. One does enjoy the arts. One does hear that Tracato is quite the wonder for such things."

"Because it's filled with serrin, who all the fucking priests here want to kill." Jaryd threw another log on the fire in exasperation.

Jeddie's eyes were wide. She cleared her throat and looked around for anyone who might hear. "Well, I'm not sure that they want *all* of them dead. . . ."

"And that's a fact is it?" Jaryd cut her off, incredulously. "You grew up in a nice noble household in . . . Tournea, did you say?" A timid nod from Jeddie. "Your priests educated you?"

"Some. But also my father, and some masters from the town."

"Well, that's good, your father seems a good man. And what did the priests teach you of the serrin?"

Jeddie looked at her boots. For a moment there was just the crackling of the fire, and the sounds of the camp. "But there must be some accommodation!" she insisted abruptly, a little desperately. "I mean, there has been so much in Rhodaan that has been successful and good, surely! My father always said so. Surely we can find some way to accommodate the best of Tracato beneath the Regent's rule!"

"You're fucking crazy—you're just like Sofy," Jaryd sighed. Jeddie cringed, evidently not accustomed to being spoken to in that tone. "Religious people, they're not interested in facts. They already know what's right, and if the facts don't fit, they'll just twist and hammer them until they do. The serrin made this place a success all right, it was such a success it's a huge black eye to the Regent, the priests, everyone from your world. They want it destroyed, that's the only way they can restore the world to the way they think it ought to be."

Jeddie said nothing.

"Don't you fear him, lassie," said Jandlys. "If our Sofy's told you anything about her people, she's told you you've nothing to fear from us lot of ruffians, we just talk a bit loud is all."

"Oh, I know that," Jeddie said hurriedly, but she gave Jandlys a grateful smile. "I know that I'm safer amongst Lenay warriors than anyone else in Rhodia."

"That's damn right!" Jandlys agreed. "Yuan Jaryd here just don't like noble Verenthanes, that's all. Old history."

"I know," Jeddie said quietly. "You used to be one, but they dissolved your family and murdered your brother." Jaryd scowled at the fire. "I'm sorry, I did not mean to speak of upsetting things. But Princess Sofy has told me."

"You know," said Jaryd, "when I was a noble, many of my fellow nobles thought me an idiot. I wasn't interested in their sophistry, I've never liked to read, and most of the plays and paintings that Sofy finds so fascinating just bore me to tears. I liked to ride and train and play lagand. And drink and chase skirts, I admit. I knew they were frauds, all my noble friends and family; I never got along with them, nor them with me. I was too unsophisticated for them. And then they went and proved me correct." He took a mouthful of food. "I'm still correct," he said while chewing, "in my disdain for everything they believe in. I'm quite certain I understand them better than Sofy ever will. Yet Sofy has more intelligence and good wit than I could dream of. And I wonder, why are the most intelligent and educated usually amongst the most stupid?"

"I don't think that that's true," said Jeddie.

"Sasha said the Tracato Nasi-Keth tortured and tried to kill her. In Petrodor half the Nasi-Keth ended up on the wrong side. In the Bacosh much of the education is handled by priests, who peddle the most evil thoughts of all. Give me a farmer's common sense and a woodsman's nose for horseshit any day. Most of the wisest people I know I've met *after* my so-called downfall, not before."

Jeddie's frown had given way to a look of intense curiosity. "So tell me, if you think the princess such a fool, why do you follow her here?"

"Well, I was ordered to."

"Lenay warriors are difficult to order if they feel their honour imperilled," said Jeddie. "Commanding a Lenay warrior away from the war is no small thing, surely?"

Jaryd shifted uncomfortably. "She needs protection."

"From whom? What could pose her so great a threat?"

"Herself," said Jaryd.

Andreyis walked beside the prisoner train, as had become his practice in the last days. His feet blistered, but that was preferable to the wagon's jolting of bare boards. The road now descended into a shallow valley, within which nestled the largest town Andreyis had yet seen in Enora. A river wound through the valley, and from this shallow height he could see several bridges, and a pair of very tall temple spires. The ground here was wet, and a cold wind blew from the north, bringing rain and low, gusting cloud.

There was little traffic on the road. At one farmhouse, Andreyis saw a family piling belongings onto several wagons, and lashing them down. Other farmhouses looked deserted. Ahead, Andreyis saw a village courtyard, and some locals gathered to throw rotten food and rocks at the prisoners. Andreyis knew he should probably climb back into the wagon—walking here alongside he might just be beaten to death. Yet he kept walking, boots splashing in the rivulets of water that ran down the paved slope.

The locals saw him, and aimed their throws. Another was hefting a heavy spade. Suddenly a rider was bearing down on them, and they scattered. From the safety of doorways, they yelled at the rider. The rider, Yshel, just scowled at them.

Out of the village, she rode on the grass verge beside him. "Best that you get back in the wagon," she said. "There will be many more like them in town."

"I heal faster walking," Andreyis said stubbornly. "What is this town?"

"It is Shemorane," she said. The name was familiar. Andreyis frowned, trying to recall. "The High Temple is here," said Yshel, seeing his puzzlement.

"Ah," said Andreyis. That was in central Enora, he recalled. They'd come that far from the border. Now they were squarely in the middle not only of Enora, but of the Saalshen Bacosh. "I'd thought the temple was atop Mount Tristen?"

"Mount Tristen is there," said Yshel, pointing. Across the valley, a lone peak loomed, its upper slopes disappearing into low cloud. "Saint Tristen came down the mountain and showed his followers what the gods had told him, here, by the riverside. That is where the High Temple is built."

Those were the twin spires in the town, Andreyis realised. He was in holy lands. Though not Verenthane himself, it raised a chill on the back of his neck.

"The Army of Larosa will be coming through this way, then," he suggested.

"And everyone is leaving," Yshel confirmed. "Now get back in the wagon, before I have one of the Enoran men come and put you there."

Andreyis did as she said.

"Doin' well what your girlfriend says, then?" suggested Hydez. Of the six Lenays in the wagon he was worst hurt, since Ulemys had died two days earlier.

"This is Shemorane," Andreyis told him. Hydez blinked at him. "Where the High Temple is."

"You're joking," Hydez said with suspicion. Hydez had fought with Hadryn forces during the Northern Rebellion. Andreyis thought it quite likely they had passed within armspans of each other during various battles, on opposite sides.

"No joke. My girlfriend told me."

Hydez struggled to sit more upright, wincing at the pain. "The High Temple is here? Can you see it?"

"I caught a glimpse, just then," Andreyis told him. "I imagine this road leads right past it, you'll get a good look."

Hydez waved Sayden aside from the opposite bench and heaved himself across with a gasp of agony. He then leaned out the side of the shuddering wagon, and stared downslope, hoping for a sight of the Verenthanes' holiest temple.

"Regent Arrosh will be leading his priests to put the Shereldin Star back in there," Sayden suggested. Sayden had long hair and thin tattoos upon one side of his face. He did not seem too excited by the prospect.

"This was always their main target," Andreyis agreed. "It doesn't look very defensible, though."

The wagon passed some villagers on the road, walking with several mules in a train, each with belongings lashed to their backs. Andreyis saw that Yshel had pulled off the road to talk to them. From the movement of hands, he guessed she was asking them where they were headed, and where the latest news put the various armies. Then she followed, red hair wet in the rain, her pale face worried.

Rounding a corner, the wagon train came into a courtyard and there before them towered the High Temple itself. Hydez levered himself as upright as he could manage on the rattling wagon, and gazed in awe as rain fell onto his face. It was no bigger than Saint Ambellion in Baen-Tar, Andreyis thought. Huge, certainly, but it was not the size that impressed. The High Temple was old . . . Saint Ambellion, like most Verenthane temples in Lenayin, dated less than two hundred years. The High Temple was so much older than that.

This is where it comes from, Andreyis realised as he looked at it. The great faith that had united the warring factions of Lenayin, even as it failed to convert much of the rural population. It was such a monumental part of the history of Lenayin, and a fact of Andreyis's life as immovable as the mountains . . . and it had all started here. Suddenly, he thought he could understand the look on Hydez's face. Not the joy, but the awe.

"The old builders built well," Sayden observed, looking up at the twin spires. The wagons clattered across the courtyard. A bridge spanned the river to the courtyard's side, and the valley's far slope rose beyond. There was traffic across the courtyard, a steady stream of wagons stacked with belongings. The prisoner train slipped through a gap, and continued to an archway beside the High Temple.

Within, the wagons stopped in a secluded square. Guards leaped from the rear and front wagons, and ordered the prisoners out. Andreyis climbed out willingly and assisted those who needed it to follow. Hydez never ceased to stare up at the High Temple.

"We're stopping here?" he asked. As though amazed that his awful captive fate had led him to this blessed location.

Andreyis saw priests emerging from the nondescript stone building facing the temple. "A monastery," he observed.

The priests, bald in black robes, talked to the guards, then gestured for the prisoners to follow. Andreyis walked supporting Sayden, as the priests hauled open large doors to reveal stables within. Andreyis smelled horses, and hay. He nearly smiled.

The prisoners sat or lay on the stable floor, which was dirt and straw with no pavings, while the priests brought food and water. Andreyis took bread and an apple and strolled, gazing over the stable doors at the horses. One stuck a long nose over the door and sniffed at his apple. Andreyis let her bite off that side, keeping the other half for himself.

"You're going to eat that?" Yshel asked behind him. Andreyis glanced back in surprise. She was following him, her bow unstrung, sword sheathed at her back. Keeping an eye on the wandering prisoner . . . but where would he escape to?

Andreyis took a bite of the remaining apple, then switched it to his bad hand so he could stroke the mare's nose with his good one. He measured her flank with a practised eye, noting the muscle tone, the shape of the hind quarters.

"She's being used as a cart horse," he observed. "Pity—her breeding's better than that. She's not very old."

A priest, passing with an armful of hay, overheard him. "Cavalry horse," he explained, in heavily accented Torovan. "She have two battle. Second battle, she nearly kill. She pull down, rider pull off, kill, very bad. She lose friend horse. Now, she no like loud noises. Cavalry, they give her to us." He pointed to the mare's other side in passing. Andreyis looked, and saw weapon scars.

"Poor girl," he murmured, empathising. He gave her the rest of the apple.

"You do ride horses," Yshel observed, watching. "How many horses did you care for?"

"Between twelve and twenty, depending on foals. I shared duties with Sasha, Kessligh, and one other. And sometimes lads from the town."

"I grew up in Li'el in Saalshen," said Yshel. "It's a city, or a large town, I suppose. A farmstead on the outskirts raised horses. I would go there and help the ranchers. Horses made me want to travel, to join the *talmaad*. I never really thought that they would take me to a war."

Back at the stable doors, there came the sound of shouting. Andreyis and Yshel turned and looked. An officer of the Steel had entered, and was looking for able-bodied prisoners. He seemed disappointed to find so few, as none of the Lenays in the group had surrendered while still able to fight.

"I'd better go," said Andreyis. "Before he tries to make the dying walk."

The Steel officer looked haggard and worn, limping with a recent injury, as he inspected the prisoners. Finally finding nine who could work, he had them escorted by three Steel regulars out of the walled courtyard and onto the main one.

Here the flow of ordinary Enorans had increased, a steady stream of families all trudging or riding in the same direction, heads down, away from the advancing Army of the Bacosh.

The Steel officer led the prisoners up the wide stone stairs of the High Temple, and past two more soldiers guarding the huge doors.

Within, the air was cool and still. Light spilled from rows of small windows across the largest indoor space Andreyis had ever seen. It felt like something from a dream, vast and echoing. To stand beneath the high roof and gaze up at the patterned glass, it seemed to Andreyis that this must indeed be a house of gods.

"Right," said the officer, tiredly. "Anyone here speak Torovan? Understand Torovan?" Blank stares from most.

"I'll translate," said Andreyis.

"Good." The officer pointed across the huge, open floor to the rows of pews before the altar. "You see those benches? I want them smashed up, make a nice big pile before the altar. Then we'll search through the back rooms and cellars to find anything else that will burn."

"Burn?" Andreyis stared at him. "Why?"

"Because we're not going to leave this place to the Larosans, that's why," said the officer. "This place, we're going to burn down."

Six

Sasha followed the rear of Damon's horse up the forested ridge road. The Lenay party emerged onto the crest of the ridge, with a wide view of rumpled northern Enora. Low, rocky hills complicated the way ahead, beneath an overcast sky and misting rain.

Koenyg halted his horse on the last patch of grass before slippery rocks became too treacherous near the edge of the cliff. Beside him, a young Rhodaani noble pointed in the direction of Shemorane. Sasha made out a distant valley, but too far, and on too gloomy a day, to see any more than that.

The Larosan party they had come to meet emerged from the opposite line of trees, waiting in the safety of cover. Their leader headed for Koenyg, and Sasha invited herself, pushing her horse between her two brothers.

"Is it true that the Army of the Free Bacosh has halted before Shemorane?" Koenyg asked sharply.

The Larosan lord nodded. "There are two bridges down on the river, destroyed by the Enorans. The Regent Balthaar Arrosh seeks to ford the river further downstream, and enter Shemorane from the east."

"With his entire army?"

"The Regent decrees that he shall enter Shemorane, and return the Shereldin Star to the High Temple," the lord insisted, solemnly. "That is his highest sacred duty. The Army of the Free Bacosh cannot progress without their Regent."

"While in the meantime," said Koenyg, "we're letting the Enoran and Rhodaani Steel not only get away, but regroup and join forces."

"The priests will have made him do it," said Sasha, in Lenay so the lord would not understand. "They've been dreaming of returning the Shereldin Star to the High Temple for two centuries. No way will they allow the army to pass Shemorane without some great ceremony."

"The priests should understand that Shemorane is not truly within their possession until the Steel and the *talmaad* are defeated. This great ceremony of theirs is a dangerous illusion," Koenyg replied. Neither Sasha nor Damon disagreed. "What news of Ilduur?" Koenyg asked the lord in Torovan once more.

"No news. It seems the Ilduuri will not come." There was a smugness to his voice.

"You've sent envoys to Ilduur," said Sasha, staring at him. "You've made a deal with them."

The lord shrugged. "My Lord Regent's policies are vast and cunning. What you describe is not impossible, though I have not heard of it."

"Fat chance he has of actually *keeping* his word with Ilduur," Sasha muttered in Lenay.

"The Regent Arrosh commands that the Army of Lenayin should continue to advance on the Steel in the meanwhile," continued the lord. "To the west, where the hills end, and open ground makes for a fast march. The Army of Lenayin is light, while the Army of the Bacosh, and the Steel, are heavy. If you move fast, you could catch them there."

Koenyg listened a little more, then dismissed the lord, and contemplated the view ahead.

"The Regent Arrosh *commands*, does he?" Sasha muttered.

"Rest it, Sasha." Koenyg had no map to hand, but Sasha had seen him studying maps every night, staring until every line and feature was memorised. "Last we heard of the Steel, they are too far ahead to be caught as the messenger suggests. They will have merged forces by now."

"The Regent hopes our pursuit will draw Kessligh's forces," said Damon. "His irregulars grow stronger each day. The Regent's army has few forward scouts, they do not survive long otherwise. I think this a ploy to make us take the lead, and deal with Kessligh."

"We *are* much better at his style of warfare," Koenyg agreed. "In that sense, Lenayin has taught Kessligh some things as well."

"They seek to bleed us," Damon countered. "Like they let us bleed in the diversion against the Enorans."

"Everyone bled, brother."

"It is garbage work. Every time they have a nasty job for someone to do, they hand it to us. They save the battles that promise great glory for themselves."

"Then we must make our own glory," said Koenyg, with a hard stare. He put heels to his horse and galloped back the way they'd come, his siblings and the Royal Guards at his tail.

Andreyis accompanied two of the Steel soldiers back to the stable to gather horses for wagons. Each took two animals, Andreyis taking the mare he'd fed the apple. If they were going to send the High Temple up in flames, he wanted her somewhere other than locked in the stable next door.

He was leaving when Hydez yelled at him from amidst the wounded prisoners. "Is it true? Are they going to burn it?"

Andreyis ignored him, waiting for one of the soldiers to control a reluctant horse. Hydez lunged past his guards, and would have reached Andreyis had his wound not slowed him. A guard grabbed him, then another.

"You're not going to burn it!" Hydez yelled at Andreyis. "You pagan scum, you're not going to help them burn it! That's not their temple to burn, it's for all Verenthanes! Don't you dare burn it!"

The guards wrestled him back to the group. Andreyis walked with the soldiers into the rain, leading the horses with his one good arm.

The vast courtyard now held a cluster of people before the High Temple. Soldiers made a wall of shields before them, townsfolk come to see, bedraggled refugees standing in the rain, halting their flight from the advancing Bacosh Army to stare in dismay at the activity about the temple.

Some carts had been commandeered, and Andreyis helped the soldiers fit the horses into the traces. Even one-armed, he was some assistance, as these soldiers knew little of horses.

Captain Ulay pushed free from the crowd before the temple and strode over. He gave the soldiers orders in Enoran, and they and one other climbed into the three carts. "You stay here," said the captain to Andreyis, "you'll be no use loading carts with one arm."

The carts clattered off, Andreyis thought, to gather more things to burn. He followed the captain back to the temple.

"Whose orders are you following?" Andreyis asked him, as the rain grew heavier.

"That's not for you to ask." The captain looked harried and worn, and walked fast, as though demons snapped at his heels.

"That's the High Temple of Enora," Andreyis tried again. "You're a Verenthane, you're going to burn down your own temple?"

"Better that than let it fall into the hands of those scum," the captain declared. He pushed through the crowd, as some Enorans called out to him, pleaded with him to stop. He ignored them and ran up the steps into the wide doorway.

Andreyis saw Yshel on the steps, in animated conversation with the dark-haired serrin lad who had also ridden with the prisoner column. The other serrin's hand went to his sword as he saw Andreyis approaching. Yshel put a hand on his arm, calming him.

"Did anyone order him to do this?" Andreyis asked her. Within the main doors, he could see broken pews piled in great stacks by the far wall. With oils such as serrin made, that would burn high. Behind that wall were rooms, and many timbers that would catch. If the end wall came down, the roof would follow.

"He says yes," said Yshel, frowning.

"Who?"

"He doesn't say."

"This is wrong."

"It's just a building," said the other serrin. "People are dying in their thousands, who cares for stones?"

"They care," said Andreyis, pointing to the crowd gathered in the rain. "Captain Ulay might be mad for all we know. Does he look entirely sane to you?"

"It's war," said the serrin. "Who is?"

"There are no other soldiers around," said Yshel. "He is a captain, he has command. These are not our lands, we do not interfere with human affairs. . . ."

"You're in this war! What's that if not interference?"

"We serrin are none of us Verenthanes!" Yshel retorted.

"Neither am I."

Yshel rolled her eyes. "That's different, you're human."

"And I think that in his human rage against his enemy, Captain Ulay is about to destroy something that his own people may never forgive him for."

"You fight against these people. Why do you care?"

"And you fight for them. Why *don't* you?"

Yshel said nothing but stared up at the spires in faint desperation.

Andreyis tried again. "Where did those carts go, exactly? I didn't hear all the words."

"They go to find the demon fire. There is a Steel artillery force encamped nearby."

"Artillery?" Andreyis asked, not believing her. "So close to the Regent's advance?"

"There are bridges down on the approach—the Regent's army makes a detour to reach us, it will take him another day or two. Kessligh Cronenverdt thinks to make a trap for his armies with artillery . . ."

"Yshel!" Her serrin comrade stopped her in alarm, and said something else in Saalsi. They argued.

"Kessligh Cronenverdt?" Andreyis exclaimed. He'd heard rumours. Kessligh had been in Tracato. It made sense that he would be leading any rearguard action to delay the Regent's advance. The Regent was obliged by holy duty to capture Shemorane and make a grand display at the High Temple. Surely Kessligh would sense an opportunity.

If Captain Ulay burned down the temple, the Regent might not come.

He would lead his army past, to stoke their fury at the crime, but he would not stay long for grand ceremonies. Ulay was ruining Kessligh's plan. Andreyis had fought against Enorans, and should have cheered at the thought. Only . . .

"Yshel, you must go and find Kessligh," he demanded. "Get a horse, ride and find him, fast. He can stop this. If you tell him what Captain Ulay is doing, he will stop it."

Yshel stared at him for a moment, then looked over the bedraggled crowds in the courtyard. And finally, up at the temple spires.

Then she ran down the stairs, and away to the stable square, and her horse.

"You wish the Regent to have his grand ceremony," said the other serrin, darkly. "With the temple standing, he will return the Shereldin Star, and his armies will gain cheer from their holy success."

"You know nothing," Andreyis snorted. "Yshel understands. Ask her."

Before long, the carts returned with loads under thick canvas. Soldiers pushed a path through the ever-increasing throng, pushing people back with their shields. With the carts at the very foot of the steps, they began unloading, with only a small distance to carry their cargo in the rain.

What they carried were stitched-leather balls, like giant wineskins except with cane ribs inserted for shape. Men carried them very carefully, two to a ball. These were the feared Steel artillery ammunition, filled with flammable oil—hellfire. The crowd recognised the shapes too, and the protests grew abruptly louder. Soldiers formed a perimeter, shields interlocked, as common Eñorans yelled and pushed, and tried to force a way through.

Supervising the unloading, Captain Ulay gave a command, and the soldiers' swords came out. But some soldiers, Andreyis noted, did not draw, and cast filthy looks back at their captain.

"No one's looking at us," a Valhanan man named Tybron murmured at Andreyis's shoulder. "We should do something."

"What?" Andreyis asked. "The captain's unpopular, but if we take him down the other soldiers won't thank us. We could run, but wounded and without horses we won't get far."

"I don't like burning no damn temple," Tybron muttered. Tybron had long hair and tattoos, and rings in his ear. "No good ever came from burning holy places."

Andreyis nodded. In Lenayin, men were more likely to kill each other over matters of personal honour, or in wars between different regions and different tongues, than over matters of faith. Lenays were a superstitious lot, and did not like to offend even the gods they did not pray to.

"Kessligh's coming," Andreyis told him.

Tybron stared. "Kessligh?" Andreyis nodded. "Yes, that Kessligh," the nod meant. Tybron whistled. "Hope he gets here in time."

They stood and waited until Andreyis could stand it no more, and then ducked inside. Within, he found Captain Ulay supervising the placement of demon fire beneath the great piles of wooden pews. Soldiers watched, as more Lenay prisoners helped—all Goeren-yai. One soldier had a small flask of oil and a flint.

"Who ordered you to burn it down?" Andreyis yelled. Everyone paused and looked. Captain Ulay saw who it was, and gave an order to two soldiers. The soldiers advanced on him. "The rest of you are just going to stand there? Your captain's gone mad! This is the High Temple of Enora, and your gods are going to hold you personally responsible for destroying it!"

The two soldiers advancing on him stopped. Andreyis saw that one, beneath his steel helm, was very young and looked very frightened.

"If this temple falls into their hands," Ulay roared at them, "it will mark the fall of Enora! We swore that we would *never* allow them to place the Shereldin Star in this place, and I will *not* hand them such a victory!"

"That which you lose you can always win back!" Andreyis retorted. "If you burn it down, you destroy your symbol of nationhood with your very hands! Why don't you just cut your own damn throats while you're at it?"

Captain Ulay yelled at the two soldiers in Enoran. They looked at each other, and did not advance further. Ulay snarled, and strode toward the soldier holding the flint and flask.

"Don't let him have it!" Andreyis yelled. The soldier stood paralysed as his captain advanced. "He has no orders, he's just making it up! He lied to you!"

Ulay took the flint from his unresisting man, and snarled orders to two other men. Those two obeyed without hesitation, and came striding for Andreyis.

Something fizzed past Andreyis's shoulder, and struck one of those men squarely in the chest. His armour was thickest there, and the arrow bounced off, but he froze in shock. Andreyis looked behind, and there was Yshel, bow in hand, reaching for another arrow even now. Behind Yshel, walking with the aid of a tall staff, was a familiar, grey-haired figure. Andreyis stared.

"You're not burning down the fucking High Temple!" Kessligh yelled. "Have you gone completely insane?" Behind him came Nasi-Keth and serrin, more than a dozen.

"Hold them back!" Ulay commanded, uncorking the flask.

A serrin man with powerful arms took stance beside Kessligh and pulled a huge bowstring with a shuddering creak. "I have him," he announced, sighting at the captain.

Soldiers ran in front of their captain, shields raised, and made an impenetrable wall. Still the serrin sighted, as though seeking a gap between the shields, with some confidence of hitting.

"I am Kessligh Cronenverdt," Kessligh announced. "You have heard of my victories against the Regent! I am the most victorious of all commanders in this war, and I command that this folly shall cease!"

"You're a Lenay pagan like all the others!" yelled Ulay from behind his wall. "You have no command here! Now clear the damn temple, because I'm going to light it, and the first flame will turn everyone on this floor to ash in the blink of an eye!"

Soldiers began to leave, ushering the Lenay prisoners ahead of them. One prisoner, limping on a bad leg, made a sudden lunge for Ulay, barehanded. His tackle brought down a soldier, and opened a gap in the wall of shields. An arrow whistled, and suddenly Ulay had a serrin arrow through his arm. He stared at the arrow. His soldiers all watched as the flint hit the ground. No one seemed to know what to do.

Then there were new yells in the temple as townsfolk began charging in. The Steel's wall before the steps had failed, the soldiers unprepared to use swords on their own people. Men and women ran in yelling, swarming past Kessligh and his Nasi-Keth and serrin, past Andreyis, then past the dumbfounded soldiers and their wounded captain.

There was no violence, for the people did not attack, but formed a human wall before the flammable pile. Numbers increased in a steady flow, and the soldiers' swords remained in their sheaths. It was over.

Kessligh's people convinced the soldiers to leave, then began removing the demon fire artillery, very carefully. The crowds of common folk cheered and wept. Andreyis went with the other prisoners and sat on the steps to one side.

Soon, Yshel emerged. Spotting him, she walked over and sat by him.

"Nice shot," said Andreyis, with a smile.

Yshel put a hand on his good arm. "You were brave," she said.

"I've fought in wars," Andreyis said sourly. "That was nothing."

Yshel shook her head, impatiently. "No, that is not what I meant. This clumsy tongue, it does not offer the best translation. I meant not a bravery of the body. Instead, a bravery of the mind. You are not Verenthane. This is not your fight, and these people are your enemies. Yet you took a risk to save something that is not yours."

Andreyis sighed. "Serrin aren't the only ones to know right from wrong."

"No," Yshel said quietly. "Sometimes you know better than us. I would have let them burn it down."

"You may have been right to. Maybe we did something stupid. But it didn't feel right."

Behind her, Andreyis saw Kessligh walking over. He climbed to his feet. Kessligh embraced him, and held him for a long time. When they parted, Andreyis saw emotion on his face. And perhaps even . . . was that a tear? Surely not.

"Good to see you well," said Kessligh, attempting gruffness. "Very good."

"No smarter, though," said Andreyis, with a nod to the temple doors.

"And I'm pleased for it. Destroying the High Temple would have been, for the Enorans, like a mother killing her own child. I don't want to be fighting with a people who think they deserve to lose." He looked over the group. "So you're my prisoner, then?"

"Looks that way," Andreyis said glumly.

"You do realise you're on the wrong side?" Coming from Kessligh, the hero of Lenayin, it nearly shocked him.

"I can't fight my own people," Andreyis said stubbornly.

"You did in the Northern Rebellion."

"You know what I mean."

Kessligh nodded. He saw the accusation on Andreyis's face, and on the faces of the other Lenays, sitting here on the steps. And he took a deep breath.

"We all have our burdens," he said solemnly. "We all must do what we must. I want a full telling from you, but I don't have the time. You'll be taken to the rear soon, wherever the rear is today. I'll make sure people know what you did."

He clasped Andreyis's shoulder, and departed. In his place stood the serrin archer from the temple. He was certainly the scariest looking serrin Andreyis had ever seen—handsome, with wild hair and green eyes, his bare arms crossed with numerous scars. Yet now, as he looked at Andreyis, he seemed uncertain. Almost shy.

Andreyis realised he looked familiar. "Errollyn!" he exclaimed, recalling the serrin who had ridden to the Northern Rebellion with his friends.

Errollyn put out a hand strong enough to crush most others, but his grip was light, in serrin fashion. "I have you at a disadvantage," Errollyn apologised. "Sasha's told me everything about you." He smiled, a rare flash of humour.

"I don't like the sound of that," Andreyis admitted.

"She loves you dearly. She told me that in truth, she has five brothers. Six, counting Krystoff."

Andreyis swallowed hard. "I know. It wasn't easy being her brother. I can't imagine how hard it is to be her lover."

Errollyn smiled sadly. "Hard when she was here. Harder still when she is not. The Army of the Bacosh pauses at Shemorane, and the Army of Lenayin draws closer. They will circle west, and perhaps take the lead in the pursuit of the Steel."

"The Regent's a coward," said Andreyis. "After the battle of Shero Valley, there's barely twenty thousand Lenays and some Torovans. The Regent must still command better than a hundred thousand, yet he falls back."

Errollyn shrugged. "Why waste Bacosh lords in pursuit when he can spend Lenays instead?"

"I hear tell of massacres," Andreyis said quietly. "Of half-castes murdered. We passed some half-castes on the road, they were frightened."

"Oh, entire villages," Errollyn said tiredly. "Half-caste or not. The Regent's lords are claiming land, they need it devoid of people. Rhodaanis and Enorans are too uppity to submit easily to feudal rule, they'll need to kill a lot of them first. And they're doing so."

To the south, behind Shemorane as the Bacosh and Lenay armies advanced, lay a wide land of rolling hills that the locals called Pirene. It was only when Damon and Sasha's formation of five hundred cavalry emerged from the hills around Shemorane that they discovered a Larosan advance party had beaten them to it.

Sasha, Damon, Markan, Lord Heryd, and Myklas galloped to the rise where a Larosan noble party awaited, surveying the lands below.

At their side, the Lenay party found a choice vantage across the Pirene. Several villages were burning, and horsemen could be seen galloping in groups. Beyond, Sasha observed larger groups of horsemen, a dark swarm against the wet green fields.

"Prince Damon," he introduced himself. "My sister Sashandra, my brother Myklas, Great Lord Heryd of Hadryn, and Great Lord Markan of Isfayen. We have five hundred horse."

"Lord Elias Assineth," said the leader. "Cousin of the Regent." He wore the full plate armour of a Bacosh knight, with his visor raised. He introduced three other lords, similarly armoured. "We also have five hundred."

"Lord Elias," said Markan, with some surprise. "My sister Yasmyn sends her regards. She says your two friends' heads made excellent lagand balls. Yours seems also an agreeable shape."

"Markan!" Damon warned him. Markan merely looked amused. Elias glared at him, but Sasha knew he had little to fear from Markan. The Great Lord of Isfayen would not steal his sister's revenge from her. "Ignore him, he's Isfayen," said Damon, as though that explained everything. "What is your purpose here?"

"My cousin the Regent enters Shemorane with the Shereldin Star," said Elias. "This southern side of Shemorane is open, and the irregular forces of Kessligh Cronenverdt threaten this flank. I intend to make trouble here, and destroy much of these fertile lands to force Cronenverdt to defend it, and thus leave my cousin's ceremonies undisturbed."

"Should we move fast, we might catch Cronenverdt and encircle him," added Heryd, with some pleasure at the prospect.

Elias nodded. "The main road from Shemorane lies ahead. Many escaping refugees are upon the road, they were delayed by the rains. If we threaten them, and cut off the road, we may provoke him to do something rash."

"Little chance of that," Damon said grimly, surveying the scene.

"I'll take the Isfayen and scout the woods to the north of the river," said Sasha.

"Wait, Sasha," said Damon. "I think we should stay together."

"Markan?" Sasha asked, ignoring her brother.

Markan shrugged. "As good a plan as any," he agreed. He stood in his stirrups and waved back down the hill. There, a hundred Isfayen riders broke away from the Lenay formation, moving about the side of the hill as Sasha and Markan galloped down to join them.

"What are you thinking?" Markan yelled above the noise of their gallop.

"I'm not!" Sasha replied.

"I'm not going to burn villages and kill unarmed poor folk! There is no honour in it!"

Sasha nodded. She had no idea what she would do. Panic seized her, but she had to push on. She could not sit in the rear and watch.

She and Markan led one hundred Isfayen across the stream, then along the bank, past farmhouses and over paddock walls. Away from the stream the land grew higher, and Sasha liked the look of that vantage. They came upon a good road leading up that way from a bridge across the stream, and Sasha guessed it would lead somewhere worth attacking. She waved them onto the road, and galloped up the slope.

Soon, she saw smoke rising ahead. It was a town, larger than the rest, nestled beneath a forested ridge. Sasha waved them off the road and into the forest. It was not hard for a Lenay to find the ridgeline, and she wove her horse through wet undergrowth, climbing all the while. Soon she had them in a line upon the ridge overlooking the town. As the Isfayen horses stopped, she could hear fighting.

This was the fighting of warriors, not of Larosan knights massacring helpless villagers. She could see horses darting through the fields about the town, wheeling in groups, evading and never quite engaging with larger formations of Larosan cavalry.

"*Talmaad*," Markan observed. "If you listen, you can hear Larosans dying." There was respect in his voice.

"The whole town's a trap," Sasha replied. "They were waiting for the Larosans to hit it. But two can play at that."

"I guess perhaps sixty *talmaad*," said Markan. "Perhaps seventy. We are a hundred."

"Markan, I want prisoners. We have the heights, we can capture some. . . ."

"Those are our allies being killed down there," Markan said blandly. "Are we not to aid them in full?"

"Dammit, Markan, our allies are burning the town and killing any remaining villagers—you just said that was dishonourable!"

"Dishonourable for *Isfayen*," Markan corrected. "As it's also dishonourable to abandon a sworn ally to death by not attacking in support."

"Markan," Sasha said in desperation, "just do what I say. Your riders are not my men to command, but these are serrin and I know them." Markan studied her, his dark eyes unreadable. "Take forty men and go straight down this ridge. Make a line so they will see you. They'll not engage another forty men, they'll run, straight for the heaviest trees in the valley yonder. Bacosh heavy cavalry cannot manage those trees, but we can."

Markan continued studying her. "If they shoot any more of my men," he warned, "I will not show them mercy."

"If we trap them in the valley, prepare to stop beyond their range."

Markan nodded and turned to shout orders. Sasha urged her horse on along the ridge, and heard many hooves following. The ridge plunged down into the valley beyond the town, but the slope was not difficult. Upon the valley floor, a small stream flowed between huge, thick trees. Sasha formed her sixty riders across the narrow valley in several ranks, a barrier solid enough to stop any cavalry less heavy than lowlands knights. Then she waited.

Water dripped from leaves high above. Mist hung in the valley air, making ghostly shadows of dark, reaching boughs. An Isfayen rider at Sasha's side made a spirit sign to his forehead, as did several others. Spirits lived here. She heard hooves and a high, keening cry in a foreign tongue. A Saalsi dialect, Sasha reckoned, a communication between riders.

A single serrin rider raced from the mist, then scrambled to a sliding halt beside the stream. The rider stared wide-eyed at the barrier confronting her, then put heels to her horse and raced back the way she'd come, hollering in that high, lilting dialect.

"They shall go around us," said an Isfayen. "The valley sides are not steep, and their horses are nimble."

"They know we are Lenay," Sasha replied. "They know we do not attack. Sometimes, serrin just know."

The Isfayen looked at her oddly. Perhaps it was the mist, and the eerie echoes, but all of those that heard her made spirit signs once more. They called her the Synnich, the oldest and most deadly of the Lenay spirits. Perhaps they thought she summoned the serrin, who were spiritlike themselves, using ageless powers. Well, perhaps she did.

The next serrin to appear were trotting, not galloping. Sasha counted twenty, but there were surely more behind. They stopped no more than fifty paces away, well within arrow range. All the serrin had bows strung and arrows nocked, yet they did not draw. The Isfayen watched them, swords ready.

For a moment, the two lines regarded each other in the silence of the valley. Then a serrin rider moved forward. She wore a wide-brimmed hat, yet it was a Petrodor hat, not of the Bacosh fashion. Beneath the brim were emerald green eyes, narrowed with a deadly intensity.

Rhillian.

Sasha also rode forward. She knew that Rhillian felt responsible for the threat that she, Sasha, represented to Saalshen. Rhillian had befriended her, then failed to kill her when they had become enemies. She had sworn to eliminate all of Saalshen's enemies, particularly those as formidable as Sasha. She had promised herself never to be so soft again, whatever it cost her soul. One signal from Rhillian, and Sasha would be feathered with arrows. Sasha could see the temptation in Rhillian's eyes. The intensity. The conflict.

Rhillian drew her blade and gestered to the ground. Single combat? Sasha couldn't quite believe her old friend now hated her that much.

Sasha drew her own blade and dismounted. She walked forward, testing the wet, leafy ground beneath her boots. Rhillian also approached. Did she wish to die? They both knew Sasha was better. Nothing was certain in combat, but in sparring, Sasha would back herself three times out of four against Rhillian, perhaps more. Rhillian knew. Sasha could see that in her eyes as well.

They stopped. Blades poised, in a hush as though every living thing in the valley now paused, and considered the many fates that had collided to make this moment finally come. Sasha took a deep breath. The scene was beautiful. The misty valley, her brave Isfayen at her back. Rhillian herself, still the most lovely face she had ever seen. The spirits were watching. This would be a good place to die.

She lowered the blade to her side, and closed her eyes.

Time passed. Too much time. She opened her eyes once more, and found Rhillian standing directly before her, and no blade between them. Her impossible green eyes were shimmering. She put a hand to Sasha's cheek.

They embraced, desperately hard, and sobbed in each other's arms. Sasha lost control of her legs, and they sank to their knees, locked together with a grip like steel. The spirits of the valley watched, and knew that all the will of kings and priests and gods could not part them. Love carved its own path, and made its own fate. About them, Isfayen and serrin cheered alike, as though the war were already won.

Isfayen and *talmaad* retreated to a forested hilltop not far from the valley, with a view back toward the stream. There, amidst cautious scenes between wary humans and serrin, Sasha sat on a fallen log with Rhillian alongside, and Markan standing by them both.

"What now?" Markan asked shortly.

Rhillian and Sasha looked at each other, and suppressed grins. Annoyingly, Sasha had to wipe at her eyes once more. She felt as though she could breathe properly for the first time in what seemed like an age. As though some crushing weight had lifted. War and suffering beyond measure lay ahead, but for the first time in a long while, life itself felt good.

"I'm sorry about your hair," Sasha said. Rhillian wore her hat at her back, held by a lace at her collar. Rhillian turned her head, to show Sasha the diagonal cut at the back.

"Look how precise it is," said Rhillian. "You swing a blade like no one else I know." Sasha reached a hand to examine the cut with her fingers.

"I'm glad you ducked," she said. They were both struggling not to cry again. Markan cleared his throat.

"I have forsaken much traditional honour to follow the path of the Synnich spirit," he said sharply. "I will not forsake more honour to follow a weeping little girl."

Sasha wiped her eyes again, and composed herself. "Rhillian, we have a task. The cause for which the Army of Lenayin has been marching has proven itself honourless. My father thought to unite the regions of Lenayin within the forge of war, as a metalsmith blends different kinds of steel in hot fire. But this is not a forge, this is a poison well, from which we all have been forced to drink. I will drink no more. I know many Lenays feel the same."

"How many?" asked Rhillian. Her eyes were wide with possibility. With amazement.

"Half," said Sasha. "At least. More will follow, with leadership. I will offer mine. I cannot promise others, but I can persuade." She looked at Markan. Markan stood tall and grim, arms folded, and said nothing.

"The Lenay lords will not follow you," said Rhillian.

Sasha nodded. "It matters no more than it did in the Northern Rebellion

—the lords do not command the respect of any but other nobility, and they are few. Besides which, I have Great Lord Ackryd of Taneryn. I will not speak for Great Lord Markan, but he is here, as you see, and his blade is sheathed."

She glanced up at Markan. Markan snorted and stared away at the view.

"You promise a reunion with Kessligh, Lenayin's greatest hero," Rhillian murmured. "Valhanan will follow you and him."

"Tyree," Sasha added confidently. "Much of Rayen, and Neysh. I cannot speak for Yethulyn and Fyden, but if we had the Isfayen . . ." She looked again at Markan.

"The eastern tribes do not love the Isfayen," Markan growled. "We have shed too much of their blood. They will do the opposite to spite us."

"They respect you, because you have shed so much of their blood," Sasha countered. "Of course, much of the nobility will not follow their common folk. And the Hadryn, Banneryd, and Ranash will fight us all to the last man."

"You would split your nation for us?" Rhillian asked.

Sasha shook her head. "No. My nation is already split. I do not do this for Saalshen, Rhillian, though that is a pleasant consequence. I do this for Lenayin. My father, and now Koenyg, wish Lenayin to be a noble Verenthane kingdom. They have seen the grand model of lowland civilisation, and they have embraced it for their own, on the behalf of all Lenays.

"I have been to Tracato, and I have seen a different vision of lowland civilisation. It is a flawed vision, but it has promise. I would rather that model for Lenayin than the one offered by the Regent Arrosh any day. Should we win, that shall be our model. And there shall little room for the Hadryn and their friends in that. We fight them now, we fight them later . . ." Sasha shrugged. "Little difference."

"Tracato left you shattered," said Rhillian.

"People there failed to comprehend what they had built. They failed Tracato. With better leadership, it can still work. It was my mistake to abandon it all in my grief. By abandoning it all, I solve no problem, I only become one."

Rhillian smiled. She looked up at Markan.

"It is not for any of us to be making Lenayin into anything," Markan said grimly. "The Lenay people are free. The Isfayen are free. We practise our old ways, and we do not let any foreigner tell us how to be."

"Then King Soros was wrong to bring Verenthaneism to Lenayin?" Sasha asked.

"That's different. He was a liberator."

"As shall we be, when we save Saalshen," said Sasha.

"These are foreign lands!" Markan snapped. "King Soros liberated Lenayin, not some faraway outpost."

"So grand battles only matter if they are fought in Lenayin?" Sasha asked him, temper rising. "Then what are you doing here?" Markan glared. "The Isfayen came here for glory and conquest, as the Isfayen have always found glory and conquest in wars on foreign soil . . . hells, your ancestors laid waste to much of Telesia and Raani . . . by your logic, why bother, if only the affairs of Lenayin concern you?"

"The Isfayen marched to war because King Torvaal asked us to," Markan replied. "He was the King of Lenayin, in case you forget. Now, that king is Koenyg. We swore an oath to King Soros, that we are Lenay, and shall abide by the word of the King of Lenayin. . . ."

"Oh, rubbish!" Sasha exclaimed. "Since when have the Isfayen actually given a handful of horseshit what the King of Lenayin thinks? Your father Faras ordered the Isfayen to war because he saw some utility in making Lenayin unite as a nation, and as a people! That's why you were sent to Baen-Tar for education, and not raised in some windy hillside hut like your predecessors . . . and now you say the Isfayen accept no ideas from foreigners? You came here fighting for a Verenthane kingdom, whether you realised it nor not. Both it *and* Saalshen's kind of civilisation are foreign causes, yet you accuse only one of being so?"

"You are not the King of Lenayin!" Markan shouted. "You are the Synnich-ahn, you are wild and untamed, like all the men of Lenayin, but you are not king! There is honour in following the king. To disobey him, and fight against him, is . . ."

He did not complete the sentence. Koenyg would not follow. Not in a thousand years. Sasha took a deep breath, and realised what she was trying to do. She would fight her brother. How many of her brothers, she did not know. Any who followed her would be in rebellion against the king. That had not happened in Lenayin since there had been a king. The Northern Rebellion had come close, but she'd been very careful then to make clear what that rebellion was *not*. This time, there would be no dressing it up as something else.

"Great Lord Markan," Rhillian said calmly. Even ferocious Markan flinched a little, to meet her stare. "I have heard it said that to the Lenay warrior, honour is all. To the bloodwarriors of Isfayen, even more so."

Markan nodded grimly. "You have heard well."

"My people are being murdered, Markan. Your warriors have slain many of my *talmaad*, yet the *talmaad* are warriors themselves, and such combat has covered all in glory, your people and mine. But you saw the town as you rode in. The Larosans set it to fire, and there were old folk there, unable to face the road, who were cut down by Larosan blades. Is there honour in such a deed?"

"No," said Markan, stony-faced. "There is honour in killing an able opponent. To kill the old, the young, the unarmed, the helpless, such is *echtyth*. It is *anath*."

Rhillian looked at Sasha.

"Untranslatable," Sasha told her in Saalsi. "But very bad."

"Then it seems to me that you must choose, Great Lord of Isfayen. What most defines the soul of the Isfayen? Is it obedience to a king? Is it faithfulness to your father's orders? Or is it the path of righteous honour in battle? If you stay your course and fight with the Regent Arrosh, you will serve with an army that murders children, that kills the old before their time, that would seek to remove my entire race—most of whom cannot fight—from the face of this earth. You will be spared the dishonour of betraying your father's path, and turning against the King of Lenayin. But when the corpses of ten thousand children lie at your feet, what honour will you have left to be stained?"

"We do not participate in that," Markan said stonily. "We fight only warriors."

"Dear lord," Rhillian said gravely. "Is this an excuse used frequently amongst the honourable bloodwarriors of Isfayen? 'I did not participate in that crime'? 'I only stood by and watched, from a safe distance, and did nothing'?"

Markan's face wrinkled, as though he were smelling something very bad. He stood for a long moment. Then he turned and strode off, kicking at a tree root in passing.

Rhillian looked at Sasha, eyebrows raised. Sasha shrugged. "I don't know," she sighed. "We can hope. I know the Isfayen have far more respect for the *talmaad* and the Steel than they do for any beneath the Regent's banner."

"Lenayin seems full of humans who respect you more for having killed a lot of them."

"Yes, but killed honourably."

"I'm very glad at the prospect of some Lenays on my side. But I can never hope to understand them."

"Nor they you," said Sasha. "It does not matter, so long as we agree that Rhodia would be better if Saalshen won, and Regent Arrosh did not." Sasha reached for and clasped Rhillian's hand. "We must have Damon. If we can persuade Damon, we shall have momentum. Many will follow."

"Damon is not the warrior that Koenyg is," said Rhillian, frowning. "The men of Lenayin will follow whom they respect above whom they like."

Sasha shook her head. "*I'm* defying Koenyg—for most of those inclined against the Regent, that's enough. If they want a respected warrior to follow, they have me, and even Kessligh. But we need Damon so that we have a royal, the next in line to the throne. Lenay men will never be royalists, but it is important all the same."

"What about you?" Rhillian asked, with a penetrating stare. "If none of your brothers will come, there is always yourself." Sasha blinked. She hadn't thought of that for even an instant. "Third in line, by my reckoning. Assuming Wylfred is still out of consideration, and your other sisters could never be accepted, where men might make an exception for a woman who fights as you do. Ahead of Myklas by birth, only Koenyg and Damon come before you."

"All the more reason to get Damon to come over," Sasha said adamantly. "What you describe is terrifying."

Rhillian smiled. "In that, I am certain I empathise. Come, we must move. How is this played?"

"I have no idea," said Sasha, rising. "I've only managed a minor insurrection before. Nothing on this scale."

Seven

Koenyg raged. He stood off to the side of the road and kicked at a low wall until loose stones fell and rolled in the grass. Then, his feet undoubtedly sore, he roared obscenities to the sky.

Damon sat astride his horse, and felt numb. The Army of Lenayin had paused in its descent down a long, rolling hill. The army was no longer a single line, but had spread wide across the hillside, as cavalry tired of being further back in the column galloped to the front.

Now, none were advancing. Hooves thundered as soldiers and officers raced back and forth between groups of men, asking opinions, demanding answers. Across the hillside yells could be heard, voices and arguments, men debating their cause.

A new thunder sounded. Down in the shallow valley, a line of clustered horsemen were galloping, small horses bearing wild-haired Goeren-yai.

"That's the Taneryn leaving," someone remarked. Koenyg stood with hands on hips by the wall and watched them go. There were hundreds of horsemen. The Great Lord Ackryd was a friend of Sasha's, had ridden with her in the Northern Rebellion, and owed his great lordship to Sasha's opposition to the previous Great Lord Krayliss. But mostly, the Goeren-yai of Taneryn had never liked this war, and had always favoured the serrin. Now, the Synnich-ahn had switched sides, and her most devoted men were following.

No one was entirely certain how it had happened. Typically, important news would arrive at the royal vanguard first, but this time it had miraculously appeared within the army's ranks before the vanguard knew of its import. The vanguard knew only that there was uproar, the breaking of ranks, and an increasing number of desertions. Now, the Taneryn left. A lot of Goeren-yai from various provinces were joining them, not waiting for their provincial fellows to decide. Most others were holding, for now. War forged strong bonds between men of the same region, and they were not leaving without consensus from their comrades. The Army of Lenayin, hardly cohesive at the best of times, was in turmoil.

"I'm going to kill her!" Koenyg roared. "No, I'm going to string her up and gut her, *then* I'll kill her!"

Damon wondered if it even occurred to Koenyg that this event said as much or more about his war and his leadership of the army as it did about Sasha. No, he thought—it probably didn't.

News of exactly what Sasha had done was vague at best. Certainly she was now riding with the serrin. Some said she'd attacked Larosan knights. Others said she'd turned on her Isfayen comrades. Others still said she'd been possessed by the Synnich spirit, and had taken flight and killed hundreds with great bursts of fire from her hands. That last seemed unlikely.

But certainly, she had defected. Around Damon, the lords of the royal vanguard looked dumbfounded. Many spoke in disbelief, wondering what madness had possessed their common countrymen. Certainly the war had become unpopular with some, and had always been so with others, but to respond like this to the defection of "that stupid girl"?

Wasn't it just like the Lenay nobility, Damon thought, to be always the last to know? Jaryd would have understood, even were he still nobility. Damon wished Jaryd were here now. Jaryd would rally support, and would ride to Sasha's side. Jaryd would urge Damon to do the same, to stand up to Koenyg, finally, and use the power of the Army of Lenayin for an honourable cause. But now, Damon merely sat in the saddle amidst a mass of confused nobility and watched the unfolding calamity. And hated himself for it.

Isfayen horsemen were galloping up the hill toward the vanguard. Nobles pointed to them. "The Isfayen have returned!" one shouted, with some relief.

"Well, that's something," said another. "That's Markan, they'll not follow the bitch now."

They parted as the Isfayen arrived. Great Lord Markan leaped from his frothing horse, and strode to Koenyg. He loomed over the Lenay king in leathers, mail and studs, his black hair flying.

"My Lord King," said Markan, and took a knee. Koenyg looked a little more composed at that.

"The Isfayen return," said Koenyg. "What do you report?"

"The Isfayen return for honour," Markan announced.

"The Isfayen are always honourable."

Markan stared up at him. "The Isfayen shall not turn against their king from a distance. If the Isfayen are to renounce their king, they shall do it face-to-face."

Koenyg stared. Silence settled across the lords, broken only by the continuing chaos further back in the column.

"Are you threatening me?" Koenyg asked, very quietly.

Markan stood. "This war has no honour. Our allies are dishonourable, and unworthy of the Isfayen. We have fought the Enoran Steel, and found them brave and skilled. We have fought the *talmaad* of Saalshen, and found them possessed of warrior spirits. And we have fought with the knights and lords of the so-called Free Bacosh, and found them cowardly. They seek glory in the killing of those that cannot fight back. They fight for gold and land. They *ransom* opponents for it. Men rise to power amongst them by title and birth alone. They grow fat with self-importance, and little hint of ability or honourable deeds."

"They are the greatest power in Rhodia," Koenyg snarled back. "Lenayin shall be great, to be allied to them."

"Lenayin's honour shall be stained. You speak of power. I speak of *tervath*. They are not the same, your tongue and mine. Men in Baen-Tar forget."

Tervath, Damon knew, was the Telochi word for honour *and* power. In Telochi, they were both the same word, as one flowed from the other. For it to work any other way, to an Isfayen, was not civilisation. There were many elsewhere in Lenayin who felt the same.

"Markan," said Koenyg, attempting calm reason. "The future of Rhodia is Verenthane."

"That is not a fact," said Markan. "That is a choice. Perhaps we choose differently."

"*You* are Verenthane."

"But I am not *this kind*," said the Isfayen, with dripping contempt. "Pray that none of us should become so."

"When the Verenthanes came to Lenayin, they brought civilisation. Before that, we were a rabble. But King Soros brought the faith, and made us one. Now, we shall grow stronger still."

"Or it shall turn us into *anath alyn* like them. I would rather see Lenayin destroyed. Should we choose such a fate, we would deserve it."

"Dammit, man, will you not listen to reason?"

"That man's cousin raped my sister!" Markan roared. "I am Isfayen, and you have no *idea* how restrained I have been to this point! No longer!"

"You want to leave?" Koenyg shouted. "Then go! It seems it was too much to suppose that Lenayin could arrive at civilisation through foresight and wisdom! You Isfayen have always had to have civilisation beaten into you, and if it has to be that way again, so be it!"

Markan took out his huge, curved sword, and answering swords came out from all surrounding. But Markan handed the sword to Koenyg.

"In avoiding one dishonour, I invoke another," he declared. "I have forfeited the honour of my father's word to your father, from the Great Lord of Isfayen to the King of Lenayin. For that, you may take my life, should you choose."

"Do it," someone muttered.

Koenyg looked distastefully at Markan's blade. "If I take your life, Lord Markan, it shall be on the field of battle. Like the Isfayen, I see little honour in killing a man who will not fight back."

Markan nodded and sheathed his blade. "So shall it be."

"You would fight against the Army of Lenayin?" Koenyg asked, disbelievingly. "Why not simply return to Lenayin?"

"The Isfayen do not run from a fight. This is a contest of honour and must be decided. We leave because one side of honour has been proven weak. The other must therefore be superior. The Isfayen are for the superior side of honour. We shall stay and see the matter resolved."

Besides which, Damon thought, if the Isfayen left, the trickle of desertions would truly become a flood. They would not be fighting the Army of Lenayin. The Army of Lenayin would be fighting Koenyg, these lords, and the northerners.

"My Lord King," shouted a noble, "we cannot simply let them leave! We have them surrounded!"

"You do indeed," said Markan, a gleam in his eye. "You would offer us a fate more glorious than any Isfayen before us. Outnumbered, surrounded by old foes, fighting to the last man. We will take at least half of you with us, and the Isfayen shall sing of us for centuries yet untold."

"There will be no attack," said Koenyg. "These matters shall be decided on the field of battle."

Markan nodded and strode back to his horse. He mounted, and with Isfayen riders at his back, he galloped upslope, toward his people's place in the column. As he passed Damon, he gave him a long, hard look.

Koenyg saw. "Have you something to say, brother?" he demanded, striding to Damon's horse. Damon stared at him. Koenyg saw that too. He knew his brother that well, at least.

Koenyg grabbed Damon's arm and yanked him powerfully from the saddle. Damon leaped clear rather than hit the ground head first, and crashed to a knee. Koenyg seized a fist full of jacket over Damon's mail, his face contorted with fury.

"Sasha tears the Army of Lenayin apart, and you sympathise with *her*?" he shouted.

"*You* tear the Army of Lenayin apart!" Damon retorted. He tried to prise free of Koenyg's grip, but his elder brother was too strong. "The men of Lenayin cannot be led against their will! The Northern Rebellion proved that, but you never learned that lesson. . . ."

Koenyg threw Damon to the ground, and landed a kick in his mailed side as Damon rolled away. "She is a traitor to Lenayin! I'll see her dead, I swear it, and I'll see you dead if you defy me!"

Damon tried to get up, but a blow struck his head. He fell, arms up for protection, and a kick struck his leg. He'd been beaten by Koenyg before, and was not surprised. Koenyg had far more tolerance for defiance from foreigners and others than he did from younger brothers.

The blows stopped. Damon looked up past raised arms at the seething king standing over him. "Look at you!" Koenyg exclaimed, before the audience of lords. "You're pathetic! You plot and mutter behind my back, you make better friends with your sisters than with me or Myklas, you spend so long with your head in girlish pursuits it's a wonder you don't wear a dress over your mail! And now, you fall on your arse and cower like a whipped dog! You're a coward, and I have no use for you as my brother!"

He turned and strode back to his horse. Damon blinked, sitting on the grass by the road. And he realised that for once, his brother was actually right. And that death would be better.

Damon leaped to his feet, drew his sword, and charged. Lords yelled warning, and Koenyg spun, blade raised in defence. Damon struck full force, and struck to kill. Koenyg retreated, fending fast, steel clashing in rapid succession. Damon saw the astonishment on his face, and the concern, to find himself nearly overwhelmed.

Koenyg reversed one hard parry and leaped upslope. Damon cut low, was blocked by the downward slam of Koenyg's blade, which reversed toward Damon's head, but Damon parried hard and cut for Koenyg's neck. Koenyg swayed aside and cut low, in that easy, balanced style Damon had seen so often in sparring, as his rhythm recovered. And he knew that the surprise was ending, and now he was in trouble.

He tried to finish it fast, before Koenyg could truly get into rhythm, but each of his strikes was blocked with increasing surety. In the blink of an eye, Damon realised he'd fallen a fraction behind in the count. Koenyg came at him quickly, one side, the other, then a fast reverse, and Damon's parrys were a little later each time. In desperation he broke the rhythm entirely and struck a glancing blow on Koenyg's arm, but the next blow crushed Damon's defence, and the last tore into his ribs.

The mail saved him, but he fell all the same, with searing pain in his side. He struggled to rise, to raise his blade once more, but Koenyg swatted it aside, and stood on his sword arm. Damon lay back, and stared up the length of Koenyg's sword as the point pressed to his throat. His brother's eyes were ablaze, even as his arm seemed hurt.

"Attack from behind, eh?" Koenyg asked, breathing hard. "Most dishonourable, little brother."

"It's the best way to kill a cockroach," said Damon, also gasping. "They're hard vermin to face, because you have to come down to their level." He was amazed at how calm his voice was, despite his lack of air. It was as though the barrier of fear had finally snapped. He'd stood up to Koenyg now. He could die happy.

"I should kill you now," Koenyg snarled.

"I never doubted you would, one day."

"I never did you wrong, little brother."

Damon laughed. Suddenly, he couldn't stop laughing. It was insane—he and Koenyg had tried to kill each other, Koenyg was about to finish it, and he'd never been so amused.

"Look at you," he said, between gasps of breath. "My big brother, trying to reason. It's like watching a bull trying to use an abacus." Koenyg's face darkened. It had been a favourite line of Sofy's, when Koenyg couldn't hear. "Kessligh always said the rulership of kings would never last. Three generations, he said. You can start with a good king, like Great-Grandpa Soros. And he has a good son, like Grandpa Chayden. But by the time father wears the crown, the vitality is already fading . . ."

"You say *nothing* about our father!" Koenyg yelled.

". . . and by the time it gets to you, it's gone entirely. Three generations, Kessligh said. A century at most. Krystoff was his attempt to prolong it, but Krystoff died, and now you prove Kessligh right."

"I am *tired* of your lofty wisdom!"

"I know—that's why you resorted to beatings when you could never match it." Koenyg moved the sword point aside. He kicked Damon's sword away. Damon raised himself on an arm. "You're a tyrant, Koenyg. You ally us with tyrants because they appeal to you."

"I ally Lenayin with the strong because Lenayin is strong! Of course you don't understand that—look at you, lying defeated in the dirt!"

"You could always best me with a blade, Koenyg. But you've the smarts of a box of hammers." Koenyg kicked him hard in the shoulder. Damon winced, but continued, "You didn't see the Northern Rebellion coming, you didn't think the Goeren-yai would ever defy you, you've no idea how unpopular the lords are, you've got no idea how much most Lenays would prefer the serrin to any of us lot, to say nothing of *this* lot in Larosa . . ."

Koenyg was apoplectic. Somehow, Damon found that even funnier than last time, and struggled for composure.

"And now," he continued, "your army runs away from you, and like a little boy who kicks his puppy, you wonder why the puppy seeks new friends." More hooves were thundering nearby, at least a hundred riders. "And who is that leaving?" Damon asked, with bursting amusement. "The Rayen? The Yethulen? Dear gods, they all hate you, and now you wonder why. Bull with an abacus indeed."

He sprawled on the ground and laughed, as lords stood about him and stared. Fuck them all. He had a few friends here, but not many. He didn't care.

"Gods, I miss you, Sofy!" he yelled to the sky like a madman, as hooves and shouts and confusion filled the air. "You were the only one of us with any fucking wits!"

The Larosans were fleeing. Sasha galloped her horse at the head of perhaps fifty Isfayen who had stayed with her, and signalled them to halt. They sat astride frothing, tired horses, and watched *talmaad* chasing the remaining Larosan cavalry across the fields, shooting arrows into the backs of any who did not ride fast enough.

It was past midday now. Larosan bodies lay sprawled at random intervals and the few surviving Larosan knights were being rounded up. Perhaps the *talmaad* would take prisoners this time. Often that was too much of a difficulty for light cavalry without transport for captured men.

Sasha waved her Isfayen toward the river, so the horses could drink. On the muddy bank she jumped down and checked her mount's foreleg for what she thought was a faint limp. As she did so, ankle-deep in water, someone else called a warning. Then she heard a mass of hooves.

From across the river, a formation of cavalry approached. They wheeled, like black starlings across a green field, and thundered toward the bank. They held no banner, but Sasha recognised that combination of powerful horses, glinting mail, and black leathers with shields. Hadryn.

The heavy horse spread across the opposing bank, perhaps fifty strides distant and far too deep to ford. The Isfayen stared back. For a moment, there was no sound but for the murmur of gentle waters, and the snort of horses.

"The tales are true, then!" called a northern-accented voice. Sasha recognised the Great Lord Heryd, tall astride his mount. "The pagan princess has finally shown herself a traitor, and betrayed her king!"

"Myklas!" Sasha yelled, scanning the opposing bank. "Are you there?"

"I'm here," came the return call. Sasha's youngest brother was not as easily distinguishable from amidst the Hadryn warriors as she had supposed. His leathers were dark brown rather than black, but otherwise he looked tall and strong like the others.

"Come with me, Myklas. Damon will, we both know it. Kessligh fights on this side, as do the greatest warriors of these lands. The ones we've been marching with until now would be rejected even by the worms in their graves."

For a moment, there was silence. Sasha's hopes rose.

"Perhaps the greatest warriors *were* on your side," Myklas replied. "But not anymore. The Hadryn ride here now."

There rose a growl of approval from the black horsemen. It rose to a cheer. Some Isfayen smiled, greatly amused by such foolishness. Others spat, or glared.

"So you're a full-fledged Hadryn warrior now?" Sasha asked. "Myk, you weasel your way out of attending temple every chance you get. You can barely recite the First Prayer."

"This isn't about that," Myklas retorted. "I've ridden with these men in battle. They are my brothers."

"Your brothers are fanatics!" Sasha's temper grew short. Myklas was young and often stupid, but she'd never thought him cruel. "Ask them what they tried to do to the Udalyn! Ask them what they will do to serrin children if—spirits forbid—they find any!"

"At least I'm no traitor!"

"Myklas, they're using you! They build you up with kind words, but the Hadryn have always sought the throne for themselves. That's all this is!"

"You underestimate your brother!" said Lord Heryd. "I said that he was the best of us in the Battle of Shero Valley, and I meant it. With little experience, and not yet an older man's strength, he showed himself one of the most formidable warriors on the field. It is to the honour of Hadryn that he rides with us. In a few years, I am certain he shall best even his brother Koenyg."

Even from this distance, Sasha could see Myklas sitting taller in the saddle to hear Lord Heryd's words.

"Myklas, you ride with murderers!" Sasha shouted.

"Look who's talking!" Myklas retorted. There was laughter from the Hadryn.

"Baby killers!" yelled an Isfayen, which set off a raucous exchange of insults across the water.

Someone splashed into the shallows at Sasha's side. Sasha looked, and found Rhillian. "Baby killers?" Rhillian asked, in mild amazement. "Have you civilised the wild Isfayen into moral paragons?"

Sasha shook her head. "It's not the baby, it's the lack of challenge the baby presents."

"Oh," said Rhillian, sadly.

"You're not too far wrong though, it's only been a generation since the Isfayen would happily slaughter entire villages. But Markan's father Faras was a wise man, he sent his children to Baen-Tar for education and he worked with the priests to change the Isfayen notion of honour. Or rather, he narrowed it, to what you see today."

"I am sad then that Great Lord Faras died by a *talmaad* arrow."

"He'd only compliment the archer's accuracy," Sasha replied.

"Speaking of which," said Rhillian, "I have some archers. I'll not harm your brother, but I'm fairly sure we could take Lord Heryd."

"No," Sasha said quietly. "This moment should be done right. Lenays need their symbolic moments, let's not spoil it."

The remaining day passed in a blur. Lenay soldiers came across the Pirene in a trickle and then a flood. First came cavalry, and then footsoldiers, formed up in larger groups for defence, with other cavalry holding back to protect them. Some told stories of harassing raids by northern cavalry and some Larosans. But mostly, it seemed that what remained of the Lenay Army, beneath the command of King Koenyg, had ceased to advance. What came on now was the new Lenay Army, and it had no king.

The rains returned, and Sasha rode from group to group, to cheers from some and dull stares from others. Always the instruction was to make for the main road from Shemorane and follow it, for its path followed the Enoran Steel's retreat. News came from messengers that the Army of the Free Bacosh had entered Shemorane, less than a day's march away. Sasha doubted they would pursue, with the ceremonies at the High Temple about to commence, but cavalry elements certainly could. The Regent's army had better than a hundred thousand men, including tens of thousands of horse. The Lenays had to put distance between them, even if it meant marching through the night.

She was talking with some Rayen cavalry when a group of galloping Isfayen caught her eye. There were perhaps twenty, yelling and whooping, swords held high as they raced through the rain. They wheeled toward Sasha's group, and Sasha saw that the main body of men were in fact surrounding a girl, dressed in men's clothes, who was holding aloft not a sword, but something melon-sized and covered in hair. Predictably of the Isfayen, it was a head.

The group galloped past, and Sasha saw that the girl was Yasmyn, her eyes blazing with triumph. It felt wrong to smile at something so uncivilised. But Sasha found herself grinning.

"I almost don't want to ask," said the Rayen man she'd been talking to, "but whose head was that?"

"Elias Assineth," Sasha said cheerfully. "Cousin to the Regent."

"You must have eyes like a serrin to see his face."

"I didn't," said Sasha. "But nothing else could make Markan's sister so happy. And Elias was commanding the forces that attacked the Pirene. She must have charged him."

As the last stragglers broke into a run across the fields so as not to be left behind, Sasha finally returned to the road. There marched the Army of Lenayin, its battle order now a total mess, with provinces mixed together, men from south, west, and east walking or riding toward the south. Sasha rode through the fields beside the road, and at the crest of a hill, gained a sight of the road ahead. The column wound through the deepening gloom, into the heart of Enora. Men of central Tyree and Baen-Tar, of eastern Taneryn and Valhanan, of southern Rayen and Neysh, of eastern Isfayen, Yethulyn, and Fyden. Only the northerners of Ranash, Banneryd, and Hadryn were missing.

Soon she found Damon and a group of nobles on a hillside, watching the army pass. Sasha hugged him, and learned of his battle with Koenyg. He was in pain from his wounded side, yet seemed somehow triumphant. The nobles numbered thirty, from various provinces, and said they knew of as many again who rode elsewhere in the column. It was only a small portion of the total nobility, most of whom had stayed with Koenyg. Many of them watched Sasha warily, as though wondering who was now truly in charge—Damon or his sister. Sasha did not think that a question she was ready to answer.

Again she remounted her horse, and rode for the head of the column. And again she was halted, as someone on a cart amidst marching warriors yelled her name. Sasha peered, as the voice was familiar . . . and her heart stopped as she saw who it was.

She urged her horse to jump a low wall beside the road, then reined alongside the cart and leaped aboard. She hugged Andreyis, and burst into tears. Andreyis hugged her back, cheerfully, then introduced her to the other wounded men in the cart. Sasha barely took in anything, demanding again and again to know how he was not dead as she'd feared.

He told her, as a serrin girl riding alongside took the reins of Sasha's horse. The girl held the reins of one other horse that Andreyis claimed was now his, a gift from the monks for saving the High Temple. And *that* was a tale, which he told with relish, his young face alive with an odd combination of enthusiasm and confidence that she could not recall ever having seen in him before. Sasha listened, and every word was acknowledged by the men in the cart. One in particular proclaimed Andreyis a great hero, and *that* man, to Sasha's amazement was named Hydez, a Hadryn Verenthane. Sasha told him he was now probably the only Hadryn in the column. Hydez replied that his honour demanded he fight at Andreyis's side.

Sasha would happily have spent all evening in the cart, but with the darkness falling, she had to get to the head of the column. First she asked for Tomli, who had been riding with the supply wagons. He'd been safe there, but would be safer here, in the company of warriors. Sasha was not willing to leave him behind with anyone, with the Regent's army still in pursuit. Then she reclaimed her horse from the serrin girl, whose name was Yshel, and had been originally tasked to bring the Lenay prisoners to Shemorane. Now, as events brought the prisoners back into the Lenay Army, she had decided to follow.

"Would my young friend with the wounded arm have anything to do with that decision?" Sasha teased her in Saalsi, yet with real interest.

"My path and his coincide," Yshel admitted.

"Or perhaps entwine?" Sasha suggested. And she could have sworn that even in the fading light, she saw the serrin girl blush.

At the column's head, Sasha found a gathering of captains, village headmen, and a few lords. No one seemed to know who was in charge. All seemed greatly relieved to see Sasha as darkness fell, and the column continued through undulating fields. Sasha ordered scouts and cavalry to fall back, to give warning in case they were approached from the rear by Bacosh cavalry. None disputed her order. Sasha did not think a threat from behind at all likely—an army the size of the Army of the Free Bacosh (or whatever they were calling it now) was exceptionally difficult to manoeuvre at night, particularly in lands where the night was owned by forces hostile to their presence. Some lanterns and torches were brought to the head of the column, and some others lit further back, or carried by roadside sentries on horseback. Cloud and occasional rain made for a dark night, yet so long as the column held to the road, all would be good for now.

Rhillian arrived from across black fields in a rush of hooves and reined in at Sasha's side. "The Enoran Steel has encamped at a river ahead," she said. "If you march all night, you should be there in the morning."

Sasha nodded. "It's a good road. I think we can forgo one night's sleep. Why have the Steel stopped?"

"We hear there is some dissension. Some commanders say that with the Regent's advance halted in Shemorane, the advantage is with the defenders once again."

"Idiots," Sasha muttered. "The Enorans beat us, but they were mauled. I'll reckon the Rhodaanis are even worse after they lost. The Regent still has more than a hundred thousand, and I'll bet further that Koenyg will attach the northerners to that army as a new heavy cavalry formation. The Steel remains massively outnumbered, and the land here is perfect for cavalry and flanking manoeuvres, which takes their artillery out of play—their biggest advantage."

"The previous plan was to head for Jahnd," said Rhillian. Sasha nodded, having suspected as much. Jahnd seemed more a place of legend than a real city. No one knew precisely how old it was, some speculated a few centuries, others far longer. It lay on the far bank of the Ipshaal River from Enora, on the Saalshen side of the border, in the foothills of the Ilduuri Mountains. It was the only place in serrin lands where humans lived, a city that had long been a refuge for humans escaped across the river from the tyrannies of their kind.

Serrin, quite predictably, had been unable to reach consensus about sending such humans back to persecution and murder, yet were unwilling to allow humanity free range within Saalshen. So they had established a city on a tributary of the Ipshaal, within which those humans had made a colony. Over the centuries, that colony had grown into a large city, about which far more fantastic tales were known than facts. What was undisputed was that the city had been called Jahnd. In Enoran, the word meant "haven."

"And Saalshen is happy to be holding the last defence of the Saalshen Bacosh on serrin land?" Sasha asked.

"Saalshen's opinion is unknowable," said Rhillian. "If by Saalshen you mean me, then yes, I think the option is best. Jahnd is protected by the Ipshaal and the Ilduuri Mountains. And we both know that the Regent shall cross the Ipshaal in time, whether we lead him there or not. You've seen how he cleanses these lands of serrin, and any trace of Saalshen's influence upon humanity. He seeks to purify humanity of us. Jahnd shall not be allowed to stand one way or another. And once Jahnd falls, Saalshen lies before him."

"How are Jahnd's defences?"

"It is protected on three sides by mountains . . . not a perfect defence, but rough terrain and favouring the defender. It has walls, which serrin told the earliest humans were not necessary, yet those humans had suffered persecution, and were terrified that their old lords would cross the Ipshaal and attack them. So they built high walls, to defend against an attack that never came. Until now."

"And how do *we* cross the Ipshaal?" Sasha asked. "Boats could move the army, but it would take many days, and the Regent shall be on our tail again shortly. And I haven't seen any boat that could navigate a river and be large enough to transport catapults."

"We have a way," said Rhillian, with a smile in the dark. "Forgive me that I do not tell you. We have not even told the Steel, save for General Rochan. If the Regent knew, I doubt he would allow his priests to delay him so long in Shemorane. He assumes the Ipshaal an impassable barrier to us, and I would rather he stays thus misinformed."

"A way," Sasha repeated, thinking hard. Boats, she supposed. Very big boats. The Ipshaal was a very big river, far too wide and strong for any bridge. Surely such large boats were possible. "I look forward to being surprised."

"You have only seen Tracato," said Rhillian. "Tracato has its amazements. But Jahnd is something else again."

Dawn broke upon wet fields and dripping trees. Mist lay across gentle hills, and the night's rain made puddles by the roadside. The light was ghostly, and Sasha felt she was riding in a dreamworld between waking and sleep. In her exhaustion, it did not seem real, what she had led her people to do. Only when the morning cleared, as the sun burned away the mist, did she see a sight that made the previous day real again.

Across a ridgeline of hills, silver ranks of soldiers gleamed in the sun. It was the Enoran Steel. Along the column, men remarked upon sighting them. Some sounded concerned. The last time the men of Lenayin had seen that sight, more than a quarter of them had died.

Sasha looked about for the serrin guides who had accompanied them through the night, and found none. Suddenly, Sasha doubted. Had they been set up? Was this merely a ruse, to lure them all to their deaths? Surely not; the Army of Lenayin was a great asset to a desperate people—not merely a depletion of the enemy's ranks, but a significant increase to their own. But still the doubt remained.

The Steel's formation demanded a reply. Sasha had not seen Damon all night, so she gave the orders herself. Again, none refused her, and word passed loudly down the column.

The army flooded from the road onto the fields opposite the Steel. There was a gentle incline, and it was not a good position. Sasha felt uncomfortable with it, and by the looks several captains, lords, and other seniors gave her, she knew she was not alone. She waited by the road, on what was becoming the far right flank of the army's front line, and watched the lines extend. Bedraggled they were, and tired, and recently humiliated, and even more recently divided and rebelling. Yet still they presented a formidable sight— many thousands of men, and thousands more cavalry, perhaps eighteen thousand by the latest count. They were, man for man, the most fearsome fighting army in Rhodia, and surely even the Steel armies of the Saalshen Bacosh could not dispute it. Sasha looked at the ranks of gleaming steel atop the opposing ridgeline, and thought that surely, beneath those shining helms, Enoran soldiers were also recalling the last time these two armies faced each other, and remembering that familiar chill of fear. Every other army they had faced had been defeated. Most had been routed, and a few, utterly destroyed.

But not this one. This army, out-armoured, out-weaponed, outnumbered when one accounted for the *talmaad*, and against the most devastating barrage of Enoran artillery, had nearly won.

"What do they do?" an officer muttered by Sasha's side, as the army assembled.

"I'm not sure," said Sasha. "I think maybe a ritual."

"They line us up beneath their ridge," said another man. "They make us occupy the weaker position. It is submission."

"If they want us to kneel," growled the officer, "then this meeting will be bloodier than the last."

"Patience," Sasha told them. Another less exhausted moment and she might have smiled, that *she* should be giving such a reprimand. "They don't even have their artillery set up."

"How can you tell? We can't see beyond their ridge."

"I can tell," Sasha lied. "Just wait."

It took a long time for the army to assemble. Finally, the last men left the road and found a place in the formation upon the field.

Several men rode forth from the Enoran formation, and came across the grass. Sasha looked around for Damon, but still could not find him. She cursed, and rode out alone. She angled left, across the face of the Lenay formation. Initially she looked for Damon, seeking to wave him out onto the field. Then she realised how bad that would look.

On a sudden inspiration, she reined her horse to a halt before a group of cavalry—Fyden men, she saw, from the features of their faces and the style of their clothes and armour.

"Who here speaks Torovan?" she asked them. A few hands went up. "You," she said, selecting one man. "Ride with me."

The man looked baffled. Sasha gestured impatiently, and turned her horse to ride out. The Fyden man followed.

Three Enorans had stopped upon the field. Sasha halted her horse before them, and the Fyden man did likewise, looking very uncertain.

"Sashandra Lenayin," announced their leader. Sasha recognised him.

"General Rochan," she said. "We meet again, on a field between our two armies."

"I had supposed you the least significant of those I met on our last occasion," said the general. "Now I see I was mistaken." He was an average-sized man with narrow features and intense, watchful eyes. He had impressed Sasha then. Now, having fought against him, and seen his generalship firsthand, she was still impressed. "My sympathies about your father. Where are your brothers?"

"Prince Damon is here," she said. "Where, I do not know. It's been a long night. Koenyg and Myklas ride with the Regent still."

"I see," said General Rochan. "And your forces of the north?"

"Them too, and most of the nobility, though not all."

"Well," said the general. He indicated his two companions. "Here I ride with Formation Captain Petisse and Artillery Captain Mauvenon."

"You had another," said Sasha, remembering. "Where is he?"

"Formation Captain Lashel was killed at Shero Valley. Captain Petisse was promoted on the field."

"My sympathies," said Sasha, and meant it. "Your men fought with courage and skill. Lenayin was impressed."

"Our artillery did you great harm," said Rochan. "We did not expect such ferocity from any army that had run through our barrage. Enora was also impressed." He shifted his gaze to the Fyden man at Sasha's side. "And who is this?"

"I don't know," Sasha admitted. Rochan looked puzzled. The Fyden man, scarcely less so. "Warrior. Who are you?"

The Fyden drew himself up in his saddle. "I am Kemrys of Fahd, son of Todyn of Fahd. I am a warrior of the Fahd Clan beyond the Idrys River, and I salute an honoured opponent. There is blood between us." The introduction seemed as strange to Sasha as to Rochan—Fyden was a long way from her native Valhanan, and the men of Fyden made formal introductions differently.

General Rochan nodded in reply. He frowned at Sasha.

"You wish to know why we are here," said Sasha, too tired for greater sophistry. "I could tell you, but any words from my mouth would be misleading. We are not like any people you have met, save perhaps for the serrin, in that we are not a people easily led. I could tell you what I think, but at the end of the day, what this common man of Lenayin thinks is of far greater consequence."

Understanding dawned in the general's eyes. And, perhaps, new respect.

"Kemrys of Fahd," he said. "You swore an oath to your king that you would ride against the Saalshen Bacosh. Why have you . . ." But Kemrys was already shaking his head. Rochan stopped, and invited Kemrys to speak.

"My oath was to follow the king into battle," he said. "I knew nothing about the Saalshen Bacosh. Still don't . . . except that you fight well, and like serrin."

"But you have now gone against your king," Rochan pressed. "Help me to understand."

"Kings are not born," said Kemrys. "Kings are made."

Sasha smiled. She knew the native wisdom of her people. Understanding dawned in the foreign general's eyes, and Sasha felt immensely, overwhelmingly proud.

"You felt he had not earned his kingship?" Rochan pressed.

"King for one day," said Kemrys, with a sarcastic smile. "Koenyg swings a good blade, but ten men in my village swing a good blade. Ten men in my village cannot be king. Maybe here in the Bacosh, kings are born to rule. In my land, kings have to earn it."

"You are in Enora now," said Artillery Captain Mauvenon. "We have no kings—our leaders are chosen by their peers."

"Aye," said Kemrys, eyeing him thoughtfully. "A good custom, I think."

"What proved to you that King Koenyg had not earned his crown?" Rochan asked.

"We heard stories," said Kemrys. "Lots of talk on the way here from Lenayin. Said the Steel armies were unbeaten, said many things about your victories. Lenays admire victory. Others in eastern provinces said they liked the serrin. . . . Now we in Fyden haven't met many serrin. But the east insist the serrin fight well, too. So already, we're wondering why we're being asked to fight for an army that's done nothing but lose for two hundred years.

"Then we fight you. Some of us say you don't fight fair, with your fireballs and such. But you won. We never thought we wouldn't win. Not even once. We see the stories are true, and we start listening to all who know those stories.

"So when we come into Rhodaan, the talk all through the column is how the Larosan priests want all the serrin dead, how they're really after Saalshen . . . and we start really thinking about what we're doing here. I mean, we're Goeren-yai. Or I am, and now that the north and the nobility's gone, I reckon five in six of us are. We'll fight for Lenayin, but not for some crazy Verenthane crusade. And we see the smoke rising from the villages we pass.

"I went with some friends to take a look, just a short gallop from the column. We saw some stuff. Lenays, you know, we like a good fight. What I saw wasn't a good fight. What I saw is the kind of thing that gets a family . . . um . . . *esseryl etych?*"

He looked askance at Sasha.

"A matter of honour," Sasha translated for the Enorans. "If a warrior commits a dishonourable deed, in some regions they consider the whole family's honour stained. It can last generations."

"Like killing families," murmured the general.

"Children," Kemrys said solemnly. "I saw children."

"Me too," said Sasha.

The Enorans seemed moved.

"And you, Sashandra?" said Rochan. "You returned to your people. And now you have split them?"

"No," said Sasha, shaking her head. "Their heart and soul are with me still, and I with them. That which opposes us now was always the cancer of Lenayin. Now is our chance to defeat it, and remake Lenayin anew."

"Your brothers Myklas and Koenyg too?"

"Aye," Sasha said quietly. "But these are also my brothers. All eighteen thousand of them."

Rochan exchanged looks with his companions. He took a deep breath.

"Well," he said. "Our armies watch us, and wonder what we say. They fear our parley shall not end well."

"Few things have of late," said Sasha, with a faint smile. "Shall we give them a happier tale?"

She dismounted. General Rochan also dismounted. And then, in clear view of both armies, they embraced.

Into the air rose a great cheer. It came first from the Enoran line, Sasha realised with faint astonishment. It had the sound of desperation to it, and wild relief. Of frightened men who had been on the verge of losing everything, who now once again found hope.

There came an answering cheer from the Lenays, and the two armies ran at each other across a field for the second time in a month. Yet this time when they met, all weapons were sheathed, and instead of blows, men of different lands separated by half the world exchanged embraces, handclasps, laughter, and tears.

It took Koenyg a while to compose himself. He took that time on his way into Shemorane, amidst the silent entourage of his remaining vanguard. The northern lords rode proud and defiant, many now holding their Verenthane stars aloft on poles or great banners brought along for the purpose. Until now, most had hidden those symbols, upon Koenyg's command. Goeren-yai in the Army of Lenayin fought for Lenayin, not for some great crusade of the Verenthanes, and Koenyg had not wished them offended to the point of anger. But now, all such concerns were gone, and some of the northern lords, instead of being angered at developments, looked actually quite pleased.

His first response was rage, yet now that he thought about it, Damon was probably right to judge his tempers with contempt. Temper would solve nothing here. In fact, what now resolved before him was opportunity, pure and simple. His father had warned him of this, numerous times. "The Goeren-yai will like this war at first," he'd said, in one of those conversations they'd dared not share with Damon, and certainly not with Sasha. "They know nothing of the Saalshen Bacosh, save that their king has declared it a land to be conquered. But the eastern Goeren-yai will not like to fight the serrin directly, and in time, their discontent may spread. Lowland honour is not highland honour, and what Bacosh men may find glory in doing will not seem so glorious to many in Lenayin."

King Torvaal Lenayin had been unsuited to the leadership of Lenayin. He had made a fine start, commanding victory over the Cherrovan invaders in the Great War, with the help of his general, Kessligh Cronenverdt. But that had been a matter of simplicity, Lenayin against the merciless invader. Clearly the gods were on Lenayin's side, and Torvaal had commanded with conviction.

Yet once the Cherrovan were defeated, few things in Lenayin were so clear. Torvaal had attempted to reach out to the Goeren-yai, and to Saalshen, with his Nasi-Keth Commander of Armies training Torvaal's eldest son Krystoff as heir to the Lenay throne. But the lords and the north had fought back, leading to Krystoff's death, Kessligh's resignation, and the departure of Sasha from the royal family. Verenthane power in Lenayin was too entrenched to accept the vision that Torvaal had proposed, and the gods had punished him for it.

Fearful of the gods' anger, Torvaal had spent the rest of his life attempting to appease them, and seeking forgiveness for the mistake that had cost him his heir. He should have known then, Koenyg had long thought, what the correct path was. And yet he had refused. Koenyg often thought that Torvaal's long period of retreat and prayer in temple was not purely about the death of his heir. Nor was it an attempt simply to regain the gods' affection for himself and Lenayin, as many suggested. His father had prayed to the gods to seek their forgiveness for the thing he should have done, and yet could not. The Verenthane faith was the great and growing power of humanity. A good king, a *real* king, would make clear to the population of Lenayin that such was to be Lenayin's destiny as well. A real king would *lead*. Yet Torvaal, devout Verenthane that he was, refused.

And now the gods had claimed him too.

Koenyg was determined that he would not repeat his father's mistake. It did not matter that much of the population of Lenayin would not willingly follow. In the new world that loomed, to be divided was to die, and he loved Lenayin too much to see it dismembered by the great new powers that would arise following the Saalshen Bacosh's defeat. King Soros had liberated Lenayin, and brought a degree of unity, but only a small degree. King Torvaal had defended Lenayin, yet in general maintained a status quo.

Now, King Koenyg would unite Lenayin, by whatever means he must. He had hoped that that unity could be achieved in the forge of war, with the willing participation of the Goeren-yai. But now the Goeren-yai refused, and sought to cling to their futile and dying ways. Well, he had known it might come to this one day, when he was king. It had happened earlier than he'd thought, and in a different location. But now, finally, the struggle to unify Lenayin, and make it strong for the challenges to come, had begun. And here in the lowlands, he had the united Army of the Bacosh to support him in his cause.

Shemorane was wet with rain. The Army of the Bacosh was filing through its main road, an endless line of men and horses. Ahead rose the great spires of the High Temple, and as the Lenay party rode toward them, even the hard faces of the northern lords began to soften, their eyes raised to the weeping sky with awe.

They emerged into the temple courtyard, and mounted knights made a cordon before the High Temple's steps, as the common men of the army marched past, kneeling to the priests who stood beside the road to bless them, their eyes also raised to the sky.

Within the knights' cordon, nobility gathered and climbed the stairs, and embraced with joy. There would now be a grand service, Koenyg suspected, for the return of the Shereldin Star. He was pleased at least that he would be present for that.

He left the horses guarded nearby and climbed the wide steps, past watchful Bacosh lords. Within, the High Temple preparations for ceremony were already underway, the hurried deployment of drapery along the walls, and rushing priests with candle holders and prayer shawls. In the middle of the long pews, talking in hushed tones with several lords, Koenyg spotted the Regent Balthaar.

Balthaar turned as he approached.

"So," said the Regent, somewhat cautiously. He had heard. They all had. Now he expected Koenyg to grovel in humiliation. Koenyg refused. "I hear it is bad."

Koenyg shrugged. "A pagan rebellion. It is unfortunate. Yet the cream of Verenthane Lenayin remain with me, and are loyal to the cause."

"More so than ever," Heryd added from behind, with hard certainty.

Balthaar's eyes flicked to Heryd for a moment, then came back to Koenyg. "You have lost . . . three-quarters of your strength?"

"At least," Koenyg agreed.

"An embarrassment."

"Pagans," Koenyg repeated. "A dying breed. Their dying shall begin here."

Balthaar's lips pressed thin. "This could create for me a problem. We outnumber them greatly, yet pagans or not, this betrayal now strengthens the hand against us. You are certain they will fight?"

"Eastern pagans are leading them, they always liked the serrin. They'll fight."

"And yet you brought them anyway," observed one of Balthaar's lords, coldly. "Even knowing how dubious was their loyalty."

"They are Lenay," Koenyg replied. "That was supposed to be enough. Evidently not."

"And now the numbers against us grow," Balthaar continued. "Enora's losses were large, and Rhodaan's even larger, yet with Lenayin to bolster them, to say nothing of those troublesome *talmaad*, whose numbers will assuredly grow larger as we draw closer to Saalshen, our difficulties increase."

"Elisse commits large forces," Koenyg replied. "Most of your allies have kept many in reserve, yet Elisse owes you everything, and sends everything. Your other feudal allies now hear word of your successes, and are terrified that they are missing out on their share of this great triumph, and thus the spoils to come. I do not know feudal manpower in the Bacosh as you do, yet I should guess at several more tens of thousands there, who could reach across the Enoran border before we cross the Ipshaal River . . . if indeed the enemy does retreat to Jahnd as we expect.

"And then there are the Kazeri. I have word of a deal between them and the Chansul of Meraine."

Balthaar looked mildly surprised. "You have sources."

"My skills are not limited solely to warfare," said Koenyg. "Should the Kazeri send the numbers being suggested, then we are in the process of building what shall be by far the largest force of men ever assembled in the history of Rhodia. Yet for all your core of strength, your primary weakness remains in cavalry, especially against the *talmaad*. Northern Lenayin remains with me, and it is almost entirely cavalry, the finest in all lands. We shall be your cavalry core. With Lenay command of cavalry, you cannot lose."

Balthaar considered for a moment. Then he put a hand to Koenyg's shoulder, and steered him away from the others.

"Brother-in-law," he said quietly in the hush of the temple's vast space, "I shall tell you of something more. My brother Prince Dafed reports from Rhodaan where we have made some great discoveries. There are workshops in Rhodaan, in towns near Tracato, where artillery is made. Steel artillery."

Koenyg stared at him in amazement. "They were supposed to destroy it all before it was captured."

"Yes, well, much to everyone's amazement, it seems that the Steel have many spare. The logistics of operating such things, I suppose, means that there are only so many units of artillery that a certain-sized force can utilise before it becomes unmanageable. These artillery were supposed to be moved by road to join the retreating army, or destroyed, as you say . . . only some Rhodaani lords hoping to curry favour with my army intervened and have now handed them over to Dafed."

He stopped, and could not restrain a smile. "We have hellfire," he added. "They were making it in the same town. We have great stores of hellfire, all captured. And even some men who will instruct us in its use, as the Rhodaani nobles have some friends who know such things."

"My gods," Koenyg breathed. "Can it be transported?"

"As soon as possible, though we may have to wait a little for its arrival."

"We shall have to wait a little for the boats to cross the Ipshaal."

"Indeed, so no loss." Balthaar was assembling a large force of boat builders and carpenters, a surprisingly simple task with such a huge force at his disposal. "The enemy's only hope is that the Ilduuri come to their aid in force, and from what I hear, I do not think that at all likely. But I would ask you, brother, do not speculate on these things too often with the other feudal lords. Some things I would rather kept just between us two."

Koenyg was astonished. He had assumed that his obvious loss of face, with three in four of his men deserting him, would result in a similar loss of influence with Balthaar. Now this. But then, he recalled, he had been hearing other things, about relations between the Regent and his allies of late.

"Your friends squabble over the spoils," Koenyg said. "Well, be assured of one thing, brother—we Lenays are not concerned with your spoils. I fight for a Verenthane Lenayin, and a strong, Verenthane Bacosh to be our ally, nothing more."

Balthaar looked relieved. "It is so nice," he said mildly, "to speak to a man whose word I can trust. Just one." Things were quite bad then, Koenyg decided. "I have a mind to put such a man in command of our cavalry, as you suggest. I understand all of the nobility of the rest of Lenayin's provinces have remained loyal?"

"Very loyal," Koenyg agreed. "This war shall reshape Lenayin, brother. The pagans shall be dealt a crushing defeat here that it was not possible to deal them in Lenayin itself. Feudal power shall be expanded upon my return, and Verenthane power too. With the pagans diminished, more warriors of Northern Lenayin shall be freed to assist you, should you need them. The north has only sent a small portion of its forces, as it faces threats from Cherrovan *and* its Lenay neighbours. Soon that number shall increase. You have seen how we fight, brother. Lenayin remains a friend well worth having."

The ceremony to replace the Shereldin Star in the High Temple was very grand, for a thing so hastily organised. Koenyg did not understand much of it, for services were in Larosan, yet the certainty of it all impressed him. Choirs sang in heavenly reverence, and priests in robes marched slowly up the aisle. Here was a force that could unite men, and cease their constant bickering. Lenayin needed this more than it needed anything.

Emerging from the temple in the late evening, the Regent's army was still filing past and paying their respects. Such a volume of men surely could not lose. Satisfied, Koenyg stretched stiff shoulders, gathered his lords about him from the crowd emerging from the temple, and walked down the steps toward where their horses were stabled at the neighbouring monastery . . . when suddenly the street erupted in flame.

Koenyg fell, as men all about fell, hands up to ward off the glare and heat. And then it was fading, Koenyg lifting himself from the steps as huge clouds of smoke boiled upward into the overcast sky. Buildings all up the street were aflame, as were hundreds of men. They ran screaming, falling on the ground, as others leaped forward with coats to smother them. Horses galloped in terror, threw their riders, and a cart team went hurtling through crowds, as more men scattered.

"Hellfire," Lord Heryd said grimly, regaining his feet.

"Kessligh," Koenyg muttered. "One might have thought our allies would have enough wits to search the buildings along their route of advance."

"He fights dishonourably," another lord observed. "To be expected, from one who fights with the demons."

"He fights to win," said Koenyg, watching as flailing, burning men ceased their struggles and fell still. "There is more honour in victory than defeat. He would like me to underestimate him, as some of our allies do. I shall not."

Eight

Sasha wanted to move, but General Rochan had other ideas. In a great intermingling, the Enoran and Lenay armies made a temporary camp across the fields by the road, while commanders from both forces gathered on the grassy ridge beneath a wide oak tree, and debated.

They had barely begun when a new party of cavalry arrived, thirty strong and mixed equally between Nasi-Keth, *talmaad*, Enoran, and Rhodaani. Most paused on the camp's perimeter, while a few continued through the throng of Lenay and Enoran men who talked, shared food, and laughed. Sasha got up to watch them approach, suspecting, but barely daring to hope.

Leading the horsemen was Kessligh. He dismounted by the oak, strode to her, and embraced her. Strangely, Sasha did not feel any tears. Instead, she felt satisfaction.

"I had a feeling," Kessligh said warmly. "When I let you go from Tracato. I had a feeling it would lead to this."

"*I* have a feeling the Army of Lenayin would have chosen this path even without me," said Sasha.

"Perhaps," said Kessligh. "Or perhaps they would simply have turned and marched home. But they knew you would never do so."

"They know this is their fight," Sasha said simply. "This is a fight for Rhodia, and coming here, they realise for the first time that Lenayin is a part of Rhodia. This war determines Lenayin's fate as much as any other. That much of my father's war they agree with. They merely disagree with him on the matter of sides."

Rhillian was there also, with a quick embrace, and then Sasha saw Aisha, with a cheerful smile, and that embrace was longer. Then there were some Nasi-Keth friends from the Tol'rhen in Tracato, including Daish, a young, freckle-faced lad with a mischievous tongue, and Sasha hugged him too.

And finally, amidst the other greetings as the party was welcomed by Enorans and Lenays alike, she saw Errollyn. He leaned on his huge bow, and gazed at her. Sasha smiled back. She put her hands on her hips, and raised her eyebrows, as though to ask, "Where have you been?" His faintly exasperated smile replied, "Waiting for you." Sasha laughed. She ran at him, and grabbed him fiercely.

"Isn't it odd," he murmured, "that as *du'jannah*, I do not feel the unspoken pull of my fellow serrin, yet with you, I need no words?"

"Odd is one word for it," said Sasha, and kissed him. That lingered, forcefully. Sasha broke away with effort, and noticed that nearby men were watching, some grinning, others astonished. Surely gossip had told of her serrin lover, yet now they saw it for real. "I'm sorry, we can't do this here."

"I know," said Errollyn. "It's hard for you to hold their respect when one of those who follows you is fucking you."

Sasha gave him an incredulous stare. Then grinned as Errollyn laughed.

"Oh, they won't mind that," she said dismissively, "they know I'm wild." She had spent the past weeks wishing nothing more than to lose herself in his arms, but now that the opportunity presented, this was all she could manage. It mattered not, he was here now, and they were on the same side once more. He seemed different, though. As though a darkness clung to him, somewhere behind the smile. But the leadership group was re-forming, and she had no time to query further.

They resumed their places in a circle beneath the oak, where stones fallen from paddock walls had been rolled into place. Damon was there, nursing wounded ribs and in obvious pain. He claimed that pain had prevented him from the jolting gallop to the head of the column, but it did not explain why he had not ridden out with Sasha to face General Rochan. Sasha suspected other reasons.

"Where have you been?" General Rochan asked Kessligh.

"Shemorane," said Kessligh. "We arranged an ambush of sorts for the Regent, I think we may have cost them close to a thousand. A large part of the town was set afire to do it, but I think it worth the price."

"You didn't burn down the High Temple after all?" Sasha asked. "Andreyis went to some lengths to save it."

"No," said Kessligh. "The flames were too far away, and the roofs all wet. The Regent's soldiers will have put it out before it spread."

"Good," said Rochan. "You cause them further confusion. We should stand here, before they resume their march."

"No," said Kessligh. "We have not the strength."

"We concede too much to them already!" Rochan retorted. "They have lost three-quarters of the Army of Lenayin, while we have gained them. We are outnumbered no more than three to one and we have triumphed against worse odds than that before."

"Our scouts intercepted a messenger," said Rhillian. "He was Kazeri."

"Kazeri?"

"The Kazeri were divided," Rhillian said grimly. "There have been those amongst them who campaign for closer ties to the new, greater Bacosh. Verenthane Kazeri, much as in Lenayin. A few weeks back it seems the Verenthanes won, and the horsemen of Kazerak ride to the Regent's aid. Kazerak is a land of horsemen. The messenger was adamant on forty thousand."

There was silence about the circle. Sasha only knew tales of Kazerak. It was huge, with hot summers and wide plains where little grew but grass. Its people were nomads, mostly horsemen, who fought largely amongst themselves. There were said to be many Kazeri, but no one knew precisely how many, because they had few towns and no cities. In past centuries, the priests had made inroads for the Verenthane faith, and Kazeri warlords had embraced the gods. There had been talk of Kazeri warlords riding to assist the Regent in his war, but no one had known for certain.

"All the more reason to stand and fight here," said Rochan, unmoved. "If we beat the Regent first, we can stand and face the Kazeri before they join forces. Better to fight two smaller forces than one large one."

"Except that neither force is small," said Kessligh. "Both are larger than us . . ."

"Size has nothing to do with it."

". . . and should we gain a victory against the Regent," Kessligh continued, "it shall cost us so dearly that the force which stands to face the Kazeri will have little chance of victory. The Kazeri are fast and skillful cavalry—neither the *talmaad* nor artillery gains us much advantage against them."

"We think they're barely a week away," Rhillian added. "It would take days just to engage the Regent, and he would delay, knowing the Kazeri ride fast."

"And the Regent has some captured artillery from the Rhodaanis," Kessligh finished. "His men will not use it well, but use it they will. The success of Steel formations has always been predicated on the assumption that its enemies shall not use such weapons back against them. One catapult alone would do terrible damage to tightly packed Steel formations."

Rochan stabbed at the turf with his sword, and said nothing. Sasha recalled Kessligh's prediction in Tracato, that if the Steel lost, it would lose badly. The Steel were accustomed to victory and advance. Retreat and defensive withdrawal were not things they had any talent for.

"We need the Ilduuri," said Kessligh. "What news of them?"

"Nothing," Rhillian said grimly. "Not even a messenger."

"I know them," ventured Formation Captain Petisse, Rochan's second-in-command. "I studied at their school, and I have family there. Leading members of the Ilduuri Council favour isolation. They have their mountains —they see no need to risk destruction to come to our aid."

"They're fools," Rochan muttered. "Do they think to make terms with the Regent and his priests once we are defeated? It may not come immediately, but one day he shall march on them, and even their mountains shall not protect them."

"The Ilduuri are isolated," said Aisha. "I've travelled there, for study and *talmaad* business. They have never favoured engagement with their neighbours."

"But I hear the Ilduuri Steel is strong?" said Kessligh.

Rochan nodded. "Strong, yes. And more friendly to our cause than most Ilduuris—Ilduur society is isolated, but their army is not; we often train with contingents they send to us. They have less artillery—it's hard to use in the mountains. Their cavalry are good, but less so than Rhodaani and Enoran cavalry. Their infantry is the best of us all. Fewer formations, more individually skilled. Longer blades. I warrant they'd give you Lenays a fair contest."

"Unlikely," said Sasha. "But good to hear."

"And no use to us at all if they will not fight," Rochan finished.

"We must persuade them," said Kessligh. "Councils are never unanimous. If Ilduur had a king, then likely his mind would already be made, and all our asking would count for nothing. But councils have factions. Probably there will be one faction that will want to help, but is currently outvoted, even if it is only the Steel."

He looked to Aisha and Petisse for confirmation. Both nodded. Rochan, Sasha noted, was watching Kessligh intently, while seeming not to. Did it rankle the great general that this foreign usurper was slowly winning command? Rochan commanded the Enoran Steel, General Geralin the Rhodaani, and Rhillian the *talmaad*. But only Kessligh could see the whole picture, and knew how to forge all the distinct forces together into a working defence. From the look on Rochan's face, Sasha thought that he was reluctantly reaching the same conclusion as she.

Now, if she could only corner Damon, and figure out once and for all who commanded the Army of Lenayin.

"We will send a delegation from the front," said Rhillian. "We can appeal to their emotion. We have seen the crimes that unfold here, and we can foretell what further crimes shall come, to us and to them."

"Who?" Kessligh asked.

"It must be me," Rhillian replied. "The Ilduuri have never liked their Bacosh fellows, not those in the Saalshen Bacosh, nor those across the hostile border. They distrust Saalshen too, yet Saalshen at least retains access to

Andal, and will be listened to. A senior of the serrinim must lead the delegation. It must be me."

"Who will command the *talmaad*?" asked Rochan, with some alarm.

Rhillian levelled a finger at Errollyn. Errollyn stared back at her. Kessligh looked thoughtful. Then he nodded.

"Excellent choice," he said. Errollyn said nothing.

"Aisha must come too," said Rhillian. "As a scholar she is invaluable. Kiel's council too I value. And I will need warriors. I think it likely there is more than merely ideological differences holding the Ilduuri back. A general may have taken power over the council, or perhaps some other tyrant. We may need to fight."

"I'll go," said Sasha. All looked at her.

"Are you not in command of the Army of Lenayin?" asked Rochan.

"Prince Damon commands the army." Sasha decided then and there. "He is better trained in large formations than I, many men are. I would do a good job, but others could do better. In the Northern Rebellion, I was surrounded by experienced warriors who did much of the thinking for me and presented me with decisions."

"I too, even now," said Rochan. "Your uman as well, I'm certain. Half the skill of good command is choosing able seconds and thirds. Admitting such a thing does not make a commander less capable."

"Have no fear, General," Sasha said with a smile, "no one who knows me would accuse me of modesty." There were more smiles at that. "I merely speak the truth. Where I have *true* skill and experience is in irregular warfare. And politics. I will be more useful with Rhillian.

"My main purpose with the Army of Lenayin is as figurehead. But men do not need to see me here every day to know I am on their side. Staying here may cause complications, as not all the men of Lenayin love me and my pagan ways. Of Damon, there can be no dispute."

Damon was watching her, grimly. Like Errollyn, he said nothing.

"She's right," said Kessligh. "She has talent for command, but her primary strength is alone. She's wasted tied down to a large formation. She can also speak for Lenayin, and the example of an army of foreigners, who now fight to save Saalshen and her friends. She can be persuasive."

Sasha caught Errollyn looking at her. Reunited for barely a moment, and now she was leaving him. Her look was apologetic. But she could see that he understood. If they were to have any future together, first they would have to win. That was all that mattered now.

The armies resumed their march, with the Army of Lenayin going first on the road, with lighter forces that would not churn the surface for those marching behind. The Lenays were exhausted, and fell out thankfully to camp that evening. As fires were coaxed from damp wood, Sasha watched Kessligh prepare vegetables with some spices for a traditional Lenay raal, and reflected how nice it was that there was no need for sentries tonight.

There was a jostle at the waterside amidst men and horses from various formations, yet from their banter, Sasha sensed the presence of something she had not felt from these men for weeks. It was not quite pride, she thought. The Army of Lenayin had split, its new king abandoned, with most of its lords and the three northern provinces in entirety. It was nothing to feel proud about. Yet there was an uprightness in the men, a confident determination, that had not been present even days before. She puzzled over it as she rubbed down several horses in turn.

When finished, she returned the horses to the nearest muster of animals on a grassy bank, and made her way through the camp. Lenays and Enorans sat together, sharing food and drink, and attempting communication. Sometimes there were serrin there to translate, and sometimes men found a tongue in common (usually Torovan) but often not. Yet somehow, it did not matter. Men gesticulated wildly, and laughed often, as attempts to make oneself understood became as entertaining as the substance of conversation itself. Sasha had often found it so in Lenayin, where barely a third of all peoples spoke the so-called common tongue. Sometimes, friendships between foreigners were easier without words in common, as all that came across was "friend," expressed in a thousand different ways. These men were so happy, and so relieved to be friends, that it was a great joy just to move amongst them, and listen to their laughter.

At camp with Kessligh, Damon, Errollyn, and Rhillian, she sat and ate. For a while they discussed provisions, roads and weather, the drudgery of command that consumed so much time yet was never retold in the grand campfire tales. Then talk turned to the Ipshaal River.

"The Regent will cross opposite Verlin," said Rhillian. "Several days' march downriver from Jahnd, there are marshes between him and it. The Verlin tributary, it flows into the Ipshaal at that point and disappears into a bog. It can be skirted, and will delay his arrival further at Jahnd, yet he will not mind so much."

"Damn," Sasha murmured. "I had hopes for a riverbank defence."

Kessligh nodded. If they could cross the Ipshaal first, and then defend the far bank as the Regent tried to follow, it could be a slaughter. But the bog that Rhillian described would prevent Jahnd's defenders from deploying in force on that portion of the riverbank, while all the Regent needed to do was find a single road to bring him onto firmer ground. Rhillian described a firm bank, with marshlands beginning just beyond. Any force defending that riverbank would be unable to make an orderly retreat across or around the marsh.

"Still tempting," said Damon. "If he lands directly on the marsh bank itself, or on the edge of it to deprive us of defensive footing, we could deploy off to the side on firm ground, and trap him in the bog."

"Maybe," said Kessligh. "Or he could build a large force on the marsh bank, form a bridgehead defended by artillery so we can't get our own artillery close enough to use without losing it, and soon we'll get stuck in a nasty, muddy fight we can't retreat from, and even if we kill him at two or three to each one loss of our own, we still lose."

"It's horrible terrain," Rhillian agreed gloomily. "Nasty to assault and nasty to defend. He'll not be so considerate as to land within range of our artillery, but manoeuvring there is very difficult; he could build up a large force before we can make any position to attack it, and then not do all that much damage even when we do. The positive side is that he'll take weeks longer to land all his forces, and manoeuvre around the marsh to Jahnd. But winter is far away, he's not short of time."

"And if we put all our forces on the opposite riverbank," Kessligh added, "he'll just land a big force somewhere else. Boats are fast, and that part of Saalshen is wild, with forests and mountains alongside the marsh. We can't move fast enough to defend it against all the possible places he might land, and though it will make his movement a nightmare too, as Rhillian says, he has time. He'll build up a bridgehead somewhere, and then we still risk being stuck on the wrong side of the marsh when we have to retreat. I'd rather defend from Jahnd, where the terrain all favours us. Presuming we can actually get across the river ourselves," he added, with a glance at Rhillian

"We can," said Rhillian with a faint smile. "Just watch."

"Oh, and Sasha," said Kessligh, remembering something. He reached into a pocket, and pulled out something that might have been a bracelet. He tossed it to her. "*En eth'athal.* You are free."

Sasha frowned, and looked at the bracelet. It was an *emyl*, a traditional Lenay bracelet, to be given by father to daughter when she left home with her new husband. Traditionally it marked the coming of womanhood, while still affirming the ties with her old family, helping her to recall where she was from. Some joked that it was a warning, from father to new in-laws, that if they mistreated his daughter, they would still have him to answer to.

Then Sasha recalled what Kessligh had said. About the fireplace, people were smiling. "Oh, come on," she exclaimed, "you have to make a bigger effort than that! You can't just cut me loose with a bracelet!"

Everyone laughed. "I got it in Tracato," said Kessligh. "From a trader who didn't really know what it was, only that it looked pretty."

Sasha pulled it tight around her wrist. It wrapped well and would not flap about, far better for a swordfighter than a necklace that would bounce around. Sasha had never worn jewellery before in her life.

"It is pretty," she said. It was made of leather strips, three bands like her tri-braid, and steel rings. And an embedded amulet, of obsidian, shaped like the sun. Nothing fancy, but heavy with meaning. It suited her well. "Thank you."

She got up and embraced him. She was no longer his uma now, and those thirteen and more years of trial had come to an end.

"I should have done it a while ago," Kessligh admitted, reading her mind. "But there was never a good time."

"And 'growing up' is always relative with Sasha," Damon added. Sasha scowled at him.

"This is a curious combination of customs," Rhillian observed. "A Lenay *emyl* with the *uma'lanin*."

Sasha looked at the bracelet as she lay in bed with Errollyn later that night, her bare arm in the air, lit by orange coals. Around them was forest, with only a few other serrin camps. Privacy, for the two of them, on their one and only night together.

Errollyn held up his own arm, with the armguard marks still about his own wrist, where an archer would always wear it. He had other marks too, deep scars. Sasha's scars were more faded, but a few would never fade completely.

"Look," she murmured. "Some couples have matching jewellery. We have matching scars."

"I think perhaps what some call 'character' is in reality just a collection of scars," he replied.

Sasha smiled. "In Isfayen, they say, 'Never trust a man with no enemies.' In Valhanan, they say, 'Never trust a man with no scars.'"

"The older I get, the more Lenay I become. How disturbing."

Sasha buried her head against his shoulder, and they lay together beneath blankets, and listened to the night wind in the trees.

The School of Arts and Music was closer to Sofy's idea of heaven than anything scripture had described. She sat in a great recital hall and listened to the most talented musicians she'd ever seen play the most wonderful compositions she'd ever heard. Her retinue sat about, clustered Tracato nobility, some high-ranking red-coats, even a few Ulenshaals from the Tol'rhen, the great Nasi-Keth centre of learning. Jeddie sat at her side, entranced.

Along the walls stood knights of her Larosan personal guard in full armour, and Blackboots of the local Tracatan militia. She had not wished to attract such a crowd, but her tours of the city were all the talk on the streets, and Tracatan society followed her, literally. She'd toured perhaps half of all the grand buildings and institutions of Tracato, and she'd been here three days. So far, the School of Arts and Music was her favourite.

"What a wonderful concept!" she exclaimed to the Tracatan Premier Chiron, who walked at her side as she reluctantly took her leave. "I had never thought to make a central place for talent in an art such as music."

"And how is music practised in Lenayin?" Chiron asked politely.

"Well, as a part of life. Music is everywhere in Lenayin, at weddings and dinners and celebrations of all sorts, but it is something passed on from father to son in villages all over Lenayin, not in the one central place."

Her mind was alive with possibilities. Imagine starting such a school in Lenayin. She should suggest it to Koenyg, he was the one who'd insisted that this war would bring civilisation back to Lenayin. Well, perhaps that civilisation could start here.

Premier Chiron walked with her to the grand entrance. He was a small man, polite, serious and dour. Sofy thought he had good reason to be dour, given his position. Tracatans still called him "premier"; as head of the Rhodaani Council he had occupied a position equivalent to king, or at least to Lord of Rhodaan. But now Prince Dafed brought word from his brother Balthaar that no councils would be recognised, and all such institutions were disbanded effective immediately.

Dafed held court in the stronghold of Family Renine, the Ushal Fortress. Sofy, however, had declined similar quarters, preferring an offer from the Tol'rhen Ulenshaals to quarter there, in that amazing building. Sasha's descriptions had not done it justice, and from there the rest of Tracato lay at her doorstep. She could not recall having enjoyed herself as much as she had these last three days. Tracato was everything a grand civilisation should surely aspire to be—wealthy, philosophical, diverse, artistic. She could not quite believe that she, the younger princess of a highland kingdom far away, was now the Princess Regent of all of this . . . and soon, if her husband's victories continued, its queen.

She could make this work. Surely she could.

Jeddie gushed to the premier of the wonders she had seen, as they emerged at the doorstep of the school's main entrance. In the courtyard before the road, crowds of people gathered. Knights and men-at-arms of her entourage held them back from several royal carriages and a large number of saddled horses, but now the people all surged forward, and cheered just to see her. Sofy waved with delight. She had not expected a reception quite this positive—these were conquered people, whose army had not lost a war in two centuries, and now retreated in humiliation to Enora, leaving Tracato defenceless. Yet now they received her as though she were their liberation.

She made her way through the jostling crowds, accepting flowers offered to her by several, waving and smiling at others. Beside the royal carriage, she found Jaryd waiting for her.

"Where have you been?" she asked with a sudden affectation of disdain. She climbed into the carriage. Jaryd followed, and a noble who had been about to join her was forced to look for alternative transport. Jeddie and Premier Chiron did join her, the carriage only big enough for four.

"Around," said Jaryd, adjusting his sword to fit against the seat. The carriage doors shut, and they clattered off. "Dafed holds council with representatives of the Elissians. I think you should too."

"Jaryd, I have no time," Sofy replied, waving to the crowds. "There is so much to learn about this city, I am quite content to leave talk of armies and such to Dafed—that was Balthaar's intention in sending him. I am here to think in larger terms, about what will become of Tracato under my husband's rule."

"Sofy, the Elissians have an army, thousands strong, half a day's march from the city. Many of them want revenge for their most recent defeat, and if they grow upset enough, you won't *have* a city here."

"Balthaar will not see this city destroyed," said Sofy. "That's why he sent me, in full knowledge of my predilections. I mean, what an enormous risk for him, Jaryd. A new wife, from a faraway land distrusted by so many of his advisors, and he grants me a responsibility so large as this. He is making a statement to his allies about how his rule shall be. He admires the power of Tracato, and wishes to learn from it. I shall help him do so."

"Sofy," Jaryd tried again, "you're assuming he has more power than he actually does. . . ."

"Please, Jaryd," Sofy cut him off. "Not in front of our guest." She glanced to Premier Chiron. "We should not discuss such things so publicly. Please take no offence, Premier."

"But of course not," said Chiron, with a slight bow. "And if I may, Your Highness, I see the Elissians not so much as a threat to us but an opportunity. All these people who cheer you, they cheer because they think you will save them from the Elissians. When Tracato heard that the Steel was defeated, many panicked and left. But most stayed, because their lives are here, and because they heard that the Regent would recognise the old feudal rights, thus placing young Lord Alfriedo Renine at the head of Rhodaan. I myself have no difficulty in stepping down from my position, and yielding to Alfriedo, if it is in the best interest of Tracato and Rhodaan.

"But still they feared that some retribution would be in order, now that the Steel was not here to defend them, from the Elissians in particular. And now you have arrived, sent by the Regent himself, and you do not preach revenge or destruction, but respect and love. The people were frightened that you would demand the destruction of so much of their beloved city, yet now you tour the great sites. The Elissian threat will rally the people of Tracato behind you, Your Highness. You are their salvation."

"Look . . ." Jaryd shook his head in exasperation. "The only reason the priests and the Black Order aren't crawling all over this city, smashing its statues and burning everything, is because they're all up in Shemorane, returning that damn holy star of theirs to the Enoran High Temple. But as soon as that's over, they'll come back here, and there's not a lot your husband can do about that. This is a holy war, being fought to cleanse these lands of any trace of serrin influence—"

"And that is why I must work fast," Sofy interrupted, "to secure an arrangement within this city before they arrive. Even the Archbishop of Sherdaine cannot argue with the word of the Regent, through me."

"I wouldn't be so sure of that."

"Besides which," Sofy continued, "I do not believe that my husband dislikes the serrin as much as some others. He speaks that language because it is the language his allies and his priests demand, but I have heard him speak of Saalshen's achievements on occasion with admiration."

"Aye, the way a bully lad will admire another lad's apple, then punch him in the face and take it from him."

Sofy glared at Jaryd. He was truly being difficult, and she didn't think there was much more to it than his dislike of her being in charge. They had had adventures together, yet in all of those, he was the man with the sword, and his way was always the way taken. Here, he was in *her* territory and subject to her command. That, of course, and the small matter of jealousy. . . .

Jeddie leaned forward. "I do not see how my people could visit a city such as this," she said earnestly, "and not be moved by all that the serrin have inspired and created."

Jaryd smiled humourlessly. "Then I suppose you also fail to see why in this city with its huge serrin population, there's not a single serrin or half-serrin come out to cheer for you today."

Jeddie frowned. "You're right, I'm not sure I do see."

"For the gods' sakes, woman," Jaryd retorted, "they think they're going to be murdered! You've convinced all the humans, but the one group of folk who most need convincing of their protection are now somewhere on the road to Saalshen."

"Jaryd, you're being very rude," Sofy said coldly. "There is no cause to speak to Jeddie like that."

"Fine," Jaryd muttered. "I'll take my concern for the serrin elsewhere, you keep on being concerned of your manners."

He opened the carriage door without bothering to ask for it to slow, and skipped easily to the ground. Behind him, in the clatter of hooves and wheels, remained an uncomfortable pause.

"Very well then," said Sofy. "There is one place in Tracato I should love to see, but have not yet visited. Jeddie, won't you tell the driver to take us to the Mahl'rhen?"

Jaryd told himself he was only venturing inside to make certain his friends were not going to end up in trouble. The brothel was to his mind a dank and gloomy place, its narrow lobby filled with bored girls dressed in poor imitation of noble ladies. Asym and Jandlys did not care, and approached the girls with the enthusiasm of men gone months without female company. The madam interposed herself, somewhat nervously as Lenay customers were doubtless rare in these parts, but Asym and Jandlys showed her their coin and made their selections, joking that it had been so long, perhaps they should take two girls each.

"And you, good sir?" the madam asked, turning to Jaryd. "My, aren't you handsome? I'll warrant it will take a particularly high-class girl to please your tastes."

She called in Rhodaani, and a girl emerged from another room, looking irritated. Then she saw Jaryd, and her irritation faded.

"This lovely girl is Elene," said the madam. "Her price is of course a little higher, but you have the look of a man prepared to pay for the highest quality."

The girl was truly beautiful: her dark hair bound up to reveal a white curve of neck and shoulder, her waist narrow in the lady's corset. She sauntered to Jaryd, and trailed her fingers on his chest, gazing up at him with sultry fire. Jaryd did indeed feel the stirring in his loins. But mostly, he thought that her cheeks were fatter than Sofy's, and her lips did not quirk with crooked humour, and her eyes did not sparkle as Sofy's did.

"I'm sorry," he said flatly. "Perhaps another day." And to his friends as they ascended the stairs, "Take your time, I'm going to explore."

"Aye," said Jandlys, admiring the girl beneath his arm, "me too!" The girl looked a little nervous with the big, bearded Lenay, but Jaryd knew she had little to fear from Jandlys. Save for what was in his pants, which he supposed for a girl accustomed to less might be somewhat frightening.

Jaryd retreated onto the road. This was Reninesenn, or Renine's Town, in literal Rhodaani. These were the docks, just a stroll from the harbour, and territory loyal to Family Renine. Those who knew the place insisted that, like most of the city, things were very quiet lately. It did not look very quiet to Jaryd, as people went about their business, a bustle of commerce and tradesmen, officials, merchants, dockworkers, and sailors.

Jaryd stretched his shoulders and looked at the clear sky. He knew he was a fool. He had coin, and like his friends, he hadn't been with a woman in months. The last woman, in fact, had been Sofy. And now here he was, passing up a high-class, if expensive, fuck because he couldn't stop thinking of the impossible.

A man was approaching him. Or was he? For a moment, Jaryd was not sure, for the man wore the wide-brimmed hat common to the lowlands, beneath the brim of which he was glancing from side to side. But now he looked straight, and met Jaryd's eyes. Jaryd put a hand to his sword hilt. The man extended his own hand instead.

"Master Jaryd Nyvar?" Jaryd nodded. "My name is Zulmaher. I am a general in the Rhodaani Steel."

Jaryd blinked. "General Zulmaher? Who led the invasion of Elisse?" Zulmaher nodded. Jaryd shook his hand. "That was quite a feat of arms, I hear. Though of course, we should be enemies."

"Many things are not as they should be," said Zulmaher. He was slightly taller than Jaryd, which was considerable for a lowlander. "You are allied to the Army of the Bacosh, whose allies—the Elissians—I defeated. But now the boot has shifted to the other foot. I hear you are a friend to the Princess Sofy?" Zulmaher's glance shifted to the brothel entrance, and the red lanterns hanging at the threshold. Jaryd wondered how much he guessed.

"I am. I hear you are Lord Alfriedo's right hand these days?"

"The Lord Alfriedo may be young, but he has two hands of his very own. I give him guidance."

"I see," said Jaryd.

"He would like to speak with you."

"With me?" Jaryd frowned.

"Your princess is walking onto very thin ice. Lord Alfriedo and I would like very much to see her succeed, but there are many others who would not. If you wish to safeguard her life, there are things you will need to know."

Sofy had never seen a place as extraordinary as the Mahl'rhen. Tracato's house of the serrin was less a building than a collection of open spaces, interlinked by chambers, gardens, paths, and low buildings that could not seem to decide where they ended and began. Sofy walked with her grand entourage along winding ways, beneath lattices overgrown with vines and dangling fruit, past semicircular courtyards overlooked by open chambers, and past public pools seemingly suited for bathing that became water features and little falls in the gardens into which they flowed.

She was taken by the pride with which ordinary Tracatans showed off this jewel. As though it were not some alien imposter within their human city as the priests might suggest, but rather an ornament for all Tracatans, human and serrin alike. There was a sadness too, Sofy thought, in that there were no serrin here. Most had fled to Saalshen, as Jaryd had suggested, though Sofy guessed that many more were merely hiding, in safe houses or with sympathetic human families. But the Mahl'rhen was not empty, for in every courtyard or open space there were people, guarding the place from looters and now welcoming these royal guests.

"Did Maldereld build this?" Sofy asked Premier Chiron as they walked.

"Oh no," said Chiron, "Maldereld spent much of her time at the Justiciary. She was many things, but she was no architect. This was previously the land of a castle and great surrounds belonging to a family wiped out in King Leyvaan's invasion of Saalshen. Many serrin wandered Rhodaan, Enora, and Ilduur for years after, and those architects with the most inspiration gathered here, and made something peculiar to human and serrin styles."

"A tapestry," Sofy murmured. "Or perhaps a fusion. The serrin mind is surely not like the human."

"No," Chiron agreed, a little uncomfortably.

"In a good way," Sofy hastened to assure him.

As they stood to marvel at a small amphitheatre incorporated into a garden and overlooked on another side by a wall and balconies, Jeddie arrived somewhat breathlessly at Sofy's side.

"Princess, there is someone you should meet. He is asking for you in person." She pointed to a doorway. "Just in here, it's perfectly safe."

Two knights insisted on walking with her regardless, and looking inside. Within was an extraordinary room, like many grand chambers save that there was a wide, circular hole in its roof. Beneath that hole was a corresponding wide circle on the floor, ringed with a balustrade. Upon that balustrade were many symbols engraved on copper and inlaid into stone, and across the tiled floor were strange shapes, like angular sculptures, some as tall as a man, but in abstract form.

Jeddie went to an old man who sat overlooking the odd circle, and murmured to him. The knights checked that there was no other way into the chamber, then at Sofy's insistence left them alone.

Jeddie assisted the old man to stand. He wore lordly clothes, a fine silk shirt and boots, and his hair was long and white. But when he faced her, Sofy could see that he was serrin. The knights had not seen his face and eyes, so long was his hair, and so human his clothing.

"Princess Sofy," said Jeddie, "this is Ambassador Lesthen. He is Saalshen's senior representative in Rhodaan."

Lesthen made a light bow. Sofy hurried to him and grasped his hands.

"Ambassador. Where are your people? Are they well?"

"I cannot say," said Lesthen, and his eyes were apologetic. And yet, quite firm. "I am sorry."

He would not say, Sofy realised. She was the princess of a people whose religious folk swore to destroy all serrin. Whatever intentions she professed, he did not trust her.

"Of course," she said. "You have decided to remain?"

"I am too old to sacrifice what life I have left on the battlefield," said Lesthen. "If sacrifice is required, I shall sacrifice here. As ambassador, it is my task to meet with you. My *uthis'ul* . . . I am sorry, there is no precise translation in any human tongue. A purpose greater than oneself."

Sofy sighed. "I have long been envious of my sister Sashandra, that she speaks your tongue and I do not. It does seem precisely the linguistic task I would enjoy most in all the world, whatever its challenges."

"Sashandra," said Lesthen with a faint smile. It wrinkled his face, with lines more dry and flat than human wrinkles. "She does speak the tongue well. Of all the humans I have met, I feel that she is perhaps the best equipped of all to understand the serrinim."

"The best?"

"You are surprised."

"Well, I admit I do not always think of Sasha as a greatly cultured person," Sofy said in humour.

"But why should it require great culture to comprehend we serrin?"

Sofy blinked at the old serrin. There was a calm to him that was mes-merising. A presence that was not fearful or anxious, nervous or embarrassed, neither wishing anything from her nor desiring to do anything to her. It was an absence of edges, she realised, the kind of sharp and uneasy edges that characterised so many of her meetings with humans. To him, she was not any of the things that she was to those people, and her being a princess affected him perhaps least of all.

Perhaps this was why Lenays and serrin seemed to get along despite their most obvious differences, she thought. Lenays cared little for rank either. Serrin neither cringed nor begged favours, and as such were perhaps the only foreigners a common Lenay could immediately respect.

"Well," she answered him, "the serrin are a very cultured people, are you not?"

"If you feel pride in it," said Lesthen, "then it is not culture." Sofy frowned, baffled. "What you call culture is like a pretty jewel to wear upon your collar to tell lesser humans that you are superior to them. There is more culture in a farmer's song as he pulls his plough, or in a sailor's game of dice on the dock front. To build it so large as humans do, to make it the preserve of the wealthy and high status, that is not culture. That is pride and power, masquerading as such."

"Yet your people build such grand institutions of culture in Tracato!" Jeddie protested.

Lesthen smiled. "Do you think that our presence here has nothing to do with pride and power? We are here to impress, and sometimes even to frighten. That much at least have we learned of your ways."

"And why does Sasha understand you best?" Sofy asked.

"Because she sees our flaws, and distrusts our wisdom, and curses us for the fools we often are, even as she takes one of us into her bed." Lesthen sighed, and leaned on the balustrade railing. "She does not gaze in amaze-ment at all we have built, rather she despairs that we have built all of this without first testing to see that the foundation is firm. As I do now."

Sofy walked to his side and gazed upon the odd shapes on the sunlit floor. "What manner of place is this? I've never seen anything like it."

"This place is to study the sky," said Lesthen. He pointed up at the rim of the circle above them. "The marks there indicate the positions of stars viewed from a certain point on the floor, at different seasons and periods. Knowing such, it is possible to tell precisely the hour, even in the darkest night.

"And these shapes upon the floor are to measure the passage of the sun by observing the movement of its shadow, and to watch the phases of the moon. If I were more knowledgeable on such things, I could tell you more, but alas, I am but a humble ambassador, and with my head full of languages and strange human customs, I have had not the time of life to learn more. And now that I am old, and the end approaches in a manner other than I had wished, I find that I regret it deeply."

"And why would you wish to know such things?" Sofy asked in amazement. "Certainly all knowledge is valuable, but this does seem a lot of intricate effort."

"All serrin thinking is obsessed with the *amor'is eden*, the great patterns. The patterns rule everything. Did you know that there are other worlds out there? All circling our sun?"

Sofy blinked at him. Sasha had once told her that the world was round, and that some serrin claimed they could prove it. Sofy had not found that speculation nearly as interesting as her latest book of poetry, and had returned to that instead. A round world sounded vaguely blasphemous.

"Some serrin speculate that there may be clues to the greatest patterns, the *amor'is eden*, to be found in the study of the motion of sun, moon, and stars. Always seeking, are we serrin. Always looking to understand. And yet, so little do we know. If only humans would understand how little *they* know, and embrace the uncertainty with joy instead of fear, things would be different."

"Do serrin believe in gods?"

Lesthen smiled. "An old serrin joke says that humans believe in gods the way that horses believe in saddles." He glanced at her. "But perhaps one must be serrin to find that amusing. Serrin believe in higher powers. Humans call those gods, and give them names and personalities. Serrin find this interesting, perhaps quaint. We do not attempt to quantify that which is so far beyond our ability to comprehend. That would be pretence."

"I had heard that serrin worship knowledge," said Sofy, "but in a strange way, it seems to me now that perhaps you worship ignorance."

Lesthen raised his eyebrows, faintly. "Perhaps you understand us as well as your sister. Many serrin say precisely that. We worship ignorance as both our enemy and our friend, for without it, we would have nothing to seek."

"Master Lesthen, I could learn so much from you. I feel we have a meeting of the minds, your people and myself. I too seek to find a commonality between all things, between my people and yours. We must have points of common similarity that can conquer all this hatred! Will you help me to find them?"

Lesthen looked at her wearily. "My child," he said, "have you heard of the serrin philosophy of the *lashka'won*?" Sofy shook her head. "The *lashka'won* describes the natural path of the world, left to its own devices, free from human intervention. Many serrin scholars of the *lashka'won* argue over its nature. Some say that the *lashka'won* is brutal, that the natural world is an endless war of living things killing and eating other living things. Sashandra's lover Errollyn is one of those, and in that odd fashion, not so different from archenemy Kiel.

"Others argue that we serrin, and indeed humans, are also of the *lashka'won*, and we love and laugh, and are capable of great affection and justice . . . as are the animals, in some ways, by some means. They describe an aspiration . . . I shan't give you the Saalsi name because it shall become too confusing, but the name means 'to aspire,' in the sense that the *lashka'won* grants us the potential to aspire to something more than the common brutality of eating and surviving."

"The gods made us with the grace to aspire to goodness," said Sofy with a nod. "Verenthanes believe in this philosophy too, Ambassador."

"Serrin philosophers debate this endlessly," Lesthen continued. "The first group of the *lashka'won*—and I am of course simplifying here—the first group are of the philosophy that gave birth to the svaalverd, your sister's fighting style. Those who practise the svaalverd understand that certain forces and momentums of the natural world are immutable, and that the greatest power with a sword comes from flowing *with* these natural forces. Strong men with powerful muscles may try to fight against these forces, but as your sister can attest, the power asserted by mere human muscle is nothing beside the power of momentum and balance properly harnessed.

"Those people argue that whatever we might aspire to become, all civilisation achieves its best results when it does not fight these forces, but rather harnesses them. The second group argue that this is a path to endless war and suffering, because all natural forces are in conflict, and the easy road of conflict is never the best road where the lives of millions are at stake. They argue that the *lashka'won* has granted us alternative paths, as you yourself now argue that a common understanding between peoples can achieve peace between enemies better than war.

"Lately I have found myself wondering what Maldereld thought. She was a great builder, and both sides of this debate have claimed her as their own. Her own thoughts from her writings, however, are unclear. She did indeed find many commonalities between humans and serrin, to build what we have all benefitted from here in Tracato and Rhodaan for the past two hundred years. Yet on the other hand, she did impose that commonality by force, at times ruthlessly."

Sofy shook her head earnestly. "Lenayin has had so many wars, yet out of those wars we have built common understandings that have not perhaps made a peaceful land, but a more civilised one than existed before. Maldereld did not allow the bloodshed of the past to prevent her from building something wonderful in her present. Our peoples are now at war, yet that does not mean that what must follow shall be tragic for all. We can find a common path, I am certain of it!"

Lesthen walked slowly through a gap in the balustrade and out onto the circular floor, amongst the sculptures that measured the movements of heaven. "For so long in Tracato we serrin have fought the nature of things," he said sadly. "We forged peace for a time. We did not build armies of our own, because the successes of the Rhodaani, Enoran and Ilduuri Steel gave us an excuse not to. If the nature of the *lashka'won* is war, then we have ignored it, as one who lives in the sea might neglect to learn how to swim. We thought that here, we had an island of peace, yet an island is nothing before the greatest of waves. We presumed to have solved the world. We lived in pretence."

He turned to look at her, leaning against a man-sized tower that Sofy now recognised as a giant sundial. Its shadow upon the ground touched markings on the tiles, denoting the hour. "I look at you now, young princess, and I see myself until only quite recently. You carry the weight of the world, two halves of the world in fact, and you try to make them fit neatly together by sheer force of will. I wish you luck in your endeavours, but I do not know that my own example can lend you much confidence."

"What would you have me do?" Sofy asked him, eyes wide in faint desperation. "What would you suggest, as the best for your people and mine?"

Lesthen smiled sadly. "If the first group of the *lashka'won* are correct, then there is no best solution for your people and mine, only for one or the other. To fight the natural way of the world is the path to endless turmoil, yet not to fight it is to give in to the ways of brutality and war. It is for you to choose. This is my philosophy, at the end of my days. It is the philosophy of sadness. And I ask you to forgive me, for pressing it upon you now."

To Jaryd's surprise, Zulmaher led him to a small temple, nestled amidst a crowd of dockside tenements. Zulmaher led Jaryd up the tight, spiral steps of a belltower, until they emerged in one of the temple's twin spires. On all four sides were arched windows, presenting an excellent view of the harbour. Against the dock were perhaps fifteen tall ships, barely a fraction of the number the berths could take. Jaryd thought it sad that he'd walked what felt like halfway across Rhodia, yet was unable to see Tracato at its finest. All the ships were gone, fearing the consequences of the Rhodaani Steel's defeat.

Seated by one window, with a large book in his lap, was a boy of perhaps fourteen years. He wore lordly clothes, and a short sword rested against the chair in its scabbard. With fine, pale features, large eyes, and longish brown hair, Jaryd thought he nearly passed for a girl. In Lenayin, such a boy would have a miserable childhood.

"Lord Alfriedo," said Jaryd, with a short bow. Evidently the meeting was here because neither Zulmaher nor Alfriedo thought it wise to invite the likes of Jaryd so publicly to the Ushal Fortress.

"Master Nyvar," said Alfriedo, and his voice was high like a girl's too. He closed the book, and lifted it with effort onto the side table, atop two other tomes. "Is that the proper form of address? Or is it *yuan?*"

"In Torovan, master will do fine." Jaryd leaned against a wall, so he could see the street. He felt more comfortable that way.

"I have been reading of Lenayin," said Alfriedo. He spoke in the manner of a very intelligent boy who was accustomed to each interlocutor hanging upon his every word. "It does seem a very fascinating land. A very savage land filled with savage people, and yet you have codes of civility that raise you far above the barbarian."

"In my experience," said Jaryd, "the only barbarians in Lenayin are the nobles. The common folk are far more civil."

"They say you were once a noble. The heir to Tyree. Only your family's rivals murdered your brother and dissolved your family."

Jaryd nodded. "My brother was perhaps five years younger than yourself. He was killed in cold blood. I demanded revenge on those responsible, but the king's law would not allow it of a Verenthane. I renounced the faith and became Goeren-yai instead."

A black-robed priest chose that moment to emerge from the stairway, carrying a tray with tea and cups. He placed it on a small table, with bread, dip, and olive oil, and departed with a smile.

"And did you win your revenge as a Goeren-yai?" Zulmaher asked, pouring tea for them all.

"No," said Jaryd. "I discovered there were things I cared for even more."

"Young men believe that what they will or won't do can change the world," said Zulmaher, handing him a cup. "Older men learn differently."

"I should like to travel to Lenayin one day," said Alfriedo, grasping his own cup. "I grow tired of only learning about the world in books. I did greatly enjoy my conversation with your Princess Sofy, though. I have met three sisters of the Lenay royal family, and found them each formidable in different ways."

"We generals were hoping the girls had inherited all the wits and character," Zulmaher added wryly. "It seems we hoped in vain."

Jaryd nodded. "King Koenyg is a warrior, plain and simple. Myklas too, to everyone's surprise."

"And Prince Damon?"

"The most intelligent of the three," said Jaryd with certainty. Knowing that Sofy agreed made him even more certain. "Perhaps the most capable, but lacking conviction."

Alfriedo looked sad, and gazed out at the harbour. Jaryd frowned. And then realised. "You were very close with the Princess Alythia?" he asked the boy.

Alfriedo nodded. "She was with us only a short time. But she became like an older sister. I never had an older sister before. She was . . ."

He did not complete the sentence. The boy had lost his mother too, in the same disturbance that killed Alythia. Jaryd was struck by how great a burden had fallen upon such slim shoulders.

"I only met her briefly, once or twice when we were all younger," said Jaryd. "Courtly circles in Baen-Tar. I recall we danced once."

"She told me much about Lenayin," Alfriedo said quietly. "Were it not for her, I do not believe I would hold your land in such affection." He sipped at his tea. "And then there was Kessligh Cronenverdt, I know he is a Torovan by birth but he considers himself a Lenay. I met him three times. He is a very wise man, yet I do not know that I agree with him in even half of what he says. He did give me many ideas for things to read about, however. I have been reading a lot of Rhodaani history, and a lot of serrin books. These books are serrin."

He indicated the books on the table beside him.

"Lord Alfriedo is wondering how committed you are to your princess's safety," Zulmaher cut in, as though concerned that his young lord was giving away too much too early. Jaryd looked from one to the other, warily.

"Utterly," he said.

"Well, I'm very glad to hear that," said Alfriedo, somewhat drily. "When a Lenay warrior says such things, I can at least be certain I believe him."

Zulmaher grimaced. "It has been a frustration," he admitted. "The enemies of Rhodaan's nobility have all deserted the city or gone to ground. It has been as though all dreams were realised . . . save that of course my Rhodaani Steel has been defeated, a terrible cost for even the hardest of hard-line feudalists to swallow."

"Not all," Alfriedo corrected scornfully. He looked angry.

"No, not all." Zulmaher looked angry too, but hid it better. "Understand, Master Jaryd, that it is a dilemma of the most challenging kind. We nobles did wish for greater restoration of noble rights, but we are patriots too."

"Not all!" Alfriedo repeated, more angrily still. Zulmaher gave him a reprimanding look, as though from an uncle to an unruly nephew.

"*Most* of us are patriots," Zulmaher resumed. "We wanted more rights, but not at the expense of Rhodaani freedom. Now our army is defeated, and some nobility regard this a terrible defeat, while others rejoice as though our salvation descends upon us from heaven."

"The Army of the Bacosh may be many things," Jaryd said darkly. "Salvation from heaven it's not."

"Lord Alfriedo shall declare his rights before the Regent," Zulmaher continued, "and to judge by the noises the Regent has been making about the restoration of rightful claims, it would be in his interest to grant it. Declaring all Rhodaani land void of noble title will only start a struggle for power amongst all his other allies who will want to claim it, and the Regent can ill afford that disunity now. By declaring old Rhodaani title legal from before the serrin came, he gains new allies here and keeps his existing ones from squabbling over spoils."

"Exactly what is Prince Dafed asking?" Jaryd asked. Within the confines of Sofy's court, he had heard only rumour.

"Just the problem," said Zulmaher. "Prince Dafed has little idea about Tracato, not our history, nor how all our institutions work. He is a warrior. Our lords now ask him what we should do with so many of our grand institutions, and he just shrugs and tells us to work it out for ourselves."

"Well . . . that's good, yes?" Jaryd asked cautiously.

"It makes them bicker," Alfriedo said shortly. "The Rhodaani lords cannot agree. Some argue to retain something like a council, so the common folk may be heard. Others wish to dispose of the Tol'rhen and Mahl'rhen. But if we get rid of all serrin influence, what will happen to all my books?"

Jaryd did not think he meant it quite so selfishly.

"For so long we have viewed these institutions as anchors about our necks, holding us down," said Zulmaher. "Now we face the prospect of losing them for good, and instead of making us happy, it makes us feel naked."

"*Some* of us," Alfriedo interjected once more. "The others, I cannot understand. I will not be sad to see Tracato without a council or a Justiciary; both were corrupt houses of pointless argument and little else. The rule of lords is far more just and efficient. But imagine if we truly tried to cleanse the city of serrin influence. Every second building would have to be demolished, they taught us much of the architecture. All of the schools. All of the arts, the craft markets, the amphitheatre with all of its plays so influenced by the serrin writers and philosophers. The libraries!"

The young lord looked unhappy. Somehow, Jaryd found himself smiling.

"You sound just like Sofy," he said.

"Yes," Alfriedo said indignantly, "well, I am most pleased that your princess shares my concerns for my city, but it is quite a different thing for a foreigner to worry about these things and for the Lord of Rhodaan to worry about them."

"Sofy is the Princess Regent now," said Jaryd. "She does not see that she *is* a foreigner. These are her lands, and believe me, you could do much worse."

"I know," said Zulmaher. "Yet there is a danger in what she is doing. Prince Dafed makes court at Ushal Fortress. Princess Sofy makes court at the Tol'rhen. One is the brother of the Regent, the other is his wife, and each seems to share a different vision for Tracato."

"But you just said Dafed cares little what happens."

"Exactly. Dafed will let the Elissians do what they will, he cares not. The Elissians are angry. I fear I have played my part in making them that way."

"You should have destroyed them when you had the chance," Alfriedo muttered. General Zulmaher had commanded the Rhodaani Steel against Elisse barely months before.

"That was not the general opinion of Family Renine at the time," Zulmaher said archly. "But it matters not. The Elissians see that Dafed is their man. And Sofy, therefore, is their obstacle."

"She is well-protected," Jaryd said. "Larosan knights; I've spoken with them. Little that I'd trust a Larosan knight, but in this instance they are committed. To protect the Princess Regent is an honour."

"She should be careful nonetheless," Zulmaher persisted. "She becomes very popular in Tracato, and at a pace that will alarm many. Many lords here see the coming of the Regent as their path to power. Others hope for a great reshaping of Tracato, and the destruction of much that the Princess Regent now champions. She makes enemies. Some of those enemies wonder just how valuable is a new highland wife to the Regent, now that the wars appear all but won. If the Regent truly loved his wife, some say, he would have kept her by his side, and in his bed."

Jaryd watched him, arms folded, and felt resentment. Toward Sofy, mostly. Resentment that he should care at all, when she was now married to another, and to interests far beyond his nonexistent status. One night they had had together . . . or several in fact, upon the road, travelling from Algery in Tyree back to Baerlyn. And then she had left, for Baen-Tar, and her regal life so inaccessible. Now he was her puppy dog, running about after her in the vain hope of a pat, or perhaps a stick to chase.

He worried and watched as she so naively placed herself into dangers that only a very intelligent girl like her could contrive to get into, all wishful thinking and girlish daydreaming. A stupid girl would think less and fear more, and be safer for it.

"I've tried to warn her," he said. "I'll keep trying. But you've met her sisters. They're a headstrong family."

"Are any Lenays not?" asked Alfriedo.

"See that she listens," Zulmaher warned. "More than merely her life could depend on it. If her enemies here dispose of her, it would bode ill for all Lenays in the Bacosh."

Nine

The party made their way to Ilduur the fastest way they knew how. Two men of the Enoran cavalry led them, knowing these roads best. They rode almost directly south, while the armies of Lenayin, Rhodaan and Enora would continue toward the southeast, and the city of Jahnd. The pursuing Army of the Bacosh would be unlikely to head this way in any force, intending the full destruction of Jahnd and its defenders.

The lands they rode through were full of people, farmers and townsfolk going about their business as they might in any other time. Sasha had rarely seen lands so beautiful, rolling hills and pasture giving way to ample forest, and some formations of land so rugged that it seemed even the grandeur of lowlands civilisation could never claim them. Several times they passed old castles, some now broken ruins unused in two centuries, others occupied by commoners who lived within the great stone walls, one family to a chamber, and used the former lordly stables to pen their sheep at nights.

The first day, Sasha argued with Pelner, the leading Enoran cavalryman, about their pace. They rode either serrin mounts or Lenay dussieh, bred for stamina more than power, but even these were not invincible. Pelner was confident they could make the Shalaam Canyon that divided Enora from Ilduur in eleven days if they were fast. From there the land rose steeply, and the Ilduuri Mountains were not territory through which any could make fast progress whatever the urgency. Another ten days at the quickest, Pelner said, and Aisha agreed, having made that journey a number of times.

To her own astonishment, Sasha found herself arguing for a more sedate pace than the Enoran wished to set. It was possible, she argued, to hold a good pace even on high mountain trails. But not if they whipped the horses first. Exhausted horses would not fare well in high, cold air, and those that did not make the transition well might die. The price was worth paying, and the party of twenty-six riders brought twelve fresh mounts with them just in case, but Sasha was unconvinced that even those would fare well without riders, and would make for slow progress at altitude either way.

Pelner disagreed strongly. Sasha suspected him, like many of the Enorans and Rhodaanis, of being in a state of shock. The Steel had been defeated and was in retreat. Their lands were falling, their civilisation ending before their eyes. With the shock came frantic haste and panic. She feared Rhillian might succumb to the same, for the loss was similar for serrin as for human, and all knew Saalshen would be next. But Rhillian, in making the final decision, sided with Sasha.

"Jahnd's defences are strong," she said. "The Army of the Bacosh will not cross the Ipshaal quickly. Four periods of moderate gallop per day, no more. We save the horses a little for the high passes, and make more time there."

Sasha spent much time riding with Aisha, learning of the lands they rode through. On the promontory of a high hilltop, the walls of an old fort overlooked the surrounding sweep of land.

"Do you know these lands well?" Sasha asked.

"You know, strangely I don't," Aisha admitted. "My nearest town of Charleren is well west, near the Larosan border. Those lands I know like the back of my hand, but I joined the *talmaad* young, and my travels took me back to Saalshen, then to Rhodaan and Ilduur and Petrodor . . . I've spent more time travelling in foreign lands than in my own."

"Where did you learn to speak Lenay?" They were speaking Lenay now, as Aisha knew Sasha liked to whenever she had the chance.

"Vayha," said Aisha. "Enora has some wonderful Tol'rhen, some certainly better than in Saalshen. But I had to go all the way to Vayha in Saalshen to learn Lenay."

"I suppose Enora never had cause to learn it before."

"Our mistake."

Sasha smiled. "Weren't you telling me before that you met Rhillian in Vayha?"

Aisha nodded. "We're nearly the same age. She was seventeen, I was sixteen. She had an important uma, much *ra'shi*."

"She told me of him."

"Even then, people knew she was different. Not *du'jannah* like Errollyn, but not like most serrin either. Not bound so tightly by the *vel'ennar* that she could not think and act outside of it. Her Ulenshaals saw the potential of that, and were grooming her for big things.

"But her languages were not very good." Aisha smiled, remembering. "I was appointed to help her. We studied together, and shared quarters. She helped me with my svaalverd. I was better at that than she was with languages."

Ahead of them, Rhillian broke off her conversation with Yasmyn to turn in her saddle and fix Aisha with a look of amused reprimand.

"Just barely," she said. "I recall teaching you to defend the high overhead, and you needed a box for your little legs to stand upon."

"I want a sword." Yasmyn interrupted Aisha's good-humoured retort. "I will learn to fight with the svaalverd."

Sasha raised an eyebrow at Rhillian. It was not the first time Yasmyn had asked. "We don't have a spare sword," said Rhillian. "And I do not think this is the best time to be learning. . . ."

"I *will* have a sword," Yasmyn said shortly. "I will take one from an enemy."

"Don't be a silly goat, Yasmyn," Sasha told her. "Men's swords are too big, I've told you before."

"I can lift one."

"Me too, but the balance is wrong—even men can't fight svaalverd with a heavy blade. Besides which, you're sixteen and svaalverd is best taught from six, or earlier. Why not learn archery instead?"

"I know knife fighting," Yasmyn said stubbornly. "I have the footwork. I can learn swords."

Her problem, Sasha knew well, was that she had never before been in the company of this many women, and been the least feared of them all. She did not like it.

Yasmyn had come because it was her best chance for glory. She had achieved her *arganyar*, which was a great glory in itself, particularly as she was sister to the Great Lord of Isfayen. All the Isfayen had cheered her, and told stories of how Family Izlar was so formidable that even its women were more than a match for "great" Bacosh knights. But now, the armies of Lenayin, Rhodaan, and Enora marched to Jahnd, to make a final great defence. That fighting promised to be men's work, and though women of the serrin *talmaad* won great glory as light cavalry, Yasmyn did not have those skills either. And so she rode for Ilduur, an emissary of the Lenay peoples, and one not unskilled in the darker arts of politics and intrigue. Sasha was not about to let her lead any negotiations, but she would be comfortable to have Yasmyn watching her back once they arrived.

They came to the crest of the hill, and the party resumed their canter. The speed was too fast for conversation, and Sasha watched the passing countryside instead, and held a careful spacing between herself and her friends. Of the twenty-six-strong party, twelve were serrin and the rest a mix of Enorans, a few Rhodaanis, and two Lenays—Sasha and Yasmyn. One of the Rhodaanis was Daish, Sasha's young friend from the Tracato Tol'rhen, and the only Nasi-Keth besides Sasha herself.

That evening they made a little distance by torchlight after nightfall, before finally halting at a small village in a forested valley. The biggest stables were at the temple, and the priests took them all in with much hustle and shouting, gathering fodder for tired horses and meals for tired riders.

Sasha washed in the stream by the temple. Donning a cleaner pair of clothes, she returned to the temple's sleeping chambers by passing first through the temple proper. It was small, with wooden crossbeams holding up the ceiling atop stone walls. In that humble silence, she found Kiel standing before the altar. He was gazing at some point of fascination—a statue, half the size of a man, atop a similarly sized plinth beside the altar.

Sasha walked to his side and looked at the statue. On its head was a garland, which Sasha knew was often used by artists to denote a Verenthane saint. Yet this woman held a book under one arm, inscribed with the words *tul'tiah ran*, or "the common law." A Justice? A practitioner of laws? Suddenly Sasha realised why the woman looked familiar.

"It's Maldereld," she said, astonished.

Kiel nodded. "It does appear to be. Not a figure regularly worshipped in Verenthane temples."

The bringer of laws to Rhodaan, Enora, and Ilduur. These lands had once been ruled by lords and priests, and Maldereld was the most well-remembered face of those who had destroyed that old reign, and replaced it with the new.

"Aisha always told me that Enora is different," said Sasha. "The most well integrated, the friendliest to serrin. The least nostalgic for the old ways."

"They worship her," said Kiel, "as a saint." His tone was faintly mocking.

"What's wrong with that?" Sasha retorted. "Would you rather the alternative?"

"I merely wonder why with humans it must be either one extreme or the other. Maldereld was a great serrin warrior and scholar. I have read many of her writings and I know that she had no love of human religion at all."

"And yet she did not ban it, as some had encouraged her to do. She saw the purpose it served. And here she is, immortalised in stone, continuing that purpose still."

Kiel looked at her. His grey eyes were unlike any of the more typical bright colours of serrin. Those were penetrating, but these were unreadable. Sasha found his stare more unnerving than that of any other serrin she knew.

Kiel had tried to kill her, on a ship in Petrodor Harbour. She had been helping Errollyn to escape at the time, after Rhillian had decided it necessary to keep Errollyn detained. Errollyn had taken that arrow in the shoulder instead, and Kiel had nearly become the first serrin in more years than all serrin history recorded to purposely kill another . . . though even that was disputable, as he'd been aiming at her. Sasha supposed it was possible he'd been aiming at her shoulder too. Somehow, she doubted it.

"Purpose," said Kiel, with faint sarcasm. "The purpose of appeal to ignorant emotion, in place of reason."

"Lately I feel that reason's high reputation has been gained unfairly," Sasha said drily.

Kiel's lip curled. "A human might think so. But a human might not understand the term."

With any other serrin, Sasha might have been interested to debate the issue further. But she knew that unlike most serrin, Kiel's words were not *unintentionally* insulting.

She looked him up and down, with the aggressive half-smile of Lenay contempt. "Fuck you," she said, and walked unhurriedly from the temple.

The women had pulled rank and claimed the stables. It would have been impolite of them to repay the priests' hospitality by bedding as serrin normally would, with men and women together . . . and sometimes in the same bed, should urge and opportunity coincide.

Sasha made a final round of the horses before bed, checking each for any sign of poor condition that had somehow escaped notice after the day's riding. As she finished the final horse, she turned, and was confronted with a tall serrin man. His eyes burned nearly gold in the dark. Arendelle.

He considered her, wordlessly. Sasha folded her arms, and said nothing. Arendelle was a friend to Kiel and Rhillian both. He had been particularly close to Triana, who moved within Kiel's *ra'shi*, and had died at Sasha's blade upon the stern of the ship, along with Halrhen, another serrin. Sasha may have fought with the svaalverd, but she was in truth a Lenay yuan. Enemies were enemies, and one did not regret their killing any more than one regretted any of the other eternal fates. But those two she did regret, no matter how rightful the circumstance.

Arendelle approached, and gazed at her face. He was not an unattractive man. Strong, in the way of serrin archers. His golden eyes gave her a shiver. Serrin eyes were never exactly alike in their intensity. Arendelle's flicked down, considering her. If he'd been human, she might have been offended.

Her heart beat faster. Should she say something? She'd killed his friend. She did not know if it was accusation in Arendelle's eyes, or reconciliation, or something peculiarly serrin and inexplicable. He put a finger to her neck and traced a line down to her collar. Then to her chest, lingering at the breast beneath her jacket.

Sasha's eyes flashed warning. Serrin or not, her cultural tolerance had its limits. Arendelle's expression never changed, but his hand hovered. Then he turned on his heel, and left.

Sasha returned to the hay, where Rhillian prepared herself a makeshift bed. Yasmyn stretched nearby, with a difficulty that suggested it was a recent habit, copied from her swordfighting companions.

"What is it?" Rhillian asked Sasha. The dim lantern light was no hindrance for Rhillian's emerald eyes. She could read Sasha's face as clear as day.

"Arendelle," said Sasha. She did not need to explain the rest. Rhillian knew. Her expression was sombre. "Should I apologise?"

"Do you feel sorry?" There was an edge to Rhillian's voice too. Triana and Halrhen had been her friends as well.

"Yes," said Sasha. "Not as a Lenay yuan—Kiel had just tried to kill me and they were trying to finish it. If we talk of fault then the fault is Kiel's." Rhillian said nothing. "But however it happened, I'm sorry they're dead."

She rolled on her patch of hay, reached and grasped Rhillian's hand. Rhillian lay back and looked at her.

"They should not have come at you with blades drawn," Rhillian said quietly. "Kiel's action compelled them. They followed his *ra'shi*. As does Arendelle, more than mine." Sasha had not heard Rhillian admit that before. "But you should not have been there to begin with."

"You took Errollyn."

"I will not apologise for it," Rhillian said quietly. "It seemed necessary, at the time."

"And I will not apologise for rescuing him. We both are what we are. Neither of us tries to hide it. That's what made us friends once. We could be honest with each other."

"And I shall be honest with you now. Arendelle blames you for those deaths. I cannot claim to know what he seeks from you—we serrin are not so alike that we can guess each other's hearts, and I do not know Arendelle as well as Kiel does. I do know that he will not harm you, unless you give him cause to."

"I know." Thinking on it, she realised she had not felt even vague alarm at his presence just now. Not for her safety, anyhow.

"I would say that he seeks to reconcile the parts with the whole," said Rhillian, switching tongues to Saalsi to better explain herself. "It is a large concept in serrin thought. The individual against the group. He seeks to understand if it is human nature that is to blame for the deaths of his friends, or merely yourself."

"Why not conclude the blame was Kiel's and save us both the trouble?" Sasha muttered.

"No," said Rhillian, with certainty. "He is within Kiel's *ra'shi*. He will not turn on Kiel."

"You mean he can't question his leader?"

Rhillian raised an eyebrow. "And humans are above this?"

Sasha sighed. She wriggled closer, and lay directly at Rhillian's side.

"Rhillian," she began, "I should explain." She grasped both of Rhillian's hands and took a deep breath.

Rhillian silenced her with a finger to her lips. "Sasha," she said gently. "I know." Sasha gazed at her. "You don't have to explain to me. Understand that as serrin, I can say that I find fault with you for something terrible that happened, and not hate you for the same. Humans find this difficult."

Sasha didn't know what to say. For some time, she had thought Rhillian her enemy. An enemy of circumstance rather than of hatred, it was true, but an enemy nonetheless. Now she was struck by the strongest doubt that serrin even understood *that* word as humans did. Kiel knew his enemies not by hatred, but by differing ideals. He hated the invading Bacosh Army though, surely he did. Did he not?

"Do serrin understand 'hatred'?" Sasha asked. She used the Lenay word, *kran*. It stood out from their Saalsi, jarringly, like some muddy boot thrown onto a beautiful green lawn.

"Rage, certainly," Rhillian said at last. "But rage is impersonal. Hatred is directed at a person. I hate the things my enemies do. I kill them so they cannot do more . . . and for justice. But serrin were always shocked at how humans place themselves before events. You hate the person, not the thing. It always seemed to us pointless. We have always held that an individual, within society, is nothing more than the sum of his actions. I may hate what you've done, Sasha. It does not mean I hate *you*."

"I'm not sure I see the distinction," Sasha murmured.

Rhillian smiled faintly. "Me neither. It is the *biel'en sheel*." Sasha frowned, not understanding. "The 'glorious dilemma.' You may call it a test of judgement. Or of character. Serrin puzzle on such things constantly."

Sasha shook her head, sadly. "It's another reason serrin are so feared by humans," she said. "Spend some time with serrin, and a human may come to fear you are better than us. Spend a lot of time with serrin, and a human may become convinced of it."

She was awoken by Rhillian, kneeling over her in the dark. Her eyes made emerald spots in the darkness, sharp and deadly, and her blade was drawn. For a moment, Sasha nearly feared. Then she realised that if Rhillian's blade were aimed at her, she'd never have woken at all.

Rhillian saw Sasha looking, and pointed to her own two eyes, then at the surrounding dark. She said nothing, crouched as though expecting death to spring from the night. Something was very wrong.

Sasha pulled her sword from its scabbard, heart thumping and hands shaking. She *hated* that, and hoped Rhillian's eyes would not see . . . but any human, awoken thus in the dark, would fear. The horses were silent. Sasha's eyes struggled to adjust to the gloom, to recall her surroundings, and make sense of the shadows. Where were Yasmyn and Aisha? She moved carefully toward where she recalled Yasmyn's bed had been, figuring that Aisha had the night vision to look after herself. Rhillian caught Sasha's arm.

"Aisha is scouting," she breathed in Sasha's ear. "We don't know where Yasmyn is. Stay still."

"What's wrong?" Sasha whispered back.

"I don't know."

"But how do you . . . ?"

Rhillian silenced her with a finger to the lips. "Just wait. Stay to my flank, I will guide you if we must move."

Sasha suffered another chill. Rhillian saw the stables well enough, but Sasha was well used to serrin night vision by now. It was Rhillian's certainty that chilled her, despite nothing more amiss than Yasmyn's absence. Sometimes serrin did this. She didn't know how. Sometimes, when something was wrong, they just seemed to know.

Something moved, very faintly, in the doorway.

"Aisha," Rhillian murmured. She touched Sasha's arm and moved, Sasha following as silently as she could, trying to stay in Rhillian's footsteps. Aisha must have gestured them forward, but Sasha could not see it.

When they reached Aisha, she looked pale. "Three dead," Aisha whispered. "Killed quietly. Assassins."

"Raise the alarm?" said Sasha, heart pounding.

Aisha shook her head. "Not yet. We're surrounded. One alarm and they'll charge."

Sasha visualised the temple and adjoining monastery quarters. The river to one side, the road to the other. If she were conducting a stealth attack at night, she'd come from the river side, where few dwellings could sound the alarm, and then . . .

"Aisha," Rhillian whispered, "stay here and find the assassins, take them quietly if you can. Sasha and I will go to the riverside. When you hear fighting, raise the alarm."

They ducked into the corridor beyond the stables and moved silently, Sasha staying in Rhillian's footsteps. Aisha disappeared into a side corridor, while Rhillian paused at tall doors left ajar. She peered within, then beckoned Sasha to follow.

It was a common room, tall stone walls with bookshelves and furnishings. . . . Sasha could barely make out the shadows, and could only trust Rhillian's sight to tell the room was empty. Rhillian paused at the next doorway, her hand gesture warning of something obstructing the way. Sasha followed her into the kitchen. In the dark she nearly tripped over a shape sprawled on the floor—a body. From the robes, Sasha guessed a priest . . . in search of a midnight snack? Investigating a noise? Even with Rhillian to guide her, she did not like this darkness. Rhillian could only see one direction at a time, and Sasha forced herself not to look behind, trusting Rhillian's vision made them faster than their attackers, whoever they were.

Rhillian paused again at the large doors leading outside from the kitchen. She tried the latch and found it locked. The assassins had entered some other way. Sasha heard a noise and spun, eyes searching the dark. Nothing. Rhillian tugged her sleeve and led her to the nearby storeroom, where sacks of grain and boxes of vegetables filled the air with musty smells.

Rhillian climbed onto some boxes to check a window Sasha had not even seen. A creak told Sasha it had opened. Again a distant noise, and a hiss, like air escaping lungs. Like someone dying. Sasha held her blade for an opening low cut, most lethal against any sudden attacker who was as blind as she and less ready to defend the upward cut than the downward.

Behind her there was a faint noise as Rhillian slid through the high window and disappeared. Sasha knew she had to turn to climb the boxes, but now there was no one to guard her back. She muttered a silent curse at her cowardice, and sheathed her blade so she had two hands for climbing in the dark. The boxes held firm with little noise, and her strength allowed her to pull herself up with little scrambling.

No sooner had she sat on the top box than she felt, rather than saw, something moving on the ground to her left. Her heart nearly stopped, and she barely restrained a panicked reach for her blade, lest that noise give her away. She saw the back of a head, long-haired, almost level with her boots. He moved carefully, crouched like a warrior, his one-handed posture suggesting a knife. If he looked up, he would see her almost on top of him.

Not a tall man. She stared, and resolved more of his clothes—roughspun and leathers, no armour, nothing fancy. Something about the way he moved said horseman. A saddlesore swagger, legs apart. Lenay? Surely not with a knife in the dark. Not only dishonourable but, against serrin, likely fatal. Lenays knew serrin too well. But there were only two serrin here . . .

And now as she sat here, he was past her, advancing into the darkness of the kitchen she'd just left. She should have jumped down and killed him, but that was awkward, and Rhillian was outside waiting for her. Aisha would deal with him. Probably Aisha was the cause of that last sound of dying. Where the hells was Yasmyn?

She slipped out the window, had difficulty sighting the ground, but jumped anyway and landed on turf. There was a little more light outside, perhaps from a sliver of moon. A large oak made a great sillhouette, and a tangle of hedges blocked the view of the river. She could hear it though, a deep murmur of water. Where was Rhillian?

Sasha drew her blade once more and edged along the wall. A wooden fence adjoined the wall, frustratingly—it was rickety, overgrown with bushes, and would be hard to climb silently in the dark. As she looked for a way over, a shadow against the fence abruptly moved, and only the emerald flash of eyes stopped Sasha from swinging.

Rhillian pulled Sasha into a crouch against the fence and pointed over her shoulder. At first, Sasha saw only varying shades of dark. Then a shape moved. Rhillian's finger moved also, to another spot. Against a tree, an odd formation of trunk . . . with legs. Another move, then another.

"I see fifteen," Rhillian whispered in Sasha's ear. "There will be more." Their scouts were in the building. If they did not return soon, they would attack.

"Who are they?" Sasha murmured.

"Kazeri."

Horsemen of Kazerak. The rumours had said they were on their way. Sasha had envisioned an army of wild men on horses . . . this must be an advance party. And she realised that if they took a direct line from Kazerak through Rakani and Tournea, it would take them directly through these lands.

"I will go through them," said Rhillian. "You take advantage of the confusion."

"One against fifteen?"

Rhillian kissed her cheek. "Remember Leyvaan," she said. "This way, there is a hole."

She led Sasha to an unseen hole in the fence, and Sasha did think of King Leyvaan, the last king of the united Bacosh throne, who had advanced too fast into the forests of the Telesil foothills in Saalshen, and lost an entire army. The fighting then had been mostly by night. For humans, against serrin, it was unwise.

Sasha crouched behind bushes as Rhillian crept forward, and lost herself in the tangle of fruit trees, long grass, and weeds. Sasha wished she could see beyond Rhillian, downstream to the town's main bridge. The bridge. Why did the thought of it make her uneasy?

She peered through the bushes. Rhillian would be killing Kazeri by now. Sasha wondered how many she would get before the Kazeri realised what was happening. But the Kazeri Army was coming in the tens of thousands, surely. Small scouting groups were one thing, but this country was notoriously unfriendly to invaders. And what were the odds that the Kazeri just happened to stumble upon them like this? What if it was no coincidence? In that case, if they knew exactly who they were after, and why, surely they'd have sent far more men than this to deal with them?

The hair rose on her arms, and the fear of knives in the night was replaced by something more. She wished Rhillian would hurry. A bell rang. Then rang again. It came from the temple to Sasha's rear, and very loudly. Distant voices shouted. Ahead of her shadows began to move. Steel flashed, and one fell.

Yells and shouts from ahead of her now, as men spun to confront the threat. Another fell, then another, with a scream, and no clash of defensive steel. Sasha ran.

Men scattered in the night, searching for the ghost that killed them. Sasha came upon one with his back turned, killed him, then nearly collided with a running second, ducking away as he swung at her in panic. She stumbled on low bushes, unseen in the dark, and saw another man coming at her from the side . . . but that man staggered as a flying knife skewered his ribs.

Another ran past blindly, then one following him was suddenly separated from his head as though the dark itself had come alive and killed him. Sasha stared about wildly, dropping to one knee to make a smaller profile, hearing now yells and fighting from within the buildings. Aisha had awoken people, or someone had. They would make for the stables, and get the horses.

She heard more shouts, from over by the river. And now she could hear hooves. Many hooves, a large group of horses, moving fast. The sound came from the bridge. *Now* she realised why the thought of the bridge had made her anxious. Any force of horses coming down that road would be on them in no time. And if these men were just an advance party to check and see if the target were in fact present . . .

"Rhillian!" she yelled, and took off running for the road, ducking between trees and bushes, and hoping she wouldn't trip on something.

She ran between the property wall and the temple building, tangled trees giving way to vegetable patches and a paved path, then emerged onto the dirt road. She accelerated to a full sprint, heading across the building's front for the stables, as new light flooded from windows. Racing footsteps behind told her she was being followed, and she looked, but it was Rhillian, gaining on longer legs. Further behind them, hooves were now thundering.

Sasha rounded the corner into the stable yards, and found two men already ahorse, wheeling circles to keep six Kazeri at bay. She raced into them without pausing, faked a swing at one to buy a rider time, then dropped to slide long in the dirt and take another's leg in passing. Another Kazeri was wrestling with a horse's reins, the horse's head between himself and the rider, as one more circled to take the rider's flank. . . . Sasha rushed that man, fake-stepped and cut him through the middle. The first Kazeri abandoned the horse's reins and retreated, only to be slashed from behind by the second rider. Another Kazeri fell to Rhillian's fast-arriving blade, and the remaining two fled.

"Big force of horses coming down on us!" Sasha told the riders—Kiel and Arendelle, she now registered.

"We'll distract them," said Kiel, and kicked his horse's sides to gallop onto the road. Arendelle nocked an arrow to his bowstring as Sasha and Rhillian raced into the stables. Some cavalrymen were there, saddling fast, but Sasha knew there was no time for it.

"Get as many as you can and ride along the river!" she shouted, untethering her own horse and leaping astride bareback. "There's too many coming, you have to run!"

"If we're separated head for Ilduur!" Rhillian added, leaping astride her own horse.

"Rhillian, you stay and escort," Sasha retorted, grasping a handful of mane. "You're no rider bareback!"

She galloped off, tearing into the street, having no confidence that Rhillian would listen. Townsfolk were on the road now, with lanterns, torches, and weapons. Sasha galloped, sword in hand, and realised that she herself was not the equal of good cavalrymen in combat, however superior her horsemanship. Bareback, she was useless.

Ahead, dimly lit by torchlight, she could see Kiel's and Arendelle's horses on the road. Both men were firing arrow after arrow into oncoming cavalry, felling several as those behind swerved. The serrin turned their horses and retreated, twisting in their saddles to fire backward as only serrin knew how, felling more pursuers. Kazeri cavalry dodged, and several collided, finding such accuracy in the dark disconcerting.

Sasha saw a chance and tore past the serrin, cutting across the road and onto a grassy verge, Kazeri startling in astonishment as she galloped by. She did not bother to swing at them, but headed for the first side road, turned with a yank of her animal's mane, and galloped on. Looking over her shoulder, she found at least five chasing her. But here away from the main road there were few sources of light, only a dull outline of winding road between squat houses.

She took the next turn, determined to get back to the temple. She nearly hit a tree, her horse startling in fear and trying to slow, head tossing and disliking running at this speed in the dark even more than she did. Sasha kicked desperately as the hooves behind came closer still.

Suddenly there were village folk with lanterns ahead at the intersection of two roads. In that spill of light, a horse stood silhouetted, and astride it, a serrin aimed his bow directly at her. It was Kiel. For a brief moment, she recalled the deck of the ship in Petrodor Harbour, Kiel's bow drawn, his arrow aimed for her heart, only missing because Errollyn took the arrow himself. Now he fired, and once more the arrow streaked straight for her, with terrifying precision. Sasha ducked, but the arrow was aimed two hands from her ear, and buzzed like an angry wasp.

Behind her, a Kazeri toppled from the saddle. Kiel drew again and dropped a second. Sasha pulled her horse to a halt, as behind her the remaining Kazeri also halted, confronted with the terror of serrin archery for perhaps the first time in their lives. Kiel drew a third time, and they fled. Kiel placed that arrow between the last man's shoulder blades with a satisfying thud.

"Follow me," said Kiel, and wheeled his horse. Sasha followed. He galloped between small houses and little groups of frightened, running townsfolk, many with weapons. Toward the main road, Sasha saw large fires beginning to burn, and heard the sounds of fighting. It was big. Staying in town was not an option, and leaving would likely serve the villagers best also, assuming the Kazeri were after their guests and not the village itself.

Kiel led them clattering down a side lane, then through an open paddock gate, past a farmhouse and barking dogs. Soon they reached the tree line and the foot of the hills. There they paused, briefly, and stared back toward the town. Still the bell clanged, and fires burned high into the night. Sasha could hear no more intense fighting, only the occasional yell, and the endless barking of dogs. Whether that was because all the townsfolk were dead, or the Kazeri had abandoned town in pursuit of their main quarry, she did not know. Neither possibility appealed.

"Probably fortunate they attack at night," said Kiel. "Horse tracks are easy to follow by day, but not for humans at night. Now we can make ground and not be followed."

Sasha wondered if their friends would be so fortunate. It depended on whether Rhillian, Aisha, and Arendelle were still with them, to guide them in the dark.

"Arendelle was well when you separated from him?" Sasha asked.

"Yes. He went to help the others. I came to help you."

"Why?"

Sasha's eyes were good enough now that she could see Kiel's dry smile.

"We are practical," he said, with irony. "You fight well."

"You too."

"Friendship," said Kiel, even more drily. "How nice."

"Rhillian will have crossed the river at the next bridge," said Sasha, ignoring his tone. "That way the Kazeri cannot trap her against the river. But it now puts the river between us and her."

"We know where she's going," said Kiel. "Let's get there before her. We cannot ambush that Kazeri force, it's too big, but we can make certain Rhillian will not be ambushed by another one. If that is just the vanguard for the Kazeri Army . . ."

"If the Kazeri Army comes down on top of us, there's not a lot we can do."

"No," Kiel agreed. "But we can make fast for Ilduur, and hope they are late."

They rode uphill in the dark, and then along the ridge at a walk. Sasha wanted to contribute a route, having had far more experience riding in hills than Kiel, but whatever moon there was hid behind thick cloud, and she could barely see the trees as they passed. She thought it was past midnight, but could not tell. The horses plodded on despite exhaustion, and Sasha wondered how she was going to be able to reach Ilduur with no saddle or bridle, no saddlebags and no supplies. She doubted any of their company would be better off, should they reunite.

By dawn, she, Kiel, and the horses were exhausted. Then it began to rain. They both decided the rain offered the best excuse to stop and rest. Kiel *had* managed to saddle his horse, and Sasha wondered if he'd awoken early as Rhillian and Aisha had. He produced a blanket from his saddlebags, and covered them both with it as they made a nest between the roots of a big tree. The leaves offered cover at first, yet soon the rain grew heavier, and the blanket began to soak. Comfortably taller, Kiel wrapped his arms around her to warm them both.

"I wish I knew how to sleep on the ground," he said with discomfort. "Errollyn can. But like Rhillian, I'm a city serrin, and I like my bed."

Sasha said nothing, fast asleep.

The morning cleared to drifting mist and dripping branches, golden sunlight fighting through the cloud. More rested than Kiel, Sasha led the horses to a stream for watering, then picked a good trail up a hillside ridge from where she reckoned a decent lookout could be gained.

Above the southern horizon, the outline of jagged mountains rose. That way was Ilduur, their destination. In the maze of surrounding rumpled forest and valleys, Sasha made out the course of the river they'd left, and where she figured the road would take Rhillian, assuming Rhillian had followed it. The Kazeri, she was quite sure, would have stopped for the night having lost their quarry.

After gaining her bearings, she prepared to remount and saw Kiel frowning toward the western horizon.

"What is it?" she asked. Kiel said nothing, squinting into the distance. Serrin, Sasha knew, saw further by day also. Sasha waited. Finally Kiel prepared to mount, looking grim. "What?" Sasha repeated.

"An army," said Kiel. "You'll not see it, I can barely make it out myself. That ridge there, beyond the yellow fields."

Sasha looked. It was not too far. Perhaps a half-day's ride. "Heading which way?" she asked in alarm.

"Northeast. Toward our retreating armies. They move along a road, I can see the road where it crests the ridge. Horsemen pass in a steady flow."

Horsemen. The Steel and the Army of Lenayin had large numbers of infantry, far slower.

"They'll be on them in a few days, if that."

"We cannot help that," Kiel said grimly. "Our mission remains unchanged; we must reach Ilduur, and hope our forces can fight their way to Jahnd."

They reached the road by midday. There were hoof marks on the turf, no way of telling whose, but headed south, toward Ilduur. Sasha and Kiel followed until a band of townsfolk arrived, all armed and frightened, with tales of a great army passing near, and none of the Steel in any position to intercept it. They moved fast, one grizzled ex-Steel cavalryman told them, too fast for warning, all ahorse and numbering in the tens of thousands. Small bands scouted ahead, causing mayhem where they rode.

Asking after their companions brought gestures aimed further up the road. Sasha risked a canter, making ground rapidly until they came to another small village nestled in the valley folds. There waiting for them ahorse was Arendelle, lowering his bow as he recognised who approached. He led them wordlessly to the town square, where gathered another nine of their previously twenty-six-strong party, dishevelled and some wounded, assisted by frightened village folk.

Sasha exchanged a relieved embrace with a grim-looking Rhillian, then Aisha, sitting with a village elder discussing the road ahead. Both appeared unhurt.

"This is all?" Sasha asked in dismay, looking around.

"Some more may turn up, like you," Rhillian said. "But we're certain of eight dead. The other six, I don't know."

Sasha exhaled hard. More than half of their party dead or missing before they'd truly begun travelling. Most of the horses were saddled; Sasha guessed they'd received some from the villagers, but their reserve horses were gone.

"Pelner is too badly wounded to continue," said Rhillian. "We'll have to leave him here and hope he survives. The village folk have camps in the hills and forests, and they can hide there for weeks. Daish is hurt, but he insists on continuing. He knows Ilduur well, so I'm inclined to risk it."

"How did they know where we were?" Sasha muttered. "I can't believe they just got lucky."

"We'll think about it later," said Rhillian. "Let's rest here for a little longer, then we'll push on. Whether the Kazeri were lucky or not, they'll have guessed where we're heading now. They'll chase us hard."

Sasha went to check on Daish. He was being tended by Yasmyn, who had herself a bloodied bandage on one hip beneath her riding pants. Daish sat shirtless, bound about the ribs with a bandage, a patch of blood on his left side.

"Stab wound?" Sasha asked, crouching alongside.

Yasmyn nodded, slicing spare cloth into bandage strips with her darak. "Past the bone, I think," she said. "I don't think it found a lung, though."

Sasha put a hand on Daish's shoulder. He smiled, wanly. "I got him though," he said. "I skewered him right through the middle, that slanty-eyed piece of shit." Then he blinked at Yasmyn. "No offence."

Yasmyn made a face. "Common ancestor, Kazeri, Isfayen. Lisan too, most likely. Long time ago, Kazeri were great warriors, spread across Rhodia. Now they're just plain-dwellers and sheep herders without even enough sense to build a roof over their heads, dreaming of ancient greatness. When they meet the Army of Lenayin, their numbers will decrease."

"Where were you last night?" Sasha asked her. "I couldn't find you."

Yasmyn showed Sasha some fresh scars on her forearm. Self-inflicted, Sasha thought. "The *arganyar*, it demands blood. My enemies' blood I have given to the gods; now I give them more each night for a week. I do the ritual outside. When I saw men sneaking. I hid."

She looked angry. And ashamed. Outnumbered so greatly, Sasha didn't know what else she could have done . . . except raised the alarm, and died immediately. But she knew Yasmyn wouldn't see it that way.

"The serrin woke up," she reassured her. "They raised the alarm, there was no need for you to sacrifice yourself."

Yasmyn said nothing and tore more strips with her darak.

Ten

Sofy trotted through the streets of Tracato, horses' hooves clattering off the high surrounding walls. She had been offered a carriage, and according to royal decorum she should perhaps have taken it. But there was fear in the air, the streets deserted save for the occasional scurrying townsman, and any protection offered by a carriage was deceptive. Amongst her entourage of armoured knights rode Jaryd and his two Lenay companions, plus Jeddie, who looked about with constant concern.

They entered a small square surrounded by very old buildings. Soldiers were camped here, horses drinking from the fountain, men in armour guarding laneways and watching all who entered. On one side rose a temple, single-spired in the fashion of old Bacosh temples. Atop its main steps stood knights in Larosan colours. These had come from the Army of the Bacosh, then. The others about the square were certainly Elissian.

The party dismounted. Jaryd took the bridle of Sofy's horse, looking warily at the soldiers. He did not need to tell her how little he liked the situation. She saw, and felt it herself, in her bones.

"Just guard the horses," she told him in Lenay. "We'll need them if we're to go somewhere fast." Jaryd nodded. His eyes flicked to Sofy's surrounding knights. They were her protection, supposedly . . . but if circumstances had changed as word had it, she'd be a fool to believe that would be their only function.

Sofy indicated to Jeddie, and the two women walked to the temple steps, accompanied by Bacosh knights, armour rattling as they went. Her knights took up station at the entrance to the temple as the women walked on, into the musty air and dull light. Sofy smelled incense, and saw that before the altar a tall chair had been placed like a throne. Upon it sat a very fat man in black robes and a tall hat. In a half-circle before him sat more priests in more chairs, beneath tall stands of scented candles.

Sofy walked toward them with gathering dread. To the Archbishop's right stood Dafed and several of his favoured lords. The priests all stood as she approached. The Archbishop stood also, with groaning effort. Sofy walked within the half-circle, and curtseyed. All bowed.

"Princess Sofy," said Aesol Turen, Archbishop of Larosa. He was the second in authority throughout the Verenthane world, deferring only to the Archbishop of Torovan. With Larosa's recent successes at the head of a conquering army, some rumoured that even that authority may be shifting.

"Archbishop Turen," said Sofy. "A pleasure."

"We shall sit," said Turen, and some men brought chairs for Sofy and Jeddie. Jeddie sat further back, while Sofy sat alone before the arc of priests. Dafed looked on, his broad face grim. "I hear interesting tales of your conduct, since your arrival in this city," the Archbishop continued in Torovan.

"The Larosan court is filled with interesting tales," Sofy replied, in Larosan. The priests all glanced at each other, surprised at her fluency. She'd been practising. Larosan was the tongue of all Bacosh noble courts, spoken by all the nobility, regardless of region. In the presence of most Lenays, those nobles would stoop to speak Torovan, the language of trade and the only regional tongue most Lenays would understand—a condescension often granted with a smirk.

Sofy's mouth was dry, and her heart thumping unpleasantly. It was a risk, to insist upon a less familiar tongue. But she could not allow them to condescend to her here, after the news that she had heard.

"Indeed," said the Archbishop. "Today I come bearing *most* interesting tales. Would you like me to tell them? You have no doubt heard rumour, by now." His tone was arch, and superior. Yasmyn had hated him on first meeting. Sofy had been more tolerant. Now she found herself conceding to Yasmyn's judgement.

"I have heard that half of the Army of Lenayin has changed sides," said Sofy. She pressed her hands firmly together in her lap, lest they should tremble. "My sister leads them."

"Changed sides," pronounced Turen. There was deathly silence in the small temple. Turen smiled unpleasantly. "Turned traitor, one might more correctly say. And rather more than half, I hear."

Sofy knew the divisions better than anyone here, save for Jaryd, who remained outside. She could guess the lines upon which the split had occurred. Led by Sasha . . . so the three northern provinces of Hadryn, Ranash, and Banneryd would have done the precise opposite. The rest would have divided largely on noble lines, the nobility with the northern provinces, the common folk with Sasha. Except (as everything in Lenayin was "except") for the Taneryn. And possibly even the Isfayen, whose nobility disliked their so-called peers and had grown recently fond of Sasha.

"Do you have news of my siblings?" Sofy asked, unable to quite keep the fear from her voice.

"Your brother the king remains loyal," Turen conceded. "The younger brother too, Myklas. The others, not so much."

Sofy let out the small, tight breath she'd been holding. "So they are well?"

"Quite," Turen pronounced, curtly. "The last I heard."

Sofy tried to think. What could have caused such a calamity? She knew that Sasha had been unhappy, as many Lenays had been unhappy. And she wasn't completely naive, she knew that her husband had been shielding her from the worst atrocities of the invasion. Lenayin had suffered greatly in battle, she had lost her own father, and Lenay morale had suffered . . . but in Lenayin, honour was all, and honourable behaviour, as Sofy understood it, did not entail changing sides in the middle of a war. Sasha's more extreme flights of emotion did not surprise her at all . . . but for the Army of Lenayin to *follow* her in such numbers . . .

What had happened to make them hate their new allies so much? Seated here before the circle, Sofy felt the wall of accusing eyes upon her. Beneath those stares, she understood her own danger.

"We would all here be most intrigued," Turen said into that silence, "to hear your appraisal of these events. We of the Bacosh had heard many stories of the fearsome warriors of Lenayin, but we had not heard that they were so *disloyal*."

"You still have a considerable portion of the Army of Lenayin with you," Sofy returned.

"As I said, rather less than half."

"A less-than-half that includes the heavy northern cavalry, always the most formidable portion." Sofy injected a note of cold reprimand into her voice. She understood very well that here she must fight, or quite possibly die. "Many Lenays fought and died so that my husband's forces could attain their current position. Indeed, our very presence in Tracato has been purchased with the lives of many thousands of Lenay warriors. It is the Verenthane code that one should never show disrespect upon ground stained with the blood of martyrs. I know that you do not mean to sound disrespectful, Archbishop Turen."

"The forces of the Free Bacosh won victory over Rhodaan upon Sonnai Plain," said Dafed, from the Archbishop's right. "I fought upon the Sonnai, and I did not see any Lenays there."

There was a muttering of approval from his fellow lords.

"You fought one Army of the Steel at odds of better than five to one against," said Sofy. "You barely won. Upon your flank, Lenayin fought another Army of the Steel at odds of one to one, and barely lost. Were Lenayin not upon your flank, you would have faced two armies of the Steel together, and been annihilated like so many of your forebears." Dafed's lords glared at her.

"By my calculation," Sofy continued mercilessly, "if you still possess the strongest formation of the Army of Lenayin within your ranks, then you still possess a force more than twice the value of all the rest of your armies combined."

"Ludicrous!" someone exclaimed.

"Ask the Enoran Steel how it is ludicrous," Sofy snapped. "All agree they came within a hair of defeat, something your Bacosh Armies have never achieved in two hundred years with many times the force. Lenays do not require odds of five to one to win *our* victories."

If they no longer need me, if they no longer fear me, I'm dead.

Observing the angry faces around her, the thought formed quite clearly. Most had never liked the alliance. Now they had true cause not to. She was an impediment, as her marriage to Balthaar Arrosh blocked access to that most valuable thing that all others craved—wedlock to the future King of all Bacosh. She had to impress upon them how important she still was, and how deadly her family and allies would be to offend.

"Now, now," said Turen, raising a calming hand. "Let us not descend into crude allegations and counter-allegations. I would hear the princess's assessment."

Sofy swallowed and calmed herself. "Lenayin is a land only recently united," she said. "There are many lines of fracture amongst my people. Many of us feared this outcome from the start. My brother the king did advocate this war in part to unite our people, to meld them together in the forge of war. He was counselled of the possibility that it may have an alternative effect. Now it seems those fears are realised."

"The pagans have all abandoned the cause, then?"

"It's not a matter of pagans and Verenthanes, Archbishop."

"And yet all those who remain loyal are Verenthane."

"And noble. That is the primary thing. This is a war about nobility, above all else."

"Interesting," said Turen. "I had thought it a war for the righteous gods against ungodly evil, myself."

"Whatever else the serrin have done," Sofy continued, ignoring the interjection, "they have abolished nobility in these lands. My husband's army seeks to restore it. Nobility is a point of great contention in Lenayin also. All nobility there is Verenthane, save for the Taneryn. I would guess that some, if not most, Verenthane common folk will have joined this rebellion—the dislike of nobility runs deep in Lenayin save in the north, irrespective of faith. Perhaps this campaign has reawakened those old arguments."

"It seems the noble families of Lenayin have not earned the love of the people."

"Possibly true," Sofy said coldly. "A fact from which *my* family remains the exception."

"I hear tales," continued the Archbishop, "that you are quite taken with these lands. With this city, and its serrin constructions."

"There is much knowledge here," said Sofy. "Things that wise rulers could learn to use, as Lenay rulers learned much from the Torovan Verenthanes who brought us the faith one century ago."

"Do you like this city?"

"I find it has its attractions," Sofy said cautiously.

"Myself," said Turen, "I feel it could be improved."

Leaving the temple, Sofy made straight for Jaryd. About the courtyard now, Elissian lords were giving orders to horsemen, who clattered away down adjoining lanes. Something was afoot.

"They're organising," said Jaryd, with a nod to the Elissians. "I think the others are coming." The Elissian Army, he meant. The one that was supposed to remain camped beyond the city limits.

"I don't like this at all," said Jeddie, pale with alarm. "What in the world is the Archbishop doing here anyway? I mean, the Army of Lenayin defects and *he* chooses to deliver the message personally?"

"My husband did not want the priesthood involved in the fate of Tracato," said Sofy. "He made it explicit: he does not trust them to make decisions."

Jeddie was shaking her head. "He doesn't *control* the priesthood, Sofy! No one does, they answer to the gods. Until now they've been preoccupied with returning the Shereldin Star to Shemorane, but now they've achieved that, they're free to start reordering these conquered lands as they see fit!"

"Balthaar had the authority to keep them out of Tracato and send me instead," Sofy muttered. "But when the Army of Lenayin broke up, that ended. His lords who opposed sending me will have revolted. . . ."

"Yes," said Jeddie, breathlessly. She was the daughter of Tournean nobility, she'd lived and breathed these manoeuvrings her entire life. "Balthaar's position itself could be under threat, he has lost face over this. . . ."

"He's just won the biggest victory in two centuries," Jaryd disagreed. "He's not about to be weakened now—"

"Listen," Jeddie said impatiently, "when a leader of a great army wins a big victory, it is judged to be a verdict of the gods. That's where his new authority comes from. Now who do you think is in charge of issuing that verdict?"

"The Archbishop," said Sofy. "He's in a fight with Balthaar over the future of these lands. And now he has a free hand here, and an army of vengeful Elissians to do his bidding." Now she was scared, in a way that threats to her personal safety had not entirely achieved. "Jaryd, I want you to ride to the Justiciary and find Maldereld's Founding. The original manuscripts, the codes of law, those must be saved."

Jaryd shook his head. "No. I swore to protect you—I'm not leaving you alone now that these idiots want your head—"

"Jaryd, I'm still a Lenay Princess, and I command you to—"

"You're not!" Jaryd snorted. "You stopped being that when you married that goon."

"Then what the hells are you doing here?" She stared at him, shoulders heaving. Jaryd stared back. The answer hung in the air, stark in their silence. Sofy's eyes nearly spilled as she looked at him. She couldn't afford this now, there were so many larger things at stake. "Jaryd, there are documents in the Justiciary that lay the foundations of a better world. A world without these *goons*, as you call them. They'll want them destroyed, they'll want all of it destroyed. Don't tell me that means nothing to you."

Jaryd looked away.

"Jeddie," she continued, "get to the Mahl'rhen, see it evacuated, see those few foolish serrin like Lesthen taken out in disguise if you have to."

Jeddie nodded and went for her horse. Jaryd indicated to Jandlys, and the huge Taneryn ran to follow. Sofy did not protest since Jandlys was obviously taken with the noble Tournean, and would fight like an animal to protect her.

Sofy grasped Jaryd's hand. "Jaryd, go. Asym can stay and protect me. Do this for me."

"And where will you be?"

Sofy smiled wanly. "Within the protective army of my husband's knights, what could hurt me?"

Jaryd arrived to find local men in urgent discussion upon the broad steps of the Justiciary. He dismounted and accosted a local to ask him what this latest commotion was about.

"Fighting," said the man, in broken Torovan. "East, east." He pointed, more northeast than east, in the direction the Elissians would come from. "Local men fight, but they many."

Jaryd ran up the steps and into the huge hall of one of the most impressive buildings in Tracato. It thronged with people, more commotion, and urgent conversation. The Justiciary was the centre of Tracato in many ways. During the troubles, the Civid Sein had overrun it, held Sasha captive here, and tortured her. Alythia, they'd murdered. No doubt Sofy was correct that any new force determined to overrun the city would aim here first.

Some hurried questions directed him to a senior Justice, talking with a local man Jaryd took to be Nasi-Keth, in a back hallway. "I'm Jaryd Nyvar," Jaryd interrupted. "I come on Princess Sofy's instructions—she has just had audience with Archbishop Turen, and she fears for the safety of the documents of law."

"I tell you, they are coming!" the Nasi-Keth man resumed berating the Justice. "The Elissians are coming, the Archbishop gives them holy sanction to enter the city and lay waste!"

The Justice stared at Jaryd for a long moment. Jaryd had seen fear before. He'd known it himself, intimately. What he saw in the Justice's eyes was not the fear for personal safety. It was more like the fear he'd known in that moment he'd learned that his fellow nobles had invoked the Sylden Sarach, and declared the dissolution of his family. The fear when an old Baen-Tar groundsman had dared approach to tell him that his little brother was dead.

It was the fear of a man who saw the one thing he loved more in the world than himself sentenced to death.

The Justice turned and led them hurriedly up some stairs to a higher hallway. They entered a grand chamber, where clerks sorted piles of parchment and books onto tables. There followed much shouting of instruction in Rhodaani, as Jaryd stood by impatiently and wondered how long it would take the Elissians to fight their way through to this point. Some ordinary Tracatans had fled the city, but most had stayed. Some of those were formerly of the Steel and retained weapons. Others were Nasi-Keth, or Nasi-Keth trained. The Elissians would not find it easy, but they had armour and organisation, and many of those opposing would be older men who had not drilled in a decade or more.

"We can't take all of this!" Jaryd insisted to the clerks who ran into the chamber from adjoining rooms, carrying yet more piles. Few paid him any attention. Jaryd fumed, and went to the window to listen for sounds of fighting.

From conversation within the room, he gathered there was a ship in harbour that could take them. Saalshen's navy ruled the waves, and once into the Sharaal Sea, a ship could find safe harbour anywhere along the Saalshen coast. But how long would such cargo be safe, if Saalshen itself were next to fall?

"This is stupid," he muttered to himself. Tracato's defenders had little time to prepare, and Elissian cavalry could penetrate faster than they could throw up blockades. They could be here any moment and they could reach Sofy too. Meanwhile he was here, guarding paper.

He stalked from the chamber and down to the main floor. Outside, he heard yells and hooves clattering. Nasi-Keth archers at the doors were loosing arrows at mounted knights who wheeled across the courtyard, running down some city folk armed only with makeshift weapons.

"Aim for the horses you fools!" Jaryd yelled at the archers as arrows glanced harmlessly from heavy armour. There were no more than ten knights, he saw—a small raiding party, advancing ahead of the main body, likely to seek the glory of first capture for themselves.

A horse was struck, and reared, flailing. A knight saw the archers and came charging toward the broad stone steps. Jaryd pushed past to the top step, sword drawn, and dared the knight to come. He did, his horse bounding uncertainly on the steps, the knight's sword readied for a right-handed swing . . . and Jaryd leaped quickly across the horse's path and half-severed its head with a huge swing.

The animal collapsed, gushing blood, its rider crashing on the stairs. Nasi-Keth were on him before he could rise, pinning his armoured bulk, stabbing with knives into the gaps between armourplate. Jaryd spun his sword several times in challenge, beckoning the other knights who'd watched to try the same.

They did, three at once, and this time rearing their horses on the steps, hooves lashing at head height, forcing the defenders back. Jaryd retreated within the doors, but those were large enough to admit even mounted riders, and now there were knights coming into the Justiciary itself, shod hooves sliding on the smooth pavings as they galloped in circles, spreading chaos.

Stupid fools, Jaryd thought, slipping outside once more through a further door—they were massively outnumbered, and the archers were now shooting at them from the walls, peppering their horses. They'd retreat or die soon enough, and weren't worth his trouble.

He retrieved his horse and galloped back toward the Tol'rhen, where Sofy was surely headed next. Those knights her husband had assigned to protect her were half of them Larosan, and loyal to their lord's lawfully wedded wife. But the other half were sworn only by word, not by blood. In the Bacosh, words beside blood were nothing.

Sofy was halfway back to the Tol'rhen when a knight fell from his horse. She heard the huge crash of metal and spun in her saddle to look. That was when she sensed rather than saw the movement to her left, a knight suddenly riding much closer than he should, and she ducked by some instinct she had not known she possessed. A large sword whistled where her head had been, and then there were yells of alarm from her Larosan guards, blades drawn, steel clashing and horses rearing and colliding all around.

She could not even scream. Having no breath in her lungs, she merely grasped her reins with her face pressed to her horse's mane and kicked with her heels in blind panic, hoping the animal would find a way through the flying bodies and blades.

Someone grasped her reins, and she fought to drag them back, but it was Asym, leading her through the mess. He lashed at one knight, and abandoned Sofy momentarily as another required both his hands. Sofy reclaimed control and found space, galloping into open road. A narrow alley appeared on the right and she skidded into it, nearly hitting the wall, barely ducking beneath an overhanging inn's signpost.

She heard pursuit behind and risked a look over her shoulder to find two knights pursuing . . . but both wore Larosan colours and the leader waved at her to keep going. She did, weaving through tight corners and across small courtyards. Then she slowed to allow the Larosans to catch up—with no armour she weighed barely a third what they did, to the benefit of her horse.

She stopped in a small courtyard by a fountain, so her horse could drink. The horse was too frightened, blowing hard, ears pricked and swivelling. The two Larosans pushed up their visors, looking anxiously behind.

"Your Highness," said one, gasping. "I do not know what happened . . ."

"I do," said Sofy, and her voice was not nearly as unsteady as she'd feared. "My husband's dear allies have decided to end our marriage. Nothing like some more Tracatan unrest to cover their crime, they could claim anyone did it."

Then came the sound of more hooves, echoing at some uncertain distance. The Larosans readied their swords. Asym cantered into view down the alley, his blade raised again at the sight of two more knights flanking Sofy.

"Asym!" Sofy shouted above the racket of hooves, her hands raised. "No!" Asym stopped opposite the fountain. "Larosan knights, Asym. Balthaar's allies, sworn by blood."

Asym spoke only a little Lenay, but he knew the Larosan colours, and knew who had and had not betrayed them. He nodded, narrow eyes grim.

"Five Larosan dead," he said brokenly, showing five fingers to be sure. "More go, run. We go Tol'rhen?"

Sofy nodded. "We have to. We must tell them what's coming."

The Tol'rhen courtyard when they reached it was filled with Elissian knights and soldiers.

"What are they doing?" Sofy muttered, peering past Asym's shoulder. They stood, dismounted, at the corner of a narrow lane, watching the activity. There were carts arriving, and men unloading from the back. It was too far away to see properly. Elsewhere in the city, Sofy could hear shouting, and the distant clash of weapons. Somewhere near, smoke rose thick into a cloudy sky. On the wind, she smelled smoke.

Asym said something in his native Telochi that Sofy didn't understand. Behind them, the two Larosan knights stood mounted, guarding the lane to their rear.

Suddenly Asym pointed. Men in the courtyard were shouting, hands waving. On the far side near grand buildings, two had fallen. Another followed, and arrows skipped on stone. Now with a massed yell, armed men were running from the cover of buildings, swinging at those closest Elissians. The Elissians stopped what they were doing and charged. Mounted knights plunged into the attackers, striking out, scattering them. One knight was pulled down, but now Elissian foot soldiers were in amongst it, and the clashes and screams of battle echoed loudly off the surrounding buildings.

Hooves clattered behind and the Larosan knights called warning, but it was Jaryd who appeared on horseback. Sofy ran back to him, away from the conspicuousness of the lane mouth.

"I thought you'd be here," Jaryd said down to her. "They're all over— they came into the city from several directions, very well planned. Local folk are trying to organise defence, but they're outmuscled. They're going after the big buildings, the institutions. I saw that big library four streets down on fire on the way here."

"Jaryd, we have to stop them!" Sofy felt utterly desperate. "These Elissians are unloading carts into the Tol'rhen, I don't know what they're doing but now the locals are attacking them. . . ."

"Maybe you could negotiate them into liking each other," Jaryd said sourly. Sofy stared up at him. "Sofy, this city's done. Finished, understand?"

"It's not finished! We can still . . ."

"Fight them? This is the Elissian *Army*, Sofy, the locals are militia at best. I'll fight them if you order it, but I'll be dead well before sundown, as will we all. Is that what you want?"

Sofy put hands to her head in despair.

"You thought you could make peace with it, didn't you?" Jaryd looked exasperated. "You can't make peace with this, Sofy. This is power. You kill it, or it kills you. Now if you're not going to command us all to suicide, we should move, and see you out of this alive." From the Tol'rhen courtyard came the screams of the dying.

Sofy mounted, and Jaryd led them away. A panicked local stopped running long enough to tell of many more Elissians coming from the west, so Jaryd turned them back through the heart of the city, hoping to emerge south, where he thought the attackers would be fewest.

Several times they passed recently dead bodies, some Elissian, some local, and the sound of fighting. Surely, Sofy wondered, the honourable thing would be to stay, and help fight? No sooner had she thought it than a group of terrified Tracatans came running down the lane, pursued by Elissian horsemen. Jaryd charged them, with one of the Larosan knights. Sofy watched in horror as Jaryd simply swayed aside the initial stroke of an Elissian cavalryman, spurring past the horse and smashing the other man's skull with his own blade. That riderless horse made a blockage, and Jaryd used it to isolate another man, jostling his horse, taking a blow on his shield and using it to force the Elissian's weapon wide, Jaryd's own blow taking the other man's arm.

For several more moments he and the Larosan knight hacked and fought, and then the Elissians were galloping off, leaving three dead on the ground. Jaryd indicated for them to take another way, hard-breathing and streaked with blood, but none of it his. Sofy had never seen Jaryd kill anyone before. His brutality shocked her.

The next lane brought them to a road where the air was thick with smoke. On the pavings lay the remains of recent battle, men dead and dying, most of them Tracatans, with good weapons but little armour. Jaryd urged his nervous horse into the road, searching for another back lane to take. To the right, Sofy could see the dome of the Tol'rhen, emerging above city rooftops.

"This way," said Sofy, pointing in the opposite direction. "I think we'd better . . ."

There came a blinding flash. Sofy stared about in alarm, and saw the Tol'rhen dome was on fire. It was a strange and awful fire, orange and blue, and it seemed to twirl in little, spinning whirlwinds where it licked the old building's huge stone walls. Tracatans in the street attending the wounded stopped and stared. Some cried out in anguish, as though the sight of their lovely dome on fire hurt them worse than any sword.

"That's what they were loading from the carts," Jaryd said grimly. "They captured some of that demon fire the artillery use."

Sofy stared in shock. She could not believe the Archbishop had ordered such a thing. What sort of a man would order a crime against all civilisation, in the name of his gods? And what sort of men would obey him?

"Come on," said Jaryd, pulling her horse away down the street. They had not gone far when they came to a small courtyard before a grand building, its roof on fire. Sofy suddenly recognised the courtyard, and the building. It was the School of Arts and Music, perhaps her favourite in all Tracato, maybe lacking the importance of the grand institutions, but with more of the beauty.

Before she knew what she was doing, she spurred her horse toward the steps and carved stone columns, as Jaryd yelled at her to stop. She dismounted at the foot of the steps and ran up, fire now blistering the golden filigree inlays of the great wall panels beside the doors.

There was much wood used inside the main hall, with floorboards and wall panels, and lovely old furnishings. Sofy covered her mouth and squinted through the smoke as she ran, hoping only that what remained of the musical wonders had been shifted, and that some of her favourite masters had had the sense to leave before the Elissians had come.

She pushed through the doors of the grand chamber where she had heard a wonderful recital just two days before. The panelled walls about the central stage were aflame, stacked with furnishings and soaked with what she suspected from the acrid smell was oil. Black smoke gathered at the ceiling, now beginning to hide the chandelier, and burning shavings and cinders were falling about like rain.

Upon the stage sat three old men, instruments in hand. They played now, a sweet sound that rose to challenge the crackling of the flames. Burning embers fell about them, and the heat flared hotter still, yet the men played on, oblivious to all but the soaring emotion of their tune, their faces entranced with that wonder alone.

Sofy wanted to scream at them to run, to grab them from the stage and haul them bodily out the doors and into the safety of the courtyard. Yet this terrifying, mesmerising scene was the first thing she'd seen all day that made sense to her. Standing helplessly, tears flowed down her cheeks that had nothing to do with the smoke.

Jaryd burst into the room behind her. He too stopped and stared at the scene. The tune reached a crescendo, and the musicians all beamed in ecstasy. Above, the flaming ceiling groaned ominously.

"Sofy, we have to go!"

She turned and ran, grasping Jaryd's hand. As they reemerged into the courtyard, several floors of the building gave way behind, an eruption of blazing debris that burst forth from the windows and doors. A billion sparks rose skyward, glorious like the last note of a song, rising up to heaven.

Eleven

Errollyn sat on his horse and watched the Kazeri come. The wild plains horsemen were skirting the hills to the north, as Kessligh had said they would. Kazeri moved in a large, singular force, and relied upon speed and surprise. Thanks to *talmaad* scouts, they'd lost the latter. Now they'd selected the most open path across fields and foothills to close upon the rear of the retreating armies of Rhodaan, Enora, and Lenayin.

Were it not for the cavalry, it would have been trouble. Yet now confronting the Kazeri were thousands of *talmaad*, and thousands more Rhodaani, Enoran, and Lenay horsemen. The foot soldiers continued their march toward Jahnd. Kessligh had been unwilling to countenance an extended delay to face the Kazeri whilst the Army of the Bacosh resumed its pursuit from the north. The cavalry would hold back the Kazeri and hope that they could stop them here. If not, the footsoldiers would be next, forming hasty lines of defence upon whatever terrain was available. It reduced the Steel's defensive strengths greatly. Errollyn hoped it would not come to that.

He held his bow in hand, resting lengthwise on his saddle horn. Across this field, all were serrin. Behind, by several hundreds of paces, were human cavalry. He had been discussing this formation with fellow cavalrymen now for weeks—first with immediate comrades and then with Kessligh, once his ideas had fully formed. Kessligh had liked it. Now came the actual test of battle.

The Kazeri broke into a full charge, a roar of thousands of voices and even more hooves. Weapons glinted in summer sunshine, a thousand sparkles of sunlight on steel. The serrin said nothing. When the Kazeri reached a certain point on the field, they raised their bows, drew, and fired. Errollyn placed his first arrow very high, then drew quickly and fired a second on a lower angle. Then he yanked his reins and galloped away from the charging Kazeri.

The Kazeri yelled in triumph to see their foe running away. The first wave of arrows spattered across their forward rank, some falling from height, others coming low and flat, both flights arriving simultaneously. Horses and riders fell, others swerving to avoid sudden obstacles, yet their opponents were fleeing, and Kazeri warriors would not neglect to claim their prize.

Errollyn put a knee across his saddle horn in a well-practised move, placed another arrow to his string while holding himself barely off the saddle. All about him the serrin were galloping, riders firing back the way they'd come. Kazeri riders pursued in howling triumph, dying and crashing to the turf in scores, yet coming no closer.

A paddock wall emerged precisely where Errollyn had measured it when placing their formation. He took the jump, then fired twice more. All across the Kazeri front, racing horsemen were falling. Another arrow, and most of the front rank were dead, fallen, or reining up in consternation, trying to dodge and colliding with their comrades.

Now he saw the line of human cavalry before him, divided with gaps in their ranks. These were Valhanan men of Lenayin, and as the retreating serrin poured through the gaps in their line, the Valhanans roared and charged. Errollyn wheeled his horse about, and placed another two arrows over the galloping Valhanan's heads, into the faltering front rank of Kazeri. Then he stood in the saddle and held out his arm to indicate the line the other *talmaad* should assume. As they dressed their line, he watched.

All along the advancing front, Lenay, Rhodaani and Enoran cavalry ploughed into the Kazeri front. Their charge faltered; all momentum lay with the countercharge. Before him, the Valhanans spurred their horses amidst the confusion of Kazeri, some Lenay townsmen on taller horses, others on wiry dussieh. They hit Kazeri riders from high and low, and seemed to have the better of most exchanges. But more Kazeri were pouring in from the rear ranks, the huge column spreading wide as it found this route blocked. Very soon, Errollyn knew he'd be outflanked.

He gave his signal, and a serrin trumpeter blew the retreat. With astonishing discipline for hot-blooded Lenays—who hated to retreat—the Valhanans disengaged and came racing back toward the serrin. Those Kazeri who chased without support simply melted in a storm of serrin arrows. Errollyn saw a group of nearly thirty riders felled in several heartbeats, like a dandelion collapsing in a hailstorm. The main force regrouped, then yells and horn blasts cut the air once more, and they resumed their charge. Again the first rank met a swarm of arrows, and again the serrin turned tail and galloped in the other direction. It was not a retreat, and now the Kazeri were beginning to realise it. It was a moving wall of accurate archery, holding itself at precisely the correct killing range from its opponent. This stretch of fields was well chosen. If the Kazeri kept chasing until the next line of forest, half of them would be dead on the grass before they reached it.

As Kazeri further back in the formation swung towards the hills on Errollyn's southernside, he realised he was being outflanked to the north; they were trying to pin his force against those hills. Errollyn did not think that particularly smart either—if they forced him to take the high ground, he would not mind at all. Besides which, the high ground held other surprises.

Again the Kazeri paused in their pursuit. Again trumpets sounded, and the rear rank of human cavalry wheeled and galloped back through the serrin line. They hammered into the Kazeri line a second time, and held them. It was within two hundred paces of the spot Kessligh had told him to expect this second engagement. Well within the parameters of their plan, and he did not even need to give the second signal.

From the trees on the leftward slope erupted a line of human cavalry— some Rhodaani and Enoran heavy horse with a forest of steel-tipped lances, and upon the far flank, to block Kazeri retreat, the one group of Lenay riders missing from the action so far: Isfayen men, plunging downhill with black hair flying, screaming like madmen as they came.

The Kazeri flank disappeared, riders impaled by lances or knocked flying by heavier Rhodaani or Enoran horses. Once into the main body and sur-rounded by enemy, Rhodaanis and Enorans dropped lances, pulled swords, and began swinging. Errollyn could not see the Isfayen now, they were too far back. But already he could see the Kazeri folding, as horsemen turned and galloped in panic.

He indicated to head north, away from the hills, and some serrin fol-lowed, others riding up close behind the heavily engaged human cavalry to shoot available targets from their horses, or merely to loose arrows into the middle of Kazeri ranks. Errollyn broke into a gallop, amidst many hundreds of other serrin also racing this way. Ahead was trouble: Kazeri had indeed come around the far flank, and Enoran men here were fighting a desperate defence to hold them away from their comrades' rear.

Again the *talmaad* raced in, holding ground and shooting one Kazeri after another where that suited, or darting in close where the fighting was more desperate, abandoning bows for swords at close quarters. Errollyn put an arrow through one Kazeri who was locked in battle with an Enoran, then made a fast right turn to evade two more who came at him in pursuit. One of those fell to an anonymous arrow, and he pulled the blade from over his shoulder, and yanked on the rein to dart behind the second Kazeri rider, who reined up so fast his horse slipped and fell.

Errollyn abandoned him for someone else to deal with, sheathing his sword for the bow once more as immediate targets rapidly became fewer. He realised that the heaviest engagement was moving further away, and spurred after it. One Kazeri target presented himself, but fell to an arrow before he could fire. More made a spirited attack upon a group of Enoran cavalry, but the Enorans were superior, and simply cut them from their mounts with heavy blows and clever horsemanship. The rest, Errollyn realised, were running away. Men were cheering, waving swords in the air in victory. Another man, an officer, interrupted some of those celebrations by standing in his stirrups and yelling.

"Don't cheer! Chase them and kill them! Kill *all* of them!"

That would be unlikely, Errollyn knew. But men stopped cheering and galloped in pursuit, to try their best to do just that. No one knew why the Kazeri had attacked Enora, save for the predictable guesses of alliances with the new Bacosh Regent. They only knew, by long experience, that the best deterrent from such aggression was to make each episode as painful as possible for the attackers. Few captured Kazeri would see mercy here today.

If he chased hard, possibly he could spend his few remaining arrows on retreating Kazeri backs and bring down several more. Instead, he stopped, and allowed his horse to walk at leisure back across the pasture toward what had been the middle of the fight. He rode past bodies of the dead and dying, looking for surviving wounded from his side to help, and wondering on Sasha's Goeren-yai beliefs. Did she think that the souls of the men he'd killed would return to haunt him? Would they stand in judgement of his own soul when he died? Errollyn looked now across the carpet of dead and shrieking wounded, and missed her more than ever.

Most of the fallen were Kazeri. He dismounted to help stanch the bleeding of a wounded Enoran, then handed him to others as help arrived. Other friendly wounded were being collected, and the dead marked with a sword or lance point down in the turf, for rapid burial. They could not hold here long; the foot soldiers were now more than a day's march away, and the combined armies were split. The Kazeri had been taught their lesson, but could not be pursued. The Regent's army had massive cavalry too, and could race ahead of their own foot soldiers if they chose.

Errollyn found Andreyis ahorse amidst the confusion, and saluted him. Andreyis saluted back with a grin, and galloped to his side. His arm had healed enough for a fight, and now he looked the proper Valhanan cavalryman with mail and a shield—he'd fought on foot to this point for lack of a horse, but Errollyn had thought it daft for a cavalryman of his standard, and found him a spare.

"So much for the rampaging Kazeri hordes," Andreyis remarked, looking over the carnage and saluting several other Valhanans.

"Fucking fools," said Errollyn. "I hope their commander survives. If we've killed him, they might put someone in charge who knows what he's doing."

"How do Kazeri find new leaders anyhow?"

"No idea. It's tragic. I'd always thought the Kazeri an interesting people, but I'd never actually met any before today. To think that some fucking tribe leader should lead them to this in the name of alliance with the Regent . . ."

"We should take prisoners and learn something about them," said Andreyis.

"You can do that if you like." Errollyn found it too depressing to contemplate.

"I will." Andreyis looked quite certain. Errollyn wondered what he was up to. "To know oneself is to know one's enemy. Surely the opposite also applies."

Errollyn blinked, realising that Andreyis had spoken that last in Saalsi. "I didn't know you spoke the tongue," he said in kind.

Andreyis shrugged. "Kessligh and Sasha were always speaking it, I learned some. I was never as good as Sasha, though. I was embarrassed to speak it with her, my accent is terrible."

"No, it's not," said Errollyn, and meant it. A serrin rider approached at a gallop, bow in hand, and reined to Andreyis's side. It was a girl, with wild red hair. Errollyn recalled her name, Yshel. She looked delighted to see Andreyis, and he her. They embraced. Ah, thought Errollyn. "You two, talk to some prisoners. Find out more about the Kazeri, why they're here, who's in charge, what the Regent promised them. If you need translators, ask around, there's bound to be serrin who speak Kazeri."

Andreyis and Yshel nodded, and Errollyn trotted on up the slope toward where he could see command banners forming. Partway up the hill, he found Kessligh, Damon and other commanders gathered by some banners. Kessligh saluted him grimly.

"It is against all natural laws," Kessligh stated, "for a cavalry engagement to unfold that closely to the original plan. We have been lucky, but the luck was planned."

"The formations work well," Errollyn replied, unstringing his bow to save the wood. "Luck can't be made, but it can be channelled."

The alternate formations of serrin and human cavalry had been his idea. Human cavalry was more suited to close contact, while serrin were superior at range. It had made sense to combine the two in a manner that negated each weakness with the other's strength. Actually making it work had been Damon's influence, him knowing far more about the fixed formations and principles of human cavalry than any serrin's more fluid notion.

Manoeuvring the army into this position in the first place, choosing the ground, and luring the Kazeri to follow them in, had been all Kessligh's doing. The man read landscapes the way Aisha read foreign tongues—with an almost unnatural and spine-chilling fluency. Kessligh gazed across his chosen fields now, eyes narrowed. "I think we got over a quarter of them," he said matter-of-factly. "That was damn near thirty thousand total, though, so there's at least twenty thousand left, probably more."

"I think we gained a few thousand new horses," Errollyn replied. "There are easily more than a few thousand good Lenay horsemen without, so our cavalry have actually increased—we can't have lost more than a few hundred."

"And our foot soldiers decrease in the process," said Kessligh. "Don't disregard them; cavalry are more valuable now, but not where we're headed. If we're to cross the Ipshaal, I'm not even certain how many horses we can take with us. The Ipshaal is wide, and there are no bridges."

"That was you on the right flank?" Errollyn asked Damon.

Damon nodded, wiping a sweaty brow. "I nearly wasn't fast enough, they just came on like a river around that flank."

"But you were fast enough. That was expertly done, to deploy that line so cleanly."

Damon looked unconvinced. Errollyn did not like that. Perhaps it was that his two brothers remained on the other side. Or perhaps Damon was just being as Sasha had always described him—cynical, put-upon, never finding things quite as perfect or proper as they ought to be. There was, Errollyn had to concede, quite a lot about the present situation that might lead a man to find it so.

"They thought they were a match for us man-to-man," said Damon. "They'll not make that mistake again."

"No," Kessligh agreed. "Unless they're completely stupid, they'll make themselves a part of the Army of the Bacosh from now on, and join their forces to the whole. We've not seen the last of the Kazeri . . . and with them, the Army of the Bacosh regains a large part of what they lost when the Army of Lenayin left."

"No," said Errollyn. "We just proved that thirty thousand Kazeri aren't worth even a portion of the Army of Lenayin."

"Thirty thousand Kazeri poorly led," Kessligh corrected. "If I were Balthaar Arrosh, I'd put Koenyg in charge of the Kazeri from now, as most of Koenyg's force is cavalry."

"Koenyg won't know what to do with them," Damon snorted. "He'll have even less respect for them than we do."

"Then perhaps he'll spend their lives callously," said Kessligh. "But a callous spending can still buy great value. Koenyg will know how. I know him, as you do."

Damon bit his lip and looked grim.

"The Kazeri may not wear it," said Errollyn. "They'll have their own factions and leaders, and pride in who leads and why. Like you said, we must reach Jahnd first—cavalry will then be less important than foot soldiers, and twenty thousand surviving Kazeri won't make too much difference either way."

It was as optimistic a view as he had to offer at that moment.

"At least we're now assured of who's in command," Damon remarked to Errollyn as they watched Kessligh progress across the hillside, offering commendations and instruction to mounted officers who followed. His hands moved in wide arcs, describing formations of cavalry across the fields, like a lagand captain coaching his team on tactics after a game.

"You could do it," Errollyn told him.

"I'm not at his level," Damon scoffed. "No one is. The man's a legend, and it's a title well earned."

"If Koenyg loses, you're king." Damon said nothing. "I know it is hard to think on," Errollyn persisted. "For all that has passed between you, he remains your brother."

"Don't think I'd regret the victory," Damon muttered.

"Easy to say," said Errollyn. "Harder to live with. But I'm not talking about your personal battle. To the men of Lenayin who have followed you this far, you are king *now*, not Koenyg."

"They followed Sasha, not me."

"Sasha told me you were grumpy. Listen to me. It doesn't matter what you feel about what they did or did not do, or what motivates them to do one thing or the other. What matters is how things stand. That is how a king must view things, concerned only with how things *are*, not how he feels about them, or them about him.

"Kessligh commands this battle, and that is good, because he is the best of us all. With any luck, and if Sasha and Rhillian can convince the Ilduuri to come and fight, we may still win. But if we do, then Lenayin will still need a king. And the men of Lenayin shall either emerge from this trial believing in you, or not."

"Have you ever seen such peaceful lands as these?" Damon sounded almost wistful. "Before this war, it must have been wonderful. All this prosperity, achieved with no king at all."

"Lenayin is not Enora," Errollyn warned. "You still need the fair and independent hand of a higher power there, or else all the regions shall start fighting once more. . . ."

"Oh, I know, I know . . ." Damon sighed. "But I wonder. If the progression of humanity lies in moving beyond kings, can any king make such progress as to make himself unnecessary, and step down? Could I, had I been on the throne fifty years? Or will that progress always come with war, and the fingertips of royalty clutching to that bloody chair until the bitter end?"

"I don't think this has anything to do with you suddenly doubting the necessity of Lenay kings," Errollyn said solemnly.

"There's nothing 'sudden' about it. I think I've always been like Sasha in some ways, doubting the high virtue of royalty."

"Or perhaps your cynicism merely infects whatever thing is closest to you."

Damon stared at him. He seemed about to be angry. Then he smiled faintly. "Perhaps. And perhaps Sasha should do it. Be queen, I mean."

"If you inflicted that upon her, she'd be very unhappy."

"It's not supposed to be about what makes her happy, is it?"

"*I'd* be very unhappy," Errollyn added. "To say nothing of the majority in Lenayin not yet enlightened enough to accept a woman on the throne, greatest swordsman in Lenayin or otherwise."

"We go presently to war against most of those," Damon reminded him. "If we win . . ." He didn't need to finish the sentence. This holy crusade to unite the Bacosh, and to unite the provinces of Lenayin at the same time, had instead reignited the embers of Lenay conflict that had first flared in the Northern Rebellion beneath Sasha's unwitting leadership. Now those embers made a full-fledged bonfire. This was now a Lenay civil war, where certain old questions would be answered for once and all.

Whichever side won here would undoubtedly return home to continue the victory there. If Koenyg won, nobility would be strengthened and the Goeren-yai attacked, missing much of their best defence lying dead upon these Bacosh fields. If Koenyg lost . . . well, the course of action then would lie with whomever sat upon the vacant throne of Lenayin.

"Oh, come on," said Errollyn, as an image occurred to him. "Can you imagine Sasha as Queen of Lenayin? Cooped up for days mediating squabbles between lords and village heads over taxes, marriages, and boundaries? She'd go insane."

"And I wouldn't?"

"*You* wouldn't make everyone else suffer to similar degree," Errollyn said pointedly. "You don't have a temper like a wildcat in a snare."

"Just like Sasha to be rewarded for her instability," Damon said. "I don't *want* to be king. I don't want to shrivel up inside like father did. I don't want to become a tyrant like Koenyg would like to be, if he could ever gain power enough over ordinary Lenays to be so. I'm not made for that kind of power, and it's not made for me."

"So make *it* into the power that *you* wish it to be."

"It doesn't work that way."

"For men whose dreams entwine with the wild sinews of mountain lands, all is possible." It was Tullamayne Errollyn quoted. One of those lines that stuck to the memory in any tongue.

"Why is it that serrin quote more Tullamayne than Lenays?" Damon complained.

"Perhaps for the same reason that Lenays are here fighting with us," Errollyn said with smile.

Sasha reined her horse to the side of the road to gaze back across the foothills. They were not far now from the Ipshaal, and the boundary between Ilduur and Enora. But their pursuers were drawing closer.

Sasha could see them clearly, traversing a fold of hillside across the valley, where the road cleared an exposed shoulder of land. They were alarmingly close, near enough to count individual men and see the glinting decoration on saddle and bridle. But as always in such country, distances were deceiving —the valley between them was steep, and the Kazeri now faced a difficult descent, then a sharp rise up to Sasha's present position. As Sasha watched, the line of riders went on and on.

Their best guess was one hundred. Certainly the Kazeri had some idea who they chased, and to what purpose. Five nights ago they had decided to forgo sleep and cross the gap to the serrin/human camp by starlight, only to meet with serrin ambush and fifteen dead. Several more Kazeri had injured themselves falling from unseen rocks in the increasingly rugged hills . . . one, Aisha insisted, had tumbled straight off a cliff. They had not tried such a night approach again, and the two groups had camped each night a suitably safe distance apart.

Kiel had argued for a night attack of their own, and had gained Rhillian's permission to scout the Kazeri camp on several nights. But the Kazeri had selected their camps well, atop steep and exposed approaches with no trees for cover. Kiel had manoeuvred upslope and taken two Kazeri guards with arrows, but had then spent much of the remaining night returning to camp, and been exhausted the following day. Rhillian, Kiel, Aisha, and Arendelle made only four serrin in the group, and Rhillian judged that they would exhaust or sacrifice themselves in continuing such attacks, thus leaving their human companions exposed, and the entire mission in jeopardy. Whatever her preference for aggressive tactics, Sasha had to agree—she stumbled on rough ground even in moonlight and, without sight, her swordwork suffered.

Nearby, Daish was slumped on the grassy verge, looking pale. Aisha knelt alongside, helping him to drink. Sasha joined them.

"How bad?" she asked in Lenay.

Aisha just shook her head and looked worried. The most recent bandages to Daish's side were red with new blood. Constant riding had not given the wound a chance to properly heal. They could not leave him now—towns in these hills were too isolated and too vulnerable to the Kazeri warband behind. And the townsfolk they'd passed were not friendly anyhow.

"We should reach the Ipshaal by nightfall tomorrow," said Aisha. "If the border guards let us in. Then we can stop running . . . but all of this riding isn't doing him any good."

"Hey," Daish said weakly. "No mumbling about me in foreign tongues. It makes me think you're saying things you don't want me to hear."

"We are," Sasha teased. "There was a girl in the Tol'rhen who claimed she'd slept with you, and you weren't any good. We were discussing whether she spoke the truth."

Daish managed a smile.

"I think not," said Aisha, helping him sip more water. "Surely not."

"What was her name?" Daish asked after the swallow.

"Peala," said Sasha. "Long hair, always in curls."

Daish managed a laugh, weakly, so not to hurt his side. "I never touched her. I have more taste."

He clasped Aisha's hand. Aisha clasped it back and, as Daish closed his eyes to rest, she gave Sasha a worried look.

Yasmyn stood further up, scanning the way ahead. "The horses are struggling," Sasha told her and Rhillian. "We can't hold this pace much longer."

"I think our pursuers will try to push the pace," said Rhillian. "They need to catch us before we reach the Ipshaal."

"If the border guards let us cross," Sasha countered. She sipped from her waterskin and swatted at a fly. "It's hot in Kazerak; I reckon Kazeri horses will handle this heat better than ours. If we push this hard for two days, we'll have them falling dead from under us. Hills are one thing, hills and heat together are a killer."

"We'd better find someone to feed us along the way," Yasmyn said darkly, looking at the high mountains. "A climb like that takes a lot of eating for horses and people—that's a four-day pass, more if the weather turns bad. We're already low on food, and if the villages remain unfriendly . . ."

"We'll find a way to persuade them," said Rhillian.

Sasha was impressed by the sheer size of the Ilduuri Range. It began down by the border with Meraine, where foothills rose into valleys that made the land easily defendable against any Meraini attack. There were fortresses there, Aisha said, and walls guarding the mouths of valleys, manned with detachments of the Ilduuri Steel and local militia. If any attack breached that first defence, an army faced a long march up a climbing valley toward the mountains, where further battlements guarded high passes, manned in turn by reinforcements brought from middle Ilduur by signal fires set burning at news of the first breach. Looking at the mountains before her, Sasha could see why Ilduur had never been conquered. It was a natural fortress, and granted entry only to whom it chose.

She led the way down the next slope, into a steep valley with sides so rocky they would bear no human settlement. The valley floor was narrow, and earth gave way to loose rock and shale, across which a stream flowed. Now it was truly hot, with sun glaring off the rocks, and she pulled her broad-brim Petrodor hat from her saddlebag.

By midafternoon, Aisha was pushing her way up the trail to Sasha's side. "Daish can barely stay on his horse," she said. "Sasha, if we keep going like this, we'll kill him."

Sasha signalled a halt, and wheeled her sweaty horse around. Yasmyn was next behind, then Rhillian and Kiel. "We can defend this ridge," she said, gesturing around them. "It has shade, steep sides, only one approach. If we stop, we stop here and fight. But there's no water, and if we go down into a valley, the Kazeri will gain the high ground, then surround and kill us."

"Can there really be any discussion?" Kiel wondered. "I know it always falls to me to say the cruel and heartless thing, but is there truly anything to be discussed?"

Sasha looked at Aisha. Aisha looked desperately at Rhillian. "Sasha," Rhillian said quietly, "if it falls to me to decide, you know there's only one decision to make."

Sasha swore, and dismounted fast from her horse. She jogged to Daish, who slumped over his saddle, pale and sweaty, without even the strength to swat away the flies that landed on his face. Seeing him like that, Sasha recalled Yulia of Petrodor, another young student of the Nasi-Keth, who had died by the risk Sasha had subjected her to, by her own orders.

"Daish," she said quietly, grasping his arm, "can you hold on just down the next hill? I have an idea."

Daish nodded weakly. "Don't stop for me," he said hoarsely. "Get to Ilduur."

"We will," Sasha assured him. "All of us will. Just hold on until we reach the next valley."

It took longer than she'd hoped. The ridge they were on continued to climb, then wove along an adjoining ridge before finally descending. But that downward slope bore the full face of the lowering afternoon sun, and the heat rising off surrounding rocks was as great as anything Sasha had ever felt.

The valley was totally exposed. The stream here gathered into a pool, wide but shallow. Sasha and Aisha half carried Daish from his saddle and sat him in the water. Sasha pulled off his shirt and began unwinding his bandages while Aisha rummaged through her medicinal bag for those magical concoctions that serrin used to such amazing affect.

"You go on," Sasha told Rhillian. "We'll catch up. He just needs a rest."

"Sasha," Rhillian warned as her horse drank thirstily from the stream, "this is not a defensible position. . . ."

"I know that. I don't intend to stay that long, I'm a better rider in these hills than anyone else, and if it gets dark, I'll have Aisha's eyes to guide me."

She peeled the last bandage off Daish's wound—it looked okay, inflamed red but healthily so. Serrin medicines prevented infections, but infections were not all that could kill, and if his lung had indeed been punctured, even slightly . . .

"Aisha is valuable to the mission," said Kiel. "She knows Ilduur, and is a fine linguist. Sasha's sword and demonstration of Lenayin's new alliance are likewise invaluable. This is not a wise risk."

"Aye, well, you find me a 'wise risk,' Kiel," Sasha said sarcastically, "and I'll find you a pig that shits silver."

"I'll stay," said Yasmyn. She wore a serrin blade at her shoulder now, which a retired *talmaad* in a passing village had granted to her. Yasmyn was skilled with her one-handed darak, and could surely improvise some use for this. Sasha wasn't certain she didn't prefer Yasmyn bare-handed than heavily armed and overconfident.

"I'd rather Arendelle. An archer would be useful—Aisha's a better shot than me but not to his standard."

Arendelle nodded and dismounted midstream to water his horse. Yasmyn sulked. Kiel looked exasperated.

"We'll wait for you at the best defensible plateau at sundown," Rhillian told them. "Don't be late." She put heels to her horse, and the reluctant animal resumed the trail. Yasmyn, Kiel, and Bergen followed.

Daish lay back in the stream, soaking, his head on the bank. "Stupid," he muttered. "You should go."

"You should shut up," Sasha told him, and placed his hat over his face to shield it from the sun.

Aisha applied more medicine on the wound and then gave him some to drink, but there wasn't much more she could do. Mostly, Sasha hoped that the cool soaking water and the moment of rest would allow Daish's weakened body to recover. He was young and fit; she had to give him every chance to get well on his own.

She and Arendelle washed down the horses as best they could, while Aisha tended to Daish. They could not risk removing the horses' saddles, and the animals were reluctant to lie and roll in the water with them still on, but standing while flasks of water were emptied over them had similar effect. She was preoccupied with that task when Aisha called a warning.

Where the trail down the hillside broke from the trees, a pair of riders now sat. Both had long hair, and middle-sized horses of breeding unfamiliar to Sasha's eye. They stared at the scene before them.

Arendelle abandoned the horses and splashed to the bank, picking up his bow and shouldering the quiver of arrows. The horsemen conversed, and one turned back the way he'd come and vanished up the trail.

"Scouts," said Sasha.

"Yes, and ahead of what advance party?" Arendelle wondered.

The Kazeri rider cantered sideways toward the stream, putting a little more distance between himself and them. Sasha had no doubt Arendelle could hit him from here, if he kept still. But the Kazeri seemed alert and unlikely to comply.

"I could ride him down," Arendelle suggested.

"He'll run away, and you'll tire your horse to breaking," Sasha replied. "He's only here to watch, he's not worth the effort."

"We should go," said Daish, trying weakly to rise.

Aisha pushed him back down. "The last time we saw them, they were a long way behind. We've some more time yet."

They waited, Daish resting in the water as the sun sank toward the valley ridge. Finally, as the ridge shadow crept toward them, and the Kazeri scout sat astride his horse downstream, Sasha decided they could wait no longer.

Aisha rewrapped Daish's bandages and helped him into his shirt. He remounted with difficulty, and they rode toward the resumption of the trail up the far slope. The Kazeri scout followed.

"You idiot," Sasha said loudly, in Lenay. "Not too bright, this one."

She waited until they'd reached the top of the rise, horses labouring on the incline, then selected a large tree that grew at a twisted angle from the upside of the trail, angling overhead. She dismounted, indicating for Aisha to ride up and take her horse's bridle as Sasha took position behind the tree.

"Won't take but a moment," she assured her companions. "Wait for me."

They rode on. Sasha put her back to the leaning trunk, unclipped her scabbard from her bandoleer, and waited. Here on the trail edge, she was level with any Kazeri rider. This Kazeri, like most, wore no armour.

Soon enough, she heard approaching hooves. A quick glance past the trunk showed the Kazeri, plodding cautiously. He was an idiot, one rider alone, coming so close after a larger group. If she'd left Arendelle to deal with him, he'd be dead right here. Instead, she leaned back behind the tree, grasped her scabbard by the wrong end, and waited until he drew level.

Then she swung around the tree's far side and hit him in the face with the hilt, hard. He fell. Sasha unfastened the scabbard and took out her blade, standing over him. The Kazeri recovered enough to stare up at her, past a bleeding brow. A young face. No more than fourteen.

Sasha swore. She indicated the knife at his belt, and the sword. "Off!" she commanded. He unhitched the scabbard and the knife, and put them on the path, hands trembling with fear. "Up!" He climbed unsteadily to his feet, putting a hand to his head, and looking at the blood that smeared his palm. "Walk!"

Sasha gathered his weapons, then grabbed the horse's bridle, gesturing the boy on ahead with her blade. He walked around several more bends in the path, Sasha following with his horse.

Around another bend, and there was Arendelle, an arrow fitted and drawn, about to launch for the boy's throat. He lowered the bow.

"Let's get him tied and back on his horse," said Sasha. "Aisha might be able to speak enough to ask some questions later."

Twelve

Sasha sat on her saddle and gazed out at the view atop this latest ridge. They had a clear view of their trail, winding up the way they'd come, visible even to Sasha's eyes in the moonlight. Arendelle sat watching it, and the slope beyond, wondering if there were any alternative route the Kazeri might find over this ridge and around them, to ambush on both sides. Sasha thought it was possible. But the terrain was hard enough for her, a Lenay. Plains-dwelling Kazeri would take most of the night to achieve that ambush, and would be exhausted the following day. Besides which, Daish would quite simply die if they did not stop for the night, to say nothing of the horses.

"He's a *kunli*," Aisha said. She only spoke a little Kazeri, but she did speak fluent Lisan, of all things. The Lisan Empire lay across the far western side of the Morovian Mountains from Lenayin—an impenetrable barrier for most, but not for Aisha's love of tongues. "A *kunli* just means a scout; the Kazeri use young riders as scouts on the plains—they weigh less on their horses and cover more ground."

"Why have the Kazeri come?" Rhillian asked.

"He's just a kid," said Aisha, "his understanding isn't thorough. But it seems the northern Kazeri chiefs are in conflict with the southern. The northerners have been losing, so they seek alliance with the Bacosh. Rakani and Meraine, mostly."

Rakani and Meraine were the southernmost Bacosh provinces. The Rakani were related to the Kazeri, and were regarded poorly by much of the pale-skinned Bacosh. The Meraini were wealthy, but historically the least involved in the Bacosh's long struggles for power. Sasha had heard rumour that Meraine's present participation in what remained a Larosan-led war was reluctant at best.

"They'll have had to come through Meraine and Rakani to get here," said Rhillian. "Perhaps those Meraini and Rakani lords thought to have us outflanked by a sudden Kazeri attack. I'll wager they provided guides."

"With old maps," Aisha cautioned.

"Just as likely they tire of Kazeri provocation upon their border," Kiel stated, "and have invited the Kazeri to their doom. Decreasing two enemies simultaneously is surely more fortunate than one at a time."

Aisha asked the boy some more questions.

"He says there were guides from Meraine. The warriors of Zalamud—that's Northern Kazerak—were promised much gold and loot in the rich lands of Enora and Saalshen. As much as they could load into carts. And alliance with the Chansul of Meraine, against the enemies of Zalamud."

"Saalshen," Kiel said. "Charming."

"The Chansul didn't offer to marry a Kazeri chief's daughter, though," Sasha muttered, thinking of Sofy. "The Bacosh dislike of savages is only so flexible."

"Sounds like a play for power by the Chansul of Meraine as much as anything," Rhillian observed. "I can't imagine the Regent will be thrilled that his least favourite Meraini has made alliance with the Kazeri. It makes him rather more powerful."

"The Regent made alliance with Lenayin," said Yasmyn. "Probably the Chansul sees this as a way to get even. If the Regent wins, he becomes King of the Bacosh, more powerful than any since Leyvaan."

"Oh, much more powerful than Leyvaan," said Rhillian. "Leyvaan did not command such a broad alliance as this. And Balthaar is capturing our weapons and our knowledge. Surely he will find use for captured Steel artillery."

"Not everyone will like this," Yasmyn continued. "When King Soros rose in Lenayin, the Isfayen did not like it. They made King Soros prove his honour in war."

"Because defeating all those Cherrovan wasn't test enough for the Isfayen," said Kiel in amusement.

"Yasmyn's right," said Sasha. "Of all the Bacosh powers discomforted by the idea of a Larosan as Bacosh king, Meraine will be discomforted most. Meraine is the one province the Larosans have least influence in—it's too big, and too outward-looking for the Larosans to ever have truly controlled. Now a Larosan is to be king of all, and the Meraini will be looking to protect their independence from what is to come."

Rhillian's eyes flicked to Sasha, an emerald glow in the night. "Ilduur has not responded to Enora's and Rhodaan's requests for help," she said slowly.

Sasha nodded. "The Ilduuri and the Meraini have always been cordial."

"We know they have relations," Aisha agreed. "There are many trails through the mountains, some of them very old trading roads. We know that some Meraini lords have even visited Ilduur, and spent time in Andal. Some in Saalshen even toyed with the idea of attempting to spread Nasi-Keth influence into Meraine, perhaps even a quiet alliance between Saalshen and individual Meraini lords, if not all of Meraine. But others in Saalshen have blocked it, saying that even a whiff of serrin friendship will bring the priesthood down on the Meraini lords' heads, and cause more trouble than it solves."

"Well, all of this is very interesting conjecture," Kiel said mildly. "But it is one thing to go from suggesting that Ilduur is a reluctant ally of *anyone*, which is a basic historical fact, to saying that the Ilduuri may have entered into a pact with the Meraini to make common cause against everyone else."

"The Ilduuri do not want to fight," said Rhillian. "If that is their object, an alliance with Meraine would appear to protect them from further invasion, without them ever having to make formal alliance with the Regent."

"They can surrender without actually having to surrender," Sasha said drily. "What honour."

"While the Meraini will gain a powerful ally to protect their independence from the Regent," Rhillian continued. "The Ilduuri are perfect for the purpose, because they don't ask any more of the Meraini than to be left alone."

There was silence in the camp. Somewhere nearby, a bird called, sounding hot, tired, and unable to sleep. Sasha empathised.

"Why we ever helped these people . . ." Kiel remarked. And left the question unanswered.

The Kazeri boy said something. And stared about at them all from his place on the ground, huddled between them with ankles tied, in obvious fear.

"He asks us demons not to eat his soul," Aisha said tiredly.

"What's in it for me?" Kiel inquired.

"Tell him to sleep," said Rhillian, with a reprimanding glance at Kiel. "Tell him we'll let him go, as soon as we're able."

Kiel blinked. "We shall?"

"Yes," Rhillian said, "we shall. I'm not killing children *deliberately*, Kiel."

"And will you seek Saalshen's survival *deliberately*? Or will you leave it purely to chance?"

They left the boy that morning, free to await his people's arrival. Kiel was not happy, claiming that he would simply resume the pursuit with the others. Rhillian did not argue, save to say that they could not win such a fight anyhow, and one fourteen-year-old boy would hardly swing the battle one way or the other. They did, however, keep his horse.

The Kazeri had not attempted to circle during the night and ambush ahead. As the land turned to long, climbing valleys and sheer, rugged cliffs, Sasha thought that was probably wise.

The party let their horses drink thirstily at the first valley stream, but by the time the trail began climbing once more, the sun was glaring into their faces, and the heat already intense. Halfway up the next rise, Bergen's horse simply stopped. A quick check from Sasha found the poor animal in great distress, heart racing, eyes rolling.

"Overheated," she told them, as Bergen unbuckled straps and removed the saddle and saddlebags. "We have to leave him—if we let him turn back to the last stream, he may survive."

"We can't just leave him for the Kazeri," said Kiel.

"He's not walking for us or the Kazeri," Sasha replied. At those words, the horse crumpled on shaky knees and lay on the trail. Sasha's throat hurt to look at his desperate pain. She'd loved horses since she was a little girl and, unlike people, they'd never asked for a fate like this.

"He's finished," Rhillian sighed, and slid off her own horse, drawing her sword. Sasha shook her head. "Sasha, it's kinder."

"Just give him a chance. He may recover, and go down to the stream. Just give him a chance."

Rhillian looked at her for a moment. Then sheathed her blade and remounted her horse. Sasha poured water over the suffering animal's neck, then tried to make him drink the rest.

"Go that way, you big fool," she said, trying to turn his head toward the valley. The horse just lay, too distressed to move. The others rode past, and Sasha remounted to follow, wiping her eyes. Bergen, mounted on the captured Kazeri horse, offered her his flask. He was a big man, with battle scars on his arms.

"That's my seventh," he said. "I remember all their names. My son is named after my favourite."

Sasha recalled her Peg, now safe somewhere in a Pazira stable in Torovan. Thank the spirits he couldn't fit on the boat to Tracato.

The top of the ridge presented them with a view of the Kazeri following them. They were much closer now. Another valley bottom and another drink and brief wash provided more relief, but climbing out of that valley, Sasha's horse slipped and fell nose-first into the trail with a thud.

Sasha leaped off and examined the animal, but could barely find a pulse. Cursing, she pulled a few useful possessions from her saddlebags, while Bergen did the duties with his sword. Another time, Sasha might have protested that she was not so weak she couldn't do it herself. Now, she had only gratitude.

She joined Aisha, the lightest rider, and her horse perhaps the largest and fittest, but the mare did not welcome the extra weight. "They're riding our horses into the ground," Sasha muttered.

By midday, huge thunderclouds were gathering above the mountains, thunder grumbling and echoing through the steep valleys. In no time at all, the rain was on them, turning the rocky trails treacherous with wet rocks and loose mud.

Rhillian was not pleased by the change. "The Kazeri will go faster now. We'll not keel over so fast in the rain, and the Ipshaal is nearly before us."

It was indeed. At the top of the next ridge, through a mist of rain, the party looked down upon a huge canyon. Spanning it was the widest bridge Sasha had ever seen. It was little more than a road of planks, suspended from huge ropes that soared across the span, affixed to four giant stone pillars.

To the side of the bridge, and at both ends, was a small guard post with a tower and crenellations for archers. "Don't the Steel border guards have to keep to their side of the river only?" Sasha asked Aisha as they descended toward the bridge.

"Enora does not bother to defend this border," Aisha replied. "Only the Ilduuri remain suspicious enough to guard borders with their so-called friends. They can build forts on either side, no one cares."

Aisha had barely looked at the bridge or the canyon, her eyes only on Daish. "Nearly there," she told him. "Just down the hill, then you can rest."

Approaching the bridge, Sasha saw that a stone wall stretched from the guard post at the canyon's edge to the natural cliff face of the opposing slope. In the wall was a tall gate. Thus the guard post controlled all entry to the bridge, and into Ilduur.

"Hello!" Rhillian called up at the small tower, walking her horse out before the others. "I am Rhillian. Four of this party are serrin, *talmaad* of Saalshen. The others are friends of ours. In the name of two centuries of friendship between Saalshen and Ilduur, I ask passage."

There came no reply, nor hint of movement. Rain washed down the dark stone walls. Sasha had climbed rocks before, but never a wall this smooth, and certainly not wet.

"Enemies from Kazerak pursue us!" Rhillian tried again. "If we are not admitted immediately, we shall be trapped out here!"

There was no reply but the hissing rain, and the roll and boom of nearby thunder. Rhillian turned her horse and came back.

"Deserted?" Sasha asked.

"No, I saw movement through a window." Rhillian looked grim. "It seems the Steel are under instruction not to admit the likes of us."

And there was no way around, and no retracing their steps. No one needed to say it. This was the only bridge for several days' ride.

"Well," said Rhillian, with a hard exhale, "there's little choice. At least here there is room for a fight."

Sasha was exasperated. If they'd known it would be a fight, they'd have held a high pass and forced the Kazeri to come at them single file up a hill. But now they were trapped against a wall at the base of a slope, with the Kazeri coming down on top of them.

The party positioned themselves. Daish dismounted and slumped in the gateway with his sword, while Sasha took his horse and readied her shield. The four serrin took the flanks: Arendelle and Aisha to the left by the canyon edge, Rhillian and Kiel on the right against the cliff wall. Bergen held the centre, a Steel cavalryman with shield, sword and armour all suited to the task, but now on a smaller, unfamiliar horse. On his right was Sasha, on his left, Yasmyn. Their horses were all exhausted. It seemed ridiculous.

"Seven against a hundred," Sasha announced. "This has the makings of a fireside tale."

"Don't you mean a song?" Rhillian wondered.

"Lenays don't sing much."

"We Enorans like to sing," said Bergen. "Don't we, Aisha?"

"I'd love to write a song," said Aisha, testing the pull of her bow, and how much her wet fingers slipped against the string. "But I'll get Sasha to write the words. Lenays do that sort of thing better than anyone."

"Hush, you lot," said Rhillian. She glanced at Sasha. They smiled. There was no need to say more.

They waited. Thunder crackled and boomed. The rain grew heavier. Sasha heard hooves further up the trail. On the flanks, the serrin pulled their bowstrings. The hooves stopped. Then turned back. A scout, hidden amongst the trees. Sasha wondered how much he'd seen.

The attack, when it came, was sudden. Kazeri horsemen plunged off the trail fifty paces short of the trail mouth, precariously above the canyon. Others rushed down the trail, and at points in between.

The serrin drew and fired. Yelling Kazeri fell from their horses at the trail mouth, and others behind reined up in fear as the first four, then six, died quickly. Then the riders coming off the trail edge rushed in, and only Aisha and Arendelle had a good angle on those. Aisha missed once, but Arendelle never did, drawing fast and felling one rider after another.

Now the blockage on the trail was clearing, and more Kazeri charged from the trees. But their path was obstructed by the confused, riderless horses of the first wave. Rhillian and Kiel's combined fire shot more tumbling from their saddles, as those behind desperately sought a way through, evading and colliding with their fellows. Kiel had more success.

Then the Kazeri bearing down on Arendelle and Aisha came too close, Arendelle killing one last rider before both serrin were forced to drop bows and draw swords. The volume of arrow fire halved, and the Kazeri came on faster.

Bergen charged. Sasha followed on his right, and saw him crash a Kazeri straight from the saddle with a massive blow. With perfect balance, he swung his unfamiliar horse into a side step that brought him exactly into line with a second, whose sword arm was severed whilst trying to defend.

Then Sasha had a rider in her way. She ducked onto his weak side with a kick of heels, shield high to deflect his overhead whilst timing her own swing a little later, catching him on the pass. Then there were riderless horses running into hers, blocking her from the next Kazeri, one of whom took an arrow through the side as Kiel and Rhillian continued to fire.

Sasha saw Bergen locked in battle with two more, neither of whom were facing her, and steered her horse for a fast lunge through traffic to put her sword through one's back. Bergen killed the other, then drove a third from his saddle with a lunge of his shield.

The battleground was becoming crowded with horses, many riderless, all rearing, dodging, and scampering in the confusion of falling rain and flying arrows. But Sasha caught a glimpse up the trail, and saw it filled with incoming Kazeri. The numbers were overwhelming.

Suddenly the air was thick with arrows, as though the rain itself had turned deadly. Incoming Kazeri fell five and six at a time, then more as the arrows repeated. Cries of battle turned to cries of fear as those remaining turned and fled up the mountain trail. The arrows were coming from the guard post, Sasha realised, and the wall itself.

Finally the yelling stopped. Sasha made a fast check of her companions. Aisha had fallen when her horse had slipped, and suffered bruises and cuts. Arendelle had a cut on his upper arm, bleeding thickly but easily treated. Those two had been most fortunate, having been in the face of that off-trail charge. The rest of them were unscathed . . . even Yasmyn, who was exultant.

Fully thirty-five Kazeri lay dead or dying, half of those in that final volley of arrows from the walls. Sasha could not fault their enthusiasm, but felt less charitable of their tactics. It was almost as though they'd never seen archery before.

Kiel dismounted to retrieve arrows they could ill afford to waste. At one body, he signalled to Rhillian. "See? What futility is this 'mercy' you practise, with people such as these?"

Rhillian and Sasha rode to see. The body was that of a boy, no more than fourteen. His eyes were unblinking as the rain fell into his face, his forehead scarred from the recent blow of the hilt of Sasha's sword.

"We killed him fair," Rhillian said coolly.

"And to what greater moral purpose is mercy," Kiel asked in bemusement, "if its most immediate function is merely to help you sleep better at night?"

"I like my sleep," said Rhillian, moving her horse away.

Sasha looked down at the young, lifeless face, and thought that her sleep had not been helped at all.

The gates shuddered and creaked, opening slowly on massive hinges. A man in armour walked out, wearing a red surcoat and crested helm. He had the build of a warrior.

Rhillian dismounted for politeness, and shook the man's extended hand.

"Apologies for being late," said the man in Saalsi. Sasha was only a little surprised—the Ilduuri were as familiar with serrin as Enorans or Rhodaanis. "We had a small disagreement behind our wall."

"Indeed," said Rhillian, with a Saalsi word that was both statement and question.

The Steel officer looked embarrassed and unhappy. "Best you don't ask too loudly," he said. "Please, my apologies to you and your friends, we'll try to get you across the bridge with no more problems."

Sasha dismounted to Rhillian's side, and they exchanged a glance. No more problems? "Who exactly controls this guard post anyhow?" Sasha murmured in Lenay.

"Be polite," Rhillian replied in the same, "but stay wary."

Aisha joined the Steel soldiers helping Daish to his feet, as the others walked their horses through the gates. Sasha looked back up at the wall parapet from this side and saw twelve men there, all with serrin-type longbows. The other men there made for perhaps twenty-five border guards. The tower did not look large enough to accommodate them all, and there was only stabling for ten horses at most. Probably the others came from the building across the bridge.

Before the tower walls, a furious argument was in progress. A man in a green cloak was shouting at a soldier whose helm crest suggested to Sasha he might be an officer. The soldier stood sullenly in the rain, and cast the odd glance at the new arrivals as his more elegantly attired superior ranted in Ilduuri. Sasha and her companions exchanged glances, as Aisha escorted Daish to the cover of a stable berth.

"Nasi-Keth," said the man who had let them in, with distaste. Sasha blinked at him. The green-cloaked man did not look Nasi-Keth. Was there a sword on his back beneath that cloak?

"They're different here," Rhillian explained for Sasha's benefit. "They belong to the Remischtuul." The Ilduuri ruling Council, that was, as nearly as anyone had explained it to Sasha's understanding. "They take their initial teachings from Saalshen, as do all Nasi-Keth, but their loyalty is to Ilduur. We try to be nice to them, but they don't truly care what serrin think."

Sasha had heard that there was no Mahl'rhen in Ilduur, no house of the serrin, to represent the interests of Saalshen, and promote amity between serrin and human. Two centuries before, Saalshen had abolished feudalism here as in Enora and Rhodaan, and Ilduur had flourished as greatly as had its Saalshen Bacosh neighbours. So successful had Ilduur been, and so peaceable toward its new serrin administrators, that Saalshen's attention moved to the more pressing problems of religion, education, and crop yields in bigger, more populous Enora and Rhodaan. Failure there would have brought real problems for Saalshen, as only the Ipshaal separated humans there from serrin to the east. Ilduur, safe within its mountain walls, had withdrawn to manage its own affairs, and say pleasant things to visiting emissaries, and make pledges of treaty and mutual support—anything to keep the foreigners happy, and out of Ilduuri affairs.

But one would be foolish to actually trust that the Ilduuri cared enough for their foreign allies to send help in the event of actual need. Some *had* been foolish, and now learned the price.

Aisha left Daish in the hands of Ilduuri guards, and came over. "He's berating the captain for helping us," Aisha translated for them. "He ordered the captain not to help us. The captain obeyed until the Kazeri attacked, then disobeyed. The captain is now to be . . . *castaanti*." She frowned. "I've not heard that word." Then her eyes widened. "Oh, like *castaantala*, as in tribunal. He'll be hauled before a hearing of superiors. I imagine that's serious?"

She looked askance at the soldier nearby. He nodded grimly. "Very serious. Likely they'll hang him."

"For helping us?" Rhillian asked in disbelief.

"For endangering Ilduur by involving her unnecessarily in foreign affairs and disturbances." There was flat irony to the soldier's voice. "Gone crazy, all of them. Crazy with fear, fucking cowards." He spat. "The Ilduuri Steel would have marched, my friends. Most of us. But the Remischtuul says no, and the Steel follow orders. We let you down. Ilduur has shamed herself, and our leaders do not care."

Rhillian's emerald stare was intense. She put a hand on the man's shoulder. "Do all the Steel feel as you do?"

"Not all, but most. We want to fight this Regent. No good comes from letting Rhodaan and Enora fall, let alone Saalshen—we all know that's his true and final goal. But the people who join the Steel are not those who join the Remischtuul. You'll see, when you get to Andal."

Rhillian nodded. "Then we have not wasted our journey to come here after all."

The Ilduuri Nasi-Keth finally had enough of berating the captain and stalked over. He glared at the new arrivals.

"So," he said, also in Saalsi. "Now that you're here, I shall have to interrogate you. We cannot allow just anyone to enter Ilduur."

"I am *talmaad* of Saalshen," said Rhillian, "as are three others of our party. The others are Enoran, Rhodaani, and their allies. We are friends of Ilduur."

"Friends," the Nasi-Keth snorted. "You bring war to our gates. Ilduur needs no friends like you."

"If one feels that a friend is to be chosen merely at one's convenience," Rhillian said coldly, "then one *has* no friends."

The Nasi-Keth gave a look of contempt and walked for his horse. The Ilduuri captain did too. Some of his men exchanged quiet words with their captain, patting his shoulder, offering support. Some glared fury at their superior in the green cloak.

When all of the party were mounted, including Daish, the Nasi-Keth led them across the bridge. The rain grew heavier still. Thunder grumbled, and blue light flashed huge, mist-shrouded mountains into startling relief. The suspended bridge swayed beneath them, but seemed little strained at holding so many horses at once. Hooves clattered on wooden planks, and from far below came the rushing of the river. It was the first time Sasha had seen the Ipshaal; the greatest river in Rhodia descended from the mountains of Raani before it cut north, to divide Enora and Rhodaan from Saalshen. A barrier between lands and peoples that had shaped the destinies of all.

Halfway across, the soldier who had escorted them in rode up to the Nasi-Keth man's side, knife in hand, and calmly cut his stirrup. The Nasi-Keth stared at him, and asked an alarmed question in Ilduuri.

Cutting finished, the guardsman sat upright, sheathed his knife, and gave the other man an almighty shove. He went sideways, his cut stirrup offering no salvation, and fell screaming off the side. If there was a splash below, the roar of churning water smothered it from hearing.

The soldier turned to the party behind, all stopped, frozen in shock. "Gets awful slippery this bridge, in the rain," he told them. "Best watch where your horse puts its hooves."

Thirteen

In the hills beyond Tracato, the Elissian pursuit finally caught them. Riding in mid-column, Sofy heard the yells and massed hooves as they crested the ridge and came tearing across the fields. Jaryd was on them immediately, leading the countercharge. Tracatan men followed him, ex-Rhodaani Steel cavalry, some Nasi-Keth with cavalry skills, a few with the serrin art of horseback archery. Two were Larosan knights, the survivors of Sofy's personal guard, armour gleaming in the sun as their huge horses strained up the slight incline.

Wagons and horses in the column about her began to run, frightened families whipping their horse teams up to speed. Sofy went with them, as much to avoid being run over as anything, throwing frightened glances over her shoulder as she went.

She saw Jaryd hit the first Elissians so hard a horse crashed and tumbled. Behind him went Asym, the Isfayen carving men from their saddles like a cook cleaving meat from the bone. Then she was jostled by a man with children sharing his saddle, desperately fighting for space on the road. Sofy clung to her reins, seeing chaos and tangles up ahead. She was too good a rider to be stuck in this mess, she thought, and steered herself off the road, between runners on foot, and along the side of a vineyard. Then she stopped to gain a better look at the fight.

Elissians were flowing past Jaryd's defenders, who now milled higher up the slope, fighting crazily against some, but unable to contain the rest, now racing between trees downslope of the road, and others galloping along the road itself. Terror gripped Sofy to see the advance, nothing between them and the fleeing column.

On the wagons to the rear of the column, men with bows were drawing and attempting to fire backward, to little effect. Elissian horsemen came thundering upon screaming city folk, riding them down as they ran. Wagons were overtaken, their drivers hacked from their seats. Sofy stared about frantically as people ran, cried, and collided. Were there other warriors who could fall back and help? Had some fled ahead, instead of fighting? How could she think such men cowards, when she was doing that herself?

Jaryd's fighters had vanished, she realised. She hadn't seen them coming back, and now they were lost amidst the poplars and ash along the narrow valley. She kicked her horse and galloped at speed, dodging others who ran or rode here, hoping to get ahead and . . . and what? Do something valorous, while running to save her neck? But what else could she . . .

Commotion ahead cut the thought short. Wagons careened off the road, one crashing into a tree and sending passengers flying, another overturning as Elissian men fell upon the column, breaking clear of an orchard to gallop amongst the fleeing city folk with flashing swords. Panic ensued. Wagons tried to turn off the road, and Sofy dodged them madly. No one wanted to go that way, but they could not turn back. They were trapped.

Sofy stopped and peered through orchard trees, back toward a farmhouse. Could she ride toward it, and hope she would not be seen?

The Elissians were barely a hundred paces ahead of her, spinning their horses, killing in a frenzy, trampling any who were close. Some now galloped her way, back along the column, people running before them in terrified waves. Fifty paces.

A new horseman crashed from the trees and into the leading Elissian. Jaryd. The Elissian's horse jostled sideways into a collision with a wagon, and Jaryd split the man's head all over the wheels. He spun, hammering another Elissian with his shield, then a skilful spin of his horse, a quick spur and leap past the other's blade, and a cut that took that Elissian through the shoulder.

The Elissian hung on for dear life, shoulder wrecked, his horse bolting in terror straight at Sofy. There was nowhere for her to go, and it dodged first, straight into the orchard trees, thrashing and slowing in the branches.

Jaryd and now Asym were fighting back along the column, killing as they went. Sofy had never seen its like. Truly she'd never appreciated what greatness meant, as a warrior. Men had told stories of Jaryd on horseback in lagand tournaments, then remarked snidely that lagand was not warfare. Lagand had always horrified her with its unnecessary brutality. Now she watched as Jaryd, Asym, and several companions hacked and bludgeoned their way up the column, with furious violence somehow as graceful as a dance.

And then he was coming back, galloping past her, and she had a glimpse of his eyes, burning within a blood-splattered face. He barely saw her, racing to the rear of the column to deal with the attack there. About her, folk were leaping from wagons, grabbing the wounded Elissian still mired in the orchard trees, dragging him from his saddle. There beneath her mount, ordinary men and women wrestled the wounded man down, tore off his helm, pinned his arms, and beat, stabbed, and tore at him with screams of rage and fear. Soon there was blood everywhere and, as they got at his weapons, torn shreds of flesh.

Sofy set off after Jaryd, too dazed to think. Tracatans huddled amidst the trees and milled about the farmhouse walls, hugging children and staring at the galloping horsemen who went racing up and down the road, hoping they were friendly, fearing they were not. By the time she reached the rear of the column, the Elissians were fleeing. Defenders on horseback were chasing. On the road, she saw Jaryd once more, and Asym, amidst a number of riderless horses. Bodies were strewn across the road. A few were Elissians. Most were not.

In his saddle, Asym looked satisfied. He gave a yell in Telochi and clashed shields with Jaryd, a mutual salute. Jaryd looked around, breathing hard, dripping with blood that was not his. His shield bore countless new marks, and he seemed to have some pain in that arm, shaking it off even now. The huge blade in his fist was blood-streaked, and bore several new notches. He saw an Elissian still moving upon the road. Jaryd dismounted and drove the blade through the fallen man's chest with a two-handed thrust. He pulled the blade out with brutal contempt and remounted. And looked at Sofy.

Seeing him, Sofy realised something that she had never appreciated before in her life. Glory was not just some awful word that silly men invented to excuse their crimes. Glory rode a horse, and saved the helpless from terrible enemies by slaughtering them, without mercy, and with great fire. Glory was awful, and frightening. But it was real, and looked at her now with heaving shoulders and burning eyes.

Jaryd and Asym sat together on the steps of the fountain in the village courtyard. Evening shadows fell upon the pavings and a cool breeze had begun to blow, relief from the heat of the day. They ate fruit from the orchards, and some bread passed around from the bakery. There were crowds about the courtyard, people clustered before the small temple, ordinary folk frightened and tired, some with children. A few were making the rounds, tearfully, asking for this or that missing person, lost when the Elissians had attacked on the road. Past the fountain, the two Larosan knights had laid out their armour and were resting, exhausted. Unarmoured, they looked like normal men.

Many of those running from Tracato had a part-serrin look to them. Others simply feared no one was safe. All were headed for Saalshen, in hope of sanctuary. Saalshen had no fortresses to stop people from Rhodaan, only the Ipshaal River. How they would cross it, Jaryd did not know. Saalshen traded in large volume with Rhodaan; surely there were boats. But if those boats fell into Elissian hands, there would be little to stop the pursuit. Most serrin did not fight. If only Saalshen were more like Lenayin, with every man a warrior, things would be different.

Asym poured some water over the wound on his shoulder. It was not deep, though the surrounding skin was discoloured. He then poured a little more on Jaryd's back, where a blow had done similar damage across a shoulder blade. Asym's upper arms and chest were tattooed with intricate curls and patterns in black ink, from which emerged the fanged and snarling faces of animals real and mythical.

"I hope Jandlys is well," Jaryd said absently.

Asym made a face. "If he is in Tracato, then no. Jandlys not quiet man. He make fight he will not win." Jaryd nodded, unable to argue with that. "It is good. Today is a good day."

Jaryd thought of the dead Tracatans on the road, but he knew what Asym meant. They were outnumbered, and slowed by their defence of this column of civilians. The cause was good, and the Elissians would surely return in far larger numbers. The opportunities for glory were high, posthumously or otherwise.

"You should have *kaspi*," said Asym, looking thoughtfully at Jaryd's bare torso. Tattoos, he meant. Goeren-yai markings. "So that the spirits shall recognise you when you die."

Jaryd smiled faintly, chewing an apple. "What if I don't plan on dying soon?"

"Elissians may have other idea." Jaryd laughed. "But besides, you die someday. The great spirits recognise me when I die, take me back to Isfayen, to the high meadows. There is great view there, maybe I see a new place to be reborn."

"You are a shepherd, yes?"

Asym nodded. "As a boy, I take flocks from low pasture to high in spring. The snow melts, and the grass is green. I watch sheep amongst the clouds, and practise my swordwork. Here, I am far from home, but I think of the high pasture and I am happy. These," and he tapped the tattoos, "these will take me there, one day."

"Perhaps the Verenthane gods will still recognise me," Jaryd suggested.

Asym smiled, and clapped him on the shoulder. "You Goeren-yai. You great warrior, spirits all see you. And I will speak for you."

A little girl with bright blue serrin eyes stopped before them and stared. In particular she stared at Asym, with his long black hair, markings, and narrow eyes. The two Lenays watched her back, with equal curiosity. She was no more than five, yet seemed to understand far more of what she saw than any human child of that age.

The girl's mother hurried over and collected her, then hurried off. The woman had not been serrin. Jaryd wondered where the serrin father was.

"These people are of the spirits," said Asym. "It did not feel right to fight them. I worry for the spirits of men who died by their hand."

"If the Army of Lenayin fights with Saalshen now, it means the serrin have accepted them and forgiven," Jaryd disagreed. "If they can forgive those who live, they will certainly forgive those who died."

Asym nodded, thinking on it, and uncorked a flask another local had pressed upon them. Ale of a kind, he'd said, made from apples. Asym took a swig, and offered it to Jaryd. Jaryd sniffed. It was fruity and strong. A sip, and nothing. Then a change, and fumes burning his sinuses. His eyes watered and he restrained a cough with difficulty.

Asym laughed and took another swig. They invited the Larosans to join them, and soon they were all more relaxed.

Jaryd walked in the evening gloom to the temple at the courtyard's end, a shirt donned for propriety's sake. Tracatans queued upon the steps, some holding candles as the night came on, hoping for a way inside. They recognised Jaryd—from the road he supposed—and stood aside with eyes lowered in deference.

The temple was attractive, like most town temples in these parts, a long paved floor between high walls. There was a priest conducting services of some kind, and a crowd up at the front where Sofy stood. Jaryd caught a glimpse of her, the Idys Mark still plain upon her forehead, hair covered beneath this Verenthane roof, blessing those who tried to touch her while fielding enquiries from several important-looking men.

Jaryd edged forward until he stood beneath an arched windowsill near the front. Upon the sill sat a serrin woman in plain clothes, observing the proceedings with calm curiosity. She patted the place beside her on the sill, and Jaryd leaped up.

"You fought well on the road, Nyvar," said the serrin. "With Lenayin with us, perhaps we have a chance."

"Perhaps," said Jaryd.

"I'm Ysilder," she said, extending a hand. "A jeweller."

"No svaalverd?" Jaryd asked.

Ysilder shook her head apologetically. "My diamonds are occasionally used to sharpen svaalverd blades. That's all."

"What happens here?"

"Gods know," she murmured. Jaryd looked at her oddly. "Figure of speech. I've been in Tracato a long time. The people appear to believe there are blessings to be had. Your princess offers herself. Now she is cornered."

"I would have taken her to Saalshen by another route," Jaryd muttered. "But she saw all these people flooding out of Tracato and she insisted we help them."

"She does seem that type," the serrin agreed.

"I doubt we do help. The Elissians will be after her, and I don't think Prince Dafed will protest; he never liked her or this marriage. They failed to kill her when they had the chance, and if she survives she may spread embarrassing tales to the Regent of how news of her death was exaggerated by his allies."

"They'll need to kill us all," Ysilder said tiredly. "The whole column, and every village we pass through. To hide the truth. It's not beyond them."

"Oh, I know that," Jaryd said wearily. "I'm yet to be convinced that *she* does, despite everything."

"She wears the mark of the wedded still," Ysilder observed. "Does she think her marriage survives? Even should the Regent love her and wish revenge on those who have gone against him, there is no point now. Lenayin is gone for him, or at least severely reduced. And his revenge, if properly conducted, would split the Bacosh and thus his alliance, just when his final victory is at hand."

"She swore an oath," said Jaryd. Ysilder looked at him—a middle-aged woman, with weary wisdom in her gaze. Jaryd sighed. "Yes, she is that type. All Lenay girls dream of marriage, and the romance of vows. A man has a warrior's honour, a woman has a wife's."

"No fair swap," said the serrin.

Jaryd shrugged. "There has been no recognised divorce. A married Lenay woman who does not obey her vows forfeits all honour."

"You're not *in* Lenayin any longer," Ysilder said pointedly.

"You go tell her that."

"No," said Ysilder. "You."

Jaryd thought about it, then pushed himself off the sill and toward the front of the temple. Sofy looked exhausted, no longer in her riding clothes but wearing a dress, spirits knew where she'd found it. The royal ring was on her finger, a gaudy emerald the size of an eye. A man had unrolled a parchment map in front of her, and was insisting with a jabbing finger upon some point drawn there. A priest hovered at her side, another man with more maps in rolls and a village head denoted by a fancy frilled collar.

"Sofy," Jaryd interrupted.

The man with the map raised his hand to ward off the interruption. ". . . see here," he was insisting to Sofy's weary gaze, "if we follow this route, it should not take us more than a day off our course, we can rally at the town and collect those from the orphanage and school, and then head for the Ipshaal."

"We cannot afford to lose a day!" another man protested. "The Elissians will be back, they will know of the major crossings, we're not sure if the boats are available or if the serrin have moved them upstream. . . ."

"There are a hundred and thirty souls in this orphanage," the man with the map retorted, "primarily children! It is too dangerous for them to travel these roads unguarded! Our column provides protection—we can gather them up and move them in safety!"

"By losing a day for them to regroup," Jaryd interjected, "which will get us all killed."

"These are women and children in need!" the man insisted.

"Look around you, I see women and children everywhere. The Elissians will be back many times as strong now they know the nature of this column—"

"You're not in charge here!" the man snapped, turning back to Sofy. "Your Highness . . ."

"As one of those whose task it is to provide the security you speak of," Jaryd overrode him loudly, "I have charge of that defence. The women and children in that town can be escorted by others if their need is great, and probably already have been. Now stop bothering the princess with your nonsense."

"Just because you wear a blade, that does not give you the right to command everyone else!" the man shouted at him. "If you want to be a fucking coward, you go ahead, your violent ways give you no rights here!"

Jaryd punched him in the jaw, and he went down with a clatter. All activity in the temple stopped.

"That's where you're wrong," said Jaryd.

He turned to Sofy. She was staring up at him, wide-eyed, but only faintly horrified. Jaryd hoped that was progress. "Sofy, what are you doing here?" he asked in Lenay. "Go and get some rest."

"These people need me," Sofy said faintly. "Jaryd, I cannot turn my back on them."

"These people need leadership," Jaryd retorted. "They need you to do what is good for them, not what will make them happy. This man's happiness will get everyone killed—you can't please them all!"

"The serrin half-castes of Tracato are some of the finest talents in all the civilised world," Sofy insisted. "They flee from slaughter, and I will help them in my own way. It is how I am, Jaryd. Surely you appreciate that?"

Jaryd gazed at her in despair. She still thought to return to the Regent, and piece things together again. He could see it in her eyes, in the ring she wore. Still the Idys Mark weighed on her forehead, taunting him, a plea to the god of fertility to bless her marriage with child. A plea for the worlds of Lenayin and the Bacosh to come together, and make peaceful union.

If it were not so sad, Jaryd would have laughed.

"Don't try to hold up the world, Sofy," he said. "You're not strong enough. No one is."

"I may surprise you. The serrin tell us that all the world is connected. We just need to pull the threads tighter."

"The serrin are about to die. All of them. Words will not save them now."

Sofy's eyes flicked to the fallen man on the floor. "I cannot be like you, Jaryd. There must be a place for the likes of me in this world you wish to see."

"You'll never be like me," said Jaryd. "One Jaryd Nyvar in the world is enough. One Sofy Lenayin is a wonderful thing too. I just wish that she would come out from beneath this burden that she hauls, and show herself to the world once more. The world would brighten, for her to be in it. But lately she serves only others, and never shows her face to any but them. I would like to see her eyes once more, for I recall that her smile was like the sun."

Sofy's eyes softened and her lip trembled. Jaryd swallowed hard. Then he bowed, and turned and strode from the temple, people parting before him. They whispered together, searching for anyone who spoke Lenay and could tell them what had been said.

General Zulmaher followed the gaolers through dark stone passages beneath the Justiciary. Lantern light moved and swung past the bars on the wall, and prisoners winced in the glare and shaded their eyes. At the general's side, young Alfriedo Renine took wary steps. Behind him, several armed and loyal men.

The gaoler stopped before one barred cage and inserted a key. The door rattled open and light fell upon a young woman within. She looked up from her seat in the corner, her lean face smeared with soot and recent bruises, beneath a tangle of hair.

"That's her," said Zulmaher. "That's Jelendria." He walked to her and crouched. "Jelendria. General Zulmaher, we met before."

"I remember," said Jeddie. She looked past him to Alfriedo and made an effort to rise. That brought a wince, and a limp. "A twisted ankle," she answered their concern. "Not serious. I can limp."

"M'lady, it would not be decorous for a noble lady to limp all the way back up the stairs," Alfriedo declared with concern. "The general is a strong man, I am certain he can carry you."

Zulmaher smiled faintly. The boy's mother had been a vain and vengeful fool, but she'd certainly taught him manners.

He carried Jeddie back up the corridor, not as easy a task as the boy made out—she was slim but tall, and her dress entangled his legs.

"I hear you were caught in the Mahl'rhen?" Alfriedo asked her as they walked. Jeddie nodded, drawn and pale. "Is it true that the Archbishop's men destroyed it?"

"I helped some Nasi-Keth and others to save some things, books and the like. A few old serrin were still there. Lesthen, the ambassador. The Archbishop's men killed him when they came." Her voice trembled. "They're beasts," she added in a frightened, hateful whisper. "They smashed all the statues and artworks. They killed old serrin on sight. Beasts, the lot of them."

"I don't understand," said Alfriedo with concern. "Did you not identify yourself to them as the daughter of Horseth?" Jeddie nodded. The party reached the steps, and began climbing. "Why did they then throw you in the dungeons?"

"We were caught trying to save another load of books. Wonderful things, with the most amazing illustrations. Old histories of the Bacosh and its peoples, written by the serrin some seven centuries ago. They attacked us even though I told them who I was. There were too many of them. Some of us got away, but I was too slow.

"The Lenay man, Jaryd Nyvar's friend Jandlys, he did not abandon me. He fought courageously." Again her voice trembled. "He killed so many of them I cannot remember their number. Ten at least. They wounded him many times, and still he fought. Were it not for him I would be dead, he killed so many of the first attackers that they retreated, and came back with a senior man who recognised my rank and detained rather than killed me. But by then, Jandlys was dead."

"It's curious," Alfriedo said. "I was told that all Bacosh men were civilised, and all around me nodded, yet I have seen that that is a lie. I was told that the Archbishops of Petrodor and Sherdaine were godly and moral people, and religious men about me nodded, yet I now see that was a *great* lie. And I was told that the men of Lenayin were brave and fearsome and honourable, and all about me laughed and scorned. Yet that seems most true of all."

They exited the dungeon stairs and came into the Justiciary hall. Beneath the high, grand roof, Elissian soldiers stood guard, as Elissians of higher rank stood upon the pavings and marvelled at the architecture. This place, they had not burned down. There was discussion as to what it should be converted into, now that its original purpose had been abandoned. Zulmaher didn't know what business any Elissians had to debate that—Alfriedo was Lord of Rhodaan, and such decisions were his alone.

A troop of Black Order were striding across the floor, men in black robes and pointed hoods that covered their faces. A priest led them, a tall man with a tall staff, walking fast. Zulmaher placed Jeddie on the ground and supported her as she balanced on her one good foot.

"General," said the priest, stopping before them. "Who gave you leave to release this prisoner?"

"The decision to detain or not to detain persons lies with my lord of Rhodaan, Alfriedo Renine, surely," Zulmaher replied. "Do you say that it does not?"

"This person is in league with the serrin!" the priest spat. "She was a member of the Queen Sofy's court!"

"And have you arrested Queen Sofy also?" Zulmaher asked. "Has the Regent given his order that you should do such a thing?"

"We have reports that she is dead."

"Best not by your hand, sir. To murder the Regent's wife would seem a somewhat significant thing."

The priest glared. "She was a pagan and she cast her lot with pagans!"

"I have met with the young lady in question," Alfriedo interjected, "and I am most assured that she is a Verenthane. Indeed, her knowledge of scripture was rather better than mine, and my education has been extensive. If you have killed her, Father, then I shall see that she receives a proper Verenthane burial. And as Lord of Rhodaan, I shall see that those responsible give a full explanation to her bereaved husband, the Regent of the United Bacosh."

The priest paled and seethed. "I also have reports that there are many wanted individuals now taking refuge within regions of Tracato under your control, Lord Alfriedo," he said tightly. "I would ask, on the behalf of the Archbishop, that you hand over all such persons to us immediately."

"As Lord of Rhodaan," Alfriedo said mildly, "I was not aware that there *were* any regions of Tracato outside of my control."

"The regions of Reninesenn and its surrounds," said the priest, through gritted teeth. "Those regions most historically associated with your family's esteemed prescence in this city, my lord."

"Father, I can assure you that there is no one within Reninesenn and its surrounds today who does not belong there." He said it with such utter, wide-eyed innocence that Zulmaher nearly laughed.

"If my lord says it, then I'm sure that it must be so," said the priest, with more than a hint of threat. "But my lord should bear in mind that there are no higher authorities in the new Bacosh than the ancient gods. My Archbishop represents those gods, and they have decreed that all things pagan must be cleansed from these lands, for the good of all souls. No lord can dispute the word of the gods. Not even a Regent."

He turned and strode away, taking his pointy-headed army with him.

"Well said, my lord," said Zulmaher, watching them go.

"I am getting tired of being told what to do in my own land," Alfriedo said crossly. "But it is hard to argue with a priest about the word of the gods, to say nothing of an Archbishop."

"Ordinary men cannot do so," Zulmaher agreed. "But another priest?"

They took horses to arrive at Reninesenn in good time. There were a great number of armed men in the streets, many with armour and weapons that were centuries old, family heirlooms not needed for warfare since the creation of the Steel, kept in storage as reminders of old family honour. Men saluted Lord Alfriedo and General Zulmaher as they passed. Zulmaher wondered just how useful they would be in a fight. Some of them had experience in the Steel, but not many.

Jeddie departed with a guard to head for the Ushal Fortress, and noble quarters. The others dismounted before the temple. Already there was a small crowd atop the steps, some now taking a knee as Alfriedo climbed the stairs, a gesture that may have had them in trouble with the city's red-coats just weeks earlier. But no one had seen a red-coat in recent times.

A few people raised cheers for Alfriedo Renine, the new Lord of Rhodaan. Many in Rhodaan had been waiting two centuries for this, the restoration of rightful powers to the nobility, and Family Renine as the undisputed rightful heirs to that gods-given power. Yet Alfriedo only looked angry.

"Please," he said loudly at the temple doors, "I will hear no cheering. We are Tracatans and our city is occupied, ravaged and humiliated. I see nothing to cheer about."

The temple was only small, but quite lovely with its high arches and wall columns. Family Renine had long held all its important functions here, away from the Council-controlled establishments of the high city, and their lick-spittle priests. Now, some of those lickspittle priests were assembled here before the altar: thirty-two in total, the heads of each major temple within Tracato. All looked anxious.

"Thank you for coming," said Zulmaher. "Firstly, the Lord Alfriedo would hear of your concerns. The past days have been trying on us all. If he is to assume lordship of all Rhodaan, he shall start with Tracato, and if he assumes lordship of Tracato, he shall start with its temples."

The priests talked, tentatively at first, then with increasing forthright-ness. They were not happy. Their parishioners were sometimes scattered, and in a few cases slain. Many tried to organise assistance, and to provide shelter to those who required it. The Black Order did not treat the local priests with respect. High town temples, frequented by Council supporters and Nasi-Keth, were shunned entirely. The only priests invited to an audience with the Archbishop were the more traditional men from Reninesenn, and others favored by supporters of Alfriedo Renine. But those were also displeased.

"He does not listen," said one old man. "He lectures. He told us that our sins are deep and that such sins can only be cleansed by blood. I presume he means ours."

"My friends," Zulmaher said, "we are all alike dismayed, I am sure. Our Lord Alfriedo may have won back his rightful seat in the command of Rhodaan, yet that shall count for nothing if we cannot win back authority over our own land, and our own city. I am but a man, as is my Lord Alfriedo, and we cannot challenge the Archbishop's authority. But you are priests. You carry the authority of the gods. The first step in reclaiming Rhodaan from these invaders shall therefore lie with you."

Alfriedo was frowning up at him, wondering what he was thinking. The priests looked no different.

"We cannot stand up to the Archbishop," one exclaimed. "He is an archbishop, we are just common priests!"

"It is the convention within the Bacosh, is it not, that each province shall have an archbishop of its own?" Zulmaher asked. "It was the serrin who ended the practice two hundred years ago. They thought to break the power of the Rhodaani priesthood by depriving them—all of you—of a leader."

And to look upon you all today, he thought sourly, it worked.

"You will appoint an Archbishop of Rhodaan?" All the robed men stared at each other. Some fearful, some frowning, and others with dawning calculation.

"A lord cannot appoint an archbishop," said another. "Not even the Lord of Rhodaan."

"Then you shall choose," Zulmaher told them. "Surely you have not forgotten the procedures?"

The robed men regarded each other in silence. An old man cleared his throat. "I have studied the process well," he said. "In old books." And added with irony, "In a library the serrin built."

"Very well," said Zulmaher. "We shall leave you to it. This temple is yours until you have selected your archbishop. Please begin."

He retreated and took Alfriedo with him. The priests did not look convinced, and many would have pressed with further questions, but Zulmaher did not wish it to sound like a request. Priests had obeyed lords in Rhodaan for the last two centuries, as they sometimes did not in the west. He should be wary, however, of what would be created by this act.

"An Archbishop of Rhodaan will still not have the authority to challenge the Archbishop of Sherdaine!" Alfriedo exclaimed in a frustrated whisper as they walked to the temple's entrance.

"An Archbishop of Rhodaan," said Zulmaher, "with his boots upon home soil, will have as much power as his people grant him. All Rhodaanis have lost their old leaders, their Council, their Justices. They are looking for someone to stand up on their behalf, yet are afraid to challenge an archbishop for fear of their souls. This appointment will take that fear from them."

"I am not comfortable with this," Alfriedo declared. "Kessligh Cronenverdt warned me of precisely this. He said that the rule of nations cannot be left to men, it must be left to laws. Yet here we appoint men, and pathetic men like our soft and pampered priests, to make decisions on behalf of all."

"Decisions that we shall control," Zulmaher assured him.

"So you say," Alfriedo said sharply. "Can you promise it, in truth?" Zulmaher thought about what to say. "My mother promised that she could control events also. Look where that brought her."

"This time it shall be different."

"I don't believe you," Alfriedo said darkly. He turned for the door. "I don't believe anyone anymore."

The party sat in the common hall of the guardhouse on the Ilduuri side of the Shalaam Canyon. Sasha sat in borrowed clothes and ate well. Outside the stone walls, rain continued to fall and thunder rumbled a distant displeasure. Daish was in bed, resting, and needed to remain so for several more days at least. Perhaps he might follow them to Andal later.

"He would have killed you all," Rulsten explained. He was the soldier who had let them in the gate, and sent the Ilduuri Nasi-Keth to his death. His helm now removed, he looked an older man, with wavy grey hair. "Last week, we had word that two Enoran messengers who passed through this way never made it to Andal."

"You're saying someone ordered them killed?" Rhillian asked, frowning over her meal. Her white hair, newly short, was neat and brushed after her wash.

"Not someone," said Captain Aster. "The Remischtuul. It's policy."

All three lands of the Saalshen Bacosh had replaced the rule of kings and lords with something else. In Rhodaan and Enora, it had been Councils of supposedly ordinary folk. In Ilduur, it was a single grand Council, known in the local tongue as the Remischtuul, meaning "large house." One institution within which all the important factions of Ilduur would be represented— from artisans to farmers, builders to priests—every guild, every class of society, had a seat within the Remischtuul. Or so it went in theory.

"Policy to kill every foreigner?" Sasha asked.

"Every foreigner bearing bad news," said the captain. "They do not want to become involved in this war. There are many in Ilduur who disagree, but lately it has become dangerous to disagree. Those who speak out in favour of supporting our Rhodaani and Enoran brothers are called warmongers and agents of foreign powers. Some have been charged with treason, and jailed awaiting execution. Others have disappeared. The Stamentaast are everywhere."

"Stamentaast?"

"They serve the Remischtuul. They move through our cities and promote social order." There was bitter laughter from the soldiers. "They watch for unpatriotic attitudes, and recruit agents of their own. Some they recruit with fear, others with genuine belief. Lately it has become intolerable, they report on everyone, and you can smell the fear when you talk to people about them."

"I don't understand," said Arendelle. Of the four serrin present, he was the least accustomed to human ways. "Why must the Remischtuul have foreigners killed?"

The captain sighed. "We Ilduuri have never been agreeable neighbours. We have our mountains, they have been our defence. Before the serrin came, we feared them, and called them devils as others of the Bacosh do. We defended our mountain kingdom with fervour, and rarely did a non-Ilduuri even visit Andal.

"But then came King Leyvaan. In his great rise to power he cajoled and threatened, and gathered a force so large even the Ilduuri agreed we should join with it, if only because he promised to rid us of the terrible serrin. But that force, of course, met with disaster in Saalshen, and left us undefended from the serrin's retribution.

"When the serrin did come, they did not murder us and eat our souls, but remade our society. We flourished, as they did. But perhaps the serrin trusted us too well and thought us reborn in those two hundred years. We never did lose our distrust of foreigners, always it hid beneath the surface. We built grand new institutions like the Remischtuul, and the Nasi-Keth grew strong, and serrin teachings spread in Ilduur. But always it was selective teachings, the men of power learned the words that suited them best and ignored others. From what I know of serrin lore, I do not think serrin intended it to be that way."

"Nasi-Keth," Sasha said in disbelief. "I've seen Nasi-Keth in Rhodaan doing stupid things, but even after that I find it hard to believe anyone in any Nasi-Keth group could argue for letting Saalshen's enemies win. I mean, if the serrin fall, the Nasi-Keth are finished."

"They don't see it that way," said Rulsten. "They're pacifists, or so they say. Serrin teachings are of peace—"

"They are not," Kiel interrupted. "Only a fool would interpret the *uthal'es* so simply."

"Well, you said it," Rulsten said wryly. "It's like the captain said, they learn what they want from the serrin and discard the rest. They think the Ilduuri should be pure, shouldn't mix with foreigners. That means not getting involved in foreign wars, so pacifism suits them."

"Yes, while murdering their enemies with violence," said another soldier, sourly.

"Nasi-Keth elsewhere are interested in creating bonds between serrin and human," said Captain Aster. "Here, they're interested only in using serrin knowledge to benefit Ilduur. Nothing else. Some may claim otherwise, but that's the gist of it whatever they say."

"But the Ilduuri Steel think differently?" Rhillian pressed.

"Not all," Aster admitted, "but most. It goes back to the Tournean War. Only fifteen years after Ilduur came under serrin control, Tournea decided to attack. They reasoned that if they captured Ilduur at its weakest moment, they would gain a fortress from which to attack Saalshen and Enora. The Ilduuri Steel were new and untested. Rhodaan and Enora came in force to our defence, and together we won a great victory that we would surely have lost had we faced the threat alone.

"Other Ilduuris forget, but the Steel never did. We've shared officers ever since; we send cadets to learn at each others' officer schools; we make good friends in foreign lands and assist those friends in their wars. We would have liked to do more, but the Remischtuul protests, and says we must remain to defend the homeland. Over time, the city folk who hold most power in the Remischtuul stopped sending their sons to join the Steel. The Steel are mostly country folk now, who have less of a voice in the Remischtuul. Most of us here are from the lands of Saadi Maal in the east, none of us have friends or relatives in Andal. It seems almost a foreign land to us, for all we suffer to defend it."

"We must get to Andal quickly," said Rhillian. "We need to convince the Remischtuul to send help to Jahnd, our forces retreat there."

"Jahnd?" asked one of the soldiers.

"Haven," another told him, in Saalsi.

"You cannot just confront the Remischtuul," said Captain Aster. "They'll have you locked up and executed."

"Then I must meet with other captains of the Ilduuri Steel," said Rhillian. "Either way, they must march to Jahnd. If they do not, Ilduuri freedom as you know it is finished, perhaps not today or tomorrow, but soon."

"Little enough Ilduuri freedom today," someone muttered.

"The Steel are sworn to obey the Remischtuul," said the captain, frowning. "We were founded on that promise—that the strong men of war would never turn their swords on their own people. To betray that is to betray everything good that the serrin helped to make Ilduur."

"We don't ask you to turn your swords on the people," Sasha told him. "From what you say, the Remischtuul have become a tyranny. What use is the freedom that the Steel have sworn to fight for if you will not fight for it here in Ilduur?"

Captain Aster gnawed at a thumbnail and stared at the wall.

"It may be a tyranny," said Rulsten, "but it's a willing tyranny. If you could ask them, I'll warrant a fair majority of Ilduuri don't want this war either. The Steel are a minority. A very large minority, perhaps, but a minority nonetheless."

Kiel sighed in disbelief. "Your people are idiots. Ilduuri may not see themselves as a serrin civilisation, but the Regent does and so do his priests. They'll demand the Remischtuul disbanded, the Steel destroyed, to say nothing of the Nasi-Keth. They are so strong that even your mountains cannot protect you. Your civilisation is the antithesis of the world that the Regent wishes to build, do you understand that?"

"It is not me who needs to understand," Aster said sombrely. "But you speak of turning the Steel against the Remischtuul. We cannot fight our own people, however misguided they may be."

"Then Jahnd is finished," said Rhillian. "And with it, the combined armies of the Rhodaani and Enoran Steel, the Army of Lenayin, and much of the *tal-maad*. Saalshen will be next, for the Regent will not repeat Leyvaan's mistake of frantic haste. Saalshen is easy prey for a large, dedicated, and patient army, even more so now that the Regent has captured some of the Steel's weaponry, and will no doubt take the time to learn how best to employ it."

"As ever with Saalshen," Kiel murmured, "we cut our own throats."

Rhillian shrugged. "And at some stage in these events," she continued, "the Regent shall turn his attention to Ilduur. The Ilduuri Steel must decide whether it is more important to uphold a pleasant-sounding ideal, or to ensure the survival of their civilisation and their people."

"You ask the Steel to fight a tyranny by becoming one," Aster said flatly.

"Yes," said Rhillian. "Only this tyranny shall not need to murder small children by the thousand to achieve its ends. The same cannot be said of the other."

Sasha had barely bedded down in the stables when Arendelle appeared at the fodder pen. At first she thought he'd come to talk to Rhillian, but instead he clambered over the bales and lay down beside her. Sasha turned to look at him, questioningly. Arendelle put a hand on her waist. She wore only her light shirt and pants, her jacket bundled for a pillow, feet bare as she dared to hope she would not need to get up and run in a hurry.

Arendelle wore as little. His hand ran down to her hip as his golden eyes watched her with intent curiosity. There was no hostility to him, and Sasha felt unthreatened. But they had barely spoken on the ride so far, and always Sasha had sensed the tension.

"Why?" she asked him.

Arendelle shrugged. "Interest," he said. It meant more than that in Saalsi, suggested resolutions to unresolved problems.

"Is this a thing with serrin? To use sex to solve unresolved issues?"

"I seek to solve nothing. Only to learn." He leaned forward to kiss her. Sasha stopped him. It only took a gentle touch to his chest.

"You've bedded human women before, surely?"

"That is not the issue," he said obliquely. He slid a hand up to the small of her back. She could have stopped that too, but somehow, that seemed wrong. As though admitting that it could make her succumb if it continued. She held her gaze steady and firm, to show Arendelle it wasn't working.

"You dislike me," she said flatly. "Yet I'm friends with your friends. Serrin have difficulty holding such contradictions in their heads. You poke at it, as you might poke at a scab."

"Your looks are nothing like a scab," he said generously. "What matter my motivation? I can see you are aroused, and with serrin there are no human consequences."

"I'm aroused because I'm a hot-blooded Lenay warrior gone more than a week without my man," Sasha retorted. She didn't like Arendelle's answer. He was telling her to shut up and enjoy it, far below the eloquence of most serrin in this circumstance. "Speaking of whom, I'll not betray Errollyn so easily."

"Serrin barely understand the concept, in sex."

"Yes, but *I* do."

"I don't dislike you," said Arendelle. He said the word with a vaguely serrin distaste. "It is too human a concept. It is because of these confusions that I seek to understand the nature of this thing between us. Between dislike and comradeship. Between hatred and love."

Sasha blinked. She couldn't quite believe he'd used that last word. Only the serrin had so many words to describe that, and one could not be confident, in tongues other than Saalsi, exactly which they meant. A man loved wine. A man loved his child. A man loved a woman. Each was a very different thing.

Sasha sighed. "Look," she said, "in another circumstance I'd join you in exploring this conundrum. I would like to be your friend, Arendelle. Can we agree that it need not take fucking to do it?"

Arendelle considered. "Fucking is more fun."

Sasha stifled a giggle. "Well, yes. But in this circumstance, impractical."

"Arendelle," Rhillian called from the other side of a hay bale. "When you've finished pestering Sasha, why don't you come over here?"

Arendelle smiled, got up, and went to Rhillian.

He really didn't like her, Sasha thought a while later, with little choice but to listen to the activity beyond the hay bale. She and Errollyn had rarely missed a day when they were together. In their first weeks, they'd sometimes rarely missed a moment alone. Listening to Rhillian's gasps of pleasure was a new kind of torture. And she laughed at herself, a better alternative than cursing.

Arendelle finished, and left. Rhillian crept over, newly reclothed, and lay at Sasha's back and embraced her.

"I thought you'd finished," Sasha said jokingly, with no little envy.

"I like to cuddle afterwards," Rhillian said. "He's gone, you're all that's available." Sasha laughed. "Errollyn wouldn't mind, you know. I'm sure of it."

"I would."

"Humans," Rhillian sighed, and stroked Sasha's hair.

"Our families are more important," Sasha explained. "Serrin families are more open. You raise children collectively. You do everything collectively. Humans aren't made for that. Our families must be strong, so we pair-bond, and should not stray."

"Yet so often do."

"And are punished for it."

"Your explanations are so dry, Sasha. Humans think they're so romantic on sexual matters, but in truth you're all so blunt about it. In human stories, great sexual encounters are usually the precursor to some terrible tragedy."

"Yes, but it's the tragedy we find romantic."

Rhillian snorted. "Don't say those horrible human things, you'll spoil my afterglow."

The following morning, the air was cool and moist. The trail to Andal rose to a high ridge overlooking the deep cleft cut by the Ipshaal River. Guarding that ridge was a great wall, with towers and a fort, intended as a secondary defence to be occupied by Steel falling back from the perimeter. The party rode with an escort of Steel, and wore borrowed red and black uniform beneath their riding cloaks. Steel frequently gave escort to important travellers, and few passing Ilduuris spared them more than a glance.

Soon they were climbing once more, but slowly this time. Rhillian followed Sasha's advice and stopped often, allowing the animals to graze or drink. Once, upon the crest of a ridge, they gained a perfect view of the mountains directly ahead, high peaks gleaming white in the snow of last night's storm. That was their path, and Sasha thought it much more pleasant without the pursuit of a horde of murderous Kazeri.

But the slow going cost them time, and they stopped for the evening in a little ridge-top village some distance short of where they had hoped to be. Their guides insisted the inn was safe, but the serrin took their meals in their rooms regardless, and did not wander out. Descending the stairs with empty plates, Sasha saw Rulsten and the innkeeper in a corner, talking in hushed tones. Word was there had been Stamentaast through this way just two days before, asking questions.

That night, Sasha shared a room with Yasmyn. Before sleeping, they sat for a while on the balcony and looked up at the silver outlines of mountains bathed in moonlight.

"If we are to die here," said Yasmyn after a long while, "then it shall be a good place to die."

Sasha smiled.

The next day was long. They passed through several more towns, a few of them showing signs of surprising wealth for such isolated settlements. In all Ilduur's history, Rulsten explained as they rode, this had been the most hostile border, and wars against one Enoran lord or another had been relatively common. The Enoran lords were now all dead, and their line decisively ended by angry Enoran peasants, but not all Ilduuri had made their peace with the *naach ul tremich stoov*, or "tyrants of the north," as Enorans had once been known here.

The question of night lodging provoked some debate. Rulsten knew of a village, but Rhillian did not like to risk the Stamentaast's spies. They settled for camping by the trail, in a shallow valley with a small, cold stream. However nice a genuine bed might be, Sasha was glad for the chance to practise taka-dans away from the prying eyes of townsfolk, and to wash away from common stalls.

This night, Arendelle propositioned Yasmyn rather than Sasha. Yasmyn accepted. Afterward, Sasha made a bed at Yasmyn's side, rugged up against the welcome night chill.

"Good?" she asked Yasmyn.

"Interesting," Yasmyn replied. She looked thoughtful. "My first since the rape." Sasha nodded. She'd thought as much. "I wanted to know that I still can."

"And?"

"Yes," she said, with neither excitement or relief. "That is no surprise. I am Isfayen."

"I heard a tale once from women in Baerlyn," said Sasha, "of another woman who had been raped, and had never been able to enjoy lying with a man again."

"It was bad," Yasmyn admitted. "But I've seen men die by the sword. I've dealt men wounds that had them screaming as they tried to stuff their guts back into their bodies. I've severed heads, and seen the severed heads of friends. This injury was not the worst I expected to take. Besides which, his head was one of those I severed."

"I feel sorry for that woman in the tales I heard," said Sasha. "If I could not take revenge with my blade, I would probably never be able to lie with a man again either."

"The fate of women is terrible," Yasmyn agreed. "I think that Rhillian is right, that all human action comes from the need for power. But she thinks it a bad thing. Like you, I think it is the only reason I am sane. Had I not had my revenge, I would be shrivelled and dead inside."

"We are different people, human and serrin," Sasha murmured. "The rare ones like Rhillian and Kiel seek power, but do not need it, as humans need it. I'm quite certain Rhillian could find many purposes in life if she could no longer fight, and be happy with that. Probably I could too, but I'd be miserable."

Yasmyn frowned. "But serrin do not have the expectation of fighting that humans do. It is a rare thing for them—they do not fight each other, only us. So there is no need for power, when none amongst them seeks it over others."

"It should sound wonderful, shouldn't it," said Sasha. "To live in a world free from violence and pain should be the ideal of all. But I am a Lenay warrior and I honestly think I'd die of boredom."

Yasmyn grinned. Sasha gave a snort of reluctant laughter and gazed up at the stars.

"The gods and spirits make us who we need to be," Yasmyn said with certainty. "We are both born to war, so we need to be warriors. Serrin are born to peace, so they need to be peaceful. Neither should feel ashamed of what we are, any more than a wolf should feel shame at killing deer. Wolves are wild, like Lenays."

"And is that why humans resist serrin attempts to civilise them?" Sasha wondered. "Because we are all wild animals, and cannot accept serrin domestication?"

"Perhaps," said Yasmyn. "But wild animals live as the spirits intended. I think it is the serrin who are the odd ones. Perhaps they need to change to be more like us."

"And what if they can't?"

"Then they will die," Yasmyn said sombrely. "They cannot fight war with peace, any more than they can hunt bear with sticks."

They lay in silence for a moment. Sasha glanced around her and found Rhillian lying close by, propped on an elbow, watching them. She'd heard every word, and her eyes in the night were bright and hard. Sasha smiled sadly, and rolled to reach for Rhillian's hand. Rhillian grasped it and looked at those fingers, as though considering something of great import. Then she sighed and lay down to sleep.

The next morning, returning from her toilet stop, Sasha sensed movement and spun to find a large, black-striped mountain cat not ten paces from her. It was impossibly beautiful, with big golden eyes and wide whiskers, big paws, and a long tail for balance on the steeper slopes. It stared, even more surprised than she, but not especially alarmed. Sasha stared back, wanting to call others to come and look, but unable to do so lest she scare her visitor away.

Eventually the cat left and Sasha returned to camp and told the others what she'd seen.

Rulsten was astonished. "Black stripes, you say? They're very rare, they steer well clear of people usually. It wasn't frightened?"

"Not frightened at all. I think she knew I wouldn't hurt her."

"The wild and dangerous spirit attracts the wild and dangerous animals," Yasmyn said knowingly, "and each knows the other for a friend."

Rhillian and Kiel looked at each other, expressions unreadable, and said nothing.

By afternoon they found themselves beneath an enormous, towering spire of a mountain.

"Aaldenmoot," Rulsten named it. "Dragon's Tooth. Thirty people have been known to try to climb it over the centuries. None have succeeded. Half of them died."

"Why climb it at all?" Kiel wondered. "There's nothing there save a higher view."

"Ilduuri climb," said Rulsten with a shrug. "For lookouts, for signals, for manoeuvres by our soldiers to outflank our enemies. Climbing is an art, and any art must be practised."

Kiel looked unconvinced.

From the valley's end, the trail rose sharply. Soon the party had dismounted to lead the horses, as some stretches of trail became almost as steep as stairs, and the horses progressed reluctantly indeed.

Ahead, the high passes were covered with golden snow. A descent in the evening across a high, barren snowfield brought them to a mountain lake, wide, glassy-still, and impossibly blue. By its bank stood a cabin with a stable, large enough for a party twice their size.

It was empty, placed here for travellers crossing the pass, Rulsten explained. They made themselves at home, and found it warm enough once the fire was crackling with logs from the large supply of firewood that must have been brought up by cart.

No sooner had they eaten, than they heard hooves crunching the snow outside, then a knock at the door. All inside looked at each other and drew weapons. Rulsten gestured them to calm, went to the door, and opened it.

There in the fading twilight stood a man with a flaming torch, cloaked against the oncoming chill of evening. He exchanged Ilduuri greetings with Rulsten, extinguished his torch, and stomped his boots free from snow on the step before entering.

Once inside, he threw off his cloak to reveal the black robes and golden Verenthane medallion of a priest.

"Thank the gods I spotted you fools before you plunged head first into Andal," he told them in Torovan, with a thick Ilduuri accent. "A party of serrin and foreigners, traipsing through the land in hope that no one will identify you? Are you mad?"

Rhillian sheathed her blade. "Who are you?"

"I, dear lady, am Father Belgride. I have been following you for two days since a concerned parishioner passed word to me of your presence in my mountains. I can guide you safely into Andal, and give you secure lodging there. Otherwise the Remischtuul will kill you all, as plain as the nose on my face."

Fourteen

Errollyn held his impatience at bay for as long as he could stand. Then, approaching the crest of a hill, he gave in and galloped. Kessligh followed, soon drawing level on the road with an eager smile that Errollyn had never seen him wear before. Damon pursued, and General Rochan, and then the whole command vanguard, galloping away from the main formation like children testing new ponies in a race.

They descended the last hill through forest, catching the odd glimpse of wide waters ahead. That was the Ipshaal, the easternmost border of Enoran lands. Upon the far side was Saalshen. It had been many years since Errollyn had seen Saalshen, yet that was not why he galloped. Scouts ahead had brought word, several days earlier, of something remarkable upon the Ipshaal. Even Kessligh, when he'd been told, had been disbelieving. Now they were close, and all wanted desperately to see for themselves.

They rode through a town to the river edge. There were piers, to which small boats were tied, village folk hauling in nets and tending sails. Beyond lay the vast Ipshaal, perhaps five hundred strides across, deep waters glistening beneath an overcast sky. Upon those waters lay something impossible.

It was a bridge. A new bridge, to be sure, for there had never been a bridge across the Ipshaal in all Errollyn's knowledge of history. So new, in fact, that it was not yet finished. Even as he watched, it grew.

Made of wood, it ended now barely fifty strides from the Enoran bank ahead. Upon that uncompleted end, great machines of timber, gears, pulleys and winches were in motion, swarming with men. They wound great wheels, which lifted large weights above the end of pylons. At a maximum height, those stone weights would release and fall with an almighty thump onto the end of the pylon, driving it deeper into the riverbed. Upon the completed bridge behind them, horses drew carts bearing new pylons, cross-beams, and decking. In all, Errollyn thought he could count at least five hundred men on the bridge, plus seven carts and fourteen horses.

For weeks they had all wondered and worried about the Ipshaal crossing. Now they wondered and worried no more. He looked at Kessligh, and both men laughed. Errollyn had never seen him so enthralled. This man who showed so little emotion in the victory of the forces he commanded now gazed at the growing bridge with the excitement of a small boy who had just seen his first catapult.

General Rochan looked utterly astonished. "That is the most amazing thing I have ever seen."

"Twelve days," said Kessligh with amazement. "Twelve days so far, and they've nearly finished."

A little ahead, Errollyn noticed several boats at the riverbank, and men standing and discussing. He rode to them, and greetings were exchanged. The men were from Jahnd, and very pleased to see them.

"We're going to pave this part of the riverbank," one explained. "Between here and the village, so your carts and catapults can move freely to the bridge. If we start now, we'll be done in three days, when the bridge is finished."

"We'll be lucky if the Regent is more than five days behind us," Kessligh warned them.

"Plenty of time," said the Jahndi with a grin. "We would have started earlier but we did not know where you were, or if there was even an army left to cross the Ipshaal. We're glad to see we didn't waste all the effort."

In the midafternoon, a serrin rider came, and halted at the head of the column to speak to Jaryd. Sofy hastened her mount up the road past creaking wagons to hear their conversation.

"Elissians," Jaryd told her grimly as she arrived. "More than a hundred. They take the more northerly route—they mean to intercept us ahead."

"How many fighters have you?" the serrin asked.

"Twenty-six," said Jaryd. "Perhaps another twenty archers we've placed on the rear wagons where they're most use, but they're not accurate like the *talmaad*. How many are you?"

"Twelve," said the serrin. Jaryd grimaced. "Can you make better time? We can have boats on the river shore when you arrive, but at your current pace the Elissians will get there first."

"We have too many on foot," said Jaryd. "If we abandon them we may save the half that are mounted."

"We shan't!" Sofy said loudly. "Jaryd, I forbid it."

"And thus condemn everyone to death," Jaryd said with temper. "This isn't some contest to see who can think the prettier thoughts, Sofy, this is us trying to make sure that at least some of us survive."

Sofy stared at him stubbornly, her jaw set.

"We can distract them," said the serrin. "Perhaps an ambush, we may lure them away, purchase some time."

"If they're coming after us," said Jaryd, "it's because they know of this column and have been directed to kill it—they won't be easily distracted."

"We'll see," said the serrin. "Make as much pace as you can, keep on this road until you reach the village, the villagers can tell you where the river landing is from there."

He galloped off. Sofy gazed up to where giant white clouds were looming like mountains in the sky.

"A change comes," she said.

"Thunder," said Asym. "The spirits are watching. They come to collect the dead."

It was raining by the time the first in the column reached the river. They poured down rough tracks through the forest, abandoning wagons as serrin helped them into longboats. More boats were coming, serrin and some humans rowing hard from upriver, where Sofy gathered a fishing village lay.

"You should be on the first ones," Jaryd told her, shield now on his arm in expectation of the Elissians' arrival.

"I will not," said Sofy. "We have an entire column behind us and Elissians somewhere near. This could easily become a stampede. Someone of authority needs to stand upon this bank and appeal to order."

Jaryd gritted his teeth, looking at the passing wagons. People on the wagons were indeed looking at Sofy with some measure of reassurance to calm their fear. Some folks were trying to unload their belongings into the boats, and the serrin were protesting. Sofy rode over to them.

"You cannot take belongings!" she shouted over their argument. "You must abandon them, we need all space on the boats for people!"

Not everyone understood her Torovan, but enough did. People began to do what she said. But other such arguments were breaking out further up the bank, and she rode off to address them. A glance back to Jaryd did not find him. He was tasked with defending the column, he could not be distracted by boats. But Sofy knew that any delays here on the bank would make Jaryd's task impossible, trying to defend an otherwise defenceless column against Elissian cavalry. Thinking of it, she had a stab of guilt at what she had asked him to do.

Grumbles of thunder grew to great booms, and flashes lit the darkening sky. The rain grew heavier, and gusts of wind whipped the surface of the Ipshaal River as the first wave of boats rowed hard toward the far bank, laden with people. The Ipshaal was at least three hundred paces wide at this point; even with every available oarsman straining, it was not a fast trip.

As the crowds built up on the bank, they faced the problem of congestion, hundreds of frightened people queuing for the next boat in the soaking rain, and all those feet, horses, and wagons turning the dampening earth to mud. Sofy rode up and down, ordering wagons aside to make way for new ones, and finding volunteers to ride abandoned wagons back up the road, to collect stragglers and bring them here faster.

Other boats were arriving, smaller fishing craft, piloted by local Rhodaanis. They took as many passengers as they could, more than was safe, and the little boats struggled in the wind and heavy rain out into the river, waters lapping perilously close to their hull rims. Still the crowds grew as more people arrived, trudging in ankle-deep mud through the trees.

A new arrival told her of wagons stuck in the mud where the road entered the forest. Sofy put heels to her horse and rode that way to find the source of the problem—wagons queued twenty deep, with more coming from the further fields. The lead three were completely stuck, whole teams of men pushing at wheels and horses and getting nowhere.

Beyond the thunder, Sofy heard something else. It seemed to be coming from the north, fading now as the wind gusted from a different direction. And then again she heard it. Hooves and yelling. Fighting.

"Leave the wagons!" Sofy yelled at them. "Leave them and run! Run to the river, the Elissians are coming!"

People ran, grabbing children, carrying the elderly, stumbling and falling in terror. From further up the road, others were still moving at a sedate pace, perhaps unhearing of the battle. They had to be warned.

Sofy galloped up the road, yelling at all there to run. They ran, some pitifully tired from the hot days of marching. A woman tried to hold up her child for Sofy, begging in Rhodaani for her to take him ahead to the river. Sofy galloped on, cursing this situation, the storm and the Elissians both. Jaryd had told her that she could not save all these people, and she had refused to listen. But now she saw his awful logic.

She turned about and galloped back. Trees cleared to her left, and across fields she saw horses galloping. Astride them were cavalry, no knights but men in mail and leathers, with coloured surcoats. Elissians, at least twenty of them. And more beyond the field, coming up the adjoining road.

Sofy's heart hammered in fear. She spurred her horse to greater speed, and then stopped on an impulse as she passed the woman with her child. She reached for the boy, pushed by his frantic mother over the saddle horn, then set off again with the screaming child in her arms. Rain blinded her, made the reins slippery in her hands, and the boy struggled; she was not an experienced rider, and riding like this was desperately dangerous. But an encounter with the Elissians would be far more deadly.

Elissians fell from their saddles. Sofy risked a quick look as she approached the abandoned wagons and saw serrin riders pursuing on the Elissians' tails. Horses wheeled to meet them, while others raced on, plunging through the trees ahead, heading for the river.

She tore between the first trees, slowing so she wouldn't hit any . . . and didn't see the running family until it was nearly too late. She hauled on the reins, the horse protested, and the next thing she knew they were falling, and she hugged the child to her chest as the ground rushed up and hit her. Then she was stunned, smelling wet leaves and mud, hands hauling her to her feet before rushing onward.

Her horse was nowhere to be seen, and she was still holding the child, who was screaming, and heavy. Sofy saw a woman sent flying in a collision, a man cut down by a sword. She ran, slipping on leaves and mud, and heard more hooves coming, but with the child she had no hope of defending herself. A horse rushed up, and she expected to die, but it passed and killed a running man beyond, who tried to throw up his hands in defence.

Elissians wheeled through the trees, striking about them. One fell to an arrow, and then there were serrin riders, firing repeatedly. Elissians chased them, and the serrin evaded. Sofy ran, legs and lungs burning, and now her arms and shoulders too, with the child's weight. Battle crashed around her, and arrows flew through the rain. Her boots sank into mud, sucking at her feet. She passed an Elissian cavalryman on the ground, groaning and trying to crawl with an arrow through his side. Nothing mattered but the river, and putting one foot before the other, as fast as possible. She did not remember it being so far away.

Then she could see the bank, a scene of chaos compared to when she'd last seen it. Bodies sprawled in the mud, terrified people scattering, tumbling down the bank as horses galloped past. Fighting milled nearby, defending cavalry exchanging blows with Elissians, but she was too blind with fear and rain to see who was winning.

She hid behind trees as more Elissians galloped by, saw a running family slashed down with swords, children and all, severed limbs falling. Then she ran, clutching the child tightly, across that open ground before the bank, arrows zipping overhead from somewhere, then a booming crash of thunder. Mud at the lip of the bank was calf-deep and bloody amidst the bodies, some of which still moved and shrieked.

Then the drop-off to the water, down which Sofy was about to throw herself with careless desperation . . . but there she saw mounted Elissians below at the water's edge, chasing unarmed Tracatans into shallow waters now red and floating with bodies. Several more Elissians had dismounted, and were pursuing others into the water, killing without mercy as those mounted riders indicated others who might get away.

They did not know which was the Princess Regent, Sofy realised. Even now, she could see them singling out the women for death. They did not know which was her, and so they killed every woman they could, and everyone else in between.

More arrows zipped in, coming from the river. Serrin boats were approaching, unable to find a place to land, archers firing from middle range at the Elissians on the shore. Swimmers were thrashing into deep water, trying to reach the boats, dragged aboard by the crews.

Sofy heard more hooves, and looked. Three Elissians were galloping at her. A young woman holding a child, she was the only immediate target, but their attention switched as two new horsemen arrived. One was Asym, not bothering to cut, but simply using his shield to bash an opponent from his saddle. The man hit the bank and tumbled down to the water.

The other rider was Jaryd, who chased the remaining two as they rode straight past Sofy, slashing one who was too slow. That man hit the mud ten paces from her, head-first and neck snapping.

"Sofy!" Jaryd yelled at her, and pointed upriver as he wheeled back. "That way, there's a boat!"

She looked, and sure enough a longboat had pulled into the shallows, surrounded by refugees. Jaryd turned back as more Elissian riders came at him . . . he didn't have time to pick her up. She had to run. The pain of exhaustion was worse than anything she'd ever felt. But so was the fear.

Sofy threw herself into a feet-first slide down the embankment, and hit the water with a splash. She struggled up, regathering the child with stiffening arms, and ran on. The water here was shallow. But the Elissians, previously below her in the water, were now behind.

Even as she threw a look over her shoulder, she could see them coming. There were two on horseback. Another few strides and they'd run her down.

A horse and rider appeared on the lip above, and simply fell off the edge. Jaryd, Sofy realised in midplunge. The horse hit the leading Elissian horse right across the saddle, crushing it and rider into the riverbank. Jaryd fell in the tangle, disappearing under rolling horses.

"Jaryd!" Sofy screamed, and turned back. He fought clear of fallen horses as they struggled to rise, one with a broken leg and thrashing. The second Elissian circled into deeper water, but the thrashing horse connected with his own, which reared and panicked. The Elissian fell with a splash, but came up just as fast.

Jaryd had lost his shield, and came at him in knee-deep water with a roar, but his leg was dragging. The Elissian survived his first two attacks with fast parries, then swung back. Jaryd ducked and drove forward, but his wounded leg was slowing him badly. The Elissian hit him with his shield, Jaryd grabbed his sword arm, and then they were both flailing and wrestling in the shallows.

For an instant they disappeared, then reappeared in a frenzy of splashing. The Elissian was on top, arm about Jaryd's neck in a grip he did not seem able to break. He was driven underwater as the Elissian fought for a knife to replace the sword he'd lost.

Sofy found herself running through the shallows. She did not recall putting the child down, nor pulling the almost forgotten knife from her belt, but as the Elissian drew his own blade she threw herself onto his back, put her knife beneath his chin, and cut as hard as she'd ever cut anything. Blood spurted, and he thrashed, throwing her off then landing on her. She kept stabbing and slicing as water filled her lungs, now frothing red and foul.

Then Jaryd was dragging her up and pulling her on along the bank. But his leg was slowing him, his limp severe. His own horse lay motionless, neck broken, the other still flailing with a snapped leg—they would have to run. Sofy thought Jaryd might drag her straight past where the child sat wailing in the shallows, but he picked up the boy without a word, his other arm about Sofy's shoulders as she supported him, and together they fought their way toward the boat.

"The Princess Regent!" Jaryd yelled as they approached the boat. Men were pushing it into the water, as still more people tried to surge aboard, nearly up to their shoulders now. Jaryd tried waving, and nearly fell as he abandoned Sofy's support. "The Princess Regent, hold the boat!"

Several cavalrymen were heroically holding the bank beneath the cover of arrows from this boat's stern and several other boats in deeper water, nearly overflowing with people, but holding position to provide cover with their archers. But even now, a cavalryman fell to an Elissian attack, and the remaining man looked to be overwhelmed.

Asym arrived with a yell, cut down one Elissian, collided with another's horse, and sent several more wheeling away. Arrows found one, and he reeled in the saddle with shafts through chest and thigh. Sofy could see Asym gesticulating at her and Jaryd to get aboard, but could not hear what he said.

Jaryd led them splashing into deeper water, as people trying to get aboard actually paused to help them, waving frantically at them to hurry. The water closed in, and the current was stronger than Sofy had expected. Screams came from the bank as blades clashed and horses thundered once more, and then Asym was down, tumbling down the embankment.

Jaryd reached the boat, thrust the child into waiting hands, then boosted Sofy clean out of the water. "Asym!" he yelled toward the bank. "Get your Isfayen backside out here!"

Asym was backing into the shallows, one arm dangling, the other holding his sword before him. Unable to urge horses down the treacherous embankment, Elissians dismounted and pursued on foot. The boat was not dislodged from the bank yet; if it were not shoved free, they would be stuck here at the mercy of the Elissians. Even now, more of them were arriving.

"Jaryd!" Sofy shouted, leaning back out of the boat to grab at his arm. "Jaryd, you have to get in!"

"Asym!"

The Isfayen threw them a look over his shoulder through wet black hair, and smirked. An Elissian came at him in the shallows, and one-handed Asym swayed aside an attack, and hacked through the other man's shoulder. Another came, exchanging blows, then fell in a spray of blood and teeth as Asym cut through his face. He roared something in Telochi, hammering his hilt to his chest, and dared the other Elissians to come and die.

Jaryd watched silently. Then he turned and, without any assistance, clambered aboard. Men in the shallows kept pushing, dislodging the boat bit by bit as its vastly increased weight pressed it down. Squeezed against one wooden side, Sofy and Jaryd watched as Asym killed two more Elissians, then another. Many more stood back in fear, and stared at the bodies floating about Asym's legs, and the blood that turned the water bright red. Lightning flashed, glinting off Asym's blade as he pointed it to the sky, and challenged his enemies once more.

Upon the embankment, an Elissian emerged with a loaded crossbow. Asym laughed at him, and yelled abuse. In there somewhere, Sofy was certain, was the Telochi word for "coward." The man with the crossbow aimed, and Asym spread his arms toward him.

Sofy closed her eyes.

Then they were moving out into the current. She was shivering in the pouring rain, and Jaryd's arms were about her. She heard him murmuring something, but did not understand the words. It sounded like a Goeren-yai chant, a call to the spirits to come and claim their fellow hunter. Jaryd's face, white with pain, bore no tears, only pride for his friend.

Sofy buried her head against his shoulder, and waited for Saalshen to arrive.

Sasha left Father Belgride's temple along a series of rear plankways upon the shore of Lake Andal. Rhillian and Aisha were with her, the three women keeping their feet dry past the walls of lakefront buildings, and across the rampways and piers to which boats were tethered.

Above pointed rooftops the sky was bright and blue, though the altitude made the air only warm rather than hot. As the road turned, mountains appeared in the gaps between buildings. The peaks had Andal and its lake surrounded, happy prisoners of a beautiful land.

People were plentiful on the streets, neatly dressed and handsome, as it seemed in all of Ilduur. There were more blond people here than Sasha had ever seen before, and Aisha assured her it had been so long before the arrival of serrin. They went about their daily business unarmed and carefree. To walk amongst them, Sasha wondered if they'd even heard that there was a war. Yet for all there was to like about the picturesque surroundings, the mood on the streets was of nervous tension.

Sasha had her own discomfort. To fit in with the local folk, the women had to dress like them. That meant dresses. They were neat and simple, of pleated dark cloth and white blouses with loose sleeves and tight cuffs. Sasha would much rather have walked the streets naked. Without her sword, that was how she felt anyway.

Rhillian knocked Sasha's hand down as she tugged in frustration at one hip as they walked. Rhillian, of course, made her dress look wonderful. She'd even braided her hair into twin tails like the local women, that odd diagonal cut finally dressed straight, and her white hair was similar enough to the frequent blond that she did not stand out here as much as she had in other cities. Her eyes, though, and that fine, angled cut of jaw and cheeks, could not be disguised. She wore the red brooch of an eight-pointed Verenthane star upon her breast, as did Aisha, who might have passed for straight human had she tried. But Father Belgride had insisted that it was not worth the risk. The star was a sign that a priest had vouched for a serrin, knew personally of his or her family, and their origins in Ilduur over many years. It signified that a serrin was a local Ilduuri, and not a foreigner. Without the brooch, it would not be safe for any serrin or part-serrin to walk in public.

Even so, they had barely walked three full blocks before someone spat on them.

"Sasha, don't glare," Rhillian said calmly, wiping the offence from her sleeve with a handkerchief she'd brought for the purpose. "Don't Lenays say you should not pick a fight you can't finish?"

"I'm remembering faces," Sasha muttered. The offender was a portly lady, whose pleasant features were contorted with disgust at the sight of one serrin, one half-serrin, and their human friend.

"Don't be concerned for us, Sasha," Aisha reassured her quietly. "We have more important matters afoot than dignity."

"There *is* nothing more important," Sasha seethed. "A people without dignity and honour deserve to be left to die."

"You sound like Kiel," said Rhillian. They spoke Saalsi, which though foreign, was common enough amongst Ilduuri serrin, and even some Ilduuri humans.

Sasha also wore a hat, broad-brimmed yet stylish enough for Andal's ladies, to hide her tri-braid, and the unfashionably short cut of her hair.

Their first stop was a market stall, which thrived upon a courtyard overlooking Lake Andal. They shopped to fill the baskets they'd brought, purchasing from several stalls to avoid suspicion, then stopping for a lingering chat with a particular fruit seller Father Belgride had recommended to them. The moustachioed man made an effort not to seem too friendly, but his eyes twinkled at them as he talked, before darting about the market to see who was looking. Sasha did not understand a word, but Aisha was fluent, and Rhillian somewhat, and both seemed to like him instantly.

"Poor fellow," Aisha explained to Sasha as they walked on. "His son has an affliction: strange fits and seizures. Serrin treatments help, but now the Stamentaast have stopped his serrin healer from treating non-serrin Ilduuri. His son's condition grows worse, and many of the healer's patients have appealed to the Remischtuul directly, but nothing happens."

"So many cowards," said Sasha. "I'll bet many of them feel as he does, and if they all spoke out together, their voice would be powerful. But their fear keeps them divided and weak."

"Most Ilduuri are not warriors," Aisha cautioned. "They have the Steel, but ordinary folk are not armed as Lenays are. Speaking out is dangerous for such people."

"Sheep," said Sasha, fingering the knife she'd strapped to her thigh beneath the dress. "If not a shepherd then always a sheep, that is the way of it."

Several passersby said rude things to them in Ilduuri that Aisha did not translate. Most of them seemed more angry at Sasha than the serrin. To be friends with the foreigner, it seemed, was worse than being the foreigner.

Then came a pair of Stamentaast, in green vests with swords at their belts. They stopped the women, and asked questions, but Sasha was not particularly alarmed—it had happened many times in the past few days. Aisha did most of the talking, and Rhillian gave curt, short answers, and her accent was good enough that the two men did not seem to suspect her. Sasha they did not bother to question. She was human, and they assumed her an angry local who did not like Stamentaast. That was common enough, and not punishable. Or not yet.

"It's insane," Sasha muttered as they were allowed to move on. "Serrin made this place so wealthy. Now being serrin is nearly a crime."

"Not as much of a crime as being Lenay," Rhillian cautioned. "Serrin have many friends and ties to the population. Of us three, if they knew our true identities, it would be you in worst danger."

"Even with a knife I'd take a half-dozen with me," Sasha snorted.

In the next square, they found a different scene. Two men were hanging by the neck from a pole and gantry. A town crier stood beneath them and shouted to the passing crowd, some of whom regarded the hanged men with curiosity, some with contempt, and others with fear.

"He says that these two men were guilty of conspiring with foreigners to force Ilduur into a foreign war," Aisha translated as they walked on. "He says to be wary of all who would force the peaceful people of Ilduur into terrible conflicts that shall bring them only suffering and death."

"Who could possibly imagine that such conspirators exist," Rhillian said mildly. "Honestly, the paranoia of these people."

Sasha left Rhillian and Aisha at their meeting with senior Ilduuri serrin. She did not want to sit in their furtive gatherings and listen to their puzzled questions and fearful astonishment that the lovely country that had been their home for so long could turn on them so suddenly. Sasha could defend many of humanity's faces from serrin question, but she could not defend this. This was inexcusable.

She seethed on it as she walked back to Father Belgride's lakeside temple. It wasn't as though the Ilduuri even had the excuse of religious stupidity. Indeed, the priests here were amongst the loudest in calling for the Steel to march, to save their brothers to the north. The Ilduuri priesthood had gained a measure of independence from Petrodor and Sherdaine over the last two centuries, and had grown to enjoy it. The faith had moved on, to become inclusive and philosophical in a way that the haters and howlers of the Regent's army would never understand. Father Belgride sheltered serrin families whose houses had been burned, and took great personal risks to assist those who opposed the Remischtuul. But the hold of the priesthood over the minds of ordinary Ilduuri was limited.

Ilduuri saw themselves as separate. As a single race whose language and customs were more different from their neighbours' than any other of the Bacosh peoples. Even in the good times, when serrin had ruled Ilduur and the Ilduuri had come to see that serrin ways were wise, intermarriage had been frowned upon. Many Ilduuri were friendly, but most simply did not wish to share their lives with the strange and foreign serrin.

Now, many Ilduuri felt that they owed Saalshen nothing. Some even felt slighted, as though the past two centuries had been a terrible endurance of occupation and humiliation, and all its benefits were somehow the miraculous achievements of the Ilduuri themselves. Sasha could not empathise, and felt in no mood to even try. In Ilduur, the people had been shown the most outstanding merit of serrin, and had tossed it aside in favour of the familiar, the safe, and the ordinary.

Sasha paused to look at some knives on sale, and glanced behind her. Was the man in the long jacket following her? She'd acquired some instinct for crowds from Petrodor and Tracato, but she still did not trust that instinct.

She took a side road, to see if he followed her. Ahead, where several streets joined, she heard a commotion. An elderly serrin, walking with a stick, was surrounded by three young men. The young men were taunting him. The old serrin stood with reserve and dignity, and made no effort to defend himself. He tried to walk on, but the men blocked his path and laughed, and knocked the hat off his head.

Sasha did not understand what they called him in Ilduuri, but she did not need to. She was almost pleased, in fact, to have stumbled upon this scene. It suited her mood entirely. Several passing Ilduuri walked on, ignoring the old man's plight.

One of the Ilduuri men snatched the serrin's cane away. He raised it, as though about to hit him with it, expecting the old man to be frightened. The old man simply stood, with weary resignation. The three Ilduuri men laughed.

Sasha headed for the man with the cane. His friend saw her coming and stepped into her path. He leered, predictably, looking her up and down. Sasha punched him in the mouth.

He stumbled, and his friends stared, all frozen in shock. Sasha would rather have had the cane, something swordlike that she could swing. It would be a short fight then. As a brawler, she was more limited, especially with the dress preventing her from kicking. But she could see from the build of these men, from the way they stood and reacted with hesitation and shock, that they were not fighters. She was.

The man with the cane swung it at her. Sasha ducked and drove her shoulder into him, knocking him backwards. His balance gone, she laid into him, left and right fists with no great style, but the ones that connected were painful enough.

The man she'd punched first now kicked at her, a feeble effort, too far out of range. She took the blow, caught his foot, and tried to nail him with a right, only for him to scamper out of range, trip, and fall on his backside. The other two came at her pushing and swinging. Sasha ducked and covered as best she could, took several hits on the body, then blocked and caught one man's arms as Errollyn had taught her, pulling him forward and off balance as she stepped back, and dropped an elbow on his head. It only glanced, but stunned, so she hit him again with a crosswise elbow. He fell, blood pouring.

The last man tackled her down, and they hit the road together, him on top, trying to pin her. Sasha pinned one arm, fighting for leverage, then simply overpowered him, to his utter astonishment. She rolled on top, sat up, then began to beat his head into the road with her fists until he stopped moving.

She got up, and the last man grabbed his bleeding friend and dragged him stumbling away. Sasha examined her knuckles. One was raw and bleeding. She'd hit her head on the road when she'd fallen, and that stung. A bruise to her ribs throbbed. Overall, she felt wonderful.

The elderly serrin man was looking at her with more curiosity than gratitude. Sasha picked up his cane from where it had fallen, and handed it to him.

"Hmm," said the old man. "Not from around here, are you?" Sasha blinked. He'd spoken in Lenay. Then she realised her hat had fallen off, and her tri-braid was free. She scampered to her hat, beside the groaning man she'd beaten, and put it back on, tucking the tri-braid into place.

"There," she said cheerfully in Saalsi. "That better?"

The old man sighed. "I think you'd better come with me."

The old serrin's name was Tershin. He'd been *talmaad* in his day, and had served Saalshen in all the Saalshen Bacosh provinces, as well as Torovan, Telesia, and Lenayin. When his *talmaad* service was ended, he'd returned to Saalshen, had two children with the same serrin woman, then moved to Andal. It had always been the prettiest place he'd been to, he said, and the mother of his children ("wife" had no equivalent word in Saalsi) had accompanied him, and enjoyed the clean air. She was dead now, but Tershin had old serrin friends here, and a few human ones.

"I did warn them," he said, as Sasha sat at his table and sipped fragrant tea. "There was not enough debate within the Remischtuul. Maldereld never paid Ilduur the attention she did Rhodaan and Enora, and the Ilduuri will always cling together like mud when threatened. Maldereld no doubt thought that useful, compared to the bickering in other human lands. Serrin value cohesiveness too much; only too late have we learned of its dangers amongst humans."

"I do wish that everyone today would stop blaming everything on Maldereld," said Sasha, sipping her tea. "I think she did a wonderful job for the most part. But she was only one woman, and whatever mistakes she made were made by all of those who helped her. She was no tyrant, and serrin make no decisions alone."

"True," said Tershin, eyeing her curiously. He placed some fruit and cheese on the table. "My old uman knew Maldereld. He'd met her several times as a boy, when she was an old woman."

"Truly?" Sasha was impressed. "What was she like?"

"An unusual serrin," said Tershin, easing himself slowly into his chair. "She loved to ride, even in her old age. She liked to be alone, more than was typical for serrin. She was no great linguist, very unusual for a leading *talmaad*. And she had little patience with the long debates more typical of our people."

Sasha smiled, thinking of Rhillian. "That sounds like someone I know."

"Those three boys today. You did not need to beat them up on my account."

"Who said I did?" Sasha retorted. "I enjoyed it enough just for me."

"You are Sashandra Lenayin, aren't you." It was a statement, not a question.

"I might be."

"It takes no great genius to see it. Though fortunately for you, even many seniors of the Remischtuul will not have heard the name. Only we who care about the world outside have cause to find interest in such names. Why do you not fight with the Army of Lenayin?"

"I do," said Sasha. "The Army of Lenayin defected. Or most of it did. We fight now with Saalshen."

Tershin stared at her. They did not know. She had travelled in this direction as fast as any news could, and was the first here to spread the knowledge. To Sasha's surprise, Tershin's eyes filled with tears. He wiped at them.

"Oh, Lenayin," he sighed. "Such a strange attraction we serrin have for your land. We have never been a warlike people, yet we are all astonished to find that the one land in all Rhodia that understands us best, has the most warlike people imaginable. It is a conundrum that has kept serrin returning to Lenayin for centuries."

"The north still fights with the Regent," Sasha added, lest he get too romantic about it.

Tershin made a dismissive gesture. "Hardly surprising—ask three Lenays for their thoughts, and you'll get ten different opinions."

"Just like serrin," said Sasha with a smile. "As you said."

"And so you come here. With friends, I suppose." Sasha nodded. "To talk the Remischtuul into fighting? It cannot be done, my girl. Their minds are decided, and most of the people agree with them."

"The Steel don't."

"And so you must convince the Steel to break with the Remischtuul. To do that, you must discredit the Remischtuul."

Sasha shrugged, not truly wishing to divulge more detail to an old ex-

talmaad. Tershin seemed a good man, but Rhillian and Aisha were meeting with many of those more significant Ilduuri serrin. If Tershin was not one of them, then he must have removed himself from that circle on purpose—serrin were too sociable for there to be any other explanation.

"I never told you what I did for a trade, once my *talmaad* days were over," said Tershin. "I was a moneylender."

Sasha frowned, and looked about at his house. It was clean and simple, but without the grand view or ornamental expense that she might have guessed of one in that trade.

Tershin smiled. "You have a preconception of the trade. Serrin break the preconception, and this explains our success. We are fair, and charge only a small percentage for ourselves."

"Don't tell me there are no serrin with expensive tastes. You're not all saints."

Tershin's smile grew broader. "True, but we share. I have enjoyed the acquisitions of wealthy friends as much as I have enjoyed a few of my own. But listen to me. Humans do not trust each other with money, the powerful in particular, as money amongst humans is power. But they know that money, though valued, does not mean the same thing to serrin. The powerful in Ilduur have often preferred to use serrin moneylenders, and serrin book-keepers to manage their accounts."

Sasha had heard the same thing in Rhodaan and Ilduur. "They trust you because they know serrin will not steal, or reveal their secrets to their competitors."

"And a misguided trust it sometimes is," said Tershin, "because though we will not sell them to their enemies, neither will most serrin tolerate corruption or theft from those who employ us. It is *fuin'is*, disruptive of the great balance."

"A *fuin'as tal*," Sasha agreed. A disharmony.

Tershin smiled at her grasp of the tongue. "But it does mean that we serrin are often wound tightly into the finances of the powerful, in cities like Andal. Even those amongst the powerful who dislike us discover that they like the safe management of their accounts more. As it so happens, my latest employment was to manage the books and accounts of the Steelwrights' Guild."

Sasha frowned. "Aren't they allied to the Steel itself?"

"Certainly, certainly. They are distrusted within the Remischtuul. Understand that the Remischtuul is comprised of guilds, primarily. It brings them all together, and they discuss, and vote. Now, a little over a month ago, there appeared in the Steelwrights' Guild's books an entry for nearly ten thousand silver talons." Sasha shook her head, not knowing that currency. "Those are used in Meraine, issued by the Chansul of Meraine himself. My task as keeper of the books was to convert those talons into Ilduuri gold marks—understand that talons are commonly converted in Ilduur, but are prohibited from general exchange."

"Go very slowly," Sasha warned him. "Accountancy was never my strong point."

Tershin leaned forward on the table. His old hands were firm in their gesticulation, and his eyes as intent as those of a much younger man. "The Meraini pay for their trade with Ilduur in talons. Some even use our marks, but of course, trade with any member of the Saalshen Bacosh is supposed to be prohibited. . . ."

"The priesthood would have an offender killed," said Sasha, understanding that much.

"So, the Meraini learn to be discreet," Tershin agreed. "They have traded with Ilduur for many centuries, Maldereld's arrival here did not stop it, and the Meraini priesthood keep silent because they receive a tribute."

"A cut," Sasha translated.

"Just so. Talons are received and used to purchase Ilduuri goods. Merchants selling those goods accumulate talons, but many of those who sell to Meraine do not buy from Meraine. They will trade talons for marks, with those that do. There is a market price for trade between talons and marks. Too many talons, and the price falls. They're easy to acquire, do you see?"

Sasha nodded. She wasn't quite *that* slow.

"Too few, and the price rises. Now, a sum of ten thousand talons is quite large. So I went to see the men who fix the price of trade. To my astonishment, the price had plummeted, a full fifteen talons for each mark. Typically the price is four or five to a mark. The most I have ever seen it is nine or ten to the mark, and I have lived and worked in Andal for thirty years."

"Andal is flooded with Meraini talons," Sasha said slowly. Tershin nodded, with great meaning. "Trade has been good lately?"

"Not that good."

"So someone in the Remischtuul is receiving wagonloads of talons from Meraine, and paying them out to the guilds."

"It would seem the only answer."

"To gain their loyalty?"

"Their silence," Tershin said grimly. "And those young men that you assaulted, I fear, were sent to me by the Stamentaast, as a reminder to me to keep my mouth shut. The Stamentaast knows all those who work within the trade. Lately, several of those setting the trade of talons and marks have disappeared. Yesterday, a new price was announced. Seven talons to the mark."

"They're fixing the price?"

"Yes, while the black market is now offering a price of eighteen. The Sta-mentaast chase the black-marketeers, and the number of disappearances grows larger."

Sasha exhaled hard. "By helping you, I seem to have put you in greater danger. It's a bad habit of mine, I apologise."

Tershin smiled. "There is no need. Indeed, you seem to have offered a solution to my problem." Sasha raised her eyebrows. "The Meraini will not send wagonloads of talons through the mountain passes unaccompanied—Ilduur is relatively peaceful and law abiding, but there are watchful eyes, loose tongues, and common criminals here as anywhere else. Such a large sum, as tribute to the Remischtuul members, will come accompanied by a senior person of Meraine."

"An ambassador," Sasha agreed, thinking furiously. "A close relative to the Chansul of Meraine himself, I'd guess. Perhaps a brother."

"Yes, but he dare not enter Andal publicly," Tershin reminded her. "The Remischtuul declares that all foreigners are equally evil. To be acting upon the bribes of the Meraini, in planning for future allegiance and a common front against the Regent in the new Bacosh, would seem hypocritical."

Sasha smiled darkly. "We must find this ambassador. If I were to throw him at the feet of the Ilduuri Steel, their attitude toward the Remischtuul might change."

"Getting this ambassador may not be easy."

Sasha shrugged. "I don't need all of him. His head will do."

Fifteen

Shuen Vaal meant "Steel Town" in Ilduuri, meaning that its residents were mostly soldiers, or ex-soldiers, and their families. Battalion banners and pennants decorated windows and walls, streets were named after battles and markets featured military gear—boots, shovels, ropes, everything a soldier might prefer from regulation Steel kit. Bergen was delighted, and stopped to enquire about weapons in his fluent Ilduuri. The shopkeeper beckoned him to a rear room, and pulled some swords from a locked chest—the Steel issued regulation swords, but were sometimes slow to replace old or damaged ones, and some men preferred a different weight or grip, depending on the tolerance of their immediate commanders.

Sasha had to drag Bergen on, for the afternoon was late, and the Andal Valley shadows creeping in on the city.

"Ridiculous that weapons cannot be sold freely," she muttered. "Soon the Remischtuul will forbid people the use of their own fists." She hated more than ever being unarmed, though she did feel safer amongst so many soldiers in civilian clothes. The Stamentaast had few friends here, and those she'd seen moved in larger groups and were not so bold as to stop and question anyone they pleased.

Yasmyn had not been pleased to be told to remain at Father Belgride's temple, but there was no choice—serrin in Andal were common enough, and all the others save Yasmyn could pass as Ilduuri, but Yasmyn's eyes gave her away. Rhillian and Aisha were still at their meetings, and Kiel and Arendelle likewise on some other lead, so this task had fallen to her and Bergen.

At the market stall Tershin had told them of, Bergen asked for Haast, Master of the Steelwrights' Guild. The stall owner sent his daughter running, and they waited, browsing over good knives on display and some axes, hammers, and other tools. They did not have to wait long. Sasha noticed the men before Bergen, four of them, all with the build and walk of warriors, however plain their clothes. She nudged Bergen, who picked up the axe he was examining. Sasha took a knife and gave it a clever twirl. The men stopped, save one who came forward.

That man demanded something in Ilduuri, and Sasha heard the name of Haast once more. Bergen answered, and Sasha heard the name "Tershin" in his reply.

The men beckoned for them to follow. "They're Steel," Bergen murmured to Sasha as they followed, two men before them, two more behind.

"They said that?"

"They just look it," said Bergen. It *was* the Steel's part of town, and Sasha reckoned if anyone would know, Bergen would.

They were led to some stairs up the side of a building, like a single, vast house, but with narrow stairways about the walls and across odd angles leading to living quarters on different floors. These stairs led to a common balcony, then up again to the attic atop the building.

Within was a living space, a kitchen built around the common stone chimney that rose through all the floors below. Two women prepared food, while another nursed an infant. Two older children played with wooden toys. Spread across a wall, Sasha saw a battalion pennant. Upon a high cabinet, out of reach of children, a long sword.

The men ushered them onto the balcony. Upon the nearby lake edge rose rows of smoke stacks, some belching black soot. Furnaces, she realised. This was the steelwright's district, after all. And those furnaces made serrin steel, an art unknown outside of Saalshen and the Saalshen Bacosh.

The leader of the Ilduuri men introduced himself. Arken, Sasha thought she caught his name.

"This is Sasha," Bergen replied in Saalsi, "and I am Bergen." The men frowned. Arken looked suspiciously at Sasha, clearly suspecting that she was the reason for the shift in tongues.

"Tershin sent you?" Arken asked, also in Saalsi.

"He did," said Bergen. "On the trail of too many Meraini talons."

The men's eyes widened. They exchanged glances. "You're from the north?" one asked, trying to place Bergen's accent.

"I am," said Bergen. "I saw that one of the pennants on your wall was of the Second Battalion of the Enoran Steel."

Arken folded his arms. "You have the look yourself. Infantry?"

"Cavalry."

"Which unit?"

"First Company. Enoran Cavalry."

The men's eyes widened. "Ah," said Arken. "*That* far north. Your accent is good."

"I've served with Ilduuri units," said Bergen. "And there were Ilduuri merchants in my home town. Several are friends."

"I've served in Enora," said another man. "Our commanders used to send small Ilduuri units to Enora to gain experience. Enora has been attacked far more than Ilduur over the years. But our commanders stopped the practice last year."

"Or rather, the Remischtuul replaced our commanders," Arken said bitterly. "Our good ones, anyhow."

"We heard," said Bergen. "Though we did not think it so serious."

Arken considered him for a moment. "You took some risk coming here, friend," he said. "You've seen the men hanging in the squares?"

"They're only the beginning of it," said another, bitterly. "Others have disappeared. They're not coming after the Steel yet, because they are afraid of making us angry. But give it time."

"You seem angry enough already," Bergen observed. "Yet the Ilduuri Steel remain silent, while the Rhodaani and Enoran Steel fight for their lives."

"There are not enough of us," Arken muttered. "The Remischtuul have removed many of our senior commanders. Nasi-Keth replace them. A few have battle experience, but most only know svaalverd. Most Nasi-Keth are loyal to the Remischtuul."

"I've seen," Bergen agreed. "What of your most senior officer? General Daani?"

"He does nothing. He does not speak to his men, and the men grow alarmed. We do not know what his opinion is. Some say we should wait until General Daani acts, and others say we should force his hand. Daani has always been a friend to Saalshen, Enora, and Rhodaan in the past."

"A false hope," said another man. "If Daani were on our side he would have acted already. He leaves it far too late."

"The stall owner said that you are Haast's son?" Bergen pressed.

"My name is Arken Haast." Arken, Sasha could not help but notice, was very handsome—blond, square-jawed, blue-eyed, and built more like a Lenay warrior than a lowlander. "It seems that Tershin sent you looking for my father, Taaner Haast. He is Master of the Steelwright's Guild. He works in the furnaces there." He pointed to the smokestacks by the lake.

"And you will succeed him when you leave the Steel?"

Arken shrugged. "Perhaps. But if the Regent Arrosh defeats our northern brothers, Ilduur may not survive that long."

Bergen looked at Sasha, perhaps wondering why she remained silent. Sasha found it useful to see how men behaved first with men, before introducing a woman into the mix. Perhaps she was maturing, finally. A few months back, she could not have found the patience.

"And as Master of the Steelwrights' Guild," Bergen asked, "your father has a seat on the Remischtuul?"

Arken nodded, cautiously. "He is just one man, of a hundred and thirty-five seats. But Tershin keeps the Guild's books, and father told me he'd noticed the Remischtuul's payments in talons."

"From where does the money come, do you think?"

"There's a Meraini company in town, isn't there?" one of the others said darkly. "With wagon loads of Meraini coin." There were sullen nods from all present. And burning anger.

"Ilduur has not declared itself neutral," Arken stated. "It has been bought, by the Chansul of Meraine."

"Is that it over there?" Sasha asked, pointing across the rooftops. "Is that the Remischtuul?" There was a grand building at the base of the valley slope, overlooking the city. Huge and wide, it looked like a palace, yet too large and new for some feudal monstrosity. That, and it seemed to have no defensive walls.

"It is," said Arken, frowning at her. "Your accent is not Enoran or Rhodaani. Where are you from?"

"Lenayin," said Sasha. Men stared at her.

"Lenayin fights for the Regent," one observed with menace.

"Not anymore. I led them to change sides."

"I said her name was Sasha," said Bergen. "Her full name is Sashandra, and you already know her last."

Arken grinned. "You're having a joke," he said to Bergen.

One of the others scoffed. "Sashandra Lenayin? The warrior princess?"

"The same," said Bergen.

"What did you think I'd look like?" Sasha wondered aloud.

"You're too small!" another man declared.

"And Lenayin would never change sides," said another. "They are barbarians. They love only to fight and care not who they slaughter. To change sides is for them dishonourable."

"How odd, Bergen," Sasha said mildly. "These men claim to know more of my people and myself than I do."

"This is Sashandra Lenayin," Bergen said firmly, "and I warn you not to anger her or she may give you a lesson none of you could survive. She fought with her people against my Enoran brothers at the Shero Valley, where we gave the Lenays a hard-fought loss."

"That much news has reached us," Arken admitted.

"At Shero Valley, she led her people in a great defection, where perhaps three-quarters of them abandoned the Regent to join us. We were enemies, but in Enora we embraced as brothers. The Verenthanes of the northern Lenay provinces remained with King Koenyg, but the rest followed Sashandra Lenayin, by her action and choice alone."

The Ilduuri men were silent. Suspicion battled with hope in their eyes.

"I am Enoran cavalry," said Bergen, drawing himself up to his full, considerable height. "I lost friends to the blades of Sashandra Lenayin's comrades at Shero Valley. I swear to you on their graves that I speak the truth."

"I also lost friends to Bergen's comrades," Sasha said solemnly. "Possibly to Bergen himself for all I know. One man who died had been as an uncle to me from since I was a little girl in my home village of Baerlyn. Yet the Enoran Steel fought with courage and skill, and they earned the respect of Lenayin. Later, as we advanced into Rhodaan and then Enora in the wake of the Regent's Army, we saw the devastation left behind, and we began to question.

"You have heard only half-truths of Lenay honour. Yes, we are loyal, but mostly we follow our code. The code says that there is only honour in the fighting of worthy opponents. We all saw too many dead children upon the road to Shemorane to believe any claim by the Regent to be fighting in honour's name. The Enoran Steel, on the other hand, was judged in battle and found worthy. My people decided on their own, according to their native values. I merely gave them a nudge."

"You *are* Sashandra Lenayin," Arken said quietly. There was a light now to his eye. Hope, full-fledged and burning. "You have the steel I have only seen in serrin women of the *talmaad*. So few human women fight. I do not see who else you could be."

"Why send you?" another asked. "If the Army of Lenayin follows you, why risk you to come here?"

"Because if Ilduur does not join this fight, we are all finished. My brother Damon leads well, and my uman Kessligh Cronenverdt even more so." There were nods at his name, enthusiastic and wide-eyed. Sasha had not quite expected this, but she sensed an opportunity. She had to grasp it. "But I cannot convince Ilduuri to do anything that Ilduuri will not decide to do for themselves, in their own hearts. And that is up to you."

"I have little hope for the hearts of most Ilduuris," said Arken. "Those here in Andal have no interest in the world outside. They have convinced themselves that foreigners are nothing but trouble and do not deserve our sweat and blood. But the Ilduuri Steel are different. We wish to fight, but the Remischtuul has removed all our leaders, and scattered them to the corners of Ilduur."

"The Remischtuul will not let us leave," said another man. "And however much the Steel wish to fight the Regent, they will not fight the Remischtuul, and the Ilduuri people, to be able to do it."

"So what would it take?" Sasha asked. "To convince the Steel to ignore the Remischtuul's orders? To defy them?"

Arken smiled darkly. "Finding this Meraini party would be a good start," he said, seeing the direction that she led them to. "Then presenting their treacherous heads to those of our comrades yet to be convinced. Would you help us?"

Sasha smiled back. "It would be my pleasure," she said. "How will we find these Meraini puppet masters?"

Jaryd tested the strapping on his calf and found it tight. Yet it lessened the pain, which the healer had assured him was nothing worse than torn muscle, and would heal so long as he treated it well.

He made his way carefully up the stairs from the lakeside, away from the serrin village upon its shores. Forest grew thick, and small cabins nestled amidst the trunks. Serrin wandered about various tasks, or sat on verandahs and talked, as seemed their way. Birds flitted overhead, and their calls echoed high and far across the canopy of leaves.

These cabins were odd in that they did not seem well suited for any trade or business. In Lenayin, woodsmen would build amongst the trees like this, but out in the wilds and not so close to a village. And even then, they would have adjoining space for leather tanning, or butchery, or woodcrafts, or however such folk made themselves a living. These cabins seemed to have little purpose save leisure, and sitting on verandahs in the tree shade, and listening to birdsong.

A small stream trickled nearby through the undergrowth as Jaryd limped up the stairs. Suddenly someone arrived at his side, placing his arm about their shoulders to help with the steps. To Jaryd's astonishment, it was a serrin woman, a total stranger, who smiled at him, and took some weight off his bad leg.

"Thank you," he told her. "What is your name?"

The serrin said something in Saalsi, uncomprehending. These were not *talmaad*, and the woman was unarmed that he could see. If she did not speak Torovan, certainly she would not speak Lenay. For all their linguistic talent, most serrin did not speak human tongues, and devoted their language skills to their own multiple dialects.

The serrin woman arrived at her path to a cabin, and said what was obviously an apology for leaving him. She walked to a cabin half-hidden amongst trees. She was wearing pants and a shirt, not so unlike what the men wore. Somehow Jaryd found that most astonishing of anything he'd seen in Saalshen so far. He'd assumed that *talmaad* women were merely abandoning their traditional, feminine garb for something more practical. Now he was finding that serrin women wore pants in Saalshen too.

At the top of the path he found the trail he had been directed to, and followed it through the trees. Suddenly it opened onto a small lake on the hillside. On either side of the lake were grand wooden buildings with pointed roofs. They reminded Jaryd of some Lenayin training halls, where men would practise swordwork. These looked more peaceful, and those serrin he could see wore robes. Priests? he wondered, as he limped on around the lake. Within the templelike buildings, the walls were lined with carved symbols he had never seen before, and decorations like wind chimes dangled and swung about the doorways.

Jaryd followed a path between wooden temples and thought that he had never seen a place quite so lovely. He had never been one to be interested in spiritual contemplation, but here he could feel the calm, could almost breathe it, like a scent on the air.

In a small pool before a smaller building, he came upon two women. They sat on a shallow step in the water and talked, their light robes wet, their hair tousled. Jaryd fought back a smile—if Saalshen had one thing to recommend it, it was this. Serrin women were not shy.

One woman looked up at his approach, and nudged her companion. That woman looked, and . . . Jaryd nearly stopped in astonishment. It was Sofy. Her hair was much shorter, still long, but now barely past her shoulders. The Idys Mark on her forehead was gone. There was no jewellery on her neck or fingers. One hand bore a bandage, cut with the knife she'd wielded to save his life, back at the Ipshaal crossing. She looked . . . new.

"Hello," she said simply, and the serrin woman climbed from the water with a knowing smile. "Sit," she invited him.

Jaryd wore only light clothes himself, good for both the warmth and his various recovering injuries. He removed his sword belt, placed it and the sword beside the pool, kicked off his sandals, and climbed in beside her. The water chilled pleasantly, and he leaned back against the poolside.

"What is this place?" Jaryd asked.

"You know, I'm not entirely sure. Kels is *talmaad*, she speaks Lenay well, yet somehow with serrin it's never entirely clear."

"It looks like some kind of temple complex."

Sofy nodded. "Oh, it is, for certain. But these people here, they're not priests or monks. Kels said they are all normal serrin, come from all over Saalshen. I think perhaps some of them have had tragedy in their lives, and they come here for solace."

"I didn't think serrin had religion," said Jaryd, gazing up at the forest canopy high above.

"Sasha once told me that serrin do not separate things into the spiritual and the nonspiritual. She said it made more sense to say that because the serrin do not organise religion, they find the spiritual in everything, not merely in temples. I think I understand now what she meant."

Jaryd nodded. "Everything is a small ritual to them."

They sat in silence, with only the sound of birds, wind in the branches, and the nearby tinkling of water into the pool.

"I never thanked you for saving my life," said Jaryd after a moment.

Sofy smiled. "After you'd just saved mine five times over."

Jaryd shrugged. "I'm a warrior, it's my duty. You're no warrior, yet you've saved mine twice now." The first time was in Algery, when Sofy had ridden in to save him from the cavalry that had surrounded him. "Even if you did forget to leave me a stirrup."

Sofy splashed at him lightly. "I was still learning to ride then. Though I did fall again just now."

"That was brave, taking that child. Stupidly brave. The kind of bravery that Sasha has. That I have."

"You have the 'stupid' right. It nearly killed me and the child both. If his mother had hidden, he may have been safer left behind."

Jaryd shook his head. "Never doubt courage. I was wrong to criticise it in you before. Courageous leaders make mistakes. Cowardly leaders make worse ones."

"You were correct to criticise me. Good leaders must listen to those who know better than they. You know fighting far better than I do. Far better than most men. I cannot make good decisions entirely on my own. I do not think that any leader can. Nor any person, in any part of life."

She seemed almost serene. Jaryd had not expected that.

"Why the hair?" he asked her.

"Do you like it?" she asked with girlish pleasure.

"I do."

"Kels cut it for me—she said that women in the *talmaad* have evolved many styles for shorter hair, since long hair is so inconvenient for them."

"Sister Mardola would not like that," he ventured.

Sofy laughed, very loudly. It was a lovely sound. "No," she admitted, with dancing eyes. "I daresay she would not."

"And the Mark of Idys? The Royal Ring?"

Sofy sighed, and swished her feet in the water. "Oh dear. It's so silly. All of it's so silly, isn't it? It's like you told me, I was carrying the weight of the world on my shoulders. And now I arrive here, in this place, and suddenly everything makes sense."

"Explain it to me, because I could use a little more sense in my life."

"Some things are good," Sofy said simply. "Other things are bad."

Jaryd blinked at her. "That's it?"

"Well, no. But what the Elissians did to us, what they did to all of those people, was bad. Evil."

"No argument here."

"And what we were trying to do for them, in helping them to safety in Saalshen, was good. I risked my life to save that child, and to help the rest of them. That was good. What Asym did to allow us to escape, that was even better."

"Eslen," Jaryd gave the formal agreement, and made the spirit sign at his forehead. To his surprise, Sofy did the same.

"He killed a lot of Elissians, yet I cannot deny the goodness of his actions," Sofy continued. She paused a moment. Then added, "I killed one Elissian, and I did not feel sad for it. That stunned me more than the killing itself. I mean, this is *me*, Jaryd." She laughed again. "The girl who used to scold the palace cat for killing a mouse. And so when I was dumped on the far Ipshaal bank I set about searching through my own soul for the horror that I expected to find at this awful thing that I had done with my own hands." She looked at her bandaged hand, floating in the cool water. "But I found nothing." She gazed at him with large dark eyes. "I was not sorry, Jaryd. I think I was even glad."

"Perhaps you are a warrior like Sasha after all," Jaryd said with amusement.

Sofy shook her head, adamantly. "No. I'll never be a warrior, I have not the discipline to learn skills that disinterest and frighten me. Nor the aptitude, no doubt. But I have realised for the first time what is wrong, and what is right. My old values mean nothing now. This new understanding has swept them away."

"There's nothing like seeing a slaughter first hand to rearrange your priorities," Jaryd said sombrely.

Sofy nodded. "I've seen killing before. I was with you and Sasha on the ride north . . ."

"I remember well."

"But here . . ." She gazed up at the trees, and at the surrounding temples. "It's so beautiful. My husband seeks to destroy all this. I had thought to excuse him, thinking that he has the right to an opinion, being the representative of so many. But I come here, and I remember the killing in Tracato and now upon the Ipshaal, and I realise that he and all his opinions and his priests and his lords can jump in the sea for all I care. No one is entitled to that opinion. Let alone to act upon it with an army of a hundred thousand."

"One fifty," Jaryd said quietly. "At least, if the Meraini come, and now the Elissians."

Sofy glanced down, with sudden fear. "And to think that I might have helped to make such a thing possible . . ."

Jaryd caught her hand. "You have the kindest heart of any person I have known. You always think of others first. It is not in your nature to condemn and wish death upon people. But you walk the path, and you learn."

"I still don't wish death upon them," Sofy murmured. "But I do want them stopped."

"And there is no other way but war," Jaryd completed.

Sofy looked back to him, and her eyes were clear. "I know," she said simply. And she smiled, and looked around in exasperation. "It's foolish. I am committing to a fight we probably can't win. Most likely we'll all die a horrible death, me especially for betraying my lawful husband. But I don't care anymore." She beamed at him. "I feel free."

Unadorned and water-wet in her robe, she looked free. Jaryd had never seen a woman more beautiful.

"And what *of* your marriage?" he asked her.

Sofy made a face. "The serrin say that life is a road strewn with obstacles. This obstacle I shall manoeuvre around somehow. Perhaps talk to the priests, consider the possibilities."

"Whoever wins the war," Jaryd added, "the other is unlikely to survive." His heart was thumping, with the dull excitement of possibility.

"That is certainly true," Sofy said.

"In which case," he obliged, "it makes little sense to be religiously observing marriage vows now."

Sofy made a conceding dip of her head. "We are in Saalshen after all," she agreed.

"Where marriage itself is a rare and foreign concept," Jaryd added. He glanced about. "And would you look, I cannot see a priest anywhere."

Sofy threw her head back and laughed. Then gave him a look that was pure devilry, and went straight to his groin. "I don't want to talk of husbands anymore," she said, and climbed onto Jaryd's lap in the water. She brushed wet hair from her face, lips nearly touching his. "Such a pointless distraction, when there are better things to think about."

Their lips touched. Her body enfolded to his, cool and firm, her lips and breath and eyes so familiar, as though they had never been apart. As though things had always been this way. She smiled at him, and kissed him again, and again. Some serrin may have walked past. Neither they, not their human guests, thought to mind.

It was late evening upon leaving the Shuen Vaal, the shadows of the surrounding mountains darkening the streets even as the sky above remained blue. Sasha heard it first, the sound of shouting, and then of glass breaking.

"Trouble," she murmured to Bergen. They rounded a corner and found several people standing before a house whose windows had been broken. Beyond, people were running, and shouts came louder. The house bore a red star on the front door—a serrin house.

"Let's just get back to the temple without any trouble," said Bergen. Sasha felt into the pocket of her dress as she walked, for the incision that made the knife strapped to her thigh accessible. Nearby, she could smell something burning. Bells clanged alarm, and city folk opened high windows to peer out and stare across the rooftops.

Stamentaast came running, green-vested men wielding torches and swords. People on the streets stood aside for them, and Stamentaast paused before another star-marked house to throw stones at the windows. Two men broke down the door and rushed inside. Bergen grasped Sasha's arm and dragged her on. He sensed that her hand was itching toward her knife; surely his own did the same.

Further along, the scene became worse. A house was fully ablaze, threatening to take its neighbours with it. City folk were crowding a wagon arrived from the lake with basins of water, throwing bucketfuls onto the flames. Sasha thought that if half the city burned, it would serve them right. A half-serrin family huddled by a street side with two children, defended by several city folk, as locals spat and threw kicks and stones at them. The children were terrified and crying, the parents desperate.

"We have more important things to do than die needlessly here!" Bergen snarled at Sasha, tightening his grip. Sasha fumed as Bergen dragged her past. Further on, Stamentaast had gathered more serrin and part-serrin, rounding them up with kicks and threatened swords. There was some argument over what to do with them. A young man, with bright blue eyes like Aisha's, shoved at a Stamentaast who kicked his mother. The Stamentaast ran him through with a sword. The mother wailed and screamed as he collapsed.

Again, Bergen dragged Sasha past. She was crying. Stamentaast saw, but the street was full of smoke, and some were holding their own handkerchiefs over their mouths. Further ahead were wagons, empty now, driven rattling over the cobbles by more Stamentaast. Soon they would be full, no doubt. Where would they take the serrin they caught? Where was Tershin?

And then, "Rhillian and Aisha," Sasha muttered. "Bergen, we have to see to them."

"Likely they're back at the temple already," Bergen replied, finally letting go of her arm.

Sasha took a right turn. Bergen followed, striding fast. She broke into a run on a stretch of empty street, then walked again as more Stamentaast appeared, running from doorway to doorway, checking on residences. There was a body on the cobblestones, lifeless in a pool of blood. An old serrin lady, Sasha saw as they passed, collapsed on her walking cane.

A little further on, two Stamentaast were driving a pair of serrin women up the street with kicks and yells. Sasha found her course shifting into their path.

"Sasha, no!"

She ignored Bergen. The Stamentaast watched her approach with suspicion. One held up his sword as she came near, pointed out to her chest, and barked at her in Ilduuri. His stance was awful.

Sasha grabbed his wrist on the weak side, disabling any fast swing, and drove her knife through his neck. His comrade swung at her as Sasha ducked back, but Bergen tackled him from the side, then set about with his own knife until the other stopped moving.

"Run!" Sasha hissed at the two women. "Up the side streets, find a place to hide!" They did, and she grabbed the man she'd stabbed under the armpits, and struggled to haul him into an alley mouth. He wasn't dead yet, despite the blood that spurted, but he wasn't about to start shouting for help either. Bergen dumped the other body, and they continued as before.

Sasha felt better now. Calmer. She saw further horrors, yet had no more tears. The emotion came from helplessness. If she could fight, she was calmer. She would need to be calm, to get through this. It seemed there was a lot more fighting to be done here than she'd suspected.

She followed the street to where she'd left Rhillian and Aisha, a large building facing onto a city square. The square was swarming with Stamentaast, and there were wagons loaded with prisoners. Sasha stepped against the cover of a wall and leaned there with Bergen, watching. Serrin were being forced toward a new group of wagons, hands bound behind them. Astride a horse, Sasha saw a man directing Stamentaast, with a sword strapped diagonally to his back. Nasi-Keth.

"Dear spirits," she muttered.

Bergen saw where she was looking. "They forget everything," he said. "They forget who made the Nasi-Keth." Sasha did not understand how that institution could turn on the people who had inspired its creation. And then on second thought, perhaps she did.

"Loyal to blood, not to reason," she murmured to herself in Lenay. It was something Kessligh had said to her once, about the difference between human and serrin. "They serve the primacy of Ilduur, and always have."

Then she saw Aisha. Clearly it was her, hands bound, climbing with difficulty into a wagon, amidst the other serrin.

"Oh, no." Sasha felt cold dread to see her. Where were the wagons bound for next? Bergen also saw, and muttered a curse. "Can you see Rhillian?"

They stood and watched as the wagons were filled, but could not see any tall, white-haired woman amidst the prisoners. Sasha did not know whether to be relieved or terrified.

"We have to find out where they're taking these wagons," she said. "With any luck they're deporting serrin to Saalshen. If not, they'll just dig a mass grave and kill them all."

"Why?" Bergen asked tersely. "Why do the Remischtuul do this now?"

"Fear. Something's afoot—they fear agitation from the serrin, possibly to make the Steel move against the Remischtuul. They cannot strike against the Steel, so they strike against the serrin instead. They'll purge all Ilduur of serrin if they can."

Some Ilduuris had been waiting two centuries for the chance, she was quite sure.

Rhillian hid. She lay atop the roof tiles and peered down on the courtyard. Wagons were rattling away, driven by green-vested Stamentaast, loaded with serrin. This was a predominantly serrin neighbourhood, made so not by the insular nature of Ilduuri serrin, but by the unwillingness of many Andal residents to sell property to serrin elsewhere.

This house belonged to the Rontii family, prominent amongst Ilduuri serrin for their wealth and charity. Moneylenders, of course, with friendly ties to the priesthood, and no small influence in the Remischtuul itself. But not enough to prevent this. Across the rooftops of Andal, fires were burning, the crackle of flames rising with cries and screams into the darkening evening.

Rhillian watched the wagons leave, noted their direction, and guessed from what she'd learned of Andal's roads the way they would take out of the city. And where then, she did not know. The possibilities chilled her. Aisha had been downstairs when the Stamentaast came, talking with the servants, who knew the city from their own unique perspective. There'd been children downstairs, too. Rhillian watched the wagon holding Aisha rattle away, and thought that the presence of children may have saved Aisha's life—she'd not have fought, armed only with a knife, if there were children to be caught in the fighting.

Something hit the roof tiles alongside where she lay, and Rhillian spun. A coin, perhaps? Her eyes found the attic window of the adjoining house. It was open, and two residents within were beckoning to her, fearfully. Both were human—a man and woman, perhaps husband and wife. The rooftop was close, and she could jump it easily. They were offering her shelter, she realised, knowing she was serrin. Many Andal humans did live in this serrin quarter, some even by choice. These were neighbours, and friends.

Rhillian waved, and put a hand to her heart in thanks. But instead of moving toward that window, she moved away, keeping low as she'd learned how in many nighttime ventures in Petrodor, so that her silhouette did not show against the rooftops. The slope of roofs in Andal was alarming, so that winter snow would slide instead of piling. At the edge she turned, took a grip of the roof edge, put her legs over, and slid until her boots found the balcony railing from which she'd climbed up. From there it was a similar drop to the next balcony, and then the next. She'd abandoned her dress on the rooftop, for the comfort of pants underneath. She wondered if Aisha were now under greater suspicion for having done the same.

She dropped from the last balcony to the narrow alley between buildings, and instinctively melted into the shadow of a wall. She crept to the mouth of a little courtyard, where the buildings crowded close. Footsteps came hustling, and she pressed to one wall, but it was servants who came past, human women clasping serrin children in their arms, and whispering at them to be silent. They moved up the alley, then fumbled for keys at a doorway. The door opened anyway, and they were ushered inside. Rhillian realised it was the same house from which her own offer of shelter had come.

Then came more footsteps. These moved less quickly, as though uncertain of their surroundings. Rhillian crouched in the shadow of the low balcony as two Stamentaast came past, swords out and searching for whomever had come this way.

Rhillian stepped behind the second and calmly cut his throat. The first heard the sword fall from the dying man's hand. He spun, and Rhillian threw her knife, hard to miss at this range. It hit him in the neck, and she picked up the fallen sword and ran him through to be sure. No armour, she noted with satisfaction as he died. She pulled the blade free, recovered her knife and faded into the dark.

The alley opened onto a road, where Stamentaast gathered in the aftermath of their successful raid. A group stood here, to guard this side of the Rontiis' grand house. Soon a Nasi-Keth man came, trotting on a horse. He dismounted and joined their conversation—Rhillian caught only snatches, her Ilduuri was barely average, and these men had a regional accent.

After a short conversation, the Nasi-Keth came directly toward the mouth of her alley. Rhillian faded back, and let the darkness claim her. The man undid his pants and began to relieve himself. He had barely finished when he received the shock of his life, to look up in the gloom and find a pair of deadly emerald eyes staring back at him.

He died as the borrowed sword ran him through, and Rhillian took the serrin blade from over his shoulder as he fell. Its balance was light and pleasant. Six Stamentaast turned in astonishment as she came at them from the alley. Two died immediately. Two more managed at least a parry before the whistling angled blade cost them limbs and lives. The fifth managed an attack, the arc of which Rhillian stepped inside and cut through. The sixth simply stared, frozen in terror.

"*Pial'a shom est*," she explained to him, in her most eloquent Saalsi form. *You should not have.* Then she killed him.

It all happened very fast and rather quietly, so that the Nasi-Keth's horse seemed more puzzled than alarmed. Rhillian stroked his nose, then mounted swiftly and set off in pursuit of where she thought the wagons were heading.

Sixteen

Sasha and Bergen arrived back at Father Belgride's temple via the rear planking and found Yasmyn waiting impatiently by the pier.

"What's going on?" she demanded. "Where have you been and how bad is it?"

"What do you think's going on?" Sasha muttered, walking past her to the rear doors. "They're rounding up all the serrin. They have Aisha for certain, I don't know about Rhillian."

She emerged into the rear-quarters dining hall and found it filled with serrin. These were no *talmaad* warriors, they were regular Ilduuri, some having ancestry in these lands for two hundred years. They sat on blankets against walls, or on tables in the absence of enough chairs, or stood in huddled groups and talked, their voices hushed as though frightened that men beyond the walls would hear them. They were of all ages, including many children. Some appeared barely more than quarter-serrin, and a few entirely human . . . mixed families, Sasha thought, and doubted the Stamentaast would have more mercy on the humans who wedded serrin than the serrin themselves. If she were to wed Errollyn, this would be her. And their children.

"Father Belgride has been taking them in," Yasmyn explained. "They all come here, and some priests have been taking a cart around. Stamentaast will not search the cart if the priest gives his word there is nothing to find. Priests are carrying wagonloads of serrin here, and lying to Stamentaast. Another priest takes a boat along the lakeshore."

"And these aren't the only wretched wanderers the priests are taking in," came a new voice. Sasha looked and found Daish, upright and walking toward them. She stared in astonishment, then embraced him with relief, remembering at the last to be careful of his ribs.

"You got better!" she observed, as Bergen repeated the embrace.

"The Steel border guards took good care of me, and those medicines were amazing," said Daish. He looked remarkably healthy, Sasha thought, with the colour back in his cheeks. "A few of them were coming this way and offered to hide me amongst them, clothed like them. And Bergen, come, look who else has returned."

He led them from the dining hall, down narrow stone passages past the kitchen and washrooms, to the stables. Before one of the stalls he stopped, and gestured. There stood a big cavalry horse, munching on fodder.

"Tanner!" the big Enoran exclaimed, and ran to his mount. "How in the worlds . . . ?"

"Two days after you left," said Daish, "I awoke in my chamber in the Steel guardhouse, and I was feeling much better. No sooner had I thought it than a soldier knocked on the door and said that I should come down to the stables. Tanner was there—they'd found him outside the walls on the other side of the canyon. He must have recovered after he collapsed, gone back to the river as Sasha said he would, then followed when he was stronger. The retreating Kazeri would have gone straight past him."

"Always a chance," said Sasha, with renewed determination. "Never count a fighter out." She turned to Bergen. "We have to go after Aisha and those other serrin. That's Family Rontii, the Remischtuul's just concluded they're to be removed, and I doubt they'll just cart them to Saalshen."

"I'll go," said Daish and Yasmyn simultaneously. Daish had been told about Aisha, Sasha saw. He looked determined.

"Someone should stay and defend the temple," said Bergen.

As though to echo his point, Sasha heard a hammering from beyond the stable doors. She strode that way, down the passage that adjoined the stables to the temple. Father Belgride leaned upon his main doors, lit by wall lamps, shouting through the grille at a man outside. With a final yell, he slammed the steel plate over the grille, and noticed Sasha.

"Stamentaast," he said grimly. "They say I have serrin inside. They threaten to storm the temple."

"Would they?" Sasha asked disbelievingly.

"I don't know," said Belgride, rubbing his beard. "I say the gods will curse them if they come in here with swords. But I don't know. Maybe."

"That's it," Sasha muttered, striding for her chambers. "I'm tired of my enemies and this dress making common cause against me. I'm getting changed."

"I will have no fighting in my temple!" Belgride called after her, warningly.

"Tell that to them!" Sasha retorted over her shoulder.

She was fighting the uncooperative dress over her head when Yasmyn hammered on her door. "Sasha, there's a man at the rear wants to talk to you!"

Sasha pulled on jacket, bandoleer, and sword, and strode through the stone halls, now filled with many bewildered and frightened serrin families. A man of mixed-race appearance stopped her.

"This is your fault!" he accused her in Saalsi. "The Stamentaast spoke of traitors, spies, and infiltrators—they were looking for you! You and your friends, someone tipped them off to your presence and . . ."

"Someone like you, probably," Sasha said coldly. "Someone who will not fight. Someone who weasels up to tyrants in hope of gratitude."

"Don't you pretend that you're doing this for us!" the man snarled. "You have no love for Ilduur or Ilduuri, you bring fire and death down on our heads for the sake of your precious foreign war and foreign friends!"

"You sound just like the Remischtuul," Sasha said incredulously. "Why don't you go and join them, if you have such a meeting of the minds? I'm sure you'll enjoy their company far more than mine and my foreign friends," if you don't mind them killing your children and raping your women."

The man grabbed her in fury. Sasha punched him in the face, and he fell. About her, the crowd recoiled in fear and shock. Sasha glared at them, readjusting her jacket where the man had grabbed her, and stepped over him on her way to the rear warehouse.

"Who's the tyrant now!" someone shouted after her.

"If you don't like it," Sasha yelled over her shoulder, "go outside and play with the Stamentaast!"

At the rear warehouse, she met Yasmyn on the point of entering to check on the commotion. "Trouble?" she asked.

"No," said Sasha. "Sheep are never trouble, that's why they're sheep."

In the dim light of a lantern, by the rear entrance from the lakeside pier, stood Arken Haast. He wore dark clothes, and an Ilduuri Steel-sized sword through his belt. He talked animatedly with Bergen, leaning against sacks of grain. Sasha thought he must have rowed here, across the lake.

"My father would not tell me," he said to Sasha. "Until the Stamentaast attacked, that is. The Stamentaast sent messengers to the Shuen Vaal quarter to tell us to remain in our houses, and that anyone found sheltering serrin would be punished. They say all serrin are collaborators with foreign forces. My father was furious—I think he went and threatened some of his Remischtuul colleagues to tell him where the Meraini are. Now he says they're in the Altene. It's a big old feudal castle atop Dirdaan Mountain, it used to belong to Family Altene before Maldereld came, back in feudal times. Now it's a residence for Remischtuul masters."

"Defences?" Sasha asked.

Arken's eyes narrowed at her. "You mean to attack it?"

"Depends on what you tell me its defences are. The Stamentaast are all tied up here. The Steel are confined to barracks, or on home leave like you. Who else is there?"

"The guilds are powerful. The Remischtuul is made up of guildmasters, with many allies in the various guilds. They make a lot of work at the residences, servants, guards, grounds and kitchen staff, that sort of thing."

"And even more now with Meraini talons paying for it," Bergen observed.

"So how many defending this Altene residence?" Sasha pressed.

"The Altene," Arken corrected. "That's what it's called. Perhaps two hundred."

Sasha's eyebrows raised. "That's a lot of defence for a united people at peace with themselves."

Arken snorted. "They're scared of the Steel, and they're scared of Saalshen. The *talmaad* don't always fight fair, and they can infiltrate Ilduur's high roads by night, and attack from the shadows."

Sasha nodded. "I saw plenty of that in Petrodor. But I learned how to do it too. And unlike the *talmaad*, I now know where to attack. Can you gather some men, without raising an alarm? Trustworthy men?" Arken looked uncertain. "What's the problem?"

"The Altene is a very hard target," said Arken. "There is only one road, and high cliffs surrounding."

"That means we have them trapped," Sasha retorted. "What *really* troubles you?"

"What if we succeed? What then?"

"We expose the Remischtuul for the frauds and liars they are. We show that they don't truly believe in Ilduuri independence, that they're prostituting Ilduur to the Meraini for fear of fighting a war they aren't sure they can win."

"Destroy the Remischtuul?"

Sasha shrugged. "Your decision, not mine. Expose them, for certain. Let the Ilduuri people decide."

"The Ilduuri people will not want this war regardless of what happens to the Remischtuul," Arken said. "I warn you, do not hope to win the love of the people for your cause, you won't get it."

Sasha folded her arms. She wasn't here to make friends. Arken was wondering where this would lead, and where she would lead them. Or if he was crazy to help her to take charge of anything. She was a foreigner, as the Remischtuul charged, and had foreign interests foremost in her heart. But if the Steel's leadership was purged, and none other amongst their ranks here in Andal could motivate them . . .

"Look," she said, "there are costs to every action. I can't promise that you'll like the outcome of this action. I can't promise that all will end well for Ilduur. I have no idea what will happen should the Remischtuul be exposed. I have no idea what will happen should the Steel march away to war. Quite possibly nothing good, for the odds are not with us. All any of us can do is what we are certain is right. And we can hope that if there is any foundation that makes a nation and a people worthy of a decent future, it is that its leaders are men and women who do the right thing when it needs to be done. I'm not naive enough to think that that is any guarantee of a happy future, but there are far worse foundations to build upon. And right now, it's all I have to offer you."

Arken considered her for a moment. Then he nodded, curtly. "I'll gather some men. We must be plainclothed. We cannot move on the Altene in force and in Steel uniform before we have exposed them, or it will be us making the first move in civil war. That way lies ruin."

Sasha nodded. "I agree. But we'll need a way to get up the mountain, as high as possible, without being seen. Is it far?"

Arken shook his head. "Down the valley and turn right. Two days if on foot all the way, less if we have transport to the base of the trail."

Sasha blinked. "There's a trail? You said there was only one road?"

"I wanted to see that you were serious," Arken said with a faint smile. "It seems that you are."

"Lad," said Bergen, "you have no idea."

There were no Stamentaast away from the town centre, and Rhillian rode through the ramshackle outskirts of Andal at a trot. She headed for the southern valley slope, where she thought she could gain a vantage across the southern edge of the city, and see a line of wagons along one of the valley roads. There was a full moon, and the east–west orientation of the valley meant that there were only two directions the wagons could go.

Certainly they were headed out of the city. If the Stamentaast were intending what she thought they were, they could not do it in the city, surrounded by witnesses and with no place to dispose of the bodies.

Andal's buildings ended, and Rhillian rode upslope amidst the paddocks of outskirt farms. Upon a hillock, she stopped. Probably the column would come this way, to the east, as westward along the lakeside was narrow, with fewer options. One could not dispose of many bodies in Lake Andal. Bodies floated, and the lakeshore was well populated. The Remischtuul could not be so sanguine of the goodwill of the Ilduuri population as to let the bodies of murdered serrin come bobbing along the lake in their hundreds over the next few days.

Rhillian could see small roads emerging from the city, winding their way up and along the southern slope. There was not even a single traveller out in the night. The few fires in the city had not spread, small orange glares and climbing trails of smoke, most of them clustered together in the tight serrin neighbourhoods.

She looked away from the lake, to the east, where the valley forked in two. One fork went northeast, and that way she could glimpse a town about the inflowing Andal River. That was Andal Garrison, home of the Ilduuri Steel. It would be barely an hour's march, once mobilised. But the road looked clear, with no glint of massed armour beneath the glare of the moon. Beyond the garrison, Aaldenmoot rose like a white tooth in the pale night sky, highest of the ragged northern range.

Then she saw it. A column of wagons, emerging from trees on the southern outskirts. A larger column than she had seen at the Rontiis' House—possibly it had detoured to add more prisoners. Rhillian watched it come, inching its way upslope, now disappearing behind a fold. She would not despair. She did not know what one serrin alone could do.

The wagons reappeared, closer now. The road would pass above her on the slope, she realised. No more than a hundred paces, but there were trees here, and she would not be seen. Between herself and that road was a small park, and a pillar monument to the fallen heroes of the Ilduuri Steel, crossed swords emblazoned on its side. Rhillian wondered if the Stamentaast would appreciate the irony.

Soon the wagons did pass, a rattle of wheels and hooves. When they were far enough ahead, she followed. She held to the lower road for a while, past grand houses, gates locked and window shutters firmly fastened. This way, the column would progress along the eastern valley fork, its land rising all the time, up into the eastern ranges. Across those lay Saalshen.

She spurred the horse up a grassy hillside onto the higher road, then found another way to climb up to a trail higher still. Houses here were fewer, replaced by farmers' shacks and pens for sheep or cattle. Looking down from her high trail, Rhillian could see the entire column—twelve wagons, each crowded with perhaps twenty prisoners; some guards riding on the wagons, others riding horses alongside.

As the column neared the trees, she thought she glimpsed movement behind a farmhouse just upslope of the road. Something glinted in the moonlight, like steel. Her trail began a bend where she lost sight of the column, and she pressed her horse to a reluctant canter. Out of sight, she heard yells from the column. Then screams.

Finally she reached a part of the trail that afforded a good view. The wagons were stopped, one now careening down the hillside, scattering bodies off the back, others pulled aside, men leaping from the back. Horsemen from the column were galloping uphill, skirting the ambush point, which seemed to be focused upon the farmhouse. Rhillian kicked her horse's flanks, and galloped on the diagonal down the grassy hillside, fighting to control the protesting animal.

As she drew closer, she could see archers firing from the farmhouse and from amongst the trees. Dead Stamentaast were lying on the road, others sheltering behind their wagons, others still trying to grasp control of the wagons and turn them about . . . but rutted roads, precision arrow fire, and the confusion of jammed and now colliding wagons made that difficult.

The horsemen flanking the farmhouse were now directly uphill of it, just barely out of range of an upward-firing archer. Instead of charging, they were debating. The archers must be serrin, Rhillian thought, to be attacking so successfully by night. The horsemen were debating whether it was worth charging into that arrowfire, knowing its deadliness.

They were still debating when Rhillian came down on them. They looked about in confusion, assuming first that a horseman must be friendly, then seeing too late that she was neither man, nor Stamentaast. They broke, and Rhillian missed the swing on her left, but connected well to her right, and that man fell from the saddle. Rhillian dodged another, then wheeled while looking over her shoulder—there were five left, all of them coming about to chase her. She took off downslope, toward the farmhouse, keeping herself out of the line of fire. Sure enough, at half range, arrows sped uphill. Behind, a horse stumbled. Riders abandoned their pursuit, one making the mistake of halting completely. An arrow took him through the chest, and the others galloped off, zigzagging madly.

More horses pursued, but these were ridden by bow-wielding serrin. They fired at the fleeing horsemen. Another fell. And that, Rhillian knew, would be that. None of those riders would survive.

She rode down past the farmhouse to see if she could help at the column, but it was all over. The only ones now living were serrin; those with weapons who had set the ambush were helping prisoners from the wagons, cutting their bonds and tending to wounds. Downslope, some prisoners had fallen from the back of wagons trying to flee, and some seemed hurt. There was very little talking, no wailing or sobbing, just some relieved, quiet tears and murmured conversation. Serrin in groups. Rhillian could feel the pull, the force that had led her up this valley to follow the wagons, and now drew her in amongst her people as they needed her.

A familiar figure approached, longish hair and tall, with a bow in hand. Arendelle. Rhillian dismounted and embraced him.

"Who are these *talmaad*?" Rhillian asked him, as men and women with swords and bows hustled about.

"They came across the eastern border, weeks ago," said Arendelle. "The border is weak, folks there do not mind serrin, and they know the back trails. They came across the peaks to Andal, moving by night. Along the high trails."

"It was *vel'ehil*?"

Arendelle nodded. Serrin did not talk about it much with humans. Sasha had encountered it before, when Errollyn and Aisha had travelled to Lenayin to assist in the rebellion. Rhillian recalled her argument with Errollyn and Aisha then, though it had been Tassi who had invoked *vel'ehil*.

No serrin truly understood it. Some said it was the sight of the future, but often those who invoked it did not find what they expected to see. Errollyn and Aisha had ridden to Lenayin in the certainty of some troubles, and had arrived in time to join the rebellion led by Sasha. They had only known that some trouble was brewing that could benefit from serrin insight.

Some serrin supposed it might be what the humans called "magic." Errollyn believed that it was merely a product of the serrin mind, an instinct for approximation, that if enough information was put in, possible outcomes would emerge. Stationed in Petrodor, he and Aisha had followed all information from Lenayin studiously, and with concern. A human might have guessed, from that information, that trouble was brewing. But that supposition, serrin felt as emotion, as the *vel'ennar*, like a tide.

Rhillian found Aisha where she knew she would—helping others, with little concern for her own cuts and scrapes. Rhillian embraced her with relief, then left her to her work and headed for the farmhouse.

Kiel was there. *Talmaad* surrounded him, gathered about a central table. A single lamp cast enough light for gathered serrin to read a map spread across the table. They talked of Andal and its neighbourhoods and made plans in dialect, known for precision and numbers.

Kiel was leading the discussion. Rhillian knew she should join them, but something made her pause. The farmhouse was neat and simple. This main room was combined with a kitchen, little jars in racks, and big jars for flour, and rolling pins for bread to be baked in the big, open oven.

Yet the little space seemed somehow wrong. A chair was poorly aligned. There by a kitchen bench a pot was broken, spilled grain and pottery shards swept into a corner. The frame of a doorway was marked by a deep sword cut. On the floor, a spattering of blood. There had been a fight here. But against whom? Where were the farmhouse's occupants? The place looked lived in, but Kiel had commandeered it for ambush against the wagon column. What had he done to the family that lived here?

One door adjoining the main room was shut. Rhillian walked to it.

"Rhillian," Kiel called from behind. Rhillian stopped and looked over at him. Kiel smiled at her, faintly. "I am glad that you came."

Rhillian stared at him. For a moment, their eyes locked. Rhillian turned and opened the door. It was dark within, and it took a moment for her eyes to make out the shapes. A bed. Some drawers. A small table, upon which rested an oil lamp. Upon the floor, between beds and table, were tangled bodies. Rhillian counted five. An old man. A younger man and woman. Two children. All human.

Rhillian stood in the doorway for a long moment, taking deep breaths. In the group about the table, no one spoke.

Then Rhillian turned. She looked at Kiel. Kiel made a small shrug. "The house was perfectly situated for ambush," he said. "We needed it."

Rhillian just stared. From the expressions of many about the table, it seemed that humans were not the only ones to find her eyes intimidating.

"There was a shortage of rope for bonds," one explained, "and a shortage of time. The column approached even as we took the house. One human escaping to alert them and the ambush may have failed, and all our Ilduuri comrades lost."

"Some of Saalshen's Ilduuri comrades are human," Rhillian said quietly. "Humans in Andal were risking their own lives to shelter serrin children when these prisoners were taken. I saw it—they offered to shelter me, too. How do you know that these would not have done the same?"

"We have saved perhaps two hundred lives here," Kiel said calmly. "If you join us now, we will save more."

"Kiel," Rhillian said slowly, to make certain he understood the gravity of this moment. "Children."

There was a silence. "It was necessary," said Kiel, unperturbed. "The Ilduuri have abandoned us, and we owe them nothing."

"And now what do you plan? To attack Andal directly? And how many friends will that gain Saalshen, now when we need Ilduuri friendship more than ever?"

"You think me unsubtle. We are stripping Stamentaast uniforms from the men outside. We have captured some others. The Stamentaast are unpopular amongst the Ilduuri Steel, yet the Stamentaast know this, and do not dare inflict any atrocity against the Steel directly.

"We will dress the men amongst us as Stamentaast. All here speak fluent Ilduuri, and in the night can pass for Ilduuri men if well disguised. We will head to the steelwrights' district, where there are many Steel-dependent families, and we will inflict such damage as the Ilduuri Steel cannot ignore. The

Steel will take revenge against the Stamentaast, thinking they are responsible, as they are responsible for so much else on this night. And with the Steel on the rampage, and the Remischtuul's attack dogs dismembered, there will be nothing to stop the Steel from declaring themselves the new rulers of Ilduur, and marching to the war as is their preference."

"Damage." Rhillian felt cold. "What damage?"

"Damage that will invoke a fitting and vengeful reply."

Rhillian turned, and looked at the atrocity in the bedchamber behind. "You mean to kill more families tonight. Families of our friends, the Ilduuri Steel."

Kiel shrugged. "If that is what it takes to motivate them onto our side, it is but a small price to pay. We speak of the survival of Saalshen, Rhillian. Many will die to achieve it, should it be achieved. When all is done, these few lives will seem like a small drop in a very large bucket."

Sasha had warned her that Kiel would come to this one day. Errollyn had, too. The *talmaad* about him seemed to share in his conviction, sombre yet determined. It was the *vel'ennar* once more, and Kiel's own *ra'shi*. He had status with them, in that way that serrin would choose leaders from their midst, by the demonstration of logic and argument. Kiel had found them, and now swayed them to his side. When serrin followed, they followed like the tide. In crisis, it could be a powerful strength. Yet now, it led them to this.

"Now is not the time for weakness," Kiel insisted. "The serrinim must be strong, and strong together. You have accumulated great *ra'shi* amongst the people, Rhillian. We would all follow you. Will you lead us?"

Seventeen

Rhillian stood by the roadside and watched as the rescued serrin gathered once more on the captured wagons and were driven into the forest of the high valley. Several amongst them who could fight had stayed, *talmaad* or former *talmaad*. The men amongst them now donned light armour and green vests, captured Stamentaast uniform, and tested the weight of unfamiliar Ilduuri swords. Steel helms with brow ridges and nose guards covered their hair. Likely in the dark and confusion that would follow, none of those attacked would recognise them for serrin. Or rather, none who did recognise them would live.

The moon now sank toward the western mountains, bathing snowy flanks in silver light. Beneath the glare, upslope of the farmhouse, a small figure emerged from the forest tree line, walking fast, shoulders hunched. Rhillian walked to meet her halfway. On the farmhouse verandah, serrin dressed as Stamentaast watched her go in silent contemplation.

Aisha was upset. She hugged her arms to herself as she walked, hiding the rope burns on her wrists. Her face was swollen on one side from the rough treatment of Stamentaast who had now paid with their lives. But that was not the cause of Aisha's emotion.

"It's not right," she muttered, blue eyes shimmering with tears.

"No," said Rhillian.

"They deserve a proper grave."

"Yes."

They walked back to the farmhouse. Aisha and Rhillian had helped to dig the graves of the farmhouse family, a hundred strides into the woods. Aisha had wanted a grave behind the house, but Kiel and others insisted that if this deception was to work, events here should be hidden, for some time at least.

"They need not have died at all," Aisha insisted, her voice quavering.

"No," Rhillian agreed, eyeing the commotion about the farmhouse ahead. The fake Stamentaast would ride and march into town shortly, to the steelwrights' district, and would commit more such crimes in the name of saving Saalshen.

"You can stop it," said Aisha. "You have the most *ra'shi* of all of us in these matters."

"No," said Rhillian, shaking her head. "Can you not feel it?" Aisha said nothing, walking head down. "The tide flows to Kiel. It is his tide that rules here, that drew these *talmaad* across the border from Saalshen. I make my displeasure clear, yet they do not care."

The moon made stark shadows on the grass before them as they walked. "Errollyn has always said the tide of *vel'ennar* will one day make us like the very worst of humanity," Aisha said quietly. "It unites only its own kind, and excludes the rest. Soon any who are not within the *vel'ennar* shall be the enemy. I feel the *vel'ennar* myself, but I no longer recognise my own people."

Rhillian nodded. She could feel it too, a pull so powerful it bathed the night like the moon. She saw serrin, and she yearned to be with them, to join them, to serve their needs. Most here tonight would follow Kiel, and by the yearnings of *vel'ennar*, so should she. And yet there was revulsion. Kiel would lead them to a monstrous place, a place that serrin had not been since millennia past. Tonight, did she serve the instinct that defined the serrinim, and made them separate from humanity? Or must she ignore it, to serve the serrin themselves? And did she have the right to inflict her own will upon her people, who wished to move another way? Serrin moved collectively, not alone, and no appointed serrin leader would defy the majority will of her own people . . . the *vel'ennar* itself ensured that she could not. Here, she could feel it pulling her toward Andal, while she herself struggled to hold her feet, and fight another direction, one lone serrin against the raging flood.

Serrin in Stamentaast uniform now gathered before the farmhouse. They assembled about Kiel, listening to his final instruction. Up the road that the wagons had followed, horsemen came galloping. They were the same who had set off in pursuit of the escaping Stamentaast Rhillian had fought. And now, they seemed to have caught another.

Between them was a human rider, yet he was not dressed as Stamentaast. Rhillian frowned, seeing that familiar position in the saddle.

"Daish!" she exclaimed.

Aisha ran to the road, Rhillian close behind. But the riders did not stop before Aisha, and continued off the road and upslope to Kiel and the gathered serrin. There they dismounted, Aisha scrambling to catch up.

"Hey!" she shouted at them, as two *talmaad* escorted Daish roughly from his horse. Daish looked to Aisha, relieved to see her yet now alarmed as his serrin guard dragged him toward Kiel, his weapons removed, one *talmaad* holding each arm.

"He's with me," Rhillian declared, stepping forward, sensing something bad. The ground itself seemed to tilt, and it was not the sloping hillside that made it feel so.

"And with me," Kiel agreed mildly. "Hello, Daish. You got better, I see."

"I did," Daish said breathlessly. "I said I'd follow. Why are you all dressed as Stamentaast?"

"A secret," said Kiel. "We're about to do something no human can know of."

"Hey!" Aisha yelled, arriving amongst them at a run. In her anger and confusion, her human half seemed dominant for the first time since Rhillian had known her. "This is my friend damn you, you don't ride past me!"

She embraced the young man, and Daish would have replied in kind, but a *talmaad* held each arm still. Aisha scowled at the guards and grabbed to remove one's grip. The other shoved her away, hard.

"He said he was looking for Aisha," that serrin said. "To rescue her, and the others."

"That's right," Daish agreed, indignantly. "Sasha came back to the temple, she said what had happened, and I thought I had to come and . . ."

"And where is Sasha now?" asked Kiel.

"Gone," said Daish, warily. Hiding something, it was obvious. Not knowing if Kiel was the right person to share anything with right now.

"Ah," said Kiel, hooking his thumbs into his belt as he strolled a little closer. "So much does Sasha care for her friends, and for the serrin."

"So little reason some of us give her," Rhillian said coldly.

"She's doing important things!" Daish retorted to Kiel. "She wanted to come but this couldn't wait."

"And neither can we. No human can know." Kiel turned, as though to consult the half-circle of serrin faces behind him. The men in helms, the women unhelmed, unable to participate lest their build give them away.

"Fight!" Rhillian wished at them, furiously. But their expressions showed little of that. Their eyes were only for Kiel, calm and trusting. The tide led to him, and so he would lead them. *Ra'shi* and *vel'ennar* combined, flowing together to make a mighty torrent. Rhillian felt as though her balance would give way. She squeezed her eyes shut, breathing hard, trying to fight it.

"I'm sorry, Daish," said Kiel, turning and drawing his blade. "I do regret this. But it is trust that the serrinim cannot afford to place upon a human right now. When even some of our own number are wavering in their resolve . . ." and he glanced at Rhillian, ". . . then how can we trust one of *you*?"

Daish stared at him, dumbfounded. A blade came out in reply. Aisha's.

"No," she said, her cheeks tear-streaked, staring at Kiel past the edge of her blade. "No, you will not."

"Aisha," Kiel said sternly, his grey eyes narrowed. "You forget yourself. You are one of us, Aisha. Are you not?"

Aisha blinked. Her blade wavered. She struggled to hold her ground, as though the valley itself were shifting under her.

"Aisha," came a new voice, and now Arendelle was emerging from the surrounding serrin, green-vested and helmed like the other men. He approached her slowly. "Aisha, you must listen. Can you not feel it? Can you not feel the pull?"

Aisha struggled for breath. Her arms trembled. She tried not to look at Arendelle as the tall man approached.

"Aisha, his knowledge risks our plan. We cannot trust one outside the vel'ennar, Aisha, he is not bound to us as you are. You know this. You know that the survival of our people comes first."

Arendelle's hand closed on Aisha's wrist. Aisha was crying. She could not look at Daish. She could not move her blade. She knew how this would end, and now the horror of her own helplessness was reducing her to tears.

"You cannot use that blade against us, Aisha," Arendelle murmured in her ear, leading her slowly aside. "No serrin ever has, not in two thousand years. You have human blood in your veins, yet you are one of us. Come and join us, Aisha. Do not look back."

Behind her, the talmaad kicked the back of Daish's knees and made him kneel. Daish struggled, but he was too weak still from his injuries to do anything against his strong guards. Kiel approached, blade drawn, and stood to one side. When Daish's head was down in the correct position, Kiel's blade raised high in the moonlight.

A blade whistled. Kiel's sword did not. He dropped it midstroke and clutched at his throat. There his hands closed on the hilt of a knife. Blood flowed thick and fast. His grey eyes looked up, with blank astonishment. Rhillian stood not ten paces away, hand extended in the expert release of a marksman. Kiel saw, and did not comprehend, for what he saw was impossible. He fell with a puzzled look, and sprawled on the grass.

Arendelle charged, blade whipping clear. Perhaps he hesitated, as the fractured vel'ennar reasserted itself in one final gasp, and reminded him that it was a serrin at whom he swung. Or perhaps it made no difference now. Steel clashed on steel, once fast, then again with a slide of counterstrike footing, then a final ripping cut. Arendelle hit limply and slid downslope, blood staining the grass a moonlit, silvery red.

Rhillian held that final killing pose, low on one knee, bloodied blade extended. The serrin holding Daish backed away, eyes wide with horror. A hundred serrin faces stared at her, with all the disbelief and shock of a people who had just seen their worst collective nightmare come to life before their eyes. A hundred pairs of hands itched to reach for blades, and fight back against the one who had killed two of their very own. And yet the one who had killed them, impossibly, unbelievably, was also of the serrinim.

Rhillian stood slowly, and cricked her neck. Her sword arm circled, then came about to find a comfortable ready stance. Her emerald eyes blazed at them all, bright like the moon and cold as death.

"So," she said to her people. "Who is next?"

Sasha and Yasmyn faced off beside a stream in a grove of trees. In each of their hands was a long stick, scavenged from the surrounding woods. Sasha never sparred with real blades. She trained as she fought, and the way she fought, people died.

Bergen watched nearby, and waited for Arken's men to arrive. Daish had remained in Father Belgride's temple, not in physical shape to attempt climbing a mountain. Sasha did not have much faith that that would stop him trying to find Aisha, however.

Yasmyn had talent, and applied herself with an intensity like the burning sun. Sasha kept it simple, and built on Yasmyn's knowledge of knife fighting, which gave her a foundation in stance, footwork, and simple combinations. Two-handed svaalverd, however, was rather more complex, and deadly. Yasmyn kept walking into combinations that Sasha could finish in her sleep, simply not seeing what lay beyond her immediate stroke. Talent meant nothing without experience, and if she encountered a half-decent swordsman in an even fight, svaalverd or not, Yasmyn was finished.

"Shields," Sasha said then, and presented her left forearm as though wearing a shield, holding her stick right-handed. "Horrible things. Most guardsmen in Ilduur, defending a fixed position, will use them."

"Useful things," Bergen countered, leaning against a tree with eyes on the road past the shore of Lake Andal. "I can crush your head with a shield strike alone."

"Horrible things because," Sasha continued, "if you let them, they can be intimidating. They interrupt natural swordwork, they can confuse fundamentals, take space from you. You treat them with contempt because that's how you beat them—with aggression. Once you start retreating, you've already conceded."

She showed Yasmyn how shields limited a fighter to a one-sided reach from the one shoulder, and how his opposite side became a refuge where a two-handed fighter could stand in range, but where the shieldsman could not reach.

"You have to be close," she told Yasmyn, demonstrating. "He'll try to crowd you with his shield, to take away your space, so that's not easy. But if you're close enough, and he swings, you step . . ."

"Underneath and to the side," said Yasmyn, seeing immediately. Now behind Sasha's shoulder, and with a clear strike to Sasha's exposed side.

"Exactly. The sword arm is the weak side, like the underside of a porcupine. Shieldsmen like to defend with the shield, they lose the art of defending with the blade, and since they can only really attack with the forehand across their body, that rotation takes their shield out of play, and if they miss, they're dead. Also, I don't care if he's as big as your brother Markan, a one-handed grip can never defend as strongly as a two-hander because the wrist folds like this, you see? A two-handed grip creates a cross brace, like a good builder making a cross brace for a temple roof. That's another reason shieldsmen can't defend with a blade against a two-hander."

Yasmyn's eyes gleamed as she understood, and practised the duck and slide across Sasha's sword arm several more times.

"Just don't let him hit you with the fucking shield," Sasha continued, demonstrating with the invisible shield, aiming for Yasmyn's head. "He'll go high, like this, but with his weight into it. . . ."

"If I go under it," Yasmyn decided, doing that, "he's defenceless."

"Yes. Cut him through the middle as you go." Yasmyn's stick slapped Sasha's stomach, and she spun out and away. "Remember, heavy weaponry is good for mass combat, not for single combat. Weapons are only as useful as the tactics they allow you to employ. A naked warrior with a spoon can defeat a knight in full armour if he has the tactics to exploit a weakness."

"Men coming," called Bergen. Sasha walked to his side and looked out through the trees. Along the road, a group of men approached on foot. They wore the clothes of regular Ilduuri, and seemed armed.

Sasha noticed Bergen looking down at her. "What?" she asked.

"I heard infantry friends describing that for real, from the receiving end." He jerked his head back toward where she'd been conducting the lessons with Yasmyn. "No wonder we lost so many."

"I heard infantry friends describing Steel shieldwork to me," Sasha replied. "They'd never seen such teamwork. No wonder *we* lost so many."

Bergen nodded slowly. Sasha clapped him on the arm and walked to the edge of the tree line to welcome Arken and his men.

She led them in amongst the trees for cover. She counted twenty-three; with her, Bergen and Yasmyn they would be twenty-six. Against two hundred? she wondered. If they got it right, they could do it with ten. If they got it wrong, a thousand would be insufficient.

"Two boats," Arken described their transport. "No Stamentaast on the water." They were a half-day's walk down the valley, near the opposite end of the long, thin Lake Andal. One of Father Belgride's priests had rowed their own transport back to the temple pier himself, after transporting them here overnight.

The men were all Ilduuri Steel, strong men, most young, a few as old as forty. Their swords were long in the Ilduuri style, and nearly half carried shields on their backs—smaller than Enoran and Rhodaani Steel shields, as Sasha had heard. Considering the heights the Ilduuris had to trek up and down, that was not surprising.

They looked at her now, some with suspicion, others with curiosity, a few more with the wide-eyed intensity of men confronted with a legend come to life. Some Ilduuri, it seemed, did pay attention to events beyond their borders. Particularly the Steel.

"Are you as good as the stories tell?" one asked her.

"That depends on what stories you've been listening to," said Sasha. "I was the uma to Kessligh Cronenverdt, who is assuredly as good as the stories you've heard. Lately I've become a better swordsman than him, though it did take a crossbow bolt through his leg to do it. He says I would have surpassed him anyway, but I suppose we'll never know."

Eyes turned to Bergen for confirmation. "She's easily the best swordsman I've ever seen," said Bergen. "No contest. When we were on opposite sides at Shero Valley, word spread through the lines that she'd commanded Isfayen cavalry to break our flanking lines and destroy a contingent of our artillery. That has rarely happened in all the history of the Enoran Steel. So, yes, she can command, too."

"Who is senior here?" Sasha asked them.

Men nodded at Arken. "He's formation sergeant," said one. Sasha was slightly surprised that the older men were not more highly ranked. Perhaps they were ex-Steel rather than active service. Or perhaps they were simply not command material. Promotion in the Rhodaani and Enoran Steel had been based on merit, not age.

"You have no higher ranks who could be trusted?" she pressed.

"A few we might trust," Arken admitted. "But at this moment, we agreed that *might* is not qualification enough."

"The Remischtuul have been playing games with officer promotions for years," another man said. "There aren't many officers we trust."

She could win these men. There had been a time when she might have felt unnerved at the prospect. But she had led enough men in battle to know that that time was past. They were good soldiers, as all Steel were good soldiers, but they lacked her experience. They had not seen the battles that lay beyond Ilduur's borders, and they did not know how that fight would go.

She did. She had been taught by the greatest. She knew mountains from her homeland, and lately cities and plains as well. She fought like serrin, but was herself very human. And now, these men who wished desperately to save their land from evils looked around for someone who knew all these things, and could lead, and found only her.

Twenty-three men of the Ilduuri Steel. Was it enough?

If they succeeded here, she reckoned, against vastly superior numbers, and brought down the corrupt and cowardly fools who led Ilduur to such ruin, then twenty-three would be more than enough. It did not take a lot of men to create a legend. The fewer of them there were, the greater would be their glory, a glory that could sweep the Ilduuri Steel all the way to Jahnd.

It was a steep hike from the valley floor, up a zigzagging trail through pine forest and across sheer slopes. A rocky cleft enfolded them as they continued to climb, legs aching on steep steps cut into rock, until they emerged onto a new world of height above the Andal Valley. Here ahead rose more mountains, mostly hidden from the valley floor, yet now dominating the sky. The Andal Valley had looked so large from down inside it—now on top of its flanking walls, Sasha could see how small a space it carved for humans amidst these great, soaring peaks.

"Pretty," Yasmyn remarked in good cheer, looking about as the trail levelled off to wind its way along a ridge of smaller trees. "Very much like Isfayen. Not as rugged, though." Yasmyn's legs were in no difficulty on the climb, and her mood seemed positively buoyant the higher they went. Perhaps she would prove useful after all.

The mountain ahead was Dirdaan, the old name of some pagan god no longer worshipped. At a clear spot on the trail, Arken paused and pointed halfway up the mountainside. There, perched upon a rocky shoulder, she could see a building, at too great a distance to make out any detail. How in the world anyone had managed to build it up there, she did not know. It looked impossible.

"The Altene," said Arken. Sasha repressed a laugh, and shook her head. "What's amusing?"

"We're going to try and attack *that* with twenty-six men," Sasha said cheerfully. "What's not amusing?" Men who overheard laughed, and kept walking.

"Odd place to command from," Yasmyn suggested as they resumed.

"Not a command," Sasha corrected. "Two days' journey from Andal in good weather won't allow it. It's a retreat, a place in which to hide and be safe, yet close enough to the centre of power for influence. A good place to store a hoard of Meraini talons and its keepers."

"You speak Lenay?" Arken asked in Saalsi, not understanding a word. Yasmyn, of course, spoke good Lenay and average Torovan, in addition to her native Telochi. That gave her two tongues in common with Sasha, half-a-tongue to meet with Bergen's broken Torovan, and none at all with the Ilduuri men, for whom Torovan was nearly as foreign as Lenay. Yasmyn had picked up a few phrases of Saalsi since she'd come to have serrin as friends, but Sasha had been struggling for fluency with that tongue for much of her life, and was still not entirely there.

"Yes," said Sasha. "How many of your men speak Saalsi?"

"Ten speak it well enough," said Arken. "The others all speak some—it's quite common amongst the Steel."

"Then we'll use it for our attack. I have no Ilduuri, and we've nothing else in common."

"And what about her?" asked Arken, looking at Yasmyn as the Isfayen girl walked ahead.

"She'll stay with me."

"Are you talking about me?" Yasmyn called back in Lenay as they walked.

"Aye," Sasha affirmed. "He wonders what you'll speak in the battle."

"Tell him the Isfayen need only the language of blood," said Yasmyn.

"And he's looking at your arse," Sasha added. Yasmyn threw a look over her shoulder and smirked at Arken.

Arken frowned. "What did you tell her?"

"That you were looking at her arse."

"It's hard to avoid at this angle."

"She's the sister of the Great Lord of Isfayen," Sasha added. "Men have died terrible deaths for less."

Sasha did not think she could keep up the banter all the way to the Altene. But if this group of foreign men were to trust her enough to follow her orders, some bonding was in order. Men she'd known a long time could overlook the fact of her gender, but for men recently met, it was impossible to ignore. Better to use her gender, and the unique position it gave her, to make amusement with them.

There were a lot of trails through the mountains, and this one crossed several of them. Any in the Altene fearing assault could not guard them all, but Arken was concerned they might post a wandering guard or two, or recruit locals to the task. He sent two men to walk ahead, unarmed and passing for locals, in case the trail was watched.

The main trail up to the Altene was on this near face, Sasha learned from talking to a man who knew the area best. But that face was sheer, and the trail's various bends climbed in clear view of the Altene's windows and towers. Even if they ascended at night, the full moon would surely give away their approach. But at the rear of Dirdaan, he insisted, there was a way up.

"You've climbed it yourself?" Sasha asked him.

The Ilduuri, a wiry man named Eirden with a thick blond moustache, shook his head. "Not me. I've a cousin who climbs. He knows all the climbing trails to these mountains."

"And he's climbed it?"

"Well, no. But he knows there is a way up."

"Says who?" Sasha persisted, with growing concern.

"Common knowledge."

Sasha distrusted common knowledge as much as she did common wisdom. But she kept her dismay to herself.

They passed between Dirdaan and the flank of its neighbour, a narrow pass beneath the sheer drop from the ridge upon which the Altene sat, very high above. It was late afternoon, and Dirdaan's opposite, northern side was in shadow. The peaks beyond, toward the Enoran border, lit up the horizon with sunlit, jagged outlines.

Soon they turned off the trail and through trees in the mountain's shadow. The Dirdaan flank above them was a vertical cliff. Sasha didn't much fancy the prospect of scaling it by daylight, let alone in the approaching darkness.

One of the two scouts ahead came quietly back, and indicated that they should all move off this narrow trail and into the trees to one side. After some moments of silent, cautious approach, they found the second scout by where the trees ended, directly at the base of Dirdaan's cliff.

There was a narrow trail here, Sasha saw, climbing the cliff. Not a natural trail, though it had been carved into natural formations. It wound upward along the sheer rock face, vanishing as it went higher. And at the beginning of the trail, where it reached the ground amidst loose rock and encroaching trees, was a stone guardhouse.

"Did common knowledge have a guardhouse here, too?" Sasha whispered to Eirden. Eirden scratched his moustache, and reluctantly shook his head. Sasha crawled to the first scout. "How many guards, do you think?"

"It looks large enough for five," said the scout. "I've only seen one, though. He came out the back and relieved himself over the edge."

The trail was well above them here, as they looked at the rear of the guardhouse. The building made a wall in an arc about the trail mouth, from cliff face to cliff face, with a gate beneath a small, two-person tower. Obviously it wasn't going to stop a determined attack from ten or more men, but that wasn't its purpose.

"I've seen these backdoor guardhouses in Petrodor," she murmured. "They're only here to slow us down, and usually they have an alarm. Can anyone see a rope or cord running up the cliff face to the Altene? Or perhaps they'll have a loud bell in that tower that can be heard from above."

No one could see anything. But all agreed that if they were to take this guardhouse, they would have to do it quietly.

"We climb the cliff here," said Arken, "and get up to the trail, then come down on them from behind."

"They can see this whole face from the tower," Sasha cautioned. "If we climb here, we'll have to do it by night. How many of us can do that?"

Arken looked around, then up at the cliff. It seemed very sheer. Sasha had tried climbing such faces herself, with some success—she did not weigh much compared to the men, and was strong for her size, and relatively unencumbered. But this face was four times the greatest height she'd ever attempted, and a fall from above the halfway point would most likely be fatal. The closer to the guardhouse they climbed, the shorter the distance up to the trail, but the more likely the guards would see them, even in the shadow of moonlight.

"We need only one person to reach the trail with a rope and secure it, and then the others can follow," said Arken. "We need not attack the guardhouse at all."

"No," said Sasha, after a moment's thought. "The day is clear, the night will be clear too, and even in the mountain shadow, the full moon will be bright. For twenty-six of us to scale the cliff this close to the guardhouse without being seen is too much of a risk, and if we climb further from the guardhouse, the ascent increases. Two or three people would be less likely to be seen and could take the guardhouse unaware, as they won't be looking back up the trail. And also, if they do have some secret cord to ring an alarm up at the Altene, by taking the guardhouse we can at least know if we were spotted, and thus if the Altene will be expecting us."

"Those windows look small," Yasmyn interjected in Lenay, guessing their conversation. "Someone small should go, who could climb easily, and fit through one of those windows."

"She says she could fit through one of those windows," Sasha translated to Arken. "I agree. Me, her, and you."

"Both women?"

Sasha raised eyebrows. "If Yasmyn can fit through that window, I can too. We may need a tall man to boost us up. Who would you pick to do all that?"

Arken thought about it. Then conceded. "Fine. We wait for night?"

"We wait for night."

That evening, more guards came down the cliff-side trail and replaced the guardhouse watch. There were only three, it seemed. But it only took one to raise an alarm.

Arken was a good climber, the skill well practised by some in the Ilduuri Steel. He went first, and hauled himself up without difficulty. Yasmyn followed, light and wiry, and seemed as unperturbed as Arken.

Sasha watched where Yasmyn put her hands and feet, and found those holds easily enough in the not-quite-dark. But still it wracked her nerves, as the ground fell away below, to know that if she missed a hold, she would be badly hurt. Soon that knowledge changed to the certainty that if she missed a hold, she would die. Her heart thudded hard, and she forced herself to concentrate as though it were a sword drill with Kessligh, watching only for the next move and the next placement of hands and feet. She'd never had a difficulty with heights, and had assumed that would hold her in good stead on this climb. Now she discovered that enjoying a good view from a relatively safe peak and clinging to a cliff face like an insect above a lethal drop in the dark were two different things entirely.

When she hauled herself onto the path, she was shaking. She lay for a moment, winded, breathing deeply, and willing her muscles to some kind of recovery. Then she stood, and discovered with further alarm that the trail itself was not wide enough for comfort during the day, let alone at night.

They descended the trail cautiously, shoulder-hugging the cliff to one side, feet wary of loose stones. It was darker than Sasha had expected, making their footing more precarious, but lessening the chance of being seen. The stone against their sides was dark, like their clothing, and with blades sheathed lest a stray gleam of steel give them away, Sasha did not think it likely any in the tower, looking out into the trees, would notice them.

They descended past the encircling wall, level with the tower. Within the narrow windows, lamplight gleamed, and voices could be heard. Stupid, Sasha thought. Looking out from a lighted room onto darkness made vision impossible. But guard duty was boring, and guards lit lamps when their superiors weren't about, by which to play dice or otherwise pass the time.

Sasha led, padding softly to the base of the short tower, and slowly tried the door. It was open. So much for crawling through windows then. Yasmyn was eager, and Arken grimly determined, so she let them go first, and waited. She was in no mood to kill surprised and defenceless guards. They went up the stairs while Sasha guarded the doorway below. Then a commotion, and some shouts. Then footsteps coming back down.

Three guards emerged, frightened and bewildered, stripped of their weapons. Sasha opened the gates to let the others in while Arken guarded the prisoners, and Yasmyn tied them with rope.

"A large bell," Arken told Sasha. "In the tower, to be rung if there was an attack."

"We'll leave the guards outside the gate and shut it, in case they wriggle free," said Sasha. "Probably they could climb back over eventually, but it would take too much time to matter."

"Killing them would be safer," Arken suggested.

"Yasmyn," Sasha asked, "will they get free?"

"Not before morning," Yasmyn replied, biting her lip as she worked.

"They live," Sasha told Arken. "I don't want the angry spirits of men dishonourably killed chasing me up the mountain."

Arken gave her an odd look.

As they began climbing the narrow trail, all discovered why the night was darker than expected. With a speed found only in the mountains, the weather was closing in. Soon the wind began to gust, and rain to fall.

The rocky trail became slippery and hard to see in the darkness. Arken led the way, then Eirden, then Sasha and Yasmyn, all keeping as close to the cliff face as possible. In places the trail narrowed to barely the width of two boots. In such places, Sasha forced her attention inward, and pretended she was performing one of Kessligh's balance drills atop a wooden fence in the pouring rain. She tried not to recall that, even then, she'd fallen occasionally. Then, she'd had only a little distance to fall to soft grass. Here, moonlight spilled occasionally through gaps in the cloud, and fell upon the rugged terrain beyond Dirdaan, a long way below.

The trail grew a little easier as the cliff face met the broader bulk of Dirdaan's middle, and great, rounded domes of rock closed in about them. But as the cliff face ended, the trail became steeper, often requiring hands and feet together, and a spider-like climb up clefts between boulders. Several men slipped in the rain and dark. Thankfully none fell.

Finally, and after a long, exhausting climb, the trail emerged onto a shelf that overlooked the Altene. Ahead the trail wound downward, and onto the exposed shoulder of mountain on which the building rested.

It was a keep, Sasha supposed, having less experience with Bacosh-style fortifications than most. Such buildings were rare in Lenayin. It was like a small castle, with walls rising directly from the cliffs that surrounded on three sides, leaving no space to stand beneath them. The fourth wall, facing them, had a drawbridge opening onto the road that climbed the opposite, gentler face of Dirdaan. That drawbridge seemed the only way in or out.

Built into the northern walls was a tower that occupied perhaps a quarter of the total walled space.

"The walls are not so high," Bergen observed as they crouched low behind an outcrop. "Perhaps a rope and grapple thrown over a wall, then we climb up?"

"They'll see us," Sasha disagreed. "With all the troubles in Andal, they'll be alert by now. There's no taking this place by stealth—we must go through the front gate with force."

"Twenty-six of us," Arken reminded her. "Perhaps two hundred of them."

"They're not Steel," said Sasha. Arken thought about it. Bergen nodded approvingly. "Militia at best. Can you guess the layout?"

They remained crouched while Arken scratched lines on wet rock with his knife, indicating where he thought the inner walls were, and the main, enclosed building and stables. The rain grew heavier, and the wind gusted. Thunder grumbled, and men looked about in some dismay. Sasha did not mind the weather at all. In fact, she thought it could help.

"It's like a snail shell," Bergen advised. As an Enoran, he'd know more about castles than any of them. "It has four quarters—you go in the main gate and it forces you through each of the three-walled sections, each with their own barred gates, archer slots, and so forth, before you get to the tower."

"By which time we're all dead," someone observed.

Sasha peered out into the rain, at the dull grey outline of the keep against the hulking mountain opposite. "Two hundred guards?" she said dubiously. "How many horses? That's a long climb from Andal on foot. They've Meraini nobility here, so there's servants aplenty, senior Remischtuul too, which means more servants, personal guards as well as Altene house guards. Cooks. Stable-hands, especially to handle all the wagons going back and forth just with food."

She looked questioningly at Bergen. The big Enoran nodded.

"They'll have five hundred folks packed in there, easy. It's not built for more than two-fifty, to look at it."

"We're certain it's two hundred guards," Arken said stubbornly. "My sources don't lie."

"No, I believe you," Sasha agreed, understanding his caution that she might be engaging in undue optimism. "But that's their problem. Where do all the horses go? And the wagons? I remember when my family had grand functions in Baen-Tar, the crowds of people would jam all the palace ways, and gates that were meant to be barred and guarded stayed open. I don't see how their inner gates can be closed and guarded if they're bursting at the seams.

"They're expecting a serrin attack, see? They're scared of Saalshen's *tal-maad* crossing the border and climbing mountains. The *talmaad* will scale their walls in the night and climb through their windows to slit their throats in bed. They don't expect an armoured thrust straight through their main defences."

"No," someone agreed, "because anyone trying it would be insane."

"These far two quarters of the courtyard will be open," Sasha continued, pointing to Arken's scratches on the rock. "I reckon this first gate beyond the main gate is closed, but the next two will be open to accommodate all those damn horses. Here, smell the air."

They did so. The cold, wet air blew into their faces, directly past the keep. Sasha raised eyebrows at them expectantly.

"Horses," said Arken, with a slow nod. "Lots of horses."

"That's the smell you get when you've too many of them and you're not cleaning up properly after them all," said Sasha.

"Not enough stable hands," said Bergen with a slow smile.

"Because they don't have the space with all their guards," Sasha agreed. They were understanding now.

"Too many guards is a good thing for us?" Eirden wondered. Well, most of them were understanding.

"It's not the numbers," Sasha explained, "it's how they're deployed. At least one of their inner gates is not shut. The courtyard is crowded with horses. If attacked, they can't use the courtyard, it's blocked."

"We can't use it either."

"Yes we can, we have the initiative of attack, and we are fewer! Defenders need to make a line, attackers only need to get in amongst them and stop that line from forming."

"The horses will cause confusion," said Bergen, with growing enthusiasm. "We get to the main tower keep and once inside, it's man against man and their numbers mean nothing. We are far superior man-to-man."

"Yes, but we need to get past the first and second gates," Arken added with some frustration.

"It's dark," said Sasha. "It's raining and thundering, and the wind is blowing. Guards hate it. If just a few of us can sneak in with the next wagon through those gates, we can hold open both gates for long enough that you can get through."

"Who?"

"Me," said Sasha. "Yasmyn is quick up a ladder and not easily seen. And Arken, your two best shieldsmen."

"Myself and Danel," said Arken.

Sasha nodded. "Good. Now we wait for a wagon. With all the men inside, I doubt they'll stop even for dark and storms."

They waited. Wind howled across the mountainside, making the light rain sting. Sasha thought some more about her plans, then grew bored of that and lay on the rock, pulling Yasmyn down beside her so they both had some warmth.

Arken shook Sasha awake. Sasha rolled and crawled immediately to their viewing outcrop. There on the road winding up to the keep gates was a pair of wagons. Drivers carried torches guttered and flamed by the wind. Even now, the drawbridge was lowering with a rattle of rusty chains.

"Let's go," Sasha whispered, and ran. Even through the clouds, enough moonlight lit the rocky trail to show them the way. Sasha, Yasmyn, Arken, and Danel scampered down the rocks. There rose no cry from the keep walls—in this weather the guards were inside, and would be lucky to spot dark shadows flitting across dark rock.

Sasha reached the keep wall and hugged to it, crouched and moving fast. Ahead, the drawbridge hit the ground across a ditch barely more than waist deep. The wagons began to clatter across it. Sasha leaped into the ditch, ducked low, and scampered directly under the wagons' wheels, and up on the drawbridge's far side. Atop the wagons, torch-wielding drivers with eyes narrowed against stinging rain looked only to the archway ahead, and shelter.

Both wagons crossed, and the drawbridge began to rise. Sasha jumped onto it and slid within the archway, aware that Arken was directly behind, Yasmyn and Danel on the opposite side. Above them, a portcullis was beginning to fall, a further grinding and clanking of chains.

The four infiltrators ducked beneath before it came down with a clang. Amazingly, there were no guards on the ground behind the entrance. The wagons clattered on ahead toward the second gate. All the guards, it seemed, were on the walls above, and not looking for shadows creeping along the ground.

There was a ladder up the wall to the drawbridge and portcullis mechanisms above. Sasha looked up, saw no activity high on the wall, and began climbing. She moved fast, Yasmyn just as fast behind her, as the two men in chain vests and with shields on their backs struggled. The winch mechanisms were under cover atop the wall, and guarded by two bored men in chain mail and helms.

Sasha cleared the ladder and slithered low on hands and toes, pressed to the shadow of a wall. In an instant, Yasmyn was beside her, darak gleaming in her hand. Sasha nodded at one man. Yasmyn nodded back.

They moved together, Sasha drawing her blade, sneaking three steps about the drawbridge winch, and striking off her target's head. Yasmyn's guard went down more messily, with a cut throat and flailing limbs. Sasha hated it, this brutal murder of unwatchful men. But the need for speed and silence left no other choice.

Yasmyn was already winding the drawbridge down, a huge handle for a small woman. Up on the trail, the other men would be moving now. Arken and Danel arrived—Sasha indicated for Danel to raise the portcullis, and stared at where this wall adjoined a fortified guardpost between them and the main keep tower. If men came rushing from there, as they might at any moment, this position would be overrun.

"Hold here," she told Arken. "Keep them off until our people are in through the gate. Then fall back. I'll get the other gate."

She turned and ran along the wall top, past archer crenellations to her left, and rounded the corner. Here was a long stretch of battlement to the second defensive wall ahead, and the guardhouse within which the portcullis winch was housed. These walls all made a box around the wagons below. Now paused before the second wall, the wagons were being inspected by guards who emerged from doorways. And here above them, two crossbowmen came from the guardhouse to stand, one on either side, and watch in case of trouble. If either happened to look up right now, Sasha knew she was dead.

She sprinted. Her boots were soft, and with no armour she was faster than the men could have been. Someone yelled, but the crossbowman on the wall before her took a moment to realise his peril. Then he looked up in astonishment.

Sasha slid feet-first beneath the crossbow as he tried to bring it to bear, and took his leg with the sword. Then she was up, nearly overbalancing off the high wall's edge. On the opposing wall, the other crossbowman fired, the bolt whizzing past her nose. A big man with a shield leaped from the guardhouse entrance ahead to block her way. Sasha dropped her left shoulder into the shield at full sprint, knocking him into his wall, then thrust her blade beneath the raised shield to stab a leg. He yelled and swung as she ducked back, thus taking his shield out of play, and Sasha slashed his exposed shoulder.

He stumbled, and Sasha simply hurdled him before one of his comrades could stick a crossbow through the guardhouse crenellations and shoot her. The guardhouse was open, with archer crenellations and a roof mounted on poles like an afterthought. A crossbowman backed away swiftly, shocked to find her so close, and a guard with a shield interposed himself and swung hard. Sasha slid and ducked left to his exposed side, and killed him.

A second did the right thing and charged her, shield first. With no available target, Sasha tried to dart around but there was no room—the shield hit her and crashed her sideways against a crenellation. She fell, and the shieldsman tried to come down on her with a stab, but Sasha swung at his leg, which he barely defended with a downward crash of his shield, and stumbled back. Sasha rolled up and away, in time to find another onrushing guard trying to impale her with a spear. She spun inside it and took his head, then another guardsman took a crossbow bolt through his back from one of his own archers on a further wall. Men were yelling in confusion and anger across the wall defences.

Two without shields tried to rush her with only one-handed swords—Sasha killed one instantly, the second scrambling back in terror as the shield-sman who'd charged her now tried to corral her toward him and the cross-bowman who was hiding behind the portcullis mechanism. Sasha smashed his shield once and again, trying to provoke an attack. A third time, and this time he swung back, and Sasha met it with full force. Her two-handed grip send his one-hander spinning through the air, whereupon she simply grabbed his shield in frustration and tried to wrestle it aside, while he tried to stop her.

She abandoned that fight as the other swordsman came back at her with a new and foolhardy courage, and died for it. And now Arken was crashing into the guardhouse. She left the unarmed shieldsman to him while seeking the crossbowman behind the portcullis winch, finding him sobbing in fear, too frightened to even threaten her with his weapon.

Arken beat the shieldsman to the ground with raw power and rammed a blade through his throat, then came striding to the crossbowman and killed him, too. Sasha stood in helpless horror, breathing hard, bruised from her fall and bleeding from the head where the shield had rammed her into the wall. The crying cross-bowman gushed blood and kicked as he died. Sasha wanted to throw up.

"Get the winch!" Arken roared at her, taking up a shield position at the guardhouse entrance. A crossbow bolt struck his shield as he crouched behind it with practised balance, and awaited the next rush.

Sasha sheathed her blade and winched hard on the portcullis mechanism. From the boundary wall, two more shieldsmen came rushing into the guard-house. Sasha stopped winching and drew her blade as Arken came under attack from his side also, blocking that way in with shield and thrusting sword.

Danel chose that moment to come rushing through the other boundary wall entrance and crash into the shieldsmen with superior shieldwork and crushing blows, a bolt through his arm that did not seem to slow him any. Then Yasmyn, ducking past to wind at the winch . . . and behind them, Sasha saw with a glance back, guards pursuing across the walls.

Only now there came the sound of fighting below. Danel finished his two opponents and blocked the guardhouse entrance to others, and Sasha risked a look over the wall beyond this portcullis.

Down there she saw horses running crazily, pouring beneath the wall, out toward the main gate. And a tight phalanx of Steel, some shields above their heads to ward archers from the high walls, others with shields before to guard archers at ground level, and all pressing through the crazed mass of horse-flesh, and turning toward where the third gate would have to be open, to accommodate all these horses. Sasha saw men over that way, scrambling atop that wall to lower that portcullis, but the mechanism did not allow that to happen quickly. They would not make it in time. She ducked back as a bolt fizzed by her head.

The defenders trying vainly to break past Arken's defences were now falling back into the tower itself, directly adjoining this wall.

"Get in!" Sasha yelled at him, pointing past with her sword. Arken charged out of the guardhouse along the wall, Sasha after him, and crashed shield-first into the tower door. It burst open, and Arken was then pressing down the stone corridor beyond, a one-man barrier taking up all the space, absorbing blow after blow with his shield and leaving defender after defender dying underfoot as he pressed on. Sasha had respected the Steel before, but now that respect reached a whole new intensity.

Behind her came Yasmyn, then Danel guarding their backs . . . only now the defenders seemed to vanish as those before Arken died or fled, and those behind diverted to the main skirmish, against the small knot of Steel infantry now well within the keep's walls.

They emerged into a major hall, elegant dark stone, tapestries, and rugs lit with lanterns. Some servants saw them and ran in terror.

"Let's find these fucking Meraini," Sasha growled. "Where would they hide?"

They found the Meraini barricaded within a regal suite at the top of the tower. Sasha stood just out of sight of the suite's main doors down a hallway, as Arken continued to keep watch, leaning around the corner with his shield for protection from the occasional crossbow bolt that came his way.

Yasmyn removed the bolt from Danel's arm and helped wrap the wound to stop the bleeding. Danel wanted to go downstairs and help with the battle, but Sasha told him what any with ears could now begin to tell.

"No need," she said, leaning by a window and listening. "Once a formation of Steel got into the tower itself in good order, it was over. They know it, I hear them surrendering."

She sent Danel and Arken to guard the hallway stairs while she watched the Meraini's suite with just one eye exposed to crossbows. As she'd thought, some men retreating from the fight below came rushing up the stairs, and in the enclosed space, Danel and Arken sent them crashing back down. She heard further yells from below, panicked men thinking they were trapped, no doubt telling their superiors that the upper floors were held by entire battalions of Steel.

They may as well have been. The local guards could fight, but with nothing like the skill of Arken and Danel, and their equipment was not to the Steel's quality. One Steel infantryman in these hallways could block the entire passage and force opponents to fight him one-on-one, a contest that nine times in ten they would lose. Seeing that, with militia of less than full commitment, demoralisation set in fast. The moment the Steel phalanx had made it past the second portcullis, the fight had been won.

Soon Arken was being summoned downstairs to accept terms. Then a pause, as prisoners were disarmed and rounded up. Then Bergen climbed the stairs and came over, grinning to see Sasha and Yasmyn guarding the Meraini's location.

"So you girls got them boxed in, huh?" His shield bore many new marks, and a bolt stuck through the steel and wood. He looked unharmed, though sweaty and tired.

"How do you like real fighting, cavalryman?" Yasmyn asked, seated against a wall with a view of the Meraini's doors. Sasha knew she'd probably been wrong to include Yasmyn in the first wave—atop the walls and guardhouses, she could have used another man with a shield, and Yasmyn's speed and climbing hadn't been as useful as she'd thought. Still, Yasmyn had done well, and would never have forgiven Sasha if left behind, for she certainly could not have taken a place in the Steel phalanx.

Arken returned with Danel and Eirden. "We have three dead," he told her. "Two more may not live, several more are injured but not seriously. We count a hundred and thirty-seven prisoners." To Sasha's surprise, he fought back a grin. "They could not believe it once they'd surrendered, and counted how few we were. They thought we were hundreds."

Sasha nodded, not really surprised. "Good," she said. "Now someone else is going to have to talk sense to the Meraini, because I don't speak the tongue, and they probably only speak Ilduuri besides." And if they have to surrender to a woman, she didn't add, they'll probably throw themselves out the tower windows for shame.

"It's an amazing victory!" Arken continued. "I confess I did not think it could work. How did you know?"

"Practice," said Sasha. The hero-worship was nice, but she was impatient to be out of here. Petrodor Riverside had been the first time she'd killed people and regretted it. The Altene was the first time she'd attacked and killed men who had not attacked her first. She could not get the terror on the weeping crossbowman's face out of her mind. He couldn't have been more than twenty.

Arken started shouting at the grand doorway at the end of the hall.

Indignant shouts came back in Ilduuri. Arken began to translate to Sasha, but she made a face.

"I don't care," she said. "Tell them we'll take them willingly or unwillingly."

More Ilduuri Steel came up the stairs as Arken continued. A number were staring at Sasha in amazement to see that she was still alive, having charged alone along the walls and guardhouses with no shield or armour.

Arken soon became tired of what he was hearing and arranged six men in two lines of three. Shields overlapping, they rounded the corner at a walk, took several bolts through the shields, then ran. There followed a lot of crashing, hacking, and finally screaming, as more Steel followed their comrades in.

Sasha walked in to see, and found a broad regal chamber now strewn with the bodies of several men in chain and black embroidered shirts of a style she had not seen amongst the others. One man the Steel had down on his knees, disarmed with hands held behind him as he struggled. He had a black goatee, long dark hair bound at the back, and quite a lot of jewellery.

"Jeffensen of Meraine, he says," said Arken, leaning on his shield. "Second son of the Chansul. He says we have committed an act of war against Meraine, that we have the blood of thousands on our hands from the battles that will follow."

"Thousands of *yours*, you cock," snorted one of the Steel. "Doesn't count, see?"

There came more scuffling from the adjoining chamber, and some swearing by the soldiers. One of them called Arken, who went. Sasha followed.

In the next room, a man was being dragged from a bedchamber. He wore the clothes of a high-class townsman: silk shirt and tight breeches. He stared at Arken, and Arken stared back. Then Arken began laughing. Surrounding soldiers seemed grimly amused.

"What?" Sasha asked in confusion.

Arken shook his head in disbelief. "General Daani," he explained to Sasha, with the mocking little bow of a man making an introduction, "Commander of the Ilduuri Steel."

Eighteen

They could have waited the night but Sasha knew she had to move fast. She had her men (because they were assuredly *her* men now) commandeer enough wagons and horses for them all, plus their wounded, Jeffensen and several more Meraini, General Daani, the several senior Remischtuul found in adjoining chambers or trying to hide in the kitchens, and all the boxes of Meraini talons they could find, the stash revealed to them by one of the Altene staff, hidden in a dungeon vault.

Now they rattled down the road from the Altene, a far more pleasant descent than the way they'd come up, with torches and moonlight to show the winding way down. Sasha climbed into the rear of her wagon and slept.

She expected to be reawakened as soon as they encountered Stamentaast or other unfriendly patrols, yet as the dawn bloomed pale above mountain peaks, she awoke to find the wagons rattling along the road up the Andal Valley, with the city outskirts approaching ahead. The city was silent, and the streets as they entered were deserted. Sasha did not particularly fear Stamentaast; they only moved in smaller groups and this party was eighteen strong and able to defeat militia many times that number. Bergen and another man with cavalry experience rode in the saddle, and they'd brought additional horses tethered behind the wagons. Two more men they'd sent riding ahead to reach the Steel garrison up-valley, and tell them what had been discovered in the Altene. Sasha had no expectations of what the Steel would do when they heard, but thought it might be nice if she did not have to do all the persuading and motivating herself for a change.

She did *not* expect that the column would be abruptly stopped on the deserted city road by a group of serrin *talmaad*, all with arrows nocked to bowstrings, and all looking dangerously ready to fire.

"Stop, stop, stop!" Sasha called up to the lead wagon, and they reined to a halt. And to the serrin, "I am Sashandra Lenayin! To whom is your *ra'shi?*"

A serrin woman came around a corner, beckoned to them, then she walked back the way she'd come. The lead wagon driver looked back to Sasha, who indicated they should follow. Not liking the wagon when a saddle was available, she leaped off, untethered one horse from the rear, then mounted. Ahead, the serrin woman also retrieved a horse hidden in a lane, mounted, and the pace accelerated.

Andal was deathly quiet. It had been two days since the night of the Stamentaast's attack and the purge of Andal serrin. They passed market squares where morning trade should be commencing, past bakeries whose chimneys should have been smoking with the fires of morning bread, all barred and shuttered. Yet the serrin woman ahead rode with confidence, and did not fear ambush.

Sasha took the lead on her horse, ahead of the first wagon with Bergen beside. They passed familiar streets now, near the lakeshore where Father Belgride's temple sat, on the easternmost edge of the lake where the city was densest.

Finally they entered a large square, deserted like all the rest. Deserted, that was, save for *talmaad*, who sat beneath the large central tree and prepared breakfast, and trained, washed, or slept. It was a camp for a serrin army, and Sasha guessed there were at least eighty men and women here. She wondered how many more that meant there were throughout the city.

Another woman came out from the tree to meet them, and Sasha dismounted fast before her wary soldiers, ran to Aisha, and embraced her. "I'm sorry I couldn't come after you," she said with emotion. "Something came up."

"We stopped the riders you sent," said Aisha, releasing her with a smile. "We heard what you did. Then we sent the riders on their way, to talk to the Steel."

"What happened here?" Sasha asked, gesturing for her men to dismount, and gazing about at the *talmaad* camp. "These came across from Saalshen?" The defences of the Altene were so strong in fear of precisely that, she recalled.

Aisha nodded. "The Steel guarding the eastern border have basically retreated to garrison and stopped patrolling the border. And the locals are all friends to serrin out there, so there was no one to stop them. These *talmaad* were about to hit Andal, but Kiel got word and rode out to find them. Arendelle, too."

"What happened, where are they?"

Aisha looked over her shoulder, as Rhillian appeared, with her familiar, swinging stride. "I think I'll let Rhillian explain."

Sasha embraced Rhillian also, and made an introduction to Arken, who cautiously shook her hand. "Bring your wounded down so we can treat them," Rhillian told him, and gestured to some serrin to help. "Then some breakfast—you must be hungry. A serrin named Tershin came to tell us where you'd gone, and I've been waiting for you. If I'm to move any further, I'll need your help."

Rhillian explained events over breakfast and a small fire. Sasha couldn't believe it. For a long while she could think of nothing to say.

"How did you do it?" she finally managed. "I mean . . . the *vel'ennar* . . ."

"I know," Rhillian said mildly. Her eyes had a faraway look. Thoughtful, and faintly sad. Yet not regretful. "I'm unsure. Errollyn is not the only serrin born with unusual instincts. You did tell me in Petrodor that you'd once thought he was the strangest serrin you'd met, only to become convinced that it was me."

Sasha remembered that day, sitting atop dockside buildings in the sun with a view of the harbour. "I did," she recalled. "But serrin cannot fight the *vel'ennar.* I've seen them try. It's paralysing."

Rhillian shrugged. "He deserved it."

Sasha blinked in amazement. The strangest serrin she'd ever met indeed. "And Arendelle?"

"That I regret," Rhillian said sombrely. "Yet he was at an untested moment also. The *vel'ennar* led him two ways at once, to fight Kiel's killer, yet the killer was me. Kiel's *ra'shi* evidently won that conflict, and left me with no choice."

"And all these other *talmaad?* All in preference to Kiel's *ra'shi* at that moment? They just accepted your actions, and went along with you?"

"Oh, no," said Rhillian. "Quite a few of them wanted to kill me. Yet they could not. Most serrin cannot. Evidently I can, to my own astonishment as much as anyone else's. It does place me in a unique position of influence."

"Obviously." It was coldly phrased, put that way. Rhillian had influence because she could kill other serrin, but they could not kill her. Such a person could have unfettered power in Saalshen. All were defenceless before her. Sasha suddenly understood the thoughtful, faraway look in Rhillian's eyes.

"So how is it that you can?" she pressed her friend.

Rhillian's emerald gaze fixed on her. "Kiel's plan was evil," Rhillian said, as though it were the most obvious thing in the world. "I do not do evil. Should Saalshen begin to do evil, Saalshen should cease to be worth saving."

"There were times in Petrodor when I heard you reject such logic."

Rhillian shrugged. "I've been through a lot since then. Life is not worth having if it does not serve some greater purpose. Perhaps this is a new phase of the serrinim, a new direction of our people. It is good that the *vel'ennar* unites us, that unity has served us well. Yet if it can also drive us to commit horrors, unthinking and unresisting, then that is no good thing at all."

"Morality over unity," Sasha murmured.

"Exactly."

"You've done it now. If Saalshen enters a new age of the individual above the group, you'll find that each individual's morality is different. And that, my friend, is why humans are always fighting."

Rhillian sighed. "We'll see. I think that the *vel'ennar* should remain intact enough that we do not all suddenly leap at each others' throats. In time, we may come to see that it is not my behaviour that was the aberration, it was Kiel's. I surely could never have done what I did had not Kiel forced my hand, and probably had not Errollyn's previous actions given me many thoughts to ponder. Our fates are interlinked, and not merely amongst we serrin."

"And so what happened then?" Arken asked. "After you killed those two?"

"That will be discussed for many generations in Saalshen, I'm sure, should we survive," Rhillian sighed. "There was a rupture in the *vel'ennar*, for certain. A confusion, a *tul'an aehl.*" Arken looked askance at Sasha, who shrugged and smiled. "A lot of us simply stood around in shock, or sat and could not speak. A few fainted. It took a while to resolve. Some of those most aggressive took to arguing, as though by argument they could bring Kiel and Arendelle back to life. I told them that any attempting to carry out Kiel's former plans would also die. When the shock of *that* faded away, I argued plans with them. You know serrin, we argue like rabbits fuck.

"Finally they were convinced that their only course of action was my course, and so we scouted Andal instead. I found Tershin, or rather he found me, and told me where you had gone. I decided that you could quite possibly succeed, you being you and all . . ." she gave a faint smile that Sasha returned, ". . . and that in the meantime, I had to save as many Andal serrin as possible, and try to get the Steel out of their barracks one way or the other.

"We came in and cleared the streets. The Stamentaast aren't much for fighting really, certainly not against us, and not in the dark. We must have killed several hundred for only a few losses, and the rest have barricaded themselves in around the Remischtuul, and Heroes' Square. Most regular Ilduuri here hate us, but those who attack us die, and the rest stay inside. We make no friends, save those in Steel Town; a few of them help us but even there they do not like to see serrin occupying their city."

"How many are you?" Sasha asked.

"More come every day. We're nearly a thousand now. The Stamentaast and allied forces are at least double that."

"Allied forces?"

"Militia. A few ex-Steel, but not many, mostly just local men who have found weapons. A few Nasi-Keth too, but a lot of the Nasi-Keth here hate the Stamentaast, and seem to think it justice that serrin should kill them for what they've done. But the area around Heroes' Square is open, they have many crossbows and even more shields—if we attack into that we'll have heavy losses. *Talmaad* are not good for such direct actions. We need the Steel."

"You want us to help you take our own city," Arken said bluntly. And flinched as Rhillian's stare found him.

"This is *your* city? Do you claim its recent actions as your own?"

"No," Arken muttered.

"Then is it *not* your city?"

"Just because the Steel and those minded like us are not in control of the Remischtuul," Arken retorted, "that does not make what you ask any easier. Andal is the capital city of Ilduur, and . . ."

"I'm sorry," Rhillian interrupted, not looking at all sorry. "We serrin do not truly understand this concept of belonging without responsibility. If something is yours, you are responsible for it. You either accept Andal as yours, and its actions as yours, or you reject them both. Now, is Andal yours, or not?"

Sasha sensed something unspoken behind Rhillian's words. "How many serrin dead?" she asked quietly.

"Oh, we don't know yet," said Rhillian, with the distraction of someone being deliberately vague to avoid confronting too powerful an emotion. "They took a lot of prisoners in that first night. Ordinary folk, many families. When we began to fight back, they needed men for fighting, and could not spare guards for the prisoners. So they herded them into houses in Remischtuul district. When the fighting began to go badly for them, they set some of those houses alight, with the prisoners still inside. We think about a thousand."

Her stare might have burned holes in Arken's eyes. He looked away. Then he turned to Sasha. "You have led us this far. What do you suggest?"

"That you come to realise that you can either be a loyal Ilduuri, or that you can do what is right," said Sasha. "You cannot have both."

More horses were arriving in the courtyard, a Steel cavalry, including one man with an officer's crest onto his helm.

"A formation captain," said Arken, as they all stood. "Looks like Idraalgen."

He led Sasha and Rhillian over as Idraalgen dismounted. He was a man in his midforties, dusky-featured for an Ilduuri, and lately unshaven. He and his two lieutenants looked about in unease at the serrin that filled his courtyard.

Arken walked up and saluted, and Sasha recalled that even the lieutenants outranked him. "Lieutenant Arken Haast, sir."

"Just the man," said Idraalgen. "The scout told me you were up to something. The Altene, he said."

"Yes, sir," said Arken. It sounded odd in Saalsi; "*rah*" was a borrowed Larosan word, as serrin had no concept of "sir," and were never likely to. "I discovered Meraini emissaries ensconced at the Altene, controlling the

Remischtuul with bribes from the Chansul of Meraine. Thousands of Meraini talons."

Idraalgen frowned. "And you have proof of this?"

"Yes, sir. The Meraini emissaries, prisoners from the Altene. One is the son of the Chansul himself. In the company of several Remischtuul chairs, also taken prisoner, with many chests of talons."

"And how did you acquire all these from the Altene?" Idraalgen asked with a dry smile. "Walk to its gate and knock, and ask politely?"

"No, sir. I and twenty-two volunteers stormed the Altene, and took it."

Idraalgen just looked at him. "You took the Altene with twenty-three men?"

"Not me, sir. Her." Arken pointed to Sasha. "Sashandra Lenayin. Sister of the Lenay king. The finest commander and swordsman I've yet served beneath."

Idraalgen and his lieutenants stared.

"Twenty-six men," Sasha admitted. "I had two more of my own."

"You hold the Altene?" Idraalgen evidently could not believe it. "With all their defences?"

"No, we gave it back," Sasha explained. "We only wanted the Meraini and their talons, to show the likes of you what was going on. Three heroes paid with their lives."

"You took the Altene with twenty-six, and only lost *three* men?"

Captain Idraalgen left them to talk to the Meraini, and the captured Remischtuul, and came away livid. Soon he was roaring orders to Steel soldiers newly arrived, and men on horseback went racing away toward the city outskirts, and in the direction of Steel barracks further up the valley.

"Yesterday," he later explained to Sasha as they climbed stairs within a nearby tower, "some Stamentaast came riding up to our barracks gate and demanded we march to Andal at once. Serrin were attacking Andal, they said. We laughed, and went back to our lunch."

Sasha decided not to mention what Kiel had nearly gone and led these very same serrin to do.

"We don't take orders from Stamentaast," Idraalgen continued, "only the Remischtuul. And the last we'd heard from the Remischtuul, they'd told us to remain in barracks. *Talmaad* in Andal seemed like justice, from what we'd heard. But now we've heard there are locals organising to attack the *talmaad* and support the Stamentaast. If your friend Rhillian stays here too long, she'll find local Ilduuri will start to fight her."

"That would be courageous of them," Sasha said drily. "Fancy picking a fight with someone who can actually fight back."

They emerged onto the tower's heights and surveyed the southern slope of the valley. There the Remischtuul building sat huge and wide upon the lower slope. Before it were large, grand buildings, similar to what Sasha had seen in Tracato. Between them and the Remischtuul, Heroes' Square. The surrounding neighbourhood, she'd been told, was wealthy, and filled with Remischtuul families, merchants, and various functionaries.

Rhillian was already atop the tower with Aisha, Arken, and several newly arrived Steel officers. "All the approach roads are barricaded," Rhillian explained. "We think there's about four thousand by now, half Stamentaast and half militia. But more join them constantly.

"The slope behind is quite steep, making flanking manoeuvres no more than a nuisance for them. They have almost no cavalry, but they couldn't deploy it even if they did. Most have shields by now, and even the militia seem quite well protected. Spears too, which will make a direct assault down the streets problematic."

"Archers?" Sasha asked.

"Lots," said Rhillian. "Mostly crossbows. They put them in the buildings and behind the front shield wall."

Sasha considered it for a moment. She couldn't see the defences from here, they were down amongst the buildings, out of sight. But she thought she had a reasonable idea. She looked at Idraalgen, questioningly.

"Far be it from me to make decisions ahead of the conqueror of the Altene," Idraalgen replied to her unasked question. "The Steel have always promoted on merit, and my experience in battle is not half of yours."

Sasha felt uneasy. What Idraalgen said made sense. She knew that she could command respect from fighting men, and Arken's men had certainly given her that. But even so, this was Ilduur, she was a foreigner, and this rapid transference of trust seemed hasty to say the least.

Still, she had no choice. "How many are your battalion?" Sasha asked Idraalgen.

"Eight hundred foot," said the formation captain, "two hundred horse. We've summonsed the other garrisons with word of what has happened, and the closest of those could be here in another day . . . but that's only another four hundred in total. The big garrisons are on the borders, obviously."

"I'm not waiting another day, let alone several," Sasha muttered. "Half the city could rise up. Why not simply leave? Take the Steel and march to Jahnd?"

"Without first taking the Remischtuul?" Idraalgen darkened with fury. "Those scum have betrayed Ilduur and they shall pay. Besides which, we cannot leave our families unprotected. The only way to preserve order in

Ilduur is to remake the Remischtuul anew, after this lot have been swept out and punished."

Sasha looked at Rhillian. Rhillian gazed back. Sasha recalled accusing Rhillian of making a mess of this kind of thing in Petrodor. Rhillian's gaze was unaccusing, yet Sasha sensed a judgement there, wondering how much better her young friend would do in a similar circumstance. Still she felt uneasy. She did not know Ilduur well enough, and surely she was missing things. She wondered exactly what she was walking into.

Her only goal, she decided, was to march to Jahnd with as many of the Ilduuri Steel as would follow, as soon as possible. After that, Ilduur could stew. It was out of her hands.

"Well," she said, "how are the approaches to these buildings on the east of Heroes' Square?"

"Closed and protected," said Rhillian, with the certainty of recent scoutings. "Steel could attack up them."

"So we take these buildings, and gain a platform of fire for the *talmaad*," said Sasha, pointing. "That allows us to disrupt movement across the entire square, and fire down onto neighbouring barricades."

"It will be a slow way to attack," Idraalgen warned. "Taking those buildings will be time-consuming, and we cannot shock them with our force of arms if we move so slowly."

"Hardly matters," said Sasha. "Force of arms is a Steel strength, but their one chance is to meet us with superior numbers and defender's advantage, and stop us. I'd rather grind them down—inexperienced troops hate it and we have a big advantage in archery with the *talmaad*. Let them try to redeploy their reserve under *talmaad* fire, we'll put soldiers in the base of those buildings to keep them safe from counterattack, and let them waste men trying *that* under fire if they choose.

"Then we go up the main roads here and here from the lake, force them to engage the barricades there, then a small force to feint from the west, no more than a hundred, I think. That will spread them . . . no, look at the size of that space they're defending, under fire at the eastern end: that should use up most of them. And this road here . . ." she pointed along the base of the hills, ". . . what is this?"

"That's Meadow Road," said Arken. "It will be defended."

"It is," Rhillian confirmed.

"Against cavalry?" Sasha asked. "Two hundred you said, Captain?" Idraalgen nodded.

"You'd send cavalry onto those cobbles?" Rhillian asked.

"I would if there's no one left to defend that road," Sasha explained.

"Even if they've double what you say they have, inexperienced armies simply do not redeploy well under pressure and under fire. If we press them like I say, I can't see how they'll keep enough force on Meadow Road to stop two hundred cavalry getting through. And if two hundred cavalry get through there, that's a knife in their heart, they'll have cavalry in their rear . . ."

"The killing blow for sure," Idraalgen agreed. "If it works."

"Aye," said Sasha. "If it works."

She held Aisha back as the others descended the stairs, so they could talk on the way down. She could see with one look that Aisha had much to tell her. Aisha knew Ilduur better than any non-Ilduuri here.

"Talk," Sasha said simply, in Lenay.

"Three-fourths of the Steel are eastern," Aisha replied in kind. "The east of Ilduur is distrusted elsewhere, for close relations with Saalshen. The Remischtuul has kept them from power and tried to recruit other Ilduuris to the Steel, but in this land of isolation, few save the easterners want to be part of an army that is friendly with foreigners."

"Do you think Idraalgen and those like him want more power for the east?"

Aisha nodded. "This is their chance to remake Ilduur. No bad thing, save that if they try for a great reform, there will be resistance, and the Steel will be required to stay and put it down. We need them in Jahnd, not putting down disturbances here."

Sasha nodded grimly as they descended the spiral stairs.

"Another thing," Aisha said hastily, "they embrace you very quickly for a foreigner . . ."

"I was just thinking that."

"Good, you noticed. The same thing happened when Saalshen first arrived two hundred years ago. They exalted us as a great wind of change, and there was much worship of the great foreign lords. It puzzled us too, but then when things began to go less well, we realised what it was. Whether you are a great foreign hero, Sasha, or a hated foreign invader, what are you not?"

"A common Ilduuri," Sasha realised.

"Exactly. Outsiders are useful to be hated, useful to be worshipped, and can be discarded either way. Never mistake the worship for acceptance."

"If it all goes wrong, they can blame me and cast me off," Sasha summarised. "But as an outsider, I have freedoms of action Ilduuris do not, making me useful."

Aisha nodded. "Just don't believe what they tell you. Now it all gets crazy."

It was crazy. As morning moved to midday, Steel infantry arrived in the square. Sasha briefed the assembled officers, who then departed to spread the plans further. There was a lot of yelling and urgent excitement. The *talmaad* were calmer, stocking arrows and testing bowstrings. They gathered about Rhillian and listened quietly.

To one side of the courtyard, a small group of Andal locals gathered to yell obscenities at Steel and *talmaad* alike. A few tried pleading with Steel officers, and were shrugged off. Some others threw cobblestones plucked from the roads. A Steel officer grew tired of it and sent cavalry to ride into the group, scattering them. A horse's bridle was grabbed, and the cavalrymen began striking. People scattered back into the streets and alleys, leaving several dead on the ground.

Five soldiers came across the courtyard at a run, straight for Sasha. "M'lady," said their leader, "best that you have a guard. This city is hostile, any watching this action from a window will soon observe you giving orders, and any fool can fire a crossbow."

He handed her a shield as well. Another time, Sasha would have refused. But today, she could feel the city simmering. She took the shield and beckoned her personal guard to follow to where the Ilduuri Steel was beginning to assemble, direct from their march from Andal Garrison in gleaming ranks of armour, shields, and helms.

Sasha wanted to lead the cavalry in, but was advised against it. Steel cavalry had their own commands and signals, and would not understand her. She could not accompany the *talmaad* as they would be hidden and firing arrows, while she needed to be visible, and was an ordinary shot anyhow. And to accompany the infantry would have been as pointless a waste of her talents as using a svaalverd blade to chop firewood, besides forcing another ten soldiers to divert themselves for her protection.

She settled uncomfortably for commanding on horseback down a main road just short of Heroes' Square, her five protecting guard mounted about her, in the further midst of a hundred men on foot in reserve. She could hear the yells and clashing steel echoing down the winding roads, yet could see nothing. Periodically a man on horseback would clatter into view to shout some recent progress, which others would relay to her, then clatter off once more. It was disconcerting to command a battle that she could not even see. It was even more disconcerting to ask others to fight whilst sitting in the rear with her sword in its sheath.

She received word that the eastern buildings overlooking Heroes' Square had been taken, and *talmaad* were pouring fire into defensive positions. Then came word that the defenders' counterattack had failed. There was no word from the northern feint, but she guessed it should have engaged by now. As for the cavalry thrust along the grassy bank of Meadow Road further up the valley slope, she supposed that they were unwilling to spare a horse to send word of what was happening.

Noise of the fighting began to fade. Sasha frowned. Why was it fading? There was only one logical reason it might, but it was far too soon for that.

The thought was interrupted by a horseback messenger appearing up the road, and waving them forward, frantically. Sasha yelled for the reserve to advance, which a commander repeated, and a hundred men in tight formation went jogging up the road, armour rattling and shields overlapping. Sasha held her horse to an impatient trot behind them, as they wound between the buildings. Ahead were the scattered remains of barricades, piles of wood, stone, and even an old wagon, strewn across the road as though struck by a giant wave.

She saw the bodies: dead Stamentaast, dead men in plain clothes, with brutal, recent wounds. These first barricades had fallen, and the second barricades, higher even than the first, were just as useless. More dead men, tangled in piles, some still moaning, some screaming and crying, and the cobbles all slippery with blood.

The road opened onto a series of courtyards that ascended the valley slope like a giant's steps, each joined by more human-scaled flights of stairs. Heroes' Square, with statues and monuments in between, flanked by grand buildings that housed the new rulers of Ilduur that Maldereld had helped install. The bodies here were feathered with arrows, and yet more cut down with blades. Steel cavalry circled great clusters of surrendering men, forlorn and frightened with heads down, casting their weapons into growing piles. Far ahead, she saw Steel formations ascending steps to the Remischtuul itself, pressing with ceaseless discipline beneath the grand entrance pillars and archway.

"Secure the courtyard," Sasha shouted at the captain in charge of the reserve. "I want these adjoining buildings cleared, I want Remischtuul chairs and their assistants arrested, I want none to escape the square."

A cavalry captain clattered toward her as the other man shouted her orders in Ilduuri, and men ran to fulfill them. "M'lady!" he shouted, and saluted with his sword. "My apologies for attacking early, but your plan worked far too well! They were beginning to collapse even without our charge, so I galloped in to finish them!"

"An excellent decision," said Sasha, staring upslope to the Remischtuul. "Now use your cavalry to ring the Remischtuul on the open slopes—I don't want important men escaping across the fields."

He saluted and galloped to do that. Sasha cantered her horse across the rough pavings, slowing to let the animal find its cautious way up the steps to the next level. *Talmaad* were treating several wounded Steel, but besides a few fallen men at the barricades behind, she could see no more friendly casualties than that. Surely it had not been so easy?

The main Remischtuul steps were too steep for horses. She dismounted with her guard, left the horses to soldiers on duty there, and ran up the steps, her guards flanking her with shields ready. The grand hall reminded her of Baen-Tar Palace, where she had spent the first six years of her childhood. A high ceiling and old dark stone . . . only here there were chandeliers of gold, and crystal decoration, and great paintings in a lowlands style.

Here were more bodies on the ground, and blood pooling on slate tiles. Further down hallways she heard shouting and fighting, as local staff were rounded up by yelling soldiers, sent scurrying down stairs like sheep mustered for market. Sasha kept striding, past older men in pompous robes and wigs now terrified and cowering, and serving staff pressed to a wall at swordpoint while roughly searched. The grand institution of Ilduur, the centre of power established by the serrin to replace the rapacious feudal families of old, was falling to the forces of its own creation.

She saw a grand doorway ahead and went through it, into a great amphitheatre of seats surrounding a table upon a stage. Here was the heart of the Remischtuul, where all the peoples of Ilduur would be represented. Now it was filled with soldiers, arresting more staff, beating those who resisted. A statue against one wall was toppled with a crash, to cheering from soldiers who apparently did not like the man it portrayed. Sasha felt like she'd slipped whilst climbing a steep hillside, and now skidded downhill with no control or direction. It was a giddy feeling, equal parts horror and glee.

Men saw her enter, and cheered and raised their swords to salute her. It was a roar of lust and power, of men who had corrected some longstanding indignity, of old wrongs righted. And it was the respect of men who had expected a hard fight against difficult numbers, and had instead received an easy one. Such men could come to believe that she could do anything. That she could lead them to such victories as had yet to be written in all the history of the Ilduuri Steel. She dared not break such a belief, for she needed it now, at Jahnd, where it could help to save the future of everything she cared about in all human lands. And yet . . . was this what it cost?

She strode down the amphitheatre between rowed seats, and leaped up onto the stage beside the table. Here the senior men would sit. Robed ushers held at swordpoint against a wall stared at her in horror, this pagan barbarian who stood upon the centre of their civilisation's power with a sword in her hand. From here she could see the mural on the ceiling, painted by a Tracatan artist's hand so that only the most powerful here on the stage could see it clearly—all the Verenthane gods amidst the clouds of heaven, pointing and kneeling and exclaiming in wonder at the holy light radiating from Aaldenmoot, the symbol of Ilduur and its people. The symbol of their freedom from feudal overlordship. The freedom of all people to live their lives as they saw fit.

About the chamber, conquering soldiers raised their swords at her and cheered anew. Sasha raised her sword in reply, and knew that she was now, as she had never been before, truly the barbarian warlord the Bacosh peoples had always feared her to be.

A second Steel contingent arrived from the east the following morning, and declared themselves in accordance. Messengers had been sent, bearing a bugle seal, a directive of general recall, ordering all of the Steel's arms to Andal. The furthest, Captain Idraalgen told her, would take seven days, including the time the message took to reach them. Sasha sat now upon the edge of a desk in chambers atop the Remischtuul's western wing, watching the fall of morning sun upon the far mountains and scowling as she considered remaining in Andal for another week.

"My people wish to evacuate Ilduuri serrin to Saalshen," Rhillian told her, leaning against the window frame to consider the splendid view of lake and city below. "I think we can agree it is not safe for serrin in Andal today."

"How many of your people will that take?" Sasha asked, chewing a thumbnail.

"Half," Rhillian admitted.

"And they'll need protection," Sasha added. "How many serrin to be evacuated?"

"In all Andal, we think there are nearly five thousand. And others who are their friends, whose lives may now be in danger. The populace is angry, and . . ."

"I can't allow it, Rhillian." Sasha was almost surprised at the calm certainty in her voice. "You've four hundred *talmaad* now, I can't lose half of them. The Steel will need wagons for its own provisions and to move five thousand civilians you'll need most of the wagons in Andal."

"I told them as much," said Rhillian. "But I did not want to preempt your decision."

"Will they listen to you?"

Rhillian looked at her for the first time. "My *ra'shi* holds," she said. "Their motion and mine make a shadow from the light." Sasha frowned. Rhillian had become somewhat more . . . vague, since Kiel's and Arendelle's deaths. As though she had retreated to ancient serrin philosophy for comfort. "Where then should serrin be kept? We have reports of angry mobs even today, roaming Andal searching for stray serrin. They seek revenge."

"I know. I have Steel on patrol. Troublemakers are to be arrested, killed if necessary."

"It will get worse," Rhillian said calmly. "You rule them now. A foreigner."

"I've invited city leaders to meet our Meraini prisoners," Sasha said darkly. "They'll see what's happened, and know who is to blame."

"Do you truly believe they'll care? Sasha, you fight for freedom, yet you will take it from them."

"Are you on my side or not?" Sasha snapped.

Rhillian smiled faintly. "Always on your side, Sasha. Merely exercising the serrin prerogative to test a position in the hope of strengthening it."

Sasha sighed. She didn't need to apologise. Rhillian knew. "I really am in charge now, aren't I?" she said glumly.

"A true Lenay warlord," Rhillian confirmed. "All conquering and terrifying."

The Remischtuul chambers were in uproar when she entered. City men sat or stood in unaccustomed places about the amphitheatre and shouted outrage at Captain Idraalgen, who remained senior of all Steel present. More soldiers stood about the walls and upon the stage, ready to make a wall of shields before her should any of the hundred or so Andalis present have smuggled a weapon past the searches.

Idraalgen stood aside for Sasha, who half-seated herself upon the grand table edge and waited for the shouting to die down. Men stared at her with some consternation. It looked odd, she supposed. The Steel, deferring to a woman. But she was used to that, and well past caring to try to put herself in their all-too-masculine boots.

"You've met the Meraini," Sasha said to the chamber. "What say you?"

"You could have plucked them off the street!" one shouted.

"Unlikely, since you've been killing all the foreigners," said Sasha.

"You got through!" that man retorted. "You and your serrin friends, you could have brought these Meraini actors with you!"

"I'm told many of you have close relations to Remischtuul chairs," Sasha said coldly. "Your pockets, I'm sure, lately have weighed heavily with Meraini talons. You've also seen the boxes of those we recovered, doubtless from the same mint."

"You hold this Remischtuul prisoner!" another yelled at her, changing the subject. "We demand all of this body's representatives be released at once! You will pay dearly for any harm that has come to them."

"Well, I think we already killed a couple," Sasha said sarcastically. "They were fighting with the Stamentaast outside, after the Stamentaast declared war on this city's serrin population and tried to kill them all."

"The serrin attacked *us!*" came the reply. Sasha rolled her eyes. "You came with them yourself! They crossed our borders and attacked us, and now our own traitorous army takes their side against their own people! We Andalis were just defending ourselves, and . . ."

Sasha did not hear the rest. It was pointless arguing, she realised. These people would believe what they wished to believe. "Let me tell you how this is going to work," she shouted over them, and silence descended. "You're going to go back into the city, and tell the residents to go about their daily lives, and do nothing else. The Steel will be assembling outside the city over the coming days, and once it has been assembled, it shall march to Jahnd, to defend this land from the very worst enemies of Ilduur that the previous Remischtuul somehow neglected to fight."

There was much shouting and disagreement at that. "You'll leave us defenceless!" one protested.

"I'm sure that's what this Remischtuul said before they dropped their pants and bent over for the Meraini, in the hope that would gain them some protection," Sasha retorted.

"You cattle fuckers never bothered to join our ranks and defend this land in the first place!" Idraalgen snarled over the upset that followed. "Small right *you* have to complain where the Steel should or should not march to next!"

That degenerated into a shouting match in Ilduuri. The eastern regions, Sasha knew, were settling scores. They dominated the Steel, and not all of their grievances against the rest of Ilduur dated to merely within the last two centuries. Kessligh had taught her much about Lenay history that royal tutors in Baen-Tar would never have dared, about how her great-grandfather King Soros Lenayin had made a huge mess following his initial successes, because he had simply supposed that all the fractious parts of Lenayin would unite within the new reality he had imposed, and that the old arguments would disappear. He had been wrong, of course.

Ilduur was nothing like as complicated as her homeland, yet Sasha could see something similar emerging now. Assuming rulership of a foreign land was fraught with dangers, particularly in how many such old arguments she did not know, and was unable to stop from spilling out of control.

Aisha now came across the stage to translate for her, but Sasha held up her hand with a weary look.

"I've told you how it's going to be!" she shouted across the chamber. "You will either comply, or you won't. Be warned, I have no sympathy for people who murder serrin families in their homes, and have so little honour they cannot tell old enemies from old friends!"

"And where will you lead our Steel once you have finished in Jahnd!" came another shout amidst the noise. "Back to Lenayin, to install yourself as queen? You claim to fight for freedom here, yet you tyrannise the people of Andal, and if you win in Jahnd you'll be second in line to the Lenay throne!"

"Some liberator!" yelled another. "She's another fucking tyrant royal! We thought we disposed of all our royals two hundred years ago!"

"Tyrant!" screamed others. "Murderer!"

Sasha repressed a sigh, and was darkly amused that the irony did not seem to touch them. Ilduur had disposed of royals and feudalists because of the intervention of the serrin. Now they tried to dispose of those same serrin and all their wisdom, and protested against those who stopped them for imposing upon Ilduuri liberty—the liberty to murder serrin families. And not for reasons of religious fervour as the Regent's forces did, but in the vain hope of peace, and the cowardly desire for the world to pass them by.

Well, if taking away a people's liberty to behave like scum was tyrannical, then she was a tyrant. So be it.

"Many are saying that, about you becoming Queen of Lenayin," said Aisha as they strode to Heroes' Square with Yasmyn. Yasmyn had been looking into the Remischtuul's books and accounts, another unexpected skill the former Great Lord of Isfayen had taught her. "They say that you and Koenyg are the natural leaders of King Torvaal's children, and that Damon will not measure up."

"Torvaal is an Ilduuri name," Sasha mused. Soldiers walked with them in rattling armour, her regular guard. "I'd never given it thought before. I know there was a man named Torvaal who fought with Great-grandpa Soros in the liberation of Lenayin, an Ilduuri who had sought fortune in Petrodor and volunteered for the Lenay crusade. Soros named him Chayden's godfather, who in turn named father after him."

Aisha watched her as they walked, curiously. "Do you miss him?"

"I'd like to," Sasha admitted. "But I can hardly miss someone I barely knew. I'm sad he's gone." They emerged onto the grand steps overlooking Heroes' Square, now an encampment of tents, soldiers, and horses. Beyond, the city approaches were guarded. Growing ranks of soldiery drilled formations, hundreds of men moving and shouting in unison. Soon it would be thousands. "Certainly I feel today I understand him better than I did."

"The burden of true power lends a curious perspective, yes?" Sasha nodded. They stood upon the top step, and contemplated the view for a moment. "Sasha? I know you love Damon, yet if he is not to become the leader that Lenayin needs . . ."

"He is," said Sasha. "He just doesn't know it yet."

"Sasha, you walked into Ilduur a nobody. Barely two weeks have passed, and you are Queen of Ilduur by default." Sasha didn't like that word at all. "Very few in all Rhodia could have done it," Aisha persisted. "I know you do not want to contemplate it, but I know Lenayin well enough to know that it needs a strong ruler, and of all the people I can think of who could fulfill that role . . ."

"Aisha, enough."

Aisha sighed. Sasha went quickly down the steps, face grim, toward where Arken was waiting for her below, in full armour, some of his new command in tow.

"Visitors," said Arken without preamble. "Awaiting on the square, demanding to see you. Nasi-Keth." Sasha nodded. It was bound to happen. The one remaining fighting force left in Ilduur was not going to take the Steel's actions lying down.

"What of your Nasi-Keth officers?" Sasha asked. Arken was now a formation captain, replacing one such officer who had abandoned his post.

"Three gone," said Arken. "One remains, and professes loyalty. Those three are now making trouble in the Tol'rhen, clear as day."

"I'd rather they make trouble there than within the Steel," said Sasha. "Let's go." Sasha's personal guard led the way across the square, Arken's men behind, the new captain, Sasha, Aisha, and Yasmyn walking together.

"Aisha is right about Lenayin," said Yasmyn. "Only a strong leader can unite the provinces. You are that leader."

"Considering that we'll be outnumbered at Jahnd by the Regent nearly four-to-one even *with* the Ilduuri Steel," Sasha said testily, "I think it's a little premature to start planning my rule over Lenayin."

"A warrior either expects to win, or expects to lose. Should you expect to lose, why bother fighting?"

"Because running away makes one a coward," Sasha retorted. "Besides which, a warrior expecting to win should not immediately pick fights with every man in town. Or else he will start losing, and fast."

"Should you lead the town to victory in battle, all others would follow you and not fight you," Yasmyn said stubbornly. "Should you win in Jahnd, all Lenays would follow you. . . ."

"Enough, Yasmyn!" Sasha exclaimed, spinning on her and Aisha as they walked. "Both of you! If we win in Jahnd, Damon will be king, and he will make a good king!" She spun back as they kept walking. "I never thought I'd see *you* two agreeing on a matter of violence."

"Violence?" asked Aisha. "No one is suggesting you should *fight* Damon for it."

"Just how fucking naive are you, Aisha? What do you think happens when rivals fight for a throne? Have you paid *any* attention to the past few centuries of Bacosh history?"

"To win in Jahnd, you should have command there," said Yasmyn, unperturbed. "To have unchallenged command, this should be settled first. Isfayen will back you."

"I will fucking beat you with my fists if you don't shut up," Sasha fumed.

"And I will repeat it nonetheless," said Yasmyn. Sasha had no doubt that she would. Uncomprehending, Arken watched them with a frown.

"We debate a Lenay matter," Sasha told him, in Saalsi. "Have no fear, we gang of Lenay speakers will not discuss Ilduuri matters in any tongue Ilduuri cannot understand. This is your land, not ours."

Arken nodded, and said nothing.

One of the Nasi-Keth awaiting them by the edge of the square was dressed as an Ilduuri Steel captain. Soldiers surrounding him appeared tense and angry, a few with weapons drawn. This was one of the Nasi-Keth men the Remischtuul had promoted to command within the Steel at the expense of experienced and respected officers, Sasha realised. Now he stood defiantly, two companions at his side. Those two were dressed as town men, though their garb was loose and flexible in the right places. Fighting clothes, for svaalverd fighters. At their backs, they wore serrin swords on the diagonal.

"Captain Rael," the officer introduced himself.

"Not anymore," said Arken. The two men glared at each other. Rael was nearly as tall and blond as Arken, with pale eyes.

"You have committed a grave crime against Ilduur," Rael told Sasha, arms folded, standing to his full height. There was no sword in his sheath, soldiers having taken it from him. They stood at the base of a statue, with further guards observing the flanking buildings for archers in the windows, shields at the ready in case of a long-range bolt.

"I have done nothing to Ilduur save to show the Ilduuri Steel a path," Sasha replied. "It was the Steel who chose to take it."

Rael scoffed. "You idiot girl, can you not see you have been taken for a ride? This is a grab for power by the easterners. They wish to rule Ilduur themselves. I hear you are fighting the Regent in the name of freedom. Tell me—how much freedom shall there be for Ilduur when we majority Ilduuri have no representation in the Remischtuul, and one of these eastern friends of yours rules us like a king with an iron fist?"

"I don't care," said Sasha. "The people of Ilduur are free, and in their freedom they chose evil. Freedom is not wisdom, nor is it kindness, nor honour. Ilduur freely chose to make war on Saalshen and its allies, and now it pays the price."

"War?" Rael looked aghast. "What is this war that you speak of? We seek only to *avoid* fighting a war, as is our right!"

"You swore an oath to your brothers in Enora and Rhodaan that you would defend them against . . ."

"The *Steel* swore an oath!" Rael retorted. "An oath now centuries old, meaningless to most Ilduuris, nurtured by the Steel only to preserve their power and status over we majority Ilduuris . . ."

He might have said more. Sasha stopped listening and looked across the courtyard, at soldiers watching, at others guarding the roads and lanes, at the pointed roofs of buildings overlooking the square. At some point, Rael must have stopped speaking, because there was silence. Sasha looked back to him, and some of her utter contempt must have shown, for he paled, though with fear or anger she could not guess. Perhaps both.

"I am Lenay," she said in a cold voice. "If all Ilduuri think as you do, then I admit, most Lenays would not care if this civilisation *dies*." She let it sink in. "You are a land of cowards, and I feel nothing for you. If the eastern regions are the only regions that will honour their oath and fight against the evil that gathers to enslave us, then I am with them."

"You fool!" Rael rasped. "You cannot bring freedom by inflicting tyranny!"

"I can," said Sasha. "I will."

"The Nasi-Keth will not stand for it! The Ilduuri Nasi-Keth have been protectors of the Remischtuul for two centuries; even now we gather former Nasi-Keth from all walks, common city folk who train still with the svaalverd, and will fight to regain it. I am warning you, we can gather more Ilduuris who are not afraid to fight, and even the Steel cannot stand against the might of all Ilduuris together, fighting for their freedom."

"Would be the first time you ever felt the need to do that," Arken remarked drily. "Until now you've left that all to us."

"Don't be stupid," Sasha told Rael. "You are not warriors, you've shown that already."

"Any man can be a warrior," Rael growled, "if he is deprived of something that he loves so dearly as his freedom."

"If you'd arrived at that conclusion a century or two ago, I might believe you. But this love of freedom you profess, this is an old and shrivelled thing, like an old man's sword arm, withered from lack of use. What you describe is passion. Love for something larger than yourself. This is something you must practise, like swordwork itself. Like courage. You cannot just rediscover courage when it suits you, or honour, any more than you can neglect svaalverd for years and expect it to all come rushing back from memory when you need it.

"You must work at it tirelessly, and with discipline. This is true for great warriors and for great civilisations; even the serrin do this, serrin who believe mostly in peace—they *practise* it. They debate and philosophise, and they learn arts and study and heal, they know that peace is a difficult and elusive thing that must be pursued relentlessly and with passion. You don't have it. Or perhaps once you did, but now it lies long forgotten."

"We shall see," Rael growled. He signalled his companions, and they turned to stride away. Sasha watched them go.

"You *must* become Queen of Lenayin!" Yasmyn said with fierce satisfaction. "It is your destiny." Yasmyn, of course, had not understood a word Sasha had said.

"Many are upset to see the Remischtuul fall even though they were not upset merely to see Stamentaast dying," said Arken. "They did not come out in numbers then, but they may now, with the Nasi-Keth leading. They may not believe that the Steel will kill them, and if there are so many, I fear they may be right."

"There cannot be an uprising," said Sasha, with certainty. "We will not have reinforcements from the rest of the Steel for days. We cannot allow it."

Arken nodded. "What is your order?"

The sun had barely moved in the sky when several hundred Steel and *talmaad* fell upon the Tol'rhen. Great gatherings of locals, Nasi-Keth, and Stamentaast scattered before the fast thrust of armoured soldiers from the surrounding streets, moving at a full run so as not to give the lookouts more than a moment of advance warning.

Arrow fire came back from across the courtyard, as startled men with bows sought vantage atop steps or from Tol'rhen windows. Most arrows or crossbow bolts cracked off the Steel's massed shields, and did not slow them. Sasha moved in the rear, surrounded by her own company of Steel infantry, eleven strong including herself. She could not see much as they crossed the courtyards, her small shield filling a space between the big ones that protected them from random arrows. It was not as easy as it looked, to move in formation, to make oneself an identical brick in a wall of bricks, and not allow any gap. She was here to command, not to fight, but from behind the wall of shields she could barely see.

In frustration she moved her shield aside enough to see ahead: men were running up the Tol'rhen stairs before the leading line of Steel, others fighting and falling, arrows zipping and clattering about. Around her, men panted harder than she, for running those roads in armour was testing.

The first wave of Steel simply ran over any defenders on the steps and plunged into the Tol'rhen. Now from behind came a mad sprint of *talmaad*, serrin with bows in hand and swords on their backs racing across the pavings in the Steel's wake. Sasha stopped her squad behind the trees of a courtyard garden, and from that cover sought a view.

Then she saw them—the cavalry, emerging from the courtyard's far side, slipping on the pavings yet blocking the crowd's retreat with their charge. Now most townsmen were running rather than fighting, some huddling for cover, cowering with arms over their heads amidst thrashing hooves and stomping boots. Others fought, and were cut down. Someone was blowing a trumpet, in a vain attempt to muster defenders on the southern side of the courtyard, furthest from the lake.

"There!" Sasha yelled. "Trumpet! I want cavalry on the left! On the left, over here!" The man with the trumpet blew some ear-splitting notes, and repeated, and repeated. Sasha could not see any immediate response—cavalry had their hands full stopping the retreat from the first attack, as had been the initial plan. Cavalry soldiers seemed to be looking for their officers, for confirmation of the trumpet call, only to find their officers busy, or to not find them at all.

Sasha swore. "Go, go! Let's get into them ourselves, the others will follow!" Her men redeployed quickly, herself in the middle, holding her spot in the line. Eleven strong, they made a line abreast, and charged. It was not a mad run like Lenay warriors might make, but a crouched run with small steps, balanced so as not to let the shields bounce around and expose them to arrows. Sasha glimpsed past her shield a force of men running at them rather than standing and waiting.

"Five!" yelled her squad's formation sergeant, and Sasha, warned of this technique, sprinted the last five steps and threw herself into that collision with her shield. She hit someone, felt him stagger back, heard yells and falling bodies as their opponents reeled, caught off guard by the wall of shields that suddenly accelerated into them. Her comrades were moving and striking, jostling her as she tried to control her shield.

She tried an overhead strike, yet now their opponents were coming back, many armed with shields of their own, and an impact sent her reeling back a step.

"Hold!" yelled the man next to her. "Hold and push!" Stab, and a shriek, a man falling bloodily. "Hold and push!" He might have been yelling at her,

Sasha thought, but she could not tell. She complied, and an opponent slashed under the shield, she barely slammed it down in time, then a shoulder ram drove her back again . . . only the soldier beside her anticipated it, and drove his blade through that man's neck.

Something else hit her shield with force enough to jar her arm, and she tried to coordinate a stab with the movements of the man to her right, but he was fast, and the target uncooperative. A spear thrust nearly took her eye out, and a sword edge left a deep gash in her shield rim, and she realised they were being pushed back, eleven against whatever-it-was, and surely now in danger of being outflanked . . .

And suddenly there were cavalry ploughing through their opponents, striking left and right, and men were scattering. For a moment she thought it was over, until she saw that only a few horses had made the break to assist, and though some men had run, others were circling and coming back, shouting for their comrades to stand firm.

"Circle!" yelled the squad sergeant, and the formation's flanks swung neatly about to make that shape with their shields, as enemies now ran around and at them from behind.

"Fucking stupid!" Sasha announced her displeasure with that, and shrugged the shield off her arm with relief. Free at last, she ran at her opponents on open ground before they could form up. She fake-stepped one, killed him when he guessed wrong, danced out of range of a second's swing, ducked easily inside a spear thrust and ripped him at close range. Uncoordinated attacks came at her, Nasi-Keth now, seeing the chance to claim her outside the shield wall and mistakenly thinking that made an easier task.

There was so much space, after the confines of the formation. She couldn't believe how much, as she danced and tore her way through three in quick succession, then a fourth who had just begun to question the wisdom of being there at all. Some shieldsmen who might have troubled her now backed up in panic, seeing what she'd done, and she faked one into a defensive block that didn't come, took his sword arm instead, then hit another's shield with such force he fell backward, and ran past him as he screamed and begged for mercy. But the others were running now, as more Steel arrived at a run, and the enemies who had encircled her squad died upon those shields, or ran away. A newly arrived formation ploughed into the main body of gathering militia ahead, and so began the next front.

Sasha's squad again encircled her, one now limping, as defenders ahead resisted with commendable stubbornness, surrounding themselves with shields, arranging spears behind those to stab at the advancing Steel, and at the repeated thrusts of cavalry. The cavalry weren't much use against that tight block of defenders, Sasha saw—their horses were slipping on the pavings, and riding into those spears at speed was suicide. Infantry had better success, fighting inside the spears and coming shoulder-to-shoulder, as the Steel liked best. But still the defenders resisted, backed against the mouth of a road, blocking it like a cork in the neck of a bottle.

Sasha looked about from within her phalanx, seeing the rest of the courtyard apparently under control and wondering who she could redeploy to assist here . . . and then there were arrows flying out from the Tol'rhen, arcing over her head, and landing amidst the defenders. That rain of arrows increased, no inconsiderable range across the width of the courtyard, but the *talmaad* were judging it to their usual perfection. Unlike the Steel, these defenders did not have enough shields, nor enough aptitude in their use, to cover themselves entirely. Men began falling with terrible regularity as their formation fell apart like a castle of sand in a rainstorm. The remainder dissolved and ran.

The battle was over, but the clean up went on all day. The surrounds of the Tol'rhen, it became clear, were havens of resistance and friendship to the Remischtuul. The rulers of Ilduur had purchased the Nasi-Keth's support with offers of power and money, and the neighbourhood was as wealthy as any Sasha had seen in Andal. Steel now went house to house, breaking down doors, asking after known men and some women, killing any who resisted with force.

Sasha found it far more awful than the battle. She wanted to retreat to some safe place and hear of events by messenger, as some commanders would. But she forced herself to walk the streets past sobbing women and angry, frightened men, past groups of wailing children ushered away for safekeeping while their parents and elder siblings were questioned, often roughly. She saw men beaten, who gave the Steel harsh words. She saw rooms and entire houses ransacked in search of incriminating evidence and hiding places. She saw one young man draw a blade in fury at a soldier who shoved his mother, only to be impaled by another, and die slowly in his screaming mother's arms.

She recalled the serrin youngster whom she'd seen killed the same way on the Night of the Knives, as it was now called, and how she'd wanted to kill the man who did it, and the one who'd given him orders. Now, that last was her.

Weapons were confiscated—stockpiles of swords and armour uncovered in attics, crossbows bundled in chests beneath piles of winter cloaks. Certainly she had averted an uprising here, of major proportions. She walked the streets from one site to another, being seen by the soldiers, and seeing them in turn. As she stood in one room, observing a new cache, she overheard one of her guards in the corridor outside, talking with another soldier.

"Six, she got. Threw off her shield and charged them down, six in as many heartbeats. Most Nasi-Keth, some of them damn good too. Never seen its like—I wondered if she was as good as the tales, turns out she's better."

Sasha paused before that man on the way out. "What do you think of my shieldwork?" she asked him with a wry smile. It was the same man who had been guarding her right side in the battle.

"Could improve, ma'am, with practice," he said diplomatically.

"Fucking stinks," Sasha summarised, and all the men in the corridor laughed. "If I never have to fight in a shield line ever again, it will be too soon. You stick with yours, and I'll stick with mine."

"If we could get the Regent's army out of formation and with no shields," the soldier replied, "I reckon you could end this war on your own."

Sasha's smile vanished as soon as she left the corridor. About her was the misery of the worst thing that she had ever done. Yet she had secured control, and made certain that the rest of the Steel would not arrive in Andal to find the city risen in revolt against her. That would look awful; those men would not be confident to follow her, finding that she did not have this situation in hand.

These men who had fought with her would mingle with the new arrivals, and tell them what kind of warrior and commander this strange girl from Lenayin was. They would tell them of comfortable victories against difficult odds, of battles that should have been painful being unexpectedly painless. And they would tell of those six kills outside the Tol'rhen to prevent her squad from being surrounded, and likely that number would rise with each telling.

She would bring the Ilduuri Steel to Jahnd, and not beneath some uncooperative commander who wished to do things his own way, but under her command, and hers alone. These men would follow her now. Many of them to their deaths, even if they won. And all of them to their deaths if they lost.

Nineteen

The lands of eastern Ilduur reminded Sasha of the eastern foothills of her native Valhanan, save that where Valhanan descended in great ridges and valleys into Torovan, Ilduur emerged through even more rugged lands into Saalshen itself. These were sometimes called the buffer lands, the only place where serrin and human lands met without the divide of the Ipshaal River. For centuries, even before the rise and fall of King Leyvaan, humans and serrin in this wild place had intermingled, intermarried, and traded, with no apparent discord. The people here called themselves the *saaren saadi*, which she gathered meant in Ilduuri the "children of heaven," and in several days of marching through these lands, she had come to see why.

The foothills were steep, and the road wound along ridgelines and often precariously sheer faces. Everything was green, and even now in late summer it rained every day, sometimes heavily. Little villages perched on grand hill-tops, with views of the lands about them that made even a proud Lenay catch her breath. Drifting clouds and mist made these places seem to be floating amongst the clouds, and many hillsides were cultivated into terraces the like of which Sasha had never seen before. They grew rice, she was told, and other crops that required much water. When the sun struck an ascending stack of flooded rice terraces at just the correct angle, the whole hillside would gleam like silver.

The *saaren saadi* welcomed the Ilduuri Steel with cheers, food, and wine. Camping was difficult, the seventeen thousand-strong army stretched along an entire ridgeline exposed to the elements, but there was simply no flat ground upon which to muster a camp. The men did not seem to mind—a good three-quarters were native to these lands, and many passed through home villages, and embraced family along the way. Sasha was not surprised to see serrin here, and many of the Ilduuri humans seemed more than passingly serrin, a hint of exotic colour to the eyes and hair, a pronounced shape to the cheeks.

She was further intrigued to see temples and pagodas atop many peaks, and an abundance of flags above the terraces that she was told were partly for worship, and partly to keep the birds off. This was a native religion named Taanist, after the man who had begun it many centuries before. Some said he was serrin, others said human, and others still that he was of mixed race. Yet his teachings were of cycles and patterns, and seemed to Sasha like the attempt of a human to structure serrin philosophies into forms more easily comprehensible to humans. Emphasised were peace and meditation, and the great cycles of life. Sasha thought that if only it were not such a long journey, Lenay Goeren-yai would come here on pilgrimage, and learn of these people. In all her time away from home, she had never been in any place that reminded her so much of Lenayin, yet with such striking foreignness.

As soon as the high foothills ended, Saalshen truly began. Through thick woods and rolling hills the Ilduuri Steel marched, and serrin came out to watch, offer food and drink, and walk alongside whilst asking questions. Clearly they did not fear the Ilduuri Steel, and had received warning of its arrival. Yet their welcome was, to Sasha, vaguely disappointing, compared to the cheers and enthusiasm of the *saaren saadi* of the higher mountains. On the other hand, she reminded herself, serrin so rarely went for that kind of enthusiasm in anything. They were pleasant, yet measured, in most things. And here, seeing a grand army of human warriors in steel armour, marching through their peaceful lands, they were perhaps understandably wary.

The approach to Jahnd became mountainous once more, as the Eastern Reach extended further into Saalshen from Ilduur. It was a range of low mountains, like a wall before them, climbed in a day through a single pass.

Finally, twelve days after leaving Andal, the way ahead dropped into low hills and the most thickly cultivated land they'd seen so far. Before them, on the right side of the valley mouth, a city climbed the hills to sprawl across that promontory of land. Beyond it more hills rose steeply. Sasha smiled faintly as she rode, gazing intently at every rise of rock and cluster of trees, trying to get a sense of the land. Jahnd was built on a hill slope overlooking a river, in a valley surrounded by hills. So far, it looked very promising for a defence. How promising, she'd have to wait until she arrived to determine.

In the valley, crowds had gathered to cheer their arrival. These were mostly human, local villagers spread through the small fields between the trees, a few waving flags that Sasha did not recognise, but guessed represented the city of Jahnd. As the valley grew wider, they passed more farmhouses, then small villages, then large ones. They crossed the river at a stone bridge through a pretty town, and hundreds of townsfolk hung out of the windows, festooned with flags, and showered them with flowers.

Sasha saw many people pointing, at her in particular. She rode alongside a collection of the highest-ranking Ilduuris—a gesture she thought important, as she did not wish to appear the aloof foreign conqueror. Behind her in the vanguard rode Rhillian and Aisha with some other officers, the rest riding at the head of their particular formations back in the column. A few of the *talmaad* rode along. Many others remained in Ilduur to help escaping serrin or half-castes from those lands. The serrin had not been keen to follow Rhillian, and Sasha wondered how she'd be received amongst her people in Jahnd.

Nearing the mouth of the valley, she got her first good look at Jahnd. It rose up the rounded promontory in a slope that seemed as steep as Petrodor's, an amazing bristle of detail, clustered rooftops, and spires. Yet even from this distance she could see the wealth of its buildings, with none of Petrodor's crumbling decay. About the base of the slope, great walls loomed, arcing out of sight about the front of the promontory. But well before those walls, the city sprawled away from the slope and out across the valley floor to the river and across.

Approaching that sprawl now, they crossed open fields and yards filled with cattle and sheep. And here, astride the approach road, waited a small welcoming party.

Sasha recognised Kessligh immediately. Yells sounded out across the Steel column behind, and trumpets blared. Colours went up, a great unfurling of flags and pennants. Sasha's new horse had been selected from the Remischtuul stable, a young stallion who reminded her a little of her beloved Peg, in build if not in unremarkable chestnut colour. Clearly he'd been trained for display, for now with the flags and trumpets, he tossed his head and pranced a little. And was disappointed, for Sasha's style was not to prance, and she made him stop.

She let an officer call the halt, and rode forward to greet Kessligh on her own. He looked good, perhaps a little more weathered than usual, but mostly from squinting into a lowlands summer sun on horseback. His companions included several lads from Tracato's Tol'rhen whom she recognised, and some well-dressed city men she didn't.

His expression as he looked her up and down was quizzical. Sasha nearly grinned. "You brought the Steel, I see," he remarked.

Sasha shrugged offhandedly. "Oh you know. Just those I could find." Kessligh's look held a good-humoured reprimand. "Seventeen thousand," she answered his unasked question. "I'm told there could be another two or three thousand trailing. Three-and-a-half thousand cavalry, the rest infantry. Almost no artillery, just a few wagons of ballistas; the Ilduuri don't use them much in the mountains."

She could see Kessligh doing fast calculations. "It's good," he told her.

Which meant that it was unlikely to be anywhere near enough, but he was pleased anyhow. "All three Steel armies combined will give us about thirty-five thousand. Lenayin brings us closer to fifty, then there's all the *talmaad*. Our defensive position is strong."

Sasha frowned. "They can't have more than one hundred and fifty—if their advantage is only three to one, our position should be good enough. What's the problem?"

"They have artillery now. Quite a bit of it, captured in Rhodaan and Enora."

Sasha looked at his grim expression, and her heart sank.

"The Ilduuris. They follow you?" Kessligh asked.

Sasha nodded. "My rank is general. Honorary, yet real enough."

Kessligh's smile was pure pride. And nothing at all of surprise. "Finally the world comes to see what I first saw," he said.

Sasha smiled, edged her horse alongside, and embraced him, one soldier to another. From behind, the Ilduuri Steel gave a cheer. To them, Kessligh Cronenverdt was a legend. They had been following his pupil until now, per-haps his successor. Now the legend commanded them too. Sasha thought that in their cheer, she could hear some relief that they had not chosen unwisely.

Kessligh introduced her to Tallam, a council leader of the city of Jahnd. Together, the three of them led the way into the city outskirts, Sasha in the middle so that she could benefit from their conversation.

"The walls are more than five hundred years old," said Tallam, a strong-looking man of middle age, balding but long-haired at the back. He wore the colourful shirt of a townsman, yet underneath was mail, and he had a sword at his hip. "We've kept them in good condition, but as you see, the town now abuts directly against them."

"Buildings will need to be demolished to give archers a clear field of fire," said Kessligh. "But some townsfolk resist."

Sasha did not even bother with exasperation, it was too predictable. "Five hundred years," she pondered instead, gazing at the walls above the encroaching rooftops and cheering crowds. "How old *is* Jahnd?"

"Serrin records place the first settlers here at the year eleven hundred before Saint Tristen," said Tallam.

Eleven hundred years before the Verenthane faith, that was. "Seventeen hundred years?" It was an extraordinary number. Many Verenthanes claimed it had not been that long since the gods had made the world.

"They were small settlements in those days; freehold farmers scattered across these valleys and hills. Serrin still lived upon the western side of the Ipshaal, on what is today the Bacosh. Humans and serrin were intermingled for a long time, and living quite peaceably together, to read the serrin records. But humans became stronger, and drove the serrin back across the Ipshaal, thus forcing the serrin to become more organised for the first time.

"Some humans of the Bacosh saw human settlement on this side of the Ipshaal as an invitation to claim these lands also for humans, but this time the serrin fought back, and evicted from these lands all humans who had helped in the invasion. But the humans living in these valleys had always been friendly to serrin, and were allowed to stay. As feudalism gained strength in the Bacosh, and then the Verenthane faith, there came more and more wars; peasants and persecuted peoples escaped across the Ipshaal, and were directed by serrin to settle here. The first truly great wave was during the Wars of Five Kings—those people feared pursuit by their former masters into Saalshen, and so built the walls."

"The Wars of Five Kings," Sasha murmured, recalling an old history lesson. The dates fit. She lost sight of the walls momentarily as taller buildings intervened, an upper-floor window crowded with cheering Jahndis.

"But the pursuit never came," Tallam continued. "Saalshen's *talmaad* grew strongest in that period. Over the centuries we have built a city that sprawls far beyond the city walls."

"How many people, do you think?" Sasha asked.

"At last reliable count, nearly a hundred thousand," said Tallam. Sasha whistled. Barely a fifth the size of Petrodor, she thought. Perhaps a little less than Tracato. Baen-Tar, capital of Lenayin, had barely eight thousand, or so people said. Being in the lowlands for this long had taught her to think differently on the scale of human civilisations.

"I don't suppose you've taught all of them to fight?" Sasha asked wryly.

"Some," said Tallam. "But understand that we are guests in Saalshen, and do not take any measures that may offend serrin sensibilities. Serrin have argued for centuries whether it is a good idea to nurture such a large human city in their midst. We are required to keep records on every resident, to ensure that our one hundred thousand does not become two hundred, then five hundred.

"So, naturally, they do not like us to have a large army, and become involved in affairs across the Ipshaal. We stay secluded, so that we do not draw other humans into the affairs of Saalshen, and give them excuse to attack the serrin."

"A nice hope while it lasted," Kessligh remarked. "But like all vain hopes, likely to achieve the opposite effect to that intended, only at a later date."

It was an attractive city, Sasha thought. In the Bacosh, this sprawl of settlement about the defensive walls might be little more than a slum of peasants and landless, huddled close to a castle for protection and refuse scraps. But in Jahnd, these people seemed prosperous. Buildings here were low, more like the simple timber and wood structures of a Lenay town, yet everywhere were workshop yards and storage lots. She saw inns with stables, an ironmonger about a great chimney, and a leather-tanning yard nearer the river. There were butchers, millers, and bakers, and, here on the right beneath some shade trees, an entire courtyard for the sale of spun cloth.

They came upon a great dedicated stables, this one for wagon horses, its yard filled with more wagons than Sasha had ever seen in a single place. The smell of many horses was thick in the air.

"Jahnd does a lot of trade," she observed.

"No more than Petrodor, on a person-to-person basis," said Kessligh. "It's the quality of what is traded that sets Jahnd apart. There are craftsmen here who make the finest produce of Petrodor look like cheap junk."

Sasha left the army to make camp in the main valley beyond the city outskirts, as there were no accommodations anywhere for so many soldiers. Yet she first sent officers scurrying to arrange good food, and with instructions to allow them all leave in shifts, to explore the city they were to defend. And it occurred to her that probably the reason why everyone in Jahnd looked so busy was that they were flat out providing for an army that now totalled half the city population.

She made her way with Kessligh, Tallam, and the command vanguard beneath a great arch in the city's walls, and up the main road of Jahnd. It climbed the steep hill face in a huge, curving zigzag, and here the buildings did stand tall and grand. Sasha had never seen such buildings. They were no grander than in Tracato, perhaps, yet the architecture! There were spires and odd-shaped minarets, great overlooking balconies and enormous windows. There seemed no consistent style, as though the city were the work of a thousand wild imaginations, with no single identity. Small roads climbed or descended the slope off this main road, very much like Petrodor, often breaking into stairways where the road became steep. And to the left now as they climbed, there was the view.

"That's the Dhemerhill Valley," said Kessligh. "The small valley you came up is the Ilmerhill Valley. The Ilmerhill is just a small tributary into the Dhemerhill, and the Dhemerhill just another tributary into the Ipshaal. If you look behind, you can see the Ipshaal from here."

Sasha turned in her saddle to look back. Down at the valley's end, amongst rolling hills, she could glimpse the wide expanse of water, glinting beneath overcast skies. Not far by horse.

Across the Dhemerhill Valley were hills. Kessligh saw her looking. "Almerhill Hills," he said. "The tongue is Enoran, like the first settlers here who named everything."

"They don't look steep enough," Sasha said grimly.

Kessligh shook his head. "Dhemerhill gives them a narrow approach, but the Almerhill Hills are not sufficiently steep to really box them in. They can deploy formations for depth up that slope if they choose."

"Cavalry," said Sasha. "Wonderful place for a cavalry reserve, should we have need to charge into them."

She thought it sad that she had arrived in such an interesting place, yet had no time to admire it. Her primary interests now were hills, approaches, and natural lines of defence. Already she itched to ride into the valley and seek out all the lines of sight, so that she would know what an enemy would see from that vantage, and how he might be inclined to deploy.

But first, she needed a high view.

Windy Point provided it. Here was the best vantage in Jahnd, directly on the tip of the promontory, and high. Parts of the city rose higher, yet Windy Point was central, the natural point of command for the battle to come.

Sasha leaned on a stone balustrade, and gazed across the valleys. She could see straight down Dhemerhill Valley to the Ipshaal beyond. Upon her left was the Ilmerhill Valley, smaller and narrower, its mouth almost entirely consumed by Jahnd's sprawling settlements. To the right, the Dhemerhill Valley continued into the depths of Saalshen. Only it turned slightly, and widened, creating open fields upon the promontory's right flank. Beyond Jahnd's walls rose several higher peaks, upon which buildings clustered. Worse, the hills leading down from those peaks were more gentle, and she could see a number of roads continuing down into the valley from those heights. It wasn't nearly steep enough on that side to stop determined infantry or cavalry. Or even artillery, she feared. Upon the open valley floor to that side was a small village, nestled against the Dhemerhill River.

"We have a right-flank problem," Sasha observed, as Steel officers, city officials, and *talmaad* stood about and looked for themselves, not standing quite so close as to obscure Sasha's view.

Kessligh nodded. "We'll be defending on two fronts. One force will come up the Dhemerhill from ahead, the other will make its way around to the right flank."

"There's a road that allows this?"

"Yes, northward." He pointed, across the Almerhill Hills. "A wide road, well known to all."

"We could block it," Sasha suggested.

"Balthaar's becoming wise to our ambushes."

"*Your* ambushes."

Kessligh shrugged. "If we send a force to block that road, I'm not sure we could kill more than one-and-a-half for every one we lose. He'll be leading with cavalry, either heavy Larosans, or perhaps even Lenays."

"Koenyg," Sasha muttered.

Kessligh nodded. "The logical way to clear a road, and travel a longer distance than the main army. If we can't kill them at three to one or better, it's not worth the cost. They'll outnumber us by that many or more, so anything less than that is a win for them."

"And we won't stop them achieving their objective anyhow," Sasha concluded. She pointed into the valley. "What is that town on the river?"

"Haller."

"We can't stop them gaining it, but we should make them pay for it. They need it badly; it controls the approaches up our right flank. If we have artillery for cover on these hills over here . . ." and she pointed to the peaks on that side beyond the walls, ". . . we can give protection to anyone defending Haller."

"You're not thinking widely enough," said Kessligh. "They'll come down the Dhemerhill from the east in a full force of cavalry. That's where we'll defend from, one long cavalry line, falling back all the way to Jahnd."

"So you'll be using *talmaad* to shoot at any pursuing force?"

"And I have just the man to command them."

That tore Sasha's gaze away from the troublesome right flank for a moment. "He's here?" she asked.

"Out scouting," said Kessligh. "He told me you'd either have all of Ilduur in flames by now, or the entire Ilduuri Steel would come marching out of the mountains with you at their head."

Sasha smiled faintly. "He knows me well."

"He's also the best battlefield commander the *talmaad* have," Kessligh added. He glanced around, but Rhillian was in conversation with some officers. "His strangeness from other serrin gives him a creative and a brutal streak. Will Rhillian object?"

Sasha shook her head. "You know serrin, very little ego. If I were to decide who should rule Saalshen, I'd put Errollyn in command of its armies, and Rhillian in command overall. She has the long vision, but Errollyn is better equipped to solve the problem before his nose. I think it should be so here as well."

"So," said Kessligh, "I have overall command. You have the Ilduuris. Errollyn has the *talmaad*."

"And Damon has Lenayin," Sasha said comfortably. And smiled. "How can we lose?" Kessligh did not agree. Sasha's smile faded. "What's wrong? Something with Damon?"

She'd barely made it to her quarters in the Great City Hall when she was accosted by Great Lords Ackryd of Taneryn and Markan of Isfayen. She exchanged warriorlike embraces with each, as she considered both friends, and received a particularly ferocious one from Markan.

"My sister brings you back safe, I see," he observed, releasing her.

"Yasmyn was magnificent," said Sasha, as servants carried her saddlebags into the enormous bed chambers. "She learns svaalverd. I admit I thought her too old to start learning, but she knows much from knifework already, and her skills are good."

"Ha!" laughed Ackryd. "If she learns svaalverd well, even her brother may not be able to best her soon!"

"Unlikely," said Markan. "We come to talk of Prince Damon."

"What about Damon?" Sasha asked cautiously, walking over to consider the view from her massive windows. It was extraordinary, looking clear down the valley to the Ipshaal.

"He is a good commander," said Markan. "Competent. You are better."

"And more respected," added Ackryd.

"Most of what men follow in me is more legend than fact," Sasha replied. "I am good, but command of armies is not like swordwork. I doubt I am better than Damon."

"Your results have been more extraordinary."

"Men will follow you," Ackryd insisted.

"Men will follow Damon," Sasha retorted, with a sideways stare. "What's the difference?" Ackryd looked frustrated. "Besides, I command the Ilduuri Steel. They trust me and only marched on the promise that I would command them. Lenayin already has a good commander—to abandon the Ilduuris so that you can fulfill this childish whim is stupid."

"You could command both," said Markan.

"You would be hard-pressed to find two forces more unalike than Lenayin and Ilduur," Sasha snapped, feeling her temper slipping. "Combining them would be folly. What is this really about?"

"It is about gaining the best commander for Lenayin at the most important time," Ackryd insisted.

"Don't you be dishonest with me," Sasha accused him, stepping forward to stare up at him. So good she'd become at holding her temper, compared to the past. Amongst foreigners, temper was not always useful. But now she was amongst Lenays once more, and Lenays expected fire. "I'm not some foolish girl to be lied to."

"There is talk that you should be queen," said Markan, blunt and unafraid as ever. "Men would prefer it."

Sasha swore, a string of very bad words even by Lenay standards. She strode back to the window and stared out, trying to calm herself. "Damon will be king, when Koenyg is defeated," she said.

"As he will be," said Markan. "No one is speaking of replacing Koenyg now; the battle to come shall decide the rightness of any change of kings. But this is the question. Battle shall decide which Lenay side in this conflict shall inherit the Lenay throne, and that is good. But battle shall not decide the order of its claimants. On our enemies' side, Koenyg is first and undisputed over Myklas. But on this side, there is no such certainty."

"Damon is older and first in line," Sasha snapped. "That is *entirely* certain."

"Lenays have always elevated the man not the rank, nor by order of birth."

"Markan," Sasha said coldly, turning to face him fully so that he understood her seriousness. "You and I have fought battles together. We are fellow warriors, and I love you as a brother and comrade. But if you are intending to create some conflict, so that I and my blood brother are forced into deadly contest, then I will kill you well before I kill him, I promise you."

The brash girl of past times may have exaggerated. This was not that brash girl.

Markan nodded, with calm acceptance. "I understand. Yet the men of Lenayin in battle shall not be denied. The question has been put, and men have spoken. You have achieved more in battle and in command than Damon, it is undisputed. By Lenay custom far older than royalty itself, the place is yours."

"And I decline, as is also my right," Sasha said coldly. "It is an unwise allocation of resources. Ilduur will only fight under me, and I cannot believe that the honourable men of Lenayin would force me to break my oath to them. I am unavailable to command Lenayin, Markan. Damon is available, and talented, and natural heir besides. It is settled."

"It is not." Markan's arms were folded, his slanted eyes deadly serious. "You love your brother. That is honourable. But this is far bigger than you. This is Lenayin. All of Lenayin."

"I promise you," said Sasha, "I will *never*," and she paused for emphasis, "be Queen of Lenayin. I do not want it, would not be good at it, and would be the immediate cause of civil wars present and future. Custom is nice, Markan, but custom can be stupid."

"You are wrong," said Markan, turning to leave. "Custom is strength, and this custom selects the strong. That is you. Lenayin shall be led in battle by the strongest. It is the failure of nations to follow such customs that leads to their destruction."

Sasha wanted to go and see Damon immediately, yet no sooner had Markan and Ackryd left than a delegation of Jahndi officialdom descended upon her. This was headed by none other than Ju'verhen Mali, the first word being a local word for premier, the second being his family name. This was the leader of Jahnd himself then, Sasha realised after a moment's initial confusion. Tallam, her earlier guide, was just a councillor.

Mali was tall and intelligent, and seemed very nice, but lords, he liked to talk. Sasha had to, once again, give a brief account of her adventures in Ilduur, all the while wondering why the number of servants in her previously empty quarters was steadily increasing, and the number of officials seemed to grow larger. Mali announced that there would be a banquet tonight to honour her and the Ilduuris, and she would be presented with the Guardian of Jahnd, a medal, and would that offend any of her religious beliefs or cause any protocol difficulties between her and her Lenay people, or the Ilduuris?

Sasha thought it nice that they'd think to ask, but now her Ilduuri captains were striding in to find her, and she apologised to excuse herself and gather news of her army's campsite in the Dhemerhill Valley. It seemed that there were inadequacies with food—her men had expected good fresh food upon arrival at such a rich city, but now it seemed they'd be living on old rations for several more days at least.

"Well, that's no good," she exclaimed to the captain who brought her the news. "Kick some heads if you have to, I want them fed properly. How is the campsite?"

That seemed no better. Sasha resolved to ride out immediately and see for herself. But now there was the head servant of these high-class quarters, asking her if she'd like to inspect her personal staff. Staff?

She went downstairs and did so, a line of well-dressed maids and menservants, and said yes, they'd do fine, and fended off further questions about the timing of her evening bath, her morning bath, breakfast in her chambers, perhaps musical entertainment arranged at short notice for guests?

"I'll tell you when I know what's going on," she said harriedly, and was stopped immediately by a Steel lieutenant, stating that Generals Geralin and Rochan of the Rhodaani and Enoran Steel required to meet with her at the earliest.

"I'll send Captain Arken instead," she said, heading back upstairs to inquire after Damon's whereabouts.

"The generals were quite insistent that it should be you," said the pursuing lieutenant.

"I'll tell Captain Arken to talk in a high-pitched voice," she retorted, climbing stairs. "I will attend to the generals as soon as I'm able."

In her chambers she found several men in robes, attended by her servants, who told her that it was customary that a service should be held for newly arrived guests, and that the Ilduuris should be received in Jahnd with offerings to the gods, and blessings from the monks. Those were the holy men of the Taanist faith in eastern Ilduur, the native faith to many of the Ilduuri Steel; in addition to the Verenthanes, Sasha hadn't realised that faith was well established here in Jahnd.

She delegated to Captain Arken, and asked a servant to send a messenger to inform him to arrange it all. She would have to attend personally, of course. Sasha gritted her teeth and smiled.

Far too much time had elapsed when she finally left to meet Damon. Yasmyn now walked with her, having come to inform her that Lenayin's leaders had arrived to hold a rathynal in nearby gardens. She walked downstairs from her chambers and across a courtyard, all of which seemed very regal for city like Jahnd. She'd have thought that a people fleeing the persecution of feudalists would not style themselves as nobles in their new land.

These grand buildings clustered upon the peak of what the locals called Mount Jahndi, and were thronged with Steel officers, other uniformed soldiers Sasha took for local city guard, *talmaad*, and well-dressed officials and servants, all scurrying back and forth between various meetings and functions. Sasha walked with two Ilduuri guards, two local messengers in case of the need for rapid communications, Yasmyn, and, now running in pursuit across the courtyard, Daish.

"Compliments of Kessligh," he said, recovering his breath. "He wants us to have a liaison. That's me."

"Excellent," said Sasha, and meant it. Kessligh would need good communication with each of his commanders, and that communication would best be conveyed by messengers who understood what was being said. Daish had strong knowledge of battlefield tactics, and personal friendships with both her and Kessligh. Words lost in translation, in the height of battle, could cost everything. "How's your injury?"

"Good," said Daish. "There are excellent hills here for running. Care to join me?"

"I'd love to, but I'm beginning to realise why Kessligh said being Lenayin's Commander of Armies reminded him more of a prison than a profession." She had gotten off her horse and run every day on the trip from

Ilduur, joined by Daish and some others, always uphill. The infantry had loved to see it. "Where's Aisha?"

"With Rhillian, meeting local *talmaad*. Explaining what happened to Kiel and Arendelle, no doubt."

"Interesting meeting," Yasmyn said drily. "The gardens are just up these steps and beyond."

They climbed stairs between buildings, then emerged onto lovely green gardens. A narrow path took them through cultivated lawns divided by banks of flowers and ornamental trees, and over a little footbridge across a rocky stream and a pool filled with fish. Ahead were shade trees, where Sasha could see many people gathered, most with long hair in Lenay-style leathers.

"Nice place for a meeting, at least," she said, relieved to be outside. To the right, there was a tremendous view across the valleys, with a faint glimpse of the Ipshaal River in the distance. All Lenays would agree this a far superior place for a rathynal than some chamber.

Men stood aside as they approached, forming a wide circle with a space now for Sasha on one side. On the other was Damon. He looked well, dressed closer to battlefield garb than most lowlanders would, as were they all, save for the absence of mail. Surrounding him, Sasha recognised a number of his lordly friends—mostly young men, amongst the few nobility who had not remained with Koenyg. Most of those now had family on the other side. Sasha admired their bravery, and their loyalty to Damon, yet did not think that their circumstance made them reliable.

She stopped at her place in the circle and exchanged the formal greeting for such a gathering, with a fist raised to all in salute. The others returned it. Across the circle, Damon did too, somewhat warily.

She broke the circle and strode to him for an embrace. Damon returned it. There was a murmuring of men about the circle, whether in consternation or approval, or something else, she could not tell. And did not particularly care.

"I'll *never* be Queen of Lenayin," she murmured against his shoulder, low enough that others could not hear. "I told Markan that if he tries to make a conflict between us, I'll kill him first."

Damon squeezed her harder. When she pulled back to look at him, he wore a smile of wan relief. Sasha grinned crookedly and gave him a light whack on the cheek, for reprimand that he could ever have doubted her.

Then she looked about at the circle of faces. "I heard some of you want me to be queen," she announced to them. Many faces registered shock. There was protocol to be observed, formality in such gatherings. One did not simply dive in head-first. "Who amongst you?"

She gazed about, demanding an answer. All eyes turned to Markan. His arms were folded, his eyes calculating. Back on Sasha's side of the circle, his sister Yasmyn watched on intently.

"These are the oldest Lenay ways," said Markan. "This is the *brohyl*, the primacy of might. The throne of Lenayin is open to claim for the first time in its history. Noble tradition states that the heir to the throne shall be determined in descending order of birth amongst sons. But as you can see, there are very few nobles here."

Sasha's eyes narrowed and she folded her arms in reply, walking slowly to the centre of the circle. Markan and Ackryd were the only great lords of Lenay provinces to have joined the defection, and both were respected. Ackryd was a former commander of the Red Swords, a formation of Lenayin's small standing army. But he could not take Markan in a fight, and everyone knew it.

Respect naturally shifted to Markan as the most senior Lenay on this side of the fight, beneath Damon and Sasha. And Markan, being Isfayen, had brought all of the Isfayen's old misgivings of royalty with him. When Sasha's great-grandfather Soros Lenayin had liberated the nation from the Cherrovan, it had been the Isfayen alone who remained unconvinced of his right to rule. They'd had to have the respect beaten into them by an admittedly much larger force before they'd consented to royal rule from Baen-Tar.

Now Markan found himself kingmaker, quite literally. Sasha only recognised about half of the faces of the other men surrounding her—these were not lords, as most of those remained with Koenyg. These were respected warriors, elevated from their status as leaders of towns and villages, with honour earned in recent battle. Sasha's eyes widened a little as she realised what had been happening.

"These men," she said, turning a slow circle to face all about her. "They are now . . . what? Honorary great lords of their provinces?"

"For now we call them lord yuans," Markan confirmed.

"And how were they selected for this honour?"

"Each province held a rathynal of its most senior leaders. There was debate, and the most honoured were nominated. Some provinces held a vote. Others conducted a *tymorain*."

A ritual combat, that was, with stanches instead of swords. Sasha thought it a stupid way to select leaders in battle—the ability to club someone with a stanch said nothing for their ability to lead large formations in war. But now was not the time for that argument.

"So you believe that this same concept should be applied to determining the true heir between royals?"

Markan nodded. "We do. We have voted." There was a murmur of assent from those surrounding.

"To what purpose?"

"To determine the true leader of Lenayin," said Markan.

Sasha nearly laughed. "An Isfayen says so? You who made war upon my great-grandpa because you didn't think Lenayin should have any single leader at all?"

"Isfayen has changed," said Markan, impassively. "The royal family has been good for Lenayin. The royal family is impartial and favours no province above others. The Isfayen believe in the honour of a fair contest, and we would see this honour continue in Lenayin."

"Yet now you challenge the method by which that royal family determines its heirs."

"Your brother Wylfred," said Markan. "Would you have him lead Lenayin ahead of your brother Damon because he is older?" Sasha frowned. Wylfred barely knew one end of a sword from another. His best chance in battle would be to lecture his enemy to death. "Of course you would not. Of those two, Prince Damon is by far the most worthy."

"Well, thanks so much," Damon murmured. Sasha nearly grinned.

"Yet here, Lenayin has two contenders to be heir," Markan continued. "Of the two, Sashandra Lenayin has shown herself the greater with a blade, and the greater in command. This is no dishonour to Prince Damon—few in Lenayin, if any, could claim otherwise. The *brohyl* in Lenayin is built upon the selection of who is best, not who is next. So should it always be."

There were growls of strong approval about the circle.

"You're an idiot," Sasha told him. "You're all idiots. Courageous and honourable idiots, but idiots you remain. This is no time to declare war on the nobility. What you're doing is changing the way Lenayin works. Now that's a nice idea, but not here. This is not that fight. This fight is for Jahnd and for Saalshen, in the belief that their survival will make Lenayin stronger and more prosperous than were they to be destroyed.

"The purpose of a royal family in Lenayin is to make stability. What you seek to do is to make that family unstable. If an heir can be challenged, then nothing is certain. The challenger will also be challenged. And hells, why stop there? There are countless men across Lenayin who could probably rule better than Damon, or I, or Koenyg, or anyone here. What you presume to introduce is a custom by which any of them may feel entitled, by virtue of simply being a good warrior, or having a very large head, to prove himself worthy. How could a king rule, if half the people question aloud whether he is truly the most worthy, and the other half are challenging him in person?"

"This is nonsense," said someone else. "We speak only of a contest between family members, not outsiders."

"So you would set brother against brother?" Sasha asked, rounding on that man incredulously. "Or against sister? My family is strained and crazy enough without the prospect of someday having to break each others' skulls with sticks.

"Furthermore, customs change. The serrin insist linguistic and historical proof exists that the Isfayen people are descended from the Kazeri. Today, they are vastly different from the Kazeri. Even in towns across Lenayin, old men tell of days when customs were different. What you seek to introduce here is not a custom, but an ideal, and over time the rules of custom always bend before the power of ideals. The ideal is equality, which is a nice ideal, and I admit I find it attractive. But a royal family's purpose is not equality, it is stability. I promise you that if you make this precedent of discarding the certainty of a fixed line of succession, you shall indeed introduce a new era of equality to Lenayin—we shall most of us be equally dead, the survivors equally regretful, and our neighbours and enemies equally delighted."

There were grumblings about the circle, men looking dissatisfied. Sasha glanced at Damon, who nodded, quite impressed.

"You are not queen yet," said Markan, unmoved. "These matters are not for you to decide, and for us to obey. Lenayin is about to embark on its greatest ever trial of blood and steel. The men of Lenayin who shall write this history, shall also write these laws."

"You don't own me, Markan," Sasha said with a deadly stare. "I will not merely go where you direct me."

"If you presume to be our leader, you will. No leader can rule Lenayin without consent of the ruled."

"I don't *want* to be queen. It is you who presume to make me your leader, without my consent. So desperate are you to be ruled, free spirit of Isfayen?"

That finally got a reaction, a fire in the big man's eyes. "All men are ruled, higher powers than men have chosen so, and it is beyond the will of men to oppose them. I do have a choice in *who* shall rule. And I shall use it."

Twenty

Across the Dhemerhill Valley, a wall was rising. Sasha rode before it, observing the rows of sharpened stakes that sprouted from the ground like some evil forest, and the deep trench beyond them. The wall itself was now taller than her as she sat on her horse, but even short ladders would scale it. Her initial optimism to see Jahnd's excellent defensive terrain began to fade.

"It's not very big," Yasmyn observed at her side. Her messengers were also with her, and Daish, and several Ilduuri captains including Arken. She'd ridden with them all up the Dhemerhill to the Ipshaal River and back. It was a relatively clear path, a fertile valley with lands cleared about the river for crops and irrigation. The valley was wide enough that ten thousand men could stand shoulder-to-shoulder, and though field walls and fences criss-crossed it, those would be dismantled by the advancing army in moments. The Ilduuri captains looked grim, and Sasha shared their sentiment.

She climbed the far valley side until the shallow slope found a road, then followed the road as the slope rose sharply. Upon a crest that made a good lookout, she joined Kessligh, seated ahorse with Lenay, Rhodaani, and Enoran commanders.

"What do you think?" Kessligh asked her.

"I'm hoping they don't know how to use that artillery they captured," Sasha replied. She spoke Saalsi, which all senior Steel spoke competently. A *talmaad* translated for the Lenays, who nodded grimly.

This lookout stood directly above the wall. To their right, the Dhemerhill Valley was joined by the smaller Ilmerhill Valley. Across the Ilmerhill, upon the opposing slope, was Jahnd, protruding into the Dhemerhill from that intersection of the two valleys.

"How far is our artillery range?" she asked.

"See that mill down by the Ilmerhill River?" Kessligh said, pointing. "If we have catapults on the walls, that's their range."

"Can't even shoot beyond our own city," Sasha surmised. "Some of the roads looked good enough for hauling catapults. We probably can't haul them back up the slope, but we could forward-position some out here in the valley, then once this new wall is breached, they fall back within the range of our city-wall catapults."

"That's the plan," Kessligh agreed. "We can only fit about a quarter of our artillery on the walls anyhow, and those can be easily avoided. I want to create killing zones where we force them into unavoidable losses."

"Which is why you're sitting up here."

"Exactly. There are a couple of crests along this side of the valley with road access from the ridge behind. I want to put a bunch of them along here and force them to take this ridge. My artillery captains tell me these roads aren't quite steep enough to stop us retreating from here down into the Ilmerhill. We'll hold the mouth of the Ilmerhill even after this wall here is breached; there are good natural defences. So we can get artillery from this position down into the Ilmerhill for a new defensive line there."

"You'll need someone to hold this ridge," said Sasha. "You can't concede the high ground above the Ilmerhill, even if they can't get catapults up this way. Ilduuris would be ideal."

"Are they that much better on the hills?"

Sasha smiled. "They climb like mountain goats and their armour and shields are lighter for the purpose. And they read the high terrain excellently, they know which passes need to be defended, and which the enemy is simply wasting his time on."

"I'd thought to use your Ilduuris on the right flank, too," said Kessligh. "Which means you'll have to split in two, defending the high-left and high-right flanks."

Sasha shrugged. "I have good captains, I can delegate. But we'll lose this ridge eventually, and from there we'll certainly lose the Ilmerhill."

Kessligh nodded. "Yes, but it will cost them dearly."

Behind the new wall across the Dhemerhill, armies were camped along the valley floor. The Rhodaani, Enoran, and Ilduuri Steel, or what was left of them. And the Army of Lenayin.

"There's one other thing," said Sasha. "We cannot simply fight this as a defensive action, retreating all the while and making them pay for each step taken. If they have as much artillery as is being said, we can't win that way. We have to try and take out some of that artillery."

"I know," said Kessligh. "You've fought against artillery. What do you think they'll do?"

"Well, assuming they're not stupid, and I don't think they are considering artillery has killed so many of them in the past . . ." She paused, thinking about it, looking from the ridge upon which they stood, to the valley below and back again. "Well, see, they have to take this ridge first. With artillery up here, we can hit them but they can't hit us. The first fight will be here.

"If they want to use their artillery against this wall, they'll have to risk losing it to our artillery on this hill. So it wouldn't surprise me if they simply try to take the wall without their artillery—hit this ridge and the wall simultaneously, but hold their artillery back so they don't lose it. It will cost them a lot more men that way, but better that than lose artillery."

"If they leave it back by the Ipshaal in safety . . ." Kessligh said thoughtfully.

Sasha nodded vigorously. "Exactly. We must risk a thrust into their rear to try and get their artillery first. Otherwise, well, I heard the stories of what the Rhodaani Steel did in Elisse to lords who cowered inside defensive positions; half a day and there was nothing left. We won't cave in half a day, but once they've taken this wall, these hills, the Ilmerhill behind us . . . we'll be stuck in Jahnd, under bombardment, and everything will burn. We won't last three days."

"Good," said Kessligh, gazing across the scene, deep in thought. She doubted she'd told him anything he hadn't already thought of. It was more that ideas, like the vegetables he'd taken such time and care over on their ranch in Baerlyn, needed to be nurtured.

Upon the road up the valley side, Sasha saw a new group of horsemen. These moved light, like *talmaad*. One of them was breaking away from the rest, in unreasonable haste. Sasha grinned. It could only be one person.

"He's been amazing," said Kessligh, with a little irony. "You should know that he has quite a following here now, amongst the *talmaad*. Perhaps to rival Rhillian's."

"Yes, well, we'll see about that," Sasha said. "You heard what she did?"

Kessligh nodded. "Extraordinary. Serrin civilisation has always evolved far more slowly than humans, but even so. They did fight and kill each other once, long ago. It seems the instinct is not entirely dead."

Sasha shook her head. "That's not it." And to Kessligh's querying look, "I'll explain later."

"One last thing—Errollyn has struck up quite a friendship with Damon in our ride here."

"Hmm," said Sasha. "You've heard about our issues with Damon too."

Another nod. "Now go to him before he kills his horse coming up that hill."

Sasha took off back down the road, giving the stallion enough freedom to find his own pace down the hill. She met Errollyn at the first elbow where the road turned back on itself, but the horse did not slow fast enough, so she had to haul him back and around. But Errollyn had leaped off, so she leaped off too, and then she was in his arms. His grip was strong, almost painful, and she clung desperately.

"Hey," she said, muffled against his shoulder.

"We shouldn't make too much of a scene," Errollyn suggested. "I mean, I'm *talmaad* leader here, and you're general of the Ilduuri Steel. People are watching."

"Fuck them," said Sasha, and kissed him.

There was another wall being built across the Dhemerhill Valley upstream from Jahnd. It was no taller than the other, cutting through paddocks, grain fields and orchard groves like a great grey scar. Facing it, trees were being cut, and farmhouses demolished. Riding along it, Sasha recalled a time when she would have felt excitement at the prospect of the greatest battle in Rhodia for several centuries at least. Now, seeing the destruction for its preparation, and pondering the destruction to come, she felt only sad.

"It's a day's detour to come through the hills and into the Dhemerhill Valley upstream," said Errollyn, riding at her side. "We've some ambush ideas along the way, but there's nothing we can do to stop them."

"I don't like this at all," Sasha muttered, looking back over the wall at Jahnd, rising high up its hillside. "Once they take this wall, they can hide behind it as we do, on the reverse side. We block our own avenue to a counterattack, and give them cover from our own artillery."

"Little choice," said Errollyn. "We must make them fight for position in the valley, and subject them to our artillery on the high slopes. It's our main chance to inflict serious casualties, because once we're forced back to Jahnd and under *their* artillery fire, the casualties will be mostly ours."

Errollyn took her east, upriver where the valley turned slightly across Jahnd's right flank, making a wider valley floor. Here the river widened, and the fields were open, and more clear of trees. This was cavalry country. Above it, Jahnd's buildings spread beyond its old defensive walls and along the high ridge. Paths led down to the valley from there, steep in parts, but not too steep for an army to climb. This would be Jahnd's right flank. *Her* right flank. It was high ground, which made it Ilduuri ground, plus whatever artillery was put up there. The Regent would have no choice but to capture these ridges, to prevent terrible fire from being rained down upon his forces with impunity.

"If we lose that ridge," said Errollyn, looking up as they rode, "we lose Jahnd. The city itself is in range from there."

Sasha shook her head. "If they mostly come down here with cavalry, they'll not be scaling that ridge quickly. That's infantry work, and the infantry will be coming up from the Ipshaal on the other side. That's where I'll be, so this will be your fight—a cavalry fight. And once they come down here, you'll be boxed in with nowhere to run."

"The only way into the valley is far ahead," he said, pointing. "We're headed there anyway, I'll show you. I can lead them on a chase down the length of the valley—it's beautiful ambush country." Sasha bit her lip. "What troubles you?"

"Errollyn, *talmaad* fighting is 'run away' fighting. I do not mean that as an insult; the *talmaad* are perhaps the most lethal warriors I've seen, man for man. But mounted archery requires distance from the enemy. You cannot close and fight nose-to-nose as regular cavalry can. And there is no room in this valley to always run away."

"I know," Errollyn said simply.

"And this is Saalshen's peril," Sasha continued with real concern, "because Saalshen has never fought nose-to-nose. Saalshen fights from the shadows and at range. You can inflict terrible losses that way, but you cannot hold ground. The army that attacks you here will hold ground, clear it, and move forward slowly and repeat. You need forces that can hold ground, Errollyn, or Saalshen itself will be lost."

"I know," Errollyn repeated. He looked sad. "We have had this discussion too many times before, Sasha. Saalshen wins here, or is lost. As are all my people. We cannot fight this way. We have always refused to learn."

"Why?" Sasha asked in despair. It was the great question, the one she had puzzled over for most of the last tumultuous year.

"Come," said Errollyn. "I will show you."

Tormae was a pretty village at the far end of the Dhemerhill, where the valley began to fade into rolling hills and patchwork forest. She and Errollyn dismounted where a diversion from the river made a small lake, fronted by several timber houses. Each had small paddocks, with a few cows and goats grazing beneath large shade trees. Sasha saw serrin men and women working in nearby vegetable gardens, and thought that the scene was not so different from human villages she had seen.

They left their horses tied to a rail by the lake and walked. She had told the entourage to leave them for a while, so they could have this time alone together. The road here seemed more trees and hedges than houses. Several small bridges crossed streams cutting the road as it wound back and forth between patched sunlight and dappled shade. Birds sang and darted from bushes to treetops, and here and there were serrin walking the road carrying bundles of crops, or odd woven baskets suspended from shoulder slings, filled with vegetables and fruit.

The locals greeted them cheerfully, several exchanging longer words with Errollyn in a dialect Sasha did not understand. Soon Sasha began wondering where the town centre was.

"This is the town centre," Errollyn answered her. "It's all like this."

Sasha frowned at him. "No industry? How is wood worked, or tools made, or leather tanned? There needs to be a grouping of people and skills in one location, surely?"

Errollyn shook his head. "You know serrin. We have many skills, we do not specialise. Thus we have no need to cluster."

Sasha stared about her, pausing as they crossed another small bridge. "You mean, these houses here were . . ."

"Mostly constructed by the people who live in them, yes." Errollyn leaned on the railing beside her. "Most serrin know woodwork. Many know stone. Most grow their own food, at least in part. Many make their own bread, and tools, and sometimes even clothes. We do not specialise. Insects specialise. We are not insects."

Sasha barely noticed the implied insult. "But there are larger cities, yes? Uam? Shea?"

"Yes, but they're quite small compared to Tracato, and certainly compared to Petrodor. All are on the coast, and only grew large on human trade. That trade is how we have such a strong navy. But Jahnd is the largest city in all Saalshen, and it is not even serrin."

"Oh dear lords," Sasha murmured, feeling slightly dizzy. She did not know whether to laugh or cry. She spun on Errollyn. "You've been lying to me!" she accused him. "You've never explained Saalshen like this! You implied the cities and towns were larger!"

"You never asked too deeply," Errollyn replied, with no more than a faint frown. "But yes, I was vague. Sasha, we don't talk about it much, with humans. Even a *du'jannah* like me can see why it is not a good idea. Can you?"

Sasha turned back to the view across the little stream, through thickets of small trees to several more pretty timber houses. "You don't forget," she murmured. "Your memories are so much better than ours. You learn a skill and remember it. So you don't specialise."

"No," Errollyn agreed patiently.

"So you are more self-sufficient. You do not need to employ a builder to build a house, you build it yourselves, because you learn how and remember, quickly. You do not need specialist tradesmen. Serrin know all trades themselves."

"Well, not *all* trades," Errollyn admitted. "But many more than humans do."

"So you don't need big settlements," Sasha concluded. "You like small towns. Villages." Suddenly it dawned on her, looking about, that for all the wildness of this place, the wildness seemed a little . . . predictable. "Oh wow, all this village is landscaped, isn't it? It only looks natural, it's actually all been sculpted. These trees, lakes, fields?"

"This stream," Errollyn agreed, indicating the water that flowed beneath their feet. "The streams are all artificial, flowing from the river, and back into it. We manage watercourses like humans have not learned how. This village could have been here for a thousand years or longer. Serrin have little urge to grow things bigger as humans do. We have all we need here, so we are not compelled."

"And so you have no industry," Sasha sighed as it truly dawned on her. A lump grew in her throat. "No great steelworks to outfit an army. No great stone quarries or lumber yards to do works of engineering, to build defensive walls."

Errollyn nodded. "And we have so little free labour. These people are happy and want for little, but they're busy. Serrin work hard—that is the way when we do everything ourselves and are self-sufficient. Armies require a surplus of men to go off and fight, and a surplus of food and provisions. . . ."

Sasha rolled her eyes and gazed skywards in exasperation. "You fools," she said sadly. And smiled at him. "You've been bluffing us for centuries, haven't you? That's why humans were never welcome to visit here."

"That and the small matter of humans thinking this the land of devils," Errollyn said sarcastically.

"But you can't actually maintain an army at all, can you? Just the *talmaad*, who are so talented as individuals that they make an intimidating impression, but even they cannot stand and fight in force."

"We would have to change our entire civilisation," Errollyn sighed and gazed across the stream. Further along were some fishing nets, woven onto a wooden frame with an elaborate mount that would dip the nets in the water. "We would have to specialise, and live in cities, and make a surplus of labour for fighting and building, and maintain them with a central leadership that gathered taxes. We don't even have leaders, Sasha. No central organisation at all, or nearly none. This is what we were debating, up until King Leyvaan's time. And after his fall, and our capture of Rhodaan, Enora and Ilduur, we had human lands to do all this for us.

"Our human allies gave us our army, gave us the Steel, and the engineers and builders, and the wealth to maintain it all by taxes, and serrin decided we did not need to change the way we lived at all. And so we went back to our old ways and stopped worrying about it so much. In truth, we were better prepared to defend ourselves two hundred years ago than today. Now we are helpless like children, and hoping only that our human friends will save us. For if they do not, we have no way of saving ourselves."

The building was a gathering space in Tormae, like a council room, though Sasha had not encountered the word before in Saalsi. It had no walls, polished wood floors, and exposed beams across a high ceiling. The centre of its floor stepped down to a hole, within which was a small garden of smooth rocks, little plants, and a pool of water. More water trickled beneath the floorboards, and all about the exposed sides were more plants. Sasha had only ever seen a building like this before in the Mahl'rhen, the serrin house in Tracato. That had been grand. This was intimate, green, and even more lovely.

She and Errollyn left their boots at the floor's edge, and interrupted the debate within. Before the central garden, Rhillian sat alone, one bare foot teasing the surface of the pool. Or nearly alone. Aisha sat one step above her, cross-legged and concerned. About the room, some seated, some standing and leaning, were *talmaad*. Amongst them were a few plain-clothed serrin, these in a light robe, tied at the waist. All appeared concerned.

Errollyn went straight to Rhillian, and she rose. Errollyn embraced her. Sasha saw her face over Errollyn's shoulder, her expression a little surprised and quite relieved.

"I'm sad about Arendelle," Errollyn told her as they parted. "But not Kiel. I would have done it earlier, had not consequences forbidden it."

"This is not a matter to be spoken of so lightly," another serrin said gravely.

"No one asked your opinion, Hsheldrin," Errollyn cut him off, eyes not leaving Rhillian. The *talmaad* named Hsheldrin looked quite displeased. "Kiel's plan was evil, as was much of Kiel's path of late. If we do not oppose evil, we oppose nothing. If Arendelle was ensnared by Kiel's *ra'shi* at the time, then his death is also an unavoidable and necessary sadness. You did right and well."

Sasha went to sit by Aisha, who offered her a bowl of biscuits.

"What happens here?" Errollyn asked the gathering, challengingly. "You all look like someone died."

Discomfort swept the room. Even Rhillian gave him a faintly warning look, resuming her seat by Aisha. Errollyn paced, slowly.

"We discuss *vy'tal air*," replied a serrin.

"Banishment," Aisha whispered to Sasha, in Lenay.

Sasha frowned. "From what?"

"Saalshen. The serrinim. Everything."

Sasha stared across at Rhillian. Rhillian met her eyes, and smiled faintly.

Errollyn was laughing. "*Vy'tal air*," he said. "Seriously? You're not joking?"

More frowns. Errollyn spoke Saalsi with deliberate bluntness, like some vandal using a porcelain statuette to break down a door. Hearing it was enough to make more sophisticated serrin wince.

"If *vy'tal air* is not invoked by this act," said another serrin, "then for what should it be invoked?"

"I don't know," Errollyn replied. "How about for something *wrong?*"

"No serrin has intentionally and in good mind murdered another serrin in millennia!" came the angry reply. "She murdered two!"

"Firstly," said Errollyn, "Rhillian did not murder anyone. Kiel murdered a human family, and was about to murder many more. Rhillian stopped him. In the course of this stopping, Kiel lost his life, as did Arendelle. A fair trade in any moral tongue, I think.

"Secondly, we are about to fight a battle for Saalshen's very existence. The *talmaad* have two truly proven commanders in this fight. I am one, Rhillian is the other. She commanded with excellence in Elisse; few if any could have done as well. This discussion can wait until after the battle, if there is an after. If there is not an after, it will be because we are all dead, thus rendering all of this most excellent hot air of yours wasted."

"This is the most serious crime against the serrinim in a millennium!" another serrin said angrily. "And you treat it as a joke!"

"I treat *you* as a joke," Errollyn corrected. "All of you. Killing a murderous serrin is evil, yet murdering human families is nothing? Is evil only evil if it is committed against a serrin? Morality cannot be equivocated. Morality is consistency. Wrong is wrong no matter who the victim.

"The only crime here was committed by Kiel. Serrin do not kill each other because we rarely do enough evil to warrant it. If you wish to be upset by someone breaking a long-standing tradition of the serrinim, be upset by *that*. Rhillian, let's leave. If this mob does not understand even that much, they are not worth our company."

"You can appoint her as commander of *talmaad* if you wish," a serrin said darkly. "Whether any serrin shall choose to follow her is another matter."

A small group of buildings clustered along the stream. One was a mill, its waterwheel squeaking in the rush of downhill water. Sasha wondered if the slope of the ground had been shaped by serrin many hundreds of years ago, or if they had chosen this slope to make the water run faster.

"Now you know how it feels," Errollyn said to Rhillian as the four of them walked along the bank.

Rhillian sighed, thumbs tucked in her belt. She was greatly upset, but showed it little. Sasha put a hand on her shoulder. "We are all four of us exiles, in our way. My father cast me from Lenayin, Aisha cannot return to Enora, Errollyn is *du'jannah*, and now you."

"I will not leave," said Rhillian, gazing at the mill. "The threats of a people who cannot punish their own mean nothing."

"I need you on the right flank with Sasha's Ilduuris," said Errollyn. "If they will not follow you, they'll have me to answer to. I don't trust anyone else to do the job."

"Arjen could," said Rhillian. "Mirelle."

Errollyn shook his head. "Rhillian, we have been having this argument since Petrodor. Serrin do not think flexibly. We follow. The *vel'ennar* is our peace and harmony, but it is also our shackles. I have no *vel'ennar*, so I see things that others miss. And now there is you, a normal serrin, who has become somehow stranger even than I. Before you took Kiel's life, I would not have trusted you with command as I do now."

Rhillian gave him a wary stare. "I am a killer of my own kind."

"Like me," said Sasha. Rhillian rolled her eyes.

They stopped on a small bridge that crossed the stream to the mills. The building adjoining the mill had a chimney, and Sasha could smell the most wonderful bread baking. Serrin unloaded sacks of grain from a cart. One recognised Errollyn, and shouted greeting. Errollyn waved back.

"What chance do you give us?" Rhillian asked Sasha as they leaned on the rail.

"If we can take some of their artillery early, a reasonable chance," said Sasha. "If not, very little."

Rhillian nodded reluctantly. "Immobility is death against Steel artillery. A fate much like Saalshen's. We are immobile. Human civilisations change, yet we remain stuck in one place."

"They weren't supposed to capture our artillery," said Aisha. "But no one really knew what would happen in a defeat. The Steel had won only victories in two centuries. Defeat was never planned for properly."

"And now we equip our worst enemies with our deadliest weapons," Rhillian finished. "But it was always going to happen. Things do not stand still upon the western side of the Ipshaal. Saalshen's enemies were always going to learn to use that weaponry one day."

"You should have invaded them all when you had the chance," said Sasha.

Rhillian shrugged. "The oldest argument, the oldest regret. Serrin are who we are—we thought that by not invading, we were being kind. And now our kindness will kill us."

"War is not the worst thing." Sasha thought of Markan, and Damon. Thought of pending battles, against enemies and friends. "Sometimes it is the lack of war that creates a worse disaster."

Rhillian looked at her. "What are you going to do about Markan?"

Sasha was not surprised that Rhillian could guess her thoughts; Rhillian knew her well. "I should do what is best for Lenayin," she replied, without conviction.

"Perhaps a woman to rule Lenayin would be good," Aisha suggested. "Perhaps it would improve things."

"Not even for the blink of an eye," Sasha said sombrely. "Do you believe in that old nonsense of women acting more kindly and gently? This is me we're talking about, Aisha."

"That is true," Aisha conceded with a smile.

"The north would rebel," Sasha added.

"The north rebel anyhow," said Rhillian. "What difference?"

"Many more would join them. I am a Goeren-yai figure, so the Veren-thanes would be threatened. And worse, the methods that Markan seeks to use to elevate me mean that every mad fool in Lenayin who feels slighted that the gods or spirits did not grant him an earlier birth will challenge his brother to battle. I agree that Lenayin needs a means of passing power from one man to another without the endless shedding of blood. I refuse to add to the bloodshed in generations to come."

A boy of perhaps twelve came running to the bridge from the bakery. Errollyn greeted him, and the boy showed him the bow he was carrying. It looked newly made, and the right height for a boy that age.

"Well, they seem quite adamant, Sasha," said Aisha. "I do not claim to know Lenayin as well as you, but I know it quite well for a foreigner. There does seem to be a desire for you to lead them, and I do not think they will simply allow you to refuse."

"You know most peoples quite well, Aisha." Sasha sighed. "They have superstitions. Some say I am the Synnich. I was Kessligh's uma, I am Goeren-yai, as are three-quarters of this army, and yes, I have achieved some things. Common Lenay folk have always disliked the Lenay nobility because the nobility hold titles that they did not earn. It is not the Lenay way. Now the nobles fight with the Regent, so naturally they strike against the ways of nobility, to elevate me above Damon."

"You could lose to Damon on purpose," Rhillian suggested. "In a *tymorain*."

"You don't think they'd notice?" Sasha retorted.

"Or you could fight Markan," said Aisha.

"My ally." Sasha thought about it, frowning. "I'm not sure what it achieves. Nor if I could beat him at *tymorain*. I may strike him four out of five exchanges, but he's huge. He only needs to hit me once—he can kill much bigger opponents than me even with a stanch."

"There is that," Aisha agreed. "But Sasha, you said you wish to do what is best for Lenayin. These Lenay men have settled upon a stupid custom, and . . ."

"It's not a stupid custom," Sasha retorted. "It is the elevation of the most capable, and more nations should follow it. It's just stupid to apply it to royalty."

Sasha was interrupted by Errollyn, drawing the serrin boy's bow and firing an arrow into a nearby tree. He spoke with the boy, impressed. The boy was pleased.

"It's newly made," Errollyn explained to her, seeing her watching. "I showed him how to make it a week ago."

Sasha blinked. "He made it in a week?" Errollyn nodded. Sasha knew serrin bows were far more complex than anything humans used, comprised of several kinds of wood, moulded together in ways that dramatically increased power, accuracy, and range.

"You people are extraordinary," she murmured.

Rhillian smiled, and grasped her hand. "Many of *you people* are just as extraordinary. So many of you have come to fight for us foreigners."

Sasha shook her head. "We do not just fight for you. Everyone wishes to make a better world, and we all believe that the human world would be far better with the serrin still in it. We fight for ourselves."

Twenty-one

Sasha dreamed a terrible dream.

Then, with a start, she awoke. The first thing she saw was Errollyn's eyes, gazing at her on the pillows from barely a hand's breadth away.

"You dream," Errollyn said softly.

"I dream of fire," Sasha whispered. "And of rain."

"Your people believe that a warrior's spirit guide will visit him before a great battle. Do you also believe?"

"*Believe.* That word is not the same from your lips and mine, even though we speak the same tongue. Serrin do not believe as humans do."

"Do *you* believe?" Errollyn pressed.

Sasha recalled the fire, and the sea of raised spears and swords. Recalled the pouring rain upon the hillsides, quenching the flames. Fire and water, the primary place of spirits. Serrin had taught her to think clearly. Yet whatever else she was, she remained Lenay, and Goeren-yai.

"Yes," she murmured.

"Perhaps you are the Synnich," Errollyn suggested, sliding a hand to her waist beneath the sheets.

"No. I'm me."

"Yet you believe in forces beyond the control of us all."

"As do you."

"I may be in the grip of one such force right now," Errollyn agreed. He kissed her. Sasha kissed him back.

A knock on the door interrupted them. Sasha wrapped a leg about her lover and ignored it. The door opened a crack.

"A thousand pardons, sir and m'lady. There are visitors."

"Better be good," Sasha murmured against Errollyn's cheek. "Who?" she called more loudly.

"Your sister," came the reply.

Sasha's eyes widened. "Sofy?" She scrambled from the bed, found some of her favoured thigh-length woollen underwear and a shirt, and just in time as a slim girl in loose pants and a floppy shirt came tearing into the chambers with no decorum at all, and charged at Sasha with a squeal.

Sasha grabbed her and they tumbled onto the bed. When Sasha let go to look at her, she could scarcely believe her eyes. Sofy's hair was nearly short. Not completely, but now it barely fell past her shoulders, a scandalous cut indeed for a girl who had always worn it halfway down her back. And she had odd braids in it, several to either side of her face, to wild and unpredictable effect. In Sofy's loose travelling clothes, Sasha could see no other sign of jewellery or decoration, save that she smelled lovely, like flowers.

"Good lords!" Sasha exclaimed. "What have you done with yourself? What happened to the Princess Regent?"

"Oh, I have tales!" Sofy explained, with a faint sadness through the joy. "But later. Look at *you*! You look fit and well, and I see few scars anywhere!" They hugged again. Sofy looked up from the bed to find Errollyn, who had dragged on a pair of pants for modesty. "Errollyn!"

She leaped up and hugged him too, then exclaimed at his remaining scars, a clear but fading tracery across his body. As they talked, Sasha felt an unexpected emotion. When Sofy's attention returned, she was surprised to find Sasha wiping tears.

"Sasha, what's wrong?"

"Everyone's here," Sasha explained, helplessly. "Everyone I love. Or nearly everyone."

"But we're going to win, right?" Sofy grasped her hands. "And when we win, how better than all together?"

Sasha sighed, and nodded, with what she hoped was conviction. Sofy did not yet truly know war. She did not consider how dearly even victory would cost them.

They exchanged tales, as servants brought breakfast.

"So where is Jaryd?" Sasha asked.

"With the army," Sofy explained. "We reached Tormae last evening; we could have reached Jahnd that night but the villagers said there would be grand events for you, so we thought we'd wait until morning."

"We were in Tormae just yesterday," Sasha confirmed.

"Yes, they said. Isn't it lovely? Errollyn, Saalshen is so beautiful! And your people! I've yet to meet any who were fearful or unkind, even once they learned who I am."

"You should see the star festivals," Errollyn said sadly. "The next is in a week, if I have my calendar right. Only I fear it will be skipped this year."

"I would love to see everything Saalshen has to offer," Sofy enthused, breaking bread and spreading butter. "I would love to spend a year here—I'm sure even then I could barely scratch the surface."

"Sofy." Sasha drew her attention, cautiously. "So you and Jaryd are . . . ?"

"Fucking, yes." And Sofy laughed at the look on Sasha's face.

"Sofy . . . you're still married."

Sofy chewed her bread. "What's your point?"

"To the Regent."

Sofy shrugged, determined to finish her mouthful before answering.

"I like this new development," Errollyn admitted, very amused. Sasha was too incredulous to respond. What in the world had happened to her very respectable and proper little sister?

"I could not reconcile it for a very long time," Sofy said after a swallow. "I mean, I love people, and I love all the things about people that make them difficult. Gods know I had enough of it with our family."

"No argument there."

"Yourself included," Sofy added pointedly, but with a sparkle. Sasha nodded impatiently. "And I got so angry with you sometimes, because you fell in love with all these things that the mindless head bashers in Lenayin love so much. You know, duelling, warfare . . ."

"We are a nation of warriors, Sofy."

"We," Sofy retorted with sarcasm. "Well, I'm not. And I've never accepted that people are evil, because that's just the excuse these mindless brutes use to justify killing each other. So I could not believe that Balthaar was evil, and for the longest time I refused to accept that he could do all these evil things that you and others accused him of. But then I saw Tracato. And I saw what the Elissians did to those innocent townsfolk we tried to save, and . . ."

"But none of that was Balthaar directly," Sasha interrupted, watching Sofy intently. "Tracato was set afire by the Black Order. And the Elissians follow themselves."

Sofy smiled. "But this is the point, Sasha. I realised it did not matter that Balthaar had not ordered these things directly. This is not a question of personal responsibility. It's a question of ideas. And beliefs. Balthaar's ideas led to that. He shares those beliefs. He thinks them innocuous enough, and godly, and right and proper, as he's been taught. He is not a bad man, and he genuinely believes that what he is doing is right, and will lead to the betterment of all the world, and all the people in it."

"Except mine," said Errollyn.

"Yes," Sofy agreed. "In his mind, serrin are not 'people.'" And she reached a hand to grasp Errollyn's in apology. "It's only what he's been taught—he does not know any better."

"How tragic for him."

"It is," Sofy agreed. "Because his wife has now realised that none of it matters. Him being good, many of his people being good, it's irrelevant. We have to stop them. Kill them all if we must. There may be no evil people, but there are certainly evil ideas and evil actions. It is very sad if good people must be killed to prevent their evil actions, but there it is. It's really quite stunning how simple it is when you realise it."

"So what will you do now?"

Sofy looked faintly surprised at the question. "Well, I cannot fight, but I can stand on a rampart and wave a banner. I can declare before all friends and enemies that the Princess Regent is so convinced of the evil of her husband's actions that she has turned against him."

"And against Koenyg? And Myklas?"

Sofy looked sad, but she did not waver. "Yes," she said simply.

Sasha let out a breath. She looked at Errollyn. Errollyn nodded. "It's going to be horrible, Sofy," she said. "The most horrible thing ever. Far worse than what you saw in Tracato, or in the Udalyn Valley."

"I know."

"Jahndis are evacuating their children and old folk. Many others are joining them, those not needed for preparations. I'd rather you were with them."

Sofy smiled. "I'd rather *you* were with them. But here we are." Sasha sighed. "Now, what are you going to do about these fools who wish to make you queen?"

Sasha blinked. And could not resist saying, half joking, "You don't think I might make a good queen?"

Sofy laughed. "Sasha, don't be silly. You must stop them."

"And what if they do not listen?"

"It seems that all of your friends and loved ones have been forced to fight their own people recently: Kessligh, Errollyn, Jaryd, your friend Rhillian, and now me. When will *you* start?"

Sasha cantered toward the centre of the Lenay camp, with Yasmyn close by. All about were Lenay campsites, mostly open fires, a few tents, many bedrolls or blankets donated by grateful Jahndis or nearby serrin. Men watched as she passed, some pausing in their tasks of washing, mending kit, or preparing food. In far fields, men trained in large ranks, coordinating manoeuvres with great yells.

The valley was wide enough that fifteen thousand Lenay warriors and their horses did not feel particularly cramped for space. Soldiers spread up the hills in search of wood and game, or roamed into Jahnd, or nearby serrin villages. Even here she saw serrin, many bringing food, others cooking or in conversation with these ferocious strangers. Many more serrin were arriving from elsewhere in Saalshen, Sasha knew, and most of them could not fight. Rhillian and Errollyn were at a loss to know what to do with them all.

Ahead, tents clustered near a small bridge across the Dhemerhill River. Men were waiting, having heard her message to assemble. Yasmyn had helped Sasha make the spirit marks on her cheeks, three lines for the three levels of being, like the tri-braid in her hair. She wore a bloodred cloth tied about her head, a *krayhal* the Isfayen called it, the declaration of a blood-warrior on the path. A second *krayhal* she had tied about her waist. Sasha let the stallion prance, and the young horse obliged, delighted.

Men parted as she rode into the central space between tents. There she found Markan and Ackryd, and a number of lord yuans, as they were now calling themselves. Her allies and friends, men who would die for her, and she for them and their ways. Yet now she pushed all such thoughts aside and rode straight to Markan, and reared the stallion.

His hooves lashed, and Markan backed up. When the stallion grounded, she saw Markan glaring up at her, only too aware of the insult she had paid him, in forcing his retreat before these men.

"*You* do not own me!" Sasha yelled at him. She drew her blade and pointed it at his chest. "I am Sashandra Lenayin, once uma to Kessligh Cronenverdt! I am Synnich-ahn, and the great spirit has driven me through walls of enemies, and I have drunk of their blood!" Spirits signs were made in a flurry about the circle, but Sasha did not cease. "*You* seek to put the Synnich in a cage, with a crown on her head! I am not made for cages, I am made for war! Who will fight me, and dare to show me my *place*!"

She wheeled the stallion, and ran him in a circle. Men scampered back as she tore before them, then back again. The horse reared again, and she let him, glaring all the while with a blade in her hand.

Markan, she thought, seemed almost to be smiling. Many stared awestruck, yet Markan knew this game. Worse, he liked it. He bowed a little and looked quite pleased that he had driven her to this at last.

"The men of Lenayin dare not place the Synnich-ahn in a cage," he replied. "We seek only for the Synnich to lead us to victory!" A huge cheer raised in reply.

"The Synnich does not care for victory!" Sasha snarled. "The Synnich wants only blood! Be careful what you wish for, little man, for the dark spirits care nothing for your glory."

"The Synnich-ahn should be warned," Markan intoned. "I am Crast-ahn, led by the greatest of the old Isfayen spirits. We of the Isfayen know you, Synnich, drinker of blood, destroyer of worlds. We see that you have chosen a servant in this world, and we see that you have chosen well. But the servant is only flesh, and may fall as others fall. I am only flesh, and I will make her fall, if she cuts at my honour and the honour of my spirit guide too deeply."

"You will die," Sasha hissed.

"There is no need for death. *Tymorain*. Tonight. All shall come, and honour shall decide it."

"The Synnich-ahn does not fight with sticks," Sasha said scornfully, as the stallion fought for his head. "Only steel drinks blood."

"The Synnich's servant is smaller than I. Sharp steel evens the odds. *Tymorain* then, yet the Synnich-ahn shall fight armoured, while I shall be bare."

"Done," Sasha snapped. "You claim to offer me power, yet you clasp the true power to yourself. You make new laws, and insist that others shall follow them. If you truly wish to follow me, you will let *me* make the laws, for all of Lenayin."

Sasha spun the stallion fast and galloped from the scene and across the bridge, men scattering before her. Yasmyn followed.

"How was that?" Sasha asked her once they had cleared the camp's perimeter, and slowed to a canter heading for Jahnd.

"Perfect," said Yasmyn. "My brother was impressed. Some others were frightened."

"Wonderful. Now if I can just figure a way to beat that giant in a headbashing contest." She glanced at Yasmyn when she did not reply. "Do you think I can?"

Yasmyn shrugged. "Against my brother? With blades, very likely. With stanches? I doubt it."

Damon had a surprise for her, and they waited in a noisy yard near a flaming furnace and bellows while the armourer went and fetched it.

"You're crazy," Damon told her, for what Sasha figured was the ten thousandth time in her life. "You're challenging him for the right to make law? What would that make you, if not queen?"

"Royalty in Lenayin makes all law save for those laws that apply to royals," Sasha replied. "Those, the people make to rule *us*. Grandpa Soros made it that way."

"I'm beginning to wonder if Grandpa Soros didn't waste his time," Damon said sourly. "All his efforts and we're still a pack of barbarians."

"With potential," Sasha insisted.

"Nice facepaint," said Damon. Sasha exhaled hard, and slumped against a post. "Look, I appreciate you making this effort on my behalf, but . . ."

"If there's one thing I'm *not* doing," Sasha snapped, "it's acting on your behalf. As much as I dislike the nobility, they did take a land of barbarians who were always at each others' throats and settle it down to some kind of civility. Now Markan and company want to return it to its previous state. Succession by family lineage can be pretty silly too, but at least it's stable."

"If you beat him, and they grant you the power to make laws, you could put a council in charge," Damon suggested. "Like here, or the Saalshen Bacosh. Abolish royalty."

"Damn I'd love to," Sasha muttered, "but I don't think we're ready. Do you?"

Damon made a face. "If I were king," he said, "I'd build institutions first. Institutions like you describe in Tracato . . . And I like the idea of those red-coats. An independent administration . . ."

"The lords will never let you."

"If we win," Damon replied, "there won't be too many lords left." Sasha shrugged in concession. Such discussion had the offhanded quality of gallows humour. "Tol'rhen. I'd love there to be Tol'rhen in Lenayin."

"So you build institutions that bring Lenayin together," Sasha summarised. "Then you try establishing councils after that."

Damon shrugged. "Maybe. It's an idea. But that's the problem—Lenayin until this date has never been anything more than 'just an idea.' It needs to become a fact before there can be any alternative to kings. Or queens."

Sasha considered him. "You'll make a good king."

"Ha. Said the peasant girl with muddy feet."

Sasha grinned. "We only have five impossible things to achieve to make it happen."

"At least six—defeating Balthaar counts for at least three on its own. Including making Markan and his friends see reason. I'm not sure I could hit him hard enough with a stanch to hurt him—you have no chance."

Sasha shrugged. "We'll see."

"So what law *will* you write, if you win?"

"I'm not sure yet. I may ask Rhillian for advice." Damon looked suspicious. Sasha grinned. "And you, of course. My liege."

"I hope he hits you hard."

Damon seemed in good enough humour, despite the indignity of the Army of Lenayin preferring her at their head than him. Damon was no egotist. He knew that his natural support, as royalty, lay amongst lords and Verenthanes—a minority on this side of Lenayin's division. These were naturally more her people than his, and circumstance had made them more so. He knew at least that they did not hate him, and many respected him greatly . . . just not so greatly as her.

They were interrupted by a new arrival moving between hammering blacksmiths with a limp. In a loose serrin shirt and long hair, Sasha took several moments to recognise Jaryd. He hugged her hard.

"Thank you for looking after Sofy," Sasha told him, with feeling.

Damon embraced him in turn, then gave him a light slap on the cheek and a mock-warning look. "That's for looking after my sister a little too closely," he said.

Jaryd smiled crookedly. There was no smirk, no cheeky humour. "It honestly wasn't my idea," he said simply. "I did try to explain to her that there was sure to be a penalty of death in there somewhere for me, but she asked me who would carry it out, here in Jahnd."

"You mean, aside from me?" said Damon.

"Well," said Sasha, exhaling hard. "I mean, she's right. The entire structure of rulership will change depending on the battle to come, and the only people who care that you're fucking the Princess Regent are on the other side. Besides," she added, "everyone knows you two have always wanted each other."

"Speaking of those on the other side," said Damon, "they're the ones who stripped you of your noble title. When I'm king, I will restore it. You'll need it, if you're to marry Sofy."

For a long moment, Jaryd was unable to speak. "I *thought* marriage talk would do that to him," Sasha observed wryly.

"I . . ." Jaryd managed after a moment. "I'm not certain I can accept."

"Listen," Damon said firmly. "You're my friend, but if you think you're going to continue to share my sister's bed without an imminent marriage, you're about to learn differently."

"I had two companions on my ride with Sofy," Jaryd replied. "One was Asym, Markan's favoured man. The other was Jandlys, son of Krayliss of Taneryn. In my time with them they spoke to me often of their beliefs, as Goeren-yai. I do not know that I have ever felt the old ways as strongly as I should—my change of faith was always a matter of convenience more than belief. But now, both Jandlys and Asym are dead."

Sasha swore softly. She'd liked Asym, and though she hadn't known Jandlys, she felt somewhat responsible for his father's death. Now, his heir had been killed too.

"I am their witness," Jaryd explained. "I bear news of their deeds to their comrades here. That is where I have been all today, telling their stories. There was a *myala*, and . . ."

Damon looked askance at Sasha. "A ritual for the dead," Sasha explained. "To assist in the passing of their spirits to the spirit world."

"I cannot say that I do believe this or do not believe that," Jaryd continued, "yet I can certainly say that what I feel for the Goeren-yai is something that I never felt for my faith when I was a Verenthane. It feels real to me. It lives and breathes. Sasha knows."

Sasha nodded. "I do."

"And if you make me a lord . . ." Jaryd did not complete the sentence.

Damon smiled. "Who has said that you must become a Verenthane once more to be a lord?" Jaryd frowned. Damon sighed. "Jaryd, I'm a prince. I'm the highest royalty in this Army of Lenayin. . . ."

"Assuming I win," Sasha reminded him.

"As *Prince* Damon, I'm ruler of this Army of Lenayin. I can make whomever I choose a lord. Goeren-yai or Verenthane."

"A Goeren-yai lord?" Jaryd wondered.

"Taneryn's full of them."

"I'm not sure Taneryn's much of a recommendation."

"In fact," Damon continued, eyes brightening with possibility, "this might be just what we need, for morale. We announce a wedding. I make you a lord, which should not offend anyone since you've been one most of your life, then announce your marriage to Sofy!"

"Needs a divorce first," Sasha said drily.

"Hmm." Damon thought about it. "Damn. Well, killing the husband surely qualifies? Can't we announce an engagement pending that?"

"Oh, that's a great precedent!" Sasha laughed. "'I now declare myself the fiancée to this wedded woman, now excuse me while I kill her husband.'"

Damon shrugged. "Unusual times, unusual methods."

"And if I don't beat Markan," Sasha repeated, "you'll not be deciding anything for anyone. Now where's this damn surprise you promised me?"

Markan's idea for a *tymorain* was to hold it in Jahnd's largest amphitheatre. Sasha walked in the middle of her escort through the theatre district, where tenements stood tall to house all the visiting serrin who came to see the plays, and busy lanes abounded with costumers and makeup artists. But now the crowds thronged for a different purpose, as hawkers yelled prices, and lines formed at stairways where city folk hoped to push their way inside.

A tunnel took her beneath the stands, then up steps and into the arena. There came a ritual yell from the Lenay crowd, and a clatter of swords as thousands stood as one. Sasha gazed about the open circle, her eyes avoiding the crowd. The amphitheatre made good use of Jahnd's hillside, located perhaps halfway up the slope with the audience looking down onto the circular stage. On the downslope side, the stage was open to the valley, with only a raised platform and a wall separating performers from a steep drop. The sun was setting, the sky above streaked with orange cloud. Shadow crept across the valley below, casting the western side of the amphitheatre's audience into gloom.

Lenay men stood about the circle, which was paved with smooth stone. At the circle's far side stood Markan. Sasha ignored the sacredness of the space, and the holyman who came to her to discuss proceedings, and walked to the Great Lord of Isfayen.

"You're an idiot," she told him, looking up to his face. "You want it *here?*"

"Where better?" said Markan with satisfaction. "You have a new shirt. It suits you."

The shirt was chain, made from serrin steel, and woven into a traditional Lenay battle jacket of hard leather, shoulder guards, and elbow pads. The chain itself was barely half the weight of any chain she'd experimented with then thrown off in disgust. The armourer had assured her it was no less strong for the lightness, and it felt remarkably gentle upon her arms.

Given the choice in single combat, she'd have preferred to fight unarmoured, as in the svaalverd, speed was life. Yet in the battle to come, she would be commanding from a horse in a world filled with flying projectiles, and required some protection from things the svaalverd could not save her from. And now, this warm and glowing evening, she was about to enter a bashing contest with a man who looked like he could bend steel barehanded.

"I do not wish to harm the Synnich-ahn before a great battle," said Markan. "It would be simpler if you would comply to be queen."

"Simple does not interest me," said Sasha. "Only right."

"Very well," said Markan. "Will you fight *eldyn* rules?"

Sasha scowled. "Why not just tie one arm behind my back?" *Eldyn* rules did not allow head strikes.

"As I said, I do not wish for you to be harmed."

"And I do not wish to be the loser before the contest even begins. If you take from me the chance of a headstrike, you take my best chance of victory. *Pryal* rules."

Markan inclined his head. The stupidity of it was now making Sasha angry. She had a war to fight, and her foolish people were so obsessed with their protocols that they'd see two of their most important leaders beaten black-and-blue instead of preparing for victory. And if a headstrike came too hard, it could be far worse than that.

She turned her back on Markan and strode to a central spot from which to face the crowd. A holyman blocked her way.

"There are procedures," he said with a scowl. Sasha stepped around him. He caught her arm. Sasha hit him with a studded glove to the head. He stumbled, and the crowd gasped.

The loudness of the gasp surprised her. She had not truly looked up yet at the crowd, not wishing the distraction. Now she did, and saw thousands. And more thousands, as she turned her head across the semicircular stands. More than half were Lenay, dangerous-looking men in full battle dress. A good portion of the Army of Lenayin were here this evening. Many of the rest were Ilduuri, watching their new general with concern and intrigue. Remaining places, up in the far reaches, were crowded with Jahndis, townsfolk just recently learned of these events, and desperate to see what craziness these foreigners brought to their city.

The holyman might have come back at her, a big man with a heavy beard no more than stunned by her blow. Sasha drew her sword as she faced the crowd, and with that view of her back, he thought again. The craftsmen of Jahnd, with astonishing artistry, had decorated the dark leather on her back with a pair of evil, blood-red eyes. They stared now upon the holyman, and he did not approach. They were the eyes of the Synnich, a lowlanders' imagining of a Lenay spirit previously unknown, yet no Lenay could see those eyes upon her back and deny to whom and to what they belonged.

"Welcome to the show!" she snarled at the crowd. "A parade of fools for Lenayin, the most foolish of all nations!" There was an uneasy shifting. Ilduuris looked concerned, and wondered what she said. "I am Synnich-ahn, and I do not care for your protocols! You seek to make me queen because power must be held by the most powerful? I seek true power now! I seek the power of law, law over you! When I win here today, I will tell you your laws, and all this stupidity will cease!"

"Not even kings can write the laws of Lenayin!" someone yelled. "Kings *obey* the law, if they want to live!"

"Then come and kill me, you fucking moron coward!" Sasha yelled. "You choose me as a ruler, well, this is it! I don't play your game! My great-grandfather Soros Lenayin brought Lenayin freedom and law and a king! I will bring Lenayin a future!"

She turned and strode back past the dazed and wary holyman, and handed her sword to Yasmyn. She guessed that all her friends would be in the audience, but it did not even occur to her to look for them. She had only felt like this once before in her memory, before the one and only duel of her life, before the walls of Halleryn in Taneryn. She had killed a Hadryn lord that day, and challenged all that the Hadryn peoples had believed, about who she was, and the infallibility of their own gods. Today she challenged all her people, friend and foe alike. Lenayin was divided, all structure was broken, and anything was possible. There were no rules any longer. She would make some.

Yasmyn handed her the stanch, and she strode to the circle's centre.

Markan did likewise. He made a faint bow. Sasha did not, and took a fighting stance. The wood felt slightly heavier than steel, and far more ungainly, but she was used to that. Markan suffered the same disadvantage. He took a similar stance, and his reach, as Sasha had already guessed, was nearly a forearm's length more than hers.

Markan waited, studying her. He knew that without the svaalverd, his disadvantage was great. Perhaps he hoped that her new shirt would slow her a little. But surely he realised that if it did, she would refuse to wear it. Markan had sparred against her before. He was fast and powerful, but he was also clever.

Sasha did not feel impatient. She just waited. And waited. Each moment was of no greater significance than any other. Sashandra Lenayin, long impatient and short of temper, could now wait until nightfall if she must.

Markan exploded into attack, which Sasha angled away with a shift of wrists and feet, and drove forward, smacking him across the middle as she came through. Markan could have crushed her skull with the next blow, but *pryal* rules were clear, and her stroke was a kill. He accepted with a nod, and they prepared again. There came a roar from the Lenay crowd, in many tongues. The regions had their separate traditions and words for a strike. Markan looked unbothered. Sasha knew she'd have to hit far harder to cause him pain.

Again he waited. This would take a long time, Sasha realised. Chopping down Markan would be like a small man felling a large tree. She would have to hit him many, many times before she won . . . unless she could get an open head strike, or something equally debilitating. Yet Markan's first attack had been conservative, perhaps aware that the svaalverd would grant her a simple opening in reply, but that that opening would not be painful for him, and could not win her the fight no matter how many times she was presented with it. Svaalverd was a method of counterattack as much as anything, using the momentum of an attacker's strike to unbalance him, and kill him with the second stroke. But with wooden sticks, she could not kill, and so it went on and on. If Markan waited long enough, perhaps her concentration would falter, and Markan needed far fewer openings than she.

Not only strong and fast, she thought again grimly, but clever.

He attacked again. Sasha parried twice and ducked away, finding no opening. Markan pressed, again somewhat predictable and not as powerful as she'd have expected. The easy option presented and she took it, but again the strike was not powerful, partially deflected by Markan as he took it on his arm and stanch together. Again he nodded, and they separated. He was not giving her any power to work with, no momentum. Sasha loved to use her opponent's power against him, and Markan refused to grant her any, despite all his formidable size. And so, deprived of her asset, she had nothing to hit him back with in turn.

That left one option.

She attacked him in a flurry, five rapid swings that he parried in fast retreat, eyes wide with surprise. She saw a three-combination move that could end in a hard blow and flashed into it, yet Markan met her setup stroke with confidence and their stanches each struck hard on the third. It knocked Sasha off her feet with astonishing force, but she rolled on the stones and came up as the crowd roared. Markan windmilled his left arm. That had been by far her hardest strike yet, though not as hard as his. Her ribs ached on her left side, but her mail had saved them from breaking, and she flexed her arms and prowled forward.

Again she attacked before Markan had even settled, but this time he was not surprised, and met her with a crashing blow that shocked her arms, then hammered her midriff even as she tried to force her defence down to meet it. She sank to her knees, unable to inhale. Markan backed off and watched, winded himself. Sasha waited for the breath to come back, aware of pandemonium in the crowd, experienced Lenay warriors knowing only too well the risk that she attempted, and astonished to see her attacks so brazen. Most exchanges she could win five times out of six or better. Now she opened herself to strikes for the chance to do real damage herself. A few more strikes like the last one, and she was finished.

Her breathing returned to normal, though her stomach hurt like hell. It was merely one more sensation, for the battle lust was with her, and single thoughts or feelings meant nothing at all. The dark spirit was with her, and wooden stick or not, it sought blood.

"Just one chance," her eyes said to Markan as she stared at his centre, absorbing all of him in that look.

She attacked again, inviting the obvious cross-swing in reply, with which she took a huge risk and ducked rather than parried. That put her ahead in the count. He knew it, hurried to catch up on the next swing, and a foot skidded. Just a fraction.

She saw the combination it presented immediately. The high-right overhead forced his balance back right, weight on the off-balance foot. His foot failed the next transition back, and she cut low and took his knee hard enough to buckle it. On one knee, his balance failed completely, his defence weak as her final blow crashed through it and snapped his head back.

Markan hit the ground limp, and did not move. The crowd erupted. Men rushed to check on him. Yasmyn held back, face impassive—it would not do at all for any woman, least of all a sister, to rush to a fallen warrior's aid and sully the moment with softness. Markan stirred, groggily, blood flowing from a badly split cheek. It spoiled his good looks, and made Sasha angrier still.

"Synnich-ahn! Synnich-ahn!" men were yelling. Sasha went to Yasmyn, handed off her stanch, and reclaimed her blade. "Synnich-ahn! Synnich-ahn!"

Sasha walked back to the centre of the circle, and waited for calm. At the stage-side, she spied Damon, watching with arms folded. Beside him was Kessligh. Damon looked displeased. Kessligh merely thoughtful.

She did not think Damon jealous of this support—like most Verenthane nobility, he had never particularly admired this rural, pagan half of Lenayin, nor gone to lengths to seek its affection. But now her actions whipped them to a frenzy. She could see from his face that he wondered how in the world this would serve to elevate him as the natural commander of the Army of Lenayin, and challenger to its king, their brother Koenyg. Well. It was a question.

Sasha held up her arms, and the noise began to fade. Finally, there was silence. Immediately broken, when someone yelled "Queen!" and a roar of approval followed. Sasha was unimpressed.

"I'm not your queen!" she shouted, once the noise had fallen. Angry cries came back at her. She nearly laughed. Lenays would argue with Death himself, and spit in his face, if he did not play by their rules. "But if you will fucking listen, for just one moment, you mob of lunatics, I will claim something far more powerful!"

Silence fell. Sasha glared at them all. "You know me! You know that I am Nasi-Keth. I have defeated one of Lenayin's greatest warriors here tonight *only*, and I stress *only*, because I am Nasi-Keth. Nasi-Keth taught me how to fight. This man," and she pointed to Kessligh, "Kessligh Cronenverdt, taught me how to fight. If you will grant me power by my swordwork, then grant also that the credit is due to him, and his ways, and the Nasi-Keth that he has served all his life."

"We will accept Nasi-Keth as queen!" came a yell. Growls and shouts of approval.

"Nasi-Keth do not accept the power of one man or woman!" Sasha replied. "You've travelled through the Bacosh. You've seen the wealth of the Saalshen Bacosh, where serrin and Nasi-Keth ideas have been in place for two centuries. These are not places ruled by a king or queen, they are run by councils."

"No councils!" yelled another. "They're a fucking mess!"

"Like a mob of old women on the verandah with their knitting!" came another. Laughter roared.

"In command of all Lenayin, yes!" Sasha agreed. "But to advise the king?" Silence from the crowd. "An idea. A council. Not in charge. Not with the power to make war. Not with any power, in fact, except the power to oppose an action of the king it does not like, and the power to suggest alternatives, which the king may take or discard as he sees fit.

"A council run according to the rules of debate long established by the Nasi-Keth. A council always governed by a Nasi-Keth, or perhaps even a serrin, should we find one crazy enough." Laughter from some, and thoughtful frowns from others. "What happens today when the king makes a law we do not like? Or when some new law emerges that lords wish to write? We have a rathynal. And what do we all think of rathynals?"

Sounds of general disapproval.

"So make a council like a permanent rathynal, with representatives in place for all provinces and regions, and put the Nasi-Keth in charge of it. That is what I propose."

"This is horseshit! We are here to win a war, not to debate. Lead us in battle!"

"And I've just told you why I can't, and won't," Sasha said patiently. "Appoint an independent commander of your armies if you will—my father did it with Kessligh many years ago. But you all know that you have no need. Damon is as accomplished a commander as you will find, and my command is needed with the Ilduuri Steel. Nasi-Keth will never rule Lenayin. But we will advise. That is our place, and our task in the world. If you truly respect my victory over Markan, you will respect that, for it was granted by the Nasi-Keth.

"And I advise," she continued, before discontent could erupt into turmoil once more, "that you are all missing the point. The old ways demand a contest of leadership. As the Nasi-Keth advisor to Lenayin, a role that Kessligh played so ably before me, I advise that there is a challenge of the old ways that is in order. A challenge for the true kingship of Lenayin, not this petty squabble over the order of lineage.

"King Koenyg approaches. His rule is unworthy and dishonourable. Prince Damon is both honourable and worthy. *He* shall challenge. He shall duel the unworthy King of Lenayin, and beneath the gaze of our ancestors shall defeat him in honourable single combat. I am Synnich-ahn, I have been granted by my victory in *tymorain* the right to make law, and I say that there shall be a duel, between brothers Damon and Koenyg, for the right to rule Lenayin as king!"

There were loud yells of approval, yet not so loud as before. Many still grumbled, insistent that by the old ways, she should lead, as she was strongest. But there were enough who cheered now, liking her notion and the red meat she had thrown to their ancient tradition, salve for the insult she had paid in rejecting it herself. She had divided them, and now they would argue and complain, but the momentum to install her upon a throne irrespective of her wishes was blunted.

Only now she could see Damon, standing by Kessligh's side amidst the noise and argument, staring at her, pale-faced, as though she'd signed his death warrant herself.

"I didn't have a choice." Sasha sat on the verandah of a farmhouse in the Ilduuri camp, sipping tea by lamplight. Kessligh sat alongside. "I just proved myself strongest, and shoved their tradition back in their face. They needed some affirmation of the old ways, and that was it."

"Koenyg probably can't accept the challenge anyway," said Kessligh. "It's a Goeren-yai tradition, he's Verenthane, and not bound to accept. And arranging it would mean delays—Balthaar's warplan may not allow it."

"But he won't like refusing the challenge," Sasha said sombrely. "It has implications of cowardice for any Lenay. It may cost him support, it may make divisions between him and Balthaar if he presses Balthaar to allow it, and it may make him angry. Koenyg can do silly things when he's angry."

"Wouldn't count on it," said Kessligh, sipping his own tea. Activity continued about them in the light of lamps and campfires. The Ilduuri Steel were particularly pleased to see her here amongst them this night, and Sasha regretted now having taken even one night in the city. It had seemed necessary, to mingle with the powerful and learn the lay of things, yet her true place was here, amongst the men who would fight and die at her command. She had memorised all senior ranks down to formation sergeants, over two hundred men. But there were many more she wanted to learn—not merely their names, but more importantly their experience, reputation and character.

"Damon's furious at me," she said. "Sofy too. Damon has rarely bested Koenyg at swords. Few men can. If Koenyg does accept the challenge, and Balthaar lets him . . ."

"Then one more of us will die in war," said Kessligh. "There will be plenty, the method matters not."

"If Damon dies, Markan commands Lenayin," Sasha said quietly. "But Markan cannot be king. An Isfayen king would be less popular than a Cherrovan one."

"In which case, it had better be you after all," Kessligh concluded.

Sasha nodded, absently. "If Koenyg kills Damon in single combat because of a duel I set up, I suppose I'll deserve that punishment and worse."

"Nothing you can do about it now," said Kessligh. "The risk is great, but the reward is worth it. That was a nice idea, though. A Nasi-Keth role for

Lenayin. Of course, it has its own concerns," he added. "If the Nasi-Keth have a powerful role as independent advisors to the crown, who advises the advisors? And who watches that they do not grow too powerful? We've seen the Nasi-Keth in too many lands straying from the wisdom of their own teachings, Ilduur most recently."

Sasha shrugged. "Something to think about if we live. We have more pressing matters now."

"And I've been working on those matters all day and my mind needs a rest." Kessligh shifted in his seat, seeking a more comfortable position for his stiff leg. "In the Great War, I would spend evenings talking poetry and ballads with my commanders. A mind can think on war too long, and forget what it fights for."

Sasha smiled faintly. "You were my age then."

Kessligh nodded. "Roughly. And alarmed at how fast I rose from nothing to command, mostly because some of my very brave and stupid superiors were more interested in displaying their honour by charging the Cherrovan head-on rather than by manoeuvring. My horsemanship was poor, but none of them could best me with a stanch. That gained me great respect, and when gaps appeared in higher ranks, I was chosen to fill them. Repeatedly."

"Victory of the strongest," Sasha murmured. "*Brohyl*."

"Lenayin's greatest tradition," said Kessligh. "And its most troublesome." A runner emerged from the dark, leaped onto the verandah, and murmured something in Kessligh's ear. Kessligh nodded, murmured something back, and the man saluted and left. "Your own rise here echoes mine in Lenayin, somewhat. A few then were even cheering for me to be king."

"I know. I've spoken with some who remember. But the north, and the lords . . ."

Kessligh nodded. "And just as well, for as you've said, if every strong swordsman feels entitled to challenge for the throne, Lenayin should drown in blood. Feudalist instincts for stability are not all bad."

"Stability can be achieved by other means, I'm sure," Sasha said sourly. "Did you consider it?"

"Kingship?" A private smile passed between them. "I'd have gone crazy. We have that in common. I was Nasi-Keth. I explained the concept much as you did today. I would be independent. I could not build a strong Nasi-Keth foundation in Lenayin as the lords would not allow it, but the leadership in Torovan and elsewhere required me to stay where I was for the influence I exerted on your father, and I was happy enough, so I did."

"And you had many female companions," Sasha said mischievously. "I heard."

Kessligh smiled, with the wry acceptance of a father whose daughter teased him. "Court ladies are awful. Entertaining enough for a young man with nothing better on his mind, as Jaryd could tell. But no company at all."

"It must please you then to be in Saalshen. Beautiful serrin women everywhere, and all quite receptive to your odd fancies."

Kessligh nodded, and looked faintly melancholy. Sasha's smile faded. "In truth," he said, "I've been thinking that if we win, I will stay here. I've always wished to spend time in Saalshen."

Sasha sighed. She was not surprised at all.

"And," he added, "you will be able to achieve so much more for the Nasi-Keth in Lenayin than I ever could. You could make it an institution of true power in Lenayin."

Sasha thought of their ranch in Baerlyn, where Lynette awaited them, and many horses. That time when they had fought, and reconciled, and then Kessligh had left for Petrodor . . . that had been the last time he had seen his home. It seemed another age. And it would quite possibly be the last time he would ever see it, whatever the conclusion of the battle to come. It was nothing to be sad about, she told herself. She would be pleased enough if he lived. Where he spent the rest of that life was a trivial concern.

"Speaking of Nasi-Keth concerns," she said, "Yasmyn has asked me to be her uman. Repeatedly."

"The Isfayen respect the Nasi-Keth, tonight more than ever."

"The Isfayen respect the *svaalverd*," Sasha replied. "That's different."

Kessligh shrugged. "Not really. It's like you and Errollyn—you came for the body, but you stayed for the man." Sasha gaped at him. Then grinned, and mimed throwing her tea on him. "It doesn't matter how you attract the Isfayen to the cause—if they like one aspect of the Nasi-Keth, you can then sell them on others later. And to have the sister of the Great Lord of Isfayen as your uma would be a good start."

"She's quite good, too," Sasha admitted. "But I'm not sure about the old arrangement of uma and uman. We need to make a school, a Tol'rhen in Lenayin. And train thousands, in all sorts of things, not just svaalverd."

Kessligh's eyes twinkled. "Ambitious," he said, with great approval.

"Oh, I have plans." Sasha stretched, groaning. "Great plans." She relaxed, and considered the army about her in the dark. "Pity we're all about to die."

Kessligh nodded, and sipped tea. "Isn't it," he agreed.

Twenty-two

Sofy found the feast more surreal than anything she'd seen since coming to Saalshen. There were tables of amazing food, and after eating, music, acrobats, and performers Sofy knew of no word to describe. Always at her elbow there was some Jahndi nobility (or however such people were described, as there was no noble title here) telling her the exquisite meaning of this dish, or that performance. Jahndis seemed to take great pride in being unique to all humanity and Saalshen too. An island of uniqueness in a serrin sea, and oh-so-sophisticated for it.

Sofy was astonished at her own cynicism. Jahnd was an amazing city, and at any other time she would have been delighted at all that she saw. But there was about to be a great war for the survival not only of Jahnd, but of Saalshen too, and so many people here seemed to barely notice. And shouldn't all this food be stored for the coming siege?

Perhaps it was the dark looks that she received from many Jahndis, born of the fact that she was still Princess Regent, and whatever the moral victory of her defection to this side of the Lenay divide, ongoing bonds of marriage meant as much to most Jahndis as elsewhere in human lands. She was the wife of the man who attacked them, and that was that.

And there were very few serrin. Jahnd only existed as a city on the tolerance of serrin, who had extended far more kindness to humanity here than humanity's treatment of serrin might have warranted. Yet this great feast in opulent halls atop the Jahndi slope was an almost entirely human affair, with the only serrin Sofy could see being those there on official invitation.

It was Jaryd who rescued her from her little corner of Jahndis who *would* talk to her, and hovering servants.

"Your sister wishes to speak with you immediately," he lied, with grave earnestness. Mention of Sasha brought wide-eyed looks and murmurs from those surrounding, who bowed graciously as Sofy apologised and excused herself.

"Oh, thank goodness," she gasped as they emerged into the courtyard, and the warm summer night. "I've been so free the past weeks, I don't know how I can ever tolerate court again."

Travelling through Saalshen with Jaryd, and a few curious serrin guides who changed every few days, had been one of the more wonderful times in Sofy's life. Serrin did and dressed as they pleased, and seemed bound by little of convention as humans understood it. Now, to be back, even in some place as liberated as Jahnd, seemed stifling.

"I've found a place far more entertaining," said Jaryd with enthusiasm. "Come with me."

"But I can't go anywhere in this stupid gown!"

"You're beginning to sound like Sasha. Come on, stop at the quarters and get changed first."

Sasha's quarters were Sofy's, now that Sasha had decided to stay with her army down in the valley. Sofy changed into the plain clothes she'd been travelling in, and followed Jaryd's lead.

"Where are we going?"

"Downslope," said Jaryd, limping a little on his bad leg. "The thing I've discovered since becoming Goeren-yai is that you have to get away from the money and nobility to find the really good stuff."

"Here," said Sofy, and put his arm about her shoulders for support.

"I'm not going to lean on you, don't be stupid."

"Then put your damn arm about me like some wench you met at a tavern," Sofy retorted with amusement. "At least you'll make it less likely I'll be recognised."

But there was little chance of that in common clothes, as so few Jahndis knew her face. Jaryd took her all the way down the hill, and slowly the stately silence of grand buildings gave way to the livelier clusters of smaller ones. At one shoulder in the road, they gained a wide view of the Ilmerhill Valley below, a sprawl of lantern lights and small fires. Down narrower lanes they passed night markets doing a busy trade, many of their customers soldiers. There were inns with great balconies overlooking the lower defensive wall, and crowded with revellers. Conversation roared and music played, and Sofy stared about in delight at all there was to see, hear, and smell.

They bought delicious pastries at a roadside stall, laughed at a street performer's tricks, and stared at amazing glass baubles on sale at a stall. There were serrin here, some *talmaad*, others not, seeming to enjoy this human confusion as much as anyone. To them, Jahnd was an amazing place they would occasionally take their children to visit, as Lenay villagers had often taken their families to see the wonders of the nearest city. This was an odd place where the humans lived and made all kinds of colourful things.

Jaryd exchanged cheerful salutes with passing Lenay soldiers, and more formal yet equally friendly ones with Enorans, Rhodaanis, and Ilduuris.

Everywhere were little groups of soldiers, stopped to chat or direct each other to the nearest interesting thing. Some singers on a corner made a wonderful chorus, with harmonies utterly foreign to Sofy's ear. Some teenage boys showed off a serrin barehanded fighting technique, with flying fists, leaps, and spinning kicks.

"This is the Low Quarter," Jaryd explained in her ear, "where the entertainments for the common folk are held. They're kept open so even the labourers working through the night can take a break now and then, and come here to relax for a while. I spoke to some hellfire brewers earlier. I reckon they could use a break."

"Hellfire! Where is that made?"

"Out of the city, away from houses so no one else gets hurt when it goes wrong. People die making it—it's very dangerous. Most folks only work a few years making hellfire, then do something else. Even then they get a medal, and some inns grant a hellfire brewer free meals. Lots of poor folk do it—it means they won't ever starve."

They came to a small courtyard where a crowd gathered beneath a big tree. Music was being played. Sofy and Jaryd went and found a spot on a stone ledge to sit amongst the other listeners. There were three drummers, all Lenay, with hand drums not so dissimilar to the Lenay kind. And there were three serrin musicians, one with a long, woody-sounding pipe, another with a middle-sized, seven-string guitar, and the last seated with a huge, four-string bass.

Sofy found what they played both familiar and utterly strange at the same time. The rhythms were Lenay, yet the serrin had put them to haunting, lilting harmonies and melodies that had never accompanied such rhythms before. The bass guitar played an underlying, repeating pattern, and the two other serrin played competing melodies over the top of it all, sometimes duelling, and sometimes coming together in apparently spontaneous harmonies. The effect was utterly mesmerising, and the rhythm infectious. Even Jaryd, whom Sofy had never known to be the greatest appreciator of music, was soon swaying back and forth and tapping his feet.

"What do they play?" Sofy asked a *talmaad* warrior seated alongside.

"Nothing I have ever heard before," the woman admitted with amazement. "The serrin musicians play traditional serrin forms, yet I have never heard them put to such amazing rhythms."

"I think they've discovered a new musical form," said Sofy. "Wonderful things happen when your people and ours come together."

The serrin smiled at her, a flash of turquoise eyes in the lamplight. Serrin had travelled to Lenayin for many centuries, Sofy thought. Strange that it took this great gathering, and a war, to produce such a fusion. The Army of Lenayin had been in Jahnd for many days now. Who knew what new wonders would emerge, should they stay longer?

Then she saw it, what Sasha had seen, and Kessligh well before her, in coming to fight for Saalshen. Koenyg saw that the future of humanity must be Verenthane, and strictly so, for that was what humans had built themselves, and was native to them. What the serrin built and inspired in cities like Jahnd was deadly to that, and must be destroyed if Koenyg's vision was to thrive.

But here was a new possibility, for all humankind. It was not so much a question of what the serrin could do for humans, but rather what they could inspire humans to do for themselves. Serrin were really quite simple beings. They did not build much, and much of what they did build was as individuals, not collectively as humans did. But what serrin had were ideas, forms of thought and wisdom shaped over the centuries, born of minds that knew little of primeval human hatreds and emotions. And where humans came to embrace those ideas, it unleashed something in humans, too. Something creative and dynamic, as humans had always been creative and dynamic in war, bigotry, and death, but now directing that dynamism upon something far more positive.

Saalshen was humanity's well in a dry desert. There was little doubt that humans could fill in the well, if they chose, for it was fragile and its waters finite. Yet if managed with care and love, the well could be sipped from for many generations to come, and make a better future for all. Koenyg thought to make the strictest teachings of the Verenthanes the rock upon which to build the future of Lenayin. Sasha and Kessligh insisted that that foundation was here, in the very place that Koenyg's vision sought to destroy. Jahnd was not perfect. Even Saalshen was not. Spirits knew, Lenayin was not either. But what they could make together, in the spirit of fusion and not annihilation, was worth fighting, and even killing, for.

The music played on, in endless variety. Musicians and drummers sparred back and forth, sometimes reaching a crescendo that brought spontaneous applause and cheers from watching humans, and gasps of delight and expansive hand gestures from the serrin. Sofy watched the crowd, as intrigued by their willing acceptance of this strange new thing as by the music itself.

Suddenly she spotted a young, familiar face. It was Andreyis, Sasha's long-time friend from the ranch in Baerlyn. With him was a striking serrin girl, with pale skin and flaming red hair. They sat intimately, arms about each other, her head on his shoulder as they swayed with the music.

Jaryd followed her gaze. "Her name is Yshel. She was his captor when he was prisoner after Shero Valley." Sofy looked at him, impressed. Jaryd shrugged. "I came to this war partly because I swore to Sasha I'd look out for him. But he no longer needs looking out for."

"Sasha will need messengers," Sofy suggested. "I heard men say. They said it's best to have people who know her well, so there is no possibility of miscommunication."

"She has Daish, the lad from Tracato."

"And on this battlefield, how many do you think she'll need?"

Jaryd thought about it. Then nodded. "Interesting," he admitted. "You know it's no safer a position than the one he'd be leaving?"

Sofy nodded. "But it is prestigious. None of us will be safe. If we are to fall, best we fall with honour."

"Now you're thinking like a warrior." Jaryd put his arm about her and they swayed together in time with the rhythm.

Alfriedo Renine wandered the road in the serrin town called Tormae. How his people knew its name, he did not particularly want to know. The Army of Northern Lenayin, as it was now being called by some, had come through here earlier, having ridden the forest road to reach the eastern end of the Dhemerhill Valley. Thankfully, they did not seem to have destroyed anything yet. General Zulmaher walked at his side, in the full armour of a Rhodaani Steel officer. That disconcerted some of the Rhodaani nobility, a few of whom also walked with them.

There were no serrin to be seen. Again, Alfriedo thought that probably a good thing. He turned off the road and walked up a path beneath great stands of trees that he could not identify, and emerged onto the shore of a small lake. Several houses flanked the lake, the nearest with a decking that crept across the water. Gardens surrounded.

"Not a natural lake," Zulmaher observed, shielding his eyes from the glare of sun on water. "I don't see how any of these water features can be natural."

A fish jumped in the water. Ducks paddled, and a heron stalked through reedy banks. Alfriedo walked along the bank to the house, and climbed stairs to the decking.

There he found something odd. A wooden chair faced the stairs, flanked by potted flowers. From a roof beam overhead overgrown with vines dangled a small object that glinted brilliantly in the sun. Upon the chair itself was draped a lady's dress.

Alfriedo looked up as Zulmaher came beside him. "What do you think? Some sort of offering?"

Zulmaher frowned, and walked forward to examine the dangling object. It was glass, yet it gleamed like a jewel. There was a sphere, with a gold pin through the middle and circled by metal bands. The metal bands in turn held a smaller jewel, also spherical, or nearly. A diamond. Zulmaher suddenly retreated a step and made a holy sign as he recognised the object.

"What is it?" Alfriedo asked, frowning.

"It is a serrin representation of the world," said Zulmaher. "The serrin world, spherical. The diamond is the moon."

"Hand it to me. It is high, I cannot reach."

"You should not touch it."

"Hand it to me," his young lord commanded. "I aim to be a learned man, and I have no regard for your silly superstitions."

Zulmaher reached, and touching only the suspending cord, removed the object. Alfriedo took it, and examined it closely. The glass sphere was inlaid with many colours, in different kinds of glass. He did not see how it was possible. For humans, it was not. He recognised the shape of one outline—the coastal map of Rhodia itself. This jewel was the world, complete with all known coastlines. Serrin had many ships, he knew, and sailed far. In recent readings he had discovered references to serrin maps of all the world, yet those books he had not found, and all the serrin who might direct him to them had fled from Tracato.

"Magnificent," he pronounced. He placed the globe in a safe belt pouch and turned his attention to the dress. Serrin women did not wear dresses any more than serrin men did. Those robes were called *ki'jo*, to be worn indoors and at leisure by serrin of either sex. But this was clearly a dress, as human women wore, and tailored to a woman's shape. Why would serrin make such a thing?

"For the Jahndis," he guessed, lifting the dress across an arm. The fabric felt like silk, yet it was interwoven with golden thread, and in no simple pattern either. These patterns were like flowers, curling and intricate, gold lines through rose-red fabric. "This is also impossible," he said with wonder. "How do they make such arts? Even in Tracato I have not seen the likes of this. It must be worth a fortune. I am surprised the Lenays have not taken them."

"The men of Northern Lenayin are not here for loot. They fight for the holy cause, and will regard such objects as cursed."

"So the serrin have abandoned their town, but left such objects as these for us to find." Alfriedo gazed across the lake. "Do they seek to make peace?"

"I think they merely wish to be remembered," Zulmaher said sombrely.

Alfriedo gazed up at his mentor. He gave him the dress to examine, and leaned upon the railing. Below, the water was thick with lilies.

"Do you believe the serrin are evil?" he asked the general.

"No," said Zulmaher. "But I did not believe the Elissians were evil, and I made war upon them all the same. It was necessary, for Rhodaan. As this is necessary, for the same."

"I have read on many of the things that were suggested to me by Kessligh Cronenverdt, since we met."

"I would not place too much store by the word of Kessligh Cronenverdt," Zulmaher said warily.

"He challenged me to consider my position. A brave man does not shirk a challenge. And I should not like a Lenay warrior of his station to think me a coward."

"My lord is no coward."

"No," Alfriedo agreed. "He said that Rhodaan's rulers have not always been wise and just. The serrin have many books and records that do suggest so, and that much of what my mother taught me of the history of my illustrious family is not true."

"The Family Renine has always ruled fairly."

"Always?" Alfriedo frowned up at Zulmaher. "Always is a long time."

"And Saalshen's councils of the past two centuries have been scarcely more just."

"A different matter," said Alfriedo. "Kessligh told me that men losing an argument always change the subject." Zulmaher was displeased. "My family has not always ruled wisely, this is plain. Brave men, and wise men who aspire to leadership, must be prepared to separate their personal desires from their quest for truth. The two are not the same, he said."

"It is very difficult," Zulmaher said acerbically, "to argue against both you *and* Kessligh Cronenverdt, particularly when he is not here."

"Oh, I think he is," Alfriedo replied with a faint smile. He pointed beyond the lake, to the west. "Just down the valley, in fact. We'll meet him shortly, and regret it."

Alfriedo and Zulmaher returned to where armoured riders waited, holding their horses, mounted, and rejoined the road. They made greater speed through the rest of Tormae, and emerged into the beginnings of the Dhemerhill Valley. There awaited the Holy Army of Rhodaan, as it was now called. They had needed to call it something, as the only army Rhodaan had known in the past two centuries had been the Rhodaani Steel, and they fought now on the other side.

All the men were mounted, and stood in ranks as Alfriedo, Zulmaher, and their accompanying lords approached. These were the great families of Tracato and Rhodaan, now restored to nobility by the Regent's victory. Their banners flew high against the green of the valley walls, and to a man they sat proudly in the saddle. Most had dreamed of this day since they were old enough to understand the tales their parents told them, of god-given entitlements unfairly stolen, and of destinies to be fulfilled. Alfriedo shared their joy and pride in part, for it was his own, born in him as it was in them from the moment he was old enough to understand his mother's stories. And yet the cost had been immense. He did miss the serrin libraries of Tracato. And in light of what he had lately been challenged to read, he rather missed the serrin themselves.

Ahead of the Rhodaanis massed Torovan cavalry. All who had come along the forest road were cavalry, as foot soldiers would have taken too long, and been exposed to serrin ambush at night camp in the forests. The Torovans gathered in their various provinces, none of which seemed to enjoy each other's company. Many Torovans had fought with the Army of Lenayin in the Battle of Shero Valley, and some Alfriedo had spoken with were resentful that the Lenays had used them more as a reserve, save for some heavy cavalry action on one flank. Others were exasperated that the Lenays, their previous allies, had divided against themselves, as though such an event were as predictable as dogs fighting over a bone.

Somewhere further ahead of the Torovans, lost amongst the trees, were a huge mass of Kazeri. No one understood the Kazeri. They had nomadic tribes, and many had grown up travelling grassy plains, and fighting other Kazeri tribes. Some now claimed the Verenthane faith, and the great Kazeri chiefs allied themselves with the Chansul of Meraine, to the disgust of the Regent's closer allies. Meraine had fought Larosa for as many centuries as humans could remember, and now the Meraini brought the Kazeri onside to strengthen their position. The Chansul of Meraine also claimed that Ilduur would not participate in the defence of Jahnd. Without Ilduur, Jahnd's defenders would be outnumbered by a ridiculous margin, and surely their defence would be very short indeed. Such a victory could be claimed as a great victory for the Chansul and Meraine, to the Regent's further displeasure. Some already spoke of a possible war to follow this one, as Balthaar asserted his dominance over the upstart Meraini Chansul.

But the Army of Northern Lenayin did not rate the Kazeri as warriors. The Army of Northern Lenayin, in truth, did not rate any who were not Lenay as warriors. King Koenyg now led the advance, far ahead up the valley, and warned that the outer defence of mounted serrin archers would be best faced by his horsemen alone. Many further back in the column grumbled, but few with any force. The northerners were not many, no more than six thousand. King Koenyg's self-opinion was vast, for a man whose primary force had abandoned him to humiliation. Few here would mind to see the *talmaad* cut him down to size a little.

Errollyn waited. He could hear the riders coming, a great, thundering wall of noise across the Dhemerhill Valley. Trees broke any line of sight across the valley fields, with trails and farmhouses making a patchwork unsuitable for any single, massed formation.

About him, *talmaad* steadied their horses and readied their bows. There were several hundred here, hidden behind trees on the lower slope of the northern valley slope. Behind more trees, several hundred strides ahead, were Enoran cavalry. Thus were Jahnd's cavalry forces dispersed across the eastern valley, divided into small groups, and hidden, at least initially. Further east, the Regent's advancing forces would have encountered the first such group, and been encouraged by their lack of numbers. That drew them into a pursuit, much favoured by *talmaad* cavalry. Smart commanders amongst the enemy cavalry would surely recognise the tactic, and perhaps prevent their forces from charging headlong into the obvious ambush. But could they stop their hot-blooded men in a roaring charge?

He could see *talmaad* now, racing down a road between fields. Others went cross-country, jumping fences and weaving through trees, slowing now to allow others to come by, and attackers to gain range. And here were the pursuers, galloping hard to catch up with the retreating serrin. As soon as they made range, serrin archers fired, straight backward. A horseman fell, then another.

But there were not many. Errollyn frowned, and peered through the trunks and leaves of their limited cover. Here were the others, a larger mass of cavalry, leather- and mail-clad riders on big horses. He recognised several of the banners, and realised why this ambush was not progressing as he'd hoped.

"Lenays!" he called to the *talmaad* about him, and felt rather than heard the intake of breath that followed his announcement. Cavalry of Northern Lenayin. Men in black with silver steel, Hadryn, Ranash, and Banneryd, mixed with the Verenthane nobility of other provinces who followed their noble king. These were not men who would fall for tricks. Likely they'd have tricks of their own.

Some *talmaad* level with their position were now waving to Errollyn from down in the valley, and pointing across to some near place that he could not see, along this valley wall. From hand gestures, he realised that Lenay cavalry were sweeping these lower slopes, to guard against precisely this sort of ambush. He directed his force into the trees, progressing far enough forward until he could see the Lenays coming ahead. Already the range was good, and he yelled for a charge.

Talmaad burst from the trees and hurtled toward a Lenay force of several hundred. Trained as *talmaad* were not to waste arrows from range, they waited for a closer shot. The Lenays, in response, did an utterly un-Lenay-like thing, by turning to bolt.

They raced away down the slope, building that momentum on fleet horses. Several of Errollyn's *talmaad* got close enough for a good shot, but arrow range chasing after an enemy was not as good as when he was chasing after *you*, and most arrows fell short. And now the main columns of Lenays in the valleys below were getting close, and Errollyn knew that to continue the chase was to become cut off and pinned against this valley wall.

He signalled a turn, and they wheeled away from their prey, angling downslope across the riders below. Immediately the men they'd been chasing followed them and pursued, always holding just beyond the optimum range. Errollyn muttered as he steered his horse between outcrops of trees, then over a paddock fence. Lenays played lagand, and though he'd never seen a game, Sasha had described it to him often, and shown him some of her skills. Lagand was mobile strategy on horseback, and Lenays played it well.

Below, a mass of Lenay horsemen had galloped ahead of their main body and were sprinting now to cut Errollyn's force off. Errollyn angled his riders into a rough line astern, with still some height advantage over the men now racing parallel to him down in the valley. By holding this line, he dared them to come up to him, at a slow angle uphill, and give his archers targets. The Lenays declined, jumping now to cross new fields, splitting and pouring around a farmhouse and a small dam.

Suddenly there were *talmaad* in their rear, riders hidden behind the farmhouse chasing after them, loosing arrows into men's backs. Lenays fell, and others wheeled about to face the threat. The forward half of the Lenay line continued. Errollyn indicated with a yell, and charged downslope.

Seeing that line of *talmaad* coming downhill onto them, the Lenays turned away. And now the first group Errollyn had tried to ambush was charging across the slope onto *his* flank, as *talmaad* over that way broke and ran, firing back over their shoulders. Some Lenays fell, and then a *talmaad* too, though Errollyn could not see how that happened.

Now the Enoran cavalry broke from cover upslope, and came pouring down the hill. The near group of Lenays broke away and ran downslope, while those deeper in the valley raced back and around, hoping the Enorans would charge past them and expose their rear. Errollyn had to admire the coordination—even surprised, Lenay cavalry coordinated well to turn tables on their ambushers.

Errollyn let the Enorans come down past him, then yelled for a charge. He led his force across the Enorans' rear, blocking any pursuit, standing now in the stirrups to loose an arrow at the Lenays, who were also charging, knowing a head-on scenario to be a good option against *talmaad*. And it was, for Errollyn only got off two shots before Lenay and *talmaad* forces collided, and he drew his blade while steering with his bow hand, ducking and weaving between the big Lenay horsemen.

Their formation was fragmented, and most *talmaad* made it through, but with swords out for parrying, *talmaad* were unable to fire arrows at point-blank range. Errollyn got a good swing at a passing Lenay who swatted the blow calmly with his shield, ignoring him to focus on a serrin who barely ducked the swing.

And then they were clear, Errollyn sheathing his sword once more to draw another arrow, but already the Lenays were galloping at full speed out of range. He considered a high shot, but did not want to waste the arrow, and put it back in his quiver instead. Serrin formed up around him, and then the Enorans, moving back to make another line. The Lenays had exchanged blows with them, briefly, then pulled back and dared the Enorans to chase, straight toward the main Lenay force. The Enoran lieutenant had wisely pulled back instead, minus several of his number.

"They're good," the lieutenant said grimly, reining in at Errollyn's side. "Damn good. I lost five; I think we only got two."

"Northern cavalry are feared even in Lenayin," Errollyn agreed.

"They've got crossbows," said a *talmaad* arriving at his side, steadying her horse. "Some of them. Not our range, and difficult to reload on a horse, but dangerous enough if we let them get close."

"They take away our extreme range, and our close range," Errollyn surmised. "They limit our options, and when they find themselves in our kill-zone they retreat. At this rate we're unlikely to kill very many of them before we run out of valley."

His plan had been to draw them into a series of pursuits along the valley, which would in turn be ambushed by group after group of hidden *talmaad* who would appear in their midst, as the serrin behind the farmhouse had done, and shoot them down. Enoran and Rhodaani cavalry then complicated the picture, charging to close range to hold the Lenays in place, allowing *talmaad* cavalry to close in and pick off targets.

But the northerners weren't falling for it; they evaded the *talmaad*'s preferred shooting range while manoeuvring easily around regular cavalry ambushes, and when they did come to blows in close, neither *talmaad* nor Steel cavalry could match them for sheer ability.

He needed to make a dent in their numbers, but even now he could see the main column of Lenay cavalry advancing behind, at no more than leisurely pace. Probably they would send out columns like these to chase and harass for a while, and spring *talmaad* ambushes before they could do any real damage, and then rotate those columns back into the main force while sending out fresh columns to replace them. They could do that all the way down the valley, and suffer very little. Errollyn thought he smelled Koenyg's planning in this.

"He thinks he knows how we fight," he said grimly. "We'll have to show him something else."

Sasha sat ahorse on a bluff overlooking the western mouth of the Dhemerhill Valley. Before her lay the Ipshaal River, wide and calm. Immediately beneath the bluff lay the small, human town of Hama. Saalshen allowed human occupation of towns in the western Dhemerhill and upon the Ipshaal banks here, to give Jahnd access to the river and trading routes to Enora. Typically it would be surrounded by small fields, trees, and farmhouses, but now it seemed an island before a sea of soldiers.

Sasha recalled the Battle of the Udalyn Valley, where the sight of so many soldiers had astonished her. Then she had fought with the Army of Lenayin at Shero Valley, and that had been many times the scale of anything she'd previously seen. Compared to what she saw before her now, Shero Valley looked like a skirmish. The army spilled in both directions along the Ipshaal bank, as far as she could see. Hills rose steeply on this bank, becoming low mountains to either side, and providing no passage to Jahnd. The only way in was the Dhemerhill Valley, and now more than one hundred thousand men were massing upon the bank to organise in advance of moving into the valley.

"They know it's a trap," said Arken, seated at her side in full Ilduuri armour. "That is why they hesitate."

"Traps can be smashed with brute force," said Sasha. "They come at us from both ends of the valley, and it is we who are trapped in the middle. We must make them pay for every advance they make, and hope that their losses are so grave by the time they reach Jahnd that they cannot trap us within."

"Perhaps they'll try to force open the valley without first capturing these heights."

"I hope they're that stupid. But they'll know we have artillery up here, and a wall down the valley, and if they get stuck up against that, they'll be slaughtered. They have to capture the heights first, and no commander ever won a war by hoping his enemy would commit suicide."

She looked across to the opposite side of the valley, wishing she could have artillery on those heights also. But the hillsides there rose steadily steeper and steeper, with no bluffs or flat ground on which to place even archers, let alone bullock-drawn catapults and ballistas on wheels. They had enough of that on this side of the valley that perhaps half of the valley floor could be covered, thanks to the extra range that height provided. It should be enough, as no commander could afford to cede half the battlespace to his enemy. But they had to hold these heights from attack.

"Look," said an Ilduuri captain, pointing below. "Stars."

Verenthane Stars, he meant. They were carried by horsemen in black robes, mounted atop long poles, galloping before the near rank of teeming soldiers. Men cheered as they passed.

"They think the gods are with them," said Arken. Several officers muttered rude things in Ilduuri to hear that.

"Lenays think the gods and spirits want a good fight," Sasha said loudly. "Today they're going to get one." That met with loud approval.

She turned and considered her position. Her Ilduuris were back from the edge of the bluff, on the off-chance that the Regent really was stupid enough to attack down the valley without capturing these heights first. That, and she did not want him to see exactly who was up here. Ilduuri Steel had smaller shields and lighter armour than the Enoran or Rhodaani armies, and when arranged in a shield line, that difference would be visible from below. She did not mind showing herself and her officers, however. To imagine that the Regent might believe there was no one up here at all would be stretching credulity.

"Should I go?" asked Daish at her side, looking wide-eyed upon the Regent's army.

"Not yet," said Sasha. "Wait until they attack, then we'll have something to tell Kessligh that he doesn't already know." Kessligh supervised the defence from the eastern end of the valley. That concerned him most, as it was certain to be a cavalry attack that, if not stopped, could overrun their rear and end the defence of Jahnd before it had even begun. This western side, effectively, was Sasha's to command. Ilduuri were mountain soldiers, they held the heights, and so controlled the battle. Whatever happened here would not happen as fast as in the east, and so was safer to delegate to a junior commander. Yet even so, as Sasha considered the scale of what confronted her, the enormity of her responsibility felt like the weight of the world.

Aside from Daish, Sasha had Andreyis and Yasmyn for messengers. She and Kessligh were separated by the entire battlefield and some steep hills, and there were other commanders she would also need to communicate with. Even three might not be enough. All were good riders, knew her well, and knew battle well enough to not miscommunicate a message. She hoped.

"Here," said Arken, indicating below. "Here they come."

Formations were advancing toward the little town below, thousands of men. "So many different Bacosh forces," Sasha observed. "The nobility speak Larosan, but the common folk don't. They won't communicate easily."

"They're trying to find the lightest forces to assault these slopes," said Arken. "If heavy steel were good for climbing, mountain goats would have shells."

Men were now pouring into the town, disappearing beneath red-tiled roofs. More were following. And now others were heading off to the left, searching for other ways up. The Ilduuri had prepared this defence for days, and knew all such ways.

"That's not enough, you fools," said an Ilduuri captain with a smile, watching the activity below. "You'll need more than that."

"Let's hope it takes them a while and a lot of casualties to figure it out," said Sasha. "Artillery Captain!"

"Commander!"

"Prepare your ballistas! Save the catapults for now!"

"Yes, General!"

Men emerged from the near side of the town, and began climbing the slope directly behind it. Some followed the path, but officers were directing others straight up through the trees, realising that the path would take far too long for them all to climb. They needed to come up in a swarm, and as the captain had observed, there were not yet nearly enough of them.

Yells went back and forth in Ilduuri, artillery spotters shouting back. They'd tested these ranges before also, and knew exactly the required elevations for each ballista and catapult to hit a specific patch of hillside. Ilduuri artillery soldiers had their own language for it, and while they used primarily ballistas and not catapults, they'd incorporated these borrowed Enoran and Rhodaani catapult teams into their ranks easily enough.

"Deploy the archers?" Arken wondered.

"Not yet," said Sasha. "Let it take a little time for them to figure out just how many we are. The longer they take to realise the strength of our defence, the more men they waste."

Sasha found herself thinking of Regent Balthaar. Balthaar thought they were only Enorans, Rhodaanis, and Lenays, plus *talmaad*. He did not count on Ilduuris too. Jahnd had a domestic militia, but those would serve as defence only and, if the Regent's forces surrounded Jahnd with their own artillery, would probably all perish without so much as swinging a blade in anger.

Balthaar would presume there to be *talmaad* in the valleys, supporting Enoran and Rhodaani Steel in their well-suited blocking formations. But to hold these heights as well, at both ends of the valley, would dilute the strength down in the valley. Right now, he would be wondering how the defenders could possibly find enough people to serve both purposes at once.

The Ilduuri Steel would be a shock to him. Possibly not a nasty shock, but a shock all the same. Was it possible that he could overreact, and send too many men up this hill? The rest of these men by the Ipshaal were very confined, between water on one side and steep hills on the other, stretched very wide and thin along the bank. If they were sending men by the thousand up the hillsides, and not preparing for a major thrust . . .

Sasha smiled. She knew just who to send to make that work. "Brother-in-law," she murmured, "your size is great, yet your stance is weak. If we can reach the Ipshaal, we cut you in half."

The artillery captain indicated to her that the ballistas were ready.

"Fire!" she yelled.

Koenyg was becoming alarmed at the lack of opposition in the Dhemerhill Valley when he saw the mass of horses charging from the trees ahead. Immediately captains were yelling, men deploying wide, others shouting to bring the rear ranks forward as fast as possible, all without the king having to utter a word. Koenyg tore clear his sword and steadied his snorting warhorse.

This time the serrin were coming all at once. He'd expected them to change tactics when their initial ambushes hadn't worked, but he hadn't expected it quite this soon. Forest made a break in the fields ahead on either side of the Dhemerhill River, but only the formation on this side of the river seemed to be under attack. They were racing now, leaping fences and weaving about obstacles, spreading to widen their line.

"Look to me!" Koenyg yelled, standing in his stirrups and holding his sword aloft. "Look to me, charge on my signal!"

He wanted to hit them head-on, so they had no time to fire. If he charged too soon, they might halt, gaining them an extra shot or more. If he charged too late, they'd get their extra shot anyway. The first serrin were approaching another fenceline, and he half expected them to stop short, but they leaped over without slowing, readying arrows on their bowstrings even now. Such horsemanship could only be admired.

"Now!" cried the king, and kicked his heels. The Lenay formation sprang forward, thousands strong, with a roar like an avalanche. The serrin fired, and halted, and for a moment the air was filled with zipping arrows. Men and horses fell left and right, and Koenyg covered with his shield, confident enough that at this range he might lose his horse, but nothing more. But his horse remained unscathed, and ahead the serrin were turning and running.

A poor predicament for him, given how the serrin loved to cut down those who chased by shooting behind them, but in the confusion of the turn, these serrin had misjudged their approach and turned too late. Koenyg's heart pounded with excitement as he saw how fast he and his men were closing. The horses of Northern Lenayin were swift, and the serrin struggled to get back up to speed after turning around. Koenyg urged his horse faster, grinning as he selected a target, unarmoured as all serrin were unarmoured, and too busy trying to gather speed to turn and fire his bow. . . .

And suddenly the serrin were evading, gaps appearing in their formation as new horsemen came rushing through, a second rank of men in gleaming armour, and these men were not stopping. Steel cavalry, with lances lowered.

They hit with fatal power, bodies flying, lances snapping, and horses careening, and suddenly Koenyg's world was filled with racing enemies. He deflected a lance with his shield, yanked the reins to dodge another, then manoeuvred to slash at a third. He wheeled about to pursue the last of them, but now the serrin were firing into the backs of those exposed Lenays. Men were hit through the back as they turned, falling with screams and thuds as powerful arrows punched holes through armour. He needed his enemies around him and fast, for cover.

He tore back in amongst the Steel, lances dropped and now swinging with swords. He crashed in on one unawares, reeling him in the saddle with a blow. And then it was chaos, crashing swords and yells and jostling, shrieking horses. He hit another Rhodaani hard, took repeated blows to his own shield, then had a kill robbed from him by a Banneryd warrior he did not recognise. The Steel men fought with skill and bravery, yet there were little tricks of horsemanship in such close quarters that Lenays seemed to know that these men did not.

Koenyg gave one man a jostle at just the right moment, upsetting his balance right before a swing, then thumped him with his shield. The man grabbed for his reins to rebalance, and Koenyg killed him with a downswing before he could recover. He manoeuvred in tight space toward a new target, but that man died before he could reach him, the Ranash warrior responsible joining his king's side to hunt for more.

All about the pattern seemed the same: Steel fighting with skill enough to best most cavalry forces, but not those of Northern Lenayin. Soon the survivors were breaking to run, pursued everywhere by howling Lenay warriors, eager for more blood. Only now as they chased, serrin arrows cut them down, or pierced horses through their necks, as *talmaad* took advantage of the confusion to dart in at truly affronting range, and shoot Lenay men and horses from close enough to throw a boot.

Koenyg yelled at his men to leave the Steel and get the serrin—one dead *talmaad* was surely worth three Steel—and his men complied. Serrin evaded with breathtaking cheek, yet some were not fast enough and were cut flying from the saddle. Others abandoned bows for swords, and slashed at Lenays in passing, yet had little luck getting past the Lenay shields.

Koenyg chased several, had a partner struck point-blank by an arrow to the face, then two serrin he chased were cut off and killed by intercepting Hadryn men. The remaining serrin fled, and Koenyg urged his horse to join the chase, yet it did not respond. In fact, his horse was slowing, and seemed unsteady. Koenyg pulled the stallion to a halt, sensing something wrong, and no sooner had the horse come to a stop than it collapsed.

Koenyg jumped off before the rolling animal could trap his leg and strode about until he saw the expected—an arrow, protruding from the horse's throat.

"Damn," he muttered. "I liked that one." He pulled his blade and ended the horse's struggles, then waited for one of his comrades to find a replacement from amongst the hundreds of milling, riderless horses. The animal they did find was a dun-coloured mare—Koenyg preferred stallions but the animal looked like quality, so he mounted and surveyed the battle.

Serrin were now running, scattering wide across the valley. Lenays were reluctantly not pursuing; those who forgot that most basic serrin tactic soon died for it, or their horses did.

"We may have taken as many as a quarter of the Steel," said a Hadryn lord. "A good fight, our losses are light."

"The Steel cavalry will think twice before charging us again," Koenyg agreed. "But I wanted more *talmaad* dead—we took only a handful, while they took quite a few of us."

"It was only the sacrifice of the Steel cavalry that presented the demons with such easy targets," another lord protested. "A few more engagements like that and the Steel cavalry shall be no more. Without them the demons' archery shall be less effective."

Koenyg frowned. "That wasn't their whole force—they're holding a lot back. I want to lure them out. We stand aside for now, let the Kazeri have some fun."

The lords looked shocked. "Stand aside for barbarian Kazeri? And cede the honour to them?"

"We wear the serrin down," Koenyg explained. "We keep them harried, we water our horses, we take some food, while allowing the serrin and Steel cavalry none of these things. Then after the Kazeri are half-dead, as I expect they soon will be, we resume the lead once more."

The lords did not like it, but knew better than to argue. "What of the prisoners?" another asked.

"Keep them," said Koenyg. "These defences are clever; no doubt there is more cleverness to come, considering who commands them. I would know more, if they will tell us."

"Oh, they'll tell us," said another lord, grimly.

"A good horse," Koenyg complimented the man who had found his new mount. "Whose was she?"

"Lord Talryd's," came the reply. "He was killed."

"Commendable," said Koenyg, with a fisted salute to his chest. The others echoed it. "Most commendable."

The Regent's opening attack had failed. The first soldiers had retreated down the slope to seek cover and await a proper massing of their forces, leaving scores of bodies on the grass and rocks. Sasha rode along the first line of deployed Ilduuri archers, and listened to the yells of massing soldiery halfway down the slope below.

"They're mustering archers!" one Ilduuri sergeant called up to her as she rode past.

"They'll be firing uphill!" Sasha yelled so most could hear her. "You'll be firing downhill! They'll have to get so close to hurt you, you could spit on them!"

Men laughed. It was not humour, but confidence and spirit. Her Ilduuris looked confident, archers now wielding shorter Ilduuri bows, and some with huge serrin ones they'd traded for. Ilduuris typically fought light, but here some had figured a larger bow would be worth the trade in weight and awkwardness.

Further ahead, away from the valley mouth, a steep shoulder of hillside was being massed with soldiers. Had they not artillery primed on that site, it would have been alarming. An artillery captain followed her, with a trumpeter to his side, awaiting her order. Andreyis and Yasmyn followed after— she'd already sent Daish racing back to Kessligh to tell him what unfolded. Now she summoned Andreyis to her side.

"Andrey, go to Damon. Tell him that Balthaar is spread thin all along the river. Their artillery is not here yet. Our one chance to do him massive damage here is for the Army of Lenayin to charge, and split him in half. Tell him that I can see all the Regent's ranks from up here, and I think the Army of Lenayin can actually reach the river, and divide a force ten times their size. Tell him to go immediately, before they acquire more depth. I do not expect we shall have any spare artillery to help him, but if we do, we shall. Got that?"

"I've got it."

Sasha was almost surprised at his calm confidence. But truly, it was more pleasure than surprise. And pride as well. "We can do this, Andrey. The Army of Lenayin can do it, tell him that."

"I'll believe it if you say so," he replied. "Prince Damon will too." He turned and urged his horse to a gallop, back through waiting ranks of Ilduuri, fast along the ridgeline.

Sasha considered the hillside once more. The ground in the middle was rocky and steep, with little chance of advance there. The attacking forces were mustered primarily to the far left, where a broad shoulder of tree-covered land made a natural path across the face of the slope, and here directly above Hama town, where a riding trail climbed a manageable ascent. If she lost either side, she would rather it be the left, as the trail back along the ridgeline behind, overlooking the Dhemerhill Valley, came directly above the town, and could be cut off. But better if she lost neither.

Then, with a crescendo of yells, they were coming again. Thousands of men erupted from cover and scrambled uphill.

"Second rank!" Sasha yelled, and a new line of Ilduuri archers rushed forward to join the first rank already in position. The first rank kneeled, and moved a little down the slope so that the second could stand above them, and aim down. Suddenly the men below were faced with twice as many archers as they'd thought there were. "Artillery, all fire!"

The artillery captain sounded a rapid tune on his trumpet. A moment later, the air was filled with whistling ballista fire. Heavy bolts arced high into the air, then fell at a steeper angle—ballistas were firing crosswise over the slope, to accommodate that sudden drop in trajectory that would otherwise make targeting the far side of a blind slope impossible. Given that all of the artillery was behind them, upon the ridge overlooking the Dhemerhill Valley, it meant that here upon the right flank, there could be no close support from artillery fire without the risk of dropping some short on friendly heads.

"Fire!" yelled the archery captain, and now the air filled with arrows. Men coming up the slope tried to hide behind shields that were quickly feathered, but others fell in tens and dozens, the lighter armour that had made them suitable for climbing having little chance against the downward velocity of Ilduuri arrows, and less still against serrin bows.

Men with bigger shields formed protective clusters and kept coming, some bravely holding place despite arrows through exposed legs. Other men formed up behind those, and climbed higher behind that line of protection.

Upon the left flank, Sasha could see huge numbers advancing well, thrusting up toward the Ilduuri line. Only now, the real artillery arrived.

Burning hellfire hit squarely in the midst of those advancing on the left, and Sasha shielded her eyes against the horror. When the glare faded, hundreds of men were burning and shrieking, entire sections of hill ablaze, whole trees flaming like torches. A great many attackers were too close to the Ilduuris to be safely targeted, but they were now alone, as those advancing behind abruptly died, and those behind them recoiled in horror.

Ilduuri archers on the left flank fell back, and the first wave of attackers crested the hill with a mixture of triumph and sheer relief to be clear of the hellfire . . . and ran headlong into the line of Ilduuri Steel infantry that they had not yet seen in their advance up the hill. Ilduuri fell upon them in a wall, and in a short flurry of blows with sword and shield, the first attacking wave were falling back down the hillside, leaving many dead on the ground behind.

Another wave of hellfire landed, this time further down the slope, turning more men and trees to flame. Before Sasha's own position, here on the right flank above Hama, there was no hellfire, as there was no suitable flat ground over to the left upon which catapults could rest.

The catapults could shoot further, however, and now did, dropping hellfire onto Hama down below, and beyond it. A house exploded in flame, then a field to the left of the town. Then the central square took a hit, and columns of men still advancing through it, or sheltering behind its walls from ballista fire, took to running. It was sad to destroy a pretty town the Ilduuris would much rather have saved. But there would be far sadder things to see before this fight was done.

With bigger shields to the fore, and no hellfire to decimate them, enough attackers coming up the slope were surviving to press home the advance. Arrows began soaring up from below as archers finally got close enough to put fire onto Ilduuri positions.

"Archers back!" Sasha yelled. "Shield line, front rank, forward!"

She wheeled her horse through a gap as they came past her, and the archers faded back from the edge. With a roar, hundreds of attackers began cresting the ridge, followed by thousands more, across a stretch of hillside several hundred paces wide. As on the left, they came headlong onto Ilduuri shields and swords, and so the new form of dying began.

"She wants us to charge?" Damon stared at the messenger—Andreyis, he recalled the young man's name, Sasha's friend from Baerlyn.

"They are spread across the valley mouth but thin," Andreyis repeated urgently. "The river is at their backs, and their artillery is not yet present."

"It is perfect," Markan agreed. His cheek bore a nasty cut where Sasha's stanch had sliced him, but the swelling was now gone sufficiently that he could wear a helm. "They do not expect it, and their position is weak. The Synnich-ahn's judgement is sound."

It was too predictable coming from Markan, and Damon did not trust it. From this far up the valley, the Army of Lenayin could barely see the valley mouth or the forces that gathered there, but they could hear them. It was the sound that an awful lot of soldiers made when they moved and shouted orders all at once. A distant roar, like a singular mass. Attacking one hundred thousand men with fourteen thousand was crazy.

And yet, as a tactic, Damon could not fault it. Dangerous tactics were only wrong when there were better options available. Sitting back and waiting for the Regent to get organised was far worse, particularly if his artillery made the journey up the valley with him. The Steel was an army built for defence, but the Army of Lenayin was not. It was best on the move, and preferably on the attack, where momentum could shatter an opponent's formation and create the fighting space within which individual Lenay warriors excelled. Attacking was desperate, but then, the situation was desperate.

"We go," said Damon. He turned to the serrin woman who commanded the *talmaad* forces at this end of the valley. "We will need the *talmaad* to break up their cavalry as we go in."

The woman nodded. Rhillian was her name, another of Sasha's friends, though Damon only knew her a little. Other serrin regarded her with a mixture of anger and fear that he had never seen serrin direct upon one of their own, but left little doubt as to her authority. It was awe, he supposed. Her face, above her light mail and leathers, was strikingly beautiful.

"As we have practised," Rhillian agreed. "We will go first, your cavalry behind."

"Just keep *their* cavalry off our formation, that's all I ask."

Rhillian nodded, turned her horse, and galloped away.

"Damn," said a lord from Tyree. "Best-looking woman I ever saw in my life."

Another laughed. "If she lives, I'll marry her."

"Do serrin women marry?" asked another.

"Aye, sometimes. *Handsome* men."

"That rules you out."

"We go now." Damon cut off their cheerful debate. "No waiting. My sister says we can reach the river. If we do, we may win this war early."

They departed with a rousing yell. As the provincial lords, real and de facto, galloped away to their formations, Damon considered his position. Behind, looming wide across the valley, stood the Dhemerhill Valley's western wall, still not as high as he'd have liked, yet serviceable. Before it, ranked in gleaming thousands, stood the Rhodaani Steel. Behind the wall, out of sight, was their surviving artillery.

The wall had no doors or gates, yet armies before it could retreat behind by ascending the flanking hills and going around. Obviously an attacking army could do the same, but would funnel itself into two narrow approaches on climbing ground that could be targeted by artillery, archers, and ground defences alike. If the Regent's army came around the wall that way, they'd be annihilated by hellfire one rank at a time. But that did not mean any retreat by the defenders to move behind the wall would be a simple matter either.

Ahead, the valley was wide, at least a thousand paces, turning gradually to the right as it approached the mouth and the Ipshaal River. High to the left, on the bluff overlooking the valley mouth and river, Damon could see a gleaming silver rank of warriors—the Ilduuri Steel. There seemed to be fighting, but the distance made it hard to tell. Beyond the ridge black smoke rose, and burning artillery made arcs across the sky. Damon hoped Sasha's artillerymen had practised all their angles well in advance, and were not dropping rounds short as those confounded catapults were liable to do. He still did not trust those things, and less so since he'd seen a catapult crew die two days earlier when a round erupted prematurely. Though he also hoped that the Regent's crews were struggling to master what would be for them foreign and unfamiliar contraptions.

The approach toward the Ipshaal was cultivated farmland, broken with trees, fences, barns, and the Dhemerhill River itself. Strict formations would be difficult here. But that suited the Lenays far more than the Steel, or the Regent. Lenays were like serrin in that they loved to improvise—the more fluid the circumstance, the better it suited him.

"Andreyis," he summonsed the lad, "first go and tell the Rhodaani commanders what we do here. Then get back to Sasha and tell her that as our attack should take much of the pressure off her front, I'd appreciate as much artillery as she can grant us." Just because he didn't trust it, didn't mean he was fool enough to reject it where available.

Andreyis nodded. "She says you can do it," he added. "You can see the whole battlefield from up there, and she's certain you can reach the river."

He turned and galloped back toward the Rhodaanis. Damon wheeled his own entourage, and cantered to his command position at the rear. Across the valley floor, fourteen thousand Lenay fighting men ran or galloped to form their lines, and find their positions in the ranks. To the east, the Rhodaani Steel began to realise what was happening, and that Lenayin was preparing to charge. There arose from their ranks an almighty cheer and a clashing of sword on shield that stirred even Damon's sceptical soul.

Twenty-three

When Errollyn reached Kessligh's perch overlooking the eastern Dhemerhill Valley, he was dejected.

"There are too many of them," he said tiredly, waving a hand back across the valley. "We fared averagely against the Lenays the first time, but then came the Kazeri, and we dealt with them harshly as always, but then came the Torovans, and after that the Lenays again . . ."

"You did excellently," said Kessligh. "I'd feared we may be overrun at this end, but you've held them up to reconsider their position. I could not ask for more."

His command vantage was on a bluff several hundred paces beyond the easternmost of Jahnd's defensive walls. From here he could see all across the valley's rightwards twist, and the broad expanse of valley floor it created on Jahnd's entire right flank. Along the ridgelines here were arrayed a small portion of the Ilduuri Steel and a whole host of catapults and ballistas, the furthest upon bluffs and ridges several thousand paces up the valley.

Down below, and behind Kessligh's position, was the eastern-facing wall across the valley. Before it were arranged the Enoran Steel in huge, gleaming squares. Before them, now, were a great mass of cavalry—mostly Enoran and *talmaad*, having been driven back down the valley from its far end by the invaders.

The invaders now made an even greater mass across the valley beyond, stretching well to the east, darkening the green fields with the sheer weight of horseflesh. Almost entirely cavalry, their order of battle held the Army of Northern Lenayin first, the Army of Torovan second, and the Army of Kazeri last . . . though the Kazeri probably did not see it like that. Also down there somewhere, Kessligh reckoned, would be one or two thousand men from the Holy Army of Rhodaan, led by Alfriedo Renine himself. Though General Zulmaher, formerly of the Rhodaani Steel, would be in actual command. Something to bear in mind, if command were to change.

"Koenyg leads them?" he asked Errollyn.

"Almost certainly," said Errollyn. He took a long swig from his water flask, dishevelled and sweaty in the warm sun. "The *talmaad* are strong. We have lost perhaps one in five, dead or wounded. The Enorans . . ." he made a face, "they fought bravely, perhaps too bravely. I wanted them to disengage more quickly. They only needed to tangle their enemies for a moment to present the *talmaad* with easy shots, but often they stayed too long. They did well against the Kazeri and Torovans, but by the time the Lenays attacked again, they were exhausted, and those fucking Hadryn and Banneryd are just too damn good."

"I know," Kessligh said sombrely. "How bad?"

"Half," said Errollyn. "We've lost half. Brave men."

"Brave men," Kessligh echoed. "We must ensure they did not die for nothing."

"We killed perhaps three for every one we lost," Errollyn added. "But the gold weight of those were Kazeri—we did less against the Torovans, and nowhere near enough against the Lenays. There's still about forty thousand left, I'd guess."

"Fair guess."

If those numbers were right, *talmaad* and Enoran cavalry would be down to about ten thousand. The Enoran Steel infantry were another twelve. Of the Ilduuris—only about four thousand—Sasha needed the bulk of them down at the western end, where the mass of the Regent's foot soldiers was about to be hurled.

"We can't cover the entire valley approach along this side," said Kessligh, indicating the right side of the valley. "The Ilduuri have scouts out all along, and will make that approach as difficult as possible, but Koenyg can find a way to get cavalry up onto this ridge, if he wants."

"It's not cavalry terrain," Errollyn replied.

"No, but they can dismount. Lenays often fight that way, using horses only as transport then dismounting to fight on foot, especially in mountains. We may not be able to hold them off these positions."

"Which opens the Enorans to attack below, with no artillery cover save what's behind them."

Kessligh chewed his lip. "We can do it," he concluded finally. "The question remains how well the Regent has learned to use his captured artillery in the time he's had it. Without it, we would probably win this conflict—we have a strong defensive position to assist our lack of numbers. But I don't think the Ilduuri can hold the Regent off those ridges once he realises how important they are—he'll throw everything he has up the slopes and overwhelm them."

"Which opens the valley to a similar attack," Errollyn concluded. "And if he has free range to use his artillery against the wall, or gets some of it up onto Sasha's ridge . . ."

"The Rhodaanis on the ground are fucked. And it all unravels from there, including here, because we'll have to pull so many forces off this side to reinforce the other that this side will collapse as well."

Hooves thundered, and Daish arrived in a cloud of dust. "Sasha sends me—the attack begins!" he announced. "There were a hundred thousand at least, mostly foot soldiers, though some cavalry also. She speculates that most of the cavalry was sent around to this end of the valley."

"She speculates right," Errollyn said wryly.

"The Regent's initial attempts to gain the ridge have been weak," Daish continued. "They are repelled comfortably, with casualties. But Sasha suspects it will not last, when the Regent sees the necessity of gaining the heights."

"He will," said Kessligh.

"Sasha speculated that she may send the Army of Lenayin to attack up the valley. The Regent is spread thin against the Ipshaal, and his artillery is not yet in position. But I left before she had given that order. Perhaps the next messenger will carry it."

"Oh, I think she will," said Errollyn with a faint smile. "Sasha's not the defensive type."

"Good move if she calculates it right," said Kessligh. "Get back and tell her that Koenyg commands on this side, we've halted his advance short of our main defences, but Enoran cavalry has suffered heavily. I expect Koenyg to send dismounted troops up to capture these ridges soon. Oh, and tell her that Errollyn is well."

Daish grinned, saluted, and departed in a hurry.

Kessligh resumed his gaze out across the valley. "Come on, damn you," he muttered. "Attack."

"You're that certain we'll hold them?" Errollyn asked.

"Not the point. We must hold forces here to guard against such a huge cavalry opponent. If those cavalry break our lines on this side and get into our rear . . ."

"We're finished."

"But Koenyg barely needs to attack. His main purpose is to force me to hold troops here, leaving my lines weak against the Regent's main force in the west. I'd rather he comes at us and gives us the chance to secure this flank by dealing him a defeat."

"You just told Daish you were confident he would attack."

Kessligh shrugged. "Aye, the main thing I wish Sasha to know is that she'll have no help from me any time soon. Precisely what happens here, she's far too busy for it to change anything."

Jaryd might have liked to ride with his native men of Tyree, but his place was at Damon's side and he knew it. Not that the prince seemed to be lacking in popularity as he rode to the front of the Army of Lenayin's formation to the cheers and yells of the men, but in this mood, Lenay warriors would cheer anything.

Now they awaited the infantry's arrival behind, having cleared the patchwork forest dividing fields at this end of the valley. The infantry made their position at a run, and *talmaad* were forming on open fields in front, several thousand serrin on horseback, bows at the ready.

Beyond them, a huge mass of feudal soldiery was forming, amidst yells, waving banners and blasting trumpets. They seemed in some confusion, yet they were further advanced into the valley than Jaryd had hoped, and not pressed as far back against the Ipshaal as Sasha's message had seemed to indicate. Had she misjudged? Or were the Regent's forces organising faster than she'd thought possible?

As though summonsed by the thought of Sasha, a burning artillery round flew arcing over the enemy formations from the bluff to the left of the valley mouth. It fell, and erupted with a great, rolling fire. Lenay men cheered, yet the Regent's forces did not waver. Even the horrors of hellfire were lost amongst such a huge number of men. They would not want to stand under it for a long time, but already most of the formation was deploying over here, upon the right side of the Dhemerhill River, furthest from the artillery's effects. The left flank, across the river, was more sparse.

"The Dhemerhill River is fordable here," said Jaryd to Damon, "a hundred paces up from this farmhouse." He pointed with his sword. "The locals showed me a number of places, and I checked them myself; river levels are unchanged since then."

Damon looked, grimly tightening the arm strap of his shield. There were bridges over the river too, but they were narrow. A proper fording could cross a large number of cavalry without slowing to swim, or to fit across a narrow bridge. A smaller force of Lenay and *talmaad* cavalry were deployed upon the left side, against a similar size of Bacosh cavalry and infantry. Damon wanted the Regent's men to think he was merely engaging them head on, force against force. Instead, a charge across the river and up the exposed left side, under cover of Sasha's artillery, could put them halfway to the Ipshaal.

"Deal with their cavalry first," he said. "Then we cross." Jaryd wasn't certain if it would be possible to coordinate such a move on so little notice. Well, they were about to find out.

Ahead, the serrin began to move, and Lenay cavalry followed. The canter slowly built to a gallop. Jaryd could not see past the line of *talmaad*, and focused only upon holding his place in the line. The Lenays left gaps in their line for the *talmaad* to fall back through. Closing them in time to make contact would be a challenge.

They wove about trees and leaped a low fenceline, and then the *talmaad* were rising in their saddles and pulling on bowstrings. They fired together, arrows flying high, then pulled a second arrow in unison and let fly at a lower trajectory. And then they divided, bunching into groups to make large holes in their formation, those who could get a clear shot now firing a third arrow as they did so. They turned, each bunched group of *talmaad* aligning upon several "flankmen" whose job was to watch the Lenays behind, and steer back through the holes left purposely in their ranks.

Jaryd steered across, and for a moment horses jostled . . . but then the serrin were flashing by, and a line of armoured Bacosh cavalry were rearing ahead, wavering with shock, no more than fifty human paces away. As usual with serrin, the timing was perfect.

More arrows flew past Lenay riders as formations clashed, men and horses falling, colliding at speed, lost lances careening into the air to crash into unsuspecting riders. Jaryd found himself racing through the first rank of knights and other cavalry without finding a target, then spread the line further to approach the second rank. These were less heavily armoured, and he parried past one with his shield whilst crashing through a second's defence on the other side. He reeled, and Jaryd spun with his comrades to pursue—these were mostly Damon's friends, a close company of Verenthane nobles who could easily have remained with Koenyg, but had not. Like Jaryd, they'd been raised on horses since before they could walk, and were at no disadvantage against even the men of Northern Lenayin.

Bacosh cavalry came back at them—Jaryd saw Damon smash one from the saddle, saw a clever lean and duck from his companion stab through another's side, and accelerated onto another's blind side himself to cut through his unprotected neck from behind. He could see back to the first rank now, some dividing, very unwisely, to chase the *talmaad*, and others galloping back to reengage the Lenays. Many of those were being followed by *talmaad*, shooting men in the back whose armour would not stop it, and shooting the horses of those where it would. The combined force of human and serrin cavalry, devised by Errollyn, was designed to be lethal to the first enemy rank, who found themselves both engaged up close and shot by deadly accurate fire from afar and behind. Already they were panicking, wheeling about to try to clear the field of serrin fire, eager to confront the Lenays but not wishing to turn their backs on the *talmaad*.

Damon and friends yelled with triumph and charged, felling more confused and frightened cavalry, and now encountering knights whose armour remained intact, but whose horses were struggling with multiple arrow strikes and dying. Some hit the ground hard and struggled to rise once more. Lenay men generally ignored them—they would be dealt with later, and were too slow afoot to bother fast-moving cavalry.

Soon the Regent's cavalry were falling back, then retreating at full gallop. More artillery flashes erupted upon the left flank, and Jaryd spared a moment to view the bluff from which they came. No fighting was visible. Had that assault failed?

Now serrin were pursuing the retreating Bacosh men, zigzagging through the Lenay warriors with bows in hand, seeking shots at retreating backs. They looked furiously determined, striving to kill as many as possible while the chance presented. Behind them came the main Lenay army, on foot, and running. Fast.

Damon was yelling, standing in his stirrups to attract attention, pointing across the river. Already other Lenay cavalry were charging that way, and Damon followed, gathering more men as he went. Shouted orders were of no use here. The noise of hooves and massed voices was too loud for anyone save an immediate neighbour to hear. But the plan was to get across the Dhemerhill River, and up the relatively exposed left flank under the cover of Ilduuri artillery on the ridge.

Jaryd hit the water amidst several hundred other horsemen, with more hundreds following. The horses plunged and struggled for a moment, and then were clear to the far bank and running once more, skirting a large farmstead and leaping fences. To the right were masses of enemy soldiers. To this side, the way was clear, as few braved the falling artillery for the next thousand strides at least. Damon's party cleared a final fence and emerged onto rolling green fields, swords out and yelling as they charged at full speed.

Rhillian reined up further back than her comrades, holding her bow in the air as a signal for others to do the same. Bacosh cavalry were trying to escape, some fording the river to the left, others galloping off to the right, across the impenetrable line of infantry before them, *talmaad* and a few Lenay cavalry in pursuit. Those would try to run up the steep valley sides high enough to find a way around. In this valley, a cavalryman could run out of room very fast, with infantry behind plugging up his only escape.

Behind, she could hear the Army of Lenayin approaching, the deafening roar and rattle of thousands of charging men. She spaced her horse a little further from her neighbour, held him still, then placed her first arrow to her bowstring. She fired, low and flat, as other serrin did the same, stopping their horses completely. Arrows flew as the roar behind grew louder. Sporadic return fire arced high and ineffective; the Regent's forces had not yet gathered archers close enough to the front rank to make their shots count. Rhillian fired again, and thought that this form of warfare was agreeable to her. A horse could carry numerous quivers, and she had a lot of arrows. She would sit here and shoot them at her enemies until there were no arrows left, then retreat to get some more.

Suddenly the Army of Lenayin were bursting past her, and she felt as though she were mounted upon a beach, a great wave crashing across the sand. There were thousands of them, and she could feel their fury shaking her bones. The Army of Lenayin had been defeated at Shero Valley. It had lost its king, and run before an enemy. It had marched in humiliation behind the victorious Regent across Rhodaan and then into Enora, with banners flying low in shame and mourning. It had suffered the worse realisation that all along, they'd been fighting for a dishonourable cause. They'd been misled, tricked into a war that many of them might have gladly fought, but for the other side. And their so-called allies had treated them with contempt, called them barbarians, and lately tried to murder their favourite princess for daring to wed the soon-to-be King of all the Bacosh. The Army of Lenayin had borne this weight for weeks and months, living for the moment of redemption and retribution. They were not merely in the bloodlust of Lenay warriors in battle. They were genuinely, blood-curdlingly furious.

The Army of Lenayin smashed into the Bacosh first rank and killed nearly all of them within moments. Gaps opened first by serrin archers became gaping holes as flanks were exposed, and quickly exploited with superior swordwork and brute force. Lenay men dove into spaces and hacked limbs from the men *beside* them, holding off their forward opponents long enough to strike sideways and open the way for their neighbour, who returned the favour to *his* neighbour, and on across the ranks. They roared and swung and bludgeoned, with the fury of madmen and the skill of artisans, and across the valley the air was filled with flying blades and blood.

And then, when that first contact had penetrated so far that most armies would have considered it a success and paused to regroup, the later ranks of soldiers pushed past their leading comrades, fresh to the fight, and took over the charge. Beyond the packed forward ranks there was space, space enough for a Lenay warrior to move, to swing, to clever-fake and spin, and perform all the deadly tricks he'd rehearsed all his life, if only in the hope of impressing his friends and village girls at evening practice. Bacosh men-at-arms, mostly peasants and village folk with solid skills but none of the artistry, simply died, falling in horrible, screaming wrecks before a class and power of soldiery they had never before encountered. The Army of Lenayin, now five hundred paces beyond the Bacosh soldiers' front line, began to accelerate.

"Good *gods*!" Arken exclaimed in the saddle at Sasha's side, looking over the battlefield. The Army of Lenayin was flooding out from the Dhemerhill Valley, beyond its protective walls, and now churned inexorably toward the banks of the Ipshaal. The Bacosh forces looked stunned, not so much retreating as sinking like saplings in a flood, as Lenays ran through them and past them, and left the slower ones for comrades behind to deal with. "Look at them!"

Similar exclamations rose from across the Ilduuri lines. Their own attackers had faded back down the slope for the second time, and men with a vantage now gathered eagerly on this side to see the battle below.

"They're still going!"

Excited yells rose to a crescendo, and then men were hammering on their shields and roaring, chanting for Lenayin. Upon her horse, Sasha wiped tears from her eyes. Of all the moments in her life she had ever felt proud to be Lenay, all were as nothing before this. She stood in her stirrups, pointed her sword at the sky, and yelled with the rest of her Ilduuris.

Jaryd thrust and crashed his way through infantry ranks, men giving way in panic, others falling flat to escape the reach of his sword, only to be trampled underfoot. On this left side of the Dhemerhill Valley, only cavalry had attacked. Now they pierced the thin and wavering lines of Bacosh soldiers toward the Ipshaal like a dagger through the heart.

He yelled in fury as some soldiers ahead were slow to run clear and barrelled into them, his horse bounding for footing, knocking through several, trampling another. Arrows zipped past, *talmaad* mixed with the Lenay ranks behind, shooting fleeing soldiers in the back. Ahead, now visible across a final stretch of grass, was the Ipshaal. Enemies parted before it, and he nearly laughed at the ease of it, this astonishing victory, against such overwhelming odds.

The Lenay cavalry reached the bank in their tens and then hundreds, and wheeled. More hundreds poured in as Bacosh soldiers parted on either side. Damon's noble friends were whooping and yelling as though the war was over. Damon, Jaryd saw, merely stood his horse upon the bank, and looked along the river in either direction.

Along each bank was an endless sea of men. Further up- and downriver, entire armies were barely even aware they had been attacked. Jaryd's joy died upon his lips, and the look that Damon gave him was wary.

"We can't hold here," he said. "We can't push in either direction along the river. The forces in the other direction will move in and cut us off from the valley. We'll be trapped. We must withdraw."

"Withdraw?" Jaryd didn't like the sound of that. Damon was often grim and worried—this seemed like capitulation. More arrows zipped through the air, only these ones were incoming. Archers in the surrounding ranks were organising. "Look, let's at least clear the hill in front of Sasha's bluff. . . ."

"There's no room. They were thin before the valley mouth but if we press them tighter along the riverbank they'll have nowhere to retreat to and we'll get stuck. . . ."

"Their disadvantage, surely!" Jaryd protested.

"And ours when we can't make it back to the valley! We had a good run, we killed a lot of them and made them wary, let's get back before our triumph turns and bites us."

"Surely we can . . ."

A whistling buzz interrupted them, like a swarm of wasps, followed by rapid thudding, and further across the grass a horse was smashed into the ground like a bug. Then another two, and a rider clubbed from the saddle by something big and fast.

"Ballistas!" shouted Damon. "Their artillery is trained on us!"

"Dammit," Jaryd muttered, spinning his horse to stare up the riverside once more, searching for the source of it. "It'll be a few hundred paces up that way, if we can just . . ."

A flaming ball came through the air directly before him—they were out of range from Ilduuri artillery on the bluff, so it could only be enemy fire.

"Hellfire!" someone yelled. It hit the fields further from the river, riders scattering, not so concentrated there to be affected. Two more shots came, one hitting a tree and engulfing it, the other erupting near the bank of the Dhemerhill.

Upon the opposite side of the Dhemerhill, more flaming balls were arcing through the air. These were coming from further up the Ipshaal bank to the north. And these were heading straight for the Lenay infantry.

"That's it," said Damon. "We're getting out before we get slaughtered." He turned and galloped back the way they'd come, waving his sword and yelling for men to form up on him. "Get me a trumpeter and get our infantry back! Full retreat!"

Sasha swore, watching the artillery land. Great plumes of fire rose from amidst the Army of Lenayin's ranks. Likely it was killing surviving Bacosh soldiers in there as well, but the thought did not comfort.

"Get them out of there, Damon," she muttered. "It was a great victory, now fall back and live to fight another one."

Here on the near side of the Dhemerhill, Lenay cavalry were indeed falling back. That would be Damon himself, though she could not make him out. Artillery fire was landing amidst the horses here as well, though less effective on the open ground. It was coming from just before her left flank.

She wheeled and rode fast along her lines, where Ilduuri men who had been cheering now stood and watched with grim concern. They knew how fast hellfire artillery could turn any exposed and tightly clustered army to cinders. Soon she reached a spot on the harshly contested left flank where black grass still burned from Ilduuri artillery and piles of charred corpses smouldered, while others lay strewn underfoot, having fought right up and even past the Ilduuri shieldline. To her left, amidst the trees, wounded Ilduuris were treated by comrades, and a small number of dead lay silent.

At the bottom of the slope, and perhaps fifty paces beyond, she could see the Regent's captured artillery. Great arms swung from the backs of huge wheeled wagons, pulled by large teams of bullocks. With each crank and crash, they hurled another flaming projectile downriver. Her position was safe from them up here; neither catapults nor even ballistas could reach this altitude from that position. But the Army of Lenayin was another matter.

"Give me a thousand," said Arken at her side, "and I can get them."

Sasha stared at him. His return stare was deadly serious. "There's still a lot of men halfway down this slope," she pointed out. "You'll have to fight through them."

"With downhill momentum it's no problem," said the confident Ilduuri.

"Then after you hit them, and destroy the artillery, you have to run back up here under fire, in full armour, with half the Regent's army on your heels."

"We are the Ilduuri Steel," said Arken, blue eyes blazing. "You see how we fight, we run up mountains in full armour every day before breakfast." It was true, they did. "In Ilduur, and here today, you have shown me the greatness of a Lenay warrior. Today we shall show you the greatness of the Ilduuri warrior."

Men nearby who overheard him gave a bloodthirsty yell of agreement.

Sasha thought about it, for the short moment that was all she had. She could not afford to lose a thousand Ilduuri here, and it was certainly possible that if a thousand ran down this hill, barely a handful would return. But she and Kessligh had both agreed that if the Regent's artillery remained intact for the entire fight, their chances of final victory were slim. Even now the artillery threatened to turn Lenayin's great triumph into carnage. This was the chance she had to take.

"Do it," she said. "Write me a war tale, Arken. Write me a war tale that warriors will tell around their firesides in Lenayin, of how the Ilduuri Steel is feared by its enemies."

Rhillian dashed across carnage, her horse bounding and skittering to avoid bodies underfoot, some still moving. Most of them were Bacosh men, but now there was artillery falling all around. Eruptions of flame engulfed unsuspecting men, and ballista fire thumped steadily to the ground with a sound like giant hailstones, here and there taking a man with it.

She found a Lenay officer beneath a banner and raced to his side. "Get your men out of here!" she yelled at him. "Sound a retreat before you lose half your force!"

"We are winning!" the officer shouted back defiantly. "A few cowardly fireballs won't stop us now."

"Fucking fool!" Rhillian shouted. "They're just getting their range in, you're losing *hundreds* of men even now!" Ballista fire hit very close. Then a nearby horse was hit, straight through the head, crushing its skull and upending it into a somersault.

"You are serrin, you do not command here!" Looking about, Rhillian saw he didn't have a trumpeter anyway. Nearby she spotted another group beneath a flag, and galloped toward them instead. She was halfway there when they disappeared beneath a wall of flame. She threw up her hands and her horse reared. The next moment, she was on the ground.

She rolled to get up, staggering on bodies. She could barely see, blinking desperately to restore her sight. The air stank of fumes and burned flesh. Where was her horse?

Hooves approached from behind, and then Aisha's voice. A big shadow came across in front, and her reaching hand grasped a bridle. She mounted by feel as Aisha asked urgent questions.

"I'm not hurt," she explained, "I just can't see, that hellfire was too close. How's my horse?"

"Looks okay," said Aisha, "just try not to fall off again." Aisha had as little respect for her horsemanship as Errollyn had for her archery. "We have to get them out of here—these brave fools don't know when to retreat!"

"Can you see officers and trumpeters?"

"Um . . . yes! Just follow me, can you do that?"

Rhillian waved her ahead and followed the blur that was Aisha's horse. More ballista fire hit, unnervingly close by the sound of it, then the flash of another fireball. Rhillian thought that temporary blindness was not such a bad thing, so she did not have to see men burning.

Her vision was clearing by the time she reached the officers, still advancing behind their men toward the Ipshaal. "Full retreat!" she yelled. "We don't stand and fight beneath hellfire, that was already decided by Kessligh himself!"

"I've had no orders from Prince Damon," the officer retorted.

"And you won't for a short while more, because he's fighting too! But in that short while, you're going to lose your army!"

The officer chewed his lip, barely flinching as two more rounds struck ahead.

"Trumpeter," Rhillian shouted, "sound full retreat!" The trumpeter looked askance at the officer. Finally, the officer nodded.

The trumpeter raised his horn to his lips and played high notes. It repeated, several times, and then other trumpeters took up the call. And not a moment too soon, as in the midst of the fifth repeat, the Rhodaani trumpeter was struck by a ballista bolt that pinned him to his horse and killed both.

"Let's pick up some wounded and give them a ride back!" Rhillian commanded. "If we're fast we can make several trips before the infantry make it back."

Hellfire rounds burst across the downhill slope, and then with a roar the Ilduuri Steel were plunging over the edge. Archers stood before Sasha and fired ahead, but with little chance of doing more damage than the hellfire had already done. The great wave of Ilduuri men ran fast and sure despite the slope, and even held a rough formation as they plunged downhill through the dying flames and smoke of hellfire strikes.

Across the wooded ridge behind, Ilduuri officers yelled for men to take up positions, now that the great mass of twelve hundred had gone. They were separate battalions from different regiments—Sasha had not wished to lose an entire formation from any one regiment, as many were from the same towns and regions. In the Army of Lenayin, village men now spread themselves across different formations, so the menfolk of entire towns would not disappear in a single hellfire strike.

There were yells and clashes from below as the downhill plunge encountered men milling at midslope and below for the next uphill attack. But here on the left flank Ilduuri artillery had been heaviest, and there were not so many still living.

Yasmyn galloped in from her right, and came alongside. "Lenayin pulls back," she announced. "The Regent pursues."

"We must give them cover. Tell the artillery to put every available unit to fire on the Regent's forces if they come within range. And then come back fast, because if Arken's men are pursued back up the slope, they'll need cover, too."

Yasmyn nodded and disappeared at a gallop, running Ilduuri replacements skipping aside from the cleared path. Sasha had nineteen thousand Ilduuri in total and nearly four thousand of those were cavalry, now divided between Enoran and Rhodaani forces down in the valley. They'd been reluctant to part from their infantry, but she simply had no use for them up on the ridges, and the other Steel armies had need for more horsemen.

That left fifteen thousand infantry. Kessligh had four thousand guarding the ridges on Jahnd's eastern flank, and she had nearly one thousand manning artillery. Ten thousand fighting men. If none of these just departed came back, she'd have nine. Casualties so far were only in the dozens, but that would change when Balthaar truly got his act together, claimed the Dhemerhill Valley mouth, and forced her to widen her line. If he came up in all places at once, holding could become nearly impossible.

The Army of Lenayin would need to fall back and regroup. The Rhodaani Steel could then move up the valley to defend her right flank and pressure the Regent's left, but they would have to do so without much of their artillery, as the defensive wall across the Dhemerhill Valley had been built without gates for weakpoints, and the valley sides around the wall made it very difficult to haul heavy artillery up and around. And once up the valley, as the Army of Lenayin had just discovered, they'd be exposed to the Regent's own artillery fire.

She had to get some of that artillery here. Dare she send more men down the slope? If she lost too many on such risky charges, she'd never have enough to hold this ridge for even a short while, and if the ridge itself fell quickly, so would the entire heights back along the south side of the Dhemerhill Valley, outflanking the Rhodaanis and their defensive wall completely.

And worse, looking out at the Regent's army beneath her, she'd begun to suspect that she'd underestimated his numbers. If his cavalry were all coming from the east, that should leave him with about a hundred thousand here, mostly infantry. But now, as she tried to count, she thought it was probably more.

Yells and cheers arose from the Ilduuri as the charging force reached the bottom of the hill and laid into the Regent's forces with a distant clashing that sounded like a thousand pots and pans being bashed together. Sasha wished there were more space upon the ridge to deploy artillery further forward, but there was not. Arken's men were now beyond his own artillery range, and exposed. More hooves came toward her, but it was Daish, not Yasmyn. "Kessligh says forty thousand cavalry, led by Koenyg," he told her, steadying his sweating, gasping horse. "The *talmaad* did well, but the Enoran cavalry got smashed, lost about half."

Sasha nodded grimly, not especially surprised. "Well, he can't have any horses from here, we're going to need them."

Daish shook his head. "No, he's not asking, they've stopped them cold but dear gods there are still a lot of them. But they've the Enoran Steel before them now, plenty of *talmaad*, a defensive wall plus artillery on the ridges overhead."

"Koenyg won't attack directly," Sasha said with certainty. Her brother could be a hothead, but not where military victory was in question. She stared at the battle below as she spoke. Arken's men were pressing through the Regent's massed ranks, closing on the artillery. Artillery teams were trying to move, but were hemmed in by men on all sides. "He'll wait and force Kessligh to hold many forces to the rear. Tell him to get down to the western wall, that's where the action will be."

"Now?"

"Now. Go find someone down in the valley to get a report on the Army of Lenayin's status on the way, and tell him that the Rhodaanis are going to be in big trouble if they have to move up to defend my flank, and get hit by the same artillery that hit Lenayin. I'm trying to get some of that artillery now," she pointed below, "but I can't afford to lose huge waves of men attacking from this position. And tell him I think we've underestimated their numbers here by maybe thirty thousand."

Daish paled. "You think?" He looked along the riverbank.

Sasha nodded. "I don't know how, but we did," she murmured, staring downward. Arken's line was nearly at the artillery now, but having penetrated into the Regent's force, his flanks were under pressure. A thin silver wall of men fought hard to keep the tide at bay.

Daish galloped away, and passed Yasmyn as he left. "The Lenays are crossing the river as they pull back," she informed Sasha when she arrived, "they're coming under our artillery cover. The Regent's forces pursue, but not hard; they seem shocked."

"Lenayin does that," Sasha agreed.

Yasmyn smiled ferociously. "The artillery captain tells me that any who pursue them beneath his fire will regret it. How goes the fight?"

Sasha merely pointed. Yasmyn watched for a moment. "Courageous," she said. "Should you send more?"

"In very little time I'm not going to have enough," Sasha replied. "Even with what I have now."

"Like trying to plug twelve holes with ten fingers."

Sasha nodded. "Soon we'll be using toes."

Jaryd made his second run back at a canter, holding a Valhanan man with a slashed arm before him in the saddle. The Valhanan had insisted upon walking, but lost a lot of blood, and his comrades had insisted he take a horse. Jaryd rode with him in front so he could be caught if he fell.

The Army of Lenayin retreated in good order along the south side of the valley, beneath heights held by the Ilduuri. Many were frustrated, yelling aloud to any commander who would listen that they should turn about and go straight back. No doubt enough of them remained in good enough shape that they would win yet another glorious victory, and then perhaps another, if they wished. But after a few more such victories, the Regent's army would simply continue to advance, while the Army of Lenayin would fairly much cease to exist.

The Rhodaani Steel now advanced in gleaming squares up the valley centre, men on the near flank sending cheers to the retreating Lenays, who saluted back in good humour. No doubt the Rhodaanis were somewhat cheered to see that despite obvious losses, the Army of Lenayin still appeared strong and in high spirits. Jaryd looked at those tightly packed squares of Rhodaanis, and wondered if the same would stand for them, when the hellfire rounds began falling.

He joined other cavalry heading upslope and around the valley wall, and then down again to the far side. There, a hospital was working feverishly in the yard of a farmhouse, and he was assisted by Jahndi women in taking the wounded Lenay from his saddle. There were many serrin here also, men and women, villagers from across Saalshen who had come to help, yet could not fight. Many of those were learning archery, which could certainly be of use in later defence, even if poorly aimed. Others made arrows, or ballista bolts, or even hellfire, prepared further defences, and helped to tend the wounded.

On a horse nearby he saw a familiar figure directing a steady flow of wagons that now trundled out from Jahnd, and threatened to make a blockage as they churned up the valley roads. Jaryd smiled, as she talked to some hard-of-hearing individual who had aroused her displeasure.

"No!" Sofy was insisting loudly. "Dismantle the fence—you can't fit all these wagons through that gate. Bring the fence down and then you can move as many wagons as you like back and forth, otherwise we'll never move wounded as fast as they arrive!"

She was about to go on to the next trouble spot when she saw him. And smiled with a delight that set his heart to thumping, even despite all the thumping it had just done for different reasons. She trotted quickly over.

"I heard they were magnificent!" she said.

"Lenayin's finest hour," said Jaryd. "Pity Koenyg wasn't there to be part of it."

Sofy's eyes fell, and she swallowed. Jaryd regretted he'd said it. "You're well?" she asked, recovering quickly.

"I'm well, Damon too, most of his friends. Casualties quite light, all things considered, but still too high."

"Better than it could have been," said Sofy, with feeling. Jaryd nodded. "Jaryd . . ."

"I know," he said, and smiled. He wanted to kiss her, but she looked so busy, and there were wounded all around. She had done this kind of thing before, and with her authority, she could make things happen. "You take care."

"And you," she said. "Is Sasha . . . ?"

"She's fine. Don't worry about us, Sofy. You save some lives."

Sofy nodded with determination, spun her horse, and cantered off to supervise more arrivals. Jaryd looked around.

A steady stream of wounded continued to arrive, many of them on horseback. Jaryd saw a serrin man with two Lenays balanced on his horse, and three Lenay infantry, big, ferocious-looking men, one of whom carried a small serrin woman with a wounded leg. So many stories, he thought. So many hopes, friendships, and tragedies, unfolding upon these lands. He imagined the Army of Lenayin, marching triumphant back to their homeland, with a number of serrin wives accompanying them. A few serrin women at least might find the idea appealing . . . provided their new husbands promised them lives filled with more than that of a traditional Lenay wife. And he imagined himself, arriving back in his homeland, a new noble title to his name and with Sofy in a saddle beside him.

Jaryd sighed, shook his head to clear it of unnecessary thoughts, and cantered off to the path along the wall, and his army beyond.

The Ilduuri were running back up the slope. Exhausted, some half-carrying wounded comrades, they struggled and strained up the grassy hill, around rocky outcrops and charred trees. Arrows streaked up and into them, lower velocity on the upward arc, but still fast enough to pierce exposed flesh and mail. Running men fell, and were helped up by comrades, but the Regent's men were pursuing behind, and those in the rear were fighting a desperate rearguard.

"Lowest slope!" Sasha yelled at her archers. "Let nothing fall short!" Arrows streaked away, and then fell, a long, fast plummet toward the bottom of the slope. "Yasmyn, get back to the artillery and tell them to fire only at the lowest slope, nothing falls short!"

Yasmyn galloped off. Sasha did not trust the trumpet now to call artillery—its notes did not allow for enough precision, and she was desperate to avoid killing her own men with those terrible weapons.

A new, whistling, thudding noise drew her attention back down the slope. Ballistas by the Ipshaal River were firing uphill. They could not elevate enough to hit the ridge, but their bolts were streaking by the score straight into her struggling, retreating men who were now approaching midslope. She saw them hit, smashed, and pinned into the turf, armour and all. She saw men trying to retrieve fallen comrades, only to find them literally stuck to the ground. The screams were a horror, and she could see their faces, eyes up toward the ridge, desperate to reach that safety.

And now, at midslope but further to the right, clustered beneath their shields for protection from Ilduuri archers, a large mass of Bacosh soldiery was preparing to hit those climbing men from the side.

"Captain Dalen!" she yelled. "Form another three companies and sweep down this ridge! Clear those scum off our mountain!"

Captain Dalen rushed to do that. Some fast orders and men sprinted from amongst the ridgeline trees to make new lines. More ballista fire tore into the retreating party. They were not nearly so fast now as on their morning runs. The Ilduuri Steel were tough and talented, yet they had not seen heavy battle in a long while, and perhaps had not realised that fast manoeuvres in training, and fast manoeuvres after heavy fighting were completely different things.

With a roar, the new Ilduuri line went over the edge and plunged down the slope. Archers sent arrows whistling ahead of them as Bacosh soldiers appeared from cover and tried to make a line. On the downslope, against Ilduuris desperate to cover their comrades, they had little chance. Still some of the Bacosh line was engaging the climbing Ilduuris, exhausted men fighting hard just to get through, until their comrades arrived and sent the Regent's soldiers fleeing down to the bottom.

They clashed too with the soldiers who pursued them, forming a rearguard that was fresh and full of fight. Heavy clashes followed, lines of Ilduuri men repelling great waves of Bacosh soldiers, and killing many with the great advantage of skill, armour, and height. Finally, the artillery was resuming, first ballista fire spattering across the lower slope, and then the blinding flashes of hellfire.

Retreating Ilduuris made the ridge and collapsed to hands and knees, gasping for air. Comrades helped them, and moved them back into the trees so they did not block the way for others coming up. Some came up wounded, helped by friends, some with arrows sticking through legs or arms, and some with worse. Sasha remained out of their way, doing some rough counting. Downslope, Bacosh men were falling back fast. As they did so, Bacosh artillery resumed firing at their newly available targets—the second wave of Ilduuri soldiers now at midslope. More were hit, with brutal force.

"Trumpeter!" Sasha yelled. "Full retreat, get them back up here!"

The exhausted, battered Ilduuris looked dejected. They'd overrun several ballistas and a catapult, but had been unable to do much damage before the Regent's forces had overwhelmed them. Dead crews would be replaced, and little would change. Now those same ballistas were killing their friends.

Sasha leaped down from her horse and walked amongst them, whacking shoulders and shields with fierce appreciation.

"Magnificent!" she told them, moving from one man to the next. "Brave as all hells! Formidable soldiering, Lenayin could not have done better!"

"We failed you," a sergeant mumbled, face streaked with sweat and blood.

"You failed no one!" Sasha shouted for all to hear. "You gave them a fucking thrashing. I see their blood all over your swords and shields! It is my fault. I gave you an impossible task and still you nearly pulled it off! You are heroes, each and every one!"

It seemed to have some effect, as men sat to rest, and drink, and check on their friends. Sasha continued walking amongst them, determined to put a hand on as many shoulders and a word of encouragement in as many ears as possible. Now the second rank began returning, some of them wounded, and she walked amongst them as well.

A lieutenant came to her, having made a more precise count. "Six hundred and thirteen missing," he said quietly. "Another hundred and five too wounded to fight." Nearly all of those in the first wave, he did not need to say. "Captain Arken is amongst the missing, several say they saw him fall."

Sasha kept her face stony calm. "Get the wounded to the rear, and put the first wave survivors in reserve for now, they deserve a rest."

"You had to try," said the lieutenant. Evidently her attempt at calm was not convincing.

"I know," she said. "Thank you, Hanser."

Lieutenant Hanser nodded and left. Sasha stroked her horse's nose for a moment. That had always calmed her in the past. It failed to do so now. She recalled Arken's handsome blue eyes when she'd first met him, the tall blond man who looked so much the Ilduuri ideal, and yet trusted the foreigners that so many of his fellow Ilduuri hated. They would laugh at him now, and consider themselves proven right, as his faith in the foreigners had killed him after all.

Sasha recalled Arken's young family left behind in Andal, and hoped that it was worth it. For a brief moment, nothing was.

Twenty-four

Kessligh galloped past lines of hospital wagons, and others loaded with ballista bolts for the artillery. He rounded the Dhemerhill Valley's western wall and found the Rhodaani Army in preparation to advance, and General Geralin in final discussions with his officers.

"Balthaar hits the Ilduuri with everything," said the general. "He attacks not only along their front, but now up the valley sides as well. We must advance, to pressure their flank, or the Ilduuri will lose the ridge."

Kessligh nodded. "You will be advancing without artillery. You must change the formations—an open formation, as we discussed."

The general frowned. "We are not accustomed to such formations. They disrupt our pattern of battle."

"The Regent's artillery will disrupt it more. Your forces are so close together that single hellfire rounds will destroy entire portions of your formation. Should you attack in such a manner, the Rhodaani Steel may be destroyed in its entirety."

General Geralin had not liked this idea when Kessligh first suggested it, and he did not like it now. The Steel had introduced hellfire into their artillery nearly one hundred years ago, and despite a century of trying, various enemies had failed to discover the secrets of its making. Now, things had changed.

"The Lenays made their attack in good order," stated another officer. "Their losses are light. The Regent's forces have not mastered their new weapons—they are not such easy things to use."

"The surest way for commanders to lose battles is for them to presume that they are the only ones on the field who know what they're doing."

"You are Lead Commander," General Geralin said sharply. "You are not in command of the detailed affairs of the Rhodaani Steel. They are mine to command, as I have risen from foot soldier to generalship across my thirty years of service, and I am certain I know them far better than you."

"You are right," said Kessligh, "you know your soldiers better than I. But I know something of your enemy, and his capability with that artillery, and I know that he will kill all of your soldiers if you let him."

"Your broken formations will not contain a force of their number . . ." the general tried again.

"My *broken* formations will allow you to absorb punishment from their artillery for a considerable time instead of being destroyed as an effective fighting force within the first few salvos."

"And I will not engage the enemy in a formation that does not allow my men to effectively close with and kill the enemy! Now good day, sir, I have a battle to fight!"

He and his officer wheeled and galloped to their formations, a few of the lower officers with misgiving looks at Kessligh as they went. Kessligh refrained from swearing.

He summoned a messenger. "Go to Sasha, tell her that if the Regent's artillery is employed in good order against the Rhodaani Steel, the Rhodaanis are about to get hammered. They're advancing with the old formation, not the new. Go!" The messenger left in a hurry.

Rhillian arrived on horseback and reined alongside. "What is that fucking idiot Geralin up to now?" she said succinctly. "Those look like the old formations."

"I want their command party shadowed," Kessligh said grimly. "If the general is killed, and pray that it comes soon, then Captain Aile should be in charge. Make certain that he is—I know he agrees with me."

"You can't reorder formations in close contact and under artillery fire," Rhillian replied. "Once they're in, it's too late."

"No, but he will manage an orderly withdrawal before they're all dead."

"I have an archer in my group," said Rhillian, emerald eyes unblinking. "Some say that he is Errollyn's equal with a bow, though there is some dispute. Many chaotic things happen under artillery fire. No one will see everything."

Kessligh exhaled hard. "I'd have relieved him of command, but the Rhodaani all follow him. If they catch you shooting their general off his horse, they may leave the battle. Better we take our chances. He may get lucky."

The attacks now made those previous seem like mere skirmishes. The Ilduuri line was assaulted across its entire front, and well down the Dhemerhill Valley. The Regent's forces had followed the Army of Lenayin's retreat into the valley, keeping at first beyond Ilduuri artillery range. Then they had attacked along a valley front more than a thousand paces wide. There had not been enough artillery or archery to so much as slow their approach this time, and now as a sea of enemy soldiers swarmed up the hills like ants upon a carcass, Sasha's entire line was engaged hand-to-hand in furious action.

"The Rhodaanis are coming!" Sasha yelled at her men as she cantered along the ridge trail behind their line, weaving through the trees as Ilduuri ranks fought and exchanged places to her right. "The Rhodaanis are coming, hold the line!"

She had no archers now, for there was no room to shoot. To her left, away from the valley, the ridge was level in parts and thickly forested, preventing any archery. Then it climbed, far more steeply than the valley walls. Their foothold upon this ridge was like a thin path upon the lip of a cliff, the enemy below and mountains behind. Any breach along the line would cut off those further along. The line had to hold, or she'd lose the whole formation.

She passed her artillery position, a ridge that ran from the mountain behind. The great contraptions swung and sprang, shooting swarms of bolts or burning hellfire rounds streaking through the sky. That would protect her far-left flank overlooking the Ipshaal, the scene of all previous action. But it was her near-right flank that worried her most.

She reached the bluff at the corner of the valley mouth and turned left. The fighting here was again heavy, and the sea of men below apparently inexhaustible. Flame and smoke roared into the air from hellfire impacts—catapults were poor for firing short range as their abbreviated swings were inaccurate, a terrible risk firing over the heads of friendly forces with hellfire rounds. They were only reliably accurate at long range, meaning this far flank. Ballista fire now fell across the middle and right flank, searing low over the Ilduuri line's heads to scythe through men coming uphill.

Seeing that the line held, she turned, careful to dodge men moving across her path. Coming back down the valley, she could see the Rhodaani Steel advancing. There were great squares of glinting silver, formations that had once terrified feudal armies far smaller than this one. But this army advanced without its artillery, while the feudals, even as she watched, were beginning to fire.

Rounds leaped into the air from down the valley, where artillery had advanced on the far side of the Dhemerhill River. She'd sent Andreyis to tell General Geralin of its position, but evidently he hadn't listened. As many as ten rounds at once soared into the air, trailing thin smoke. The Rhodaanis were packed so tightly together they could not possibly dodge.

She stopped at her artillery position, not even bothering to watch the enemy's rounds landing. The artillery captain came running down to her, shield above his head as he left the protection of a near catapult in the light rain of arrows that nearby archers were directing at his contraptions.

"We're about to lose the ridge!" Sasha yelled. "Pull all your units off the ridge at once, and get them back to Jahnd!"

"If I stop firing now our left flank may fold!" he shouted back above the din of battle.

"We're going to lose it anyway!" Sasha retorted. "Your artillery is more valuable, you've done all you can here—now it's time to leave!"

He nodded and ran back to his men, yelling orders. Sasha turned and spared a look down at the Rhodaani formations. Black smoke rose, and fires spread. It was hard to see the formation clearly, just glints of steel through the smoke. On the wide flanks, Rhodaani cavalry was charging, accompanied by *talmaad* and Lenay cavalry back for a second charge. It met little opposing cavalry, but gathering now before the Regent's artillery were great rows of pikemen, apparently organised for just that purpose. Their pikes were huge, and their lines bristled like a porcupine. Cavalry hated that. It seemed the Regent had put some thought into how to protect his artillery from cavalry at least.

Andreyis came racing back from his latest mission, and Sasha sent him on a new one. "Tell Kessligh we're pulling off the ridge! We'll protect the artillery and try to make a new line for them to pass, but if we stay here we'll lose everything."

He left. Yasmyn had been sent to carry another officer's message, and she had no idea where Daish was. Sasha turned and galloped up the line once more, to where her left flank was about to find itself without artillery cover.

She'd just reached the bluff when yells and running men alerted her that the line behind her had been breached. She spun her horse and saw a swarm of men-at-arms pushing through the Ilduuris and across the path she'd just ridden. Rear ranks were peeling off the adjoining lines to attack them, but as they did so, a second portion of newly thinned line also collapsed. The line now dissolved into a mass of fighting, flailing men with no semblance of order. The chaos extended a hundred paces across, and was growing wider. She, and everyone on this side, was now trapped.

An officer ran to her with wild-eyed desperation, shouting questions she could barely hear. She did not bother yelling back, but instead gestured with her hands—a firm line to hold along the ridge so they did not get cut off again, and this new front upon the ridge itself should fall back past the bluff and contract upon itself to make a pocket. She did it as calmly as she could, despite the fighting barely twenty paces from her side, and the officer seemed to absorb that calm, take deep breaths, then turned to run back and yell orders.

Sasha spun and galloped about the corner and onto the Ipshaal front. Soon she was met by Captain Idraalgen, senior officer on this flank.

"We're cut off, the middle just folded!" she yelled at him, dismounting from her horse. "We're about three thousand stuck on this side, and our artillery is retreating!"

Idraalgen did not look very surprised. "Do we attack?" he asked cheerfully.

Sasha laughed. "Yes, but backwards! Those trails up the mountains, can we use them?"

"Any trail is enough for Ilduuri," he replied. "We'll contract into a tight pocket and funnel men up the trails from behind. They can chase us if they wish, but the trails are narrow—one Ilduuri can stop a whole army if positioned well."

"Then that's the plan!" Sasha shouted, and slapped him on the shoulder. But she couldn't take her horse. Probably she should have had the stallion killed so that the Regent would not gain another mount, but she had a man take him off beyond the left flank and tie him to a tree. Killing horses was bad luck, and she was superstitious enough to think that a worse threat to this battle than her enemies gaining one more steed.

With her shield on one arm, Sasha took position by one of the trails where it began to climb through steep rocks and precarious trees, shouting for the rear ranks to make an orderly ascent. They came running past her, slinging shields to their backs and swords into their scabbards, then onto the trail at speed. After long fighting, battered, sweaty, and bloody, they *ran* up the trail, climbing fast in the knowledge that in single file, one slow man condemned every man behind.

Soon the extended right flank of their pocket was falling back from the bluff, amidst triumphant cries and yells from the Regent's men. Directly before her she could hear Ilduuris yelling back, a few in Saalsi, words to the effect that all the piled corpses at their feet did not look like much of a victory.

The pocket drew closer, armoured flanks closing in on all sides, and arrows began to fly more thickly as the Regent's men identified the source of the trail above. Sasha found shelter behind a tree trunk, her shield raised, and figured her men were down from three thousand to just a few hundred. Now it became tricky.

A sergeant alerted her to the endgame, racing from the line now only ten paces away, waving frantically at her to run. Sasha slung her shield and ran straight up the path. Arrows struck about her, and she realised the other advantage to having the shield on the back as Ilduuris wore it while climbing. She'd been in the saddle rather than fighting on foot, so her legs were relatively fresh, yet still it hurt. Fifty paces up she paused where Ilduuri archers had halted to sit just off the path, with an increasingly sheer drop below, and expend their remaining arrows on the men who now closed about the remaining Ilduuri.

Sasha took a knee alongside them and looked down upon the final act.

Wounded men, she realised, seeing the last formation of perhaps twenty men fighting amidst the trees, their balance unsteady, clearly too wounded to make this retreat. The last healthy Ilduuri made the trail and climbed, and a gap opened behind him as the wounded men fought, and fell, one, then two, then two more. They could not have gone first—the path was too narrow and they'd have slowed the entire Ilduuri retreat if their comrades had carried them. That would have cost far more lives than just these twenty.

Sasha drew her sword, and yelled an old Lenay war cry. The spirits of these mountains would hear, she was sure of it. The last Ilduuri fell, throwing his blade at an enemy in final defiance.

"Get those fucks when they come up the path," Sasha told the archers, and left them with a whack on the helmet. The archers put arrows to bowstrings and loosed downslope as men-at-arms tried to follow.

Sasha resumed running, confident that they would not be followed for long. The path was strictly single file, and treacherously steep to any who left it. Five Ilduuri, mixing bows and swords, could hold it indefinitely against any number of foes. In Ilduur, they trained for precisely that, shutting off large numbers of remote paths to invaders through the mountains. A few dozen determined men here could stop armies.

The path angled up and across the mountain face, trees growing sparsely, affording her a view of all the battlefield as she ran. Below to her left was the ridge above the Dhemerhill Valley. Ahead was her artillery position, now vacated save for one huge blaze that blocked the way—one of the hellfire ammunition wagons set afire to block the retreat. Behind it, the ridge was all feudal soldiers, many now pointing and looking up at the Ilduuri retreat, but with no way of stopping it.

The valley below was seething with the Regent's army, and the banks of the Ipshaal were now clearing, as men found it safe to enter the valley. Ahead of them, toward Jahnd, silver-armoured men were falling back across the valley in scattered groups. The land behind them was ablaze, and even now swarming with cavalry. Those were friendly, covering the Rhodaani Steel's retreat. A large force of horsemen, but too light of build, and lately too tired, to make any great impact upon the walls of infantry before them.

Her breath came hard as she found her running rhythm, climbing higher and higher across the face of the mountain. It seemed almost as though she were flying, high above the greatest battle in the history of all humanity, in the company of thousands of newly liberated souls.

General Geralin was not dead. Nor, Kessligh observed, was he feathered with serrin arrows. He dismounted before Kessligh's command party, ashen-faced and soot-streaked. One of his accompanying officers had to be carried from the saddle, bleeding profusely. There were only two such officers, where there should have been an entourage.

Geralin looked about at the army that retreated past him. Men who had marched so upright and proud, in perfect lines and squares, now limped and straggled in small groups, their shields battered, their armour blackened in parts by smoke and ash. There were not nearly so many of them here as there should have been. Not so many at all.

He looked at Kessligh, and at Damon, who sat in his saddle alongside. Damon had come hoping to see far more Rhodaanis returning than this.

"How'd your plan go?" Damon called to him, in brutal dark humour. In his eyes was not amusement, but something closer to hatred. Damon hated fools above all else. Wallowing in a village duckpond, they were harmless. Leading armies, far less so.

General Geralin looked once more at what was left of his army, then drew a knife and cut his own throat. He fell awkwardly, then lay still. Hardly anyone noticed.

"That bad, huh?" Damon asked.

"Should have done it myself," said Kessligh.

"They'd have all left and wouldn't have cost the Regent anything at all," Damon replied. "This bought us something, at least. I want to go and welcome Sasha. Back soon."

He left at a canter, messengers and several juniors following. Kessligh remained in his dust, contemplating the body of a once proud general, and wondering if humans would ever learn as serrin did to see what was truly before them, instead of what they wished to be so.

The path descended onto a flat shoulder where a small town overlooked the convergence of the Ilmerhill and Dhemerhill Valleys. The town was full of activity, Ilduuri men bustling through, wagons on the hillside road hauling ammunition to the artillery's new position. Sasha arrived at a walk, within the tail of her army, and received a rousing cheer from the Ilduuris gathered there.

She saluted them without enthusiasm. "Wounded heroes remained behind and gave their lives to guard our retreat!" she called to those who cheered. "Save your cheers for them—they fell to the last man and went down swinging."

At the base of the slope she looked about at the town and drew a few more deep breaths—they'd slowed to a walk once it was clear they were not being chased. The walk had given her a good look at the battlefield, and she'd left several of the best runners behind on the trail to bring back reports of the Regent's advancing formations.

Captain Idraalgen was waiting, and filled her in on the Ilduuris' new position, at the wooden barrier wall they'd built earlier in parallel to the stone wall across the valley below, a fallback they'd all known was coming.

"We've good artillery position just up from the town too," he added, "but not close enough to the wall, so the range will be lacking."

Sasha made a face. "Artillery's not built for mountains. How many did we lose?"

"A third of it. We sabotaged most, set it on fire; I think they only captured one working ballista. . . ."

"Look, we're not going to be able to fit more than a portion of the force up here, so let's make preparations to move most of them down to defend the wall. And I want them fed."

Suddenly Damon was riding up the road between wagons, horsemen, and soldiers. He dismounted at her side, as Idraalgen hurried off to see to her orders.

"So how's your day been?" Sasha asked him wryly. He looked very martial indeed in full armour, sweaty and rugged with blood droplets on one cheek. Not his own blood, Sasha noted with approval.

"Oh, fair." His lip curled. "Not dead yet."

"But the day is young." Actually the day was getting quite old, shadows long as the sun set in the direction of the Ipshaal. But it was the traditional Lenay exchange for such circumstances. They tapped fists. "Rhodaanis?"

"Smashed. General Geralin killed himself."

Sasha snorted. "It was a bad position, but *fuck*. Solid squares? What was wrong with him?"

"Nothing his own knife couldn't solve, apparently. We're not going to hold this wall."

"Were never going to. Let's just hold it today, give them a night to think about it."

"I know Rhillian's got all kinds of ideas for what the *talmaad* can do by night," said Damon.

"Aye, well, she's not going to kill this army by sneaking a few arrows in the dark."

Damon nodded grimly. "One of your messengers was telling me you think we've underestimated their force. How many do you think?"

"Here?" Sasha wiped hair from her face. "One thirty."

"We missed thirty thousand?"

Sasha shrugged. "How many Bacosh lords do you think heard of the victory at Sonnai Plain, concluded they were missing out on the greatest triumph of Bacosh history, and sent in all the force they had to link up with Balthaar?"

"You think?"

"All I know is that there's well more than a hundred thousand here. I've seen a lot of big forces lately and I think I can guess."

Damon sighed. "Well. It was near impossible to begin with, what's another thirty thousand?"

"Damon," said Sasha, drawing his attention. Then she smiled. "Biggest battle ever. I mean in all the history of Rhodia. We're Lenay. We're in it. Where else would you rather be?"

"Anywhere," said Damon. Sasha laughed. She knew Damon didn't embrace that sort of thing; she was merely needling him, as he now needled her back. "You haven't asked after Lenayin yet."

"I don't need to." For a brief moment, Damon seemed genuinely touched. "And I saw them withdraw in good order."

"We lost a bit more than a thousand. Light under the circumstances."

"Aye. Light."

Damon's eyes gleamed. "We must have taken at least ten times that. Twenty times, maybe. It was extraordinary."

"And you led it, King Damon." Damon stared at her for a moment, eyes still gleaming. *That* was what Sasha had been looking for from Damon. Perhaps for the entire time she'd known him. Only now did she see it. The look of a Lenay king at war.

"Tell it to Koenyg," he replied.

"I fucking will. And so will you."

Alfriedo Renine walked gingerly along the bank of the Dhemerhill River, General Zulmaher and a handful of other Rhodaani lords accompanying him. The Rhodaanis were camped between the Lenays and the Torovans, a small group of perhaps two thousand noble cavalry squeezed between much larger forces. They had not yet seen battle, though Alfriedo's thighs felt as though they'd been through a war. He'd always liked to ride, though in Tracato he'd had the luxury to dismount and rest when he chose. Not here.

His short sword felt heavy against his leg as he walked. Men along the riverbank washed or gathered water by torch- or lamplight, as the river, barely twenty paces across at the widest, gleamed with the reflections of fires, dotted like the stars in the night sky above. Clusters of horses whinnied and munched on the grass, and food cooked on a thousand campfires. On either side of the valley loomed hillsides and mountains, upon the sides of which no man now dared to venture. The night belonged to the serrin, and cavalrymen here in the eastern Dhemerhill made their camp as close to the central river as possible. Up the hillslopes the trees grew more thickly, and serrin could move unseen and unheard. Sentries stood watch the length of the campsite's long, winding flanks tonight, and no man envied them the duty.

With the Lenay king's tents still a distance ahead, they approached another large tent. Seated within a roughly fenced enclosure between trees were prisoners, guarded by Lenay men in black armour. Alfriedo slowed to look. Some prisoners were serrin, others human. Enoran, he guessed. All were tightly bound, many wounded. In the river itself, more prisoners had been tied to stakes, so that only their heads were above water. From within the adjoining tent came screams. There were no campfires near the tent. Even hardened Lenay warriors preferred to seek their rest further away.

King Koenyg's tent was near a small bridge across the river. Many Lenays stood guard around it, or sat about nearby fires to eat, drink and talk, yet never did they cease to be alert. Many in particular kept an eye on the river, for there were rumours through the camp that serrin could float downstream underwater, breathing from sheepskin bladders, and emerge within the camp to slit men's throats as they slept. Alfriedo did not think it possible, an air-filled bladder would surely float, and the campsites along the river stretched several thousand paces at least, all watchful with sleepless men. Yet for gods-fearing Verenthane men to be invaders here in the land of the serrin could be an unnerving thing, particularly now that the sun had set. Men told stories, and believed things that were not proven true.

The guards before the tent flaps showed no signs of admitting new visitors. From within, Alfriedo heard conversation, and saw shadows cast against the tent walls.

"They won't let you in," said an accented voice to one side, in Larosan. Seated against a tree by the riverbank was a man in Torovan armour. He was young, perhaps twenty, with a mop of untidy hair recently flattened beneath a helmet. His legs, sprawled before him, were long. "King Koenyg likes to make everyone wait."

Other Torovan nobles sat or stood nearby, some talking, others sharing a smoking pipe. Alfriedo walked to him, and the tall man climbed achingly to his feet.

"I am Alfriedo Renine, Lord of Rhodaan," he introduced himself.

"Carlito Rochel, Duke of Pazira."

"You are a friend to Sashandra Lenayin," Alfriedo observed as they shook hands. Carlito frowned, as though he thought the young lord was accusing him of something. "I was a friend to Sashandra's sister Alythia," he explained. "She told me something of Sashandra's adventures with your father, Alexanda Rochel."

"Ah," said Carlito, with dawning realisation. "Alfriedo Renine. The boy lord of Rhodaan, of course. Please, we shall sit, my legs are killing me."

Alfriedo smiled and joined Carlito beneath the tree. "Please, gentlemen," the duke addressed the other Rhodaanis, "sit on the grass, share some wine. We have good Pazira wine, none of that Petrodor horse piss that is all you Rhodaanis seem to drink."

A skin was unstoppered as the Pazira men gave hospitality.

"So," said Carlito. "Princess Alythia Lenayin. I heard what happened to her, very sad."

"She was like a sister."

"Very sad. Sashandra was very sad too. I know her a little, yes, from when she was with the Army of Lenayin, and before."

"Some may argue that she is still with the Army of Lenayin," Alfriedo said drily.

Carlito stared at him for a long moment, then looked about, to be certain of who else might overhear. "I know Lenayin a little," Carlito said in a lower voice than before. "Pazira shares a border with Valhanan Province. My father dealt kindly with the Lenays there, that is how he befriended Kessligh, and Sashandra."

"My condolences on his passing," said Alfriedo. "I heard nothing but good of him."

Carlito inclined his head. Whatever his languid manner, he seemed a serious and thoughtful man. "I thank you. He told me it was foolish to think that Lenayin could ever be a Verenthane kingdom. He said that it did not matter what the King of Lenayin thought—or what the Archbishop of Petrodor thought—Lenayin would always be pagan at its heart. It was crazy to invite them to this war, and expect them to fight for a Verenthane cause. This split they have made should only surprise men who have not paid attention."

"I have been reading much of Lenayin lately," Alfriedo admitted. "I even have some books in my saddlebags. Kessligh Cronenverdt challenged me to do so, and I have accepted. What you say may be true."

Carlito sipped from his wineskin. "Sashandra, you know, she killed some Verenthane men even when she was on our side. I saw it. Friends of the Regent himself, big, noble men, they threatened her and called her a whore. She killed them."

"She seems to do that quite a lot."

Carlito shrugged, in that very expressive way of Torovans. "Some say she loves blood. But I met her before, when she came to Pazira with Kessligh to see my father. She did that twice." He smiled a little. "Very strange girl. But kind of pretty. You know?" He glanced at Alfriedo, teasing. "No, you are too young, you do not know."

"I know," Alfriedo retorted. "I'm not *that* young."

Carlito put a hand on his shoulder, apologising. "Anyway. She had a temper, but she was not . . . you know, a killer. I think maybe she kills because people keep attacking her."

"There is a great warrior in a tale told by Tullamayne, Lenayin's greatest storyteller," Alfriedo recalled. "Tullamayne writes that he was asked once, 'Why have you killed so many men?' And he replied, 'Because so many men deserve to die.'"

Carlito smiled. "So Lenay, yes? I've read Tullamayne, my father forced me to. He said I could not understand Lenayin had I not."

"This seems rather like a Tullamayne tale today, I think."

"Indeed. Perhaps we are all living inside one of his great heroic tales, Lenay warrior brothers all fighting each other. Only he did not envisage a warrior sister."

"A modern twist."

"Of course."

The camp seemed strangely peaceful, despite the ongoing noise of forty thousand men and horses at rest. Water bubbled and splashed over nearby rocks. Alfriedo thought of the prisoners tied in the water upstream.

"So why are you here?" Carlito asked. "Certainly you are very brave, but it does not seem reasonable that a boy should be expected to ride into battle for the Regent."

"For two centuries Rhodaani nobility has been dreaming of reclaiming its noble rights," said Alfriedo. "To do so we must swear allegiance to Regent Balthaar Arrosh. With my mother dead, I am the heir to Family Renine, and thus Lord of Rhodaan. I must be here to claim our place in the new world to come."

"I too," said Carlito, with a heavy voice. "My father did not wish to join this war, yet there was no choice. Patachi Steiner of Petrodor declared himself King of Torovan in the War of the King, and now we independent dukes of the provinces must declare our allegiance or be overthrown. I am here for Pazira, and for my family. It is my responsibility, as Duke of Pazira, and so I come."

"A serrin philosopher named Rihala once argued that a person has three great responsibilities. One responsibility is to himself, and one is to his neighbour, and the last is to the truth. It's complicated, with serrin it's always complicated, but he argued that of these three responsibilities, the last is the only one that matters, and all other responsibilities flow from that."

Carlito frowned. "How is that?"

"Because if you do not look for truth as your main responsibility, then neither you nor your neighbour shall ever be free. Serrin have an idea of freedom, it's not like humans think of it. Freedom for serrin is truth. Lies are slavery."

"Serrin," Carlito sighed. "I don't understand."

Alfriedo smiled. "As I said, it's complicated."

"Yes," Carlito said drily, "well, if we win here, in this glorious campaign, I shall never understand because they'll all be dead. Eventually."

"The Regent may stop at the Ipshaal after all," Alfriedo said quietly.

Carlito took a long swig of his wine. "You are not such a boy that you believe this thing." Alfriedo said nothing.

Tent flaps parted and King Koenyg emerged with some other men. He farewelled them, then walked to where Carlito and Alfriedo waited. All present climbed to their feet.

"Duke Carlito," said Koenyg. Carlito was taller, yet Koenyg was powerful. His square face and chiselled jaw were, at this range, impressive. "Lord Alfriedo. Good of you to come."

"As instructed," said Carlito, drily. "What matter concerns you?"

"Serrin," said Koenyg. "It has been brought to my attention that your Pazira men have come into the possession of some serrin prisoners. I understand that they may have information that could prove valuable. I require you to hand them over for interrogation."

"No," said Carlito, quite calmly.

Koenyg frowned. "Then my interrogators will come to your camp and conduct the interrogation there."

Carlito thought about it for a moment, quite unhurried. Then he shook his head. "No," he repeated.

Koenyg's face hardened. "Explain yourself."

"I have seen your tent, up here." Carlito indicated the tent upriver, holding the prisoners. "We do not do that in Pazira. It is not our way."

"Duke Carlito, we are at war."

"And war is the place for honourable things. This is not our honour."

"The Regent Arrosh has placed me in command of this formation. I command you to hand the prisoners over."

Carlito scratched his scruffy hair. "My father taught me that if I did such a thing, I would go to the hells. Perhaps you do not fear the hells because you are already there."

Koenyg did not look impressed, but neither did he lose his temper. He did not seem particularly surprised, as though he had been warned to expect such behaviour from this lanky Torovan. "I understand that you did not see much action today."

"Your Highness did not see fit to bestow upon us such an honour," Carlito agreed.

"And you will see little tomorrow. This men's business of warfare is clearly beyond you."

"Real men kill men who fight back," said Carlito. "My father taught me that, too. He said it was a popular notion, amongst the *common* men of Lenayin."

Koenyg dismissed him with disgust. Carlito bowed, summoned his men, and left. Koenyg looked at Alfriedo.

"Torovans," said Alfriedo, as though that explained everything.

Koenyg smiled. "Indeed. In fact, that is what I wished to speak with you about."

"Oh yes?"

Koenyg put a hand on the boy's shoulder and steered him toward the tent. "As you are aware, Lenayin has access to only one great sea port."

"Petrodor," said Alfriedo with a nod.

"Exactly. And that is some journey from Lenayin. Petrodor, you will no doubt note, is full of Torovans."

"Quite."

"Now, not all Torovans are as troublesome as our Pazira friends, yet there is a new king in Petrodor, and we do not know yet what relations shall bring. I should like to know a lot more of Tracato, as I've heard that its trade is nearly the rival of Petrodor's, yet it has so little trade from Lenayin. In the future, I would think that it would be of great benefit to both our peoples should this absence be addressed, don't you agree?"

Sasha galloped from the eastern wall and into the dark valley. Her party rejoined the road, lit by a solitary scout ahead, while she trailed behind. The road passed fields and farmhouses, and clusters of trees as yet undamaged by war. Beyond Koenyg's initial advance down the valley, there had been little further fighting.

Ahead she could see the massed fires of the enemy camp, with several great bonfires forming a perimeter. Guards lit those fires partly in fear of a stealthy serrin approach, and partly in the hope of disrupting sensitive serrin night vision. It was a sensible move, and effective . . . if serrin wished to try anything so obvious.

The scout stopped short of some horsemen in the middle of the road. Errollyn reined up at Sasha's side, and stood in his stirrups to scan the fields and trees ahead.

"Nothing," he said. "But I'll watch that low wall to the left, that's the only possible location."

Sasha pressed her new horse to a walk and Damon moved up on her right. Behind them, four more riders, two of them *talmaad*. The scout with the torch peeled off as they approached, confident as Errollyn was that no ambush awaited.

On horseback opposite them sat Koenyg and Myklas, before a number of senior northern Lenay lords. Amongst them, Sasha recognised Great Lord Heryd of Hadryn, a longtime foe. There were no flags of truce raised. In Lenayin they were often disdained—a man's word was supposed to be enough.

"You're losing," said Koenyg, without preamble. "Give up."

"My Ilduuris scored at better than ten for every loss today," said Sasha. "The Army of Lenayin did perhaps even better, and with far worse positioning, while you sat here for most of the day and drank tea. You have an interesting notion of 'losing.'"

"*Your* Ilduuris," Koenyg said flatly. He hadn't heard, Sasha realised.

"My Ilduuris. The Ilduuri Steel, the one you thought would not come. They hold the ridges above the valley mouth, and slaughter the Regent's men who try to displace them."

"They do not hold it any longer. We have eyes." The far side of the valley was high, and would afford them a view. Koenyg may not be in direct communication with the Regent, but he could see what happened up at the valley's western end. "The Rhodaani Steel charged the Regent's artillery. Their losses looked severe. Now the Army of Lenayin and the Ilduuri Steel are all that stand between Jahnd and overwhelming force on that side. Your position is hopeless. And believe it or not, I would rather not kill either of you."

"Feeling's not mutual," said Damon. "I challenge. This dawn, with blades."

Koenyg smirked. "Nice. Offer a challenge you know I cannot accept for tactical reasons, to make me look cowardly when I refuse. You're desperate. No one here cares for your silly plots. And no one here believes you could beat me even were there five of you. I lose no face because I have nothing to prove to you, little brother. Nothing."

"Nothing save honour," said Damon.

Koenyg stared. Damon stared back. Hold firm, Sasha willed Damon. Damon had truly stood up to Koenyg just once, in all his life, when he had led what remained of the Army of Lenayin away from the northerners and nobles remaining loyal to Koenyg. But Koenyg had won that contest of swords also, and Damon had only survived by Koenyg's mercy.

"Be careful what you wish for, little brother," Koenyg murmured.

"*Tymorain* is a stupid tradition anyhow," Damon replied. "Swords at dawn is no way to select a leader of nations. The men I lead required me to challenge, for formality's sake. But when deciding the leader of nations, outcomes of leadership matter more."

"You're leading your army to its death. The cream of pagan Lenayin shall die with it. Verenthane Lenayin shall emerge victorious, and our strength in Lenayin shall be doubled when we return with our Verenthane allies."

"You'd lead a new Verenthane invasion of Lenayin?" Sasha asked in disbelief. "Hold the Goeren-yai at swordpoint? Convert or die?"

"I didn't want to do it this way, Sasha, but this is what you have forced me to. The faith is the future of humanity in Rhodia, and your pagan ways shall fade, as pagan ways always do, Lenayin's and the serrin's."

"I'm going to fucking kill you," said Sasha, and meant it. "I may not enjoy it, but I'm going to do it."

Koenyg snorted. "You and what army?" His nobles laughed.

"Don't you wave your cock at me," Sasha said coldly. "There may be only a handful in Lenayin you can't best with a blade, but I'm one of them. You inherited your army. I won mine. You show respect or I will fucking kill you right now, and there's not a damn thing any of you can do to stop me."

At her side, Errollyn flexed his bowstring. There was no arrow against it yet, but that could change in the blink of an eye. Behind them were more *talmaad*.

"This is a truce," Koenyg said flatly. "You are not so dishonourable as to kill blood relatives with cowardly arrows beneath a truce."

"I command respect, by the ancient codes that you and your poorly bred ilk have forgotten," Sasha snarled. "I am Synnich-ahn, and you are *not* my equal." She rode a little closer, daring him with her eyes. "Or do you dispute it? Do you think you can take me?"

Koenyg said nothing, watching her coldly.

"This is a field of truce, not a field of challenge!" a lord said angrily. "Cease this posturing!"

"What does a man with no honour know of truce?" Sasha spat. "What does a man who sides with the murderers of small children have to say of honour? What do you do with serrin prisoners even now, brother? Treat them kindly? Treat them with honour?" Koenyg stared past her, stonily. "You offer us a safe surrender, but that's a farce too, isn't it? Tell me, if I surrendered to you, would you stick the knife in yourself? And would you stick your cock in first? I bet you would, you're just that kind of man, aren't you?"

Koenyg nearly went for his blade.

"Come on!" Sasha yelled at him. "Come on, you coward, let's do it! Right here, right now, let's make a circle where I can fucking end your miserable life!"

"Sasha, no!" came a desperate cry from behind. "Stop this now! I'll not let you pick a fight!"

"He's picked every fight he could since he was a boy," Sasha retorted. "I've only refrained from challenge for politics and manners, and both are now used up."

But Koenyg was ignoring her, staring past her shoulder to the voice behind. "Sofy?" he asked.

Sofy edged forward. She threw back her hood, and torchlight caught her face. "Brothers," she said.

"Good gods!" Myklas exclaimed with youthful enthusiasm. "Where have you been? We've had reports that Elissians and the Archbishop of Sherdaine plotted to kill you, and other reports that you plotted against the Regent. . . ."

"It was Archbishop Turen and the Elissians," said Sofy. "I wanted to preserve the riches of Tracato for the Regent's rule. The Archbishop wished to cleanse Tracato of all serrin influence. I voiced my disapproval, and he tried to have me killed."

"And when did this happen?" Koenyg asked drily. "Perhaps directly after Sasha and Damon turned traitor and betrayed all semblance of honour?"

Sofy nodded. "It was directly after the defection of their followers from your command, yes."

"This is *your* fault!" Koenyg declared, pointing a finger at Sasha. "An army like that which the Regent maintains is a mass of competing interests, yet *you* unbalanced the entire formation! You set those of the Regent's allies who never wished to see this union with Lenayin directly at Sofy's throat, and look what fortune that she is still alive! Sofy, I had no idea, I was worried. Please allow me to return you to your husband."

"No," Sofy said calmly. "I stand with Damon and Sasha."

"No!" Myklas shouted, in sudden anger. "No, I won't allow it! Sofy, we're your brothers. . . ."

"As is Damon."

"And he's a traitor! He betrayed you!"

Sofy looked at him sadly. "Dear Myklas. I love you dearly, my sweet brother, but you are a child. You have bonded with the men you fight alongside, as young men will in battle. Do you not think that the Cherrovan who invaded Lenayin felt the same for their comrades? Such bonds do not make men right, and they do not improve the cause for which they fight.

"Koenyg believes that the Verenthane civilisation for which my husband fights will make Lenayin strong. I believe that he may be right. But I can now see that it will only do so by killing every good and noble thing in Rhodia that will not conform to its strictest rule. I saw those things burn in Tracato. I've seen them die in the villages across Enora and Rhodaan. I now see you, dear brothers, trying to destroy them here in Jahnd, and doubtless beyond into Saalshen after that."

"But we're not going to . . ." Myklas began.

"Ask him," said Sofy, pointing at Koenyg, and then pointing again at Great Lord Heryd. "Ask him as well. The strength of their faith is its unity. Its solidity of purpose. Serrin will destroy that solidity, as is their nature, by asking too many questions. The serrin perhaps have not realised this—they are innocent and do not mean to destroy anything. They do not realise how dangerous the asking of inconvenient questions can be for men whose belief will accept no disagreement. But the only serrin who does not ask questions is a dead serrin. The Archbishops know this, and, dear Myklas, the men you ride with know it too."

Myklas looked at Koenyg, frowning. Koenyg did not look at him.

"Sofy," he said, "you are lawfully married, before the gods themselves. You shall shame all Lenayin should you now choose to fight against your husband."

Sofy looked him calmly in the eye. "Lenayin fights with me," she said. "True Lenayin. I do not know what you are, but you are an imposter upon my land. And my husband, and all who follow him, shall always be its enemies."

Sasha walked through her army's camp behind the western wall. Men sat by their fires and talked, or repaired damaged gear, or prepared to sleep. Most did not wear armour, not fearing a sudden attack in the night. Any force that included the *talmaad* would own the night, and the Regent's men knew it.

She exchanged greetings and words of encouragement as she walked to the small town where the Ilmerhill and Dhemerhill Rivers converged. Here Sofy had arranged a hub of wagons moving supplies and wounded. Upon the spit of land between converging rivers there was a grand house of several storeys, and a garden. Spilling onto the garden were many *talmaad*, Ilduuris, and Lenays who had heard a rumour that good food could be found here.

Sasha could smell it as she approached the kitchen, fresh bread and cooking meats. Within the kitchen, she found mixed human and serrin staff, mostly women, preparing meals that were certainly not an army's standard ration. Soldiers queued though the night grew late, thinking a delicacy—perhaps a final delicacy—to be well worth the effort.

Directing it all, Sasha found Aisha, of course, moving amidst the cooks while suggesting spices and tasting sauces. She saw Sasha and smiled, her eyes a little red. Sasha hugged her, and Aisha seemed to collapse for a moment in her arms.

They'd found Daish's horse during the Rhodaani Steel's retreat, dead in a charred circle of hellfire. His body they'd not identified, though someone had thought it significant that a messenger had died, and reported the loss. It seemed that a Rhodaani cavalry commander had sent him to carry an order to the main formation that trumpets could not deliver—no one knew what, for the commander was now dead too, like so many Rhodaanis. But Daish had galloped forward when the Rhodaani cavalry had been retreating, and given that his horse was reported as being little more than charred meat, death would have been instantaneous. Sasha hoped.

Aisha released herself, wiping her eyes. They did not need to speak of it.

"Did you hear also Bergen?" Sasha asked gently.

Aisha nodded. "In the first engagement with Lenay cavalry, I was told. And three dear friends in the *talmaad*, serrin you have not met."

"Where's Rhillian?" Sasha asked.

"Hunting," said Aisha. In the dark, with a serrin's eyes. Many serrin would sleep little tonight. "I thought I could make a better use of my time here. I always cook when unhappy. And there's nothing like a war to remind people to appreciate the sweet things in life."

"Just don't make it too sweet or they'll not want to fight at all." Aisha smiled. "I'm looking for Kessligh—have you seen him?"

She found Kessligh up at Liri, the small town overlooking the western wall from the southern junction of where the Ilmerhill Valley joined the Dhemer-hill. He sat on the balcony of a house filled with officers, discussing the day's battle just passed, and how it might be improved upon tomorrow.

Sasha drew up a chair and sat beside him. The night was cloudy, and there was no visible moon. Across the junction of valleys and rivers, the campsites of the defending armies sparkled with thousands of fires. Upon the far side of the Ilmerhill Valley, Jahnd itself was alive with lantern and torch-light, with great fires burning bright atop its defensive wall. Across the valley floor, the city's outer sprawl was lit with less magnificence, yet here above could be heard the unceasing hammering of the workshops.

"How's Koenyg?" Kessligh asked, with faint irony.

"Didn't take my bait," said Sasha, putting her feet up on another chair. Kessligh poured her some water. He did not like to drink anything stronger in battle. Sasha accepted her cup, and drank. "Nearly, though. I made him pretty angry."

"You have that gift with quieter tempers than Koenyg's. Would you have killed him, had he accepted immediate challenge?"

"Yes," said Sasha. "You?"

Kessligh shrugged. "In Lenayin a man does not speak of killing another man whose sibling is present. Family deals with family."

"Don't worry," said Sasha. "If I can, I will." She sipped again. "Sofy was wonderful. But her appeals are wasted on the Army of Northern Lenayin, I think. Koenyg is only more convinced that we pagan-friendly royals are a cancer to be cut from the body of Lenayin. Myklas is troubled. I should be sad to kill Myklas."

The words nearly caught in her throat. She coughed with annoyance, and covered it with another drink.

"He is a naive, misled boy," Kessligh said quietly. "But a good lad. We always wondered when he would find something meaningful in his life—the last-born son always struggles for purpose. Unfortunately he has found his meaning with the Hadryn." Kessligh paused. "You think to use Sofy against the Regent himself? Request a truce flag and have her speak to the Bacosh lords?"

"I'm thinking on it," said Sasha, "but I don't know what she could say. Few of them have any sympathy for her. Her defection only convinces them that the allegiance with Lenayin was a mistake. It certainly makes Koenyg's position with the Regent precarious, but only after this battle is over, which doesn't help us at all."

Kessligh agreed. "They tell themselves they fight for a future of peace and unity, but if they win it will be back to the old feudal squabbling and a new war for every season, just like the old days. But no, however weak the Archbishop's and the Elissians' defiance in trying to kill Sofy makes Balthaar look, it doesn't help us now. They'll postpone that argument until after we're all dead."

"We had a good day today," said Sasha, "all things considered. Tomorrow will be much worse: we've lost our best position."

"I was speaking with the Ilduuris," said Kessligh. "That defence of the ridge was one of the best demonstrations of battlefield command they've seen. Your senior sergeants are the ones holding the formation together, and always the hardest to please—I've spoken to several this evening who would happily die for you. That says everything."

"And after today," said Sasha, "I for them. I was not impressed with Ilduur when I first arrived there. But after today, a part of my heart shall be forever Ilduuri." She smiled at him. "Coming from one as blindly in love with Lenayin as I, that says everything."

Kessligh sat forward in his chair and indicated the valley before them, lit with campfires. "I wanted to ask you then," he said. "From one who has just forced the largest army in history to pay a far bloodier price for a bit of high ground than they'd wanted to, look at the valleys before us, and tell me what you see."

"Armies," said Sasha, tiredly. Kessligh had done this to her often, when she was his uma. Asked questions in the form of a lecture. She'd thought she was a little beyond that now. "Darkness. Walls."

"Exactly," said Kessligh. He wasn't looking at her. He was staring into the night, as though seeing something that other eyes could not, in the way that Errollyn might see something in the night that was to her invisible. "A great commander sees it. Armies. Darkness. Walls. What do they remind you of, put together?"

Sasha did not think too hard. She thought she knew what Kessligh was striving at. "Prison," she said. "Dungeons beneath Tracato. Pain." Alythia's severed head lying at her feet in a cell. She squeezed her eyes shut.

"Confinement," said Kessligh. Sasha opened her eyes once more, and stared at him. "We have been looking at this space before us all wrong. We have been trying to defend it, to keep them out, to make them pay for every part they capture. We expect to lose it eventually, and to retreat to Jahnd for a final defence. And then they'll have it. And it's a big space, well large enough for the Regent's entire army even before he began to take casualties. We've thought of how he might hold it, and how he might manoeuvre within it."

"He'll ring us," said Sasha, also leaning forward. "We'll be trapped in Jahnd. Koenyg will break through from the other side, we'll have to leave the valley or be overrun from two directions at once, and hide in Jahnd for protection."

"Because we'll have the stationary position and they'll be closing down on us. In daylight."

Sasha's breath caught. She opened her mouth to speak again, then closed it. And shot him a hard look.

"No," she said. "No, we couldn't manage that. It's too hard, combining serrin and human forces, and with the additional losses we'll have taken all through tomorrow . . ."

"Not once we get back to Jahnd," Kessligh said. "We'll have walls to defend us then, and the city outskirts."

"Which will begin to burn very fast once they line up their artillery on us."

"Which will take them time to arrange," Kessligh countered. "We just need to survive until tomorrow night."

"Damn," said Sasha. "That might not be easy. How would we force a hole in their line?"

"There's no telling," said Kessligh. "Some things cannot be preplanned. But I tell you now because I trust your mind, and I want you to think about it. If there is any chance at all of making it work, I'll need all the help you can give me."

Twenty-five

The next day began well enough. In the east, Koenyg still did not attack. In the west, the Regent's forces moved their artillery close enough to the defensive wall that they could land volleys of hellfire upon it, and set it ablaze in many parts across its length. Kessligh had the Ilduuris and what was left of the Rhodaani Steel manning the wall, as they were better armoured for a static defence than the Lenays, yet when the hellfire began to strike, he pulled them off. The Regent's forces poured forward, but discovered their first mistake in using the catapults—a structure you'd just set ablaze was no easier to assault than it was to defend. Men could barely approach the burning sections, let alone lay their ladders and climb. Those who did climb the unburned sections were too isolated, and quickly cut down by archers and ballistas from the ground below.

Soon the fires went out, and the Regent's forces retreated beneath heavy defensive artillery fire to regroup and try again. They tried rolling their artillery forward to gain range to shoot *over* the defensive wall and onto the lines of Steel and Lenay soldiers waiting behind, but Kessligh had thought of that, and his artillery returned fire with solid shot-balls of stone. Unlike hellfire, these hit and bounced with considerable momentum, and kept bouncing. Observers on the flanking hills reported several catapults struck by bouncing rounds, and one badly damaged. The Regent's men quickly withdrew their precious artillery back to a safer range.

Observers counted twenty-three catapults and sixty-two ballistas, all wheel-mounted with separate ammunition wagons. Defensively, the Steels could muster twenty and fifty-six, respectively, in reply. It seemed an even match, until one considered the astonishing size of manpower that the Regent possessed to back it up. The Regent could absorb the casualties caused by artillery, and could exploit the havoc it wreaked in once orderly opposing formations. The defenders could not, on either count.

Next, the Regent's forces began probing the hillsides above the wall in force. Those thrusts were met with Ilduuri men, far more skilled in battle on the high passes, and repelled. Small groups of the Regent's men had been scouting for trails across flanking mountains, Sasha's men reported to her. Each time they'd found a small group of Ilduuri, sometimes only three or four men, blocking a narrow pass by practised methods, and causing many casualties.

At midmorning, the Regent's officers arrived at their best plan yet. They brought the catapults just close enough to fire *over* the defensive wall by only a short margin, braving return solid shot artillery to do so. The hellfire burst just beyond the wall, making great blasts of flame between the Steel lines and their wall, thus preventing infantry from rushing to man it as the next attack came roaring in. This had been thought of, however, with long trenches dug just behind the wall—protected from most hellfire save that which hit directly upon the wall's crest—and roofed in places with wood, tin, and tar to protect it from flames. Those men sheltering within were able to scramble up the wall quickly as they heard the attack coming in, many now armed with long pikes fashioned for the purpose.

Others joined them, braving the shifting hellfire rounds for a dash through the kill-zone—the valley was wide, as was the wall, and even twenty-three catapults could only make sporadic fires along such a long line. Defensive artillery replied, and caused far greater carnage upon the clustered ranks of men-at-arms who attacked. Sasha rode along the line to be certain the defence was holding where the Dhemerhill River flowed beneath the wall, but that archway was defended first by great steel poles through the water, barely wide enough for a small man to squeeze between without armour, and tantalisingly trapping many who tried. A small group of archers trained serrin bows upon the gap, and feathered any who got stuck. It was far easier to take a ladder and climb over or go uphill and around.

The noise was incredible. Acrid smoke from erupting hellfire singed the nostrils as outgoing artillery creaked and swung, and ballistas and archers released, and artillery crews yelled and wound and loaded their mechanisms. Tens of thousands of voices roared before the wall, as fighting broke out along its length, a clattering of steel that sounded like a wagon load of cutlery tumbling down a cliff. Archers braved the incoming hellfire killing zone to loose volleys blindly over the wall, while others sheltered more closely behind the wall, where incoming artillery would not fire for fear of killing their own men, stepping back just enough to fire almost straight up and over.

The air was thick with outgoing artillery, ballistas, and arrows, fire erupting beyond the wall in concentrations sometimes so close, Sasha was almost pleased she could not see the result. Defenders upon the wall signalled with flags to artillery, indicating where they needed support most direly, and artillery men would struggle to manoeuvre oxen and great wheels, to push their contraptions into position to hit those targets.

It could not last, Sasha knew—there were too many attackers. But they'd succeeded in doing the one thing they had to—bringing the attackers within the killing range of defensive artillery and holding them there for a long period of time. The carnage upon the far side of the wall must be horrific by now from hellfire alone. The Regent would have this wall, and eventually all this valley up to the walls of Jahnd, but he would pay an obscene price for them. And the defenders would move this artillery back as they retreated, and force the Regent to pay yet a higher price to breach the walls of Jahnd itself. With any luck, the plan was that he might have so few men left, they might recoil in horror and refuse to press home the final assault.

What Sasha did not expect was to hear commotion from behind, and turn in her saddle to find that the eastern wall had broken with no warning at all, and tens of thousands of enemy cavalry were foaming across the valley toward her like a giant wave.

"Retreat!" she yelled, and was horrified at how shrill her voice sounded. It sounded like fear. Which of course it was. "Trumpeter, full retreat, all ranks! Back to Jahnd, back to Jahnd!"

But her force was spread wide across the wall, and some of them up the hills to either side of the valley. Cavalry moved fast, and charged into their rear. There was little hope of regrouping now, but she had to try, or all was lost.

Then she saw Kessligh, riding out to the left bank of the Dhemerhill River, with a signalman to wave his flag and indicate a new line, a retreating line, with the river on the right flank and the left to face the oncoming infantry . . . thank the spirits for Kessligh, she thought with relief. They had to get as many of those on the northern end of the wall down and across to this southern bank as possible. The river protected them from the cavalry while the left flank could hold off the infantry as they pulled back toward the city.

But they had to save as much artillery as possible. Thankfully all of it was situated south of the river in fear of precisely this eventuality, and the need for a fast retreat to Jahnd. She galloped to the nearest artillery line, yelling and waving madly, as their crews looked about and stared.

Errollyn was not entirely certain how it had happened. Only that one moment, Koenyg's forces had been engaged in a full-frontal assault against the Enoran Steel's formations, then somehow they pivoted and came in massive strength around the left flank, and straight about that end of the defensive wall. He suspected a trap, but he had been engaged upon the right flank and had not seen it happen. Sometimes in war it was all over so quickly, and now it hardly mattered.

He raced back around the defensive wall, taking *talmaad* and Enorans with him in a headlong sprint. The Dhemerhill River was now between him and the main assault, and these were the lower reaches of Jahnd itself, criss-crossed with roads, little clusters of farms, houses, and industry, with temples and bridges as well. Open cavalry terrain it was not, and his force slowed to leap fences and cluster onto access roads. Errollyn quickly headed toward a bridge across the Dhemerhill, and the wider fields upon the far side.

Here galloped a steady flood of horsemen of all descriptions—attacking Lenays, Kazeri, and Torovans, mixed in with *talmaad* from the left flank who were pursuing, weaving amidst the attackers and shooting them down, trying to slow their headlong charge into the rear of those who opposed the Regent's main force. They had to be slowed, or Jahnd was lost.

He fitted an arrow, turned left across the galloping formation, and drew with his left hand across his body. It was his weaker side, but not by much. Several men closest had shields raised on their left side, so he selected a man further on and put an arrow through his neck. Around him, fellow *talmaad* did the same, arrows peppering shields and horses, some falling, riders behind swerving to dodge tumbling men and animals.

Cavalry on this side of the formation quickly began to break up, unwilling to run straight while being picked off by the parallel formation of serrin riders. Suddenly a group of Lenay cavalry were breaking and charging directly into the serrin line, scattering them. Errollyn shot one man through the shoulder, turned quickly across two more, drew and shot another man through the back. And then there was a forest patch forcing a merging of the two lines of cavalry, and things became crazy.

He dodged past incoming cavalry, ducked a close swing, shot a Torovan through the chest, then drew a blade to gallop fast through a gap between five more, deflecting two swings as he went. The next gap abruptly vanished, and he cut in front of a Kazeri rider on the opposing side and half-collided, his horse skittering as he fought for balance. Everywhere were galloping riders and swinging blades. He was directly in the middle of the enemy stream, and if he stayed here, he would die.

Jaryd tore into the oncoming cavalry front on, accompanied by every sur-viving Rhodaani, Lenay, or *talmaad* cavalryman who still sat ahorse. What followed was insanity. Men and horses collided at full speed, bodies were sent spinning in horrid collisions. He thrashed at enemy bodies, took blows on his shield, and dodged his frantic horse as best he could, unable to see the results of his strikes and given no time to care. He saw men killed on all sides, saw bodies rolling underhoof, saw a serrin girl who had no business attacking Lenay cavalry with a blade die horribly. Another serrin aimed her horse for deliberate impact with a group of hurtling Lenays that smashed bones and sent riders cartwheeling through the air. The serrin knew the stakes. To lose here was to lose everything.

He cut a Kazeri man through the side, took a blow across his left shoulder, then smashed a Torovan's face with the edge of his shield. He found some space, where several evading *talmaad* had managed to find time to fire arrows. He wheeled to protect them—accurate *talmaad* in this melee could kill far more quickly than he. They fired, and men racing past fell from the saddle. Some Torovans now charged the serrin, who shot, bringing down one man and toppling another's horse. Jaryd performed a fast dodge and reverse to charge up an unexpected side and take another Torovan through the neck with an overhand chop, then wheeled back to chase off several more.

More serrin joined the first group, numbering more than ten now, firing arrows in all directions, toppling enemy riders from unexpected angles, without the time to bring their shields into play. Jaryd waved his sword at others, Lenay and Rhodaani men coming to join his defence, forming a line to block those who charged the serrin, allowing the serrin to shoot sideways at men who could not defend themselves.

It lasted until a small group of Hadryn riders hit his defensive line from the side, killing Rhodaani and Lenay defenders with brutal strokes, then ploughing into the serrin before they could fire, scattering them and killing several. Jaryd chased, smashed the skull of one Hadryn who did not look behind in time, then barely dodged another who tried to do the same to him. He needed eyes in every side of his skull to counter this madness. Everywhere riders were dying who never saw what hit them. Still more fresh attacking cavalry charged in. There seemed no end to their numbers.

Rhillian led her line of *talmaad* galloping north, to where the far end of the wall's defenders, Ilduuri and Rhodaani Steel, were now retreating at what was more of a mad sprint than an orderly retreat. On one side the Regent's men pursued them, a running tide of feudal warriors who had suffered awfully beneath the defensive artillery and had blood on their minds. On the other side, the charging mass of attacking cavalry mostly headed past Rhillian's position to hit the gathering infantry formations upon the far side of the Dhemerhill River, but some now charged in to finish these straggling defenders, caught out of position by the rapidly changing circumstances.

Her *talmaad* formed two lines, one to engage the cavalry and one the infantry. Rhillian joined the infantry line, lacking confidence that her archery would be effective against fast-moving horsemen, urging her horse into space between the running Steel and the sea of pursuing infantry. Standing low in the stirrups, she drew and fired repeatedly into that running mass of men. Other serrin, more accomplished than she, manoeuvred closer and cantered before the tide, drawing and firing, killing man after man with ruthless precision, swinging back and forth for the best angle and never quite letting the next infantryman catch up with the horse.

For a short time it was a killing spree. Mounted archers against unsupported infantry was a deadly weapon. Soon the infantry wave was halting, men pausing to shelter behind their shields and form defensive walls, supported by pikes that the *talmaad* had no intention of charging. They simply switched targets to those who were still running and thus relatively defenceless, often cantering alongside running men with insolent disrespect and shooting until all were dead, or crouched defensively. Shield walls were harder to penetrate, but neither were they any threat to the Steel men in retreat.

Then the attacking cavalry broke through.

Rhillian wheeled fast, seeing serrin scattering before a wall of charging horsemen. Well, she'd known that by placing herself between two enormous enemy forces she was likely killing herself and everyone with her, but the situation was what it was. They'd bought enough time for some of these defenders to make it back to their main formation. Now for the price.

She stowed her bow in the canvas bag behind her left leg and drew her blade. This, she was better at. Attacking men fell, hit by arrows, then the shooters were killed in turn, swords in their scabbards. Rhillian dodged around several attackers, accelerated past some more, blocked a blow, swerved an attack, hurdled a falling horse, ducked another strike, then split a Kazeri's head with an optimistic lash that was more the sharpness of her blade than any true power.

She was doing rather well, she thought, until a big Banneryd horseman came crashing past, found her passing too fast for his blade, and so stuck out his shield instead. It was like riding into a wall, at speed. For a moment, she was flying.

The river saved them. It was the biggest cavalry charge in the history of anything, but it was strung out across the valley, only a portion of it striking in the first wave. And to hit the rapidly assembling lines of Rhodaani and Ilduuri Steel, and the Army of Lenayin, it first had to cross the Dhemerhill River.

Only twenty paces wide at this point, the river was still deep enough to make horses stop in a lunging spray of foam, and struggle forward through the deepest part before reemerging. And when they did, they hit a wall of impenetrable shields.

Sasha rode up and down her line of shieldsmen, manoeuvring to pass behind the archers now shooting over their comrades' heads into the charging cavalry. The river disappeared beneath their numbers, a solid mass of horse-flesh and waving swords. Now there were ballistas firing into them, their mobile wagon mounts twisted even as they retreated, raining heavy, fast-moving bolts into the horses' midst. Cavalrymen bashed and hammered at the wall of steel, and men in the shield-line leaned into each other as the whole line shook and flexed beneath the assault. But for all the things cavalry could do, it could not ride through walls.

Sasha took a moment to stare toward the wall, now flooded with enemy soldiers. There was no river protecting them on that side. But there was the Army of Lenayin. Those men-at-arms who now ran howling toward the waiting lines of Lenays were likely from the rear ranks, with no experience of what had happened to the first forces into the valley, when Lenayin had hit them end on. Now they would learn. But this was a defence, and the Army of Lenayin was not built for defensive actions in the open. In such tight lines there would be no space, and no momentum. Even the Army of Lenayin could not stand such an assault for long. And on the far side of that wall, the Regent's forces would be bringing up his artillery.

Rhillian found herself awake. It was an odd awakening, from a floating, dreamlike state, like swimming underwater, and then the water was gone, yet the floating remained. There were groups of serrin philosophers who would travel to high mountains and meditate for sometimes years on end, in search of that dreamlike otherworld that grew upon the far side of consciousness. Those serrin, upon returning from their meditations, insisted that one could bring back the spiritual essence of that otherworld, once visited, and return it to the real world. Perhaps that was what she felt now, aware that she was awake, yet not entirely conscious. Some serrin speculated that wakefulness and consciousness were two different things. Or, depending upon the tongue being used, perhaps ten different things, requiring a hundred or more different words in combination.

She smiled. She should tell such serrin, if she saw them again, that one did not need to meditate for years to reach a dreamlike state of being. One need only fall off a horse.

She opened her eyes. A blur resolved itself into the confines of a tent. Daylight spilled through an open flap. Nearby, she could hear voices and commotion. But not battle. Merely activity, men and horses, a rattle of harness, a gruff laugh.

A soldier came in and looked at her. That was when she realised that she was lying on the grass, her head level with his boots. He looked down at her. A Lenay, she thought, though short-haired and smooth-faced, unlike the wild men of the Goeren-yai. She was a captive, then. Of the Army of Northern Lenayin.

The soldier left. Rhillian tried moving. Her wrists were bound above her head, and tied to something. Her ankles were similarly bound. She lay stretched and immobile. Breathing hurt—it felt like a broken rib. Probably she'd discover worse if she could move.

Another man entered, broad and powerful in leathers and mail. His left cheek bore a deep cut, recently cleaned, yet he wore it with unconcern. There was blood on his leg, Rhillian saw, as he pulled across a small chair and sat, eating fruit. She did not think the blood was his.

"You're Rhillian," he said. "The one the Torovans call 'the white death.'"

She'd been recognised. It was always a danger in battle, with her white hair. Most *talmaad* did not wear helms as they blocked their vision.

"I'm Koenyg," he added around his mouthful, and washed it down with a swig of water. "King of Lenayin."

Rhillian studied him from her place upon the ground. She'd heard him described, yet never seen him face-to-face. He looked like a king. And yet he wore no symbols of status as most kings would. Even the Verenthanes of Northern Lenayin, and those like Koenyg who naturally allied with them, did not hold with the lowlands faith in symbols of status. Koenyg Lenayin was clearly a warrior and a leader, and amongst his people that was all the status he needed.

"Sasha spoke to me of you," he continued, speaking Torovan. He needn't have bothered, she spoke Lenay quite well. "She spoke highly. Said that you were nearly her equal with a blade. I'm nearly tempted to let you free just to see for myself."

"Please do."

Koenyg smiled, and bit another mouthful. "I said nearly. Are you hurt? Would you like some water?" He drank some more. "It's not poisoned, as you can see."

Rhillian realised that her mouth was very dry. It was tempting to reject his offer for spite, but that made no sense. If she could possibly escape, she would need what health she could muster. She nodded. Koenyg kneeled, placed the skin to her lips, and upended it. He let her drink as long as she needed. Then he resumed his seat and, meeting her eyes with an unworried gaze, drank from the same skin. He did not fear that she would give him some disease. Many of the men he rode with would not do the same. Rhillian gazed at him, not knowing what to make of this man, this brother that Sasha alternately loathed, then grudgingly respected, in turn.

"The battle goes well for us," he said, without bothering to ask if she wished to know. "They did manage a masterful retreat within the walls of Jahnd; Kessligh's doing, no doubt. But their losses were great. We captured another third of their artillery that they were not fast enough to take with them or destroy in leaving. They move their artillery behind Jahnd's walls, which we cannot bring into range with our own artillery without losing it to theirs. But we are moving catapults up on the eastern flank, to occupy heights above Jahnd. I doubt they'll last until morning."

Rhillian thought it all sounded quite probable. Koenyg seemed far too direct to be the boasting kind. "And then?" she asked him.

Koenyg shrugged. "Then we return to the Bacosh to consolidate what we've gained. I will return to Lenayin, with the Army of Northern Lenayin. I expect trouble there, when word arrives of what the traitors did. I will bring Bacosh allies with me. We shall set about expanding the Verenthane base of power in Lenayin, which is surely in Regent Balthaar's interest, now he sees how we fight. The pagans have shown that they cannot be trusted with power. They have little interest but personal honour, but the Army of Northern Lenayin fights for a grander civilisation."

"You will kill two sisters and a brother in this quest."

"They kill themselves with their choices," said Koenyg. "I am with history, and history waits for no man, nor weeps for them when they die."

"And Saalshen?"

Koenyg shook his head. "Not my concern. Perhaps the Regent shall forgive your intrusion into human affairs these past two hundred years, and your desecration of the faith. Perhaps he shall let you all off with a warning. But then, my sister Sofy told me just last night that Verenthane civilisation and serrin civilisation cannot coexist. I think she may be right."

"And so we all shall die," Rhillian said quietly. "Thanks to you."

"I am on the side of history," Koenyg repeated. "And history weeps for no man."

"History sides with no man," said Rhillian. "It watches from afar, and laughs at his claims of ownership."

Koenyg shrugged. "I'm winning." He shifted in his chair to look at her more closely. "If you wish, you could return with me to Lenayin. Learn our ways. Convert to the faith. That would be a novelty, to be sure, perhaps even sufficient to impress the Archbishops."

"I decline."

Koenyg raised an eyebrow. "I don't think you realise quite what I'm offering. Most of these men would simply have you killed, and painfully. They think you're evil. I don't. I just think you're in my way."

"And proud to be so."

Koenyg smiled. "I'm offering you a chance to show the world of men that your people are not evil. That you can be civilised. That you can embrace the gods, and learn to live as we do. You would be the perfect model of such a display. From there, you could become a spokesperson for your people, and could travel to Torovan and the newly united Bacosh, beneath my banner. But it could only be possible in Lenayin. As I said, here, they'd just kill you. But Lenays do things differently, and find other paths. It is our strength."

"Ours too," said Rhillian.

Koenyg nodded. "Then you'll consider it? It is no small offer. The protests I would face from my strongest supporters would be intense. The unholiness of Saalshen has been a core teaching of the Torovan and Bacosh faiths for centuries now."

"Made more so in recent years for political gain," Rhillian added.

Koenyg shrugged again. "Perhaps."

"What you're saying is that you will try to help me save my people, who are about to become defenceless if this battle is lost, by helping us all to convert?"

"Yes," said Koenyg. "With you as their figurehead and representative, to prove the possibility to the doubters, and backed and protected by the King of Lenayin. Any invasion of Saalshen will take years to organise. Perhaps there were plans for it to happen rapidly after Jahnd's fall, but losses have been too severe here, nearly a half of the Regent's total force has been lost so far, a staggering cost. Saalshen is defenceless without the Steels, and there is no need for mad haste. I think you could have a year at least, perhaps two, within which to make arrangements for your new circumstance in Lenayin."

"And in return for our mass conversion," Rhillian continued, "we will be required to abandon our freedom of thought? Our questions? Our philosophies and arts? Our instinct to take human ways and thoughts that we find intriguing, and blend them with our own to find new and interesting expression?"

Koenyg smiled. "Exactly."

Rhillian met his gaze quite clearly. "I think that my people will tell you that they would rather you killed us all down to the very last child." Koenyg's smile faded. "Which is where this is most likely headed anyway, in time."

Koenyg sighed. "I offer you a chance to change that course, yet you spit on it."

"No," said Rhillian. "By making such an offer, you spit on *us*."

Sasha stood atop the defensive wall and watched Jahnd burn. About her were Ilduuris, worn, exhausted, and battle-stained. These were not her familiar names, for after Arken, Captain Idraalgen was also dead, as were numerous others she had known in Andal. Those remaining stood together and watched a new artillery shot come whistling in, and land a hundred paces from the wall in a bright flash. New fire consumed buildings, adding to the blaze that already burned, and blocked out all view of the Dhemerhill Valley behind choking smoke.

Perhaps that was just as well. The Dhemerhill, and now the adjoining Ilmerhill, was entirely occupied by the Regent's men. They burned all the town adjoining the city walls, to create a clear approach for assault, if it were needed. Given the reports of artillery hauled up the rear, flanking slopes to hit them from behind and above, Sasha did not think it was necessary. This burning was mostly for distraction, and for spite.

"I am sorry, my friends, if I have led you to this," she said heavily.

A sergeant put a hand on her shoulder guard. "We came willingly," he said. "And it has been glorious."

"Aye," said Sasha. "Yes, it has."

Now it was late afternoon, and the shadows grew long. Artillery would fire from the high slopes and set the upper end of town afire. Walls would be undefendable and, when cracked with heat, could probably be breached with stone shot from the catapults. They would not last the night if they stayed here.

She left her men to head down the stairs to a street below, where she reclaimed her horse. Yasmyn was there, having acquired a new horse, her old horse dead from a ballista bolt as she'd raced back and forth amidst the carnage of the retreat, attempting to convey orders and warnings from one commander to another. She was grim and blackened with smoke, yet sat proud in the saddle.

Andreyis was missing, but alive, tending to Yshel who, word was, soon might not be. She'd been too near a hellfire round that exploded, and was burned.

Rhillian was missing; Aisha had been near her at the time, and her description did not sound promising. Of the thousand or so *talmaad* who had followed Rhillian on that mission to cover the retreat of the wall's defenders, barely half had returned.

Errollyn was missing, too. Sasha willed herself to be like stone, and set off uphill, with Yasmyn close behind. She could not grieve now. Errollyn was too good at surviving for her to believe the worst without evidence, and no one had seen him fall. Besides which, she had the conclusion of a battle to wage, and if it went the way things now suggested it would, and Errollyn was dead, she'd be joining him soon enough.

Wait for me, she willed him as she urged her horse uphill past lines of ascending, battle-scarred soldiers and frightened townsfolk. Don't leave for the spirit world before I get there. I'm coming.

At Windy Point, she found Kessligh, Damon, and Jaryd, standing before their horses to survey the scene. Jaryd was credited by some as having saved the retreat. He'd plunged into the first attacking wave of cavalry, then led many to regroup on the far side, and swung back to hit those lead cavalry again. The distraction had forced their attention aside from assaulting the retreating Steel, and bought them enough space to fall back to the outskirts of Jahnd, where cavalry could not follow.

"The night is our only chance," said Kessligh. Sasha nodded. It was what they'd discussed in Liri, last night upon the hillside. These valleys made a confine. The only thing the Regent's men feared now was the dark, and the serrin who prowled beyond the reaches of their fires. Serrin cavalry could fight at night, their horses trained to trust that their riders could see better than they. In the dark, such riders could kill and not be killed in reply. But first, they had to escape this trap.

"How do we make a hole?" Jaryd wondered, gazing down at the valley. The Regent's forces made a giant circle about Jahnd, and across the mouth of the Ilmerhill Valley. They had occupied the Dhemerhill Valley at first, to drive out opposing forces, but now they'd pulled back and made a great ring of steel across it instead.

"If they'd stayed in the valley," Sasha observed, "in amongst the buildings, we'd have done well. In the dark we could get in amongst them on the streets, it would be single combat, and Lenayin would kill them. But it seems they've thought of that."

Kessligh shook his head. "They'll be expecting a final breakout attempt. They'll make us come at them across open ground. Night vision will count for nothing if they know precisely where we are."

"Lenayin is at half strength," Damon said tiredly. "We've more than that for a defence, but many are wounded, and not up to an attack."

"We've enough *talmaad*," said Kessligh. "Barely. But as Jaryd says, we need to find a hole. If we can get through them . . . somewhere." His eyes searched the encircling lines, hungrily. "Look here, they place their catapults too close together. The Steel space them out more—those ammunition wagons can sometimes catch fire, and if one goes up, the flames kill everything within a hundred paces. Those catapults are barely sixty paces apart."

"Great," said Damon. "We only need to cut our way through walls of soldiers two hundred deep supported by thousands of archers and all of their ballistas to reach them."

"We have to punch a hole," Sasha said solemnly. "It will be nighttime, they'll only see poorly, we can feint them and hope they do not realise our trick."

"They'll know the first feint is a feint," Damon muttered, "it's the obvious thing to do in the dark."

"Then we'll try to make it convincing. But they're not going to just let us through. They know it's our only hope, and they'll be ready for it."

"This many *talmaad* in the dark," Kessligh muttered. "If they can just break the lines and escape the encirclement, they can kill without being killed themselves. They'll force the Regent's entire force to squeeze up against our artillery just to escape."

"Not quite," said Damon. "They've artillery, they'll use hellfire to light up the night, plant big fires everywhere. The *talmaad* will be visible as though it were daylight."

"So get the artillery," Jaryd concluded. "Same plan as before."

"Only it didn't work last time," Sasha said solemnly. "I sent a thousand men to try, they got nothing, and more than half didn't come back. This will be much worse."

"Dammit," said Kessligh, jaw clenched. "There *must* be a way."

Twenty-six

Evening was falling, torchlight flickering upon the walls of the tent. Rhillian lay on her back, her wrists now tied before her instead of above her head. It left her somewhat more free, yet still completely hopeless. Her broken rib made any attempt to sit up agony, and periodically a Lenay warrior would peer through the tent flap, just to be sure.

Now someone entered the tent once more, carrying food. But this was no Lenay man, this was a boy. And not just any boy, Rhillian saw as he kneeled beside her on the grass. It was Alfriedo Renine, her old sparring partner from Tracato.

"I heard it was you," Alfriedo said, with a faint smile. "I thought you might like some food?"

Rhillian nodded. If it gave her the strength to bite off King Koenyg's nose, it would be worth it. Alfriedo assisted her in sitting up, as she winced in pain, and rested her back against a chest. With the plate on the grass beside her, she could take food two-handed to her mouth without assistance.

"Where have you been fighting?" Rhillian asked as she ate.

"I haven't," said Alfriedo. "I am here to fly the flag for Rhodaani nobility. Some of my nobles were very keen to join the fighting at first. Since then they have seen its nature, and many have changed their minds."

Rhillian nodded. "Astonishing that some men still seem to dream of a pleasant war."

"There are places about the western wall where bodies carpet the ground so thickly, you can walk from the Dhemerhill River to the bottom of the southern slope without touching the ground."

"Where the Regent's men hit the Army of Lenayin," said Rhillian. "The first time in this battle Lenayin has been hard-pressed."

"The Lenays are extraordinary warriors," said Alfriedo. "The men of Northern Lenayin are unsurpassed as heavy cavalry, and now the foot soldiers of Goeren-yai Lenayin show their superior swordwork against a huge force. Whichever side wins here, the legend of Lenayin shall only grow."

"They're not all Goeren-yai," said Rhillian. "Quite a few are Verenthanes, including the prince who leads them."

Alfriedo nodded. Riding in the rear of a great, advancing army, he had been observing carnage for two days now, and looked as pale as the boy who had always loved to eat ham, but had now been given a blade and told to go and kill the pig himself.

"Your mother never told you it would be like this, did she?" Rhillian asked.

"I did love my city," Alfriedo said faintly. "I did truly love it, Rhillian. I loved all of it, not just the human parts. My mother told me that I was born to be lord of all of it. She told me that it was my destiny, ordained by the gods. And I thought that was wonderful and good, for my love was pure and true. How could the gods be wrong? How could my mother, and all the noble families, and so many centuries of tradition?"

Rhillian stopped eating, and just watched him. "You thought that the gods had blessed you," she said quietly. "Now you see that it was a curse."

"One man can make a great difference, she told me. I was to be that man. And I studied and learned, and I was always very good with books and learning. I have learned many things, Rhillian, but only since I met Kessligh and yourself did I begin to wonder if I had learned any of the right things."

"Knowledge is not wisdom," Rhillian agreed. "Acquiring knowledge is easy. Using it wisely is hard."

"Would you place a peasant boy upon the lordship chair of Rhodaan?" Alfriedo asked her. His big eyes were faintly desperate. As though he sought something from her. "Would he do a better job than I?"

"He might," Rhillian said. "It depends on the boy. He might know only a little, but he might have judgement. A man with no judgement may know everything, yet understand nothing. What do *you* know, Alfriedo?"

"I know that my cause is flawed." Alfriedo's voice trembled. "I know that there is no certainty that what comes to replace how Rhodaan was ruled in the past is an improvement."

"No *certainty*?" Rhillian stared at him. "Is that all?" Alfriedo could not meet her gaze. "They're going to kill my people. All of my people. The Regent will not make Leyvaan's mistakes again, he will be methodical. Perhaps even by the time you are a full-grown man, there will be no Saalshen left, and very nearly no serrin.

"Alfriedo, we *built* Tracato! We made it everything that you love. These men hate ideas. They hate the creative mind. They hate everything that you love about the way Tracato was."

Alfriedo sat for a very long time, his head down, knees drawn up. For the first time since Rhillian had met him, he looked like a boy, lonely, frightened, and a long way from home. Finally he looked up, eyes red and cheeks tear-streaked. "But I can do nothing," he said weakly. "I am just a boy."

"Today, you are Lord of Rhodaan. Within those city walls, Kessligh stands, and observes these lines. What does he see, Alfriedo? And what would he tell you, if he could speak to you once more?"

Jaryd ran down the streets outside Jahnd's defensive walls, his shield raised to ward off the heat from blazing buildings. More hellfire erupted somewhere near, with a great whoosh. Townsfolk ran by carrying wounded, sweating and wincing. Many had cloths and shirts wrapped around their heads against the heat, and to keep flaming embers and smoke from their eyes and lungs.

At an intersection he found Sofy, nearly impossible to recognise in her mail shirt and wrapped headscarf, hurrying from patient to burned patient amidst the smoke.

"Sofy!" He grabbed her arm, and she shook him off. "Sofy, you have to go! One hit on this road and everyone within thirty paces dies!"

"So what?" she yelled at him, eyes determined. "If you want to help me, help me! Otherwise go away!"

Jaryd helped her. Some folks in this part of Jahnd, outside the defensive walls, had been slow to evacuate. No one had expected the collapse of the eastern flank so soon, nor the onslaught of catapult artillery. Many had still been racing to collect families and relatives when the hellfire began falling.

The burns were terrible. Bodies were laid out in rows, treated by fast-working humans and serrin who cut burned cloth away from bodies with blades, often taking chunks of skin with it. There were serrin lotions to be applied, and wet bandages to wrap, but for many there was nothing to be done. Sofy organised hand-drawn carts, and city folk hauling wheelbarrows. Some of those with handcarts were wealthy men and women, clothes scorched and faces blackened, working alongside their more plain comrades. One of those leading the most daring excursions down side streets to find new victims was a well-known merchant, one of the wealthiest men in Jahnd. Now he was coming back, bringing one last column of rescuers up a burning road, yelling encouragement and struggling under the load of a man he carried on his back.

Sofy directed several final wagons to wait for this last load, as flames grew hotter from the south. The wind was shifting, and they had to leave. Down a nearby street, wood facades and masonry crumbled in a roar of erupting sparks.

A hellfire round exploded directly upon the returning rescue party. Sofy, Jaryd, and all fell flat, arms covering their heads. On the road, Jaryd looked up to see the dark shapes of rescuers and their loads flailing amidst the flames. As the fire dimmed, several burning figures emerged, staggered a few steps, then fell.

"Sofy, we have to go!" Jaryd yelled. For once Sofy did not protest. She yelled at everyone to leave, and took her place pushing the most loaded cart. Jaryd joined her, shield slung on his back, as they pushed and bumped over the rough pavings, through choking smoke so thick they had to close their eyes and hope those in front could see the way.

It went on interminably, and then the defensive wall was above them, and they were beneath the main gate. Jaryd nearly fell with exhaustion, but Sofy caught him, led him aside, and made him drink from a waterskin as soldiers and townsfolk rushed about the wagons, carrying wounded away. Jaryd poured water over his head, and rubbed at his face.

"You shouldn't have come after me," Sofy scolded him. "We're all taking risks; you can't protect yourself, your men, and me all at the same time. Look at you, you've nothing left."

"I'm okay," Jaryd murmured, arms on knees. He coughed, throat irritable with smoke. "You're braver than me. I hate fire."

Sofy sat alongside him and put a hand to his chin. "No," she said with a smile, "that makes you braver than me." She kissed him.

Jaryd put an arm about her, and they sat together in the fading light amidst the chaos of the lower defensive wall. Compared to the events of the day, it was a moment of contentment just to be together.

"When we marry," Sofy remarked, "you'll be a prince of Lenayin."

"Your husband's not dead yet."

"The night is young."

"Aye," said Jaryd, "that it is."

Damon trotted his horse down Jahnd's main street. It was crowded with cavalry, tired men on tired horses, battered and grim. He stopped often, exchanging salutes with officers, lords and others he recognised. Here on the higher slope, he found Jaryd, leading the last third of the horsemen assembled.

They clasped hands. "I hear you rescued my sister again," Damon quipped.

Jaryd shook his head. "She rescued a bunch of townsfolk from death, I only helped. She was doing well without me."

"She's a good girl," Damon said sadly. "If I could find another girl as good, I'd marry her."

Jaryd smiled wryly. "Prince Damon, it's been an honour."

"The honour is mine."

Damon continued downhill, past the assembled thousands. Their numbers were well down, less than their original total. It still made a very large force of horsemen, but it was nothing compared to what lay beyond the gate. Jaryd would lead the last group out, the ones who, if desperate plans went anything according to form, would try to hit the enemy artillery, some of which had been captured just earlier that day. But for that to work, the first wave had to succeed.

In the middle of the formation were the serrin. They would follow the formation's spear as it tried to punch a hole in the enemy lines. *Talmaad* were not armed for such a thing, and their horses were light. The point of the spear had to break through the line, and once through, good things could happen. Jaryd exchanged salutes with the serrin man who had been appointed *talmaad* leader. He hoped the man was as competent as Errollyn had been. And he thought of Sasha, and how pained her heart must be right now.

Down on the lower slopes of Jahnd were arrayed the heavy cavalry—Rhodaani, Enoran, and Lenay. These were big horses, some Steel cavalry with lances, most with sword and shield. At the very base of the slope, before the wall, were the meanest cavalry of all, some Steel, and others Lenay. Leading them was Great Lord Markan, his black shield battered with more strikes than could be counted, and with notches in his blade that even constant sharpening could not hide. He bore several wounds, his armour torn in places, his face tight with pain. Yet somehow, he looked happy.

"Command is yours," he said with a salute. "King Damon."

Damon smiled. "My brother will protest." Markan spat, to show what he cared for Koenyg's opinion. "You know," said Damon, "it will be nice to be king for just one evening. The shortest reign in Lenay history."

"And the most glorious."

They both knew what would happen. They would charge the artillery, which was not so silly on horseback. What *was* silly was charging the wall of infantry, backed by cavalry and archers, that now surrounded Jahnd. If Sasha's earlier estimation had been right, the Regent had begun the fight with close to one hundred and eighty thousand men and cavalry. The defence had been truly magnificent, and whittled them down to a little less than half of that. Which left—Kessligh estimated to look at them—eighty-five thousand. All cavalry forces combined, here along Jahnd's main road, made barely ten thousand. They would probably break the line briefly, but then the line would close, half the attacking column would be cut off, the other half pursued by the cavalry behind the defensive line, vastly outnumbered, and killed. And that would be that. But they had to try, because there were no other options left.

Far above and behind, the upper wall of Jahnd was under attack from infantry and artillery that had climbed the hills behind the city. The grand buildings atop the slope were burning, while the southern wall was assaulted by enough infantry to keep significant Enoran and Rhodaani Steel troops occupied.

That left Lenayin and Ilduur to advance out into the Ilmerhill Valley at night, within the cover of the valley's city sprawl. It was cover from which to attack, as none of the Regent's forces were foolish enough to occupy that part of the city at night, where serrin could pick them off and Lenay swordsman outclass them up close. But it was a good place for a trap if the plan worked, and a good start for a futile last charge if it did not. Sasha led them, commanding Ilduuri and Lenay soldiers on foot. She was more use on foot than on a horse, she said so herself. Damon hoped that when it all failed, she might retreat up the Ilmerhill and escape back to Ilduur the way she'd come in. But if the Regent won, there would be nowhere any of them could hide in the long run. And knowing Sasha, he knew there was no way she'd run.

"Well," said Damon. "No speeches. We all know why we're here."

"If we all die tonight," said a Rhodaani man, "it will still have been worth it."

"Still?" said Markan, eyes blazing. "I would have ridden across the known world in search of such a death."

Alfriedo sat upon his horse at his place in the line. The Rhodaanis were on the left flank, facing Jahnd, and up against the hills. Flanks were usually reserved for the best forces, but this flank was against a steep slope, and was not a direct line from Jahnd's main gate. Behind them was a patch of scattered forest, and behind that, the Dhemerhill River. It was not likely that any attacking force would come galloping this way.

He walked his horse to the side of a group of Torovan nobles, also ahorse. The nobles looked across to him, and General Zulmaher at his side. They nodded. Their leader, Duke Carlito Rochel, brought his horse across to stand beside the Lord of Rhodaan.

"It seems we are expecting an attack," said Alfriedo. All the army stood ready, a huge force of men, shields in place, making a great wall, flames from the city reflecting in polished shields and helms.

"Yes," said Carlito, drily. "And it seems that we have been relegated to the side, we Pazira and our fellow outcasts." His noble companions smirked without humour. Members of the Rochel clan, Alfriedo guessed, and their allies.

"It will be a desperate charge," said General Zulmaher, gazing at the walls. "They will try to punch a hole through our line with cavalry. *Talmaad* will ride through that hole. Once they get behind us, in their thousands in the dark . . ."

"We cannot fight serrin in the dark," Carlito muttered. "Not here. At night in Saalshen we cluster like a ball; here we are spread out between two forces, Jahnd and serrin."

"The breakout will fail," Zulmaher said confidently. "These lines are far too strong, and their forces too depleted. And our artillery will turn about and light up the valley with hellfire. If we can see serrin, we can fight them."

Carlito nodded gloomily. He showed no joy at the prospect of victory. Nor did his noble friends. Before him were arrayed ranks of Pazira cavalry, and a small number of Pazira infantry. Largely unblooded, they'd lost barely a man. Alfriedo's Rhodaanis too were mostly unscathed. A trivial number they'd made between them, Paziras and Rhodaanis, when the battle had begun. But now, nearly three thousand men combined to form a significant chunk of this left flank.

Alfriedo recalled what Rhillian had said. He gazed up at the heights of Jahnd, its grand buildings silhouetted in flames. The architecture reminded him of Tracato. Was Kessligh up there watching? Of course he was. The counterattack was about to happen. And what was this that he felt, when he should have been terrified to be having these thoughts? Why did the prospect of what he was about to do fill him only with calm?

"My dear Duke Carlito," Alfriedo pronounced, quite mildly. "I cannot escape the feeling that our combined forces are poorly located for this coming battle."

Carlito laughed bitterly. "If they wish to die in the main fight, let them. I am pleased to sit this one out. I want no part in this stupid man's war."

"My thoughts exactly," said Alfriedo. "I also think we should sit this one out. I suggest that we do so. Perhaps three thousand paces in that direction."

He nodded toward the far northern side of the valley, lost in darkness. Carlito nearly laughed. Then frowned. He studied Alfriedo's face more closely. Alfriedo met his gaze with complete seriousness. There was a moment of utter and complete silence.

Carlito's eyes slowly widened. He looked about at the encircling army. Eighty thousand at least, infantry first, then cavalry. In the middle of the formation, the great, swinging arms of catapults, now mostly silent as the fires took hold without them. And then back to this, the left flank. It was not a difficult flank, easy to hold even for lowly rated forces. Anyone attacking here would pin themselves against the hills, a terrible place to be.

But what if this flank were to simply disappear?

A thousand emotions tore across Carlito's face. Alfriedo could guess them all, for he'd felt them too over the past hours of deliberation. Duty to his family. Duty to Pazira. To family tradition that went back centuries, and would all be taken from him if this failed. It was a poor flank to attack, but a deadly flank to leave open. Here they guarded the throat, and to leave would expose it.

And yet the cost if they won. Alfriedo had recalled Alythia telling him Sasha's tales of Alexanda Rochel, Carlito's father. Alexanda had hated this war. Hated the Archbishop's vile ravings about the evil serrin, and hated most of all the rise of the greedy and powerful merchants in Petrodor, the Patachis, that stripped all Torovan of the good and wise rule of the eldest families. Carlito was surely his father's son in such matters. But could he risk everything Family Rochel had built in Pazira over many hundreds of years, his own life and those of all his relatives, on a matter of principle?

For a moment, Alfriedo felt the fate of the world swing upon a thread. One man, his mother had told him, can make all the difference. "Yes, Mother," he thought. "Now I believe you."

Astride his horse, Kessligh's eyes widened. He peered through a tube, a serrin invention with glass lenses on either end, that could help him to see distant things. Yasmyn did not know what he searched for, the Regent's formation was quite fixed and highly visible, shields and armour alight in the glare of flames before Jahnd's wall. They would not shift. They had all of Jahnd trapped, and they would not move for anything.

"They move," Kessligh breathed. He peered intently through the tube, mouth open. Yasmyn stared into the dark, seeing only lines of soldiers. But now, there on the far right, up against the hills of Jahnd themselves . . . was that a line breaking away? Several lines, in fact? Her own eyes widened. What in the world were they doing? "I see a banner. Oh dear spirits, it's Alfriedo. Alfriedo and Carlito!" He turned to Yasmyn. "Message to the front! Tell Damon that the far-right flank retreats! Rhodaan and Pazira have made us a gap, do not attack them, they're on our side! Go now!"

Yasmyn spun her horse and galloped, horseshoes sliding on pavings across the high courtyard. Upon her right, great buildings were ablaze, and the sound of fighting raged.

She reached the main road and skidded about a corner, heart in her mouth as her horse nearly fell . . . please the gods and spirits old and new, she could not fall now. The road ahead was filled with cavalrymen, blocking the way.

"Messenger!" she yelled, thrusting past them, making space by force where she had to, crashing them aside. "Messenger, urgent message!"

Ahead, cavalrymen turned to look, then pulled their horses aside. Space appeared and she accelerated once more, dangerously fast on the slippery ground downhill. Men were shouting ahead now, and cries of "Messenger!" flew downslope faster than she could manage at a gallop.

She passed the serrin at the midslope, then finally reached the lower slopes and heavier cavalry. Before the defensive wall, she saw Prince Damon with a group of commanders, waiting for her. Beside Damon was her brother Markan, with an expectant frown.

She could barely contain her excitement as she told them. Prince Damon simply blinked at her, astonished. Her brother Markan laughed, reined to her side, and kissed her roughly. Then he yelled, and all the horsemen yelled back. Most of them had not heard what she said, but they saw the news was good, and cheered that fact alone.

Markan yelled again, and this time, Prince Damon joined him. Then he turned, and galloped out the gate. The combined armies of human and serrin followed him, in a constant, deafening rush.

Damon took a right turn out of the gate and along a weaving city street. Visibility was no issue here, for fires made the street as bright as day, casting crazy shadows across unburned facades. Buildings turned abruptly to smaller houses, then disappeared completely as he emerged from the city. Here were fields, and walled pens for animals. Beyond them, far wider fields, occupied now by a massive and impenetrable wall of armoured men. But as he looked right, up against the valley's southern slope, there was a gap. It was a large gap, quickly filling as men from the adjoining line flooded in. They would have to hurry, before a new line formed.

He cleared the animal pens, angled right again, and drew his sword. A roar ripped the air, yet it did not spring from his own lips—suddenly he was being overtaken by cavalrymen, one of them Markan, swords also drawn. From his peripheral vision he saw artillery rounds streaking into the night sky. Huge fireballs erupted upon the fields behind him, on either side of the racing cavalry. Ahead, running men and some horses scrambled and yelled and waved arms and weapons, trying to dress their line. Damon yelled with a furious bloodlust that he had not truly felt since the battle's commencement. He wanted to kill them all. Gods willing he would.

His horse simply leaped through the infantry line, unimpressed with the obstacle they presented, and he leaned from the saddle to hack a man as he passed, feeling a satisfying jolt through his arm. Ballistas fired, but whizzed overhead. Damon cut toward them, as other cavalry rushed forward on his left to do the same. Men leaped from the back of ballista wagons to escape the swinging blades, only to be trampled underfoot by big horses trained not to dodge.

Damon indicated with an arm out to keep turning left—he had to protect this flank for the cavalry column still racing through the gap, and get them all behind the Regent's lines. Men followed him, yelling to form up, but it was dark. Very dark, he was realising now. There was no moon in the night sky, and in less light than this, a man riding at any speed off-road would shortly come to grief.

Cavalry were counterattacking now. Most of the Regent's cavalry had been behind the lines of infantry, in case of precisely this sort of break-through. But they were scattered, having had no time to gather in force. Damon hit one man across the shield, accelerated hard to hit another in the shoulder, then swung about to help an Isfayen man engage an armoured knight. Swords made little impact upon the knight's armour, but with him squeezed between them, Damon simply hit him in the visor to stun, then pulled him hard from the saddle. He fell with a crash, and Damon wheeled to look back at the racing cavalry line.

Several thousand were already through, and now the serrin were passing. They loosed arrows into those infantry trying to close the gap, and men fell in droves. A steady stream of serrin were passing, firing one shot from range, then another up close, and Damon could see ranks of feudal infantry dis-solving. Men stopped trying to advance and either sheltered behind their shields or ran. Those who ran quickly fell with a shaft through the back. Those crouching behind a shield lasted longer, but these were feudal men-at-arms, not heavily armoured Steel infantry with their enormous body-covering pro-tectors. These shields were small, often little wider than a man's forearm was long, and serrin accuracy, deprived of killing shots, found other gaps instead. Arrows punched through stomachs, thighs, and hips, and men fell screaming, clutching at shafts that, at these ranges, only plate armour could stop.

And now the serrin were wheeling left, still in a long, weaving line. Damon felt somewhat chilled to watch it, for a line like this, cutting across behind their ranks, had ended the Army of Lenayin's battle against the Enoran Steel at Shero Valley. Now it aimed at a common enemy, and new ranks of oncoming cavalry fell beneath a storm of concentrated arrow fire. Other cavalry broke and tripped on walls or ditches, some horses protesting at being made to run too fast on ground they could not see. They slowed, and made easy targets of their riders, who fell in turn to serrin fire.

In previous battles, *talmaad* had scattered before charging feudal cavalry. Now they held firm and cut them down with contempt. Cavalry cleared, the line continued on, winding leisurely behind the Regent's formation, unleashing a broadside storm against the rear ranks of infantry. There were five thousand *talmaad* in this attack, each one frighteningly accurate. Arrows now flew like rain, close range and aimed, not merely sprayed from distance. Men fell in their hundreds, and kept falling, all along the line.

"Horseback archery done right is not warfare!" Markan suddenly appeared to yell at Damon's side. "It's murder!" For all the Isfayen's prefer-ence for honourable warfare, he was grinning ear to ear.

"Come on!" Damon shouted. "We can still help them with the cavalry!"

They charged after the serrin, more of whom still flooded past even now. Suddenly Damon saw incoming artillery fire ahead, and pointed. Hellfire hit in the serrin's midst, engulfing riders and horses, turning animals into flaming meteors, running across the grass until they crashed and died. Damon wove past the flaming grassland and bodies and saw that the night here was now day. The catapults had been turned and were firing from the middle of the formation, back over their infantry's heads. Upon the left, infantry ranks were re-forming, bigger shields to the front, archers behind. With clear targets now to shoot at, feudal archers were returning fire with accuracy. Ahead and about, serrin riders fell, and horses staggered as they were struck.

More hellfire erupted, serrin trying to dodge wide of the incoming fire, many failing. As the glare faded, Damon could see a great mass of horses gathering ahead. The Regent's cavalry was being regrouped for a charge. With all this fire, the night would not bother them. And if they bottled up the attack on this side of the formation, the artillery would keep falling until they were all dead.

As Jaryd's cavalry raced toward the Regent's artillery, some *talmaad* ahead of them peppered the surrounding defensive lines with arrows. Some fire came back, and *talmaad* fell, but they did not break or dodge, merely continued to walk up and down, taking down pikeman after pikeman. The catapults were surrounded by such terrible bristles to guard against precisely this. But long pikes required two hands, leaving none for shields. Many pikemen wore breastplates instead, but even in the dark, serrin shot for faces and throats.

Only when Jaryd's cavalry were bearing down did the *talmaad* split to allow them through. And then there were pikes rearing up in Jaryd's face, still enough to cause a flash of fear, and a sudden maneouvre to keep from being skewered. The line of horses crashed in, animals rearing as pikes impaled them, riders falling, poles snapping into pikemen's faces. Jaryd found himself inside the line of spikes, and wheeled his horse to force a wider gap, hacking about him with his blade.

Other cavalry forced their way within, Lenays on smaller dussieh, typically less frightening for infantry but harder to impale on giant poles. They got in amongst the pikemen, and did not need to reach as far to strike. The forward rank of pikemen began to collapse, men abandoning poles to reach desperately for shields and swords. That made more space for cavalry, and soon there were horses trampling everywhere through their lines, and men fleeing in panic.

Suddenly there was artillery ahead of him, great wagons on huge wheels, pulled by teams of oxen. Even now, their huge arms swung, hurling flaming balls toward the rear of the left flank.

Archers defended them, and fired at oncoming cavalry. Jaryd felt a jolt through his shield, then his horse screeched and stumbled. Another jolt, and the horse fell, but at slow speed. Jaryd rolled off as a lifetime playing lagand had taught him, while other cavalry tore past and laid into the archers without mercy.

Jaryd ran, still limping on the leg he'd hurt crossing the Ipshaal weeks ago, and found his way up onto the nearest catapult, blocked by a shirtless crewman who grabbed a polearm. Jaryd warded off the blow and cut the man's legs from under him. He climbed up over those bloody screams and killed the next two crewmen, several more abandoning the massive winches and pulleys to run away, only to die amidst the cavalry.

Looking at the catapult mechanism, Jaryd realised that it would take some time to disable one properly with a sword. Ropes could be cut, but there was spare rope stored in loops, for they snapped quite frequently, and could be repaired fast if need be. But behind was the ammunition wagon.

He climbed onto it and looked down. The wagon's sides were like a giant box. Inside were racks, within which were stored the leather balls of hellfire rounds. There was a system of water, fed by a large trough at the back, that dripped down over the leather balls to keep them cool. When the catapult arm was wound down, a loader would take out a ball and place it in the cup, while another poured on a smear of hellfire, and lit it.

Both loaders had fled, and he was alone up here and under fire, as arrows zipped in, impaling the wagon. He looked about, and from this vantage of height, saw something shocking. This was the only portion of the artillery defences that had collapsed. Even here, his cavalry were now fighting a losing battle to hold back the teeming tide of infantry that regrouped and charged the far side. Archers peppered them with arrows, and horses were falling. Very soon they would be overwhelmed.

The great torch upon the wagon's rear that lit the final rounds was still in its sconce, and burning. Nearby catapults were still firing, incinerating serrin riders, and the last hope of victory. Jaryd realised what he had to do, for Lenayin and everything that he loved. For Sofy, who would surely die with most of Jahnd if this attack did not succeed.

He grabbed the torch off the wagon's rear and fell flat atop the wagon's storage rails. Below, a hellfire round had been arrow-struck, and was leaking badly. He pushed the torch toward it, and held it there.

"I'm sorry, Sofy," he murmured. "You can't save me this time. But I can save you."

His ears were filled with the Goeren-yai war cries of his cavalry around him, battling to grant him more time. They'd be joining him in the spirit world, his brothers-in-arms, and that suited him fine. His last thought, as the fire lit, was of Tarryn.

"Hello, little brother. How've you been?"

The fireball was the brightest thing Damon had ever seen. It pierced the eyes with heat more white than orange, and every serrin on the battlefield turned completely around to save his or her vision. Flames roared through infantry in the middle of the Regent's formation and engulfed a neighbouring catapult, which also erupted. As did the next, and the next, and the next, a chain of fire like a rolling wall, engulfing men by the thousand.

When it died, the battlefield seemed paused, as though in shocked silence. Serrin stood their horses off, blinking and dazed. Across the Regent's army, men stared in disbelief.

Too close together indeed, Damon thought, recalling Kessligh's observation. Far too close. And a second thought, as he realised how many attackers had surely been within range of those fires. Jaryd was one of the best horsemen and warriors in Lenayin, and one of the most determined. Surely he'd been in close. Suddenly, he knew with certainty that his friend was dead. It was a certainty like serrin sometimes had, of things they could not possibly know about each other. He just felt it.

Damon did not cheer in triumph, or salute the bravery of fallen heroes. He gathered as many men as he could, and charged the nearest enemy cavalry he could find. Then he began killing.

Sasha stood on a rooftop in the sprawl of buildings that was the Ilmerhill Valley part of Jahnd. Gazing across the clusters of roofs and streets that separated her from the mouth of the valley, she could see a wall of infantry moving at speed toward her. Tens of thousands of men in armour, yet their formation was broken, as though they were fleeing. Somehow, it had worked. No one down in this valley, far from lines of communication, knew how it had worked. But all had seen the fireballs that had turned night into the brightest of days, and knew that the attackers had lost the majority of their most feared weapons.

The infantry that advanced upon them now behaved exactly like men who had *talmaad* at their rear, in the dark. Their artillery gone, their centre in flames, their backsides peppered with arrows from the night, they retreated to where they had cover. The city in Ilmerhill Valley, where they could hide behind walls, and *talmaad* could not see them. But where Lenays and Ilduuris could.

She turned and faced the yard behind. It was an animal yard, leading to a small slaughterhouse. Fitting, she thought darkly. It was crowded with

Lenay and Ilduuri infantry. The past hour, they'd been discussing tactics, playing to each others' strengths, here amongst the buildings.

"Listen!" she yelled at them, and they quietened. "They're coming! We know how many they are, but think! Five thousand *talmaad* attacked and broke through. You've seen how they shoot. A single *talmaad* can easily kill ten men in a fight. That's fifty thousand. Our enemies retreat here because they're *dying* out there, by the thousand. They can't fight what they can't see, and what applies to serrin applies to us here as well.

"Their only advantage is numbers. But here, we force them to fight man on man, and numbers mean nothing. Like the *talmaad*, each of you is worth many of them. Forget tactics. Forget clever games. I want from each of you only one thing. I want blood!"

There was a roar, then fast silence. She had them. "Kill them all! Show them no mercy! You are warriors such as they cannot match without the assistance of numbers, cavalry, and artillery. I want each of you to make a personal tally. I want you to compete with your friends for kills and heads. Remember what they did to our fallen friends! Remember what evil they fight for! Remember what the serrin did to King Leyvaan the Fool and his army, two hundred years ago! They forgot that lesson then! We will teach it to them again!

"I am Synnich-ahn, the most deadly of the ancient spirits, and I want to *drown* in their blood!"

"Blood!" her army roared. "Blood! Blood! Blood!" They punched the air with their swords. Sasha seethed, drinking it in. She meant every word. She wanted to slaughter, this deadly night. She could feel the ancient spirits in her veins, urging her to more than mortal cravings. It was as though the spirits of all the recently departed were driving her, seeking revenge, wanting this fate that had befallen them to befall their enemies as well.

Aisha saw *talmaad* cavalry wheeling ahead, though she felt the urge to turn well before she saw the turning. She rushed that way, adjusting her seat upon the saddle, confident her horse could still see in the great glare from behind. The feudal cavalry were closing on big, fast horses, and the serrin line was too disorganised from evading artillery to cut them down in force.

She ran with the main group of *talmaad*, heading out to the Dhemerhill River as the light upon trees and fields grew dimmer, and shadows darker. She stopped near the bank of the Dhemerhill, as others stopped about her and looked back. Feudal cavalry were slowing now, though she could not see precisely. They appeared to have closed upon the *talmaad*'s rear ranks, where fighting continued at close range. But now, light from the great fires was fading.

Hellfire burned fast and hot, and would continue to burn for long periods after the first eruption. But that first eruption was by far the brightest and hottest, and the long fire that followed would be dim by comparison. Human cavalry had chased them all the way out here across the fields with blood on their minds, without a thought as to where the light that allowed them that chase was coming from. Now, moment by moment, that light was fading. The shadows were closing in and human riders slowed in concern, horses protesting at shapes in the dark, at trees and stumps and ditches.

Not yet, Aisha thought, walking her horse forward. She could feel a new momentum building, an inexorable tug, as with a large boulder beginning to roll from a high slope. Not yet. Noise from the oncoming charge continued to fade, in concert with the light. Now there were cries from the humans, as they realised their mistake. Calls to regroup, to form into lines. But they could not see each other to make that happen. Not yet.

Suddenly, the urge began to build. Now. Every serrin moved at the same instant. There was no need to move faster than a canter, but suddenly those ahead were filling the night with arrows, and men were screaming. She came across a trail and around some trees, and there they were, feudal cavalry, some knights, some Northern Lenays, milling and ordering and trying to re-form like blind men grasping about in a dark room. Serrin were firing into them on all sides, and they were falling.

Now they charged, knowing they had to do something other than stand there and die. Riders came toward her, but several did not see the low fence ahead and toppled over it, another horse reared in fright and dumped its rider, and others slowed to a fearful jog. Aisha sighted one whose shield was not properly in play, drew quickly to her chin, and released. She'd wanted the throat, but hit shoulder instead. The man yelled and was hit by a second shaft an instant later, straight through the jaw.

Holes opened amidst the human lines. Aisha urged her nervous mare into no more than a canter, weaving between some panicked, riderless horses, cautioning the mare to some bushes, then slowing so she did not stumble on rising ground. The mare trusted her. Now she was in amongst the cavalry, where she would be dead in moments during the day. But her enemies stared at her and past her, unable to tell this horseman from the others.

Aisha smiled, selected a Lenay man barely ten paces to her left, and shot him through the neck. This range suited her well, she thought, quickly drawing another arrow. There was a choice between two Torovans and another Lenay. Common sense chose the Lenay, and she put this shaft through his face. Even Rhillian could have scored kills in here.

One of the Torovans died to another serrin. The other tried to gallop, and rode headlong into a tree. He fell, and as he lay on the ground, a serrin rode to stand over him and shot him through the chest.

All about it continued, feudal cavalry now trying to run, attacking friends mistaken for foes, trying to form up. Aisha saw ten Lenay cavalry make a defensive group, unaware that two of their number were actually *talmaad*. They killed four of the other eight before they were recognised, and simply danced away when the Lenays came after them. One of the last four fell in pursuit, two more fell to other serrin arrows, and Aisha rode quietly up behind the last as he stared about him in panic, and shot him through the back from five paces.

"*Elay esc'tah!*" the serrin called to each other in Saalsi, almost laughingly. "We can see!" was perhaps the closest translation in any human tongue. It was a taunt, as serrin rarely taunted, an insult born of fury. The words rose in the air with a lilting high note, and humans ran before those alien, haunting cries.

Remaining human cavalry galloped, as fast as they dared, back toward their lines. Half the *talmaad* pursued. The other half ignored them and set off across the Ilmerhill River, to lay into the infantry on that side, before the Ilmerhill Valley mouth.

Sasha crouched in wait behind the fenceline of a small yard, surrounded by her Ilduuris. She'd chosen for them the eastern part of town nearer the Ilmerhill River, while Lenays took the western side, across the main road. There was no confusing either group with feudal men-at-arms, and Ilduuri were far more suited for this city fighting than Rhodaani or Enoran Steel. Smaller shields and longer swords, and a superior ability to fight alone or in small groups. There would be no great shield walls here, only small ones blocking streets and alleys. And, given the numbers that approached, lots of fast manoeuvring and improvising.

Those numbers were now running down the main road across the yard. There were shouts, officers directing men to look for enemy, to check for ambush. Many men did not seem to be paying attention, and were more concerned with putting distance between themselves and the pursuing serrin.

Sasha waited, knowing that a longer wait was better. There would be no signal to attack—the first ambushing force to be discovered would start the fight, and everyone else would join in. She waited longer, as more men and a few horses came crowding along the road. Some now came into the yard, amidst carved masonry in half-finished blocks. Perhaps the first ambusher to be discovered would be her . . . but these men stopped, exhausted, and gathered together to talk of what they'd seen. They sounded disbelieving, and concerned, but not yet completely terrified. That would change.

Suddenly there were yells and clashing steel. Men with her echoed it, as all about the roar of thousands of men rose above Jahnd's roofs, and they ran into the yard. Fighting erupted. Sasha stayed where she was, with several Ilduuri, concerned about a countering flank onto this narrow road. Sure enough, within moments, men-at-arms were racing out this way in numbers, getting clear of the crowded main road. Ilduuris ahead sprang from the shadows and attacked.

Men rushed from the adjoining alley, and Sasha killed one before he saw her, a fast move from a blind side, a lesson learned in Petrodor. Others came at her, and the Ilduuris with her hit them, felling several, and then there were more breaking through, and Ilduuris from the yard falling back, and everything was chaos.

"This way!" Sasha yelled as horsemen came up the alley, and they fell back down an adjoining alley, then across a closed courtyard, pursuit close behind. In the courtyard Ilduuris made a second ambush as pursuers crashed into that line. Sasha raced ahead and checked the new street, where fighting had not yet reached.

One of the horsemen rounded the corner just then to cut her off, a knight in gleaming armour, but with visor down at night, how could he see? He charged her, and Sasha darted across the front of his horse so he swung on the wrong side. A cavalryman was with him, and sprinting men-at-arms behind. The cavalryman crashed into Ilduuris emerging from the alley behind, and then Sasha had fully ten men-at-arms coming about the intersection at her, with shield, sword, and spear.

She danced right again, out into the intersection, as Ilduuris behind engaged. She tore the sword from one man's hand, forced another to defend with his shield, then went low and slashed his leg. His balance failed, his shield dropped, and she removed his head, but another nearly impaled her with a spear as she ducked away, backward down the road.

Suddenly the spearman fell, an arrow in his side. Sasha took the opportunity to entice another swordsman into attacking, ducked across and split his exposed side. Another man shrieked as an arrow took him, and the others were now spreading out, looking about in fear. Sasha attacked another, and he defended three straight blows, scampering backward past a comrade who did not adjust in time, so she killed him instead.

But she'd advanced past one more, who circled behind . . . and fell with a shaft through the neck. Sasha was laughing. She did not know this humour, she had never laughed before to see men die. But there was only one man with such archery in a close melee, and she could feel him with her now.

One more backed against a wall, hoping the shadows would hide him, and was skewered there by a shaft that pinned his neck to the planks, leaving him gruesomely hanging. The survivors ran, and a last man fell with a shaft through his back.

Still grinning, Sasha turned and saw a dark shape emerging from the shadows, broad-shouldered and shaggy-haired, a huge bow in hand and a big quiver at his hip. His eyes gleamed green in the dark. He stood before her, and his breath was warm on her lips.

"Hello, lover," said Sasha with a smile.

"You told me to wait for you," he murmured back. "I did."

Sasha stared into those amazing eyes. She had told him to wait for her. She'd thought maybe he was dead at the time. Had he heard her?

"Where were you?" she asked.

"I lost my horse. I hid for a day on the far valleyside, cut off. When dark fell, I came back."

"And how did you find me?"

Errollyn smiled, a gleam in the dark. "I have no *vel'ennar* with other serrin, it's true," he replied. "But I share it with you." Sasha felt paralysed. His nearness was intoxicating. But it did not seem as before. She could *feel* him, somewhere beyond where senses could perceive. "I see you, Synnich-ahn. You are a beacon in the dark. You are hunting for blood this night, and I have answered your call. Let us spill some together, and save our peoples."

They returned to the road where her Ilduuris had fought and found them triumphant over both mounted riders. The knight had been pulled from his horse, and now they sat on him to hold him still while another sought to find a gap in his armour, and finish it messily.

Then they returned to the main fight. Errollyn remained slightly behind, preferring his bow to the sword on his back. He and Sasha fought together, and even in the worst confusion, it was as though they had one mind. Two men attacked them, and while he shot the left, she killed the right. There was no wasted energy, no miscommunication. She was the right hand, and he was the left. Together they made a tally such that the Ilduuri men fighting with them would tell tales of it for generations, and which Lenays would repeat and say proudly that they were there too.

Lenays and Ilduuris killed until those who were not dead were running for their lives. They ran into the night, and those who reached the Ipshaal began searching for boats. But these nights were filled with serrin, and the lessons of King Leyvaan echoed now as they had not done in two centuries since. All who attacked Saalshen must die, with none to survive to reach their homes, for if fear was all that humanity understood, fear must be Saalshen's final, awful protection.

The Ipshaal was wide. Beyond it lay Enora, filled with angry Enorans only too happy to assist in exercising Saalshen's final lesson. Perhaps a few, very lucky souls would live to return to the feudal Bacosh, but those could be no more than one for every few thousand who had marched.

And so the second great feudal army in two hundred years marched into Saalshen with much glory and fanfare, and disappeared with barely a trace. Gods and spirits and higher fates willing, the victors prayed, it would be the last.

Morning rose across the valleys, grey like dread. Smoke lingered in the air, and singed the nostrils. Damon walked, for he could not bear to make his poor horse take another step, the animal was so spent he would take a week to recover. It was in pasture now, belly full of grass and water, washed clean of sweat and dirt, cuts and bruises treated, and likely fast asleep. Damon wished that a prince of Lenayin might also take such liberties.

A King of Lenayin.

He walked across fields of dead. Tullamayne had spoken of such fields in many a tale, and though his tales were always steeped in epic melancholy, that melancholy had never felt quite so epic as this. Humanity lay as refuse upon the ground. Damon had always been like Sofy in that he loved the things that made life good, yet unlike Sofy in that he expected people to do everything opposite to achieving those things. Today, his view of affairs had triumphed over his sister's, yet the thought of it was only bleaker still.

City folk picked their way through the dead, many with wagons. Friendly wounded were already collected. Now they piled friendly dead, with as much reverence as one could accord a scene of mass slaughter. The enemy dead they ran over with wagons, and occasionally stole a piece of jewellery. The crows were following, and would soon arrive in swarms. Damon did not think there were enough crows in all of Rhodia to consume all this.

Finally he arrived at a scene. The Ilmerhill River was nearby, bubbling happily away. Great Lord Markan was here, as was Sasha, kneeling by a man who lay on the grass, two serrin arrows through his body.

Damon stopped beside the man, and looked down upon the dying King of Lenayin. Koenyg looked up, squinting against the overcast sky. And smiled, with bloodied lips.

"Brother," he whispered. "You won."

"I won a great pile of corpses and many dead friends," Damon replied. "It's not much of a prize."

Koenyg shook his head. "No," he said, and coughed, weakly. "No. You have won a great victory. Now you must consolidate it."

Damon frowned. He looked at Sasha. Her jaw was tight with intense emotion. He had not thought that Sasha would grieve for Koenyg. But now he kneeled, reluctantly, and took his brother's hand.

"There is no choice now," Koenyg continued, weakly but with determination. "I do not like this path for Lenayin, but events have fallen your way, not mine. Saalshen must be the foundation of our future. Rebuild it. Rebuild the Saalshen Bacosh. Rebuild Lenayin in its image. Declare war on the north if you must. They will oppose you with every breath. Be steel against them. You have chosen your path, and Lenayin's. Now you must walk it."

Damon swallowed hard. "You counsel me to attack your closest allies? The family of your wife and son?"

"Damon. Brother." Koenyg's hand tightened with unexpected strength. "All that I have ever done, I have done for Lenayin. I tried to unite a divided land. I thought the north was central, and the rest should be made more like them. I still think it. But that is not to be, and now you must unite Lenayin *your* way.

"Let nothing stop you. No weakness, no fecklessness. No elder brother intimidating you, even beyond the grave." He smiled. Damon struggled to hold his gaze. "Let not even the love of your other siblings stop you from doing what you must for your people. I never did. Not even when it caused me such pain as these arrows can only imagine."

It hurt. Damon looked at Sasha, as she wiped at tears. She knew what he meant. Damon did too. They had never been friends, but family was not friendship. Family was family, even in hatred and feud. As leaders of nations, they did not always have the luxury to put each other first.

"Myklas lives," said Damon. "Wounded, but recovering."

"Sasha told me," said Koenyg. "It is good."

"Kessligh thinks to let the wounded live," Sasha added. "To send them across Saalshen, to see what they attempted to destroy. A new convert is a more powerful believer than one born to the faith, he says. To gain thousands of such men, and send them back to their homes in the Bacosh after some years amongst the serrin, could be a strong example to others."

"A good idea," Koenyg whispered. "Myklas is fortunate. I should have liked to do that myself, had the *talmaad*'s aim been less accurate."

"I should have liked you to fight on our side from the beginning," Sasha retorted, attempting stern reprimand. "I should have been proud to fight alongside *all* of my brothers."

"For a moment there, you did." He clasped her hand. Sasha nodded, mutely. "Damon. Two last things. Promise me you shall look after Lenayin as I have said."

"I shall," said Damon. "I promise."

Koenyg sighed a little, and looked relieved. He gazed up at the grey sky above. "And promise me that you will not leave. I would not like to die alone."

"I shall stay," said Damon, and sat properly upon the grass to do that. "And I shall never forget that you made me who I am."

Koenyg managed a smile, recognising a backhanded compliment. But he liked the irony, it was clear. "I shall see Father again," he said dreamily.

"And Alythia," said Damon.

"And Krystoff," said Sasha.

"And hopefully," Koenyg added, with fading strength, "none of the rest of you, for quite some time."

King Koenyg Lenayin died gloriously upon the field of battle, surrounded by his siblings and the bodies of his enemies. By his death, a new world was born.

Twenty-seven

It was more than a year before Sasha returned home to Lenayin. But return she did, at the ripe old age of twenty-two, and breathed the crisp air of early winter as she rode with friends along an achingly familiar stream, icy with the white dust of recent snow on the ground. Two years away from home was a long time, she reflected as she rode.

More than half of that time, it was astonishing to think, had come after the great victory at Jahnd. Kessligh, as soon as the victory was complete, had begun pushing for attack and reconquest, as Saalshen had done following the invasion of King Leyvaan. Many had protested. Losses were severe, they'd said. The survivors were exhausted. The lands that Kessligh proposed to conquer were vast and powerful, even now that the cream of their warriors lay dead upon the field. Most wished to return to the Saalshen Bacosh, reclaim what they had lost, and begin rebuilding.

But Kessligh was adamant. The Saalshen Bacosh, he said, can rebuild no faster than its enemies can. Matters remain fundamentally unresolved. Perhaps you will have a decade of peace. Perhaps a generation. But soon, inevitably, the forces that had driven this invasion would lead to another, fought by men for whom this great defeat was but a distant tale. It had been so close this time, when the Regent had captured artillery and hellfire. Inevitably the knowledge to build such things would spread, as it was already spreading in Petrodor, as he, Sasha, and Rhillian could attest. The next time, they'd be back with artillery and hellfire of their own, and affairs would be even worse.

Empire was the solution, he'd said, and the serrin had protested. But not so loudly this time, shaken by events, and the realisation of just how close things had been. Rhillian was firmly on his side, as was Errollyn, the two serrin to emerge from the war with the most *ra'shi* of all the *talmaad*. They would follow Kessligh, they said, though few believed that what he claimed was possible.

Firstly, Sasha had returned to Ilduur with the survivors of the Ilduuri Steel. Those numbered about half of the men who had accompanied her, though that was a considerably better number than the Rhodaani and Enoran Steel had ended with. A good number of *talmaad* accompanied her—Errollyn and Aisha amongst them, and Rhillian, who had been found relatively unharmed in Koenyg's tent after the battle.

On the way back through the Saadi Maal country, they'd gathered a great many older Steel veterans and new volunteers. At Andal itself, they found the city risen to oppose them with a strong militia, yet it folded meekly when they realised what little chance they had. Sasha told them all that things would change. She sat with senior Ilduuris and serrin, and hammered out plans for a new council to replace the Remischtuul, for independent courts such as Rhodaan had made, and for the rebuilding of the Ilduuri Nasi-Keth.

The Ilduuri Nasi-Keth would be run by serrin now, brought in from Saalshen. It was the only way to ensure the nasty tendency of Ilduuri isolationism did not reinfect the Tol'rhens, and turn the Ilduuri Nasi-Keth against the very ones who created them. For council elections, no former members of the Stamentaast or other, tainted organisations need apply. New Steel volunteers would be armed, and left to garrison Andal. All involved in the previous uprisings against the serrin would be punished. It was colonisation, pure and simple, and far more heavy-handed than Maldereld's two hundred years before.

Many protested to Sasha that it would not work, that Ilduuris would never accept it. They didn't need to accept it, Sasha had replied. So long as there was force enough in the Steel, and in the *talmaad* who reformed the Nasi-Keth and occupied Ilduur, the rest of the population could shut up and like it. The Steel would be back again soon, and in force. Any more trouble while they were gone would only lead to reinvasion and large-scale killings to make her present punishments seem mild. And then she'd gone, before the winter snows blocked the high passes, and marched north to Enora.

Enora had been a joy. Townsfolk had showered them with gifts and flowers along every road, and village choirs sang for them at every stop. They'd passed this time through Aisha's home village, and Sasha had met her serrin mother and human father, and heard wonderful tales of Aisha at age five, arguing with a local priest at communion about how the Gathering Prayer should be pronounced in Larosan.

They'd collected more veterans on the way through, and a great many young volunteers for the Steel. Many local serrin and part-serrin also volunteered for the *talmaad*. Yasmyn had asked why local human women could not volunteer for the *talmaad* as well, since light cavalry seemed a task serrin women did well. The Enorans said they'd think about it, but Sasha wasn't holding her breath.

Rhodaan was just as welcoming, though by now wet and cold with winter. At Tracato, the armies had mustered once more, Rhodaani, Enoran, and Ilduuri Steels together, with the Army of Lenayin and Carlito Rochel's Pazirans as well, who were cut off from Torovan and had stayed to fight. All had gathered many volunteers, and more poured in every day. It took a long time to train a soldier of the Steel to standard, and longer still to gather the means to provide and pay for them all, but Kessligh did not need them for battle, but rather for the occupation that followed.

In spring he took the Steels north into Elisse, and finished in a few weeks what the Rhodaani Steel should have finished alone the previous year. Elissian Lords either surrendered their powers or died, along with their armies. Elisse had lost most of their remaining forces at Jahnd, and Kessligh judged that if he sent enough force, he would barely need to fight at all. Most surrendered, and he left garrisons of serrin and volunteers behind. Lords and nobility likely to cause trouble were rounded up and taken to Saalshen. When Kessligh left Elisse and headed west, the Saalshen Bacosh provinces numbered four, for the first time since Leyvaan's fall.

Damon had been concerned about trouble in Lenayin, once news of events in the Bacosh reached them. But as Kessligh had pointed out, the only way home to Lenayin lay through either Larosa or Algrasse. In the end, it was Larosa. And of course, it always had to be.

This had been a real fight. Larosa had lost enormous manpower at Jahnd and was in disarray with the deaths of many lords, to say nothing of Balthaar Arrosh himself. But facing the loss of everything, the nobility had rallied in great numbers, and mustered all available men upon the field of battle. Nearly one hundred thousand gathered on the fields near Sherdaine, a force considerably larger than what attacked them.

But now they faced Kessligh, commanding three Steel armies replenished by retired veterans who knew this game well, a large mass of *talmaad* cavalry, Pazira, and the diminished yet still formidable Army of Lenayin. Also, they were back to the old days now, when the righteous side had all the effective artillery, and the feudals had none. It had been another slaughter, this time entirely one-sided, and Larosa had fallen to the Saalshen Bacosh.

Kessligh then pointed out to Damon that, if one looked at the map, Algrasse was also between Lenayin and Larosa. Damon had shrugged, and said, before a grand dining hall in Sherdaine full of Lenay and Steel men, "Why not?" All had cheered.

Algrasse had folded meekly, making the Saalshen Bacosh six provinces strong. The Army of Lenayin bade farewell, taking the Pazirans with them, and returned home before the northerners became truly restless—already there were reports of fighting on the borders, and northern lords refusing to accept the new, traitorous, pagan-demon-loving king. Sasha had been persuaded by her Ilduuris to stay around for the Tournean campaign at least, as Tournea promised to be the challenge that Algrasse had not been. Tournea, word was, had made frantic arrangements with southern power Meraine and westerly Rakani, to join forces and make a very big stand upon Tournean fields.

This they had done, with another force of more than a hundred thousand, but this time far more cunningly applied. A victory was won by the invaders, but a far less decisive one, with losses incurred and regrouping necessary. And then, inevitably, some of what Rhillian drily called "peace-mongers" had come from Saalshen bearing news of deals and agreements with Meraine and Rakani that would remove the necessity for further bloodshed, and Saalshen's already alarmed *uman'ilen* (as the great philosophical minds were called) went over Rhillian's head to declare that the *talmaad* would not commit to further conquest unless such proposals were carried out in full.

Kessligh and Rhillian complained, but there was little they could do—Tournea, Meraine, and Rakani were formidable enough that invading them further without *talmaad* support would be unwise, particularly in the precarious state of readiness that the Steels still found themselves in, and without Lenay support. Besides which, serrin volunteers now comprised a large part of the occupation force in Elisse, Algrasse, and, most worryingly, Larosa, and Saalshen was even threatening to withdraw support there also.

Sasha had left then, wishing to be home before the next winter, and not wanting to be mired in Tournea, enduring Kessligh's frustration as endless negotiations with scheming feudals served only to preserve a force within humanity that would be far better exterminated for good. And so, Kessligh observed wryly, the well-meaning men and women of peace in Saalshen laid the foundations for future bloodshed and suffering, by ensuring feudalism's survival in the southern Bacosh. But in truth, he was not too upset—Elisse and Algrasse were small additions, but Larosa was an enormous prize. It needed now to be transformed, as Rhodaan, Enora, and Ilduur had been transformed, two hundred years before. The task was enormous, and if successful, the remaining feudal provinces would be no match for its wealth and power in years ahead.

But neither, somewhat worryingly, would be the other Bacosh provinces. The same old Bacosh problem—Larosan domination—reared its head again, yet in a different guise. Rhillian, however, had only laughed at the prospect. "If the next generation's largest problem is a wealthy and serrin-loving Larosa wielding too much power through its elected councils," she'd said, "then I welcome them to it."

Sasha had thought it all a rather grand invasion and expansion of empire, whatever the wise heads of Saalshen thought. She was proud to be a part of a conquering army that brought freedom to the peasantry and promised to end the bigotry and hatred of the serrin that had led to these awful wars in the first place. Two centuries before, Rhodaan, Enora, and Ilduur had been transformed vastly for the better, and now Elisse, Algrasse, and Larosa would be too. She hoped. It would be an awesome task, requiring the labours of countless men and women, human and serrin alike, and a great deal of sacrifice. Free nations were hard to build, while tyrannies came easy. But if there was ever an endeavour that was worth the cost, this was surely it.

Staying a little longer had been tempting, but she had plans for Lenayin, too, and Damon needed her support. Besides which, she desperately wanted to go home.

She'd not taken the direct way home, however. She'd stopped first in Pazira, in the foothills of her native Valhanan, and called upon Duke Carlito and his family, and the Lenay garrison Damon had left there. The garrison was not especially large, but the message it sent the King of Torovan, better known as Patachi Steiner, was simple—hurt Pazira, and your reign will end. Pazira was now surrounded by hostile Torovan provinces, and a very hostile king in Petrodor, but even the king did not dare ignore the threat of Lenay invasion.

Damon could quite likely not deliver on his threat, given instability in Lenayin, but King Steiner was a merchant, and knew what constituted acceptable risk of profit and loss on his accounting pages. He would wait, and watch Pazira and Lenayin with a beady eye, if for no other reason than the death of his heir at Jahnd, Simon Steiner. Sasha's brother-in-law. Sasha would regret the losing of brothers for as long as she lived, but she would never regret the losing of this brother-in-law, whatever pain it caused her estranged sister Marya.

Politics and threats aside, she'd enjoyed Pazira immensely, and the hospitality of her friends the Rochels. Family Rochel were patrons of Lenayin now, like it or not, as was Pazira. Well, if Saalshen could have an empire, however reluctantly, why not Lenayin? But she kept the thought to herself.

Also in Pazira, she'd reclaimed her beloved Peglyrion, whom she'd been scared might not remember her. But he'd practically trampled her at the stables, which made her cry, to the amusement of all. Riding up the slopes of Pazira to the Valhanan border astride her favourite horse was serendipity. Doing it in the company of such friends was even better.

Errollyn was with her, knowing well that she'd need him, in more ways than the personal, in what lay ahead. He'd been to Lenayin briefly, loved it, and looked forward to settling down for a while somewhere far away from cities and crowds, while still doing something important. As Saalshen's senior representative in Lenayin, he would certainly be doing that, even were he not based in Baen-Tar, the traditional location of such ambassadors.

Aisha was also with her. For what Sasha was planning to start, she needed not only serrin, but scholarly and educated people. Aisha was every bit the part, and Aisha loved Lenayin with a passion that rivalled Sasha's own. Linguistically, she opined, Lenayin was the most interesting place in all of Rhodia and, with what Sasha now attempted, had a greater potential for cultural amazements than even the newly expanded Saalshen Bacosh.

Yasmyn also came, following the formal ceremony that made her Sasha's uma. She was old for a new uma, and Sasha young for an uman, but Yasmyn had recognised that the only path for a woman in her position to gain the authority and respect she desired in Isfayen was through the Nasi-Keth. Sasha did not know if these motivations were the most desirable, yet if that was what it took to gain converts in Lenayin, she would take it.

There were many she left behind in the new Saalshen Bacosh whom she was sad to leave, yet happy for all the same. There were her precious, brave Ilduuris, five of whom also rode with her now, two of those with families sent for from Ilduur itself. It was imperative, all had agreed, that Ilduur maintained contact with Lenayin, and with Sasha in particular. Sasha thought it imperative for emotional and political reasons. The men who rode with her had fought with her in the Steel. Two had been wounded and could no longer serve, and all knew construction and masonry from their civilian lives, one of them to an exceptional degree. She needed lowlands builders with grand skills to fulfill her dreams, and best of all, as Ilduuris they knew how to build in mountains.

Kessligh, she had no doubt, would spend several more years as commander of the Steel armies, yet she thought it likely that the Steel's fighting days were done, for a while at least. He'd been so long in Lenayin, required by the Nasi-Keth to be so, yet he'd always yearned to see Saalshen. He'd have the chance now, and Rhillian had offered to take him herself, to learn and see, travel and talk, to all the places that had been largely forbidden to humans for as far back as anyone remembered.

Certainly he'd travel back to Lenayin at some point and see how she was faring. Whether he'd finally settle here, or there, as his years finally began to catch up with him, she had no idea. He'd rather teach, she knew, but it was nice to see him finally getting the respect he deserved, and she had no doubt they'd eventually build far more statues of him in the Bacosh than of her.

Rhillian was the person Kessligh had appointed to put the whole Saalshen Bacosh back together, in its new, enlarged form. The wise heads of Saalshen, reappearing now that the serious work was done and frivolous concerns could rule serrin minds once more, were displeased by this, but what her own people found disconcerting in her actions only recommended her more to human eyes.

Rhillian grasped human ways and minds to a degree that most serrin could not, and though her understandings were not always perfect, she had at least learned to know her own limitations. Even as the fighting had continued, she'd been spending long hours in a tent or borrowed quarters, scribbling notes on laws, or reading books. Many long evenings they'd all sat together with her—Sasha, Errollyn, Kessligh, and others, discussing their new provinces' structure of councils, the form of laws, the raising of new Steel armies, the disbanding of noble title, and how to stop the old nostalgias from flaring up once more as they had in Tracato and Andal.

All had contributed ideas, yet it was Rhillian who settled now upon what she hoped would be a working formula—that of serrin oversight and mediation, in all human institutions, for the next generation at least, and probably beyond. Serrin would not always run human institutions (save the Ilduuri Nasi-Keth) but they would hold positions of oversight, to watch the appointment of officials, and the conduct of debates. Human powers could squabble and fight all they liked, as trying to prevent such conflicts was clearly against human nature. But serrin would mediate and make certain that honourable rules were upheld, and that all would accept the final result as final.

Humans liked things to be absolute. Serrin preferred them in balanced and nuanced shades. Humans would try to force "final" solutions, often with terrible results. Serrin would prevent them, and maintain balance by playing the ends against the middle.

"Maldereld reborn," some were calling Rhillian now, listening to her pronounce on such matters. One great female serrin general had built the first version of the Saalshen Bacosh from the ground up, and now two centuries later, another would expand on the project, and hopefully improve it. Sasha had little doubt that she would, for so much had been learned in that time, from bloody, painful lessons. Rhillian seemed utterly absorbed in her work, and Sasha found some pride in the thought that their many struggles together, both with and against each other, had shaped and prepared her for this, what would be the great defining purpose of her life.

Sasha was saddest to part with Sofy. For all her strength, Sofy had not a warrior's soul, and Jahnd's aftermath had left her shaken and fragile. Sasha missed Jaryd deeply, and mourned for him, yet as a warrior herself she knew that Jaryd's loss should be rightfully placed amongst that of a pantheon of heroes, whose glorious deeds would outlive them all. Such a death was to be celebrated more than mourned, yet Sofy did not see things this way.

She had declined Damon's request for her to return with him to Baen-Tar, and remained in Tracato, to bury herself in the task of rebuilding. The latest news before Sasha's departure from Tournea had been that Sofy was appointed by the new Rhodaani Council to the role of Protector of Rhodaani Arts and Treasures, whatever that meant. Sasha reckoned that Sofy would take it to mean more than it was intended to. She had great goodwill amongst Tracatans, as the Princess Regent who had tried to save them from her husband and nearly died for it. Even amongst the Rhodaani nobility, some still considered her Princess Regent, despite the extinguishment of noble title across all Saalshen-occupied Bacosh. Thus she could finally play her much sought-after role of peacemaker, as Rhodaani nobility attempted to resettle into their lands while weathering the understandable resentment of non-noble Rhodaanis. Princess Sofy (her reverted and more accurate title) could keep them safe, and advise them on how not to upset the resettling Rhodaani populace.

That task would be easier, of course, now that Alfriedo Renine had accompanied Damon to Baen-Tar, as much for his own protection from his people as anything else. But having abandoned his claim for the lordship of Rhodaan, Alfriedo was in need of somewhere safe to stay, and to continue his education, and Lenayin had seemed the ideal location, given his ongoing fascination with the Lenay people. Whether the somewhat fragile and intellectual boy would continue to love Lenayin, once exposed to its more brutal expectations of masculinity, Sasha did not know.

But Sofy, she was confident, would love it in Tracato. Sofy had always wanted to make things, and in Tracato she had a palette on a broad scale. There were libraries to see rebuilt and restocked, the Tol'rhen to repair, the Mahl'rhen to see resettled by serrin occupants and serrin treasures, and new masters to be found for the many schools.

And in the meantime, she could be Lenayin's representative in Rhodaan, and perhaps even the most senior for the entire Saalshen Bacosh—Damon would see her well endowed with coin on top of whatever the Rhodaani Council were granting her, and she could keep her own court and advisors, and gather a centre of Lenay power and influence in one of the Saalshen Bacosh's most powerful cities. From there she could also keep contact with the one part of Petrodor that King Steiner did not control—the dockside—and help to spread Nasi-Keth and serrin influence there, and elsewhere in Torovan. An unusual role for an unmarried princess, perhaps, but these were unusual times . . . and for certain there would be no lack of handsome and powerful male suitors. Sasha did not envy such men, however. They would be competing with the memory of one of Lenayin's finest heroes. But hopefully, some day, one of them would measure up favourably, and her little sister could be truly happy once more.

The party arrived in Baerlyn just before dark, and found a grand celebration prepared. There were introductions for her new friends, happy reunions with old ones and a tearful reunion with Lynette Tremel, who had been working Sasha's ranch the whole time she'd been away.

"Andreyis met a girl?" she exclaimed now, hearing this news for the first time.

"That's why he's not returning," said Sasha. "At least not yet. Perhaps one day." They sat together in the Steltsyn Star, having deflected promises of great tale-tellings for another day, for she was too tired, and she had so many accumulated tales it could take her until the next morning to work through them. Now the rest of Baerlyn busied themselves getting to know Errollyn, Aisha, Yasmyn, and the Ilduuris, allowing Lynette and Sasha a little time alone, in one corner of the very noisy inn.

Lynette had had a year to come to terms with her father's death, on the battlefield of Shero Valley. It had been some months since she'd learned of Jaryd's death at Jahnd, which had saddened her also, though she'd not known him long. Sasha was proud of how well Lynette coped, for she'd loved Teriyan dearly, and missed him still. It was a common fate for the women of Lenayin, to lose their men upon the battlefield, and she bore it stoically. But now she was sad to learn that her old friend Andreyis was not in Sasha's party, though pleased that he was well.

"Her name is Yshel," Sasha explained. "She is serrin and *talmaad*, eighteen years old . . ."

"Serrin!" Lynette gasped.

"And Andreyis is quite convinced she is the most beautiful girl in all the world. She was hurt at Jahnd, she had some burns to her body, but she's recovering well and her scars are fading. Last I heard they'd joined Sofy's court at Tracato. It's a new world in the Bacosh, and they're both young and smart. Who knows where they will end up?"

"A girl like that fell for Andrey," Lynette sighed. "Who'd have thought?"

Sasha smiled. "She has red hair. I'm sure you were some inspiration."

"I should have just grabbed him, shouldn't I?"

Sasha laughed. Lynette had never had any interest in grabbing Andreyis before. Women were blind sometimes, only noticing a man after he became unavailable. "I don't think Andreyis would have known what to do if you'd grabbed him before," she chuckled. "But he certainly does now."

The following morning, after a night spent at the inn, townsfolk accompanied the party out to empty fields higher up the Baerlyn Valley. Here by the little stream, Sasha's Ilduuri friends examined the site she'd been thinking of for more than a year now. The ground was sloping, but they insisted it was not a problem; they could dig a flat foundation, and build wide and long.

They loved the valley. It was steep enough to remind them of Ilduur, yet more rugged and wild. Already they were discussing plots for their own houses, to the curious enthusiasm of the locals, now contemplating the large changes that their most famous resident had brought back to the village.

"Much will change," Sasha told village headman Jaegar as they stood together on the slope, and looked over the wonderful view down the valley. Its jagged, pine-strewn ridges were even more lovely than she remembered. "A Tol'rhen in Baerlyn will mean this is not a sleepy little village any longer. In time it might even become a proper town, with wealthy folk, large buildings, and everything."

"Good," said Jaegar, with genuine approval.

Sasha was a little surprised. "You won't be sad to see such changes?"

Jaegar shrugged massive shoulders within his heavy coat. "Everything changes. Some changes are sad. But for all your rustic life out here, Sasha, you've never been poor, and you don't really know what it's like. But you've seen Torovan now, and the Bacosh. You know how poor we still are up here."

"Oh, you'd be surprised," Sasha said wryly. "In both lands massive wealth is matched only by extraordinary poverty; I saw people there for whom Baerlyn is luxury."

"Even so, folks here would rather have more. Build a Tol'rhen here, and they will. Trust me on this."

"I always do."

The Ilduuris were gesticulating as they explained to others, through Aisha's translation, what the finished building would look like. Large, seemed the general agreement.

"Besides," Jaegar added, rubbing his hands against the cold, "it's not like you're building a slaughterhouse. Should be pretty."

"I'll make sure it is," Sasha assured him. "It will probably take about five years, if we get the coin we're promised. But we'll not wait five years before opening. Saalshen's promised me many teachers—I said I'd send for them once I got here and finalised my plans. Then we start recruiting kids."

"What criteria?"

"Haven't decided yet. We need some nobility and wealthy folk, obviously, for politics. Need high folk to have a stake in the Nasi-Keth. But talent has to count for a lot, too. Willingness to learn. And I want some girls," she added, with a sharp look for emphasis.

Jaegar smiled. "I've four daughters. Take one, please." Sasha laughed. "Who pays for it, exactly?"

"The good King Damon," said Sasha. "He's promised us *gold*."

"So *we're* paying for it," Jaegar said drily.

Sasha smiled, knowing local opinion of the king's tax. "Aye, but so are the Hadryn."

Jaegar snorted a laugh. "And good luck to your brother collecting that tax up north this year."

"Aye," Sasha sighed. "Another thing to have a war over. That and Koenyg's bitch Hadryn wife claiming the throne for her son."

Unfortunately, it was most likely the truth.

After the inspection, Sasha took Errollyn, Yasmyn, and Aisha up to their new home at the ranch. There Sasha reintroduced herself to Kaif and Keef, her enormous boarhounds, who became so excited to see her they had to be restrained. And then the horses, whose number had indeed increased. Torovans had been buying a lot of horses, it seemed, and paying good money for breeding them, too. Though it sobered Sasha to think that at least a few of the horses she'd raised at this place would have marched with the Torovan army against Saalshen.

Errollyn, Yasmyn, and Aisha loved the ranch, and spent some time exploring, marvelling at the enormous views of the mountains to the south, and at the thick forest above the cleared pasture slope. Sasha told them of the animals that lived there, of the wolf pack with dens in the next valley across, and took them to see the waterfall and rock pool hidden amongst the trees to the west, freezing cold now but lovely for swimming in summer. Lynette told them that Jaryd had loved that pool when he'd been here two summers ago, before the Army of Lenayin had marched. Sasha thought she would name it for him, Jaryd's Falls, and have Jaegar and some others up for a traditional remembrance. A freed spirit liked to return to the places where it had been happy in the previous life, and in that happiness could be enticed to rejoin the living world in birth once more.

After lunch, with tea in hand, Sasha settled on the south-facing verandah with Errollyn to take in the warmth of the midday sun and admire the view, while Lynette showed Yasmyn and Aisha more secrets of the ranch. Errollyn looked utterly relaxed. He'd never liked cities much either, and at the prospect of settling here for some considerable time, he looked as though all the tension had fled from him.

Sitting beside him, Sasha knew how he felt. There was a lot of work to do, and trials ahead. Damon's kingship was not yet secure, and she was a vital pillar of his support. The north would doubtless rebel, as soon as they settled their internal disputes over who their great lords now were, and probably there would be civil strife and battle. The provincial lords had been hammered at Jahnd, yet would certainly regroup and press again at their claims for feudal rights in Lenayin. To the far north the Cherrovan threat always loomed, Torovan was now a problem rather than just a source of gold, and the new Bacosh was one giant experiment in a new form of civilisation that no one was certain would work.

Nothing ever truly ended, and returning home felt like more of a beginning than a conclusion. But there were wonderful possibilities ahead also, born of the sacrifice of so many heroes. Things that were worth fighting for, and dying for if necessary. She'd learned, these past two years, that she needed that more than anything. Something worth dying for. Something worth living for. In Lenayin, those two things were usually the same.

"That sun across the mountains is just magnificent," said Errollyn, shading his eyes against the distant glare.

Sasha nodded, smiling, and for the first time in years felt completely at peace.

About the Author

JOEL SHEPHERD was born in Adelaide in 1974. His first manuscript was shortlisted for the George Turner Prize in 1998, and his first novel, *Crossover*, was shortlisted in 1999. He wrote two other novels in the Crossover series, *Breakaway* (2003) and *Killswitch* (2004). *Sasha*, the first novel in A Trial of Blood & Steel, was published in 2007, followed by *Petrodor* (2008) and *Tracato* (2009).